THE WIND'S BREATHE

STEVEN FRANCIS MONTAGNA

Printed in the United States of America
Published by: Stephen Francis Montagna

ISBN: 978-1-970301-02-1 PB
ISBN: 978-1-970301-03-8 HB

Copyright © 2025
Stephen Francis Montagna

PROLOGUE

An endless crew of underpaid and overworked and thoroughly exhausted young and old Japanese workers alike, started their third week of blasting and digging in the ancient Kai mountain region of central Japan. Where it was believed many great battles once waged between the mightly warlords of Japan's ancient past. The time honored but long forgotten field of battle, and respect of that past time was laid out over the ancient vast Kugyo plain, and covered over by the passing time. It was believed the very place where the workers were toiling. Was where the once massive Armies of samurai warriors' loyal to their Shogun, shared their lives within Lord Kawasomeru's ocean wide encampment and battlefield as he prepared for the final battle waged between Lord Takehiro Kawasomeru and Lord Motoshige Wakatsuki's, two massive samurai armies readied themselves for the battle of their lives.

But now, the respected encampment and samurai, who fought so bravely in the past of Japan's history, and died on the reverent land the modern day construction workers were toiling on, was replaced by a crawling sea of yellow painted steel and wire earthmoving equipment. Along with an Army of modern day workers dressed in protective hard hats, overalls, and thick work gloves, and now armed with picks and shovels. The crews waged the new war, but with the earth and its bounty to discover her hidden treasures and wealth for their greedy owners.

When a rich deposit of much needed iron ore was discovered in the Kai mountain range, the age old plunder of the earth and battlefield began in earnest. With no respect or consideration displayed for Japan's honored history offered to the past times. The silenced and deadly war cries of the wildly charging samurai and their faithful steeds were replaced by destructive dynamite, deafening roar from the earthmoving equipment, and pollution of the diesel engine machines. As they assaulted the earth under the constant cursing of the angry foremen, as they screamed at their toiling workers to produce more wealth for their owners and company.

Some luckier workers uncovered numerous ancient brass arrowheads, rusted and snapped katana blades, and parts of armor once used to protect the lives of the warriors from the biting edge of the sword's call, along with scattered bones of long dead warriors and their horses.

A few pieces of discarded armor were bent or otherwise destroyed, uncovered by some workers, and saved as keepsakes. But the owners of the equipment and companies were more interested in searching for the prized iron ore, than in what they believed were worthless trinkets of the past glory of Japan's history. The account of Japan's history, and samurai who carved out a harsh living in Japan's savage past, had been forgotten. Just as all histories of other great nations, were also lost in the quest for personal riches and greed of the earth.

But on this special Tuesday morning, the work crews were ordered to blast away a certain section of low lying ridges, at the very base of the Kai pass. This work was to allow easier access to waters of the Kai River. The water would be used to wash away lose earth and debris, blasted from the earth to expose the deposits of iron ore buried in the rocks, and hard packed earth. Despite how rich modern day Japan was, she was forever forced to rely on imports of her steel and iron, to manufacture cars and various other commodities, and personal fortunes. This reliance on other nations went against the fiber of the honorable Japanese people.

As the cloud shrouded sun raised in the Heavens over the distant mountain range on this damp and overcast day, a light mist was soaking the ground they worked on. The workers knew later in the day, heavier rains were expected, and that would place an early end to their workday. So the workers set off to plant the explosive charges, and try and make the most of the morning hours, and time they had left to work and earn a living.

A massive earthmoving bulldozer was working at trying to remove the lose rock and dirt recently blasted away from the base of the ridge the day before. Many behemoth, yellow painted trucks moved in like a swarm of angry bees, as the earthmoving machine scooped up bucket loads of lose rocks and earth, and dump it in the rear of the waiting trucks for removal from the worksite as fill for other projects the company had going on.

Troubleshooting spotters kept a constant vigil before the slow moving mechanism, as the machine dug in the crumbling ridge, making certain the machine did not fall victim to an uncovered crevasse that the machine might tumble in and get damaged or stuck. This region of Japan was noted to be honeycombed with steep hidden caves and deep rivets that could trap and or otherwise damage the mammoth and expensive commercial machine of steel and wire.

By the end of the first hour of work for the crews, the fine mist slowly turned into a steady and heavier drizzle, with the lead foreman considering calling an early end to the day's work. The foreman did not want his crews getting hurt or injured foolishly, by slipping on the wet and loose stones, or mud of the site. He glanced in the sky and was about to blow his whistle to end the day's work, when one of the spotters began raising all sorts of hell by where the bulldozer was digging in the side of the mountain. The worried foreman left his perch on top of the running board of the truck he was standing on, and rushed to where the spotter was working, fearing the bulldozer might have thrown a track, or somehow got damaged or stuck on the site.

When the foreman reached the worker and looked to where he was pointing at. The older man noticed what looked to be a mouth to a hidden cave that seemed to been carved by human hand in the side of the mountain, and obviously covered by an ancient avalanche many years past.

The cunning foreman immediately ordered the heavy machine away from the opening. Then, he ordered the spotter to retrieve a flashlight from the field office trailer. There was something eerie about the cave that interested him, and he cautiously climbed into the narrow opening and peered in the dark dank smelling void of pitch blackness. In his wandering mind, he was fearful something immortal and dangerous was lurking in the mouth of the cave, waiting to drag him in and devour his soul, to give the evil a new life.

When the spotter returned with the flashlight, his eyes displayed his excitement. The foreman grabbed the light from his hand and shined it in the opening. He saw the bright light reflect off something hidden within the dank cave. Now, greed and the want for personal riches for him to enjoy, took over his once fears of the foreboding cave opening, and what might be lurking within, the foreman started to probe further into the hidden underground chamber.

Carefully placing one foot before the other, he entered the feeling of dread void of darkness and fear. Breathing was hard in the dust filled cave, because of stale air so long ago trapped in the sealed chamber of death, and dust raised by the blasting in the area. The fearful foreman pulled back as if he was frightened by what he noticed hiding in the cave opening. But his dreams of wealth filled his mind, and gave him the courage to continue on deeper into the cave.

He looked over his shoulder at the spotter, and ordered him to move the machines further from this section of the ridge. Then he sent most of the crew home for the day. The foreman Utsumi was going to keep a certain crew of chosen men he could trust with his life, to remain in case they were needed if there was anything found in the cave of worth to them or the owner of the business. His mind was spinning as he tried to look deeper in the cave.

Once the cautious foreman was certain the workers he did not trust to keep a secret to their death, were gone from the site. The old foreman Utsumi removed his handheld radio from his breast pocket, and placed a call to his boss in Tokyo. He wanted to inform him of what he believed he found on the site, and wanted to see what his boss wanted to do about his discovery, and if his boss had new orders for him over the find.

CHAPTER ONE

The young and good looking owner of the construction company, Hiromoai Hatanaka rested in his plush office on the twenty seventh floor of the luxurious elite Hatanaka Towers. The magnificent structure was built by his father when he became successful in the construction field in Japan. When the call from his excited foreman came through on his home base set, he gave out with a disgusted sigh as he glared at the phone as if it had insulted him. The youthful handsome owner of the company was enjoying his third cup of coffee, and taking time by reading the Tokyo Times, and savoring the latest copy of the comic book Shi, written by the artist Billy Tucci, he received in the mail from the United States.

Hiromoai was the oldest son of three of Hatanaka and Son's Mining Corporation, one of the oldest mining and construction companies in Japan, and possessed more money than he could spend in three lifetimes. He sat up in his chair while removing his shoeless feet from the desktop, as he answered the call in a disgusted tone as he recognized the call from his caller ID. "Yes Utsumi, what the hell do you want of me now, dammit? You seem to know when I put my feet up to rest a little bit for myself, old man. C'mon for the love of money, what the hell do you want from me already on this day? I'm rather busy and exhausted, and I don't have time to waste on any bullshit, or problems facing you on the construction site. You're the damn foreman of the site, so handle any problems that arise and leave me the hell alone will you."

"Hiromoai-san! You won't believe what we think we have just uncovered over here at the site sir. Machine Five, Three, Three uncovered something hidden in the mountains of Kai, and I think you should come out here and see what it is for yourself, sir."

"Utsumi! I don't have the fucking time or the patience to waste on this kind of bullshit, nor do I wish to drive all over Japan looking at worthless crap you have uncovered by one of our machines, old man. For Christ sake man! Have the damn machines dig whatever the hell it is up, and if it has any worth to it, bring it in with you over the weekend..."

Utsumi dared to interrupt his boss as the foreman exclaimed excitedly. "Hiromoai-san! What I believe we have uncovered out here is valuable beyond thought and belief, sir."

The excited words of the old foreman finally got the full attention of his youthful boss, as he placed his paper down on his desk covering over the Shi comic book, and then he stood with his radio phone locked in hand as he barked angrily in the handset. He knew this old worker for most of his life, and he was aware nothing ever got him excited, nothing ever interested the old man as he grumbled. "Utsumi! What the hell is it you think you might have uncovered at the site, dammit? And why the hell do you think it's so valuable you bring it up to my attention, and requesting my presence at the damn site? I never heard you so damn excited about anything, not even when I took you to the bar and we watched the strippers dancing the other week, old man. Okay Utsumi, you aroused my interest. Tell me what you think you found at the damn site?"

"Hiromoai-san! I can't believe it myself sir. I think we uncovered an ancient burial site of an honored Warrior buried who knows back when, sir. The completely intact crypt seems to be laden down with ancient armor and Katanas from what I can see from the mouth of the cave, sir. Hiromoai-san, I saw bones, bones and helmets and swords laid out respectfully sir. It looked like there were a few Samurai buried inside this crypt. According to our laws and beliefs that means there must be a real hot shot Warrior of great worth and respect buried within this tomb, sir. A find like this could mean riches beyond your wildest dreams, Boss. More than any mere amounts of damn iron ore buried in the hill can bring you, sir."

"For Christ sake, what about the other workers? What the hell are they doing, old fool?" Hiromoai asked nastily, allowing the first signs of excitement to creep into his tone.

"That's easy Hiromoai-san, I sent most of the unworthy workers home for the day, because it's starting to rain heavier, and tomorrow I'll start them working in a different section of the site, far away from this site so we can discover what's buried in this tomb in private, sir."

"Utsumi-san! That was good thinking on your part, old man. You done well, I'll be leaving in a few moments for the site. Order temporary lights strung out in the cave by the lazy electricians. I want to see everything by the time I arrive at the damn site. I should be there by, ummm..."

He looked at his Rolex watch, mentally figuring out how long it would take him to reach the Kai Mountains and construction site, as he continued with his words at the old foreman. "Utsumi! I should be arriving at the damn construction site within five or six hours at the most, depending on the traffic and rain. I'll bring out plenty of hot coffee and food with me, old man. Don't remove anything from the damn cave, and don't allow anyone else to either until I get out there old man, or it'll cost you your damn job, mister."

"Fine Boss, you got it, anything you say Hiromoai-san. No one will remove anything from the cave as long as I'm on the site, sir. This I promise you by my oath to you, Hiromoai-san." Utsumi offered as a smile slowly crossed his weather beaten lips.

"Utsumi-san! Handpick the workers you'll need to assist you on what I just ordered at the site. I don't want any word of our fucking discovery to leak out to the general public, until I'm able to remove whatever the hell I want from the damn cave first, old man."

"Right Boss, I done that before I sent the other workers home, Hiromoai-san. It's raining pretty heavy now at the site sir." Again, Utsumi looked to the sky as if seeking the approval from the gods, for his sending most of the workers home for the day and them losing pay.

He ignored the words from his foreman as he hung up and pressed the button on his intercom and ordered his secretary to cancel all his scheduled meetings for the next three days. He informed his secretary he was unexpectedly called away on an emergency situation at the Kai construction site, and he was leaving for the site to clear up the situation. Once he finished speaking with his secretary, he called downstairs and ordered his car made ready for a long trip.

The bored garage attendant wanted to know if his boss wanted his private driver to drive him out to the site, but he refused the offer stating he would drive to his destination himself. By the time he got down to the ground level of the building, his Mercedes was fueled up and waiting for him with the motor running. He jumped in the pure white vehicle, and headed for the highway driving through the heavy rain and light traffic.

The old and exhausted but excited foreman Utsumi, followed the orders from his boss to the tee, and called for three electricians to remain on the site and work in the now steady downpour. The electricians struggled to move a heavy portable generator on wheels up to the cave opening. Once it was there, the workers ran three runs of temporary lighting in the uncovered mouth of the cave, under Utsumi's stern direction of their work.

He and the few remaining laborers he ordered to stay on the site, removed the lose stones and earth from the opening of the cave, to make walking and working much easier. He could not wait to enter the underground chamber, and when he did he noticed the body of General Yoshio Kobayashi dressed in the full armor of that time. The antediluvian Kabuto helmet lay on the floor on its side, the fall bending one of the fearsome Fukigayeshi turn backs, and knocking a Kuwagata horn off the aged helmet. Obviously, it slid off the now skinless skull, many centuries ago. The body of this samurai was locked in a kneeling position of respect, forever keeping a vigil on a second body almost covered with a thick layer of dust and loose dirt that obviously fallen from the cave roof because of the construction work going on outside the ancient tomb.

Carefully, he worked his way deeper in the foreboding, dark opening. He was scared beyond words or actions he was a firm believer of the ancient gods who controlled the underworld of life for all Japanese people. He knew if someone went through so much trouble burying this warrior, there had to be a curse attached to it. Once in the cave, he blew the fine layer of dust from the samurai bones on the floor of the crypt. Here and there the glint of silver and gold could be seen.

Enforcing his beliefs this ancient samurai was one of great worth and respect, he saw the deadly katana blade lying on the warrior's shoulder. When he blew the dust from it he uncovered the skull of the horse and jumped back in fright from the sight, not knowing what to make of this discovery. In all his years, he never once heard of any famed warrior being buried with his trusted war steed accompanying him to the land of beyond and wonderment.

He reached out with a shaking hand and removed the well dated katana blade from the ancient body. He felt the heft of the once great blade as he blew the dust from it and the crumbling wood zutsu, the once gold inlaid tubular, lacquered scabbard. He tried to pull the blade free of the crumbling scabbard, but it would not budge for him no matter what he tried, and he did not want to use more pressure for fear of destroying its possible value. What he did not know was the blood of Wind held the blade tight to its wood prison.

He ordered the laborers to vacuum up the layer of the dust six inches deep in places from the cave floor. When they started working, breathing in the cave became impossible, so he moved to the mouth of the cave and kept his eyes glued to the laborers as they worked. To make certain they did not steal anything from his boss. He did not care if the dust was choking them or causing harm to their bodies that would show up years from now, as long as they continued to work.

By the fourth hour of work, most of the dust was removed from the bodies of the warriors and horse, and the floor surrounding the bodies. Everywhere he looked inside the cave, there were weapons of worth placed ceremoniously around the bodies of bones. What was so striking about the crypt of yore was the prone warrior who must have been forced to commit Suppuku, his severed head placed on his chest over what he believed would have been the gash in his belly. Where this warrior's head should have, there was a fan of highly decorative bamboo shaft arrows laid out as if they were a helmet of great respect for the dead samurai.

Utsumi was at a loss over what might have happened to this warrior of the past. But his fate did not concern him, not with the vast worth lying scattered about in the crypt, ready for his picking. He pocketed a number of kasazuri gold plates he forcibly removed from the armor of the samurai on the ground, knowing his boss would keep the rest of the treasure for himself.

At the start of the fifth hour of work, the disturbed dust began to settle down, and the air was becoming easier to breathe. The heavy rain returned to a light drizzle. He stood outside enjoying a Marlboro cigarette and some fresh air, when he noticed the glaring headlights of his boss' car charging down the dirt road leading to the site. He could not believe his foolish boss would drive such an expensive vehicle over such terrible roads at the break neck speeds he was traveling in. To disrespect such a fine machine was most insulting to the old foreman.

Hiromoai's car came to a sliding stop on the mud just before the field headquarters' trailer he jumped out of his mud covered car and looked around for the workers and foreman remaining on the construction site. He was dressed in a two thousand dollar silk suit and five hundred dollar leather shoes. He stomped through the mud and muck covering the site, without regard to his clothes or shoes as he headed for the work trailer. He flung open the door as if he was angry with it, and cursed when he discovered no one waiting inside the construction trailer. He searched the site outside, until he spotted Utsumi walking towards him through the mud and light rain.

He left the trailer in a blind rage, and intercepted his foreman midway between the cave and trailer and barked at the old man. "Utsumi, where the hell's this fucking cave you said you found on this site, dammit? It better be something and you're not just wasting my time over nothing or it's going to cost you your damn job, mister."

The old man turned and pointed towards the low ridge, ignoring the way his boss spoke to him. Even though he was a foreman, he was Japanese and he respected everyone, and he demanded the same in return from anyone who spoke with him.

"Okay Utsumi, out with it, what the hell did you find in the cave, old man?" The boss growled impatiently as he followed his foreman to the opening in the side of the mountain. "I'm certain by now you were all over the damn thing. You better not have removed anything from the cave without my permission, old man. Everything on this damn site belongs to my ass, mister."

"Hiromoai-san, I found too many things of our ancient past to describe before we reach the cave where you can see all the items we found, Boss. I'll tell you this much sir, this old bird buried inside the cave was a real wealthy shit. He was buried with a full set of armor, and had a second dumb shit killed, to watch over his ass for eternity I guess. Some hot shot Shogun from the past, must have really respected this old bird, to bury him so honorably in his own little rathole like this, sir." The old foreman spoke in the manner he was being spoken to.

They rushed up to the burial chamber in silence; a heavy mist was falling again, making travel hazardous. The racket from the generator was deafening, as Hiromoai saw the light filtering out of the opening, and increased his pace. His expensive shoes were making his travel treacherous. He was slipping and sliding all over on the rain soaked earth and lose stones.

The young owner of the construction company charged past the few electricians and filth covered laborers without speaking to them as he headed in the mouth of the cave without fear of what might be waiting inside. The second he entered the cavern, the workers inside rapidly filtered out in order to give their boss privacy to examine what they had uncovered inside the cave. He was stunned to his soul by what he saw waiting in the cave. There, lying in the center of the crypt was the body of a long dead obvious samurai decked out in his full battle armor.

The fleshless carcass of a horse rested near the warrior's right shoulder, lying on the floor. The horse had obviously been decorated in its own armor, for in the horse's neck area lay a long armor plated neck cover made of pure silver the wood saddle had long ago been eaten away by earth worms and the likes. Some fragments of the leather reins remained, and the silver bit lay on the separated lower jaw of the horse's head on the ground.

He knelt by the ancient samurai and studied the skinless skull resting inside the mighty battle helmet. He softly blew some dust from the skull then looked into the eyeless sockets staring at him so hauntingly, as if searching for this warrior's soul. Absentmindedly, he picked up a badly rusted iron throwing star, and it actually crumbled to rust in his hands. He then looked at Utsumi and barked as he continued to look in the sockets of the skull of this samurai.

"Utsumi! You did well sending the worthless workers home for the fucking day. That was wise, old man. I'll have a trailer get up here later today and I want everything you found in here loaded up in the damn thing. I don't want anything overlooked, keep a detailed log of the items and get it to me personally. Naw, fuck that shit, I'm going to stay on the site and supervise the gathering of weapons and armor myself, dammit. I can't trust any of you people to carry out your orders properly. Get over to the field office and place a call to Mieno. He's working at Site Twelve, and informed him I want the damn trailer brought to this site right now, old man."

Without hesitation or uttering a word of protest, Utsumi turned on his heels and rushed to the construction trailer they were using for a field office on the site. He placed his call to Mieno as ordered. Mieno was the driver servicing a second construction site seven miles from his site.

Hiromoai saw the six ceremonial arrows resting in the open quiver, and was surprised they were in good shape after all this time. The only thing missing from the bamboo shafts were the feathers that made the arrows ride the wind currents true to their victims. He picked up one of the tanto blades and it easily slid out of its scabbard. He did not notice the Agemaki, the six foot long ornamental bow that slid under the warrior's body long ago, obviously moved by earth tremors and blasting going on outside the underground chamber. The bow had lost its string and curve that made it an extremely threatening weapon of past times. He looked around for the swords of the warrior, and only saw the small wakizashi blade, the shorter stabbing blade. He pulled it free of the grasp of boney fingers, and tugged on the shorter tuska hilt, the gold tsuba still had some of its original shimmer to the ancient weapon.

After little pressure, the blade slid out of the sheath and looked almost new. He fingered the edge and received a slight gash on his finger for his trouble. Still holding the unsheathed short blade in his hand, he got up and went to the kneeling samurai. His helmet had long ago fallen off his skeletal head and landed on the floor by his knees, obviously slightly damaged by the fall to the ground. The threatening hoate brass face mask lay a few inches from the helmet on the ground. He could not understand why this warrior was ordered to kill himself, and yet his head was not removed. He lifted the bone hand protecting the swords lying across the haidate armor thigh guards. The swords were in perfect shape, old and obviously worth a small fortune. His mind screamed at him, 'where the hell's the honored warrior's striking sword?'

The young and concerned owner of the company returned to the bones of the warrior lying on the ground and checked out the prone body a second time; everywhere he looked he spotted another ancient weapon or piece of armor, but still no striking sword with this warrior. He thought it was strange as he checked out the rest of the eerie crypt further. There were traces of cloth he felt were once expensive kimonos, buried with this obvious highly respected warrior, and a number of wood thongs and clogs were also present inside the crypt. Everything a warrior might need for a future life shared with the gods, but still no katana blade to be found.

The old foreman strolled in the cave and announced Mieno was sending the trailer out from the other dig site, and it should be arriving on their site in a half an hour, or a little longer. He was driving the machine himself to make certain it arrived as soon as possible.

Hiromoai ignored his foreman's words as he continued searching the crypt for the missing long sword of the ancient warrior. Finally, he turned sharply and snapped angrily at the old man. "Dammit Utsumi I found one of the Kogas. (The razor sharp implements carried in the concealed pocket of the katana's scabbard). That means this one's sword was once inside the damn cave. Have you seen this one's long sword hanging around in here, dammit? I can't find the damn thing anywhere, and I can't believe these asses went through this much trouble burying these two birds, without leaving this one's killing sword with him." He pointed at the armor clad body of Wind not having the slightest idea the warrior's body he was looking at was that of a female warrior, the only one in all of Japan's ancient history.

He did not respond to his boss' question as he shifted his weight on his feet and stared at Hiromoai, trying to figure a way to inform him he took the sword while remaining out of the boss' doghouse, and keeping his job. An idea flashed in his mind and he meekly offered as his lips broke into an ugly sneering grin. "Yeah Boss, I got the damn thing alright sir. I tried to pull the blade out of the scabbard earlier, I'm afraid it's held tight, sir. I was going to bring it to the shop and have the carpenters cut the scabbard free of the blade. Then, I was going to clean it and present it to you as a gift when I got back to the office, sir." Utsumi smiled, but it was wasted on Hiromoai who glared back with a wary eye, easily seeing through the tall tale he spun.

He worked too long with construction men to be fooled by any of them. He knew they were nothing more than a pack of liars who would steal the gold fillings from his teeth, given half a chance. He put up his hand and wiggled his manicured fingers as he bitched. "For Christ sake Utsumi! Do I look like I have shit for fucking brains to you? Yeah, I was born at night, but it wasn't last night. Get the fucking sword and stop dicking me around. When the hell are you shits going to learn, I did everything you birds are trying to pull off against me, and there's no way in hell you people will stick it to me before I stick it to you jerks first. I have a mind to plant my foot up your ass. Give me the damn thing and keep your stories for your girlfriend or wife."

The old foreman let out his breath in a rush and then went outside the cave, and in a few seconds he returned carrying the katana sword he hid outside the cave earlier. He tried to save face a second time by offering to his boss, his words coming out almost as a plea this time. "Honestly Hiromoai-san, I swear on my worthless head, I was going to bring the sword to the carpenter's shop, and have the machinist there cut away the stuck scabbard of the sword. The blade won't budge an inch out of the scabbard no matter what I tried against it, sir."

He cocked his head to the side as he glared at his foreman, knowing this sword was earmarked for his mantle or for sale on the black market, once he had it cleaned and shining. Just from the tuska hilt and few decorations still remaining on the handle, he owner could easily tell the old blade was more than ancient. It had obviously had to have been made by one of Japan's greatest sword smiths of the past. He gave a few jerks on the handle, but the foreman was correct. The blade was stuck fast in the crumbling wood prison. He held the sword in his right hand and tapped his shoulder with the covered blade, as he barked a string of orders, enlisting the aid of one electrician as a laborer, to box the scattered armor and weapons in.

He sent a laborer to search the site to locate any boxes or wood to make protective crates to carry his find in. The foreman cut up sheets of plywood and made a few boxes to transport the ancient items of war in. By the time the tractor trailer arrived at the site, most of the find was packed in the hastily constructed wood boxes, ready for shipment to Tokyo. The driver was smart enough to take along three helpers who were pressed in duty, helping to make the remaining boxes needed for the rest of the ancient armor and load the other boxes.

The workers weren't careful with the brittle ancient items of war, and a few pieces broke as they were manhandled and crammed in the makeshift boxes for transportation. They worked into the middle of the night, making certain they picked up everything of worth from in the chamber. The bones of the horse and warriors were pulled apart from the armor and other treasures, and dumped unceremoniously in a heap, mixing animal and human bones together in the pile.

The young owner of the company was not interested in the days of glory of Japan's past or the worth and interest the ancient armor and weapons would be to Japan's museums and history. He was only interested in removing everything that meant any worth to him then covering over the chamber before any nosy archeologist came snooping around on the scene. All he needed was for them to get the government involved in his excavation, and close his project down for who knows how long. So the archeologists could remove the items he was removing in a fraction of time or care. He knew if the archeologists ever found out about the ancient crypt, they would claim all the items of worth for the government, and he would end up with nothing but long delays, and a load of back charges he would never get paid for from Japan's government.

These thoughts of archeologists and government officials crawling all over his site and getting in his workers way, were put out of his mind when the last of the items were packed and placed in the rear of the truck, and the doors closed and locked. He pulled the driver aside and ordered him to pull under the garage at Hatanaka Towers, and move the machine to the Tower's freight elevator. The workers were to load the boxes on it, and then he was ordered to take them to the twenty first floor and have the items loaded in the vault. He warned the driver in no uncertain terms not to allow anyone to know what his cargo was, or where it came from, or it would be his job. All the while he spoke to the driver he continuously tapped his shoulder with the sword used to kill Wind, which he kept out of the truck for himself. He intended to free the blade from the scabbard, even if he had to destroy the wood sheath to accomplish this feat.

He watched as the truck carefully pulled away from the construction site then turned to his remaining workers as the sun was preparing to climb over the mountains. This was the last sight Wind's eyes beheld before she gave up her life to her lord, for the good of Japan's future. He ordered the men to different sites in Japan. He wanted them separated so they could not divulge the secret of his discovery. No one left the site until the charges that would destroy the crypt from prying eyes forever were set off and the cave destroyed. In his mind, he placed prices on many of the items of armor he separated from the other items he planned to keep for himself.

He knew once the ancient items of war were sold or otherwise dispersed all over Japan and the rest of the world. Even if the government did find out about the ancient crypt and his discovery and missing items of wealth, all he would suffer was a number of stiff fines for his thief of the items. He could square that away easy enough on the books as a donation to officials, thus use any fine as a tax deduction. He told the workers they would receive an extra week's pay for this one day's work, providing each of them didn't breathe a word of what they discovered at the site.

Hiromoai ordered everyone from the site except for the foreman. To Utsumi he offered an extra hundred American dollars a week to his paycheck in cash, so taxes would not be taken out of it. He told the foreman he would be spending most of his time cleaning and polishing the items they found inside the crypt. The old man was pleased to be pulled out of the work force because lately his bones were constantly aching from the countless years of work in the construction field he suffered through. Even the weather was starting to affect his aging body. He was moving slower and never wanted to work on the construction sites any longer.

Once he was certain he successfully covered all his bases, he informed Utsumi he was going to catch up on his sleep using the field office. He ordered the foreman to keep all the workers showing up for their day's work away from the structure, so he could sleep. He turned and headed for the field office, using the sword as a walking stick to steady him on the sloppy mud. In his mind, he could not wait to see the steel of the blade, his heart racing with anticipation.

After he entered the construction office, he closed the door and then bolted the lock shut. Then he went to the small refrigerator and removed an ice cold Pepsi and took a good pull of the soda. Once his thirst was satisfied, he turned to the ancient sword he carried since given it by the old foreman. He laid the katana sword down on the slanted plan table as he finished off the soda and then he took a magnifying glass and scanned the entire length of the sword handle and scabbard, looking for a possible name or mark of the maker of the sword imprinted on it.

He discovered a number of small holes drilled in the scabbard where the gold and decorative inlays were once carved in the wood, but there was nothing left of them but embedded dust covering the once fine silk brocade of the hilt. Finding no name or mark of the maker of the owner, he hefted the weight of the sword in both hands. He made a few mock thrusts and chops at the air about him with the wood encrusted sword, as he grunted and threw his leg forward and up and down in the ancient ways of making war and cursed aloud as he grinned at himself, proud of the ancient sword he held in his hands.

To hold such a fine antique sword in his hands filled his body with the awesome feeling of uncontrolled power and pride, once possessed by the samurai of age-old Japan. It was a thrilling and consuming feeling, and made him want to view the steel of the blade more than bedding his young secretary. He placed the sword on the plan table, and rolled it over and tried to pull the blade free of the scabbard while allowing the sword to rest on the table, as he worked on it.

"Dammit to hell this piece of crap won't budge!" He suddenly roared as he lost his temper and turned red from the effort he was applying against the trapped sword. In angry passion, he took the sword in both hands and then tugged on the handle and scabbard as he lost his temper further with the ancient sword. Try as he might, he just could not budge the two parts free. Headstrong as he was, he tried a few more times to get the two ends apart, and he even banged the wood scabbard on the floor of the trailer, trying to dislodge the sword from its wood.

It was as if the katana blade and scabbard had minds of their own, nothing he tried succeeded against the two ends of the weapon. The young Hiromoai again took the two ends of the sword in each hand and he tried to actually rip the sword free of its wood prison. The force and hard twisting he applied against the fragile and wood scabbard was having dire effects on the ancient case. The strength of his hands crushed the fragile wood until it finally released its death grip on the sword, and it finally slid out of the wood cracked and crumbling tube.

With a roar of triumph over the sword and crumbling scabbard, he wildly waved the unsheathed and heavily marred steel shaft through the air above his head, making the sword whistle its cry of death long asleep, as he swung it through the air. He lowered the blade and then closely examined the rusty shaft of steel. This was the only weapon in the lot so badly cared for by its owner. There were flecks of wood from the scabbard still stuck to the sword blade, and he picked at it with his fingernails. As he picked at the wood fragments, he was stunned by the terrible condition of the ancient weapon of death. He carefully studied the stains marring the great blade, and suddenly realized they were not stains at all, but dried blood and the acid of the blood had long ago eaten its way into the fine, pure steel of the ancient sword.

Even though he did not care much about Japan's past that made the nation grand, he knew enough about it to know of the consuming respect the samurai showed for their blades and masters. He wondered what type of careless warrior would have dared treat his katana blade that was supposed to be his very life, with so little respect and honor, to dare sheath his deadly sword without first wiping the blade free of the blood of its dead victim.

He absentmindedly fingered the stains as he wondered whose blood it was marring the sword, and how it got there. He could not help but wonder if this warrior was killed in the heat of battle, or was he ordered to his death for some infraction he or his family committed against the Shogun of the time. He continued to examine the fine, once razor sharp edge of the deadly blade. There were numerous nicks, chips, and deep, marring scratches on the edge of the blade, testifying to the many battles the sword had witnessed in its long lifetime.

Shortly after the blade was freed of its wood sheath still in one piece but badly damaged, and after he had cleaned most of the stuck wood from the shaft of the sword, a small light slowly appeared unnoticed by him in the center of his office. He was too infatuated with working on the blade to pay much attention to the light's growing intensity.

Once the lethal sword was brought back to life by his constant picking and scratching at the remaining wood from the steel shaft of the blade, the light rapidly grew until an eerie and consuming luminescence filled the construction office. Now, it was noticed and he had no choice but to pay attention to what was going on about him. A slight, damp musty breeze developed, seemingly to come out of nowhere within the confines of the office, blowing paper, dust and cigarette ash swirling around the interior. The breeze continued to grow in its intensity until it almost worked itself into a wind of its own, trapped inside the field office.

The short hairs on the back of his neck stood on end as he stared disbelievingly at the light rapidly growing in its intensity and size, until the harsh glare completely filled the entire room of the construction office. The always believed to be fearless boss of Hatanaka Engineering's first instincts were to take off in a dead run and escape this growing glow and possible threat against him and his life. Allowing whatever it was coming out of the light to have his field office, and anything else it wanted to take while visiting the earth. His pulse increased until it was pounding loudly in his ears, and his breathing became labored as he stared out of fear and astonishment at the weird mist developing in the center of the glowing, bubbling and churning harsh light.

The floor beneath his feet shook and grumbled with the wood of the trailer groaning, and he felt an earthquake was hitting the site. Suddenly, screams, terrible screams of fighting and death, clashing samurai of long ago, filled the confines of the trailer. The glass from the trailer windows shattered violently, as if struck by unseen weapons. Loose items of light weight were picked up and tossed furiously in the air, and became dangerous missiles in flight.

The terrible loud and chilling screams of a history long past, grew louder and more intense as clashing swords and excited neighs from frightened horses long dead and yelling samurai, were heard from within the mist. For a moment,

Hiromoai could swear he could actually taste the choking dust clouds of long ago, and smell the sweat created by the wildly charging horses and fighting samurai. In his mind's eye, he could see the melee of fighting taking place as if it was happening where he stood. Ancient death was all about him and he was afraid to move a muscle, for fear of dying in the unseen Pandemonium suddenly raging about him.

Out of the center of the wild mayhem filling the office and his mind, the blinding and boiling light grew rapidly, coming to the intensity of a blinding super nova. He was forced to cover his eyes as he felt more than saw what was growing in the center of the light. The almost unbearable heat being emitted from the glow made him sweat and his skin crawl. A slight movement suddenly caught his eye as the terrified screams of the fighting past of Japan became deafening, overwhelming. From what he could see developing in the center of the light, he swore there was a form of a person, naked as the day it was born, trying to materialize. Then this apparition slowly came at him while taking no true form or shape. Male or female, it was impossible to tell.

He forced himself to remain standing in his office and steady, now more interested in what was trying to appear before him than scared of the growing apparition. Whatever the thing was, it refused or it could not take a solid form before his eyes. The formless shape remained a floating, churning mass of nothingness while trying to form some kind of shape, nothing more than a mere shadow of a human being was able to be seen in the cloud. At times, taking on a better shape and then disappearing back in the cloud as it tried to shape itself over.

The six eight foot florescent lights overhead suddenly sparked and then exploded with the force of miniature blasts, showering him in a rush of sparks and shattered glass, bathing him in sudden and all consuming darkness except for the growing light still trying to take shape before his eyes. Fear replaced what he thought was courage moments before, and it threatened to overwhelm him until he finally reacted in defense of himself. Taking the ancient katana sword in both hands to better defend him with against this approaching cloud of mist.

The young owner of the large construction company prepared mentally and physically for the fight of his life against a thought to be spirit coming after him from somewhere in the underworld of darkness and myth. Every muscle in his trembling body was prepared to fend off any hostile aggression, this oncoming spirit of the mist might display towards or against him. He felt this essence was sent against him to punish him by the gods for his indiscretion in the ancient crypt, and the terribly insulted soul of the warrior buried in the crypt.

Only when he realized the fearsome entity coming out of the mist was that of a naked and stunningly beautiful woman once it took a better form, did he lower his defenses against the shape taking true form. Maintaining the threatening stance of the samurai, he studied the image of the exquisite, youthful Japanese woman coming out of the blinding light and mist. But the form disappeared in the mass, and only the churning cloud continued to approach him. He was a long time student of self defense and was trained in the art of jujitsu and handling and defending himself with a katana, no matter how old or badly neglected it was. And in this case, he was prepared to fight against this wonderful shape trying to develop in a solid form before his eyes.

Summoning up his strength, he barked as nastily as he could at the boiling cloud, to show whatever was appearing before him, he was not in fear of its presence. "What the fuck is this shit, dammit?" He had to again cover his eyes because of the harsh glare made even brighter by the darkness of the trailer, and the spirit obviously reacting to his words of anger aimed at the bubbling mist. The glow seemed to grow more in intensity as he spoke to the boiling cloud.

A sweet, almost song like and extremely venerable voice came from within the churning mass of cloud, and spoke with the tongue of ancient Japanese. "Hai Kawasomeru-sama! It has been many years since the last time my mighty Liege Lord has graced me, by summoning me to stand before you as I have done many years ago upon the ancient battlefield of yesterday's glory of Japan. What is my Lord and Master's new bidding of this most undeserving vassal of time everlasting?" Again, the glow seemed to grow more intense in its now gentle radiance.

Scared to death and still trembling to the point of no control because of the sweetness of the spirit's voice, yet feeling the exceedingly dangerous and threatening power it possessed. The young Japanese businessman shook as he mumbled in modern day Japanese at the shape still struggling to take some kind of true form. "What the fuck are you? And where the hell did you come from? Are you an evil spirit sent to kill me dark spirit of the underworld?"

Wind's unconquerable spirit did not understand some of the Japanese words spoken by her believed to be lord and master, and she replied. "My Master of life and death over all things, everything from the universe comes of Nothingness. Nothingness is the nameless vast void of true beginning. Follow the nothingness of Yao, and you'll be like it, not needing anything, seeing and understanding the Root of everything. Lord Kawasomeru! You speak words of Japanese that this worthless Samurai are unfamiliar with to my worthless ears and mind. Please my great Lord and Master, have I been asleep for so long a time that the proud words of Japan have changed so? Please my Liege Lord! Speak of the old Japanese ways so this fool of total obedience, may better understand your commands and desires, Kawasomeru-sama."

The soft voice of this shadow was so soothing and calming that it completely erased the fear from his body, and he realized he would have to omit his colorful words and slang from his conversation, if he truly wanted to communicate with this person hiding in the churning mist. He drew in a breath to help calm down his nerves a little then he offered. "Spirit of the Mist, can you be seen? I mean can you make it possible for me to see your form clearly?" Despite his efforts to control his rampaging emotions and fears, his voice trembled and broke under the terrible strain he suffered, as sweat ran down his face and burned his eyes.

"Lord Kawasomeru, why do you act as if you're in fear of my being, your obedient and loyal servant of countless years past? I'm still your most trusted Warrior tested many times on the battlefields of the past of Japan. Did I not spend my entire life in blind obedience to you and your laws, my Lord?

Was it not by your words that bonded my soul, my spirit to this great Katana blade, and the land of the living for all eternity? I'll serve you now as I have served you in the past of Japan's birth with blind obedience and loyalty to all your demands of my person."

"Then I take it you're dead, Samurai of the old and forgotten times and ways?" Hiromoai snapped in flawless Japanese, again gaining more control over his once shaking body and words.

"Hai my wise Lord and Master, you above all others should know of this fact true. Was it not by your hand this worthless fool was sent to inhabit the Ukiyo, the Floating World of forever waiting and wanting? So peace might be returned to the lands of the realm. Were you not my honored kaishaku, my executioner my Lord? The teaching that leads to total Transformation is of Furyu Monji, not depending upon the written word. There's no teacher to ask, nor chance to be educated further by. There's nothing to teach, for I'm because of your demand, my Lord and Master of all times." Wind's unconquerable pride and strength, commanded her spirit's almost accusing words now. She never questioned who Hiromoai was. Whoever held the sword in their hands in her mind was her Lord Kawasomeru, and he demanded total obedience and respect.

He searched his mind to see if he could pull up anything written in the history books about an ancient samurai put to death in the name of peace for Japan's future. He cursed himself for not paying closer attention in his history class, because he could not recall any such warrior of the past and his, or in this case, her death. He marveled over the wonderful sweetness of the female samurai's calming voice, but still he never thought it could be connected to that of an ancient female warrior speaking to him from within the cloud of mist in the trailer.

He cocked his head to the side then stared at the bubbling mass in an effort to see if he could locate where the voice was originating from, within the boiling mass of nothing. Every once in a while he picked up the lovely form of the spirit speaking to him. His courage grew stronger and he repeated in a firmer tone this time. "Spirit of the Floating World, is it possible I may see your true form? Can you take a solid presence before me, Samurai whose name I am unaware of?"

She smiled at her young master as she offered. "Hai my Lord and Master, only if your great Katana blade is held within my most undeserving hands can I be seen by you. It's the only way for me to return to the world of the living, my honorable Lord and Master."

"Warrior! What is your name?" Hiromoai growled, growing impatient with the spirit.

"My Lord and Master, I have no true name to be known by the spirits who dwell within the living world. I live by the name you have bestowed upon my worthless body countless years past. WIND is the name you chose to address me by, my Liege Lord! I live now as then to serve you as I have lived in the past of countless years gone by, Master."

The young and confused Japanese businessman stared disbelieving at the still churning mass that seemed to becoming less violent by the moment. Then he placed the foreboding ancient blade back down on the plan table for the fourth time, and he moved slightly away from it as he ordered in a commanding tone to the spirit still hiding within the mist. "Samurai Wind! I give you back your killing sword, so that I may see what you truly look like. You'll not attack me with it will you Warrior of the past days off Japan's great history?"

For the first time since the female spirit appeared before him, a tone of anger edged her sweet voice, as she snapped angrily at her new master. "Upon a soul that's absolutely free of any and all thought and emotion, even the mighty and feared Kotora, the angry tiger finds no area in which to insert its fierce claws upon. Ieeeee... my wise Lord and Master of time everlasting! Am I now a member of the despised eta (the lowest of the low in ancient Japan) that I forgot my sacred keppan, my blood oath sworn to you many years ago on the edge of my sword of justice? Am I a filthy manure eating Ronin (a samurai with no master to display his loyalty and be commanded by him) that I'd dare dream of any such evil treachery displayed against your proud person, my true Master of light and darkness of life and death?

"If I ever contemplated such a terrible thought, the roaming Kami of the underworld (spirits and gods of ancient Japan) that float alongside me day and night, would rip my worthless body asunder, and they would have eaten of my foul innards and soul. So I could never be reborn Samurai to the lands of Japan again. I've been summoned from the Floating World by your command, to serve you as I have once served you upon the ancient battlefields in the past, my Lord. Most obediently, I remember and understand and honor my yoshi gi, my duty to all your desires and demands. I live toda chu, total loyalty to my Master of countless years past."

"Then it was I who commanded you, Samurai Wind?" He asked, trying to understand what was happening and who this spirit was, and why she chose to appear before him.

"Hai (yes) Lord! Wholly I returned to the great land of the living by your calling me to serve your every wish and demand in the living world. To vanquish all your sworn teki, (enemy) wherever they choose to exist upon this earth, my Lord. But you error my Lord, for I am General Wind. You once again summoned me from the Floating World of non-existence, by removing your great Sword of Justice from its sacred scabbard, as you have commanded me in the past. It was by the command you placed on my soul, and that of your Katana sword.

"Stop speaking, stop thinking, and there'll be nothing that you'll not understand. Return to the Root of understanding my Lord and Master, and you'll find the true Meaning of everything you desire for. Pursue the power of the Light, and you will lose its birthplace. There is no need to seek Truth, only to stop having views in your mind. All will be explained to you in the time allotted you by Karma, and by the gods who command truth and justice."

He stared in disbelief as her life force moved with lightening speed, and swiftly came out of the harsh glow and completely engulfed the sword lying on top of the filthy coffee stained slanted plan table. The blade instantly disappeared in the harsh glow surrounding the spirit, and the radiance grew more intense until he thought it was going to set fire to the field office.

Outside, his scared foreman ran wildly to the harsh glowing trailer, and banged ferociously on the door and screamed a warning, informing him he thought the field office was ablaze. The old man was scared to death when he saw the blinding luminescence from where he stood by the destroyed cave and ancient crypt, and rushed to the trailer to save his boss' life.

He did not bother to turn to the door as he ordered the foreman away from the building, after he assured him everything inside the structure was alright. He did not want to take his eyes off the spirit from the past for a second, and what it was doing with the killing sword controlled in her hands. Although he could not swear to it, but he felt more than witnessed the actions of the boiling mass. He felt the spirit living within the turmoil take a threatening stance against his foreman's voice. When Hiromoai called in concern to him over what was taking place in the trailer, and was concerned for his health and well being. Staring harder into the boiling mass of light and cloud, he was positive the spirit dwelling within the cloud, was taking a protective stance for him against the voice calling to him from outside the trailer.

He was glad he warned Utsumi away from the construction trailer, for fear of what this spirit might have done to his body with the ancient sword. If she reacted violently against the old man, if she felt he was a threat against who she was calling her lord and master.

From out of the golden and rapidly cooling glow, a lovely and naked woman's form appeared, and it promptly assumed substance and true form. The young woman held the katana blade like a true samurai of the past, and the ancient weapon somehow had returned to its original luster. It was shining like new in her hands, with all signs of rust and dried blood gone from the shaft of the blade. The keen razor sharp edge was back along with its threatening danger, and the sword seemed to vibrate with a life of its own, in the warrior's hands. He was correct and when he was able to clearly see the spirit, he was amazed it had her full attention aimed at the door to the trailer where the voice from outside was speaking at him. He relaxed when he noticed the spirit's form calm when he ordered the old man away from the door of the trailer.

This strange, beautiful woman stood around five foot seven inches and weighing a little over a hundred pounds and had lovely, round, full breasts with pointing nipples surrounded by a dark pool of captivating color. Her stunningly beautiful and pitch black silk like hair was cut short in the front, about even with the bottom of her ears. It was the ancient Kami no sagariba hair shape worn by most women of the ancient past of yukakasa, of having high value.

The back of her hair was waist length, and some fine hair hung remarkably across her breasts, and her hair moved like the breath of a night breeze softly about them, accenting her breasts perfectly while the rest of her hair hung freely down her slender back. The female spirit had no waist and long, slender, and obviously powerful legs. Her stomach was taught, strong with muscles rippling beneath her flawless skin to the rhythm of her breathing and movement. Her powerful body was obviously honed to such strength it informed him he was alive, only because this fearsome woman samurai, permitted him to continue to breathe life.

As she moved closer to his side, every muscle of her magnificent body showed, and moved perfectly with her body. She shifted her weight with all the grace and silence of a stalking kotora, the fearsome tiger ready to spring upon its unsuspecting prey, in a heartbeat to destroy it and enjoy her meal of it. Every movement of her body was well calculated, well thought out, with only one thought in her mind, to protect herself and her master's life from all harm.

As he intensely studied the outstanding form of this fiery temptress, he could not help but think she was a fine prize for any man to possess then shock set in. This samurai from the past was a female. In all his schooling years, he remembered only one slight reference to a lone woman warrior, and that came in one of the foolish Nolt plays. Comically painted actors danced on the stage like fools, trying to make everyone believe once in Japan's past, a noble woman samurai was alive. Fighting in the honored cloistered samurai caste this once supposed great woman warrior was one to be feared and respected, by the best of Japan's uncountable male samurai.

He always believed the story was a myth, a foolish story told on the stage to entertain the want to believe in fables and the fools who wanted something to believe in. It was a belief, a legend if you will, born to give the women of Japan something to believe in, to want to believe in. But yet here she stood in all her grandeur right before his eyes, naked as the day she was born and very threatening. He searched his mind and pulled up the only name he remembered from the foolish story, and offered in a calm tone to the spirit. "Ahhh... spirit of the past of Japan, your name is Tanzoka." He knew he mispronounced the name and he tried a second time. "Tanzara... errr... Tan something or other. What was your true name, spirit from the past times of Japan?"

Lowering the sword to a less threatening posture, and allowing her body to finally relax from the intrusion by the foreman from outside the trailer, she suddenly smiled reassuringly to her believed to be master as she nearly sang her words in explanation. "My great Lord and Master! Why would my worthless worldly given name be of any concern to your great Wa and mind? I remember the name that you had bestowed upon my foolish head at my Gembuku ceremony, my entering the malehood state. Wind is my name given to me by your breath, my Lord. It's the only name I'll respond to for life. I'm here to honor and serve you my guiding light. To protect your honor against all harm and against your teki, and to destroy your enemies no matter where they try and hide from my wrath and will." She saluted Hiromoai with the sword in the old way.

The owner of the construction company nodded at the respect being displayed by the beautiful young, but ancient woman warrior standing before him without the slightest concern over her nakedness. He stared at the beauty covered with flawless, golden skin standing without shame or fear. Her posture was absolutely perfect, her hands at rest by her side, the deadly katana blade held in her right hand, pointing towards the ground away from her lord's body. To display before him she was no threat to his life. She was standing proud, erect, defiant, and perfect.

The Japanese businessman understood he better stop asking so many confusing questions of the past that might cause this spirit of a woman warrior of Japan's ancient past to think he might not be this Kawasomeru fellow she thought he was. As he continued to stare at this lovely vision of sheer beauty and strength, standing proud yet defiantly before him, he went deep in thought. He tried to formulate his next question of the beautiful spirit.

She noticed the leering look from her new master even though her spirit had long ago forgotten what her Lord Kawasomeru truly looked like. Her curse did not link her spirit to his earthly form, but to that of his katana blade. Anyone who possessed the weapon commanded her being, and as far as she was concerned, anyone possessing the sword was her beloved Lord Kawasomeru.

She purred sweetly, almost sexily to her master. "Lord Kawasomeru! Is there any enemy you wish placated?" This question was posed because of her past summons by her master. Any time he needed someone vanquished silently and swiftly, he sent for her from the Floating world.

"General Wind! You'd destroy my without honor competitors and enemy, if I order? You would not hesitate to carry out my bidding, Samurai?" He asked with concern in a shaking voice.

"Kawasomeru-sama! I'll destroy all your teki no matter who they are, or where they prowl the night shadows, to hide their loathsome existence. As my blood oath taken before, professed. This undeserving Warrior is here to honor and serve your ever wish and desire and command, my Lord." She hissed defiantly as she raised her sword, and saluted him in the ancient way again.

He could not understand why this ancient warrior calling herself Wind, constantly referred to the sword as his. Did she lose her katana during battle, and the warlord lent her his katana to finish the war. For some reason the sword she held, belonged to the warlord of that time, this Lord Kawasomeru person. Shaking this question out of his mind he asked another question bothering him of this warrior. "Why did you die Samurai...err... General Wind?"

"My wise Lord and Master of everything of the earth, have the years not been kind to your great memory, my Liege Lord? Surely, you must recall the reason why this most unworthy Samurai was ordered by your breath to commit Suppuku before you?" She suddenly cocked her head to the side and then waited for her master to reply to her question.

"Suppuku!" Hiromoai exclaimed in a sort of excited voice, as he continued to stare at the face of the lovely spirit of the female samurai. He knew from his studies that Suppuku was usually reserved solely for the male samurai of the age. A female was never allowed inside the elite and closely guarded world of the samurai caste. A female was usually ordered to stab her throat and then she was allowed to bleed to death slowly and painfully. But he knew from finding the ancient crypt this female was for some unknown reason, allowed to kill herself in the ways of the male warriors, by slicing open her belly and then having a second lop off her head, so she would not suffer long. He wondered what powers this beautiful woman possessed and commanded, to allow her such a time protected honor as Suppuku. The male samurai caste would never give up their long guarded rights to any lowly female, without many problems and complaints.

He smiled as he thought he would have liked to have been a fly on the wall, when this female was allowed to commit Suppuku in the male manner, and observe the reaction from the stuffy and close knit samurai caste who witnessed the event. He could not wrap his mind around the fact he was speaking to a woman honored like the best male samurai of the time. He also could not believe he was standing inside the filthy trailer, speaking to a spirit of a samurai, obviously dead for almost as long as his name survived on the earth. There was something wrong with this confusing conversation, and he was going to find out what it was, even if it took him a week to hear this warrior's story from years past, when she live in the land of the living in Japan.

Collecting his thoughts for a few seconds, he spoke cautiously and calmly to the extremely dangerous spirit. In the most commanding tone he could possibly muster he was certain this long forgotten warlord, spoke to her in he replied. "Yes General Wind-san!" He added the 'san' to her name to add to the respect he was displaying for the female warrior, as he went on with his words. "It's true I understand why you were ordered to commit Suppuku by my command, Samurai General. But I want the privilege to relive the story of your past life, and your honorable death from your own lips, to refresh my old feeble mind, Warrior of the past. Indulge an old man by reliving the last days of your life, and what it was that caused me to sentence you to death, as I had obviously done against you, Wind-san." He let out his breath in a rush, and waited for her to begin her story of her past life for him.

"Hai my Lord and Master of light and darkness, you're mistaken by the words you spoke; for your far from being an old man who is addle of mind and body, my Liege Lord. I'll be pleased and honored to take you through a journey of my memory to the past of yore. So you might once again relive the endless days of our past glory and great wealth. My Lord, you cannot describe it, you cannot picture it within your mind, nor can you admire it, and you cannot feel it's awesome Karma. But it is your real self that has no hiding place from yourself. When the world has come to pass, it will not be of the world as we know it throughout our lowly existence, my Lord. One in all, all in one, if you understand and believe in this then there is no need to worry about your not being perfect, or will to be needed to fret over my Lord and Master. To be Zen, one must be pleased with his inner self and being, my Lord."

Patiently, she slowly began to explain why she was ordered to her death in the ancient past of Japan's great history. It was a past that would take much time to explain to her new Lord. So he could understand what happened to her, and why she was ordered to her death by her liege lord of the time. She began to carefully lay out her life in the past to Hiromoai.

CHAPTER TWO

The ancient Samurai Warrior now known as Wind knelt, and then she went in a comfortable sitting position of total obedience and respect for her new lord and master, by resting he full weight on her legs crossed at the ankles. She leaned back and placed her weight on her heels to lock them to the floor, displaying she was in no position to spring into treachery against him. Her hands resting flat on her knees, palms up in order to display she was unarmed and of no possible threat against his life. The dangerous female samurai allowed her muscles to relax as she seemed to go into a sort of trance. She sat naked, proud, respectful her head bowed forward in case her master decided to lop off her head for any displeasure he might feel she offended against him. She controlled her breathing while waiting for her master to speak further.

The extremely confused and stunned young owner of the construction company could not believe the beauty of this woman visiting him from the spirit world of beyond belief and wonder. It seemed like there was a constant light being emitting from her rock hard taut body, making her seem more god like and mysterious. The owner of the construction company could not take his eyes off her beautiful, upturned nipples crowning the firm lifting breasts that moved slightly with every breath the beautiful female warrior drew in for a minute.

Her tight stomach was drawn in and held, and her back was arched straight as it was, made her seem thinner and larger breasted. Her long, slender legs spread slightly at the knees, made it possible for him to view those hidden treasures he only dreamed about the woman of the geisha, or pillowing tea rooms of Japan's violent past possessed. She was hairless except for the hair on her head. She was absolutely stunning in every feature.

The wise but ancient female samurai understood the lustful leer she was observing being emitted from her lord and master's eyes, but it was not the first time that she had witnessed such interesting looks from the man who owned her being and soul. Many times in the past, especially when the powerful Lord Kawasomeru was getting older, he wanted to experience her captivating charms. She allowed him to use her body in any manner he pleased. She suddenly drew in her breath in anticipation of sexual requests from her lord. But when they did not come, instead it seemed her young lord and master was more interested in hearing about her past life.

She grew sad and let out her breath and then gradually began the story of her past life. She had to admit that she was terribly disappointed about his lack of interest in her sexually. It was a long time since she had last pillowed with any warrior in the living world. She carefully studied the face of the man sitting across from her for a few seconds, in her mind Lord Kawasomeru seemed much younger than she had remembered and she smiled. She was pleased with the face of who she thought to be her lord and master.

Hiromoai no longer saw the deadly blade held in her hand, and wondered how she was able to remain in solid form without being in constant contact with the sword. He stretched his neck and peered around her kneeling form. It was then he noticed the very tip of the great blade was slightly resting up against the side of her leg. Now he knew how she was able to remain in solid form before him. He figured as long as any part of the great blade touched her body anywhere, she would remain whole in the land of the living.

She was about to begin the endless explanation of her past life, when he suddenly interrupted her words and offered to her. "I see by your actions that you have to remain in constant contact with your sword, Wind-san. What happens to you if you break the contact with the great blade?"

"Two things can happen to my spirit, Kawasomeru-sama. If this worthless Warrior is involved in mortal combat with my Lord and Master's loathsome teki, and I happen to lose the sword in battle, the Kami (Gods) who consent to my return to the living world to answer your call, will allow me to remain in solid form until I carried out your order and destroyed your enemy, my Lord. Once I've been katsu, victorious on your behalf, I'll be taken back to the land of the Ukiyo World by the Kami command and honored rightly. But my Liege Lord, as you're aware, if you order me to break contact with the sword, this worthless soul shall be immediately sent back to the Floating World, to await your next summons to come to your aid again."

"Wind-san, if the Kami gods can call you back to the Floating World any time they deem fit. What happens to the sword once they command your spirit to return to their world of existence? Say, if I sent you on a mission and you lost the sword while doing battle for me?"

"I'll never be called back to Ukiyo World by any Kami until I have obediently returned and informed you that your request was carried out faithfully by my hand, Kawasomeru-sama. The Kami who control your curse are bound by their toda chu, their loyalty to your demand, to wait until this unworthy Warrior had successfully returned the great Katana sword to your honorable hand, before ordering me to return to the Floating World, my Lord." She nodded at her master while trying to figure where her lord was going with this conversation.

"Is there any way I can send you back to the land of the Ukiyo World, until I have further need of your services, Samurai?" He asked as he committed this latest bit of information to his memory. Even though he was getting used to having this spirit near him, he still didn't trust her for a second. How could he possibly trust anything that came back from the spirit world, or anywhere beyond life itself? Especially a spirit as dangerous as this female warrior seated before him seemed to be. He had no way of knowing for certain if this spirit was that of the White Heaven or the Red Hell. If this enchantress of the mist was from the Red Hell, she could turn on him as easily as she offers to kill his enemy in the economic world, and eat his soul.

"Yes mighty Lord and Master of time everlasting. There is a way you have the endowment to send me back to the Floating World, to await your next call of my service for my Lord. This is to give my Master the command and power to change your wonderful mind before employing my powers granted me by the spirits of truth and justice of the Floating World. As long as I'm in your occupancy, I'll remain in solid form, whole if you will my great Lord. Without need of my Katana sword's presence in my hand, to allow me the solid form of the living. But the instant you grow weary of my useless attendance before you, all my Lord and Master has to do is simply replace the sword back in the wood scabbard, and this worthless form of me shall be forced to return to the Floating World without hesitation or delay. The darkness offered by the scabbard will make my spirit need rest."

"General Wind-san, do you have any will to fight against returning of the Katana sword to its scabbard, or you going back to the Ukiyo World of wonderment and dreams?" The stunned young business owner asked, smiling over the awesome power he suddenly controlled in his hands, and the power he would maintain over this frightening spirit of the past, speaking so freely to him as if he was the god of the earth and she the servant.

"Huh, I never truly want to return to the very lonely world of the clouds and mist and non form of existence, my Lord.

But I have no will of my own to stop or change what has been ordained by the Kami and my Lord and Master's desires. My power to match the endowment of the Katana blade being returned to its scabbard is nothing to be measured in such terms, Kawasomeru-sama. It is the final word, the final action, the last truth that controls my true destiny and will, my Liege Lord to my remaining in the living world of smell and taste." (Sama means Lord)

"Wind-san, do I have to send for you only when I want someone dispatched? Or when I have a certain job for you to carry out for my desires? Or, can I just send for you to talk about times long ago past, or when I might have the desire to want to show you off, or impress someone I choose to join my company?" He was pressing, searching to find out how absolute his power over this extremely threatening spirit of the ancient times past, truly was.

"My Lord and Master, your control over my every thought and being is absolute, so total, so unending. My Master owns the capability to send for my form at any whim you deem fit to be destroyed or enjoyed in the living world. You control my destiny as is your right that has been ordained by the Kami who control all destinies. The perfect Samurai Warrior employs his mind as a mirror so it grasps nothing and refuses no knowledge. It receives but does not retain. This is why I'm capable of carrying out your every bidding obediently, without hesitation my Liege Lord. All you have to do is remove the Katana sword from the blade's wood scabbard, and I'll immediately be returned to the land of the living, only to serve you in any manner that you deem necessary or desire, my Master of life and death."

"How long can you remain in the living world, before you must be returned to the Floating World for whatever reason you have to return to that world is? Do you have to return to the Ukiyo at all, Wind-san?" He asked the female warrior.

"Alas my Lord, this Samurai is bound by my sacred duty to the countless Kami to return to the Ukiyo World after a certain stay and time enjoying the living world. If I try and remain on the earth past my time of allotment by the Kami who control such things, my worthless form shall cease to be a spirit in either world. My self will dry up and everything I once was will no longer exist but in memory. I'll die as a spirit and never again be able to be called back to the living world, even by your demand or your command, my Lord."

"Huh, you still didn't answer my question Wind-san! How long can you remain on the earth of the living, before you're bound to return to the world of the clouds and mist, Warrior of the past times?" He repeated, trying to get a direct answer from the crafty samurai from long ago. For some reason, he felt she was trying to dodge the answer he was seeking from her.

"I'm sorry for being the cause of upsetting you, my Lord. To answer your question, seven sticks of time, (One week). If in that time allotted I have not fulfilled your order, I must return to the Floating World for one stick of time (A day) to renew my strength. I'll be granted enough time to return your sword to you, before I must return to the Ukiyo. If I take too long to return the sword to your person, I'll become weak and endure terrible pain to hasten my speed to your presence. I'll not be allowed in the world of the clouds until you have your Katana in hand."

"General Wind-san, what happens if you have to return to the Floating World before you have carried out my demands? Is there any punishment you might suffer for your failure to carry out my orders before you were returned to the Floating World, Samurai?" He cocked his head to the side as he carefully studied her lovely face of this spirit while weighing her words, and committing the important information to his memory for future use.

"Hai my Lord and Master, I'll be severely punished by the god of my naming, for the full stick of time I must remain standing in the Floating World, before I'm allowed to return to the land of the living and carry out my orders by your command that I had failed to carry out when I was first ordered to do so by you my Master. This is the only time my spirit is capable of feeling sensation while dwelling within the land of the Ukiyo, my Lord. Any punishment of my spirit will be witnessed by all Kami present at the great meeting chamber on Mount Fuji, my Lord."

"Is this where the Floating World revolves around, Mount Fuji, Wind-san?"

"No Master, those foolish enough to seek the truth by means of intellect and learning, only find themselves walking further away from that truth. Not until your thoughts cease to exist their unending branching here and there, not until your mind abandoned all thoughts of seeking something, not until your mind is motionless as stone, will you be allowed to walk upon the true road to the Gate. Mount Fuji is only the opening we spirits use to travel from the living world to the world of the dead. There are others, but this worthless one has never used another thus far."

"Who is your naming god, Samurai?" He asked as he stared at this stunning beauty.

"Fujin-sama, the always angry God of Wind is my Kami namesake, my Lord." She announced proudly as she puffed up her chest and stared at her new master.

Hiromoai Hatanaka was surprised by the strength offered in her tone. It seemed like this female warrior was not afraid of anything she might have to face, even Fujin-sama who was well noted for his uncontrolled rage and anger and ill mannered temper. He drew in a breath and asked. "I have another question for you to answer for me, Wind-san."

"Yes my Lord and Master? If it is within my limited power to answer properly, this Warrior will be most pleased to answer my Master's wishes." She smiled at him while shifting her weight slightly and making her breasts sway barely in response of the movement by her.

"Wind-san!" He tried to sound like the commanding Shoguns and warlords he saw numerous times on TV, by barking out his questions or responses he had, or wanted and demanded from the warrior of the past seated before him.

"Yes my Lord?" She ignored the harsh tone in which he spoke to her.

"Wind-san! While you're visiting the living world as you put it in this solid form, are you able to taste, feel, and enjoy the experiences the world of the living has to offer to its own?"

"Please excuse the foolishness of this exhausted Warrior of past times, but experiences my Liege Lord? I fear I'm at a total loss as to what you mean by experiences, Lord Kawasomeru." She looked in the eyes of Hiromoai as if seeking the answer to her question in them.

"Yes, I can understand your minor confusion of my words I offer to you Wind-san. By experiences I mean are you able to feel, err... let's say, sexual pleasures? Can you taste food? Do you even require food while in the solid state of the living, Samurai? Do you eat anything while floating within the clouds? Feel the warmth of summer, and enjoy the cool breeze from Fuji Mountain in the fall. Are you able to smell the cherry blossoms in spring and feel the chill from the snow in the winter, Wind-san?"

"Hai my Lord, it is the same and at the same time it is not the same. It is different yet not different in the least, Kawasomeru-sama. Yes it is true that I am able to experience and enjoy these pleasures of the mind, heart, and soul, but only when I am in this solid state. When I soar among the clouds with the other Samurai, I see nothing and taste nothing, and have no want of anything. I have no need for any luxuries or needs of the body and soul. I think and dream of things of long ago past. Hai, I need food for fuel while I am in this solid form in the living world. The countless pleasures of the living world are reserved for the living. I am only living when I walk upon the honored face of the earth, and carry out your needs and demand, my Lord."

"And you're pleased with this situation as it exists I take it, Wind-san?"

"I have no particular thought as to this matter my Lord and Master of time. It is easier for me to reply by stating I am pleased in any manner I might serve my Lord."

"I can't believe this. If I were to tell another woman of this time how you offer to serve me, with blind, total obedience and absolute respect. She'd never talk to me again. She might even take to hating me over this awesome power I control over your fine spirit, Samurai." He grumbled as he shook his head, not certain if this development was as good as he first thought it was. All he needed was for word to get out that he was keeping a young beautiful Japanese woman for an absolute servant. He would be besieged by the local women always after him to hire more women, and place them in positions of power in his construction company.

"Please forgive this stupid Warrior, who has lived far too long within the past times, I don't understand what you are trying to say to me, my Lord?" She replied softly and then she stared at the young, good looking Japanese face of this master staring back at her with a slight smile on his lips. She was certain he was the owner of Kawasomeru's katana.

"Nothing Samurai, forget what I just uttered for the time being. I meant nothing by those foolish words of confusion, they were idle words spoken by an addle mind while trying to clear one's head of bewilderment. If I want you to understand what I'm saying I'll speak directly to you, and make certain you're following my every word clearly." He sat back on the broken office chair and then glared at the seated naked woman warrior as he drew in his breath.

Wind did not reply, instead she bowed polity when addressing her master.

"That's better you'll remember who is the Master here, Wind." He growled as he removed a cigar and lit it with his lighter. Once it was burning, he blew the smoke to the ceiling.

Her eyes grew as large as saucers as she stared in astonishment at the smoke bellowing to the vastness of the Floating World, displaying for the first time signs of fear as she bowed. The stare and sudden movement broke his daydream and drew his attention to her and he grumbled at her. "What's wrong with you now Wind-san? You're disrupting my Wa, my inner peace with this look that's suddenly on your face. I wish to enjoy my cigar while I think a little."

"This unworthy Warrior is sorry for disturbing your sacred Wa, my Lord. If it would please you, I will commit Suppuku to make amends for my disturbing of your inner peace. To upset your Wa was the furthest thing that roamed within the addle mind of this Warrior, Kawasomeru-sama." She did not move a muscle as she waited for her master's reply.

"It's an expectable emotion to upset my Wa. I wanted to know what was upsetting you, that's all." The young Japanese businessman replied to the ancient Samurai Warrior.

"My Lord and Master of time never cease to impress this worthless of his vassals. I cannot believe you are able to master the burning breath of the mighty dragon, and you are capable of keeping that unbelievable power locked within that small gold box trapped within your mighty hand. What powerful Kami do you own and command, my Lord? I see you using a weed to produce the wretched smelling breath of the mighty dragon, my Liege Lord. Is there no end to the all consuming powers that you have learned to master in your great lifetime, my Lord and Master?" She stared at the smoke still bellowing up to the ceiling.

"Ahhh... I see what's causing you this great concern, yes I see how in your eyes you must think I have mastered the dragon's breath, and locked it within this gold box. But what you see is no mystery at all, Samurai. You see, there are millions of Japanese who learned to master the dragon in the same manner as I have. Wind-san, there are many experiences that you have to witness in this new world, and I'd be most pleased to be your honorable teacher."

"There is no one other who dwells within the living world who would be better able to teach this so unworthy of students of this new life, my Liege Lord." She bowed greatly to Hiromoai.

"Fine, fine." He grumbled while taking another drag from his cigar. The odor nearly made her choke on the vile smoke. She wanted to cover her mouth with her hand, but was frightened she might insult her master further, if she balked at the smell emitting from this mystery. She never saw anyone smoke anything before in her life. She again bowed towards this young Japanese male of control over her being.

"Wind-san, a few moments ago you made mention you'd commit Suppuku for interrupting my Wa. If I ordered you to commit Suppuku, would that end your ability to return to the living world?" He rested his cigar in the astray while waiting her to reply.

"Iye, (No) my Master. Ieeee, it was a civilized offer I had merely extended to my powerful Liege Lord. This worthless spirit warrior can commit Suppuku every day of time, if you so deem it fit for me to display this great feat before your eyes."

"Would you feel the pain Suppuku usually brings to one's soul, if I ordered this of you, Samurai? I mean are you able to feel any pain while you're visiting the living world?"

"I'm afraid I'd feel every bit of the pain that goes with such an honor, my Liege Lord. As this Warrior has already informed her Master before, as long as I am allowed to walk on the living world, I am governed by the same sensations that rule the living. The same powerful laws that control nature and man control my destiny while I move upon the land of the living world. If I commit Suppuku, I'd merely die of the earth and return to the Floating World. I can only return to the living if you summon me again. I committed Suppuku once in my past lifetime, and I would not like to witness the terrible pain of the sacred act for a second time."

"But you'd do this if I so demand it of you?" He asked in awe of the respect he commanded.

"Instantly, without hesitation Kawasomeru-sama. I don't wish to endure the fearsome wrath of Fujin-sama, if I fail to obey my Master's every order or want of me. This Samurai is here only to serve, obey, and carry out your every request faithfully, my Liege Lord."

"Hmmmmm... Maybe one day I might want to witness Seppuku, Wind-san. I only read how this honorable act was carried out with blind obedience. Perhaps I'd wish to witness this great honor in person. We'll see, yes we'll see I believe. Commit this thought to memory Samurai. Remember what's in store for you if you ever fail me, Wind-san."

She was unable to hide the look of pain she remembered of her Suppuku when she was ordered to take her life by Lord Kawasomeru. It masked her beautiful eyes with hurt, and clouded her beautiful face momentarily. She stared at her new lord as he drew another breath from his fire stick, and waited for him to blow the dragon's breath from his body. The moment the smoke came from his chest, she carried out her master's request of explaining her past history. She was at a complete lost as to why her master was so interested in her past being, a past he should have been a major part of.

"Lord Kawasomeru, do you wish for me to begin my history by offering the day I was born to this earth? Or do you wish I begin my saga at a certain point in time of the past life, my Lord?" She asked sweetly as she stared at her new young lord.

"Iye! It'll not be necessary for you to go that far back in your past lifetime, Wind-san. However, I'd like to know of the year and month of your birth if you remember it, Samurai."

"Yes my Lord, I was born in the sixth month of the year of 1339 I believe. It has been so long that years mix with years until I am not certain when I was truly born to the earth, my Lord."

"That year will do just fine for my interest. I gave more thought to my request for you to tell me of your past times. I believe it'd take too long for you to begin to explain now. Tomorrow morning I'll leave this filthy mud hole for my living quarters in Tokyo. Once I'm home I'll again summon you from the spirit world, and you'll explain everything so I can understand your past life much better, Samurai. Do you mind if I return you to the Floating World until I return home, Wind-san? Then, you'll be allowed to visit me and we'll talk for many days."

She bowed politely to her new lord and master for a fourth time.

"What's the action I do to free you to the bond of this Katana Blade, Samurai?" He asked, hoping there was no way to free her of the curse placed on her head. But if there was, he wanted to know so he did not accidentally free her before he was done with her services.

"My Lord and Master, all you have to do is snap the great Katana sword in two and then pitch the two ends towards different directions of the winds. They must never again be allowed to touch, and I'll be forever forced to dwell within the loneliness of the Floating World, always waiting, always wanting to be allowed to serve your presence again in the living world, my Lord. But in the other hand, if ever the two ends once again touch, the broken sword will heal itself and again I'll be able to be called back from the Floating World by the Master of the sword."

"And if I only wanted to send you back to visit the Floating World for a short time, all I'll have to do is return your Katana sword to its sheath, for you to return to the Ukiyo land?"

"Hai my Lord, but this Warrior feels she must correct an error my Lord speaks of. You say the Katana is my sword, it is not my sword at all my Master."

He ignored her attempt to correct him and went on with his words to the ancient warrior. "Then forgive me of this dishonor I placed on your spirit, Samurai. I believe I'll return you to the land of nothing for a short period of time. I don't think it's wise for you to be so exposed in this building that has many eyes and ears stalking it. Good night Wind-san, until tomorrow when I'll again allow you to return to the land of the living, and we'll speak in private Samurai."

Again, she bowed gracefully as she watched her master walk behind her and retrieve the sword that was barely touching her leg, and then he walked over to the discarded wood scabbard. As he reached for the once crumbling wood tube, he was stunned to discover the fine inlay had returned, and the scabbard looked like it was just finished being made. The missing wood reappeared, and the cracks sealed as if repaired by some unseen force. Even the highly lacquered sheen had returned to the once nearly destroyed wood scabbard.

"What is this Wind-san?" He cried as he studied the once nearly destroyed scabbard.

"My Lord and Master, it is simple to explain for your knowledge. As long as I am allowed to visit the land of the living, all my honored weapons and equipment given me many years past by your hand, will return to the condition they were on the day of my death. It is part of the great gift you had bestowed upon my head on the day you ordered the linking of my soul to that of your mighty Katana sword my Lord." She bowed, removing her eyes from his stare.

There, again the samurai of yesteryear referred to the katana blade as his. This time he was not going to allow the statement to pass unchallenged. "There, that's another question I've been meaning to ask of you, Samurai. Why do you refer to this, what I believe is your sword, you say is mine. Explain this error as you stated if you don't mind."

He waved the blade in the air before him as he waited for her to explain further.

"That statement is as well easy for me to explain, my Lord and Master. On the day that you ordered me to report for my death, I was ordered to dress like a woman. That meant I was unable to carry my two swords in my Kimono you gave me as an honor for past victories over your hated enemy on the field of honor. Being I came to you without my Samurai guard in order for me to carry out Suppuku, I was forced to ask you to be my second, my kaishaku my executioner. That meant you had to use your great sword to dispatch my life, and free my soul from its worldly bonds. Upon my death, you cursed me and ordered my spirit to live forever within your mighty Katana, to give that blade my life-force, a force of its own if you will, my Lord." She drew in a breath as if these words were causing her distress then continued her explanation.

"That was why I was buried along with your great Katana sword resting by my side for time unending within my Kofun, my ancient tomb. Instead of my own Katana blade to protect myself with, for future battles I was engaged in. In the past times, on those occasions you summoned me from the Floating World to assist you in the unending wars against your hated and countless enemies. This unworthy Warrior was pleased to see you chose to carry my Katana blade in those many battles that plagued the Empire all the way into the sixteenth century. I cried for the vast numbers of honorable Samurai Warriors who passed through the Floating World, seeking their final destination and peace till the end of time.

"I was pleased beyond all thought and desire when the unending wars finally came to a conclusion, and the brave youth of Japan ended their dying in the mud of the Great Plains of justice. But in these last years of my floating within the clouds, I have witnessed a new breed of Samurai Warriors passing through the land of the Floating World. But their wounds are different than those suffered on the old battlefields of honor and respect, my Liege Lord. Some Samurai informed me they were killed in what they called drug wars, and battles for turf.

"I do not care very much for this new breed of Samurai Warriors. I find most of them without honor or respect. They seem to have their own interests and desires held within their heart more than those of their Lords. It is a terrible state when one's Samurai forget who they are living and dying for. I am afraid the Kami who open the doors to the Ukiyo World, are not very patient and kind with these new without honor Warriors. They are treated very harshly by the angry Kami, and sent to the lowly areas of the Floating World, to carry out those tasks no honorable Samurai Warrior are burdened with. I do not respect these new Warriors of Japan, my Lord."

"Huh, nor do I, they're warriors of little account I offer Wind-san. Yes you have answered my question to my satisfaction, Samurai. I'll return you to the Floating World for the time being." Without another word, he slid the sword home in the wood scabbard. Almost instantly, the blinding light returned to the interior of the trailer. It instantly engulfed the slender form of Wind and within seconds, her form faded until she was nothing more than a memory. All the while he stared at what was happening to Wind, he did not notice the new looking scabbard had once again returned to its ancient, decaying crumbling form.

Just as the last specks of the blinding light and her spirit disappeared from sight, he noticed the fine layer of dust in his hand and looked at the scabbard. He was shocked to see it in terrible shape. A thought struck him and he went for the handheld radios in the trailer. Finding one charged he pressed the button and growled. "Mieno, this is Hiromoai. Come in."

"Yes Hiromoai-san, this is Mieno." The driver just turned onto the highway leading to Tokyo.

"Mieno, there's been a change in your fucking orders. Instead of dropping my equipment off at the twenty first floor vault of the building, I want the crap delivered to my penthouse apartment. Once you delivered it there, you're to carefully unpack the items and leave them organized in my study for my pleasure. I have a new need for these damn items of the past we have discovered here. I'll send the old goat Utsumi out to assist you with this new order. I'll be leaving for my penthouse tomorrow morning, so this will give you enough time to do as I ordered."

"I'll carry out your orders as I received them Hiromoai-san."

He did not reply, instead he broke off the communication with his driver and bellowed for his foreman. "Utsumi! Utsumi, where the hell are you hiding at, dammit? Get your ass in here!"

Utsumi decided to hang around the outside of the trailer since seeing the blinding light flooding the interior of the beaten up work trailer. He did not like the lights he saw coming from the structure. He listened as his boss obviously spoke to something that must have emerged from the blinding light. He was afraid his boss was falling under the evil spell of a dishonored Kami who lived within th4e steel of the sword he gave him. With all the wonders they witnessed in the past few hours, his old beliefs reentered his mind in all their glory and strength.

The old foreman knew of the dreaded underworld, the floating world and the world of vast darkness and light. The White Heaven and the red hell, and finding these things of the ancient past, he was afraid one of those doors might have been somehow opened and it was going to swallow all of Japan in its gaping and evil jowls. He knew well of the evil Kami who wandered underneath the surface of Japan's earth, and he understood they were always trying to find evil ways to enter the living world, so they could take it over and eat the humans living on the face of the earth. His old beliefs told him once the humans were gone from the land of Japan, the earth would then belong to the underworld Kami, and the Heavens would be torn apart by eternal war and conflict and strife. The good of the universe would spill forth, and only the evil world would live on after that war was ended.

When the old man heard his boss screaming for him, his fears rose anew. He was certain the evil Kami he was speaking with moments ago had somehow taken over his mind and body. Now, his boss wanted to eat his soul so he could live on. Slowly, trembling, he replied with hesitation. "Yes Hiromoai-san. I'm here sir."

Hiromoai heard the weak reply from his foreman and barked angrily at the old man. "What the hell are you doing out there, dammit? Get your ass in here so we can speak old man. I have orders for you to carry out for me, old man." Without knowing it, he was using the same commanding voice on Utsumi he had used while addressing Wind moments before. The tone made Utsumi that much more afraid and uneasy of his young boss.

Slowly, the old man entered the trailer as if he was entering his grave. Seeing his boss in such disarray, he was positive an evil Kami had found a way to enter his soul. Nervously, he absentmindedly fingered his life bag given him by an old seer many years back when he was a young man. The Buddhist priest told him as long as he wore the protective bag, no evil would be able to enter his body through any of his orifices or the pores of his skin.

He saw the fear of God look on his foreman's face and laughed as he asked the old man. "What the hell's wrong with you, old fool? You look like I was the devil himself."

"Are you not Hiromoai-san?" Utsumi muttered because he was afraid to look at him.

"Don't be a horse's ass old man. I'm the same man you knew for many years, but far more wiser and much stronger now, and I possess a wonderful new power to make me a man to be feared by all. An awesome new power that's going to make me the most feared and powerful man in all of Japan. No, correct that old man, in the entire fucking world, old man. And you'll be one of the most important cogs of my machine that will take over the world. But you're going to have to work your ass off for this fucking position. I'm appointing you my assistant who'll reside in Hatanaka Towers with your entire family. Your duties will be to look after the condition of the ancient armor and weapons we found earlier today in that fucking cave. There'll be times when I'll have need of you, and you'll see wonderful things with your foul eyes. You'll be well paid for your silence and loyalty. What do you say are you ready to stop work in the field?"

Utsumi bowed to his boss, already forgetting much of his fears he suffered as he prepared to follow his boss' latest orders.

"Fine, get the jeep and get on your horse then. You have to get to the Tower before Mieno arrives with his cargo. I want the items we found laid out in my penthouse, cleaned spotlessly and waiting for me when I arrive. Then old fool, you'll see the wonders I speak of."

"I'll be leaving for the Tower immediately, Hiromoai-san?" The old man replied politely.

"You're already late for leaving for my apartment old man. Get going and tell no one of your orders, better yet old fool, speak to no one and get your ass to my apartment." He watched as the old man bowed and backed out of the trailer. Once he was gone, he gave into his body's need for sleep and turned in. He slept through the rest of the day and half the night, sleeping with Wind's sword resting right by his side. He did not want to be away from it for a minute, almost as if he had a need to be in contact with it, as she needed it for life. He planned to leave for home the next morning, but since he woke at two a.m., he decided to leave early. He felt Mieno and his crew, along with Utsumi and his family, should have everything ready and cleaned when he arrived in Tokyo earlier than expected. He almost called his secretary and ordered her to work, this was more for sexual pleasures than work, but he thought better of it. He wanted to handle Wind before exploring his secretary's lush willing body.

The night watchmen were the only people remaining on the site this early, and the only ones who knew he was leaving. The one guard opened the gate and smiled as he sped off the site.

JUNE 3rd, 1996. HATANAKA TOWERS, TOKYO JAPAN. 5:30 P.M.

Hiromoai pushed his car beyond endurance in his rush to reach his apartment and the wonderful treasures waiting there for his personal enjoyment. He parked the car at the mouth of the underground parking lot. Leaving it there for his attendant to take care of, and he jumped out and barely acknowledged the guard who called for his attendant to fetch his car. He rushed in the marble entrance of the lush building and headed right for the elevators. The service workers bowed politely to the owner of the building, but their politeness was ignored by the powerful man. Many of the stunned servants stared at him because of the terrible condition of his clothes. Mud was caked on his shoes and the bottoms of his expensive pants. Never, had any of the workers in Hatanaka Towers saw their boss with filth on his person.

He tapped his foot impatiently, ignoring the sideways glances he received from the workers as he waited for the elevator while he was tapping his shoulder with the ancient sword. He let out an exhausted sigh and entered the brass enclosure as if he was angry with the world. He stabbed the twenty seventh floor button as if his finger was a knife, and then he waited to be delivered to his living quarters. Less than a minute later, he exited the car.

The thick, expensive carpet absorbed his footsteps as the dried mud flaked off his once highly polished shoes, and left a trail of mud lying on the rug. He saw lights from under the apartment door and knew someone was working on his orders. He entered the door and saw Utsumi's wife carefully cleaning a piece of armor. She immediately stopped what she was doing and bowed politely at him. He insultingly nodded to her as he searched the room for her husband. Two of Utsumi's children were working on cleaning the many items removed from the crypt.

The young Japanese businessman had to hold his breath because of the lingering and overwhelming cloud of dust raised from the armor and weapons was threatening to choke him. Angrily, he barked out loudly. "Utsumi, where the hell are you, dammit?"

Losing face before his wife and children over the manner in which he chose to call out to him, the old man rushed out of the kitchen and bowed to his angry boss.

"What the hell's going on? You should've finished by now and the cleaning people should have had this dust cleaned. Call the cleaning people and have someone get here and air this place out. Make certain the one you choose is trustworthy and will keep everything she sees secret."

The old man nodded and did as told. Within moments, two women entered the apartment and began to clean the layer of dust from the items and floor. Hiromoai left the workers to their chores and went to the bathroom to relieve himself and take a shower. He returned and stomped in the study, wearing only a kimono that would have cost Utsumi a month's pay. On his feet was an expensive set of split toed slipper socks. He surveyed the massive room cluttered with countless pieces of ancient armor and weapons. Many broken or otherwise bent out of shape.

Utsumi's wife and children left the room the second Hiromoai came out from the bathroom.

He remained silent until the cleaning women finished. When they left, he clapped his hands together loudly, the sound echoed throughout the massive study, and startling Utsumi. Everything was as he pictured in his mind, with many pieces of the ancient armor and weapons raised from the floor by wicker baskets supporting their weight.

Everything was spotless, no dust seen anywhere. Some luster of the armor was brought back to life by Utsumi's children's hard work.

"Outstanding Utsumi! You have outdone yourself on this mission. Is everything here?"

"Hiromoai-san, everything we packed from the crypt is present and accounted for sir. I checked off each item personally from the list you written out when it was unpacked here, sir."

"When did Mieno finish with his extra work last night, Utsumi?"

"About two hours ago I guess Hiromoai-san." Utsumi reported with a grin and a slight nod.

"Fine, that's good, put him in for double pay for the entire day. Put yourself in for the same fucking pay, Utsumi. Errr... your children and wife should be well paid for their work, old man. Give your children one hundred and fifty American dollars for their outstanding work. Your wife should get at least two hundred dollars for her work as well, Utsumi."

"Hieeee Hiromoai-san, you offer my worthless family a king's ransom in pay and honor for their worthless toils they have committed on this night, it's too much for their poor efforts at cleaning the weapons and armor sir. Half that amount is more than enough for them." He bowed gracefully to his young construction boss.

"It's worth it old friend. I pay for what I want and I pay well for all who serve me and swear silence and allegiance to my projects. I trust your wife and children know why this must remain a secret." He waved his hand at the many items they smuggled out of the Kai pass crypt.

"Their silence is assured Hiromoai-san. They know if they breathe one word of what they have witnessed here today, they'll suffer my unfettered wrath." The old foreman gave him a wink of his eye to show they understood they did not see what they brought into the apartment.

"I hope it's as you stated to me old man. What about the damn cleaning women?"

"I took it on myself to reward each of the lowly whore's fifty American dollars for their work today, and their silence Hiromoai-san. They understand this well sir."

"Good, excellent, fine Utsumi. Excellent. All is as I hoped for." He grumbled as he walked slowly around the study inspecting the ancient items. Suddenly, he was sorry he was not more careful supervising the packing of the weapons and armor. Many items were bent or otherwise squashed. Some were so badly damaged by the rough handling and packing, they lost most of their worth. But this was not his concern, he wanted each item they removed from the ancient crypt laid out so he could see if each article would return to its original grandeur when he sent for the spirit of Wind. He checked his watch, it was past six p.m. and he was not only starving, but he was thoroughly exhausted and having a bit of trouble keeping his eyes open. Drawing in a breath he again barked at Utsumi. "Where the hell's my fucking cook at dammit?"

"Hiromoai-san, I thought it would be more prudent for me to send her away until your return to the apartment, sir. I didn't know if you wanted Lady Yoke to be around to see what you brought back from the work site with you, sir." The old man tried a smile but it did nothing to soften his boss' anger aimed at him.

"That wasn't the smartest thought you had today, you old fool you. What the hell am I to do about my damn supper now mister? I'm starving and besides, Lady Yoke could've assisted you and your family with cleaning up some of these damn items we found the other day, old man. I trust her as much as I do you. Maybe even more at that old man."

"Hiromoai-san, I ordered Yoke to her mother's home in Tokyo, sir. She can be back here in ten minutes if you need her. Although I wasn't certain you wanted her here, I didn't want her going home in case you wanted her to return. She lives too far to return today. I'll call her back?"

"Of course call her to return unless you intend to cook for my ass, fool."

He bowed as he rushed for the phone. Yoke was back at the apartment and cooking within twenty minutes. Utsumi couldn't take his eyes off the horde of treasures and silently cursed his boss for stealing them out from under him. After all, he was the one who found the items in the first place, so he felt he should be getting a larger proportion of the wonderful bounty. He turned and watched as Hiromoai ate as if there was nothing of great worth resting just a few feet away from where they all sat enjoying their morning meal.

Although she did not feel it was her right to ask, Yoke cautiously eyed many of the wonderful items suddenly cluttering the massive study, and she found herself wondered where he found them. But it was beyond her good manners to ask any questions of her boss. If he wanted her to know, he would choose to inform her at his leisure about them. She fluttered around the men as if a butterfly going from one bloom to another while sampling the fine nectar.

Hiromoai completely ignored all the attention the woman showered on the both of them. He was confident Yoke's tongue would be ripped from her mouth, before she would dare betray what she saw resting in his room today. But to ensure her silence, he asked her a question.

"Lady Yoke, I've been meaning to ask you, how is your honorable Mother getting along these days young lady? I know she was having some medical problems a while back. You barely speak of her any longer with me young lady. I trust she's enjoying good health lately."

Yoke did not know how to respond to his question. This was the first time he ever spoke to her as an equal. She bowed low, perfectly and held it as she replied. "Alas Hiromoai-san, my poor Mother's health is failing of late I'm afraid. I fear she's not long of this earth. She needs medical treatment and my poor Father is unable to pay for the aid she requires."

"Huh, why didn't you tell me she was in a poor state, foolish woman? I'll have my personal physician pay her a visit. He'll look after her and bring her back to good health, Lady Yoke. It might be a good idea for you to return home, so you can better look after your ailing Mother." He stuffed the cooked to perfection piece of chicken in his mouth and chewed noisily.

"Ieeeee... I'm afraid I'll be unable to pay your fine doctor for his service, Hiromoai-san."

"I don't remember telling you that you were responsible for his foul fees, Lady Yoke."

"What? You'll offer to pay for my Mother's health treatment, Hiromoai-san? Why sir?"

"Certainly, it's the least I can do for you. Just say I'm honoring you for your past years of loyal service to me." He announced as he smiled at his female helper.

Yoke did not know what to do, she was stunned by his offer, and did the only thing she could think of doing, and dropped to her knees and bowed in the old way. She bowed until the tip of her nose touched the polished floor, and held it until her boss chose to speak to her again.

"What's this all about young lady? Get up from the damn floor will you please foolish one. I'm no damn god to be bowed before, no Shogun, no fearsome warlord. I'm merely a friend trying to assist another friend's Mother in need."

"Hiromoai-san, you're truly a kind and caring Shogun in my heart, and I'll forever be in your honorable debt, sir. I owe you so much for the care of my beloved Mother, sir."

He knew he had just cemented his bond with the young and beautiful woman. This bond was going to afford him the gift of being able to call on her services day and night. He was thinking of trying to pillow Yoke lately. With his offer, he knew she would visit him in the middle of the night to repay him. He smiled at the young woman resting on her knees, and added. "I expect you to return to your Mother's home to look after her health for your honorable Father, woman."

Without knowing it, he began to act and speak much like the ancient Shoguns of Japan's past. Talking and acting much like the proud and powerful men of the past.

"Hiromoai-san, I'm deeply saddened to be forced to announce that my Mother's worthless home is just too small to support my presence, along with my Father and three brothers living there." Yoke cried embarrassingly, as she bowed so he could not see she was very near tears as she laid out her mother's health problems before him.

With each bow Yoke offered, he felt proud of his actions as he grumbled. "Well then my little wild flower, it seems we'll have to do something about that situation. Tell you what I'll do then young lady, there's a home I always use on Willow Street for special visitors when entertaining them for business purposes among other things. It has five large bedrooms and an equally large kitchen, along with a fine living and dining room. It has inside bathrooms and even a health spa to enjoy and the home is fully furnished. I haven't used this home in the past few months now. Besides, I have others that I can use for this purpose, young lady. Why don't you and your family move into this home for a little while until your mother's health has returned. You're more than free to remain there for the entire time you work for me is you care to."

"By the kind gods who work their wonderful magic to make this world spin properly within its place in the Heavens, I must have been blessed by all of them on this outstanding day. If my worthless ears can believe what my mind thinks its hearing. How can I possibly repay your generosity Hiromoai-san?" She cried as she bowed low for the third time before him.

He was certain if he removed himself from his kimono, he would find her mouth glued to his shaft in less than a heartbeat, with her Jade Gate spread waiting greedily for his pleasures. Suddenly, he felt this offer was going to work out better than beyond his wildest dreams. To have such a beautiful young woman to attend his every sexual need when his secretary was at home with her husband, could be a blessing. He smiled at her as he offered. "You're embarrassing me. Take what I offer in the manner it was offered, and think no more of it please. I want to help you, and to help you I'm pleased to help your family. Get up I'd like another glass of sake."

She rushed to the kitchen as if the devil was chasing after her soul, and refilled the cup. Before she entered the eating area, she pulled on the front of her kimono, allowing her breasts to nearly roll out the opening of the garment. She wanted to please the man offering to help her family. She carried the cup in the way she believed was of the old ways, and offered the first cup to him. She was instructed by her mother many times, who told her if she wanted to please a man, she should be attentive to the pleasure she could offer him. She lingered as she bent to serve him, the effect was not wasted as he smiled while taking in the breathtaking view she offered him.

The outstanding meal and warm sake completely refreshed his spirit, and soon his strength returned to his exhausted body. He was in his late thirties, and in fantastic shape. No fat on his body to speak of, this was because he ate only the best and most expensive of foods Japan had to offer her elite class. He worked out twice a week in his private gym, and visited it on occasion when he felt anxious or upset, or in the need to work off some trapped energy. He stood six foot three, with the jet black hair of most Japanese people. He had no chin whiskers, and possessed a fine, well shaped face, with broad shoulders and narrow waist, and a small rearend and powerful legs. He got his strong shape by working in the field for his father for seven years, before his father moved him to the office and out of the field.

Now, his father was all but retired from the company and he ran most of the office and responsibilities of the business on his own. He made all the major decisions for the entire company, only turning to his father whenever he was trapped in a no win predicament, or needed him to deal with another old Japanese businessman. The old of Japan did not enjoy dealing with the younger men who were running their father's business. His mother had died four years ago, and his two younger brothers were more interested in fast cars, and faster women than the family business. This attitude easily enabled him to cut them completely out of the business over the years, until he was the sole power for the company.

The young Hiromoai was known to be an extremely tough and ruthless person to deal with in matters pertaining to business. Any company dealing with him usually ended up agreeing with all of what he demanded of their companies. His company was large enough to demand respect and fear from many of the smaller construction companies, forced to work with his business. He was in the middle of the process of trying a hostile takeover of three smaller mining and construction companies. He was getting involved in the import and export business of late.

His other plans included trying to absorb a number of other of Japan's larger construction companies that would make Hatanaka and Sons Mining Corporation the largest construction company in all of Japan. He planned to move some of his operation across the ocean to the shores of the United States in the future, where he wanted to corner the mining world in the country of lust and greed. Letting out a disgusted sigh, he suddenly stretched his hands over his head and arched his aching back and yawned loudly.

Utsumi took this moment as the end of their meal and resting time. Seeing his opportunity to finally speak with his boss, the crafty old worker asked him in a beggar's voice. "Hiromoai-san, when we first spoke back at the work site, you offered to show me sights that were beyond my belief and understanding, sir. I'm extremely interested in witnessing these sights you spoke of, if it's at all possible for me to witness them that is, Hiromoai-san."

"Yes I did say that didn't I? And you had to remind me of my words, old man. Yes, yes as I stated, you'll be impressed over what I'm about to display for your consumption, impressed indeed old man. Yes maybe awed by the spectacle I'll unleash before your aged eyes. I can't believe it Utsumi, or the outstanding luck involved in finding this unbelievable treasure, and these weapons. That ancient crypt you uncovered at the site had more in it than you'll ever know, or even understand old man. Yes, perhaps you're right, I believe it's time I revisit Wind."

"Wind, Hiromoai-san?" He asked, slightly confused and even concerned over what his boss was speaking about, as both he and Hiromoai rose from the kitchen table, and then the pair of them headed for the great study of the massive apartment.

CHAPTER THREE

Without saying another word to his old foreman, Hiromoai got up from the table and dipped his fingers in the finger bowl then wiped them on the towel. He dropped it on the table like it meant nothing, and walked to his study which was bigger than Utsumi's first floor of his house.

Immediately, Yoke appeared from the hallway and cleared off the table. She cast a lingering glance at the man she suddenly loved more than life itself, as he walked with Utsumi.

"Wind?" Utsumi repeated cautiously, barely over a whisper in case his boss did not hear him before as he fell in line with him, and they both headed for the massive study.

"Yes old fool, Wind. Be patient Utsumi and you'll see the wonder of Wind. Right now she's dwelling within the

Floating world and will remain there until I summon her for an appearance before me and you and Yoke. Lady Yoke!" He bellowed out for the young woman to join them.

"Hai Hiromoai-san? From the Floating World sir?" Utsumi asked, really confused now.

When Yoke poked her head out of the kitchen to see what her boss wanted, he said. "You'll accompany me to the study I want you to see this wonderful gift I found as well, young lady. But what you see will have to go to the grave with you I'm afraid, Lady Yoke. You must swear this to me upon your sick Mother's honorable soul, young lady."

"I swear this on the life of my soon to be born son, Hiromoai-san." She replied as she came out of the kitchen and then she rushed to catch up with the two men heading for the study.

He smiled at her and with ill manners he asked her if she was pregnant.

"Ieeeee Hiromoai-san, there's no end to your sudden interest in my person and family, sir. But I'm sorry to offer, the wise Kami that control such things has not deemed it fit to grant me with the pleasure to be with my longed for child. Hiromoai-san, I fear I'll likely become an old ugly hag long before the first child grows within my wanting and waiting body."

"Lady Yoke, one thing you'll never have to worry about happening to you in your life is you'll never be an old ugly hag in this world or the next, young lady." He retorted as he turned from her and then he entered the study where the armor and weapons were stored.

She covered her mouth so she would not expose her teeth before him, as she giggled over the fine complement he just offered her. Now, more than ever she loved him.

They both followed him in the study through the decorated tri folding shoji doors, and took seats pointed at by their boss without uttering a word. His penthouse apartment was lavishly constructed in the same manner as the lifestyles of ancient Japan. In the study, there was a small sand garden raked to perfection, with three large rocks resting in the middle of the planter. They were given him by his father for jobs well done for the company. To the left of the garden was a four foot water fountain overflowing into a small pond equipped with coy gold fish and carp. The gently slapping water was most soothing to the Wa of the vast apartment, and those who enjoyed the room. A small bamboo stand was constructed in the corner of the room, and there were slight bird calls from unseen birds easily heard when you entered the study.

Massive columns of solid teak inlaid with brass and gold leaves reaching to the ceiling twelve feet above them. Great and intricate scenes of ancient wars painted between the arches of one wall of the study, each beautifully painted mural depicting a famous horse or foot battle of ancient Japan. His vast collection of fine antique weapons adorned the walls of the study here and there. All three people were walking in split toed socks. Once seated, he warned them of what they were about to witness on this night on wonderment.

"You'll soon see something beyond all belief, beyond all understanding and reason. I request you remain patient and silent until all is explained to you. For what you're about to see is in no way a threat to your person. Once I summon Wind from the beyond, you'll have to remain absolutely still and silent until and only if I order her back to her spirit world." He warned.

"The spirit world!" Lady Yoke cried, scared of what her boss might be speaking of.

"Will you be still for a moment, dammit? There's nothing to fear from the ancient Samurai called Wind I'll summon up on this night." He growled the strength of his tone made them settle down and be quiet. They stared with mouths agape as he made preparations to call Wind from the Ukiyo, the land of the dead. Neither Utsumi nor Yoke saw him act as he was acting now.

He moved the long flat box he carried since he returned to his apartment from the construction site, and left it resting in the study while he ate and spoke to them. He tossed the case on the lush sofa with little reverence, and snapped the both latches open. Next, he removed the ancient sword they found hidden in the aged crypt, from the silk wrapper he covered it with. When Utsumi saw the old katana blade, he again cursed his boss under his breath for taking it from him. Till the day he would die, he would always feel the sword and gift it contained, truly belonged to him.

Hiromoai held the sword out so they could see its age then spoke. "Utsumi, this sword has mystic powers linked to it beyond belief, and it'll make me the most powerful man in the world."

'So you told me robber of the old, hated thief of my good fortune and Karma'. Utsumi growled angrily in his mind as he stared at the ancient sword held in Hiromoai's hand.

"Yes, and I was able to accomplish what you were unable to consummate in the trailer at the construction site, old man. I was able to remove the ancient sword from its wood scabbard without much trouble mind you. Now behold what's not to be believed by normal thinking and eyes. For I'll now summon the Samurai Warrior from her resting place in the land of wonder and waiting." With that said, he swiftly yanked the sword out of the scabbard with one movement. At the exact moment the rusted shaft was removed from the sheath and breathed again, a light began to glow in the center of the study. Pockets of dust missed by the cleaning women were picked up and blown across the room, along with anything that weighed little.

The Lady Yoke had to cover her eyes so she would not scream out in terror of what she was witnessing taking place in the study. She feared the gates of hell had just been flung open against the world of the living, and the cursed Devil Kami was being summoned from the angry red depths of hell. Her body shook and she was scared to death, she held her mouth clamped tight and a finger resting in each ear, for fear an evil Kami might jump in her body through the openings, and then take her body for its foul needs and wants. She also crossed her legs because she heard horrible stories throughout her life about how a feared Devil Kami could enter a woman through her Jade Gate, if he saw his chance to enter her body in that fashion.

Hiromoai saw the reaction from Yoke and smiled as he turned to watch his spirit materialize from the boiling mist taking shape in his apartment. He decided to remind them before Wind's spirit appeared before them in solid form. "You must remember to remain still and quiet from this moment on. I don't want you scaring what is about to visit us on this glorious day."

This time, the appearance of the ancient female Samurai Warrior seemed a lot less violent. He did not realize his study had few items to be blown about in the strange breeze created by the spirit's appearance before them, as she quickly took solid form. The study was many times larger than the construction trailer, so the breeze was far less confined and violent. He stared at the boiling, churning cloud of confusion as it struggled to take shape. The moment the form of the woman began to appear, it instantly got the attention of all three people in the study.

Recognizing the shape was that of a female, Yoke was not so afraid of the apparition now. She gradually removed her hands from her ears, and stared intensely at the woman with captivated interest. Something about her presence was forcing her to relate to the female spirit already.

Hiromoai moved towards the boiling cloud of mist and laid the sword on the rug before the specter's feet as he bellowed in a deep, commanding voice at the spirit. "Samurai Wind-san, I order you to have audience with me! Take my Katana so it might give substance to your spirit!"

"Hai, my Lord, I shall do as ordered by my Master of life and death over all things related to the pulse of Japan, and her honorable people." The sweet, almost singing voice of the spirit replied from within the boiling mass, as her spirit instantly engulfed the great katana blade laid out before her feet. The light surrounded the sword, and it actually started to float softly in the glowing mass of turbulence. Almost at the same moment the cloud took possession of the sword, the woman's shape took on a more solid form. The golden radiance expanded until it completely filled the entire study. Only her form was seen through the glow and bubbling mist now. Many smells of the Floating World and past of Japan's great history also filled the room.

Lady Yoke leaned forward in her seat, surprised the woman was naked, stunning, and young.

The instant Wind was whole, she dropped down to her knees and pitched forward in a low bow and held it until Hiromoai responded to her presence. She inhaled deeply, filling her starving lungs with the sweetness of the air of the living, to help exorcise the staleness of the foul air inhabiting the Floating World. The golden glow withdrew from the study, leaving all three people in awe. While the radiance was engulfing the study and unseen by the others, the ancient armor and weapons scattered about the room, returned to their original luster and greatness.

Gone were all signs of any rust, dents and cracks. Gone also were the missing parts from her armor, along with any signs of age and wear. Returned was the missing gold and silver work, and any crumbling wood was anew, even the intricate paint work once decorating the ancient items of war and life was returned to the armor and weapons in all their glory. It was as if each article was just made and delivered from the maker to his apartment. The fine silk brocade was wrapped perfectly in place, held in position by the once missing gold crests of the handles of the countless weapons and armor, and everything was clean, and the lingering smell of dust and decay and age, was gone from all the weapons and armor.

"Kon banwa. Good evening. Yokoso oide kudasareta. Welcome to my house. Ikaga desu ka? How are you? I told you I was going to send for you once I returned to my home so we can speak at our leisure, Wind-san." The young Japanese businessman bowed politely towards the ancient female warrior he was calling Wind within the limits of good manners, as he asked her the first questions in a soft tone of voice and in excellent Japanese of the old world this time.

"Domo genki desu Kawasomeru-sama. Quite well, thank you my Lord." She returned the bow graciously and smiled good-naturedly over the kindness displayed by her master and owner.

"Do itashimashite. I assure you you're welcome here, Samurai of years past!" With the boring pleasantries over with, his tone quickly turned harsh and grumbled. "You're here by my request, by my command Wind-san, so you need not rely on the constant contact with the sword."

"Hai my Lord and Master." She replied as she allowed the magnificent sword to remain by her knees, as she straightened to a more comfortable position. Again, resting her hands flat on her knees, palms up, she did not even glance at the two strangers staring at her so purposefully. She remained with her eyes locked on the face of her master only. The strangers in the room meant absolutely nothing to the presence of the female warrior, and she totally ignored them.

"Wind-san, these people to my left are my closest friends. They are Utsumi-san and Lady Yoke, Wind-san. You may look upon them and acknowledge their presence with respect mind you, Warrior of past times." He warned as he glanced at the two other people in the room.

She turned to the strangers and smiled pleasantly as she bowed graciously, and then added affirmatively to them.

"Any honored Tomo (friend) of Kawasomeru-sama, has nothing to fear from my sword or my wrath. I am sworn by my sacred keppan, my blood oath given to protect my powerful warlord, and all who serve him loyally and honorably upon this earth."

"She's so beautiful Hiromoai-san." Lady Yoke cried as she returned the smile as pleasantly, no longer fearful of the woman of wonder who appeared from out of the cloud of mist moments ago. There was something about her presence that seemed to calm the fears of anyone near her spirit. What she was feeling was the power and sheer confidence the spirit emitted. The thing bothering her most was why this spirit was referring to her boss as Kawasomeru.

Utsumi did not speak instead he took time to allow his eyes to drink in the stunning beauty of this naked woman sitting before him so confidently. It was many years since he had the honor of seeing a firm, young naked woman's body, and he was making the most of the wonderful gift she was offering him. The astonishing vision of this beautiful woman was awakening emotions and feelings he thought long dead in his old and aching body, eaten away by the evil Kami.

"Wind-san!" Hiromoai suddenly growled in almost a threatening but commanding tone while trying to capture her attention once again.

She turned her attention from the strangers and returned it to Hiromoai. She bowed as she waited for her master's reason for calling her from the land of the dead and forever waiting.

He let out his breath as he began to speak. "Wind-san, when we last met I requested you take time to tell me of your past life, but then I interrupt your story. This is the reason I sent for you again. Before you begin, I'd like to see a small demonstration of your skills with the blade. Your aisu kuge (swordsmanship) I believe the correct word is. Will you indulge my interest?"

"Aisu kuge is the correct word for my skills with the sword, my Lord and Master. It is within your right to request me to display my fine skills with the deadly Katana blade, especially because it was by your orders I was so well trained with the weapon. My Lord, what is the demonstration this worthless Samurai can entertain my Master's pleasure with?"

"Utsumi-san, stand and assist Wind-san in this demonstration. Thank you."

Utsumi rose slowly, fearing for his life and what his boss had in mind as a demonstration for this witch of the clouds. He was scared to death his boss had found a way to forever seal his lips over what they found inside the ancient crypt. He was fighting his body, demanding it to remain standing erect. He ended up staring at Hiromoai with terror locked in his eyes.

Hiromoai saw the look of terror etched on his aged face and barked angrily at him. "You old fool, why the hell are you shaking so, there's nothing to be scared about. Stand there and don't move a muscle until you're finished with this damn demonstration old man." He then turned to Wind and grunted at her. "Wind-san, you see that old man standing before you?" Every word spoken in the room was of the ancient tongue of Japan's past.

"Hai my Lord! He is old and is shaking for unknown reasons to my presence, my Master."

"Fine, he's one of my most loyal and trusted employees. I don't wish any harm to befall his person. To allow this would displease me greatly Warrior. Do you understand what I ask?"

"Hai, wakarimasu my Lord and Master, I understand your warning Kawasomeru-sama, and it will be obeyed fully." She replied confidently as she gave a slight nod towards Hiromoai.

"That's very wise on your part Wind-san. If you're foolish enough to allow any harm to him in any manner I don't offer you permission for. I expect you to drop to your knees and commit Suppuku immediately Warrior, without my having to order you to do so. May the gods you dwell with, guide your fine skills for this demonstration, Wind-san." He then walked over to one of the many stands containing Wind's collection of ancient weapons, and he removed a small tanto blade, unsheathed it and tossed the naked blade before her knees. The blade was for her use if she harmed the old man with her display of swordsmanship for him.

Wind glanced down at the small blade and picked up the meaning and warning for it to be resting at her knees and she offered to the man commanding her sword, and life. "Hai my Lord and Master, may I ask what is the demonstration you desire to witness from this worthless of Samurai Warriors, my Liege Lord?" She asked proudly as she bowed again towards Hiromoai, while completely ignoring his warning threat of the small tanto blade.

"You'll soon see, Wind-san. Utsumi-san, take this and place it between your fingers, only allow a half inch of it to extend beyond them." He tossed a half used cigar to the old man.

"That's good." He said as he moved to the old man and stuffed a second cigar in his belt, and then he tucked a third piece of cigar in his breast pocket. Each cigar stuck out of the old man's clothes no more than a full inch in length. He then turned to Wind and barked angrily at her in a commanding tone. "Samurai, I wish to see you lop off the ends of my burning weeds as swiftly as you can. Please, you may begin anytime you're ready to start this demonstration, Warrior."

She bowed and offered to the young Japanese man commanding her to action. "My Master, many are afraid to empty their foolish minds of all confusion, lest they be plunged into the great void of meditation. They do not understand that their foolish mind is the greatest void to be conquered by their will and spirit. The ignorant abstain from phenomena but not thought the wise eschew of true thought, but not phenomena, my wise Master who understands all." She suddenly went silent for a brief moment and then placed her mind deep in thought and calmness. When she finished her slight meditation she rose and prepared for the assault against the three pieces of cigar. Before she began her attack, Lady Yoke moved slightly and instantly distracted Wind and Hiromoai at the same time. With anger in his tone, he snarled angrily at her.

"Lady Yoke! What the hell did I just tell you god dammit? I told you to be silent and still while I'm working with this Warrior from the past. Why have you decided to go against my wishes, young lady?" Hiromoai glared at the young woman while waiting her reply.

The stunned Lady Yoke bowed in the same manner as Wind had moments before as she offered. "My wise and honored employer, this beautiful woman is naked. Although she's a pleasure to view, I'm quite certain she might be a little more comfortable dressed in clothes."

"Hmmmm... I haven't given that problem any consideration, Lady Yoke. Wind-san, would you feel a little better about yourself if you were dressed in a Kimono? I have many extra Kimono I'm certain will fit you properly. If not, Lady Yoke will lend you one of hers, Samurai."

Although Wind was not the least bit embarrassed by her nakedness, the memory of the fine silk garment and how exquisite it felt against her bare skin, made her long for the gentle kiss of the kimono. Giving into her earthly memories and desires, she nodded yes to her master.

"Hiromoai-san, I'm certain your Kimonos will not fit this slender Warrior as well as mine would. I'd deem it a great honor and a pleasure if this fine woman Warrior would wear one of my Kimonos for this demonstration she'll soon offer us, Hiromoai-san."

He did not reply to the offer, he merely shrugged at Yoke.

The Lady Yoke was off like a shot, she had a room by the side of the kitchen to store her clothes used in her daily chores in the apartment and changed in this room. She opened the bamboo trunk and went fishing through the few kimonos until she found one that would enhance Wind's beauty. Carrying the folded kimono over her arm as if it was made from the finest porcelain, she entered the study and went over to the naked spirit. She dropped to her knees before Wind and offered her the kimono resting across her outstretched and delicate arms.

Wind was unable to hide the smile as she allowed her mind to remember the wonderful days of long ago. This woman reminded her of her sister, Estsuko. Especially because of the way she offered to assist her in her actions before her warlord. Carefully taking the kimono she handed her the sword, while she slid in the garment. For a few seconds, she enjoyed the extraordinary feeling of the silky fingers that felt as if they were massaging her body. Fond memories of her time long ago flooded her mind, but her thoughts were interrupted by Hiromoai who growled.

"That's enough of this crap, woman! I didn't call this ancient female Warrior from the Floating World here to be pampered and fussed over like she was a lowly geisha whore by you, Lady Yoke. Wind-san is here to offer a demonstration for me, for us. Wind-san! I'm waiting for this demonstration I demanded of you! Be aware my patience is wearing thin, Wind-san!"

"Hai my Lord and Master." She snapped as she waited for Yoke to return to the chair. Once there, Wind started to bounce the weight of the katana blade in her hands. Then, with the speed of an attacking kotora, she instantly lashed out in blind fury. A blur of silver slashed through the air as she roared a soul deep growl, and the cigar locked between Utsumi's fingers was cut at the very tip of them. She whirled around in one motion on the ball of her right foot, and swung her sword at the old man for a second time. With a loud whoosh sound, the ancient katana blade easily sliced through the tip of the cigar sticking out of Utsumi's pants. She then allowed the momentum of this thrust to carry her around in a complete circle, as she changed her grip on the sword while still in motion and for the third time, attack Utsumi's shaking body.

Utsumi felt the slight breeze on the side of his cheek created by the speed of the ancient sword as it sliced through the air on its way to the target. Without a sound, the sword cut in two the third cigar resting in his breast pocket.

The tip of her sword cut a quarter of an inch slice in the thin fabric of his shirt. The samurai ended up holding the sword out before her face aiming it up towards the Heavens. Her arms locked in position, elbows bent, one knee resting flat on the floor with her kimono spread out under the knee like a blossoming flower. Her other foot rested flat on the floor as well, so she could easily jump right back on the attack if ordered to do so by her excited lord and master. Her back arched taught towards her target and her muscles struggling to get control of them again. He beautiful face displayed the sheer confidence that her enemy was no longer a possible threat against her or her lord and master's life. If Utsumi was a true enemy against her master, his body would have been sliced in three separate pieces now.

Hiromoai was thoroughly impressed by her astonishing demonstration with her sword skills as he witnessed the three cigars cut in two. Utsumi slowly ran his hand over his breast pocket and felt the slightly torn fabric with his fingers, and then he checked his body for any damage. The sword only cut the thin fabric of his shirt, not his skin.

He saw Utsumi checking his chest and he growled at him. "Are you hurt old fool?"

"No, amazingly not Hiromoai-san, the sword only caught the fabric of my shirt, not my skin. I can't believe what I have just endured, sir. That had to be the most impressive display of swordsmanship I had ever witnessed in my entire life, sir. Is this creature from the past times as skilled with other weapons here, Hiromoai-san?"

"That's a good question, Utsumi-san. Wind-san! What other weapons can you handle so true as you have just handled your deadly sword, Warrior?" He decided he was going to use the san on Utsumi's name if he remembered so Wind would not think he did not respect him.

She dropped to her knees again and bowed. Her beautiful light blue kimono spread out so her bare knees rested flat on the floor. She drew extra strength from everything she touched with her skin, while visiting the living world as she replied to her believed to be lord and master. "Hai Kawasomeru-sama! I'm expert in Kajima, the skills of the bow. Hozo, spearmanship, with the throwing stars as well, Kyushin, close hand to hand combat. While I dwell within the Ukiyo World, I was taken under the protective wing of Hachiman, the fearsome Kami and King of Warfare, and he showed me many different ways of protecting my Lord and Master's life. In countless many ways I was never trained by my most honorable and well skilled Father.

"I'm always learning so that I might be the most powerful weapon protecting your life in the living world, Kawasomeru-sama. From the Ukiyo World, I am able to witness and learn new ways of waging war, and protecting one's ward. It is the only thing I am able to see and learn, from my endless stay in the Floating World. It is allowed so I might continue learning, my Lord."

"Ahhh... so, one day I'll have to witness these other admirable skills in your possession, Wind-san. Now you're with me here in the living world, are you in need of anything the living world has to offer its faithful children, Wind-san?"

"I hitouyo (require) life giving water to continue my story my Lord and Master, for I thirst so."

"Sunimasen, I'm sorry for not thinking of your personal needs, Wind-san. Lady Yoke, bring this female Samurai a flask of cold water, flavor it with some lemon for her pleasure."

Again, Yoke was up and off like a shot, she returned with a flask of cold water and offered it to the samurai. Wind took the glass and turned her back to Hiromoai while she drank. She was aware it was the height of bad manners to allow her lord to witness her drink or eat before him.

The concerned Lady Yoke moved nearer to his side and asked in a low, almost whispering voice. "Hiromoai-san why does this confused spirit from the past times, call you by a different name? Is her mind scrambled by the wonders of death and what lies beyond reality and belief? Does she not realize you're not the one she calls you, Hiromoai-san?"

He leaned closer to Yoke's ear as he whispered back at her. "Lady Yoke, it's because of the sword. Whoever possesses the blade in this Samurai's eyes is this warlord Kawasomeru. It's the only thing that controls this dangerous weapon I added to my arsenal against my enemy."

"Ieeeee... I understand Hiromoai-san. This master she keeps referring to is this warlord from her ancient past." She replied in awe of what this female spirit brought back to the real world.

"Exactly Lady Yoke, return to your seat and be still so that I might hear more of what this Warrior of the past has to say." He looked in the eyes of Yoke to rush her back to her seat.

The Lady Yoke bowed gracefully to Hiromoai and silently returned to her seat.

"Wind-san! Is there anything else you might require or want or need from the land of the living while you're visiting here by my command, Samurai?" The Japanese businessman asked the ancient warrior as he turned his attention back on her.

"No my considerate Kawasomeru-sama. This worthless Warrior thanks her Lord and Master for the kindness he has already displayed towards his most undeserving ward."

"Fine, fine. Now Wind-san, I'll wait to hear your story of the long past. Begin."

"Hai my Master." Wind drew in a deep breath, and then she began her long saga of years past. "For more years than I care to admit, my Lord and Master and the dog eating Wakatsuki were engaged in constant battles for power. It was like the ground of the earth gorged itself upon the young Samurai Warrior's blood that died for their honored Lord's interests on both sides." Wind made certain she omitted the Sama at the end of the enemy warlord's name, to keep her insult to his memory alive and well as she added. "Wakatsuki's repulsive invasions of your honorable province kept your realm in the constant state of war and anxiety and fear. It forced you to send numerous young Samurai Warriors to my honored Master Trainer Father for his special and skillful military training programs for these young Samurai to learn.

"When I came to the age of malehood, I was brought before you for the ceremony of Gembuku, when I would be allowed to enter the Samurai Caste under your banner and respect, my Liege Lord. On this day of honor and respect, I was challenged for being unclean of body, and you in your infinite wisdom, refrained from having me stripped naked as many foolish male Samurai suggested you do against my person. I was accused of have the ugly curse of filth, leprosy on and eating my body. Instead of having me stripped as a common whore, you ordered me to remove my chest armor so that I might be tattooed in order to display your ownership of my person. Upon seeing my breasts the gathered Samurai balked, and they loudly demanded my death. I was set upon by an angry Samurai who humiliated my person, by trying to shove his snake serpent, his ying in my mouth before the other Warriors. Again my wise Lord, you displayed your wisdom by allowing me to work out of this situation on my own accord."

"And you were able to accomplish this, Samurai?" He interrupted the female samurai.

"Hai my Lord and Master of life and death. I was able to do that quite well."

"Then tell me how you were able to accomplish this amazing feat, Wind-san?"

"As you must remember my Lord and Master of life and death, upon being attacked by the angry young Samurai, I swiftly removed my Wakizashi blade and sliced off the offending and ever growing appendage of the insulting Warrior. A second Samurai from the ranks came to my assistance, and he lopped the fouled mannered Samurai's head from his worthless shoulders. Then he knelt alongside me and offered to commit Suppuku before you. But you refused his honorable offer. I was ordered to remain kneeling throughout the never-ending length of the ceremony. For hours I spent pondering my worthless fate, silently praying to the Kami of the Floating World for permission to take my life. But the gods obviously had different ideas for my future fate, and never answered my countless prayers. Finally, after a short lifetime passed, you finally sent for my person. I was brought before your presence and that of your certain

Generals, and you angered them further by informing them that I was going to be allowed to enter the Samurai Caste under my proud Father's banner of the Claw.

"Although you did not take your wrath out on my deceitful head for my sin of deception committed against your person, my honorable Father paid dearly with his life. But once again you displayed great wisdom and patience that this worthless Samurai will never possess. You ordered my most honorable Father to poison my terribly ailing Mother to relieve her long time suffering. Once this was accomplished, you then ordered my father to remove the finger he once swore his sacred blood oath to your father on. My father then went to Mount Fuji and committed Suppuku under your direct order. He was seconded by General Yoshi Kobayshi-san.

"I was told by the loyal General that my father's body was slid in a vent that allowed the mountain Kami to breathe. My father's blood has forever mixed with the metals that shape the swords of your Warriors. That is why I believe we were unable to be bested on any battlefield your Samurai fought upon. How could we possibly lose a battle with my most honorable father's sacred blood guiding your Samurai's arms and blades true?" She took a breath.

Hiromoai allowed this because he was thinking about interrupting her, to find out who this General was. But he thought better of it because he was more interested in hearing her full story.

She began her story anew. "My Liege Lord, there's an old saying in the world of Zen, if you work on your mind with your mind, how can your mind possibly avoid mass confusion. Lord Wakatsuki was guilty of this terrible sin that he committed over and over again and again. For its well known that it is the mind that leads the mind astray. You must guard yourself against the mind. My Master, Lord Wakatsuki's foul Army created countless problems for one of your loyal provinces, and you ordered us Samurai out in the field of honor to hunt down this filth eater, and dispatch him along with his foul Army of god cursed mongrels. We chased the fools onto the ever expanding vast Kii plain to try and engage them in mass battle.

"Lord Wakatsuki's Army of filth was massed on one end of the great Kii plain, and our forces on the other. I took my horsemen into the narrow Kii pass in an effort to split the reinforcements Lord Wakatsuki expected to come to his aid, when the battle erupted in all its fury and death. Once I accomplished this great feat, I attacked the unsuspecting Lord Wakatsuki's flanks and my Warriors ripped into the very heart of his foul Army of fools. Thousands of honorable Warriors lost their lives from both sides. The attack lasted for more than three feathers of time, and when it was finally over, we successfully driven Lord Wakatsuki's lowly forces in total disarray into the distant mountains." Again, she paused to catch her breath. Explaining her life was making her anxious and short of breath. When she got her emotions under control, she began anew.

"Without our knowledge, the repulsive Lord Wakatsuki cried to the Shogun residing in the capital city of Kyoto, Shogun Takauji Ashikaga-sama. The foul one went so far as to dare threaten to attack the Kyoto Bakufu with his loathsome forces if the Shogun did not intervene, and act as a go between with the two warring warlords to draw the wars to a conclusion."

This time, Hiromoai decided to interrupt her by asking. The moment he spoke, she became silent and bowed to hear what her master wanted of her. "Wind-san! I fear I don't remember much about the Shogun of that time period. Dozo (Please) Wind-san, refresh my memory. When and how did the Shogun come to power at that time, Wind-san?"

"Hai my Lord, Shogun Takauji Ashikaga-sama, rose to power during the troubled time of the Hojo rule over Japan. The seat of power was the Kamakura Bakufu. The great wars between the invading Kublai Khan and his loathsome father ended, and the true Emperor of Japan the Go-Daigo was opposed and hated by the Hojo family of Regents. But the Hojo Regent Emperor could not be elevated to the true throne of Japan, because the crafty Go-Daigo Master thought to keep the Imperial Regalia within his possession. Infuriated by this evil theft, the Hojo Master was unable to be installed to rule over the lands of Japan.

"The Hojo ordered the countless attacks on the province of Kasagi intensified in an attempt to capture and kill Emperor Go-Daigo then he planned to seize the sacred Imperial Regalia. Upon hearing of these new attacks aimed at the true ruler of Japan, a great Warrior rose forth from the depths of the Samurai, to take up the fight for the true Emperor. Samurai Masashige Kusunoki-san, a well renowned fighter, prized for his unconquerable skills at warfare and his steadfast loyalty for the true Emperor of Japan. Samurai Kusunoki-san fought bravely from his impenetrable stronghold of Akasaka, in the province Kawachi situated in the foothills of Mount Kongo. Masashige-san gave safe refuge to the Emperor's son, Prince Morinaga-sama, and together they defended his encampment against the horde of Samurai sent out to destroy the Emperor from the Kamakura Bakufu under Hojo command.

"The loyalist as they came to be recognized fought honorably and bravely against such an overwhelming force of Kamakura troops. Short on Samurai and supplies to keep the few Warriors he had fighting, Samurai Kusunoki-san had only the terrain of the land to arrest the overrunning of his defenses. The inevitable happened sometime in the eleventh month of the 1331st year. The resistance by Kusunoki-san and his Warriors waned then collapsed. But instead of committing Suppuku as Samurai are taught from birth. The two Go-Daigo defenders chose to escape to Akasaka, to live long enough to continue their war against the Hojo's rule from there.

"Once the entrapped Emperor of Japan was informed he was without reinforcements coming from the feared and hated Sohei Monks from Mount Hiei. The task of protecting the displaced true Emperor of Japan was in doubt and would eventually collapse. Emperor Go-Daigo decided to flee from the Sohei Monk's protection and he tried to make his way to his son's side. On his way to join his defenders, Emperor Go-Daigo was finally captured by a wandering scouting party of Samurai sent out from the Kamakura Bakufu for just this purpose, and he was brought to the heavily defended Rokuhara Bakufu in Kyoto. After a speedy trail, the Emperor was found guilty of crimes committed against the realm, and he was exiled to the baron Island of Oki, to live out his remaining years in hardships too ugly to describe and endure, residing far away from any Army that might pick up the just cause for the true Emperor of Japan."

Hiromoai was thinking what this had to do with the Shogun of the time, and he was about to interrupt her story again. But he had to admit he was finding the history lesson of the great past extremely captivating, and he decided to allow her to continue unchecked, until she got to the part he asked her about at the beginning of her story for them.

"After escaping the Akasaka's trap, Samurai Kusunoki-san returned to his stronghold, and this time the wise Warrior placed more efforts in building an even stronger and much more easily defended encampment. The wise Warrior moved his camp even higher up the steep steps of the almost impenetrable south side of Mount Kongo. From this encampment, Samurai Kusunoki-san and his small Army inflicted devastating losses on the filthy enemy Army sent out from Hojo's Kamakura Bakufu to destroy him. The unexpected resistance offered from Samurai Kusunoki-san's so small a defending Army, surprised and completely confused the Five Regents of the Kamakura Bakufu, and the Hojo leaders were left with no other choice but to commit even more and more Samurai to reinforce the attacking Armies of the Hojo clan.

"In the troubled year of 1333, three mighty Samurai Armies were massed together, and were sent forth from the Kamakura Bakufu, to purge the rebel Imperial defenders from their mountain stronghold. The first Army led by the respected Warrior, Samurai Aso-san was ordered to attack the encampment at Kamiakasaka, along the Kawachi road. The second enemy Army being led by Samurai Osaragi-san, was ordered to attack Yoshino. Once these two Samurai Armies were successful in destroying resistance from these positions, they were to join with the third marching Army, creating one massive Kamakura Army scheduled to attack Samurai Kusunoki-san's stronghold at Chihaya on Mount Kongo. The Warriors were requested to take Kusunoki-san alive and bring him forth locked in chains to Kamakura for final judgment, then his execution.

"Samurai Kusunoki-san withstood every possible assault mounted against his fortification, and Warriors by the enemy Warriors sent to destroy them. The wise Kusunoki-san enjoyed great success in fighting off the powerful Army from Kamakura, using not only his Warrior's great skills to defend his stronghold, but the terrain of the mountain to hinder the enemy attacks against him. Huge, bone crushing boulders were tumbled down upon the unsuspecting attackers, caving in mountain passageways on them, and cutting the attackers off from the rest of their foul Army. Samurai Kusunoki-san dispatched the trapped enemy troops with great haste. He launched clouds of arrows, at times blocking out the sun as the arrows rained on the Samurai working their way up the rough terrain on the south side of the mountain.

"The highly intelligent Kusunoki-san's stronghold was never able to be breached by the enemy Warriors sent from Kamakura, and they were fought to a standstill. Honoring stories of Warrior Kusunoki-san's mighty stand mounted against such overwhelming forces spread throughout Japan, and many tales of his fierce defiance followed. Great honors were bestowed on him by even the enemy Warriors, spread across the eight Islands that make up Japan, and were instrumental in forcing the exiled Emperor, Go-Daigo's return to the mainland.

"In the fourth month of the 1333rd year, the true Emperor of Japan, Go-Daigo landed on Hoki province on the coast of the Japan Sea west of the capital city of Kyoto. The response from all who met the Emperor Go-Daigo's reappearance as he landed on the mainland deeply distressed the five Kamakura Hojo Regents. Seeing this as an added threat against their rule, the Kamakura Bakufu Commander sent out two more huge Armies to once and for all, destroy Emperor Go-Daigo and all his faithful followers before he was able to install his influence over them. The great General named, Takaie Nakoshi-san, a close and highly respected Hojo relative, was ordered to lead the Army from the east and General Takauji Ashikaga-sama..."

"Ahhh... finally, we get to the Shogun I was interested in, and what he had to do with the shaping of Japan's history, Wind-san." Hiromoai grumbled as he interrupted her story and shifted his weight and stared at the beauty possessed by the spirit Wind. He slid his tabis, split toed socks on the polished wood floor as he listened to her narration of the past of Japan. Of all he knew about Shogun Ashikaga, he never knew he was once an enemy to the true Emperor of Japan. He was led to believe General Takauji Ashikaga was one of the staunchest supporters of Emperor Go-Daigo's rule.

CHAPTER FOUR

Wind bowed towards Hiromoai and he replied with a flick of his hand for her to continue with her story. Once again, she drew in her breath then she went on.

"On his way to attack Hoki, the General from the Karakura Bakufu, Samurai Takaie Nakoshi-san was felled upon by a more superior Army being led by Samurai Norimura Akamatsu-san, fiercely loyal to the Emperor Go-Daigo. The enemy General was killed in the savage battle that took place along the road. The remaining forces of Nakoshi-san's mighty Army left the fighting in total disarray, and they returned to Kyoto where they joined forces with the second Army that was being commanded by General Takauji Ashikaga-sama, who found himself in command of all Kamakura forces in western Japan because of this situation.

"Being a great and wise General in his own right, Ashikaga-sama realized the opportunity of his to command, if he so chose to follow his destiny carved out by the Kami who command such fate. General Ashikaga-sama was aware with his family's royal lineage standing behind him, he, and he alone would be able to demand his right to become the ruling Shogun of all Japan. Ashikaga-sama was certain the title would be bestowed upon his head from the captive and grateful Emperor, if the forces of Samurai under his command were used properly.

"General Ashikaga-sama knew his future in Japan rested solely upon the shoulders of Emperor Go-Daigo, and with the weakened Hojo Regents in soft command of the northeast of Japan. Ashikaga-sama was further aware Samurai Kusunoki-san's once mighty Army was demonstrating the weaknesses of the powerful Hojo Armies for Japan to witness. So General Ashikaga-sama quickly seized upon the moment, and he changed alliances from the Hojo Rule. Now, he supported the true Emperor of Japan.

"General Ashikaga-sama turned his massive Army of Samurai from the pursuit of Emperor Go-Daigo and his loyal Warriors, and he attacked the Army defending the Kamakura Bakufu headquarters stationed at the Rokuhara Bakufu at Kyoto. The wise General Ashikaga-sama's huge forces easily overwhelmed the exhausted and depleted Rokuhara defenders, and all resistance to his devastating attacks collapsed quickly, allowing Ashikaga-sama's forces to capture the city in the name of the rightful Emperor of Japan. Emperor Go-Daigo, still retaining the Imperial Jewels, returned to his rightful thrown. But not before he allowed the Emperor supporting the Hojo Regents to live out the rest of his life in peace."

She began to rush her words now in fear of boring her lord with her unending story of the past. "When the news of the collapse of the Kamakura Bakufu at Rokuhara reached the Imperial defenders led by Samurai Kusunoki-san at Chihaya. The siege ended with many Hojo Samurai going over to the Imperial defenders there. This allowed Warrior Kusunoki-san's rapidly expanding defending forces to descend from the mountain stronghold, and go on the offensive against the Hojo Warriors. With the Hojo strengths lying only in eastern Japan, its demise were now written on the clouds that hung heavy over the Kamakura capital Bakufu.

"In the sixth month of the 1333rd year, the once mighty Kamakura Bakufu fell under the ferocious attack by an Imperial Army being led by Samurai Yoshisada Nitta-san. This leader organized other leaderless rebel clans and roaming Aamurai around the Kozuke provinces, in search of true direction. Together, they descended on the weakened Kamakura Bakufu. Nitta-san used the military tactics of splitting his army in three separate attacking forces, and the Warriors fought through the narrow passageways that afforded Kamakura its natural defenses.

"It was believed the forces of Samurai Nitta-san enjoyed the divine intervention offered by the Sun Goddess Kami, Amaterasu. It was said Samurai Yoshisada-san offered his blood soaked sword to the Sun Goddess hovering above him in the sky watching the war unfold. She took the great Katana blade with all the reverence offered and in return, Goddess Amaterasu used her mystical powers and she rolled back the waters of the Ocean, thus affording Samurai

Yoshisada-san and his Army a dry coastal route to approach and attack the city.

"From this route, the wise Yoshisada-san chose to attacked the Bakufu that made up the capital of Kamakura from the least defended position. After nine days of savage fighting through tunnels carved out by the tumbling sea, the remaining Hojo defenders numbering less than a hundred strong, along with their deposed Hojo leader retreated to the Buddhist temple to make their last stand. Cut off from reinforcements and in desperate need of supplies, and seeing their situation hopeless, the last Warriors of the Hojo Regents committed suicide, while the Kamakura Bakufu burned around them. The collapse of Kamakura marked the end of the Hojo rule, and brought Kyoto back in focus. Emperor Go-Daigo was restored to his rightful seat of power over Japan as Emperor."

"Wind-san, this is all fine, well, and good. But you still haven't gone into how Shogun Ashikaga-sama rose to power in ancient Japan. I'm waiting for this explanation and I'm becoming extremely upset because you obviously chose to dance around this part of your story for so long. How can an enemy to the thrown become one of the most powerful Shoguns to ever exist in Japan? Explain this in a hurry to me or risk my wrath, Samurai."

"Hai my Liege Lord, forgive my stupidity." She bowed correctly then straightened and went on. "In the early Muromachi period, as Shogun Ashikaga-sama's time of rule came to be known, began in the year of 1333, came the return of rule to Kyoto after the collapse of Kamakura, and the installation of Go-Daigo as the supreme ruler of Japan. Emperor Go-Daigo's return to power was far from what the

Emperor expected. Just as Hojo Regents before him, his administration was being plagued by upset Samurai making demands for land rewards for serving him, and in returning him to the seat of power of Japan. Many Samurai received no bounty. Of all the Samurai, none had more to be rewarded for, and none disappointed as Takauji Ashikaga-sama.

"The powerful General Ashikaga-sama was the direct descendent of the fearsome and extremely well respected and powerful Samurai, Yushitomo Minamoto, which assured his pure blood line to the ancient ancestors of Japan. This fact alone entitled him to lay sole claim to the position of Shogun of Japan. In reading the unrest building against him, Emperor Go-Daigo removed the General from the capital by ordering him to mass a new Samurai Army and recapture the all but abandoned Kamakura Bakufu, recently claimed by one of the surviving sons of the soundly defeated Hojo leader.

"Governed by his blood oath to the seated Emperor, the powerful General Ashikaga-sama carried out his orders without hesitation or delay, and in a short time he vanquished the rebel son of Hojo and then made Kamakura his Bakufu. Lord Ashikaga took command of the headquarters and word reaching Emperor Go-Daigo that the General was suddenly acting suspiciously towards his rule. Emperor Go-Daigo chose to paid little attention to this growing problem and warning. He was exhausted from the endless years of conquest and he was more than satisfied to have the troublesome General Ashikaga-sama well out of the capital city. Emperor Go-Daigo never suspected Ashikaga-sama would dare to raise an Army against his rule.

"But, during the second month of the 1336th year, it was reported to the Emperor that General Ashikaga-sama was marching a large Army of countless Samurai against Kyoto with one thought in mind, to place Lord Takauji Ashikaga in the position of Shogun of Japan.

"Lord Ashikaga was an exceptionally clever and most cunning General though, and he instantly seized upon the rivalries existing between the warring Monks of Miidera, and the loyal supporters of the Emperor Go-Daigo, the fearsome Sohei Monks of Mount Hiei. General Ashikaga-sama quickly allied himself with the fierce fighting Miidera Monks who were in the midst of carrying out another one of their long standing squabble against the Sohei Monks. But Lord Ashikaga underestimated the Miidera Monks long lasting hatred held against the feared Sohei Monks, and they refused to join his Army.

"General Ashikaga-sama's march his Samurai Army on Kyoto was beleaguered by countless attacks by these Warrior Monks, and his once powerful Army was soon so depleted that they were easily defeated. The exhausted Ashikaga-sama's once massive Army was driven out of the capital, and his surviving forces were pursued by Emperor Go-Daigo's forces into the narrow straits separating Honshu from Kyushu provinces, where General Ashikaga-sama was forced to cross the southernmost Island for his survival.

"From here, General Ashikaga-sama raised new suspicions against Emperor Go-Daigo, and he was successful in uniting these misgivings with the complaints of the Kyushu Samurai who received no pay for their loyal services to Emperor Go-Daigo. A number of extremely angry and upset clan members were talked into supporting Ashikaga-sama, and his Army soon grew to countless thousands of Warriors. His first action took place at Tadara Beach, where his forces destroyed Emperor Go-Daigo's trailing Samurai Army. By the sixth month of the 1336th year, Lord Ashikaga felt his Army had grown strong enough in numbers needed to offer him success in challenging Emperor Go-Daigo Armies, defending the capital of Kyoto.

"Lord Ashikaga began his long waited assault on the capital city of Kyoto with a unified land and sea attack aimed against the city. The vastness of his opening assault caused mass panic and confusion within the Imperial Court, and a fearful Emperor Go-Daigo ordered a last stand to be taken on the shores of Minato River, at the fork where the river flows out to the vast sea. The Warrior responsible for the fall of the Kamakura Bakufu, Samurai Yoshisada Nitta-san, had his land forces stationed at this exact position, and by the time Lord Ashikaga's newly regenerated Army appeared where the earth meets the sky.

The wise Samurai Kusunoki-san had warned the Emperor not to dare engage the far superior forces of General Ashikaga-sama in pitch battle. Instead, he suggested the Emperor Go-Daigo flee the capital city and seek the safety offered by the loyal Sohei Monks of Mount Hiei. Samurai Kusunoki-san offered to engage General Ashikaga-sama's forces in a harassment campaign in much the same manner he was able to defeat the Kamakura forces on Mount Kongo. He would fight General Ashikaga-sama's troops until he was able to whittle them down to a much more defeatable force to be conquered.

"Fueled by his past great victories upon the field of battle, Emperor Go-Daigo decided against fleeing the capital at this time. The Imperial Court along with the backing of Emperor Go-Daigo and his loyal forces went on with the original battle plan, and he ordered the great Armies of the Emperor to march against the rebel forces being mounted by General Ashikaga-sama. Not wishing to go against the Emperor's orders, Warrior Kusunoki-san agreed with his orders, and he rode off to share the fate of his Army.

The battle of Minatogawa began on a very hot, humid and extremely stifling sunny day in the seventh month of the 1336th year. The fearless Warrior Kusunoki-san, who was used to fighting his enemy with the mountains protecting his flanks, decided to make his stand against the rebel forces with the River Minato to his rear. Part of General Ashikaga-sama's Samurai forces made its first attack from the riverside, and these warriors were able to force a landing in the rear of the Imperial Army's unprotected flanks. Samurai Kusunoki-san quickly realized this and he fought these attackers while the outcome of the battle could still have gone either way.

"Samurai Kusunoki-san's loyal forces might have won the great battle against General Ashikaga-sama's far superior Warriors if it was not for the terribly tragic mistake committed by the unwise Samurai Yoshisada Nitta-san. Instead of standing strong and fighting by the side of Samurai Kusunoki-san's loyal troops, Warrior Yoshisada-san withdrew from the frontline battle when this second enemy Army from the river, landed in his flanks and prepared to attack his forces from their flanks. Samurai Yoshisada-san found himself hard pressed between two separate heavily attacking enemy Armies, and his forces were driven from the battlefield suffering horrendous losses to his Warriors.

With the collapse of Warrior Yoshisada-san's Samurai forces, the openings the defeat created crumbled Samurai Kusunoki-san's defenses. The defeat of Yosisada-san's Warriors allowed the Armies led to battle by General Ashikaga-sama, his son Tadayoshi, and the Army from the river led by Samurai Hosokawa-san, to surround the cut off Samurai Kusunoki-san's Army, and close in for the kill against them.

"Now, cut off from much needed reinforcements and supplies to carry on his defense of his emperor, and pressed from all sides by General Ashikaga-sama's rampaging Armies. Samurai Kusunoki-san was forced to watch in horror as his loyal Samurai Warriors were slaughtered in uncountable numbers in savage fighting against the enemy forces. Warrior Kusunoki-san, the famed Samurai of myth, decided to commit Suppuku. He chose this course of action instead of allowing himself to be taken alive, and be marched like a common criminal through the streets of Kyoto, only to be crucified at the end of his long march in front of the gawking worthless townspeople, and General Ashikaga-sama and his loyal warriors.

"Samurai Kusunoki-san, did not commit Suppuku in his previous battles when he was completely surrounded on Mount Kongo, because he had instructions by Emperor Go-Daigo to fight for the Emperor's cause against all odds, to the death of every Samurai under his command. This instruction had the loyal Warrior fighting from the mountain tops until General Ashikaga-sama turned the vast tide of war against him, by going over to Emperor Go-Daigo's alliance. But here, the fighting on this open flat outpost at

Minatogawa, Samurai Kusunoki-san was unable to defend his position properly.

"Emperor Go-Daigo instructed Samurai Kusunoki-san to fight until there was no hope of victory. This last order from the Emperor opened the door, and it allowed Warrior Kusunoki-san to commit the honorable act of obedience to his Lord, Suppuku. At the moment he believed all was lost to his Warriors and himself, and there was no sense to fight on.

"With this honorable act committed, Samurai Kusunoki-san had forever sealed his great name, and linked it to the legends that make up Japan's proud past. The highly respected Warrior Kusunoki-san died the honorable and righteous death sought after by all loyal Samurai to their Lord and Masters, and motivated by blind and unwavering loyalty and devotion to his Emperor Go-Daigo. When the forces of General Ashikaga-sama's great Armies finally located Warrior Kunsunki-san's body, it was still locked in the honorable sitting position, his legs crossed under him and his innards spilled upon the battle scarred breast plate of his armor he was forced to remove, in order to perform the sacred act of death for his Lord.

"The awe struck Ashikaga-sama Warriors did not separate Samurai Kusunoki-san's head from his body instead they accorded his death the final act of honor and total respect. Ashikaga-sama Warriors built a huge pyre fire, and there upon they laid the body of this highly respected Warrior, still clothed in his full battle armor right in the center of the great heap. They laid his breast plate across his chest, making careful not to allow his innards to fall to the ground and become polluted then the honoring Warriors set the pile ablaze. Many of General Ashikaga-sama's Warriors knelt in silent pray, and paid great homage to the fearsome and fallen enemy Warrior of the respected Emperor Go-Daigo's. They stood guard over the body for many hours until the fire had consumed every part of the body of the enemy General.

"The fearsome General Ashikaga-sama was driven on with his quest not only by thoughts of deathlessness and immortality. His sole driving force was to forward his family name, and then assume the prestigious title of Seii TaiShogun of all Japan. Once this great honor was bestowed upon his head for Ashikaga-sama's outstanding deeds on the field of battle, it'd be destined to live on and passed from one family member to another for the rest of Japan's future, thus assuring Shogun Ashikaga-sama's place in history.

"After the devastating defeat of the Imperial Armies at Minatogawa by General Ashikaga-sama's forces, Emperor Go-Daigo had no other choice left open to him but to flee the capital city, and take refuge on Mount Hiei under the protection of the fearsome Sohei Monk Warriors. Upon hearing the fleeing Emperor had surrendered the capital to him, General Ashikaga-sama ordered his Army to the mountain stronghold of Hiei, with instructions to destroy the troublesome Sohei Monks, and to take the deposed Emperor captive and bring him back to the capital city. After many months of savage and fierce fighting, with both sides suffering terrible loses on the battlefield. The Emperor Go-Daigo was finally captured when the wise General Ashikaga-sama sent word that he was going to allow the defeated Emperor to live out the remainder of his life in peace in Tosa province. But my Shogun lied to the Emperor.

"Growing extremely weary over the unending years of wars and savage battles, and mounting deaths suffered by so many loyal Samurai Warriors under his name and banner, the Emperor Go-Daigo finally capitulated to the trickery of General Ashikaga-sama. He surrendered to the ever pursuing General's Warriors. The moment he was taken captive by General Ashikaga-sama's forces, the aging and completely exhausted Emperor was unceremoniously marched to the capital city of Kyoto, where he was held captive in the Castle until he was able to escape in the first month of the 1337th year. Upon escaping his arrest in the city, the crafty but well aging Emperor fled to the mountains of Yoshino, where he ruled as the true Emperor over the southern domain of Japan.

"Yoshino was ideally suited as a defensible fortification in this region of Japan, and along with the help of his sons, Prince Morinaga and Prince Norinaga. Emperor Go-Daigo remained there in safety, easily defeating all Armies sent out by the newly declared Shogun of Japan, General Takauji Ashikaga-sama to recapture him.

"The wise Emperor, so sad to announce for your honorable ears to understand my Lord died on the third month of the 1348th year. But Prince Morinaga-sama never did succeed Emperor Go-Daigo to the long sought after thrown of Japan, as was expected by all his followers. The young Prince died the year before his great father from wounds suffered in battle against General Ashikaga-sama's Warriors by the fifth bridge on the main road that lead into Kyoto city.

This left the younger Prince Norinaga-sama alone to rule over the southernmost domain of Japan until it was finally decreed by Ashikaga-sama that the two northern and southern courts should make a peace alliance between themselves. This order finally joined the two Japans together forever, and it further cemented the true seat of power of the one true Shogun of the lands, Shogun Ashikaga-sama's honorable will over the domain of all Japan for many years to come. Kyoto remained the seat of power in Japan for countless years of my memory. Shogun Ashikaga-sama became the greatest Shogun to rule over the two Japans, and he controlled most of the wars that raged after he rose to the Shogun title."

Hiromoai noticed Wind was suffering from exhaustion and he decided to give her a break by his standing and stretching. The moment he stood, she became silent and bowed. He turned to Lady Yoke and smiled when he noticed she was having trouble paying attention to Wind's story and offered. "Tea, Wind-san?" He grunted at the female warrior of past times.

Wind looked up at him after hearing her name mentioned. Her master used the American word for the brew, and she did not know what he was offering her. He saw the slight bewildered look etched on her eyes and corrected his words. "Cha, Wind-san?"

"Hai, dozo Kawasomeru-sama. You're too kind to this worthless vassal, my Lord."

"Lady Yoke, this Warrior is in need of a break before she continues her life's story in the past times of Japan's history. Bring her tea, errr... Cha for us." He stared at her to get her moving.

"Hai, right away Hiromoai-san, it'll be my pleasure to bring us all a cup of Cha." She got up from the couch and headed for the kitchen to brew the tea.

She heard the name the woman called her liege lord, but decided her master had the right to go by as many names as he may chose. The only name seared in her memory, was the dishonored name of Tetsuo Hatanaka. He was the lowly Lord Wakatsuki despised samurai who so long ago, killed the one lover she ever shared herself with. It was told to her how this dishonored warrior waited like a dog in the night stalking a wounded deer in a pile of rocks, and charged Captain Katsunoke Seisakajo after his back was turned to the enemy warrior. Tetsuo Hatanaka never gave Captain Seisakajo a fighting chance to defend himself properly against his attack, and this was why he lost great face and was hunted and killed by her.

The ancient female samurai remained kneeling on the floor while waiting for tea. She paid no attention to her kimono, and she did not realize it was open to the waist and allowed her breasts to be seen by her liege lord, and the other two people in the room with her. She never suffered from any false modesty she deemed it a wasted virtue as far as she was concerned. The human body was meant to be seen in the manner that it was created, beautiful, well crafted she believed, and naked. After years of hiding from view that she was a woman with a fine shape, she found herself enjoying the exciting feeling of having these men trying their best to see what she possessed, and was hidden by the silk and very colorful kimono.

The tea arrived and Lady Yoke offered the first cup to Hiromoai as tradition demanded of her. He took the cup and waited to drink until Wind had a cup in her hand.

"Would you care to sit in a chair while enjoying your cha for a few moments of enjoyment, Wind-san? I think we should rest a while before you continue to explain your past life in Japan, and the version of the way it was so long ago to live in Japan." He offered and for the first time since he discovered this beautiful female warrior, there was a genuine softness in his tone.

"Iye my Liege Lord! Do you think me soft of body and mind? I'm comfortable where I am seated presently." She allowed a trace of anger to cloud her eyes for a moment.

"Suit yourself Samurai I only wanted to get you more comfortable, before you continue with your story, that's all." He snorted as he slurped his tea, ignored the kneeling samurai.

There was another phrase her liege lord used that she did not understand. But rather than risk insulting him, she decided not to inquire what was meant by what he uttered. She drank her tea in silence she knew patience was the answer to all questions. So she cast her eyes to the floor as she finished her tea. Before resting the cup on the floor, Lady Yoke was at her side and refilled it.

Lady Yoke was having a problem keeping her eyes off Wind's breasts. They were perfect, and larger than most of her Japanese girlfriends. She was enthralled by them. By no means was she a woman who loved women, but she wanted to touch them, or at least touch this samurai spirit to see if she was really sitting before her, and had solid form to the touch. Fighting this overpowering feeling off, she returned to her seat and waited for Wind's saga to continue.

"Are you in need of food, Wind-san?" Hiromoai asked in almost a demanding tone.

"Iye my Lord, I am fine, this worthless Samurai thanks her concerned Lord and Master graciously for displaying such kindness and consideration to this most worthless vassal. Do you wish me to continue with my life's story for your edification, my Liege Lord?" Wind offered as she allowed a slight smile not baring her teeth to her master.

"Yes, but you'll wait until I had a chance to finish my tea first, before you'll continue on with your life story, Wind-san. But I'll not allow you to babble along at your own pace this time around. You'll answer my questions in the order that they're asked of you, Samurai." He warned the spirit in no uncertain terms.

"Hai. All my Lord and Master has to do is nod and I'll continue with my life's story." She waited for Hiromoai to finish his tea and when he rested the cup on the table, he glared at her for several long seconds while formulating his thoughts. Finally he asked her.

"Wind-san I believe I'd like to know the reason for my ordering your untimely death? What infraction had you committed against my will and desires that had forced your death upon you, Samurai Warrior of the past times?" He was a smart man, and he refrained from asking too many question on how this Lord Kawasomeru had risen to power, or other decisions he was supposed to have been involved in.

He planned to do his own research about the ancient warlord, so he would know how to deal with this threatening spirit and weapon suddenly under his complete command. Heaven knows, there were enough books written about ancient Japan, and he was confident this Lord Kawasomeru should be mentioned in a good many of them. By asking this question, he felt her suspicions of his identify would not be questioned. At least he hoped it would not be so, he did not want to say or do anything that might make this extremely dangerous spirit suspicious of him.

Wind cast a wary eye at him, but she knew enough not to question her master's requests or demands of her being. All she understood was he was her lord and master, and as such he was within his right to ask her anything he may deem important to his Wa and interest. Drawing in a deep breath because this part of her life was extremely painful for her memory, she began slowly, but not until she allowed her shoulders and posture to sag a bit, because of the agonizing memories related to this most trying time of her life and memory.

"Kawasomeru-sama, the war was going on too long, with many honorable Samurai paying for the exhausting war with their lives. Although my Liege Lord enjoyed many great katsu, victories and success on the battlefield, my Master was cheated of his greatest conquest of all. Every time my Lord's loyal Samurai placed the dishonorable Lord Wakatsuki's enemy forces in a compromising position. The crafty lowly dog eater would squeak out of the trap laid out before him with his skin still on his foul bones. Behind our backs the manure eating dung heap communicated directly with Shogun Ashikaga-sama in Kyoto, trying to enlist the Shogun's aid in stopping your invasion of his worthless lands.

"Only when the hated Lord Wakatsuki threatened to attack the capital city of Kyoto with his powerful Armies, did the Shogun finally give in and he sent a representative to force both warring sides to the peace table. My honorable Liege Lord was aware the war was lasting endlessly, and it was only a matter of time before the Shogun decided to intercede on his behalf in the name of peace for his entire realm. My Lord came up with a deserving and prudent plan, to break the back of the dog eating Lord Wakatsuki and his foul army of worthless Samurai.

"My Liege Lord's well calculated plan was to kill the Commanding First General in the command of his enemy Lord Wakatsuki's disgusting Army of lowly dog eaters. With the valuable aid of my Liege Lord's countless spies, my cunning Lord and Master was able to locate where this well respected enemy General was scheduled to travel on at a certain day, at a certain time, and the Samurai that would surround him as the General traveled. First General Masahatsu Motoshima-san of Lord Wakatsuki's First Horse Army was ordered from his secret encampment at Hokke, the Village of the Lotus.

"The fearsome and very powerful enemy First General was to move his massive Warrior forces over to the Village of Nagashinoi to mount a sneak attack against my Liege Lord's honorable troops that were bivouacked at the southern end of your main forces. An attack here would be extremely costly for your honorable troops, and it could have drastically slowed your steady march mounted against Lord Wakatsuki's retreating forces. It was a cunning idea, and my Lord was unable to reinforce these troops, if my Liege Lord wanted to continue the pressure on Lord Wakatsuki's disgusting Army of cowards.

"It was reported by my Master's spies that First General Motoshima-san planned to move his forces down the Kai pass through the Kai mountain ranges. To move so many soldiers down such a treacherous pass carved out of the mountains countless centuries ago, by the once mighty flow of the Kai River that ran the full length of the pass, was believed to be extremely foolhardy and highly impossible to accomplish. With a well placed small Army of archers, the Army more or less trapped within the narrow confines of the pass, could be easily picked apart and savaged at will by the hidden archers. The reason my Lord and Master voted against this type of action, was because by the time my Lord was in possession of this vital information. It was too late to move the needed archers in position in time to intercept the moving troops and their feared General, and the soldiers were of any consequence in the outcome of battle.

"That was why my intelligent Master came up with the alternative plan. Once my Lord and Master finished addressing his Generals for the upcoming attack on Wakatsuki's foul Army, my Lord bade me remain behind while the Generals left to attend their troops. Once the Generals were gone from your presence, you laid out your plan to this lowly Warrior. Secretly, my wise Lord and Master informed me of the First General's route, as well as informing me on how to destroy this feared enemy General. I set out on my quest with confidence and..."

"Wait a minute Wind-san!" Hiromoai barked as he shifted his weight on the couch, and stared at the beautifully female samurai. He wanted to ask, but he wanted to be comfortable first.

"Hai my Lord I wait as instructed. Are my long winded words confusing your memory and mind, Kawasomeru-sama?" She replied as she automatically bowed to the ground.

"No, not at all, I'm not confused by any of your words, true I was there nevertheless I want you to relive everything I told you to accomplish on that day. Is that clear of what I demand of you, Wind-san? Omit nothing from your long stream of words for my ears and understanding." He leaned forward on the couch and then glared at the beautiful female warrior, displaying his displeasure over how she tried to skip over a very important item of the day in her story.

"Your order is my command to carry out to its final conclusion as always, my Lord. Please forgive this worthless vassal for causing you displeasure with her boring story of her past life. I will try to recap everything that happened on that day, and the quick days that followed which led to my death." She bowed low to Hiromoai then straightened up and looked into his eyes.

"You do exactly that Wind-san. You will carry out every one of my orders as faithfully if you know what's good for you, Samurai." He snapped angrily, displaying his boredom and impatience with her story.

"Hai. My Lord ordered me to entice this General into my web of deceit and death, by using my body as a weapon against his loathsome crusade to pillow with every woman in Japan. My understanding Lord Takehiro Kawasomeru demanded proof if I was successful on my quest to destroy this puissant of enemy Generals against his rule. The proof my Lord demanded was the General's proud snake, his mighty serpent, his swaying ying. My Lord informed me General Masahatsu Motoshima-san was in possession of a famed and mighty tattooed male member.

"The great tattoo was of a mighty serpent which wrapped its body completely around his vigorous member hanging between his legs. The mighty head of the serpent was the head of his shaft, and when the loose skin of his shaft was pulled back, the dragon's mouth seemed to be spitting out the red head of the shaft in all its anger. The long tail of the threatening dragon wrapped itself around the pair of golden celestial globes that hung below his raging and ever woman seeking shaft. My Liege Lord demanded of me that I bring him back this long sought after prize, from the enemy First General as proof of his foul and demanded death." She cocked her head to Hiromoai as if in a silent plea, asking him if this was enough of an explanation of this point that did not bring her much pleasure reliving again.

He nodded to her, but not before he glanced at the other two sitting across from him, to see their reaction to this startling story the ancient samurai warrior was telling them. Lady Yoke sat straight up with both hands covering her mouth, and her eyes opened wide. She was staring at the beautiful female samurai in stunned disbelief. Obviously knowing what was coming next in this fascinating story of Japan's savage past. The old foreman Utsumi sat with his legs crossed and his hand resting in a protective manner over his withered male member. He smiled then turned to Wind, and nodded.

She began her story anew for her captive audience. "This worthless Warrior set off to intercept the feared General Motoshima-san, with my own escort of fifty loyal Warriors. I searched the forever wandering Kai River, until I located the proper position on which to wage my assault against the enemy of my Liege Lord. I swam out to a little Island I located in the rapid flow of the river's water. There, I salted the Island with many of my weapons I hid below the surface of the water. Once I was pleased over the trap I had woven for my Master's hated enemy, I returned to the river's bank and dressed quickly, and then I rode off to see how far the First General and his guard Samurai were from this position.

I spotted them at what I believed was one quarter of a stick of time away from my tiny Island. So I rode back to my Island, but not before I secured my horse and ordered my Samurai out of the area.

"I then removed my Kimono and swam out to the small Island. Once there, I began to wash my body while waiting for the foul First General's appearance before my eyes. It did not take long for him to arrive, and when he saw my back he ordered me to turn so that he could drink in my nakedness. Upon seeing me he ordered his worthless Samurai to keep moving as he stripped himself of his armor and filthy Kimono, and walked out to attack me. His assault against my body was deplorable to endure, he moved without regard to my pleasures and desires. He used his foul teeth, fingernails, and general roughness to please his vile needs of the body.

"I had to push him off my body or he would have surely drowned me in the swift water while seeking his pleasures with my body. I stroke his shaft so it was of the proper stiffness, so I could remove the trophy for my Lord's wants. I used my left hand to stroke him while my right hand searched below the water, until my fingers touched the handle of my tanto blade. I believe that the foolish First General was waiting for me to take his offending member in my mouth. But instead I used the small blade on his great pride and woman pleasing dragon. With a swift action I removed the offending member from the repulsive General's body and then..."

The Lady Yoke could not help herself and she let out a small cry over the savagery of past times of Japan, as she covered her mouth with both hands again, and stared at the ancient spirit. She was stunned this beautiful woman was capable of being so barbarous to another human being. Her cry made Wind, Utsumi and Hiromoai glance at her, before she continued with her story once she made certain the lovely woman in the room was with no injuries.

She took the time to smile at her for a brief moment, but she ignored Lady Yoke's fear of her being, as she continued on with her story. "I believe the foul First General was so wrapped up in seeking his foul pleasure at my expense that he did not even realize what I done to the proud Warrior snake, until I sank the tanto blade deep in his throat to dispatch him quickly. One thing I did not want to happen was for the highly respected enemy First General to suffer longer than the Kami allowed. Even though he was an opponent, and a most formidable one at that, his honorable feats on the battlefield were well respected even by his enemy.

"If he was not my adversary, I would have been proud to serve with him on the field of battle. He was that good and respected a proud Samurai and soldier. Once I was certain the First General was dead, I shoved his over bloated body into the swift flow of the river, and placed his severed member in my mouth so I could use both hands to swim back to shore. I rushed back to my Lord and Master's vast encampment after gathering my Samurai guards. I handed my Master his sort after prized trophy, and my Liege Lord was pleased beyond words over the completion of my quest for him. I was overly rewarded by my generous Lord and Master for this deed."

"How so did I over reward you for your service, Wind-san? Explain how you were rewarded by me in the past of Japan's interesting history. I truly don't remember all the gifts I bestowed upon you at this time, Samurai." Hiromoai interrupted the female samurai's story again.

"Ieeeee... Am I forced to relive all the wonderful things my kind Lord and Master embarrassed me with, by heaping on my worthless and undeserving head and shoulders, Kawasomeru-sama?"

"I warn you Warrior from the past, you're causing me much anger by questioning my every request of you. Again I warn you Wind-san. Don't risk my consuming wrath by questioning my wants and demands of you further, or you'll suffer greatly by my anger. I asked you a question and I expect an answer to it, immediately at that Samurai!" He demanded while glaring at her.

"Hai my Lord and Master, please excuse my poor display of ill manners. I shall explain for your enlightenment of what you requested. Once I killed the enemy First General, my Liege Lord was so pleased he forced me to accept the rich lands between the Seventh and Eleventh Villages of his province. My Master further rewarded this worthless Warrior, by giving me three hundred kolu a year in rice. Two kiki a year in silk, and one hundred horses, three hundred Katanas, along with five thousand yabusame, mounted archers and their horses, this was the pay of a loyal land owning Daimyo." She paused for a second, even though she thought she was speaking to her Lord, during her story she always referred to everything that happened as he, or her lord and master or Lord Kawasomeru. This made her story hard for the three persons in the room with her to follow, and when she did not see any reaction coming from Hiromoai over the way she was explaining her life story, she continued on with her words.

CHAPTER FIVE

"But the death of First General Motoshima-san, did not serve the purpose that my Lord and Master had hoped. The dog eating Lord Wakatsuki, continued to retreat deeper into his lowly lands, and he carried out a scorch earth policy by destroying all villages, crops, roads, and bridges as he moved his foul Army deeper into his repulsive lands, in order to hide from his fate at your hands, my Lord. He drafted young men of the Villages on his never ending retreat, and pressed them in service in his depleted Armies. The cursed Lord Wakatsuki went so far as to enlisted the aid of women of the Villages he destroyed, by ordering them to use any means at hand to slow my Master's Warrior's march for justice against the foul enemy warlord.

"All the while Lord Wakatsuki continued his retreat deeper into his foul lands he was in communication with the Shogun in Kyoto. As I stated before, the Shogun was hesitant to get involved with his warlords' disagreements and endless battles. But when Lord Wakatsuki dared to threaten to turn his troops towards the south, and invade and destroy the capital city of Kyoto. The Shogun was forced to react against this threat from the vile dog eater.

"The Shogun was in fear a river of blood would sweep over the realm, if Wakatsuki's Armies dared to attack Kyoto. As my wise father and teacher told me on many occasions, 'A quick and overpowering victory is the main aim of any war. If the fighting was allowed to continue for too long, weapons will become blunted, and morale of fighting Warriors blanched, and the outcome soon becomes in question as to who will be the victor of the war, my Master, or your enemy'.

"At first, the great Shogun planned to send his Armies marching against Lord Wakatsuki for daring to threaten his realm. But the Shogun's Generals pointed out it would be prudent on his part to send out an envoy to Lord Kawasomeru's encampment, and a second envoy to Lord Wakatsuki's camp. Ordering the two powerful warlords to sit and speak of peace between them. The Shogun took his General's advice and ordered his envoy to broker this peace agreement, and if one was not able to be worked out. The envoy was empowered to pull the Shogun's troops in the Dewa province out, and attack any warlord's Armies who refused to agree to a peaceful solution worked out by the other warlord and the powerful General.

"If both warring sides were unable to come to agreement, my Master and the dog eater Lord Wakatsuki would be ordered to commit Suppuku while in the presence of the Shogun's General and personal envoy. General Morimoto-san would then lop off the heads of both warlords, and bring the heads with him to Kyoto for the mighty Shogun's private viewing. The powerful Shogun planned to appoint two of his most loyal Generals as the new warlords of the sixteen central provinces, and have them bring the warring provinces back to a peaceful state. I fear to offer General Morimoto-san was promised your great realm, Kawasomeru-sama.

"When General Morimoto-san arrived in your encampment, he was not a pleasure to deal with. The angry General envoy was well noted for his rash rudeness, ruthlessness, and very repulsive manners. He made rude demands for food from my Lord and Master, and actually treated my Liege Lord with the greatest of disrespect and ill manners and even open disdain. The General demanded to witness the Samurai who had killed the feared and powerful enemy First General Motoshima-san. I was brought before his and your presence at this meeting. Once there, I was forced to display my skills with the Katana for the visiting General.

"Once I was allowed to retreat from the meeting, my Master and the General began talks of peace between the two powerful warlords. During these talks, the General informed my Master that Lord Wakatsuki and a number of his Samurai were marching towards your encampment. My ingenious Master quickly entertained thoughts of attacking Lord Wakatsuki's caravan while he rode to my Master's camp. When the General heard these thoughts, he warned my Lord and Master that Lord Wakatsuki rode under the protective banner of the Shogun himself, and was not to be attacked when under this banner under any circumstances.

"My Master was forced to place these thoughts of destroying his enemy lord Wakatsuki when he was most venerable, out of his mind. The offensive Wakatsuki dared to ride in my Master's encampment as if he was the conquering champion. The nefarious and dishonorable warlord was so conceited he dared to wear the yellow Kimono which proclaimed victory over his enemy. I was furious my Master had to endure such terrible insults in the name of peace for Japan's sake.

"While the peace talks were going on, my Master's Warriors were forced to wait outside the tent at attention until a solution was worked out between the warlords and General. My Master was gracious in few demands on his vanquished enemy and his lands. General Morimoto-san seemed to be leaning towards my Master's compassionate offers. He went so far as to threaten Wakatsuki, to force him to agree with my Master's demands for peace. But the crafty Wakatsuki was not to be easily pushed around by either you or the General. Seeing he lost many requests, he made one final demand that rocked my Master's strength when dealing with this lowly dog.

"When the details to the agreement that would restore peace to the realm were sealed, and the General placed the Shogun's personal chop on it, the repulsive Lord Wakatsuki made one final demand of my concerned Lord and Master which was his right under the circumstances. He demanded the head of the Samurai who he referred to as an assassin who killed his First General in a detestable manner. General Morimoto-san agreed with Lord Wakatsuki's demand because he referred to me as a cast down lowly assassin of his General. In ancient Japan, an assassin was the lowest of the low in battle, and was not afforded the respect and protection offered to that, of the honored Samurai Caste. My wise Master tried to point out what Lord Wakatsuki was calling an assassin, was in fact a Samurai Warrior of Yukakasa, of having high value, only guilty of following his Liege Lord's demand to destroy his enemy where they were found.

"Upon seeing the evil Lord Wakatsuki had struck a nerve in my Master's body, the dog eater pressed the point further until General Morimoto-san had no other choice in the matter but to insist that my Lord and Master order the death of this Samurai turned assassin. Even though the General understood Lord Wakatsuki was speaking of my being, and he ordered my head be displayed on the wood plate before the disgusting Lord Wakatsuki for his private viewing. This was the only way peace would be able to be returned to my Master's domain.

"Only when the final chop of the Shogun was set to paper, and the seal of the Shogun placed on this agreement, did the meeting breakup. I was sent for by my Lord and Master, and you requested my presence meet with you on your meditating rock which was well known to all your Warriors of the vast encampment. You ordered me to appear there before sunrise. I did not understand the reason for this special meeting ordered by you, but I decided to wear my best Kimono, a further present given to me by my Lord and Master for my loyal service to you. But by wearing the Kimono, I was forced to leave my trusted killing swords behind because there was no place to wear them in the Kimono properly, my Lord.

"I reported to the contemplation rock as ordered, and my Lord and Master offered me the greatest respect and pleasure of sharing the wonderful sunrise with him. This was one of the greatest respects any Lord could possibly offer his lowly vassals. It is a request only dared to be dreamed of by any Samurai sworn to their master. Here I was, sitting with my Master as if I was on the same divine plain as he. The sun had to fight its way through the thick clouds of the far off sunrise before it won the battle for the Heavens. Once the sun broke free of the mountain's grasp, my Master turned to me with sadness etched in his eyes, it was then you ordered me to commit Suppuku before you. My Master again paid one of the greatest respects any Samurai could possibly dare hope for. Lord Kawasomeru offered to second my honorable death.

"With saddest of heart, I slowly prepared myself for death as ordered, but my Lord was not done honoring me as yet. Kawasomeru-sama ordered me to take Suppuku in the manner of male Warriors. I was to slice my belly. Everyone knows a female ordered to death by her Lord and Master, was to remain modest and slice open her throat and slowly bleed to death, with no second to assist the honored one on her travel into the Floating World of wonder and myth. I expected nothing less from my Liege Lord, who named my killing sword by his proud lips." She stopped speaking as she drew in a quick breath.

"What was the name I bestowed on your sword, Wind-san?" Hiromoai asked, trying to get as much information as he could from this fearsome female samurai without arousing her concerns.

"Wind's Breath was the honored name my Lord had bestowed on my Katana, my Master. You told me it was the only name worthy of my sword, because it was an extension of my abilities and arm, to strike death against your hated enemy wherever they chose to roam upon the sacred soil of Japan." She dared a slight smile to her new master.

"It was a good name." He replied, impressed with the wisdom of her liege lord.

"Yes it was Master. Drawing in my breath I slowly undid my Kimono and then allowed it to slide off my shoulders. I prepared my mind and soul for the honor to be released from my earthy duties to my Liege Lord, and to mother earth. When I was prepared to carry out your order, I further stunned my Liege Lord by asking you a question. I asked why I was being ordered to my death. I was scared I had somehow committed a terrible infraction against your will. I did not want to go to my death fearing I might have dishonored my Lord in any way. The last words you spoke to me, still ring within my worthless mind whenever I close my eyes. You bellowed in a most commanding voice I have ever heard spoken. 'Samurai Wind-san, you have honored me in ways no other Samurai could dare hope to attain, beyond belief, beyond obedience and honor. Your honored and untimely death was ordered by me in the name of peace, so that peace might once again be returned to the great lands of all Japan'.

"With that said by my Lord and Master, I carried out my final order of obedience to my Liege Lord. I plunged the small tanto blade into my belly, and then slowly slid it across my body. Despite what I had heard of the sacred act, Suppuku was surprisingly painless, that was until I turned the blade in my body, and then started to work the blade the other way a second time across my body. I must have grunted at this point, because your mighty blade swiftly fell upon my neck, and placed a swift end to my Suppuku and the pain involved in the sacred act. Strangely as I remember it as my head remained lying on the ground, and reasoning remained within my worthless brain, I heard the words spoken to my honored body by my Lord.

"While still holding the sword that had dispatched my worthless life in your hand, my Lord cursed my soul, my being, my essence to the spirit of the Katana blade forever. My Liege Lord offered in his great wisdom, 'a Samurai Warrior, who can choose the proper time of his death, can trick fate and the gods who control all things in our lives'. My spirit was ordered by my Master to return to the land of the living the moment his Sugahara-sama crafted Katana blade was released by its wooden prison and breathed the sweet air of earth again." At this point, she had to swallow to relieve the memories stalking her mind of this moment in time.

"My still seeing eyes witnessed the powerful curse placed upon my soul, and I witnessed my Lord place his blade still soaked with my blood in its zutsu, the wood scabbard. I felt when my blood was soaked up by the scabbard something of my being was trapped in the tubular prison. Slowly, my ability to reason and see betrayed me and within seconds, I found myself soaring among the floating clouds and birds in flight. As I floated among them, I was greeted by many past greatness of Japan. I met Izanagi and his beloved sister and wife Izanami, who gave birth to the eight sacred Islands of Japan. They greeted me pleasantly with smiles and polite bows.

"Izanagi was still in possession of the fabled Celestial, Jeweled Spear of true birth and beginning for the eight Japanese Islands. I saw my honorable mother and wise father and Master Trainer, as they enjoyed themselves among the clouds, free of all pain and worry. I likewise saw my dear sister Enko, slaughtered so terribly young just because her only crime was an assassin thought she was me. I found myself dancing with many great and well respected Samurai General's who laid down their lives in the dust for their Lord and Masters of the past. Everyone who was great I passed and honored as I traveled towards my final destination, to sit on the right hand side of Fujin's mighty thrown, and to await your summons to do battle in my Master's name and distinction again." She suddenly bowed towards the man who she believed was her Lord Kawasomeru, and then she awaited her next order by his mouth.

Hiromoai let out his breath in a rush, because it was hard for him to believe all he just heard from Wind's lips. He was stunned by the savagery and was in awe of the respect the samurai of the past rained down on their lords. He longed to possess such power over people. Then the thought struck him, he was in possession of such power over one being. Wind was his to order as he saw fit. She was his private weapon, and would make him one of the most feared men in the world. He leaned back on the sofa, and then he ran his hand over his chin as he stared at Wind, who was bowing low to him. It thrilled him to see the great respect she offered him.

He turned to Utsumi and grunted nastily at him. "Well old fool, what do you think?"

"About what Hiromoai-san?" Utsumi questioned as if he was confused by his words.

"About this female Warrior and all she just told us of the past history of Japan, you great fool? Do you believe her, old ignoramus?" He glared at the old man while waiting for his reply.

"Of course I believe her Hiromoai-san. What would the spirit have to gain by lying to you about her past or anything else for that matter, sir?"

"To gain my trust and..." He snapped back, but he was suddenly interrupted by Wind.

"I have your trust Lord Kawasomeru." She moaned as she remained in the bowing position.

"Huh! And how is that Wind-san?" He grunted nastily at her this time.

She allowed her head to raise from the floor just enough until she could lock eyes with her thought to be master. Then she offered as if insulted by his last words. "My Lord and Master, I have served you faithfully on the battlefield many times in the past, with your honor locked in my heart and mind. Everything I had accomplished in my worthless life, I had accomplished under your banner and desires. I successfully defeated many of your hated teki on the battlefield and elsewhere, and sent their worthless souls to the Floating World to await their rebirth. I gave up my life so your name would forever remain great and respected. I left the Ukiyo on numerous occasions, to continue my fight against your worthless teki. I shall continue to answer your summons to Yoshigi, duty whenever you summon me to do so until you release me from your ageless curse. I live in both worlds only to serve and honor my Master of life and death." Again, she returned to the honored bowing position and then she held it this time.

"Yes Wind-san, and if all I heard from your lips is true, you have indeed gained my trust and respect, Samurai." He could not control himself and he allowed a slight smile to cross his lips, as he looked down at the kneeling beautiful female warrior from Japan's past.

"May Fujin-sama tear my worthless heart out with his bare hands, and feast lustfully upon its beating flesh. If I ever entertain treachery and dishonor against my Liege Lord." She offered.

He nodded at her and then he turned and glanced at Lady Yoke. He saw nothing but the greatest of respect and awe emitting from her eyes for this beautiful female samurai warrior. He noticed in Lady Yoke's eyes she wanted to look after Wind's needs just as her own vassals must have done in the long ago past times. He realized if she lavished her attention on her, Wind's attention would be heightened for his own needs. He smiled reassuringly, knowing he was going to have the Lady Yoke serve this samurai.

"Wind-san, I bid you to stand before me!" He barked and then waited for her to carry out his last order. When she stood, she placed her hands down by her side, palms out facing her lord so he could easily see she was in possession of no weapons and was no threat against his person in any manner. In doing this, her kimono opened in the front and again, his eyes enjoyed the breath robbing vision of her naked body as he offered.

"Wind-san, I'm in fear that I might have exhausted your fine spirit, by demanding so many exhausting explanations of the past time of your life in ancient Japan. I want to look after your inner self as I choose to feed you. Wind-san, allow Lady Yoke to prepare a yu (hot tub) for you so you can enjoy a relaxing soak. Since you can enjoy the feelings of awaking when visiting the living world, allow me to show you some of the other luxuries you've been missing while wandering within the Floating World of wonder and myth. Lady Yoke take this Samurai to my bathroom and bathe her properly. Look after her needs whenever she's visiting us. Carry on Lady Yoke." More and more, he spoke in the old ways.

"Hmmmm... I'm afraid this worthless vassal has forgotten how pleasing a good yu could be for one's health and Wa. Yes my Lord, thank you for this suggestion. I long for the warm waters of a bath to encase my weary soul." Wind said while displaying her womanish side of the warrior.

He smiled as he watched as Wind fell in line behind Lady Yoke's lead silently.

The Lady Yoke lead Wind into the bedroom size bathroom with its hot tub on one side of the bathroom away from the tub as she offered to the samurai kindly. "Do you have to relieve yourself, Wind-san?"

"Yes I have that need, but I fear I see no pot in which to carry out my business in, Lady Yoke." Wind replied as she looked around the large room for a pot.

"I'm afraid we no longer use pots in this time, Wind-san. All you have to do is sit on that toilet over there and let go. There's paper there to wipe yourself with, or you can try the beday if you so desire, Wind-san." She pointed at the roll of toilet paper hanging on a rack.

Wind sat on the toilet as if she feared the light blue porcelain chair was going to swallow her soul and being. Once comfortable, she did her business. She used the paper to wipe herself as suggested and she smiled over the vast luxuries now enjoyed by the well deserving Kawasomeru-sama and all who serve him honorably in this time.

Lady Yoke gave her privacy by preparing her tub and turning her back to her. When she stepped behind her, Yoke stopped what she was doing and placed the decorative brass tray on the marble floor, and Wind stepped in the wide metal dish without being told to do so. This part of the act of bathing remained the same over hundreds of years. She removed her kimono and allowed Lady Yoke to wet and then lather her body with sweet smelling soap. Soft moans escaped her lips as Yoke washed her private areas, and lingered as she washed her breasts.

Once she rinsed the soap from her body then she took Wind's hand and helped her step into the large tub. Again, a moan escaped her lips as she lay in the soothing warm waters, and she rested her head on the overstuffed rubber air pillow resting behind her head. Lady Yoke moved to her side and dipped a cloth in the water and then ran it lightly over her face.

"By all the Kami inhabiting the Floating World, I have forgotten how soothing this is to the heart and inner soul of this Warrior." Wind moaned as she allowed her body to relax.

Lady Yoke purred in a sexy voice barely over a whisper. "Wind-san, you have such an exquisite body. Your beauty is beyond compare or description. The mere presence of you must have driven the foolish Samurai of the past to extremes never dreamed of by the great fools."

While the women were not in the presence of any males, they were at liberty to attack them at will and laugh about how they dared to insult the samurai.

"Lady Yoke, I'm sorry to offer, but this foolish woman was not allowed the luxury to seek normal pleasures of a woman offered by man. I was a highly trained Samurai, and only interested in destroying my Lord and Master's hated enemy. Nothing more, nothing less."

"Then it's I who am sorry for your well being, Wind-san. To be robbed so of one's most womanly ways, must have been extremely hard on your mind and spirit, Wind-san." Every time she called Wind by what her boss called her, she cringed over the dishonor she felt she was aiming at this female warrior from the past.

"Lady Yoke, do not concern yourself about me, I was bred to serve my Master faithfully on the battlefield." Wind announced as she put on a proud smile on her lips.

"Wind-san, you have never been with a man of the past?" She suddenly cried, fearing she never enjoyed the great pleasures of the body by pillowing with a male.

"Ieeeee... Lady Yoke. Do you think I never experienced the art of pillowing with a man in my past? To refrain from such pleasures offered by the gods to enjoy, would be to defile the honor and respect of one's ancestors. Yes Lady Yoke, I had one lover in the past time, before he met his death in a battle for his Lord and Master's sake." She turned her head to look in Lady Yoke's concerned eyes. Then she turned her head back and closed her eyes so she could enjoy the warmth feelings of the waters and dreams the Lady Yoke stirred in her being.

"What was your lover's honorable name, Wind-san? Errr... may I ask you another question please, Wind-san?" She asked the female warrior with concern lacing her tone.

Wind opened her eyes and turned slowly towards the young woman and nodded yes.

"Wind-san, what is your real name? It doesn't give me much pleasure to call you by such a cold and manly sounding name when I address your presence, Wind-san." She diverted her eyes from Wind's face, afraid she might have insulted the warrior from the past.

"Huh! It's been so long since I last heard my family name spoken in my ears, I almost forget it myself I fear. My name given to me on the day of my birth was Yuriko, Yuriko Tanizaki-san." She could not believe the great pleasure she received and enjoyed at hearing her true name mentioned before her, even if it was by her own mouth and words.

"That's an honorable and most proud name, Yuriko-san. I'd be so honored to be allowed to call you Yuriko-san in private, so as not to upset Hiromoai-san." Lady Yoke added the san.

"A wise idea, Lady Yoke, I'd enjoy the honor you offered me in private. But to dare upset one's Master is to entice one's fate to befall you. To answer your question, yes my only lover was Captain Seisakajo-san." She allowed Lady Yoke to add the san to her female name.

"I'm sorry he was killed so early in your budding relationship, Wind-san. How was he in the art of pillowing, Yuriko-san?" Lady Yoke asked of the samurai then turned red for her boldness.

Wind slowly leaned back in the tub and she closed her eyes as pleasing memories of the handsome face of the young Captain Seisakajo came flooding back in her mind. She spoke in almost a dreamy tone to Lady Yoke. "Captain Seisakajo-san was a very kind and most attentive and very tender lover, Lady Yoke. When we first pillowed together, he realized I was never with a man before. So Captain Seisakajo-san took his time when first entering my waiting Jade Gate of pleasure. Before he entered my waiting and wanting Jade Gate, and he did wonderful things to my body. He first placed his fingers in my wanting gate, to as he said help to open me for the first pleasures of coupling.

"Then my lover replaced his fingers with his ever exploring tongue. Stars exploded wildly within my confused mind, as he sent waves of pleasure washing over my trembling body. I wiggled and moaned to the motion of Captain Seisakajo's extremely skilled and most pleasure giving tongue. He played with my breasts, licking at my nipples and making love to them first." She opened her eyes and then looked out the skylight towards the Heavens above her.

The stars of the night danced pleasingly across the darkened sky, mixing in with the silhouettes of the tall building outside reflecting off the silvery clouds above her. The sheer radiance from the full moon helped the shadows shine, and the red glow of a halo surrounded the moon as if it wore a kimono of red mist for one's pleasures to enjoy. The moon's glow splendidly lit up the soft textured cloud filled sky to an eerie comfort. Wind's mind returned to the pleasing thoughts of the first pillowing she experienced with her only lover Captain Seisakajo-san.

"Yes Lady Yoke, it is very pleasing for the heart and mind to remember the good times one shared with one's lover in life. If one regards bodhi (enlightenment) as something to be attained in life then he's guilty of the sin of the false pride of one's self. Before Captain Seisakajo-san mounted me, he warned me there might be some slight discomfort involved with our first coupling, until my Jade Gate grew accustomed to the invasion of his mighty peerless pestle. But he entered my womanness with so soft and slow approach that I barely felt any discomfort at all from the act of love making, Lady Yoke. I found myself locked within the great pleasures of pillowing, and I wrapped my foolish legs around his wonderful rump, and tried to draw his whole being through my wanting Gate, and swallow him whole if I was able to.

"During our first pillowing, I was fearful I might become with child, but he removed his mighty dragon from my Gate to pleasures before the seeds of birth were planted within me. He spilled his life giving juices on my stomach. I never saw this fluid before in my life, so I touched it and smelt it then I tasted it. Nothing about it did I find unpleasant or offensive. Salty yes, but not unpleasant at all, I think my mind was so confused by..."

"Ieeeee...Yuriko-san, you have learned the way of pillowing quickly and well I see, my wicked new friend from the ancient past times. Was he a long time friend before becoming a lover to be with, Yuriko-san? Were you long time lovers I hope? Please tell me more of Captain Seisakajo-san and his abilities at the art of pillowing." Again, she blushed red over her directness with the samurai from the past, but both women were acting like girls rating their lovers.

They laughed over Lady Yoke's question, before Wind turned serious and then added. "No Lady Yoke, I'm afraid we were not long time friends nor lovers. For much time, Captain Seisakajo-san was one of my personal guard Samurai given me by the understanding Lord Kawasomeru, for my personal protection from any possible assassin attacks against my person. I barely knew of his existence for many months, because I always ignored my Samurai, and we barely spoke before the night of my first pillowing with the young Captain. Yes, it is true we rode together on many occasions side by side, but we never talked. I mean, we never really spoke about private matters, or of life and common concerns. All our conversations were about the hated Lord Wakatsuki, and how we were going to destroy our Master's unwanted enemy.

"Yes Lady Yoke, we coupled for the first time because I was in desperate need of a warm and tender heart to hide my fears in. In my mind's eye, I saw the death of my beloved and honorable father, and I cried sadly for his fine spirit's freedom from all earthly ties, and his guidance of my wayward spirit and life. It was then that Captain Seisakajo-san gained his strength and dared to knock on my shonzukuri, the Samurai long house to see why I cried so in the darkness of the building. He requested permission to enter and I gave it to him reluctantly. Upon my crying, my Kimono was displaced and I saw him stare at my breasts.

"I am so sorry to admit this to anyone my friend, but that was that, and we found ourselves locked within each other's passionate embrace and needs of the body and soul. We had been lonely for much too long a time. We made love for what seemed to be an eternity to my foolish mind, until my senses finally returned, and I quickly ordered him out of my shonzukuri nastily I'm afraid. I felt deeply betrayed by my body's weakness, embarrassed over the pleasures that I had enjoyed, shared with the young Captain. I was a fool for allowing him to leave when I needed him so much. We could have coupled many times on that wonderful but most sad night. It was a night that I shall never forget. The experience was like the great doors of Heaven were cast open, and the Army of angels flooded out. It was wonderful Lady Yoke, wonderful."

The Lady Yoke felt terrible for Yuriko, because every word she spoke sounded so much like a military command, manly. Lady Yoke almost cried for her, she felt this female was robbed of the beautiful things that make a woman, a woman to be cherished by a man's heart. How terrible it must have been for her to live and loved through the terrible times of ancient Japan as a female samurai warrior locked behind a lie of being a male soldier.

The ancient warrior noticed the sadness in Yoke's eyes and offered in a calming tone. "Lady Yoke, only when you have no thing in mind, and no mind in things, you are truly vacant and spiritual, empty and marvelous and open to things you would not normally seek, or see with a clouded heart and blinded eye. Yes Lady Yoke, you are a kind and gentle person, but please do not fret over me or my past life. It was not as bad as it must sound to your most caring ears and concerned heart. You must remember that I was a well respected and highly honored Samurai, a woman Samurai Warrior, and a woman leader of men. My understanding Lord and Master made certain the Warriors of his realm knew I was the best Warrior in his Armies. Kawasomeru-sama was proud of me, and my accomplishments on the field of battle. I was a complete Samurai…"

"But not a complete woman, Wind-san." She interrupted then regretted her unkind words aimed at her new friend as she lowered her eyes and wished she could take back her words.

"Yes you are correct in your choice of words in which to address me with, Lady Yoke. I was never allowed to be a complete woman throughout my short life in the service of my Lord Kawasomeru. I was thunderstruck with overwhelming sadness when Captain Seisakajo-san went to the Floating World and left me behind to live on. I had a very hard life true, but the pillowing with Captain Seisakajo-san was well worth all the hardships I had endured for the rest of my life. The love of one man was worth more than the entire worth my Lord and Master had lavished upon my most undeserving shoulders." She stopped speaking and let out with a sad sigh then began to enjoy the hot water of the tub and dancing clouds again.

"Yuriko-san, what was it like to be a woman of a Samurai back them? A wife I mean." Lady Yoke asked as she allowed her hand to rest in the waters of the tub, and she swirled it around absentmindedly while listening to Wind's captivating words of Japan's past.

"Ieeeee… a woman of a Samurai had to be so much smarter than her husband Samurai…"

"As it's like now Yuriko-san. The women of my time have to be much smarter than their male counterpart at all times, or the fools would lose everything they own together. They're so stupid and helpless and child like." Lady Yoke interrupted Wind sarcastically.

Both women laughed over Lady Yoke's statement, knowing it was true.

"Yes Lady Yoke, you are wise beyond your young years." Wind paid honor to Lady Yoke by adding Lady before her name, as she added to her words. "But be fearful my friend, for a person might appear to be the fool, yet not be a fool at all. He may be more cunning than your wisdom, and may only be guarding his wisdom wisely against you. Lady Yoke, the Samurai wife had to handle all money matters for her most honorable husband. It was forbidden for a Samurai to soil his hands with money, or useless transactions.

"The Samurai's only reason for being, his only reason for living, his very existence was only to serve his Lord and Master honorably. The Samurai's wife was left to anticipate her Warrior's every need and wants, whether those needs were of the pillowing kind, or of a need to have a most understanding ear in which to complain in. It was not a difficult understanding to possess if one listened to her husband with a listening ear and an understanding heart. All the wise Samurai wife had to do was to merely think about her husband, and she would easily understand his every need before he made them known to her. Samurai do not like to have to ask for anything from anyone, it was well beneath them, and that too was also forbidden of them. Especially if the Warrior's needs are for his comfort or pleasure.

"It was considered unmanly, weak of conduct and will for any Samurai to think about creature comforts for himself. The Samurai's life was dedicated solely to protecting his Lord and Master, his interest, and the Samurai's wife to think and worry of his needs and comforts were her only way of protecting his life, and honoring her Lord and Master wisely at the same time. It was the wife's duty to make certain her Warrior was clothed properly, to check him before he was called to an audience before his Lord and Master. To make certain he ate properly, and rested correctly when at home and in peace. To look after his weapons, to make certain they were clean of rust or blood, and rice powdered down so the deadly Katana blade would slide swiftly and easily out of the divine wood scabbard, when needed to defend his Master, or himself.

"Yes Lady Yoke, a Samurai's wife's work was never-ending. Not only did she look after her Samurai and his earthly needs, she had to look after the house chores, dealings with anyone who either owed her husband money or rewards, or who he might owe debts to. She had to rear the children, and make certain they were well looked after. If her husband was brought down in battle, she had to look after herself, on her own. If her Lord was of kind heart and understanding eyes, he would look after her for the rest of her life. But if her Liege Lord was of the mean spirit, and cared little for the Warrior who died on his behalf, she would receive no further rewards from him, and she was usually forced into the service of one of the Tea Houses. She would be forced to sell her body time and again to have enough money to feed herself, and her children."

"Excuse me for interrupting your most enhancing words, Yuriko-san. But would the wife of the dead Samurai be well cared for in the care of the Mama-san of the well-known Tea House of the times past?" She asked, remembering the extraordinary stories she heard about the famous Tea Houses of the past, and the services the women performed for their paying admirers.

"I am so sorry to announce for your ears to understand Lady Yoke, but any woman forced to enlist her services to the Tea House, was usually rated by the Branch of the Willow tree. If she was lucky enough to be rated a woman of the First Branch of the Willow, she would command more in price than most Samurai could possibly afford to pay for her services of the art of pillowing. Her life was usually dedicated to serving any man of worth and respect. Usually, a woman of the First Branch was ultimately bought by her Liege Lord, once she had proven her mastered skills in the fine art of pillowing to him then she would become one of his many consorts. If she was lucky enough, she might even attain to become the Liege Lord's First Consort and Lady of the Castle.

"A highly sought after honor paid only to those chosen few wild and most daring beyond compare in the fine skills of pillowing and the art of pleasure giving to the man paying for her outstanding talents. The Lord could also use the consort as a special reward or gift to a certain Samurai because of his deeds on the battlefield, by giving him the contract of the woman of the First Branch of the Willow. But if the Master so chose to keep her for his private needs, she had to look after his every need and wants whenever the Master was tired of his number one wife's pillowing technique. But, if a Samurai's wife was forced to visit the Tea House for employment, she was always rated the Fifth Branch until proven otherwise to the Mama-san.

"Here, she would be used to satisfy the lowly farmer, a himin with money if he could afford her asking fee, or attend to the lowest of the low, the hated and foul eta class. When she no longer appealed to even these lowly types, she would be driven from the Tea House, and would find her only way of making money was by visiting the lepers who always had money. Once she pillowed with one of these filth, she would never be allowed to pillow with a clean person again.

"Yes the life of a woman in Japan was not one to be looked upon with relish or pride. If she displeased her husband, he was within his right to send her away without anything to see her through her life alone, or he could kill her if he so desired. If the infraction was severe enough, a woman's life was worth what her husband placed upon it. Her Samurai could beat her every day of her life without reason, and if his soul was of the black nature and she had no one to complain to. No one to protect her, she could be starved to death at the whim of her Samurai husband, or be traded by him to another Samurai in place of a past due monetary settlement or wager.

"Anything the respected Samurai husband wanted to do to, or against her was in his divine right by the laws that governed the land. That is why I considered myself far better off than most women of Japan. I, as a Samurai was respected even feared and sought after by many male Samurai who wanted to be taught my ways of warring and battle skills. My Master treated me as his equal, going against his Generals interests for my sake. I was given a fife worthy of a Daimyo, a great person, the land barons who controlled all trade in his area of responsibility. I had nothing I wanted for, nothing I longed for, nothing to be desired or needed..."

"But that of a true lover to share life with I fear Yuriko-san." Lady Yoke dared to snap, feeling that confident she could because of the rapid bonding of the two women that already took place between them.

Wind's eyes clouded over with sadness, and a tear escaped from the corner of her eye as she fondly remembered Captain Seisakajo-san's forever smiling face and his ever exploring hands. She longed for his warmth giving touch on her body. During the eons of time that had passed in the Floating World, she never once came across his forever wandering spirit. Never finding his spirit, she believed Captain Seisakajo was reborn samurai and no longer existing in the land of the Ukiyo World. After years of searching for his spirit, she was forced to give up her quest in search of his likeness, especially when Lord Kawasomeru requested her presence before him in the land of living, as she suddenly added to her words.

"Yes you are most correct with the words you aim at my heart, never a true lover to hold near and dear and treasure, to cherish above all else for life and pleasure, it is the only gift that the living world I truly missed all my foolish life. I prayed every night to the Kami of the Floating World to be allowed just one visit by Captain Seisakajo-san until his death separated us forever. I'll forever search and destroy any foul dog eating relatives of the cursed and lowly murderer of my beloved Samurai Warrior."

"I hate to ask this question of you for fear of upsetting your Wa, Samurai. But do you know the name of the filthy murderer you speak of, Yuriko-san?" the Lady Yoke asked Wind.

"Hai Lady Yoke, I know of the evil name that haunts my memory every second of my life in both worlds I dwell within. For countless years past I repeated the foul one's name until it was burned deeply in my everlasting hungering for revenge memory. But the repulsive hated name will never cross my lips to be honored by me. I refuse to give immortality to the memory of this murderer of my lover, or give comfort to any disgusting offspring by offering his name to another ear to hear and respect. Unless I have the ancestor of the dog eating coward cowering before me and my sword, to await my justice, my revenge and hatred harbored against him and his.

"Lady Yoke, I swear I will never rest peacefully in mind and body in either world I share, until I cleansed the living world of all dung heaps sired by this immoral detestable entity of the past. As I stated Lady Yoke, I shall teach all unholy ancestors of the loathsome and cowardly murderer a lesson in the virtue of revenge. I will forever teach the abhorrent mannered offspring's of this detested nauseating murderer, a factual and true lesson in the temperance of revenge and honor for ones soul and mind. I seek my revenge leveled at anyone sired by this murderer."

A glimmer of anger flashed across her pleasing eyes and face, as she envisioned in her mind's eye the detestable face of the murderer who erased Seisakajo-san's honorable spirit from the face of the earth, and took her only true lover from her so early in their budding relationship.

The Lady Yoke noticed her words unsettled her friend's Wa, and she decided to bring the sparkle of the stars back in her lack luster sad eyes. She softly stroke her temples with her fingertips, as she allowed her body to relax in the warm water of the tub, as she closed her eyes and allowed herself to enjoy what Lady Yoke was doing for her mind and body.

Lady Yoke was an expert at bringing a person to a relaxed state with her hands and soothing words. She shifted her slender body by the side of the tub until she sat directly behind Wind's back the best she could, while she rested comfortably in the hot tub. She placed slight pressure on Wind's neck, so she understood she wanted her to sit up straighter in the warm waters.

She kneaded the muscles in Wind's neck and she shivered even though she was sweating from the heat of the tub, with delight over her touch on her exquisite body. It was too long a time since she allowed herself to enjoy the pleasing touch of another person's hands laid on her body.

She allowed herself to enjoy this warmth feeling as long as possible. Just the touch of Lady Yoke's hands on her back and neck, relaxed her more than the waters did for her spirit and mind.

Her hands slowly slid down until she worked on Yuriko's powerful shoulders and upper back. Carefully and tenderly, she carefully worked the taught muscles of Wind's strong back until she found them starting to relax under her experienced touch, guidance and light pressure. Again, she returned to working on Wind's neck muscles still tensed and bunched up. Lady Yoke applied more pressure on these muscles with her thumbs and forefingers, making Wind moan with the pleasing touch of another's hands on her body.

She leaned forward and slid her hands up and under Wind's arms, and did not stop until she gently cupped each of her breasts. Her breath was hot in her ear, and she whispered softly as she also nibbled on her ear. "Yuriko-san, please, you have the body of a goddess of even our times. I see you as being more of a threat and weapon in this world of man with these, of nature's most deadly of weapons, to be used against a man in his domain against the will he tried desperately to force upon us women." Lady Yoke lightly shook her breasts and added. "Than with the mightiest of swords made of the finest steel and silk brads by man Yuriko-san, it's said in all Japan that if the flower is beautiful then it's in need of cultivating. And with these weapons you have on your chest, you can cultivate any foolish Japanese men of our time."

Wind purred as if she was in harmony with the universe, feeling her soft touch on her body and remembering the pleasingly Captain Seisakajo-san's face, and warmth giving hands. She relaxed further, and allowed herself to be swallowed up in her experienced hands, and moaned again a sigh of memory of her first lover she ever known in her lifetime in the living world.

"Yuriko-san, I'm afraid to offer this bit of worthless wisdom to you, but with the shape you possess, you can have most foolish men of modern day Japan panting, and sitting up and begging like little children, for the mere privilege to pillow with you for one mere night of pleasure and enjoyment. You're truly a goddess to be looked upon with reverence and respect, Yuriko-san." Lady Yoke announced proudly but softly in her ear as she smiled at the dangerous female warrior relaxing so easily at the end of her fingertips in the warm water.

She turned sideways in the tub and stared at the young woman playing with her breasts. She looked in the soothing eyes of Lady Yoke, and saw a face full of mischief and respect of her and of her life. She had no choice but to begin to laugh over acknowledging her words aimed at her moments ago, as they spoke privately together in the bathroom. Wind found herself respecting her new friend, and her feelings for this woman were confusing to her fine spirit. She was being torn between the feelings of respect, and also suffering through the same feelings that she once shared for her only lover of the past. In her troubled mind, Wind suddenly found herself falling in love with this beautiful young woman, and this was a new feeling for her to labor through. Never once in her life had she ever felt love for another woman, or to dare think how it would be to share her bed and love with another woman of Japan.

Wind had to shake her head in an attempt to drive out these new and troubling feelings and she laughed, which made Lady Yoke join her and they enjoyed the light moment, as they laughed together.

CHAPTER SIX

Hiromoai and Utsumi remained in the study sipping tea and chatting together. He heard the laughter from the bathroom, and was certain that Lady Yoke was bringing pleasures to his female weapon. That was what he had in mind all along. He loved to witness that special union of two women, especially if he was in the middle of them.

When he finished his tea, he stood and slowly walked around the massive study, carefully investigating each piece of ancient armor and weapons that he stole from Wind's crypt a few days ago at the construction site. Everything was in perfect shape before his eyes, highly decorated with inlaid gold and silver. Each inlay told a certain story of the past of Japan's great history. One scene engraved on a certain piece of armor clearly depicted the great battle between the cities of Kyoto and Kamakura. An arm shield depicted the invasion and defeat of the Kublai Khan invading forces. A highly decorated Yoroi Hitatare, the heavy over armor robe showed in all its splendor, the great battle that once raged between the two powerful warlords of Kawasomeru and Wakatsuki's and the sixteen providences that made up the land of Central Japan, and their samurai forces on the vast Kai plain.

Another relief decorated Kabuto helmet covered the battle at Minatogawa. The gold and silver inlay seemed like new, as if it was just made and polished. All dents, scars and damages once marring the items was missing from the pieces of armor had somehow magically reappeared in place in all their glory. He was thrilled beyond words, because he was wise enough to have removed everything he found buried from the crypt of this ancient female warrior.

He decided to keep every piece of armor and weapons they found for his property. Because as long as Wind was in his presence, the ancient items were like new. He decided he was going to have an artist come in the next time he sent for Wind. Once the armor was returned to new, he would have the artist duplicate the intricate inlaid work and paintings on each piece. When the armor returned to its terrible crumbling state, he was going to have an Army of workers repair the articles to their original state and luster. So he could enjoy the wonderful items even when Wind was not standing before him and sharing his presence.

As he slowly strolled around the massive study in silence and deep in thought, he carefully picked up a piece of armor and gently rolled it around in his hands. He thoroughly enjoyed the outstanding workmanship of the old crafters of past times. The chilling and ugly and always sneering brass Hoate face mask with the frozen sneer was a wonderful work of art in its own right. It was surprisingly heavy, weighing nearly five pounds he figured. He wondered how the warrior would wear such a heavy piece of armor, let alone fought in it. Everything he picked up of the ancient armor and weapons filled his heart with a new pride and respect for Japan's ancient past. Pride and respect for the romantic and savage history that made Japan a power to be feared by even the modern day world.

He listened, and again he heard the two women laughing and enjoying each other's company in the bathroom. He wanted to speak to Utsumi, but he also wanted to make certain the women were occupied before he began speaking with the old foreman. Slowly, he headed to his sofa with Utsumi following him around the room like a puppy. When the old man went to sit, he stopped him with a wave of his hand and signaled to sit alongside him on the sofa.

Again, Hiromoai Hatanaka listened to the soft sounds of pleasure from the bathroom for a moment, and when he heard the women laughing again, he leaned closer to Utsumi and then whispered. "Utsumi, who is the most dangerous fucking competitor in the construction arena I must fear the most? What company do you think gives us the most trouble landing government contracts and other large jobs throughout Japan? What CEO would be missed the most in this corporation? Who should I release Wind against first? Remembering once she is sent out to destroy anyone I deem standing in my fucking way of becoming the most powerful man in the world, that corporate leader's going to meet his fate at the hands of Wind's killing blade, old man." The

Japanese business owner asked of his old foreman while looking him in the eyes.

"Hieeeee Hiromoai-san there is so many it's hard to choose the worst of the lot, sir."

"Search your feeble mind old fool if you value your fucking job in my company. Think of the damn name I seek from your aged lips, old man. I'm seeking your wisdom in this problem I'm facing; I already have my first target picked out in my mind. But I want to make certain you have the same man in mind. I fear I might have overlooked the worst of the lot, and if you agree with my pick, I'll know I was correct in my first target for Wind's justice and sword. Don't keep me waiting too long to hear of your pick, old man. I'm extremely tired and stressed out, and my patience is no long under control I warn you old man."

"Are you really going to allow Wind to kill this man you have in mind, Hiromoai-san?" Utsumi asked, not believing his own question he just asked of his boss. Of everything he thought of Hiromoai, a murderer or user of an evil assassin had never once entered his mind. He always believed that Hiromoai was a most civilized man, and civilized men never employ the use of an assassin, and especially not want to kill someone.

"Don't trouble your impotent mind with worries that don't concern you in the least, old fool. Just concern yourself with the fucking answer to the question I just asked of you, Utsumi. I asked you for a name and I'm waiting for it to cross your foul lips, old man." He allowed his voice to rise a little over a whisper, to show Utsumi he was growing angry with his constant stalling.

"Hiromoai-san, the first name that comes to mind is the Yurkowa Earth Moving Construction Company of Tokyo, sir. They have leaders working in the government eating out of their deep pocket, Hiromoai-san. They seem to get the best of jobs we bid on first, even when they come in over our declaration price, and they get the job. This company and their evil owners have cost us much profit over the years, Hiromoai-san. The fools have successfully cornered the market on the earth moving equipment, forcing us to go to the hated United States to buy from their worthless American company of Caterpillar. To acquire our needed heavy equipment, while the Yurkowa Company enjoys using the equipment made right here in Japan, and they don't have to pay the high import prices and taxes that we're forced to absorb, sir. This company has cost us much money in the past, too much to be pleased with I add, Hiromoai-san." He held his breath, hoping he did not go against his boss's first decision with his offer.

The young Japanese owner of the construction company leaned back on the sofa and clapped his hands loudly together as he fired back at the old man. "There, you see how easy that was, Utsumi-san. You're much wiser than I thought you were old man, and that brings me pleasure to realize you have picked out the same miserable dog eating dung heap I locked my eyes on. Yes Utsumi-san, the Yurkowa Construction and the old bastard running the company is my main competitor on this Island. I'll tell you something else I know you're not aware of, old man.

"I'm in possession of certain inside information which informs me that Asahiko Yurkowa's detestable son Tsutomu, plans to sell our machinery to the ever intruding and foolish Americans. If Yurkowa is successful with opening the doors to the United States to sell his earth moving equipment there, they'll surely become the largest construction corporation in all Japan. I'll assure you of this much Utsumi, that honor's reserved for me and my company alone. I'll not allow that lowly dog eating fool to beat me ever again in any transactions we're engaged in." More and more, Hiromoai was adopting phrases from Wind while using the colorful words again, but only when he was not dealing with the ancient warrior from the past.

Utsumi nodded and smiled but was reserved in his tone, and this angered Hiromoai over his lack of enthusiasm for his plan to destroy the Yurkowa Construction Corporation and the owners of that company as well. Although Utsumi saw this company as the true enemy and main competitor, he did not like being involved in murder. If Hiromoai wanted to employ Wind's services, someone was going to die by her hungry for blood killing sword. If he knew about it, and did nothing to stop it then he would be as guilty as Hiromoai and Wind was, for the unspeakable crime of committing murder. This thought sickened him to his very soul. Even thought he done countless things in his past life that were not quite legal, and he also bent the law on many occasions, he never once crossed the line this far as to contemplate murder until today. He was scared to death to be involved in such a possibility.

His happiness left his body as he noticed the terrible strained expression suddenly etched on the foreman's weather beaten face, and he snarled angrily at him. "What the hell's bothering you this time old man? You seem suddenly upset. Talk to me old man."

"I'm terribly sorry Hiromoai-san, but I just can't get used to the idea of murdering one of our main competitors, sir. What have we become, to allow the deaths of a number of fine Japanese men only guilty of trying to survive in this stagnant economy of Japan? If you allow this ancient Samurai to take up arms against your competition in your name, I'm afraid you're as guilty as she is in the act of murder, sir. With my knowing about the sin, in the eyes of the law and the gods, I'll be just as guilty, sir. I just can't be a part of this..."

Hiromoai stood with a start and kept his back to his foreman as he quickly gathered his thoughts. Displaying the disdain he held in his heart for the old man, he snarled in a savage voice at him. "Who the hell are you to tell me anything, suggest anything to my ass, you old bastard! If I wanted your advice in this matter, I would have requested it come out of your foul spewing mouth. As for your feeling of guilt in this plan, old fool. You don't have to feel anything, I'll handle Wind and her orders will come from me, not from you so you're guilt free old man.

"I warn you old man, if you dare to speak a single word of my future intentions to anyone, anyone I warn you, Utsumi. Then not only you'll feel the wrath of Wind's Breath crashing down on your worthless neck, but your entire family will pay the same price with their lives for any disloyalty you offer against me or my plans. When you signed on with my company, you swore an oath to my father that you'd give him your total loyalty. I'm demanding you remember your oath to him and myself. If you betray me then you betray my father as well old man. If you do, I'll brand you a traitor, and your life would be worthless on the streets of Japan."

He turned and threateningly stabbed his finger at Utsumi's chest as if it were a weapon, as he spat at him with anger lacing his voice. "Utsumi! You'll do what I tell you, and you'll keep your mouth shut while you're at it! I'm in no mood to have any head games played against me by an old man waiting to die. I gave you a good paying job, and gave life to you and your worthless, dung eating family. Now, I have need of your fucking services above and beyond what you originally signed on for. It's my right to make these demands of your ass if you intend to remain breathing, and in my employ old fool. This is all I have to say to your ass on this subject. You'll do as I say, or your neck will become the first flesh I'll have Wind test with her sword on."

He bent closer to Utsumi and glared harshly at him while angrily waiting for his reply.

The old man squirmed under the angry glare from his boss. He was deathly afraid of this man, he was scared he might lose his job, his very way of life. He was stunned Hiromoai would dare to threaten him and his family with death, especially at the hands of this ancient spirit samurai. He was as angry as he was scared of Hiromoai. But in his heart, he knew he had no choice but to follow his boss' orders if he wanted to live. He was about to reply when he heard the bathroom door open, and both he and Hiromoai turned to see who was coming out.

The two women walked out of the large bathroom in a pleasant mood. Lady Yoke was in the lead, and she was followed closely by Wind, who was now dressed pleasantly in a brightly colored pure silk kimono that Lady Yoke lent her. Wind's small feet were covered by cotton cloth tongs, and her silk like jet black hair was placed up on her head in the soft bun shape of the old geisha women of Japan. It was held in place by a pair of antique Japanese ivory skewers from Hiromoai's private collection. The kimono garment was open to the waist, and offered a slight glimpse of her breasts as she walked like this warrior she was, proud.

Wind looked stunning, as he thought she would look as remarkable dressed in her ancient armor. He knew no matter what this ancient spirit wore, nothing would be able to overpower her beauty and outstanding shape, and the fact she was a woman of great beauty.

Lady Yoke saw Hiromoai first, and knew immediately he was having a slight disagreement with his foreman. She immediately tried to turn Wind around and head her back to the bathroom, so the two men could continue their conversation without them interrupting them. But Wind's sharp mind instantly noticed the confrontation, and her first thought was to protect her master.

She roughly shoved Lady Yoke aside as she charged forward, forgetting that she was her friend, almost knocking her to the floor and nearly running over the top of her as she rushed into the large study. The sounds of taiko drums rumbled on throughout the room as she entered in a rush. She covered the distance separating her from her new lord and master in less than a heartbeat. She was considered to be ashigaru (fleet of foot) and she proved it by how quickly she got to her master's side, prepared to protect him from harm even if it would cost her life.

Wind moved with the speed of the blowing winds as she scooped up her killing katana blade in her right hand, and instantly took a threatening pose in one motion, and aimed the blade at the old man's chest. She would not divert her eyes from him for a second, fearing treachery. She tried to place her body between her lord, and the old fool glaring back at her master.

Hiromoai would not allow her to shove him aside as easily as she did Lady Yoke.

She allowed her new lord and master to keep her from getting at her target, but she reached out with her killing sword and its steel shaft of the weapon stood between her master, and the old man still sitting on the couch shaking like a leaf caught up in the wind. The tip of the warrior's ancient blade was a mere few inches away from the tip of the old man's nose.

She hissed in a threatening voice at his foreman. "Foolish one of great age, it is I, Wind who will drive back the eyes of this devil! If I failed to protect my Master's life for just one instant of time, Fujin-sama will seek revenge upon my offensive soul, by feeding my worthless flesh to the fowl of the air and the lowly beasts of the fields, so I will not be able to be reborn Samurai."

Utsumi was scared to death to even dare breathe. He could not believe how swiftly this extremely dangerous spirit moved against him. He looked in the angry, staring cold eyes that left no doubt in his mind whatsoever that this woman would kill him in a flash, if he made a move. He pulled his arms to his body and held his hands palm up, so she could see he had no weapons. He hoped this move would take the threat out of her body, but Wind still refused to back down an inch in her intimidating stance held against Utsumi as she glared right at him.

Hiromoai's head spun, everything happened so quickly it was not registering clearly in his mind. When he noticed

Wind rush by him and pick up her sword and hurry back to his side in one swift motion, and then she shove the blade point right at Utsumi's face. He thought she was going to cut his throat, and he was powerless to react fast enough to stop her actions.

His first thought was maybe this weapon he found in the shape of this ancient female warrior was too much of an implement of war and a danger for him to completely control properly, and she would kill anyone who she deemed a threat against his person. He was suddenly worried she might be a power that might be too uncontrollable and she could cause him great embarrassment with her attempt to protect his life from any harm like she does. This was all he needed, with his so close to the surface hair-trigger temper and constantly fighting with business partners or workers or other companies he was forced to work with. He could very well end up losing a very close friend, or a much needed worker or even a ally he could ill afford to lose.

When she did not cut Utsumi's throat, his swift mind took over his actions. Quickly, he held up his hands as he bellowed at his new found weapon. "No Wind, don't! Don't kill my trusted employee Samurai. I told you I didn't want anything to happen to him and I meant it, I..."

"That order is the only reason your teki is still drawing his foul breath in the land of the living, my Lord." She snapped nastily, but she still would not take her eyes from the old man's face.

Hiromoai placed his hand on the top of Wind's Breath and applied pressure, slowly forcing the deadly blade that seemed to be actually vibrating on his hand, towards the floor.

The ancient female samurai allowed her eyes to drift from the old man sitting in fear on the couch, and she looked to her master with questioning eyes. She permitted his pressure to force her blade to a less threatening position, and her shoulders released some tension as she calmed.

"That's right Wind-san, there's something you need to learn if you want to remain in the land of the living. Just because I raise my voice or get angry with someone, it doesn't mean that he's my enemy or a possible threat against my person. What you see taking place before you, is just a slight disagreement over a work matter, nothing more. If you killed my trusted friend Utsumi-san, you would've harmed me in ways you wouldn't understand. Wind, I have many associates that I'm forced to deal with every day of my existence. I have many arguments with the fools as much, but I cannot afford to have you go flying off the handle and killing someone I might merely be arguing with. You have to learn to keep your killing heart under better control, or I'll stop sending for you from the land of the dead, do you understand me? Do you understand what I am saying, what I'm telling you Samurai?"

He did not wait for a reply from the female warrior as he added to his words. "Wind-san, I'd like to have you remain dwelling in the living world more than you float in the dead world of wonderment and myth, so you can enjoy more of what the living has to offer. But I'll not do that any longer if you're so damn willing to kill anyone who I have a slight disagreement with. You have to understand when my life is truly in danger Wind-san, or if I'm merely engaging in a verbal argument. There are few times in your service to me when you'll have to protect my life with your killing sword.

But I'll send you out on your own to destroy those who seek treachery against me. It's either that, or I'll order you to remain in a room if you're visiting when one of my associates is here, Wind-san." Hiromoai stared at her face until what he told her registered in her mind. He knew this when she lowered her sword, and relaxed her muscles. She dropped down to her knees and bowed, fearing she upset her lord.

Hiromoai then turned to face the old man. He saw nothing but sheer terror carved in the weather beaten face, and he realized Wind made his point to the old foreman, far better than he could have possibly hoped for. His face broke out in an ugly sneer as he hissed warningly at the old man. "Utsumi-san! I trust no further words on my part are necessary for me to enjoy your total loyalty in this matter we were speaking of. I think Wind-san has shown you your errors by refusing my demands, old fool. Am I correct in these thoughts, coordinator of antiques?"

Hearing his boss was going to take him out of the back breaking work in the work field and make him coordinator of his antique weapons and armors they discovered at the worksite, he decided if Hiromoai sent him out to kill his enemy, he would do it gladly now. Utsumi bowed, allowing his own sneer to slowly cross his lips, and it immediately informed his boss he was on his side and would back him with his death.

The young Japanese owner of the construction company suddenly glanced at his watch and was shocked to see it was so late. Time had flown by while they listened to Wind's very engrossing tail of Japan's ancient past and her life at that time. When they began speaking, it was just after seven p.m., now it was twenty past two the following morning.

"I knew you'd come around when you had a chance to think over what I was saying. Wind-san!" He turned to her and added. "You'll remain where you are while I deal with my help."

"Hai my Lord." Wind answered, not raising her head or eyes from the floor.

He looked to Utsumi then at Lady Yoke, and gave them both a swift head movement, showing them he wanted to speak with them in the kitchen without Wind present. They quickly filed out of the study, following him to the other room. When they entered the kitchen, they took chairs surrounding the table then he spoke slightly above a whisper to them.

"Okay, we heard what this woman Warrior from our ancient past had to say about her life in old Japan. It's late and I think you both should consider going home, but I want both of you to return here eight o'clock sharp tomorrow morning. If I'm sleeping when you return, allow yourselves in and begin work. Lady Yoke, you'll clean up the apartment, I noticed some missed dust and packing material lying around here and there. Utsumi, you'll find some better places to display the ancient armor and weapons. Keep your eyes open for any imbedded dust.

"You know what dust can do to the fragile metal of the ancient armor. Once you two are gone, I'll continue my conversation with this female Warrior. She might think she's through with her explanation of the past. But I some got news for her little ass, she only begun her story of the past. Well, that's all I have to say for this exhausting night. You're free to go home. But you're both warned to keep your tongues still about this ancient woman and the weapons we found at the construction site. I don't want any word of this damn Samurai, or any of her equipment to get out to the public. You both swear to me you'll keep my secret to your death?"

Utsumi stood and straightened his back and could not wait to get out of the presence of this threatening warrior from the past and his boss. But he was frozen in his tracks when he noticed Lady Yoke refused to stand. Working in construction all his life, he knew about backstabbing, and felt this one had something to say to Hiromoai, and she wanted to do it in private. He could not help but think she was going to go behind his back, and maybe beg to have his new job. The old foreman decided to remain where he was standing, and see what Lady Yoke wanted from his boss. So he took his seat again and stared at the young woman waiting to speak to his boss.

Hiromoai saw the concerned look in her eyes, and knew there was something on her mind and he snapped at her in an exhausted tone. "What is it you want now Lady Yoke? I'm really done in and I want to rest as I said, dammit. I want to talk a little more with Wind for a while longer then I'm going to turn in for what's left of this very exhausting night. Come on Lady Yoke and get to it for me will you please, what's bothering you now young lady?"

She cast her eyes to the floor as she began speaking just above a whisper. "Hiromoai-san, I was vain enough to dare hope that I might stay the night, and look after Wind and your needs as you have suggested before. I can sleep in my changing closet sir. Hiromoai-san, there's enough room to be comfortable in the room. I can sleep on the floor, I don't mind at all, sir. Wind is so unaccustomed to our ways of life, and I planned to explain a few of them to her when she woke. That's if you'll allow her to remain in the living world as you call the present time, sir."

Hiromoai let out his breath in a sigh, relieved it was no concerning matter that had Lady Yoke upset as he offered in a much calmer tone to her. "Lady Yoke, I can assure you that Wind will remain for the full five days she has allotted to her by the gods of the Floating World to visit with us. I have a lot of knowledge to learn from her, as well as she from us. Hmmmm... Perhaps this might not be so bad an idea after all, young lady. I could always use a woman around here twenty four hours a day to look after my needs. But you'll not sleep in that damn closet I'll tell you. You can utilize the fifth bedroom on this floor. It has its own bathroom and shower, so you won't be bothering the main shower or me. Yes, this is a very wise idea I must admit, Lady Yoke." Noticing the old man was still standing over his shoulder, he growled angrily at him.

"Well Utsumi, what the hell are you still waiting for, dammit? I gave you and your family an apartment. There's no reason for you to remain here, especially now Lady Yoke's going to stay." In the back of his mind, he had dancing visions of making love to Lady Yoke while she made love to Wind, and all three of them lying naked on his bed, playing the forbidden games of debauchery. The thought made his mind up on allowing Lady Yoke to remain in his penthouse.

Hiromoai's master bedroom took up the entire second floor of the luxurious and massive apartment suite, and it came equipped with a large wrap around outside balcony, a hot tub on that balcony that was large enough to accommodate ten people, and a wet bar that would make any bartender green with envy. His bathroom was large enough to get lost in, with a dry sauna and a miniature pond stocked with gold fish, and a bath tub that could hold four people, it also had two long vanities and mirrors spread throughout the huge room. Three skylights allowed in the sun or moonlight, and thus enabled the user to see the stars that sparkled throughout the long night, if they were enjoying a good soak together.

Seeing Lady Yoke had no claim against his job, Utsumi bowed politely first to Hiromoai then to Lady Yoke and then he turned and walked out of the apartment proudly.

When Utsumi was gone, Hiromoai ordered Lady Yoke to prepare her room for her presence. Before she left, he requested. "Lady Yoke, you'll not come out of your room for any reason, unless I send for you. No matter what you might hear going on out here. There's a phone by the side of your bed if I need you tonight, I'll page you through it. Good night Lady Yoke."

"Hai, good night Hiromoai-san. Where will Wind be spending the night with us, sir?"

"Dammit that's not your concern, Lady Yoke. You just worry about yourself for a damn change, and straightening your room. I'll handle Wind's sleeping arrangements, young lady."

"Hai Hiromoai-san, I can't tell you how honored I feel to be invited to live within your honorable home like this, sir. I'll bring good luck and Karma to you. I want to..."

"Yeah, yeah, okay Lady Yoke, I understand how you must feel and I appreciate it. But I have pressing matters to deal with, rather than getting involved in a long drawn out thank you from you. Please Lady Yoke, I'm tired, exhausted to be exact, and the sooner I finish speaking to Wind, the faster I can catch up on my sleep. Kon banwa Lady Yoke." (Good evening)

Lady Yoke blushed at the mild rebuff as she replied. "Kon banwa Hiromoai-san. Sleep well sir." Lady Yoke bowed to her boss then turned and headed down the hallway to her new room.

When she finally disappeared in her room, he rushed in the study, sat on the sofa before the kneeling samurai and spoke pleasantly, choosing his words very carefully. "Wind-san, you may stand before me." He waited until she was standing proud, and confident.

She bowed politely to the seated Hiromoai then rose gracefully to her feet.

He returned the bow just within being polite and barked at the ancient woman. "Wind-san, I wish for you to remove your Kimono. I want to see you in the way I first found you, if you don't mind. Seeing you in this manner might bring new questions to my mind I might want to ask."

"I do not mind Kawasomeru-sama. I do not suffer the sin of false modesty, my Lord." Without hesitation, she untied the obi and allowed it to slide down her silk kimono. Instantly, the two ends separated and he saw all of her he wanted to see. To his surprise, she sexually looped the silk kimono off her shoulders, but brought her arms up so the garment got caught in the cruxes of her elbows, and creased her body with the fine garment. The exquisite fabric hung around her form like that of a light blue floating cloud, completely engulfing the lower end of her beautiful body. It was a stunning effect, worthy of such a fine and attentive warrior.

He scrupulously studied her exquisite form for several long moments, rating it in his mind as he did any project he started. She was perfection beyond belief, beautiful and free of description, not a blemish or marring mark anywhere on her wonderful, rock hard body, no wasted fat or skin. Everything about this most enchanting and extremely dangerous ancient female samurai warrior was hard, perfect, and very threatening. He moved his head in order to get some of a side profile of her wonderful body as she stood before him proud, erect.

Wind understood what her master wanted from her, and she slowly turned her body so he could enjoy his efforts and exploration of her body. She smiled over the consuming power her body commanded over her new master. He was almost drooling over her.

He absentmindedly drew in his breath in a rush as if the female spirit standing before him was robbing him of his air, never before in his entire life had he ever seen such beauty and perfection possessed by any woman of Japan. Whose exquisite body should adorn the canvasses of the ancient Masters. Her breasts turned slightly upwards, with no sign of sag to them. Her nipples were in the center of her breasts, and the ring that circled them was perfect, exquisite. From the side view, he could see she had no belly at all, just the fine hard lines of her taut stomach muscles shown through the tight skin of her waist. Her long and slender legs could have only been copied by the greatest of marble carvers of ancient Rome.

Even then, he doubted the human carvers could possibly capture such perfection with mere marble, chisel and sweat. Even her feet were perfect, small, well shaped with smooth toes and well trimmed toe nails. Her hands warned of their smoothness, but yet the strength they held. She had powerful shoulders that easily enabled her to use her sword so effectively. After a short time of drinking in her unlimited beauty, he waved a finger calling her nearer to his body.

Wind's mind tingled with anticipation and desire of what her master was going to do to her body. She was open to any sexual experience she could enjoy in the world of the living. It was too long since the last time she had the privilege of pillowing with another mortal. She moved forward until her toes were almost touching the sofa, stopped and waited for his next move.

When she did, he reached up and gently cupped a breast in each hand. He slowly rolled the fine mounds of soft, silk like flesh in his hands, pinching the nipples lightly, gently between his thumb and finger as he enjoyed her outstanding sexual treasures. A weak moan suddenly escaped her lips as she allowed herself to remember her past lover as she got completely engulfed in his masterful touch and her desires. Her body reacted to the slow motion of his hands. She bent her neck back and closed her eyes as she enjoyed what he was doing to her.

While he enjoyed playing with her breasts, he slowly worked his right foot between her feet, and then he began to move it back and forth, gently forcing her legs apart with this motion. Soon, her legs were apart far enough to give him easy access to her sex.

Her breath came in heavy rapid pants, as she waited not so patiently for what she felt was an eternity, for his hand to finally probe her inner self. He reluctantly released his grasp on her breast and ran his hand slowly down the outside of her exquisite and rock hard body, to the fine curving of her narrow waist, and the delicate swell of her left hip. Actually tickling her skin as he slid his warm hand slowly across her belly to her lovely side, he went up and down here for a few times, lightly touching and driving her wild with impatience and wanting. His hand started sliding down her long slender left leg to her knee, sending shock waves of pleasure trembling throughout the full length of her exquisite taught body. She could not believe the wonderful feelings that her new lord and master awoke within her wanting body, with the mere light touch of his experienced hands and finger tips on her sweating skin.

He slid his hand from her knee and moved it to her inner thigh, and then he slowly worked his hand towards her center. Lightly tracing out small circles with his palm and fingertips on her warm skin, as his hand worked ever upwards.

She almost came right then when his right thumb lightly flicked the very tip of her wanting womanness. Suddenly, he stood and pulled her tightly to his hard body, he kissed her hotly, greedily, with a passion and fire burning wildly within his heart and body. He opened the obi of his exquisite silk green kimono, and then he allowed the robe to slide away from his shoulders as he kissed her forehead and then her closed eyes, next he kissed her both cheeks.

His breathing made her ear get goose bumps as he blew softly in it. His breath was making a slight whistling sound as he kissed the very tip of her chin, and then he actually licked it. He forced her head back with his hand by grabbing the back of her jet black long hair, not so gently pulling it back as he kissed the hollow in her throat, licking it as well as he breathed on her neck. Again he was driving the unleashed desire wild within her waiting and wanting body. She was getting weak in her knees as she waited for his next pleasures to drive her wild.

He slid down to his knees before her, forcing her to move a little away from the couch with the weight of his body pressing against her. Then he kissed her chest as his hands returned to softly kneading her breasts gently. She relaxed her arms, and her silk garment slid silently from her arms and landed on the floor, surrounding her feet in its beautiful mist of blue silk. He kissed the top of her breasts and then he ran his tongue from her breastbone outwards until it found her nipple. He drew the tiny pearl in his mouth and ran his tongue over it several times as he sucked on it as a nursing child would after finding the waiting teat. The effect made her break out in a cold sweat, and get weaker in her knees and tremble slightly with desire.

His tongue and mouth lingered while exploring her erect nipple, pressing, nibbling without teeth, and then drawing on it and letting the nipple go, only to repeat this action a second time. Everything he was doing to her breast, made her more receptive, wanting, needing his desire to fill her. His left hand worked over the other breast, pinching the nipple gently between his fingers then rolling it between them. Slowly, he ran his tongue down her body to her belly. Going down to her belly button he lingered there for a moment, dipping the tip of his tongue into the small pond then rolling it around inside it for a brief moment, forcing her to shiver with delight and desire. He kissed it and probed the tiny opening again with the tip of his tongue.

She suddenly arched her back in an effort to offer herself completely to his fine exploration of her body. She was pressing now, wanting to begin the act of pillowing with her lord and master. But he would not be rushed by her impatience and pressing him forward. He was doing his act as if it was a sort of rite, a ritual that he needed to complete before finally making love to her. Everything he did to her exquisite body was being done with one thought in mind, giving his mate pure pleasure and desire, and sending her into that world of pure desire and lust.

Wind could not wait any longer and she started really pressing by rested her hand on the top of his head, and she tried to push it down as she remembered what her only lover had done with his tongue. But he resisted her pressure as he kissed her hip and then the side of her rearend as he hugged her hips tight to him. She arched her back so far she nearly tipped over, but he did not relinquish his pleasurable assault on her body. Instead of allowing her to tumble to the floor, he took her full weight in his arms and slowly lowered her to the floor. He slid down the length of her body and forced his head between her legs. He kissed and licked her thighs, not neglecting either. He continued kissing and sucking her skin as he worked his way to the inner thigh.

She was wiggling and moaning almost constantly now under his skilled actions and attention. In all her life, she had not ever experienced the delights he was arousing in her body tonight.

He suddenly pulled her legs up and forward so he had total access to her flowering petals. He looked at her loveliness because it was free of hair, and found himself enjoying this experience immensely. He ran his tongue slowly over the folds, and she jumped and arched her back and shivered and exploded in unashamed lust. He tasted her and she tasted good. He licked her offering as if licking a lollipop. He ran his tongue inside and then licked the walls of her inner self. He drew in the little node of pleasure and rolled it gently between his lips. He sucked on it and let it go and then drew it back in his mouth, running his tongue over the very tip of the pleasure giving center. He even breathed on it, his hot breath further driving her wild with sheer desire and wanting as she closed her eyes so tight and bent her head back again.

She suddenly cried out, her mind locked deep within the pure delights of wild passion, her breathing coming faster and faster as the next wave of overwhelming pleasure built up wildly in her mind and body and threatened to explode within her. She exploded without shame a second time. The saltiness again filled his mouth, and made him go wild with his own built up passion, as he rapidly increased the rotations of his tongue, sucking and kissing every part of her love.

When he felt he had her right where he wanted her, and she could climb no higher in the height of her own passion as she was. He suddenly slid his body up hers, stopping just long enough to nibble lightly on her nipples for a moment, and then kissing her chest as he continued to slowly inch his way up her exquisite body until he finally reached her waiting mouth. She returned the kiss with an equal wild abandonment, but did not know how to respond when he forced his tongue into her mouth. She never kissed anyone using her tongue.

She opened her mouth to the pressure of his probing tongue, and she enjoyed the wonderful meeting of them in her mouth. When she kissed him, he slid himself deep inside her and started rotating his hips slowly while pushing up, further driving her wild.

The ancient samurai locked his rearend to her with her powerful legs once she wrapped them around his rearend. Arching her back tightly to him in order to meet his powerful and mighty thrusts, she moaned with delight, pulsing with the emotion of his hard pushing, feeling the fullness of his shaft deep within her, enjoying every movement of the wonderful experience. She forgot how wonderful it was to pillow with a man, especially a man who knew how to wake the sleeping passion and emotions of a woman he was pleasing. Her cries of pleasure mingled with those of his grunts and snorts, as their bodies became one in the act of lovemaking, with their breaths mingling together in the height of passion in the art of pillowing.

Hiromoai unexpectedly pulled out of her, feeling the exquisite fruition of the action and then he dipped himself back deep inside her. He increased his speed, forcing her to join his mounting passion with wild thrusts of her own. When he felt her shake under him, he knew she came again. He suddenly pulled out of her at the last moment and stood while pulling her up roughly by the hair, and made his member dance right before her eyes.

He then guided her head to his waiting shaft by her hair, and when the very tip of it lightly touched her lips, she parted her mouth to its pressure. It was the first time in her life that she allowed a man's member into her mouth. She not only tasted him, but herself on the mighty shaft, as she slid it in and out of her mouth rapidly. She was still caught up in her own heights of passion of coupling with her new master. She had no control over her body nor did she want to control it at this time. All she wanted was to please her new master and was willing to do anything in her understanding to accomplish her and his desires.

While she licked the pulsating hard shaft, she felt it grow stronger, thicker until he finally exploded in her mouth. Being inexperienced as she was, she did not know what to do with the hot liquid surging into her mouth, so she just swallowed what she could of it but he pulled out of her mouth, shooting half his essence on the side of her cheek and lips and over her nose. It was a wonderful experience, one she was certain she was going to enjoy again and again when visiting the living world. She did not find the taste of his essence offensive, even enjoying the taste of it as she licked what she could from her lips, cheek, and his still swaying shaft.

He finally released his grasp on her silk like jet black hair, and she fell backwards to the floor, exhausted from the pillowing with her master. He dropped down to his knees, and sprawled out on top of her sweat soaked body. His body was not heavy on her, and she enjoyed the warmth and weight of him lying right on top of her naked as he was. She loved the weight of his body, she loved the sexual pleasures he showered upon her wanton spirit with. She was beginning to fall in love with her new master, and liking the feeling of his rock hard body against hers.

Hiromoai then rolled off to her side and slowly ran the tips of his fingers lightly over her breasts, nipples and taught stomach. The touch of his fingers was like a hot match being traced across her body, raising her to heights of new passion. His shaft rested tight against her thigh, and she reached down and began to stroke his shrinking member. But soon gave up because it was not responding to her touch and manipulation. She rolled over to her side so she could face her liege lord while wearing a dreamy smile with her eyes half closed, and was surprised to find him fast asleep while laying on the hardwood floor. She smiled in the closed eyes of her lord and master and now lover, feeling fulfilled as she listened to the rhythm of his heavy breathing.

She did not have need of much sleep, so she got up and pulled the thin tatami mat from under the table, and slid it up against his body. Then she rolled him onto the mat, being careful not to wake him. Next, she took a small pillow from the sofa and placed it under his head. She looked around and the only item she saw to cover him with was a richly decorated throw blanket. It was an exquisitely painted silk rendition of Kublai Khan's invasion of Japan, with hundreds of mounted samurai attacking the invading enemy forces, driving them back into the sea and their deaths. Many bodies lay trampled under the wildly charging horse's hooves.

After carefully studying the thrilling scene of the great battle for several enjoyable moments, she placed the cloth over her sleeping master. Then she curled up in a tight ball naked on the sofa, sleeping over her master's prone body for the rest of the night, taking the posture of protecting his life while he slept so peacefully on the floor. She also slept peacefully, happily remembering the beautiful coupling and comparing it to when she first made love to Captain Seisakajo so long ago in her ancient past. It was a most pleasurable joining, but she found herself wishing that Captain Seisakajo had placed his mighty member in her mouth as Hiromoai had done to her. Because she found the ways of the mouth a most enjoyable act to enjoy while in the motions of making love to a man.

She found herself feeling she had robbed Captain Seisakajo of a most pleasurable part of their first coupling. Sleep finally engulfed her exhausted body, and thoughts of failing Captain Seisakajo fled her memory as she relived Hiromoai's outstanding lovemaking to her.

CHAPTER SEVEN

TUESDAY, JUNE 4th, 1996

Yoke was the first to wake and came out of her room and brewed tea for her master and his female weapon. While the water was heating, she strolled into the study to see what shape it was in. The glistening weapons and ancient armor caught her eye first, bathed in the soft blue glow from the tanks filled with tropical fish. Then she noticed Hiromoai lying on the floor, covered with his prized relief. Her hands went to her mouth, fearing he might have gotten so drunk last night, he did not care if he ruined the expensive exquisite relief. She stepped in the study and her eyes picking up the naked but already on guard, beautiful female samurai from the past times.

Wind held the smaller, razor sharp wakizashi short stabbing sword locked within her hand, her body ready to leap on the shuffling feet she heard coming into the study moments before. She instantly relaxed her threatening stance when she noticed it was the Lady Yoke entering the room. Every muscle of her body was ready to spring into action against any unknown intruder to her master's castle, and possible threat to his life.

She bowed to Lady Yoke from the sofa as she began to wiggle her legs out from under her, and sheathed her short stabbing sword at the same time. Then the ancient samurai stretched her arms over her head, and wiggled her body to realign her backbone.

Lady Yoke returned the kind courtesy with a pleasant bow at Wind.

Wind placed a finger to her lips then cast her eyes at the peacefully sleeping master lying on the hardwood floor. Yoke smiled as she nodded and waved Wind to follow her to the kitchen.

As she left the study to follow Yoke, she retrieved her kimono from the floor. But Hiromoai was sleeping on her obi, so she allowed the robe to flow freely around her body like the morning mist. She entered the kitchen and Lady Yoke pointed to a chair pulled out for her use. Sitting in the chair was a new comfortable encounter for her. Instantly, a steaming cup of tea was placed before her, with Lady Yoke bowing to her in a morning greeting. She felt honored this woman was giving her the first cup of tea to enjoy. A privilege usually reserved for the master of the house. She slurped it noisily to display her appreciation of the offering from the other woman.

Lady Yoke was embarrassed by the god awful noises coming from such a beautiful and well trained woman. But she chose not to correct her actions, she was not certain if the noise had any meaning in the past of the samurai's life, but in modern day Japanese women did not make those noises under any circumstances, especially in front of another person. Everything a woman did was to guard themselves from being embarrassed before any male member of Japan.

She sat at the table enjoying her tea with Wind, occasionally glancing at the dangerous samurai to check on her needs. She placed rice cakes on the table, and Wind was enjoying one. The warrior caught the glances and ignored them. It was only when she caught Lady Yoke looking at her with a smile she acknowledged her stare. Without hesitation, both women giggled like children with Wind trying to hide her laugh behind the rice cake and tea cup in her hands.

Lady Yoke laughed so hard she had to place her cup on the table and hide her laughter behind the mask of her slender hand. Even in modern times, it was the height of bad manners by allowing your mouth to gape before another Japanese person. Between her laughter, she got some words out. "Well Yuriko-san, how was Hiromoai-san's lovemaking technique?"

She cocked her head to the side at hearing her liege lord was now going by the name of Hiromoai-san. She accepted this because it was Lord Kawasomeru's divine right to employ any other name he so chose to be addressed by. Coming back to her conversation with Lady Yoke, she replied to her question with excitement lacing her tone.

"Fantastic! Does Hiromoai-sama do everything as well as he does the act of pillowing with a woman, Lady Yoke?"

"Hai, he's a master at whatever he tries in life, Yuriko-san." She replied as she tried to retain her smile before the strange and beautiful female warrior of the past times.

"Lady Yoke, there are two ways of spreading light from the Heavens above, one is to be the candle that gives light birth, the second to be the mirror that reflects light and makes it grow. I'll be looking forward to the next time we pillow again. I'll make the act of pillowing grow brighter. Ieeeee... Lady Yoke, Hiromoai-sama made my teeth melt in my mouth. I never experienced such pleasures of the flesh and mind. It makes me sad I am no longer able to enjoy such happiness every day of my life. I am sorry I must dwell in the confines of the forever lonely Floating World, until I am next summoned by my Lord. I would so enjoy pillowing every night if I were allowed to share it with Hiromoai-sama. To be a Samurai is to be governed by a commanding Master..."

She stopped speaking when she noticed the cloud of sadness crossing over the lovely eyes of her friend, and stared at her with questioning eyes. She offered kindly, "please Lady Yoke do not fret so for my unworthy soul. I have enjoyed a good life in the past, and the Kami have seen fit to grant me the privilege to enjoy the world of the living more times than this worthless vassal should enjoy. I am happy beyond words and fulfillment, proud to be Samurai."

"I'm sorry, but it's not that Yuriko-san. It's..." she replied, fighting back tears.

"Iye! If not that then what is upsetting you so deeply on this lovely morning, my friend? You were so happy and pleased when I first entered this room. Could it be my worthless presence has upsets you so, Lady Yoke?" she asked as she stared into the eyes of the sad looking Lady Yoke.

"Oh no, please don't think that for a moment, Yuriko-san. I'm afraid I love you like a sister already, Yuriko-san. It's just that I find myself wanting to remain in your presence all the time, to learn more from you, and that of the old ways and to maybe teach you of the many ways of the new modern world while I'm at it, Yuriko-san." Lady Yoke again cast her eyes towards the table, as a tear escaped from her eye and ran down the side of her cheek.

Wind studied the strained face of the beautiful woman then understood what was bothering her soul, as she offered. "Lady Yoke, one cannot love or hate something that is about another, unless it rebounds something that one loves or hates about one's self. Not knowing how near the truth rests in the harmony of things to be, people seek it in the distance, always lying out of hand's reach. They are like him who stands in the midst of a clean lake, cries in thirst so imploringly. Ieeeee, to think my addle and worthless mind is so clouded and packed with manure, as not to see what is written on the sad face of my friend who is so attentive to my many needs and desires."

She looked back at Yuriko with puzzlement clouding over her damp eyes now.

"Lady Yoke, people in the world do not doubt it is the teaching that is the true beginning of confusing doubt. When experience is viewed in the ways of teachings, it presents unlimited doorways into the domain of the inner soul and peace. I'm so sorry for pillowing with your lover, Lady Yoke." She felt the fluttering of Lady Yoke's heart, and knew she was right in her assumption Lady Yoke had eyes for Hiromoai, and she was guilty of trotting on her feelings.

"Oh no Yuriko-san, I'm afraid that you're confused over what is truly troubling me. Hiromoai-san is not my lover at all." She sighed deeply.

"Huh, the best lie is the truth, and the best wisdom lies in silence. A piece of wood cannot burn by itself. Then it is your heart that wishes Hiromoai-sama was your lover, neh (isn't it) Lady Yoke?" She dared to look deeply in Lady Yoke's sad eyes while waiting for her reply.

Lady Yoke dabbed at her eyes with the napkin, but she did not reply to Wind's accusation.

"Huh! I thought it to be so I see I am correct in my assumption. Lady Yoke, you wish Hiromoai-sama for that of your feathered pillow, neh?" Wind smiled kindly at her friend.

"Yuriko-san, yesterday you accused me of being wise and understanding, now it's I who must pay the same homage to you. Yes Yuriko-san, I wish beyond all else that Hiromoai-san was my lover more than life itself. He has been so kind to me and my family of late, and it has reinforced the feelings of love that I harbored for him over the many years I've known him. I know if he'd allow me to please him just once, I can make him happy beyond his wildest dreams. I'm well trained in the countless ways of pillowing with a man, to make him forget about any other woman in the world, while he's sharing my wonderful delights for one night."

"Huh Lady Yoke, it is not what happens to one that disables him, but what that one does about it that matters in the flow of life's forces, and lessens the pains of the lonely and searching heart to endure. Do not seek to follow in the footsteps of the ancient Masters, seek what they sought in the past. I believe it shall be a fine coupling when you finally entice Hiromoai-sama into your web of wanting and desire. He is truly a well educated master when it comes to pleasing a woman on the pillows of pleasure and desire. But alas, this stupid Warrior is sorry my foolish eyes had not read what was written upon your heart, Lady Yoke. I would have found a way to have avoided pillowing with your intended lover, my pretty friend.

"It is a terrible insult I have heaped upon your most honorable soul and heart, Lady Yoke. I should commit Suppuku at your feet, to make amends to your presence and the gods who allow me to dwell within the living world, no matter how brief my stay may be here. Lady Yoke, can you find it in your heart to forgive this ill mannered and very foolish Samurai for her blindness to your heart's desires and wants? Bentatsu, the act of love is meant to be shared by the ones truly in love it is not to be celebrated for the mere sake of lust, and to fulfill the animalistic needs of the body and mind. To pillow is most spiritual and honorable, Lady Yoke."

Yoke smiled weakly at the spirit. "I have nothing to forgive you for. I have no claims on his uncontrollable heart. I fear he doesn't know I exist when pillowing enters his mind. I'm not insulted you coupled with him. In fact I'm pleased you were able to bring pleasures to him."

"Lady Yoke, it is said to learn the most confusing ways of Lord Buddha is to learn about one's own self. To learn about one's self, is to forget one's self. To forget one's self is to be enlightened by everything that makes the world exist as we know it. To be enlightened by the breathing of the world's heartbeat and understanding it pulse, is to let fall one's body, mind, and soul to be empty and pure. No matter how much we try, we think, we can only come up with but a pale reflection of true reality. Huh! If you believe that Hiromoai-sama does not even know you exist when pillowing enters his heart and mind then we shall have to do something about that very foolish belief of his. Look within yourself Lady Yoke, for Thou are Buddha.

"Yes Lady Yoke, we shall do it in most deceitful ways that Hiromoai-sama's eyes will understand what his mind is unable to see. Without going anywhere you can understand the world's secrets. Without opening your eyes, you can understand the countless ways of Heaven. Lady Yoke, the further away you go, the less you will know. Everything you need to win the heart of Hiromoai-sama is in your spirit. You have many exquisite Kimonos to choose from I believe. We must find one that compliments your body perfectly. You will serve us tonight in the Kimono we pick out, allow the obi to remain loose about your waist. Then, you must linger in your bow towards Hiromoai-sama. Allow his eyes to wander your throat and the fine swells of your lovely breasts. Once you are certain you have captured his attention, you must then right yourself and leave the room quickly. But make certain your rearend dances as you walk."

"Yuriko-san, I'm sorry to admit, but I have tried that just yesterday on him, and it did me no good." Lady Yuko complained to her fellow conspirator.

"Lady Yoke, one thing you must understand about reality, is by sitting quietly, offering nothing, spring comes from winter's grasp and the grass will grow by itself. But we must add the needed water to make nature move along much quickly in this case, especially because we are forced to deal with a man's foolishness. When you accept the understandings life brings forth before you, even though those lessons might be most unpleasant and very challenging to accept. Then you took the first step to entering the location of your true self and real purpose on this earth and life. This is when you first begin to cultivate the essential attitude of pure openness and complete understanding. Wonderful legends that allow fantasy to fly high, and to cause that slight escape from reality are all about you, if you come to see with your heart instead of your unseeing eyes. Lady Yoke, what have you tried to do that you feel has missed its target's eye?"

She chuckled softly because she was embarrassed by Wind's words as she offered. "Yuriko-san, when I went to the kitchen to prepare his tea, I loosened my obi and pulled the front of my Kimono up. I was certain he enjoyed all I could show him without being too obvious about it. Yet, he had failed to request my presence in his bed. I'm afraid it's hopeless."

"What's hopeless Lady Yoke?" A man's voice suddenly asked from the arched hallway.

Lady Yoke jumped at the sound of his voice as he entered the kitchen. "It was noting Hiromoai-san." She bowed low, correctly and held it for the proper amount of time.

"I don't believe that for a second young lady. I see by your eyes that you're sad on this morning. Besides, if it's true and it's not important then why did you choose to bring it up to Wind-san's attention and not mine? I repeat Lady Yoke? What's hopeless?" He snapped as he nodded his bow towards her then rested his hands on his hips and continued to stare at her dressed in the kimono she wore the night before. He moved his hips slightly from side to side in an attempt to try and ease the aching he received from sleeping on the hard wood floor.

"I see by your stretching your back is bothering you, Hiromoai-san. I can walk on it if you like? It always seemed to relieve your pain in the past?" Lady Yoke asked politely.

"Don't try and change the subject on me young lady. I'm wise to those little tricks you played against me. I want to know what was bothering you before I walked in the kitchen. I know I can help if you'll allow me to assist you." He moved further in the kitchen as he held her in his stare.

"Please forgive this worthless servant Hiromoai-san. You should have a cup of tea resting before you. I'll get one for you. Please, make yourself comfortable at the table." She was trying desperately to change the conversation again as she stood and pulled a chair out for her boss to seat himself, and then she rushed for the stove to retrieve a cup of tea for him.

He took the seat, he was dying for a cup of tea, but he wanted to know what was upsetting Lady Yoke. He turned in his chair and was about to growl at her when Wind interrupted.

"Hiromoai-sama, I trust that you slept well last night." She flashed her best smile, it was strange for her to use his new name, and she made certain she added the 'sama' which meant lord to his name, when addressing him; as if she used the name she called him throughout her many years of service to her lord and master.

"Huh, I see I'm not going to get a straight answer from either of you confusing women. Lady Yoke, I see you have enlisted the help of Wind-san to add to my confusion. As long as I live, I'll never understand the mystical world of woman." Giving up trying to find out why Yoke was upset, he continued. "I'll take it you two were talking about woman stuff and let it go at that."

"You're wise to believe that thought, Hiromoai-sama. Ikaga desu ka?" (How are you?) Wind asked politely of her lord understanding she and Lady Yoke won a minor victory over her master.

"Domo genki desu, Wind." (Quite well thank you.) He replied pleasantly.

With the morning politeness over, he sipped his tea. Then he glanced at Wind and smiled as he offered. "Wind-san! I'll speak with you further tonight after I returned from my boring meetings today. I am setting up a meeting with the always troublesome Tsutomu Yurkowa for later this morning. I might have need of your services before I planned to make use of them, Samurai."

Wind blushed, thinking he might want to repeat last might's pleasantries as she replied without hesitation. "My Master, my Katana and spirit are yours to command as you deem necessary." She bowed as best she could while seated. She hated to admit it, but she was getting used to the lack of attention usually aimed at the master of the house in times past. She enjoyed sitting in the chairs that supported her back. There were so many pleasantries of this living world she enjoyed.

Turning his attention to Lady Yoke as she poured his second cup of tea, he grumbled while still wondering what was upsetting her. "Lady Yoke, I'll be gone most of the day, I expect to return by seven tonight. I'd like a warm dinner when I get home, some warm sake will be nice as well."

"Hai, I'll have a fine dinner waiting you no matter when you return from work, Hiromoai-san."

"I had no doubt you would. I'll leave for my office when I finish my tea and dress..." He took a sip from his tea and then leaned back to relieve some of the pain in his back.

"Huh, you'll not be enjoying your breakfast sharing it with us this morning, Hiromoai-san?" Yoke cried, she was upset her boss wasn't going to have something to eat before starting his work. Besides, she wanted to remain in his presence as long as possible before he left for the day's toils. She felt the more he saw of her, his interest in her might grow for her treasures.

"Naw, I have to get going. I have a busy day scheduled, Lady Yoke."

"It's not a wise man who goes off to work on an empty stomach. You must have food to work for the day. Please allow me to make you something to eat." Lady Yoke warned as she almost pointed her finger at him before catching herself. She was calling on the training her mother gave her on how to please a man, and arouse his interest. She was beginning to press him with her attention, and realized she had to back off before scaring him away from her true intentions.

"Yes, I know this, but you're starting to sound more like a wife than a helper lately. I'm getting a little worried about you. First I find you next to tears this morning and now you're trying to sound like a wife. What else are you going to surprise me with this morning?"

"Me Hiromoai-san?" She asked with a shy smile as she pointed to herself and turned to him.

"Yes, you, and don't give me any of that poor little old innocent me look either young lady. It won't work this time I assure you." He retorted while flashing one of his well noted smiles.

Lady Yoke glanced at Wind and they both instantly started to giggle.

"Yes, I see by the way you're acting that you have a new partner in crime helping you play your little head games against me, Lady Yoke. I trust that you'll look after your new found friend while I'm at the office today? Lady Yoke, Wind-san is allowed to do anything she pleases but leave the apartment for any reason. Nothing is off limits to her interest inside the apartment. Make certain she has plenty of rest and food, some sake if she prefers. The old fool Utsumi will be returning to the apartment to look after the armor and weapons later this afternoon. He'll need to be fed as well I guess. If you're low on anything, send him out to the store for it."

"Hai Hiromoai-san, I'll look after everything while you're at work today, sir."

"Fine, fine, I'll get dressed then. Wind-san, Lady Yoke will give you other Kimonos to wear today. If you have need of any other clothes or needs, ask her and she'll go shopping for your needs. Don't leave the apartment under any circumstances. Do you understand my orders to you Samurai?" He warned as he stared at her, while waiting for her to reply.

"Hai Hiromoai-sama, I understand what it is you want of me and I shall follow your orders faithfully, my Lord and Master." She replied, pleased that he had the forethought to add the san on the end of her name. It was centuries since anyone thought to honor her so. Even though the san was mainly reserved for a male warrior, her position made it acceptable to use it with her name, and an honor to be addressed with the manly respect. She was able to follow most of his words because he and Lady Yoke used flawless Japanese when speaking. Some words were foreign to her, and for now she let the words she did not pick up, go. When she got to know Lady Yoke, Hiromoai, and Utsumi a little better, she would then inquire what those few words she did not fully understand meant. For now, time was on her side for further learning.

Hiromoai stood and headed for his master bedroom suite to shower and dress. He was sore from sleeping on the floor, and for a moment he considered taking Lady Yoke up on her offer to work out the nagging kinks and pains of his back by walking on it, but he decided against it. He wanted to confront Yurkowa more than he was interested in relieving his suffering. He even thought the pain would better enable him to deal with the troublesome Yurkowa at the meeting.

When he left the kitchen, Wind grew bored with the silence and she got up and went to the study. She walked over to the many bamboo baskets with her armor displayed on them, and she carefully inspected the items of war removed from her ancient crypt. She was pleased that most of her belongings were in such fine condition as she cautiously fingered one of the small protective gold Kasazuri plate hanging from her heavy Yoroi Hitatare battle robe. As she ran her fingers over the richly decorative gold plate, her mind drifted back to when she was first awarded the great armor robe by Lord Kawasomeru. It was when she had defeated the well respected enemy First General, Motoshima-san in the narrow Kai pass.

Pleasing memories of that battle flooded back into her mind, and brought a smile to her lips. How she yearned to be in command of a wildly charging Army of Yabusame, mounted archers, engaging them in war for her master's interests and desires. That was a samurai's only want his true desire, his need for life and his existence on the face of the earth.

She so enjoyed the sin of vanity as her head swelled with pride over memories, a dishonorable virtue to be displayed by any samurai of worth. Nevertheless, she allowed herself to enjoy the luxury of remembering the battle she was the cause to be won then honored so by Kawasomeru.

Lying across the armor robe was the most prized possessions of her entire stock of weapons. She looked at her Agemaki, the ornamental long bow with the highly decorated open quiver, and the set of six richly painted arrows with the brass tips of death. Everything was as it was when she was awarded the fortune of weapons and armor from Lord Kawasomeru's hand.

She slowly drifted down the row of baskets supporting her weapons and armor. Everything she looked at brought her pleasure. Every piece of her equipment had its own memory attached to it, and she fondly remembered every reason she received them from her master of the time.

Lady Yoke drifted in the study shortly after Wind left the kitchen, and was sort of follow her in silence, as she examined the complete collection of ancient weapons. She was tempted to ask the beautiful female warrior what some of the weapons were designed for, but seeing the ancient samurai was deep in thought, so she placed these few questions out of her mind for now. Their daydreaming was suddenly interrupted by Hiromoai who came downstairs from his bedroom looking refreshed and well dressed. He was smiling at the women as they walked about his massive study while looking at the many weapons now in his collection.

He smiled when he noticed them in his study exploring her armor. This was because he wondered how she would look dressed in the ancient implements of warfare. He questioned if her exquisite shape would be hidden by the bulky equipment and loaded down with the weapons every samurai warrior employed in their warring abilities. When the two women turned to him he bowed, and they returned the honor as they smiled at him.

He heard the downstairs buzzer and answered the intercom himself instead of disturbing the women's Wa, and the enjoyment they were sharing as they wandered around looking at her armor and weapons. It was the chauffeur he sent for from his bedroom while dressing.

The uninterested driver reported that his car was fueled and waiting for him in the parking lot. He acknowledged this then told the driver he would be down shortly. He went back to the study and addressed his servant before leaving for the day's work.

"Lady Yoke, I have to leave now. Take good care of Wind-san. She's your responsibility when I'm away from the apartment, and her spirit's visiting us. She's to obey your order as she would me when I tell her what to do, is that clear Wind-san?" He warned and asked her as he turned from Lady Yoke, and rushed to leave his apartment, leaving the women watching him go.

"Hai my Lord." Wind replied to his back with a smile.

"I'll assume my responsibility for Wind-san, and her personal welfare and needs while you're away from the apartment with the greatest of pleasure I assure you Hiromoai-san." Lady Yoke offered to his back as she smiled at the man who she loved so dearly now.

CHAPTER EIGHT

THE HATANAKA TOWERS, JUNE 4th, 1996

The young Japanese businessman Hiromoai Hatanaka entered the elevator and pressed the basement button. It seemed like the elevator took a century to get there. When the doors opened, he was in a foul mood and stormed out of the elevator. He barked at his driver over nothing as he stood holding his door for him. He plopped down in the rear seat and stabbed the window button. The window closed and he picked up his latest Shi comic and flipped through the colorful pages. He loved how beautiful the Tucci creator drew his characters of ancient Japan.

The young driver knew where he was going and he took off without waiting to be told where to go by his upset acting boss. Hiromoai looked up from the Shi comic and growled at his driver. "Did my secretary inform that foul mouth little pup from Yurkowa Construction that I wanted a meeting setup with him for later on today?"

He wanted this meeting between the young members of the rival companies. He did not want the old ones in on the conversation so he could speak frankly with his main competitor, and did not want any witnesses around if and when he had to resort to threatening Tsutomu. He understood he could not be heavy handed if their fathers were at the meeting. Both old folks might resort to sword play over threats leveled at, or by the younger members of the companies.

"Yes sir Hiromoai-san, she told me to inform you that your requested meeting was setup for ten a.m. at your office. She said the Yurkowa kid wanted to know what the meeting was about sir, and she replied she didn't know. The kid griped quite a bit, but agreed to meet with you, sir. At first, Tsutomu wanted the meeting to be held in his office, but your secretary told him that was impossible, you were squeezing this meeting in between other meetings for today, sir."

"Yeah, she's smart as a whip." He grumbled absentmindedly as he glanced at his watch. It was only seven thirty, so he had some extra time to kill. He relaxed and soon he was in a much better mood as he grumbled at the driver. "Stop y the damn store, I think I'll indulge in a cup of real coffee today. Maybe it'll help keep me awake, and help with my damn back at the same time."

"What's wrong with your back Hiromoai-san?" The driver inquired politely of his boss.

"Don't ask you'll not believe where I spent last night sleeping, dammit." He grumbled then let out a grunt of pain as he turned and looked out the car window.

"I could only imagine Hiromoai-san." The driver smirked over his shoulder, he was aware of the vast sexual appetite possessed by his young and good looking boss. The driver stopped the car and got out and rushed in the store and picked up two coffees. He ran back to the car and passed both cups to his boss relaxing in the rear seat. Then he was behind the wheel again. It took a few minutes longer to get over to the office for the meeting. Normally, he would have used the lush office in Hatanaka Towers. But today, he chose to use his smaller office in the center of downtown Tokyo. He was afraid to meet with Yurkowa at the Tower, because if they ended up in a shouting match and Wind heard them going at it. She might charge into his office and dispatch the young fool before he could possibly stop her attack against him.

Finally, the stretch limo pulled up before the seven story building, and he went through the brass doors to the elevators like he was angry at them. He pushed the floor button then waited to be delivered to the chosen floor. He got off on the seventh floor and entered through the brass double doors, and smiled when he picked up his secretary sitting behind the desk ready for work as he offered to her kindly. "I'm sorry I made you travel extra for today's meeting, Lady Meko. But I need the privacy of this office to speak to that pain in the ass young Yurkowa kid. You only have to say until my meeting with the damn fool is completed. Then, you're free and you can head for the Tower to finish the day off there. You may take two full hours for lunch if your care to, call it a little gift for your extra travel here for today, Lady Meko."

He did not wait for his secretary to reply as he charged through the door and headed for his desk. The air-conditioning was on full and the office was comfortable, clean, and neat. He placed what was left of his coffee on the desk then checked to see if his secretary was on the ball.

Meko had set out a carafe of tea on the hot plate, and two bottles of expensive sake sat on the counter with stem glasses and crushed ice in a silver tray. There were a number of rolls of uncooked fish and eel with toothpicks holding them together. They rested in another tray over crushed ice. Napkins were folded, and music played at the right loudness to conduct a meeting.

Hiromoai nodded to himself as he opened the drawer and checked his recording equipment. He smiled, seeing the fresh spool of tape and knew his secretary was on the ball and she thought to set the machine up for when Yurkowa arrived for their scheduled meeting. He slid the drawer closed and sat back and rested his feet on his desk as he clasped his hands behind his head and started to go over what he was going to demand from Tsutomu. He felt good about his position as he closed his eyes for a few moments and entertained the pleasing thoughts of becoming the new boss of both Yurkowa Construction, and Hatanaka companies.

Time passed quickly as he was wrapped up in thought. In the outer office, his secretary kept a close eye on the clock and front door to the office. Lady Meko rushed about cleaning the outer office to make an impression on their visitor she wanted her boss to look good before him. At five minutes to ten, Tsutomu Yurkowa charged in the office as if he was angry with everyone on the earth. He was flanked by a pair of bodyguards as tall as they were wide. Both professionally cased out the outer office in silence, even checking under the secretary's desk. Once the guards were positive the office was free of possible hired killers, they nodded to their young boss.

The secretary stood and bowed to the powerful young but very angry man as she offered him kindly. "Yoi Asa, Master Tsutomu Yurkowa-san, and how are you today si..."

"I piss on your good morning and your manners as well bitch! Where the hell is this pain in the ass of a boss of yours hiding at for hell's sake? My damn time is very valuable as you well know witch, and I have none of it to waste on the likes of him on this day or any other day for that matter. He called for this damn meeting to take place between us, so why the hell isn't he out here waiting for me to arrive? Is that his god damn office, woman?" Yurkowa pointed towards the closed and richly carved set of double doors with his chin.

"Hai Yurkowa-san, I'm terribly sorry that you're in such a foul mood on this morning, Yurkowa-san." The secretary replied pleasantly while in a state of shock by the way this ill mannered young man just spoke of Hiromoai to her.

"Fine, inform your damn boss I'm coming in that fucking room. You two goons wait out here for me and stop anyone from interrupting us while we're meeting together, or it'll cost you your damn jobs. I'll buzz you if I find myself in any fucking danger in there." Tsutomu held up a tiny radio device and tested it. It rang in the guards ears and they both nodded to Yurkowa.

The secretary was on the intercom as Tsutomu burst into his office. Hiromoai let go of the button and rose as the wild young man entered his office and offered him his hand politely.

"You don't have to stand on my fucking account Hiromoai. Look man, I don't like you and you don't like me, I can live with that easy enough. That's fine, so let's skip the usual bullshit and get down to why the hell you wanted to see me today. Is my company hurting you that much that you have to beg me for fucking favors now, Hiromoai?" Yurkowa dared to boast his company was enjoying great success over his company.

Hiromoai took his seat as Yurkowa sat down in a chair directly across from the desk, and then he merely glared angrily back at him. "Huh, I'm pleased that you acted like what you truly are, Tsutomu. A god cursed gangster! This makes my conversation all that much easier to carry out with you. Yurkowa, your company isn't hurting me in the fucking least..."

"Then why the fuck had you sent for me, god dammit? I have a shit load of work scheduled for today and here I am wasting my damn time with you. Look Hiromoai, I have important things I have to accomplish today. Unlike you, I still have to work for my damn money and living." Yurkowa hissed at the slightly older man with hatred burning wildly in his eyes.

The fuming Hiromoai sat back in his chair and snapped angrily at his counterpart. "Tsutomu, you own the foulest of fucking mouths in all of Japan, and the worst of manners as well, fool. It's a wonder you have successfully made it past puberty with your backside still intact. Yurkowa! I called you here to inform that you your wasted life is in terrible danger, if you don't do as I instruct you. Some Sake? Let me warn you Yurkowa, I'm the only man on the face of this earth that can possibly save your miserable life for you, if I so choose to do so mis..."

"Fuck your damn Sake you drink it, Hiromoai! So you say my fucking life is in danger huh? From who? You! I know you hate my ass but I never thought you'd dare to threaten my life." Yurkowa's eyes suddenly darted around the room, looking for any hidden assassins. He held his radio in hand ready to send out the alarm to his guards waiting in the outer office.

Hiromoai allowed a wicked sneer to slowly cross his lips, as he added in a chilling tone and warning to the younger man. "No Yurkowa, the threat is not from me, nor is it lurking in my office, foolish one. The threat I speak of, is I know there's a hired killer who has your name plastered in its deadly sight. I know of who hired the cursed killer, and I further know how to stop this attack on your foul hide, Yurkowa. But it'll cost you dearly my young friend."

"How the hell do you know this fucking assassin and his Master, Hiromoai? Unless it's you who has sent this bastard of a killer on its evil task aimed against my ass. Well Hiromoai, I have some fucking news for your ass too. There's no way in hell any god cursed assassin is going to get through my ring of guards I surrounded myself with. So you're wasting your time trying to scare my ass like this, buster." Tsutomu jumped up in a rush, but when Hiromoai raised no protest against his leaving the office, the suddenly scared and concerned Yurkowa thought he was not kidding, and decided to take his seat to see if he could find out a little more about this supposed assassin sent out to kill him. If Hiromoai was confident enough to allow him to walk out of his office so easily then this executioner must be of the feared Ninja Caste, and everyone in Japan knew if the Black Mask was after you, sooner or later they'll succeed on their mission. When he was seated, Tsutomu snapped. "Well Hiromoai, what Black Mask is supposed to be hunting for my damn ass? I'm not the least bit afraid of any fucking hired assassin."

"You're incorrect on that assumption young fool Yurkowa; there are no Black Masks after your foolish ass this time I assure you."

"Then I really don't have anything to worry about then, do I? If the Black Mask isn't after my ass then no other assassin in all Japan is good enough to get around my security people and live to carry out his orders. So there's nothing else for us to speak about, is there Hiromoai? I'm leaving, thanks for the bullshit warning. I'll remember it and your god damn threat."

"You'll not live through this night if you leave my office without hearing more about my warning for you. Yurkowa, don't listen to me and your old goat of a father will find himself praying to the Kami for your foul soul to be safeguarded by the gods."

Again, the confidence of his demeanor sent a chill down his back, and made him take his seat and prepare to listen to Hiromoai's words more attentively. He stared at the older man for several tense moments, before asking in a much softer tone. "What do you know of this assassin aimed at my ass, Hiromoai? And from what stable of assassins does this fucking killer hail from?"

"Don't concern yourself over this assassin or its damn stable, Yurkowa. If we can come to a satisfactory agreement between us, I'll have this assassin stopped before he comes after you..."

"Huh, then I was right all along to think it was you who was pulling the fucking strings on this loathsome killer! What the hell are you trying to pull off here, Hiromoai? You know damn well if I press this here little button, my two guards will come charging through that damn door as if it wasn't there, and I'll have them snap your fucking neck for threatening me with assassins." Yurkowa interrupted as he glared at Hiromoai seated so confidently behind his desk.

Hiromoai sat with his elbows resting on his desktop, his finger tips lightly touching against each hand. He continued to smirk nastily at the excited and scared Tsutomu.

"So you still don't believe I can have my damn guards come through those doors and snap your fucking neck in an instant, Hiromoai?" The young Yurkowa pointed to the double doors leading into his office, his youth showing because Tsutomu allowed his voice to rise and his confusion show. His darting eyes betrayed he was truly scared by his threatening words, and was only reacting like a fool to try and make himself feel better about this supposed assassin hunting him.

"Oh no Yurkowa-san, I know you can have your guards come charging through those doors in a flash. But as I stated, I'm not your enemy in this situation. I know someone hired a killer, and placed your name in his sights. If you don't want my help, fine. You're free to leave any time you please, but what I know of this assassin, she'll get to you no matter where you hide, or who you surround yourself with. She's professed to be that good at her craft in dealing out death."

Yurkowa suddenly felt as if he had the upper hand in this conversation, and he allowed his temper to get the best of him as he nearly shouted at Hiromoai this time. "She! She! My fucking so called would be killer is a god damn She? How the hell is any worthless bitch going to ever get through my two tree trunks out there and kill me? This is sheer bullshit and bad manners if you were to ask me, Hiromoai. At first I was beginning to believe your foolish threat against me, but if you want me to believe that a simple minded she assassin's coming for my head. I say good, let her try and she'll see what she'll get for her damn trouble. My guards will hold her down while I fuck her to death Hiromoai. I'm not afraid of any damn woman assassin!"

"Tsutomu, if I were you I'd be shaking in my boots over this assassin coming after me. I saw this one at work in the past, and I believe your tree trunks out there will only lose their worthless heads if they dare to try and cross her path. I'm not kidding you on this life or death warning, Yurkowa. This female assassin is that good, and she'll easily get through any defenses you place around yourself. Like I warned you, I'll be happy to help you with this hired killer, Tsutomu.

"But I expect something in return for saving your worthless life. Do you want me to continue this conversation or do you want to end it right here and now? Or do you want to rave like a wild man, while your life hangs in the balance on fate's wings. I have no further time to waste on such a child crying like he lost his favorite toy. I offer you life, and you stand before me screaming for death you fool you. If that's the way you want it, that fine with me. Leave so I can get on my work.

As much as you don't believe this, I do have to work for my money also."

The overwhelming confidence in his tone made Yurkowa go silent as he stared at the older man with fear filling his eyes. He was scared to death some assassin was stalking Tokyo aimed at killing him. He was twenty seven years old and rich beyond dreams. He had his whole life ahead of him, and wanted to enjoy it, and what his money could buy. Sitting back, he tried to get his temper under control. If he was able to back off this assassin he would give him the world.

Yurkowa searched his mind for who might have wanted to employ a killer against him. He could not pull anyone's name up. He did not believe Hiromoai would hire a killer against him. Even though they were rivals in the work field, he felt neither side would ever resort to employing a killer against the other. Drawing in his breath to help control his fear and calm his nerves, he asked. "Hiromoai-san! If you know who this assassin is, give me her name and I'll take care of this situation myself. I'll have my people handle her ass good and proper."

"Yurkowa, if your inexperienced people try to go against this female assassin, they'll be sent back to you drawn and quartered, and packed in small boxes. You have no one who can best her deadly aims against you in your employ. I'm the only one who can possibly save your life, if you allow me to do it that is." He smiled at the scared kid staring at him with wild eyes.

"Dammit! If this is true, how the hell can you stop this hired killer so easily, Hiromoai-san?"

"Simple fool of an ass, all I have to do is allow the employer of the assassin know that I'm aware of the plot aimed against your worthless life, and he'd have no choice but to call off his assassin. Because I know damn well he intends to send the assassin after me once you're asleep for eternity, fool. I assure you Yurkowa I have no intention of losing my life to an assassin."

"Am I to take it that you'll back this assassin off my shoulders, Hiromoai-san?"

"Yes, for a price I certainly will Yurkowa. Yes, for a price I'll save your worthless life for you, Tsutomu-san." Hiromoai replied while wearing a smug look on his face.

"I knew you had something on that warped mind of yours, and that price being what for me Hiromoai?" Yurkowa snapped as he allowed his temper to get the best of him again, and cocked his head and stared at Hiromoai. Feeling he was going to get the truth from him.

"Hmmmmm... It'd be so simple a matter for me to say everything you own is the foul price for your worthless life, Tsutomu. But your menial possessions don't interest me in the least I assure you, you fool you. If I were to save your cursed life, to place a worth on it, hummmm... let me see, I'd expect no less than controlling interests in Yurkowa Construction." He instantly relaxed and grinned nastily at his younger competitor.

"Jesus Christ, why don't you ask for the world as your fee for saving my life? There's no way in hell I could give you controlling interests in my Father's business, fool. My Father and brother, even though he has nothing to do with the company, my Father disowned the fool from his life, and no longer recognizes his other son's existence, would both kill me. Besides Hiromoai-san, I only own twenty seven percent of the damn stock of the company, and I can't do anyth..."

"And your worthless brother owns another twenty seven percent of your worthless business, fool of an ass. After what you told me about your useless brother, it doesn't seem to me to be too difficult for you to gain control over his shares of your company if you want, Yurkowa. All you have to do is get his shares and then combine them with your shares, and you met my price for your worthless hide, fool." He interrupted the younger man, and then continued with chilling confidence. "Sooner or later, I'll own your miserable company anyway, whether or not you're alive to witness my takeover of it. If I have to perform a hostile takeover against it, I will.

"It doesn't matter a lick to me either way it happens Tsutomu-san. I was just trying to save your foul life, and make a little profit while I was at it. But, if you don't think your life is worth your family's god cursed company then so be it fool you're more than free to leave my office at any time you so please. I do have my own work I must to attend to, Yurkowa." Hiromoai bent his head and began to fumble around with a file folder, and ignored the younger man.

Yurkowa stood violently when Hiromoai told him of his outlandish price he demanded to save his life. He was fuming, shaking, and staring at the top of the older man's head, as he began to pace before his desk, rage getting the best of him as he tried to walk off some of his anger. He began to pace faster as his temper increased, not certain what to do. Whether or not to believe his rival about this supposed assassin coming after him in the middle of the night. Finally, his exasperation got him, and the younger man exploded in a flood of curses and angry accusations, as he pointed his finger at Hiromoai.

"You lousy motherfucker you! You're the one who's behind this attempt on my life, dammit! If you want my damn business, try and get it. I'll fight you every step of the fucking way with everything I have available to me, Hiromoai. I assure you, you'll never get my business, no matter how many god cursed assassins you can conjure up and send after me. I'll fuck you and I'll fuck you good and proper if any of your hired killers are found lurking about in my future. You better start watching your own ass my friend. I might find me an assassin to send after your ass. Mark my words Hiromoai, if you come after me I'll come after you. I'm not afraid of you or your fucking female assassin. I warn you, I'll fuck you, I'll fuck you real good Hiromoai..."

The doors to his office suddenly flung open and the two deeply concerned and highly agitated guards rushed in the office with their weapons drawn. They placed Yurkowa between them and aimed their Glock 9 mm pistols right at Hiromoai's chest. The guards heard their boss screaming from outside the office and they did not wait to be summoned by him.

Hiromoai maintained control over his composure as he merely smiled over the threatening actions of Yurkowa's two large Japanese bodyguards. His secretary followed the two guards in the office and covered her mouth when they dared to aim their weapons at her boss.

With a mere flick of his hand, he rudely dismissed his secretary who was very hesitant to leave the office until he gave her the look to get out. Once the secretary was out of the office, he hissed in a controlled, yet a seething tone at Tsutomu.

"How fucking dare you, you worthless piece of vile shit! How fucking dare you come in my office and threaten me in this foul of manners, Yurkowa." Hiromoai angrily stabbed his chest with his finger as he added to his upsetting words. "You're nothing more than what I called you when you first came into my office. A lowly Yakuza! A pissass gangster! Well Mr. Yurkowa, why don't you take your two thugs and leave my presence at once. The mere sight of your flesh makes my stomach churn with pure disgust. I have nothing else to say to you until you learned the meaning of respect, Tsutomu. Respect for someone who is only guilty of trying to help a friend and opponent. And how do you repay my offer of help? By having guns aimed at me by your two gangsters, and saying I'm the man who hired a fucking assassin to kill you. Talk about biting the hand that feeds you Yurkowa. Be gone with you ungrateful little shit you."

Hearing there was a possible assassin lurking near the two guards straightened and started scanning the interior of the office, looking for any threat aimed against their boss.

"Huh foolish ones, like I told your stupid boss here. I'm not the one who he has to worry about. But the damn fool wants to waste his time threatening me, rather than worry about his worthless life. Get out of my fucking office I told you!!!" He raged at the younger man as he stood and rested his hands flat on the surface of his desk, and glared at the young scared man.

"I..." Yurkowa went to offer, but he was instantly cut off by Hiromoai

"You nothing you fool! I don't care to listen to anything further you have to spew forth from that cesspool you call a mouth of yours, Mr. Yurkowa. It's too fucking late to enlist my aid against this assassin and save your life now, you ass. You have sealed your foul fate by not taking the advice and offer I suggested to you. I'll not help you now for all the worth in Japan. You're on your own now. Don't say I didn't try to help you. Get the fuck out of my office before I call security and have the three of you asses thrown the hell out the windows! Leave, I now wash my hands of your foul presence!" Hiromoai turned his back on the three and stared out the window.

Seeing he was not going to get anywhere further with the fuming Hiromoai, Yurkowa turned and stormed out of the office as if the evil was already stalking his heels. He was not certain if Hiromoai was playing a mind game on him or not. So he decided he was going to surround himself with a ring of highly trained bodyguards, until this supposed assassin was discovered then taken before him so he could find out who she was working for. Then, he would turn her and use the same executioner against the one who sent her against him. He understood if he dumped enough money in the assassin's lap, she would forget her allegiance to her original employer, and do his work for him. His two bodyguards followed the young man out of Hiromoai's office while cautiously checking the area for any sign of a possible assassin.

The moment Yurkowa left his office his scared secretary rushed in the room and she asked him if he wanted her to alert the police over what happened in the office.

"No, Yurkowa's a foolish man about to get what he deserves from fate. Get Utsumi on the damn phone for me, I need to speak with him. He's at my apartment working on a project."

"Hai." Lady Meko bowed politely to Hiromoai and then she rushed out the office to complete her mission for him. She was still shaking from the sight of him having guns aimed at his body. This was the first time in her life she ever seen a gun in person.

Hiromoai was so upset by the young Yurkowa's childish reaction he was unable to calm down. He angrily paced back and forth behind his desk as he waited for the phone to finally ring for him. When it did rang he actually dove for it and barked into the receiver. "Yes?"

"Utsumi here Hiromoai-san. Your secretary told me to call you. What happened?"

"Utsumi-san, get out and pick up five melons and bring them down to the pistol range on the fifth floor of the building. I have a demonstration for our female visitor to perform for me."

"Yes, they'll be here when you return from the office sir. Are you still coming home around seven o'clock tonight sir?" Utsumi asked, trying to find out how much time he had to work with.

"No! This fool of an ass Yurkowa has me so upset I can't think straight. I'm going to leave the office for the day and come home by eleven. Make certain our visitor knows I want her ready when I return." He warned as he checked his calendar to see what meetings he had scheduled.

"Yes Hiromoai-san, she'll be waiting for your return home when you arrive, sir."

Hiromoai hung up the phone and began his pacing of the office again.

THE PENTHOUSE APARTMENT, THE HATANAKA TOWERS

Wind was enjoying her time helping the old man work on her ancient armor and weapons. Every trace of dust was cleaned, and she assembled the armor in the correct order it was to be used in time of battle, placing the proper weapons with the armor. She continued working while Utsumi was on the phone. When he returned, he smiled at her.

"Wind-san, there's a change in plans. Hiromoai-san's to return at eleven this morning, and he wants you ready for some kind of demonstration he's planning for you. You'll accompany him to the fifth floor, so I suggest you dress in something more appropriate to walk around the building in. Something more modern I'd suggest to you." His Japanese was not nearly as good as Hiromoai's or Lady Yoke's, so Wind was having a bit of trouble following his words. But she got the gist of the conversation and nodded in agreement as she offered to the old man.

"What's wrong with this I have on Utsumi-san? It's rather pleasing I believe, neh?" Wind replied as she pointed at what she was wearing to the old man.

"Nothing's wrong with it. You look stunning in the Kimono, but I don't believe you should be walking around the building dressed like that. I believe something more conservative would be more appropriate, so you don't draw any attention to yourself. Lady Yoke, come here please."

She came in the study from the kitchen and bowed towards the two.

"Yoke, I just spoke to Hiromoai-san a few minutes ago, he's coming home earlier than he first expected and he wants Wind to accompany him downstairs to the shooting range for some kind of demonstration. I think she should be dressed differently for her trip through the building. Do you have something else she can slip into other than what she's wearing now?"

"Hai." She replied as she put out her hand and Wind automatically came to her and she told her. "I believe I have just the dress that'll fit you perfectly Wind-san."

Wind followed the Lady Yoke to her changing room without a word.

Utsumi placed his cleaning rag down on the table and took off to pick up the melons.

The two women were having fun trying to find a dress that made Wind look conservative. It was hard to hide her exquisite figure and threatening postures, and the interesting way she wore her hair. They settled on a tight fitting black dress that came down to her knees. Wind tried on a bra but quickly removed it for two reasons. One; it did not fit her right, and the other was because it felt terrible against her skin. She came out of the room still wiggling and scratching her exquisite body everywhere. She did not like the tight fitting fabric in the least.

Hiromoai could not calm down, so he left the office in a huff earlier than expected. He spoke to his secretary and told her to cancel all his other meetings for the rest of the day. Gone, was any mention of the two hour lunch he once offered her before his meeting with the young Yurkowa. He got in his limo and ordered the driver to get him over to Hatanaka Towers A-SAP. He planned to check his messages, do some catch up work then collect Wind for his demonstration.

It was ten, twenty a.m. by the time he returned to his plush apartment. When he walked in, the first sight he saw was his female warrior dressed in the sleek, long black dress looking extremely uncomfortable and irritable. He drew in his breath because she looked more stunning in modern day clothes, than dressed in her beautiful kimono.

Wind easily picked up the lingering look and understood it and nodded thank you to her lord. She enjoyed the way he was always stared at her since calling her back from the floating World. It made her feel like a woman who was desired by her master, a pleasing feeling she thought.

"Wind-san! Are you going to be able to use your sword dressed in that thing you're wearing? Not that I mind the new look in the least, Samurai. You look beautiful as always. I believe you'll look great dressed in anything you put on your exquisite body." Hiromoai offered as he studied her exquisite shape covered by the tight clinging black fabric.

"I'm afraid I will not even be able to walk in this ill fitting outfit Lady Yoke picked out to wear, Hiromoai-sama." She moaned as she scratched her thigh, and wiggled her rearend to try and get a little more comfortable stuffed in the new and extremely tight fitting dress.

Hiromoai laughed and suggested as if it was an afterthought. "Wind-san, Lady Yoke will place your Kimono in a carrying bag, and we can take it with us. Once we're where we're going, it'll be private and you can change into the Kimono at your leisure. I'll place your sword in my case, so no one sees the weapon. If anyone speaks to you, ignore their words and keep walking."

Wind bowed correctly, acknowledging her master's latest orders.

"Lady Yoke, do you know if the fool Utsumi is back from his errand yet?"

She came out of the dressing room and bowed as she replied. "Hiromoai-san, I didn't hear him come back yet sir. I'm sorry to offer, but I don't know if he returned from his errand yet, sir. I haven't seen him since he left on his mission for you, sir."

"Shit! Never mind that old fool for the time being, dammit. Come on ladies, we have to get busy. We have a lot to do and precious little time to get it done in I'm afraid. I want to get this little demonstration finished with so I can get something done today."

Hiromoai went in the study and sheathed the sword known to him as Wind's Breath, and then he placed it in the carrying case. Immediately, Wind felt very fatigued. Lady Yoke came in the study and he told her to place Wind's kimono in a traveling bag and give it to her to carry.

She handed Wind the bag and noticed she was not right. Hiromoai saw her condition and asked with concern. "Wind-san, are you alright? You look pale, tired. You want to sit a while?"

"I am suddenly very tired Hiromoai-sama. It happened when you sheathed my sword. I feel like I lost all my strength. But I am certain it will return when the sword is again bathed in the air of the living world." She tried to smile, but she was so weak it came out as a grimace.

"Well, we'll be at our destination in a few moments and then you'll get your all strength back, Samurai. Let's go, we'll meet Utsumi downstairs when he finally returns from the store. For all I know, he might already be waiting for us downstairs dammit."

There was no one allowed on the floor of his massive apartment, or ride in his private elevator either, but when he and Wind emerged from the car on the fifth floor. There were numerous people walking around carrying out their normal work duties for the company. He totally ignored everyone they came across on the floor as he rushed Wind to the pistol range built inside the building for his and his bodyguard's private use.

Although she commanded many lingering stares of admiration from the passing men of his company, no one dared to speak with the beauty walking by the boss. She tried to keep her eyes cast down towards the floor as she closely followed Hiromoai.

The Hiromoai sons were one of the chosen few who were allowed to carry concealed weapons by the government of Japan. They used the range in order to maintain their sharpness with the weapons. That's why the brothers built a pistol range in the building. That's where he was taking her. When they entered the acoustical room built to silence the sound of weapons being discharged inside the building, he placed a carrying bag against the leg of a table they rested their arms on when aiming the weapons at the targets thirty feet from the table.

Hiromoai saw Utsumi was busy setting up the melons the way he thought he wanted them on the stands. He nodded to the old man as he placed the carrying case down on top of the table. He opened it and unsheathed the deadly Katana killing sword. Instantly, Wind's strength returned.

"Wind-san, you may change in your Kimono if you feel you can't work in that outfit..."

Before he even finished his words, she was already wiggling out of the restricting dress. He and Utsumi settled back and enjoyed the show she gave them as she squeezed out of the ill fitting dress. Naked, she pulled the kimono out of the bag and slipped in it, thinking nothing of her nakedness before the men. She tied it tight with the obi then looked at Hiromoai and nodded.

"Here, take your sword and follow me in silence, Wind-san. I want to show you something that I was concerned about." He snapped at her as if he was angry at her as he walked towards the melons Utsumi set up on five narrow wood stands.

She took the sword, Wind's Breath felt good resting in her hands again and it gave her extra strength. She followed him to the melons on the stands.

"Okay Wind-san, this is the test. How close do you have to be to attack your target? Say the damn melons are the enemy. Show me what you'll do to my enemy, Samurai."

"Huh Hiromoai-sama, you give me a test that is not a test for my skills with the blade at all." She complained as she stared at the large melons resting haphazardly on the stands.

"Do what I tell you and hold your tongue while you're at it. I caution you, never question another order from me again, or you'll pay dearly for that error Wind-san." He growled again at her as he moved back to give her room to swing her sword properly at the melon.

With the speed of uncontrollable wind freely roaming the earth, the beautiful female samurai swung her katana blade at the melon. She struck it twice before the first piece fell free from it, and then she let out her breath and waited for Hiromoai's reaction to his orders.

"Excellent Samurai! But there are new ways in the modern world that I'm certain you're not familiar with, Wind-san. Utsumi, place that piece of armor around the next melon for me."

Wind watched with interest as the old man looped the imitation ancient armor over the next melon resting on the stand. She moved a little forward and reached out and felt the material of the poorly made copy, and then she snapped as if she was appalled by its makeup. "It's very poor quality to protect ones Samurai with, Hiromoai-sama. It's not fit to be worn by a honorable Samurai or even a worthless eta, the lowest class of the low of Japan for their protection."

"Will it stop your blade from injuring the melon protected in the damn armor, Wind?"

She felt the metal and poorly stitched hemp skin of the armor a second time, and announced for her lord. "Huh, maybe the first blow it might offer a little protection, but never my second thrust, Hiromoai-sama. This armor is not worthy of a lowly Gusoku, the rustic Samurai who roam the lands in search of a master to serve. I'd never allow any of my Samurai to wear such poor quality armor. I would rather go to battle naked as the day born, than fight in this insulting armor. My Liege Lord would be embarrassed to equip his Samurai with this inferior armor."

"Look, I didn't ask you to rate the quality of the damn armor, Wind-san! I asked you if it'd stop a Samurai's blade.

You answered my question to my satisfaction, come over to the table, I want to show you something." He almost cursed, but he knew Wind would not have understood his angry words, and he was in no mood to try and explain them to her. So he tried to keep the colorful words out of his conversation with the strange female samurai.

She followed him back to the table in silence and then watched as he removed a piece of metal and locked it tightly in his hand.

She tried to get a look at the thing, but his hand nearly hid the object completely from her view.

Hiromoai turned and announced to the ancient warrior. "Samurai, in the twentieth century we have these weapons of destruction that can kill great distances from the target. I assure you Samurai of past times that this weapon can penetrate the strongest of ancient armor and..."

"I have the long bow that can kill from great distances. Is this like the bow Hiromoai-sama?" She questioned as she tried to get a good look at what he held locked in his hand.

CHAPTER NINE

"We can get through this demonstration a whole lot quicker if you remain silent and watch and learn from what I will show you." He snapped hotly at the beautiful female warrior of past times.

She bowed while taking the slight chastisement from her lord in stride.

"That's much better, I'll explain further so you'll understand this demonstration Wind-san. This weapon is like your bow because it can kill from long distances. But this weapon here can kill from greater distances, more than twenty times further than your best bowman can launch one of his arrows and hit their intended target. I'll demonstrate this great feat for you. Samurai, keep your eye on the armor clad melon."

When she looked to the melon, he fired his Colt, 9 mm pistol. The sound of the weapon fired made her flinch and cover her ears and jump away from his side in fear. But she kept her eyes glued to the melon and saw the armor and melon explode at the same instant.

"Ieeee... by the foul breath of the evil Kami that roam the stink and slime of the underworld? What devil is in possession of that piece of iron that gives it the power of thunder and striking strength of a bolt of lightning from the Heavens? I never saw such a weapon. If you arm your Samurai with such weapons, there is no Army in Japan who would dare treachery against you."

He smiled over Wind's words of confusion as he explained. "This is known as a pistol Wind-san, a firearm and they're not allowed to be carried freely in Japan by most Japanese. But they're here, everywhere in great numbers if one knows where to look for them, and is willing to pay the going price for them. This pistol is much like the ones that Tsutomu's worthless guards carry. You must be very wary of them because they can do great harm to a body, Wind-san. Tsutomu is the target I'm going to assign you tonight. With him, he'll have men that control these weapons, but only a few. The others will attack you if they discover you with their hands, or weapons much like the ones you're used to being attacked with in the past of your life. The sword and bow are allowed weapons in Japan. Let's see what it did to the armor I fired at."

"Huh Hiromoai-sama, I will have to be very Ashigaru, (fleet of foot) if I was attacked with such weapons as you have just displayed before me today, and the death they could cause to the body, my Lord and Master." She replied in an excited tone of voice as she rushed for the damaged armor, and had it in her hands before Hiromoai reached her side. The side of the poorly made armor the imitation bullet ripped through seemed like it was exploded by unseen forces. There was a hole large enough for her to easily slid two fingers into it.

She studied the shattered melon scattered about on the floor, and was shocked by the awesome power of the weapon as she asked her master. "Hiromoai-sama, I did not see what came forth from your pistol that caused such damage to this poorly made armor created by some worthless fool. If we had such weapons in Kawasomeru-sama's great Army, there would have been no enemy in the empire we would not have been able to defeat on the battlefield. I curse all closed mouth Kami for withholding such a important weapon from my Liege Lord's Army until today."

"Do you think the bullet would have gone through your superior made armor as easily as it did this piece of junk I employed for this demonstration for you, Wind-san?" He asked, not really interested in what she thought of the weapon, other than if the bullet would have penetrated her armor as easily as it had done to the modern day copies.

"Bullet?" She asked with confusion as she stared at Hiromoai's face with questioning eyes.

"Yes Wind-san, a bullet. That's what the pistol fires. It's a piece of lead protected in flight by a brass jacket." He said as he removed one from the clip and offered it to Wind.

"Ieeeee... It looks like a dragon's tooth wrapped in gold, Hiromoai-sama." She grumbled as she placed it in her mouth and bit it. "Huh, it is as hard as the dragon's tooth, my Lord."

"What you call gold is brass. Do you think it would've gone through your armor as easily, I ask you a second time?" He asked while growing impatient with his ancient female warrior.

"Hieeeee... I fear it would have easily traveled through my superior made body armor as easily as my Katana sword travels through the air, and slices through the foul bodies of your hated enemy upon the field of battle, Hiromoai-sama. I see no way for any loyal Samurai Warrior to protect himself from the bite of such a powerful weapon as this one is, my Lord." She admitted as she stared at the new weapon.

"My next question for you to answer for me is; do you think a bullet might end your life on the earth if one of the rounds struck you, Wind-san? I'm speaking of your spirit life?" Hiromoai asked the question with concern as if he was in fear of the answer, and the loss of the services of this extremely dangerous female samurai, if she were fired on by any of Yurkowa's bodyguards with one of these weapons.

"My life will never end upon the earth of the living world, unless your mighty Katana blade is snapped in two, and the two ends never allowed to again be mated together by the mere touch the two ends of the weapon together." Wind bragged proudly to her new lord and master.

"What do you think a bullet might do to your body if you were hit by one while you're this spirit from the past?" He asked as he stared her in the eyes and waited for her reply.

"I fear that I do not truly know the answer to that question my Lord and Master. I was never hit by a dragon's tooth that flies through the air unassisted and unseen by the eye of this Samurai. Ieeeee... I'm Wind your loyal vassal my Master, why do you suddenly aim your thunder making weapon at my person? You do not have to be in any fear of my person, for I am no more than your most loyal servant to carry out your smallest bidding. I do..."

Her excited words were cut off by the deafening echo of the pistol going off three times in rapid succession. Each bullet struck her square in the chest. She was knocked back a few steps, but the bullets didn't have the effect on her body he thought they would.

She felt pain momentarily as the bullets went completely through her body. She was stunned and feared the dragon's teeth ripped into her body as much as she feared Fujin-sama's unfettered wrath. But the instant the rounds traveled through her body, the wounds immediately healed over. She never once lost her senses nor balance. She looked with concern at the three holes ripped in the silk of the kimono fabric and opened it, and then she checked her body. Only slight red marks remained on her chest, and soon they disappeared. She found herself wondering what powers she possessed that could stop her from being destroyed by the dragon's teeth.

The stunned Hiromoai stared at her with his mouth hanging open and awe in his eyes. He expected her to die and disappear, and he would have to summon her again from the Floating World, once she had time to heal the wounds from the bullets. "Are you alright Wind-san?"

"Ieeeee... I believe I am fine, Hiromoai-sama. I feel nothing from the dragon's teeth now."

Utsumi stood scared to death, like his feet were stuck to the floor. He never saw anyone shot and not die from the wounds, especially being shot at so close range.

"What did you feel when the bullets first struck and then passed through your body, Wind-san? Was there any pain from the bullets to your body and was it enough pain to stop you from carrying out my orders to you if you were in the process of a mission?" Hiromoai asked as he struggled to get the stunning feeling of her not dying out of his tone.

"I felt pain for a moment, but not enough pain to stop me from reacting to the unseen dragon's teeth as they struck my body. I did not like the roar of thunder that seemed to bother me more than the dragon's teeth entering my body, and the pain they caused my being for brief moments."

"I can't believe it. Godddd, I can't believe the power you offer me by your mere existence before me." Hiromoai replied as he turned the gun, and looked at it as if it betrayed him.

"I cannot believe it myself, my Liege Lord. I feel I should be scattered about the room much in the same way as the melon and that worthless armor was destroyed. Maybe the mighty Dragon Kami is friends with the powerful Fujin-sama."

"Do you think you would've been able to continue fighting after you were hit by the bullets if you were engaging an enemy of mine? Err... excuse me, dragon's teeth as you like to call the bullets." Hiromoai asked concerned if the rounds would have caused her to not be able to carry on with her mission if she was attacked by bullets.

If she was unable to carry on with her assignment if she was attack by bullets then he was going to be forced to figure out another way to get at his rival and destroy him with this weapon in his possession from the past of ancient Japan. He did not need her to fall in his enemy's hands if crippled for a brief second by the bullets and then end up fighting him instead of Tsutomu.

"My Liege Lord, I really do not think that the momentary pain would have been enough to stop me from protecting myself, or from killing your hated teki, no matter how many dragon teeth were sent to devour my spirit. As I have already stated to you Hiromoai-sama, I was more shocked from the loud thunder that came from the weapon than from the pain of the dragon's teeth entering my body my Liege Lord. But I shall get used to the thunder for my Lord's behalf, and then I will not be affected by the dragon's teeth, or its angry roar, my Lord."

"Dammit, I can't believe the bullets didn't kill you as they were designed to do, Wind-san. It's impossible, completely impossible and absolutely amazing to believe what I have just witnessed, Samurai." Hiromoai grumbled as he continued to look at the gun as if it failed him.

"Ieeeee Hiromoai-sama, I guess I can only be dead for the period of time I get sent back to the Floating World of forever wanting and waiting, if my death is caused by the ancient weapons of Japan's great past. These new weapons of the present day Warriors do not seem to have the same effect on my body and soul as the old weapons of Japan do." Wind offered as she lifted her breast to see if there was any remaining damage to her body, caused by the three bullets. The ugly redness was already faded and nothing remained of the wounds on her body. All memory of the pain caused by the shooting was gone and forgotten from her sharp mind.

"Wind-san! If you suffered no ill effects from the dragon's teeth then I'll be pleased to continue with the demonstration of these weapons. Let's get back to the table and I'll show you more that'll fill your mind with awe and respect for modern day weapons of Japan." He said as he again looked at the pistol in his hands, as if the weapon had betrayed him.

She followed him back to the table in total silence. She had to admit that she was excited to see this fearsome weapon and how it worked and created death. Any new weapon was of great interest to her as it would be to any wise samurai warrior. It was her duty to know what weapons might be employed against her, or her liege lord.

"Wind-san, this next weapon I'll show you is called an automatic weapon. It fires hundreds of bullets in one quick breath of time. It's known as a Heckler and Koch MP-5 machine pistol. I suggest you place your hands over your ears if you're still rather sensitive to the roar of the dragon's force before I begin with this next demonstration."

"Ieeeee... What does my Liege Lord think this lowly Samurai Warrior is? A weak minded addle fool who allows the thought of controlled thunder to scare her being. No my Lord and Master, I'm Samurai, and I'll conquer any fears that this world of the living has to offer against me. I shall get used to the bark of the dragon until it no longer bothers me. As Samurai, I am bound by honor and my oath not to allow anything to turn me away from my mission. Thunder cannot harm my being. I am ready for this next demonstration by you my Liege Lord."

He smiled over her proud boast as he though we'll soon see about that boast and he pulled the trigger and sent a burst of fifteen rounds slamming into the remaining three melons, sending large chunks of ripe fruit flying in all directions. The cloud of choking smoke from the many fired rounds surrounded his head as he fired.

Wind feared the fearsome dragon of this time was devouring her master's soul in the foul smelling mist completely engulfing his face. But this time she refused to allow the thundering weapon to scare her, as she stared in awe over the staggering power the weapon possessed in its metal prison. When he was done firing, she cautiously picked up one of the spent shells. She smelled the acidic odor of spent gun powder, and moved it and wrinkled her nose over the vile odor being emitted by the casing. She kept the spent round, thinking it had some magical powers attached to it she might be able to use of later, in her battles of right for her master.

He rested the smoking weapon on the table and then offered. "There are many other types of these weapons throughout Japan. You must be aware when someone aims one of these weapons, or anything that looks like one of them at you. He's my and your enemy, and he must be dealt with swiftly. You must never leave an enemy alive, so he can come back in the future and challenge you to a fight on another day. It's that simple Warrior of the past times of ancient Japan." He warned as he watched her roll the spent shell around in her fingers.

"Hai my Lord, it is a wise warning to be obeyed, if one wishes to be successful on the endeavor one is sent on by her Master." She replied as she bowed. "You have not changed your ideals over the many years that passed my Lord. Your thoughts echoed many times in my worthless ears by my honorable father who trained me in the skills of the Samurai Warrior."

"Fine, now that we settled this bit of information for your knowledge, we must return to my apartment and speak. I have work for you tonight, and I have a lot of information to go over with you so you're aware of where you're going, and who your target is. I'll show you a picture of your target with a detailed map on how to get to my teki's lair. Utsumi-san, clean up this mess before you return to my apartment, I want all traces of what transpired here erased."

"Hai Hiromoai-san." Utsumi said the words as if a curse left a bad taste in his mouth. The old man hated being stuck with menial work, and it seemed like since they found this female samurai and her crap buried with her, that's all he was doing. He glared at the back of Hiromoai as he walked out of the range with his samurai dressed in her damaged kimono following like a puppy.

He did not realize she was still dressed in her kimono until a worker stared at her. He turned and noticed the three holes ripped into the kimono and handed her the carrying case to hide the damage fabric from view as he offered barely over a whisper. "Wind-san, keep the case held before your chest. I forgot to have you change back into the black dress."

She did as she was told and got in the elevator behind Hiromoai. In seconds, they were back at his penthouse. Lady Yoke met them at the door and stared at the holes drilled in her kimono.

Hiromoai picked up the concerned look by Lady Yoke and offered her. "I'm sorry Lady Yoke, but it seems we suffered a minor err... accident during our demonstration, and I was successful in destroying one of your fine garments. I owe you another Kimono of better worth. Please, feel free to buy yourself three Kimonos in order to replace the one that I had just carelessly destroyed on you, and place them on my personal charge account. Thank you."

"You're too kind and understanding to this most undeserving worker, Hiromoai-san." Lady Yoke replied with grace as she bowed in thanks for his kind offer.

"Nonsense young lady, you're worth your weight in gold. Take Wind to your room and give her another Kimono to wear. Then, I want to see her in the study, and it has to be in private."

She smiled at Wind and she followed her to her room. She never once asked what happened to the destroyed kimono, and Wind never volunteered the information for her. Once she was dressed in a new kimono, she headed for the massive study while Lady Yoke remained waiting in her room until, and only if she was sent for any reason.

Hiromoai had snap shots lying on the coffee table, along with a map of Tokyo.

Wind walked over to the table and sat on the floor with her legs crossed under her body, and looked at one of the many pictures. Suddenly, she was scared to death by the picture. She never saw paper with the image of a face so clearly printed on it. She was afraid that some evil Kami somehow flattened this person's being and then he entrapped that person in a paper prison for all eternity to come. She cautiously turned the picture over in an attempt to see if anything was printed on the back of the person. Then, she flipped the snap shot over again and stared at the image of the smiling face. It was a pleasing young face of a proud looking Japanese man.

"That criminal that you're looking at on what we in modern day Japan call a picture, is my biggest teki and largest threat to my person in all Japan, Wind-san."

"Then he is a filthy Ronin! It will bring me great pleasure eliminating him from your memory my Master." She replied as she bowed slightly from her seated position to Hiromoai.

"Yes, a filthy Ronin he is at that, Wind-san. He must be dealt with before he's allowed to destroy my business, or cause great harm to my person or yourself. The dog eating animal spent his entire worthless life with trying to harm me, my interests, and my company."

"Then I shall be proud to bring his unworthy ways to an end, Hiromoai-sama. A soul, who can conquer his own nerve and yet maintain his equilibrium, will be successful on any mission he is sent forth on. Rejoice in the wisdom of the mind. My Lord, when your enemy no longer fears your power, it means a bigger power is on the horizon to try and conquer your will and desires. In this case, I will teach all your teki I am that power to be so feared, and you are the most powerful warlord to ever walk upon Japan's sacred soil." She hissed as she glared at the smiling face.

"That's what I want you to do to this enemy. Wind-san, look at this map. Have you ever followed a map before in your life, Samurai?" He asked as he looked in her eyes for the answer.

"What we call results are only the beginning of our many toils in life, the wise and always testing Kami from the world of wonder have set out before us. Hai my Liege Lord, on many occasions I have studied maps of conquest and battle. During the unending wars with the filthy Lord Wakatsuki, I was placed in command of an Army of horsemen. It was my duty to place these Warriors where they would do the best good on the battlefield. Thus, I was trained in the many ways of the reading of maps, my Lord." Wind offered she could not hide the fact she was slightly insulted by his questioning her, if she was able to read and understand maps.

"That was too much of an explanation. Why can't you just answer one of my questions without adding all that fluff to it? Anyway, it should be easy for you to follow my instructions on this map. We're here this is my building, Wind-san. Here." He made certain she knew where he was pointing on the map then ran his finger across the map to a new location and added.

"This is where my foul teki dwells with the walls of his compound. He's well guarded both day and night by a small Army of highly trained and attentive bodyguards, and other security type people, Wind-san. The fool fancies himself that important to the matters that concern Japan, and the world. If you work your way across this section on the map," again he pointed to the map and then added. "You must travel up this street here, and then come out near this yard if you hope to find the building of my enemy successfully, you should end up coming out by the south gate of his filthy compound. Then, you have to get over the eight foot tall wall at this point, which is the best place to get over the protective wall unobserved by his security people, Wind-san. My enemy has many guard dogs roaming the grounds at night, so you have to watch out for them. You'll also have to deal with them, kill the dogs if need be. The dung eater you'll be searching for sleeps on the third floor of his home, with his cursed wife."

He pointed to a picture of a castle like structure then offered. "Wind-san, you're to stealthily enter his foul room from the balcony. Kill his wife before allowing him to wake because I want you to punish him before he dies. Then wake my teki and allow him to see his wife butchered before his eyes, before you painfully kill him. Do you understand everything I told you so far?"

"Hai my Lord, he who is your hated teki and anyone he loves is as well, your foul teki for all life to come. Only that day that dawns to which we are fully awake and aware of my Lord and Master, this lowly Samurai Warrior shall destroy them both to please your great honor."

"Excellent. You want me to take you for a drive through the area, so you can see the path you're going to be forced to employ on this night?" He offered to assist her on her first mission.

"Iye my Liege Lord! I'm not that addle of mind that I cannot follow simple directions printed on a map. I need no such trial run to follow my duty for your desire. I know where I am to go, to destroy your worthless teki, Kawasomeru-sama."

"Outstanding Samurai. What do you have need of for this mission, Wind-san?"

"I need only my armor and weapons to carry out my duty faithfully for you, my Liege Lord. The rest is preordained and your enemy will meet their foul fate on this night."

"You're going to use your armor, Wind-san? After seeing how easily a bullet can penetrate it, I thought you might want to travel light, and omit the use of your heavy body armor, Wind-san."

"Hieeeee Lord Hiromoai, I have forgotten what type of enemy without honor or souls we are dealing with in the living world, Hiromoai-sama. I shall take time to design my body armor more suitable for battle in the land of the living world. One of much lighter weight and easier to travel and fight in, I shall be in need of a room in which to work, and maybe the assistance of Lady Yoke also, my Liege Lord." She boasted to her master.

"You can have the room next to Lady Yoke's. She'll help you dress and I'll send her in the room with you. You can keep her as long as you have need of her service, Wind-san."

"Domo Hiromoai-sama, domo." She got up without further word and picked out certain pieces of her armor and weapons from their stands in the study. When her hands were overflowing with the items of war and protection, she headed for the room offered her by her master.

He called Lady Yoke out of her room and then directed her to assist Wind with her work on her newly designed outfit. She quickly disappeared in the room with Wind.

He sat back on the sofa and then smiled at the richly painted ceiling as he let out his breath in an exhausted sigh, feeling soon he was going to finally be rid of the always troublesome Tsutomu Yurkowa, and then he would go after his foolish father as his next target for Wind to destroy. Once the well aged father of Tsutomu, Asahiko Yurkowa was dead, he would then approach the remaining son of Yurkowa Construction he shall allow to live, and make him an offering for his company. He knew he could talk the other son into anything for greed and money.

He leaned forward on the couch and picked up the scattered pictures of Tsutomu from the floor and table, and pitched them in the marble faced fireplace. He hit the gas button and the pictures burst in flames. In seconds, all evidence he planned to kill Tsutomu was gone forever.

He got up from the couch and headed for the kitchen, he was that confident there would be a pot of tea waiting for his enjoyment. If he knew Yoke as well as he did, he was right the tea was there and he poured a cup. He spiked it with some Sake then returned to the study to enjoy his tea, and the thrilling feeling of becoming the world's most powerful businessman in Japan.

Sipping his tea, he listened to the women laughing in the other room while working on Wind's new protective armor. He could not wait to see what she was working on. Knowing Wind and Lady Yoke, and how exact she was in everything she did or said, he understood she was on the verge of creating one hell of an outfit to carry out his orders. Time passed slowly, he ended up falling asleep while waiting for her appearance, while he rested on the couch.

He was exhausted from the laborious trip to the construction site a few days ago, and removing the armor and weapons they found in the cave, and spending the night with Wind, and sharing her treasures. The most upsetting meeting with Yurkowa also served to rob his strength. He slept for three straight hours, and woke when the women came out of the room, and stood before him.

She woke him by whispering his name softly in his ear, and then smiled as his eyes fluttered open, and then he focused them on her lovely face.

HATANAKA TOWERS, TUESDAY, JUNE 4th, 1996, 8:20 P.M.

After resting and when Hiromoai opened his eyes, he was surprised by what he saw. Wind stood before him in her modified armor. She cut down the Suneate leg armor so it did not wrap around her legs, only protecting her shin and knee from the sword's kiss. The long Kote sleeve armor was changed in much the same way, cut back so it only protected the back of her forearms.

He noticed she used only the back of her forearm to protect herself during a fight to the death with the sword. Her chest and hip armor was changed drastically. She had cut the skirt part of her heavy armor short, so it only covered her fine rearend and front area of her body. The upper part of the armor robe was really thinned out, with much of the heavy bulk removed from the body armor protection. The neckline was cut low down to the center of her breasts, and the swell of her exquisite breasts filling the missing protection area. The thick collar of the once heavy robe armor was also cut down, so it afforded her neck and shoulder good protection from the katana blade's cutting edge, yet it also afforded her free movement at the same time.

The light neck piece of the newly designed armor went across her shoulders, making her look like she had shoulder pads on from the football field. The top of the newly designed outfit closed across her neck, rising up like the old day Victorian chokers. It was being held in place by a solid gold button, depicting the crest of the Claw. Her discipline and training printed on it in honor for her father and master trainer. The center of the body armor was cut in a deep vee shape, so her taut stomach muscles could be seen and work freely. There was a pair of oval holes cut in the once heavy armor, extending from the sides of her waist to the tops of her hips. Hiromoai could easily see the holes allowed her body to move much more freely.

In her arm armor, she placed a set of pointy skewers hidden in each pad on both arms. They were the Kogai, the razor sharp implements usually carried hidden in the katana sheath, she placed them in each of her leg armor within reach of her hands. Her belt had a number of throwing stars tucked in it, and her katana was slung over her left shoulder, so it was out of her way and offered her freedom of movement, yet it was also in easy reach of her sword hand.

A razor sharp small tanto blade, along with her short wakizashi stabbing blade, was strapped to her right leg. Other weapons could only be hinted at, hidden among her newly designed armor. The proud ancient Kabuto helmet was minus the wide and flashy Fukigaueshi turn back curls. They were cut down until they were only inches wide, and seemed like a set of curled ears.

The once fearsome Kuwagata horns and great plume of feathers once adorning the ancient helmet were removed, and the holes covered over with a pair of Kasazuri plates that once hung from her heavy armor robe bottom. The forever sneering brass Hoate face mask was the only thing that she did not see fit or could not change. She looked more like an angry god Kami, ready to kill the world if it got in her way. Her slender feet were covered by a pair of high leather boots, obviously given her by the Lady Yoke. Her six foot Yumi bow was slung over her other shoulder in such a way that it was free of blocking any of her movement she might need to carry out, and the side of her left boot was her quiver, for the seven bamboo shaft arrows. Her hands were covered by fingerless black leather gloves and only a simple strap looped her middle finger to keep the gloves set in place on her hands.

Hiromoai got up from the couch and slowly walked around her breathtaking rock hard body covered by her modified body armor, taking in the effect of her handiwork on the armor. She was a stunning figure to be both awed and feared. The back of her outfit was cut down to the small of her back and looped over her slender, but strong shoulders to hold the front of the outfit set in place. He could see how she would be able to move much more freely in the outfit now.

Her hair finished off the picture perfectly. Short in the front and long in the back, but her jet black silk like hair was braided in long knots, and the long hair crossed over in the center of the vee in the back of the outfit, and was fitted in a specially situated loop, to keep the hair from bothering her during times of battle or movement. At the end of the hair braid, there was a folded over gold tip, sharpened so it could become a weapon of last defense, by using her hair to wield the dangerous weapon against her enemy. She was as threatening in her modified body armor, as she was beautiful in the black dress she wore a few hours ago to the pistol range, so he could show her what a pistol and bullet could do to her body in the twentieth century.

He held his breath as he took in this stunning vision of her beauty, yet her body seemed to be vibrating, telling all who stood anywhere near that her entire being was all weapon, and not to be toyed with without risking one's life, or to be underestimated. He slowly walked around her until he was again standing in front of his sofa. He dropped down and then grumbled. "Wind-san, you're truly a most threatening figure to behold. I hope you're as good in your skills as you appear to be. Remember Samurai, I don't want you to be taken prisoner by any of these fools under any circumstances. You're instructed to fight your way out of any situation you're trapped in. I'll allow you out at exactly twelve o'clock midnight tonight. I believe at this time the dog eating Tsutomu will think he's safe for his night's sleep. I expect you to be back here by one thirty, that's one feather and a leaf on the time stick after midnight, Wind-san."

"Hai my Lord and Master, I shall return by the allotted time you have just suggested to me. I see my efforts with my body armor had the desired effect on your person, Hiromoai-sama." She allowed a smile of victory over her new outfit.

"Good Wind-san, very good indeed, I'm going to be attending a party tonight, show my face so to say so no one can accuse me of any possible treachery against this son of a milkless whore he is. You'll get back to this apartment and enter it like the breeze you're named after. You can leave from the balcony of your room and work your way down to the rooftops of the building next door. Use the building tops to get to the first road I showed you on the map. Work your way to Yurkowa's house, carry out your orders with haste and then return here, Wind-san."

"Hai Hiromoai-sama. The perfect Warrior employs his mind as a mirror and in that..."

"Please, we know you're a faithful follower of Zen and the Buddha prophecy Wind-san. But the Buddha's words are most confusing to me and my understanding. I order you to refrain from always quoting his words to everything I say for the love of Pete." Hiromoai grumbled as he let out his breath in a rush and then he glared at Wind for a long moment.

"Hai my Lord, it shall be carried out as you have ordered, my Liege Lord."

"Wind-san, Lady Yoke will inform you when it's time to leave and carry out your mission. I'll not be here when you leave, nor will I be here when you return. If you're successful against my enemy, you're free to bathe and sleep at your leisure. If you fail tonight, I expect you kneeling in the study waiting my wrath to fall upon your shoulders." He glared at the ancient samurai.

"This worthless vassal will not fail her Liege Lord on this sacred mission I leave on."

"Failure wouldn't be a very wise course of action to follow, Samurai. If you fail me on this mission, it'll have dire consequences for you to experience." With this warning issued to his dangerous warrior, he stood and walked to the stairs leading to his master suite. He changed clothes for the party when the Lady Yoke began to fuss about with the final details of Wind's body armor, moving the padding and protection to the places it should cover properly.

He came back to the study dressed in an expensive silk blue suit, and addressed Lady Yoke as he rushed by her and headed for the hand carved oak door to his apartment. "Lady Yoke! You will inform Wind when it's twelve o'clock and time for her to leave on her mission. That's when the owl cries to her memory. Wind has some work to perform on this night for me Lady Yoke."

"Hai Hiromoai-san, it'll be done as you suggested sir." She bowed towards the rushing Hiromoai as he made his way to the front door of the apartment, but he ignored her. He did not reply as he stormed out the door without looking back at the two women.

Lady Yoke glanced at the clock and then she informed Wind she had three hours to wait for her duty to begin. Wind did not understand what Lady Yoke meant by the hour, so Lady Yoke corrected by offering the ancient female samurai, that an hour was three feathers on the stick of time for the lonely night owl to cry the beginning of the new night's birth.

Wind bowed and then she filled her remaining time by checking and dusting rice power on her killing sword and stabbing blade, as if it was a mysterious ritual she performed for the pair of great blades. She also looked after her other equipment and armor, to make certain everything was in perfect order. She was preparing her mind and body for the slaughter on this pending night. She had a ritual to perform before she went out on any mission for her lord and master. She prayed to both Buddha and Fujin, and she burned incense and offered a bowl of rice and raw fish Lady Yoke gathered for her earlier in the day, to her guiding Kami, Fujin God of Wind.

Time crawled at a snail's pace as she prepared her mind and body for the battle of right about to take place on this night. She never allowed herself to think she was a lowly assassin, because she was going to rely heavily on the cover of darkness to dispatch her master's enemy. When Lady Yoke entered the study, she had to wait until Wind stopped her deep meditation before speaking to the female samurai. When she acknowledged her presence, she replied softly.

"Yuriko-san, I'm sorry to inform you, but it's time for you leave on the Master's orders."

"Hai Lady Yoke, I thank you for the information." Was all she replied as she slapped her hands together and then stood and bowed in the direction she was praying to. Next, she turned and stretched to get her muscles loose and walked to the double doors to the outside balcony.

Lady Yoke followed her to the sliding glass doors in silence, but drew her breath in when she saw how high they were from the street below her. Like the ghost she was, Wind quickly disappeared over the side of the balcony as silently as her name suggested.

In the palms of her leather gloves were a set of strong gripping claws that could easily be retracted at will between her fingers, and be out of her way when she had to use her hands for movement. She used the steel claws to help climb down the side of the tall building, until she reached the first rooftop. Like the wind, the ancient warrior darted stealth like across the first roof and leaped onto a second but lower roof, making less sound than a stalking cat. Silently, she worked her way over the roof using the shadows of the buildings to hide her progress. It took her less time to get to the road where she dropped to the ground and surveyed her surroundings.

The instant her feet were on the ground, she stopped as if rooted to the earth, and then she listened to every sound surrounding her and watched. Then she used the alleys to travel to Yurkowa's place, and only once did she come across someone lurking about in one of the narrow alleys she was roaming through. She glared at the old man dressed in filthy, tattered rags and staggering then he leaning against the wall and staring at her. She placed her finger against her lips and shushed the old and startled man scrounging around in the garbage and filth.

She smiled while trying to calm the old man a little, but the old beggar did not see it because her face was covered by the fearsome and heavy brass Hoate sneering mask. The old man was scared to death by what he thought was a nightmare brought on by some bad wine and the lack of food. He dropped the bag he was looking through for something to eat, and then he took off in a dead run the opposite way she was traveling.

Wind next looked to the sky as a cool wind was driving a mass of jagged clouds high above her head. She waited for a few seconds and then she cautiously moved out, working her way down the length of the filthy alley until she came out on an open street, standing by a six foot high stone and cement wall. She jumped up and grabbed the top of the wall and easily pulled herself to the top. Broken and dangerously jagged shards of razor sharp glass adorned the top of the wall, forcing her to be extremely careful where she stepped, or placed her hands. She noticed strings or thin wire stretched out, obviously some kind of alarm system. She stepped over the thin wires while making certain she did not snap one of them then she dropped like a drifting snow flake to the other side of the wall, where the grass was covered by fallen damp leaves.

She landed lightly on one foot and quickly knelt for a moment while lifting her head and looked around her position. She was obscured by the darkness of the area, and contours of her exquisite body were barely visible, as it mixed with the darkness of the night surrounding her being, and tall shadows cast by trees of the courtyard she stood in. She suddenly heard the dog's heavy breathing before she spotted the angry animal lurking in the dark a few feet before her.

It was a huge black animal with piercing wild looking eyes, with threatening and drooling jaws, and it was obviously stalking her. She picked up the dog's movement in the pitch darkness and removed a throwing star from her sleeve and let it fly. A soft yelp informed her that the animal was no longer a threat against her person.

She easily penetrated the compounds once thought to be impenetrable security defenses, until she spotted the first man walking down a brick inlaid walkway while watching where he was walking. She dropped down to a knee, and then she backed up in the shadows and waited for the unsuspecting security man to pass by her position. The unsuspecting security guard moved as if he was not the least bit worried about any kind of danger lurking in the underbrush before him. The guard stopped walking right in front of her, and casually lit a cigarette. Her mind worked out her attack angle, and if the man gave the slightest hint that he was aware of her presence in the brush, he was going to be dead before he could possibly react against her attack against him. Or he was able to give out the alarm of her presence in the compound.

The security guard drew in the smoke as if it gave him great comfort then blew it over his head as if he just made love to his wife, and continued walking down the walkway. She smiled, because it reminded her of the first time she saw Hiromoai light one of the terrible smelling weeds. But this one did not smell nearly as bad as his did.

The samurai committed the position of this security guard to her memory in case she had to use the same route in order to escape the compound, once she had successfully accomplished her mission for her master. She would be ready to intercept and then dispatch the guard later on, if the need arose. She ran on her toes, traveling with the swiftness and silence of a deer fleeing a pack of attacking dogs. She was unhappy with the leather boots because they were impeding her ability to move swiftly across the ground as silently as she wanted to travel. She was emphatic she was going to eliminate the boots and go back to the split toe tabis, once this mission was completed, and she returned to Hiromoai's apartment.

In her mind, she decided she was going to keep the upper parts of the boots as her quiver, and cut the souls out of the boots, so her tabis could kiss the face of the earth, and make it much easier for her to move about. In no time, she ended up leaning against the castle like building, and checked the side and found the easiest way to climb to the third floor level of the structure.

CHAPTER TEN

Wind skillfully employed the shadow of a tree to hide her climbing up the side of the building. She dropped softly on a wrap around balcony, and then she worked her way around to the set of double glass doors pointed out by Hiromoai on the picture of the structure he showed her. When she moved around a life size statue of a naked woman holding a dove out in both hands, while staring at the heavens above her, she noticed a second security man out before her. He did not notice her presence because he was looking over the compound area below the balcony, and he was also speaking into a small black box he held in his hand. She decided not to do anything until the security guard finished speaking into the box. The second the guard replaced the small radio in his belt loop, she stepped out from the shadow so she could confront him. Her sword held at the ready to begin her attack against him if he made a move at her.

"Godddd, what the fuck are you, and how the hell did you get up here! Are you a fucking throw back to a time long ago past, Mister? And what the hell are you doing up here anyhow? How the hell did you get up here? Talk to me god dammit!" The stunned security guard growled as he reached for the weapon hidden beneath his jacket for protection.

"Foolish one, if you value your worthless life and wish to see the sunrise of another day's dawn then I warn you, do not reach for your thunder making weapon. Unarmed, I shall allow you to live out your remaining years in peace and harmony with the earth and sky. Arm yourself against me foolish one, and you will become my enemy, and you shall die accordingly to the ancient laws of the Samurai code." She snapped coarsely in ancient Japanese at the guard.

"Fuck you Mister! I'm going to blow your fucking head off of your damn shoulders for..."

Her target obviously understood Japanese, but responded in English. The guard was never able to finish his threat directed at the invader. Her sword ripped through the air silently, and lopped his head from his shoulders. She stared at the headless body as its hands searched for the missing head. Slowly, the body sank to the ground, twitched until it finally stopped moving. She stepped over the body as if it was not there then she continued on for her target. She found the door she searched for, and slid one of the Kogai implements through the door and forced the lock.

She drew in her breath as she dropped low in the shadows and silently slid in the room. She allowed her eyes to adjust to the blackness then spotted the two people sharing a sleeping bed. She went to the woman and gently pulled the covers from her body. She was naked and Wind removed her tanto blade and then grabbed the woman by the hair and torturously bent her head back. She swiftly slid the razor sharp blade across her throat to end her life quickly. It was not her desire to make this innocent young woman suffer needlessly. She cut deep and swiftly, making certain she sliced the vocal cords, so the terrorized woman was unable to cry out an alarm against her as she stared wide eyed in the assassin's ghastly brass face plate and quickly bled to death. Blood soaked the bed, actually running under the sleeping man.

Wind silently moved to the other side of the bed. With the very tip of her katana blade, she barely nicked the sleeping man's chin to wake him from his slumber. She wanted him to stare into the face of his death before she dispatched his life as ordered by her new master.

Tsutomu Yurkowa eyes snapped open and blinked rapidly, trying to adjust to the darkness of the room. He felt the dampness beneath him and checked it with his hand. When his hand returned dripping with fresh blood, he looked to his wife and saw her face and chest covered with blood, her eyes staring the death glare at the ceiling.

Wind was suddenly stunned when she looked in her target's face, although she saw pictures of her target Hiromoai shown her back at his apartment, they must have been old, because she never realized this man would remind her so much of her dead lover. There was something startling about this man's face that made her pang, and forced her to breathe heavily as she carefully studied her target's handsome looking face in the darkness of the room. She held her killing sword threateningly aimed right at his chest as she continued to stare at him.

"Who the hell are you? Why the fuck did you come here and threaten me in the middle of the night? Why do you want to kill me? What have I ever done to you to make you want to take my life from me? I never done anything to harm or made any threat against you. Who the hell sent you here to kill me, dammit?" Tsutomu cried in Japanese as he tried to move out from under her harsh gaze hidden behind the heavy brass mask of hatred, as he quickly gathered his strength robbed by this invader who just killed his wife while they slept.

She stopped his movement by resting the very tip of her katana blade on his chest as she snapped, hating this man and not truly knowing why, and not understanding some of the Japanese he was snarling at her. "My Master has command's me so, dishonored one."

"I tell you assassin, your Master is a god damn criminal!" He hissed as he lied back.

"No! My Lord and Master is pure of heart and mind, a good and kind Liege Lord who commands me justly to end your worthless life, foul one."

"Then why the hell does your damn Master send your ass out to kill me from the shadows of the night? Why the hell does the lowly bastard bid you kill me, cursed assassin? He's forcing you to become a murderer for his unjust cause. If you carry out his orders to kill me, you'll become a criminal just like your god damn Master is. Look assassin, this is the fucking twentieth century, there are no more Masters to be obeyed so. Here, everyone's fucking equal to their once

Masters of the ancient times, assassin." He was saying anything he could in an effort to save his life. He had no way of knowing he was arguing with a female assassin, and wasting his words.

"Everyone has a Master in life and in death foul being with an insulting tongue and nasty thoughts. Be still disgusting and loathed one while I try and think! I'm confused, and the only reason you are still drawing breath from the living world, is because your face reminds me of someone from my long ago past time that I once..."

"It's fucking simple then murderer of the darkness, don't kill me! Allow me to live and I'll turn my back on you, and you can use the same shadows that covered your entry, to hide your escape." He begged the fearsome looking apparition so closely hovering threateningly over him.

"That request is impossible for me to obey, worthless one. I must destroy you fool, my Master commands me so, and it is my sworn and sacred oath that I must obey my Master's command without hesitation or delay." She replied to his begging even though her target was still using many words in Japanese she did not understand, or know their meaning.

"You must not kill me, stalker of the night!" He suddenly demanded of her.

"Your face." She moaned as she remembered her Captain's face smiling lovingly at her.

"Disobey your fucking Master, think for yourself for a change god dammit. He's wrong! Dead wrong, assassin of the night's darkness! Don't allow yourself to become just like he is. Save yourself from a life of crime, of being hunted down like a lowly dog by the police, hated wherever you travel for the rest of your wasted life." Yurkowa dared to reach out after he saw the slight hesitation in her actions. He tried to take the sword from her grasp.

Wind moved back to avoid his hand as she repeated. "But your face foul one."

"Stop jerking me around and give me that damn sword will you dammit!" He growled, for the first time since this specter entered his bedroom and slaughtered his wife, he felt it might be a woman hiding behind the brass mask of hate, as Hiromoai warned him.

As he reached out for her sword a second time, she slapped his hand away with the edge of the blade, nicking him by cutting a finger with the deadly blade. Her heart saddened, she could not help but feel that she had just injured the only lover she had ever known in life.

"Dammit! You! You just fucking cut me with that damn thing! See what you done to me? I'll kill you for that cut, assassin of no worth!" He roared in English as he examined the finger. He searched his mind and came to the conclusion that Hiromoai was behind this killer's actions, and he bellowed at the invader. "Hiromoai! I'll kill you for this attack on my home and family. How dare you send this worthless assassin to my bedroom to kill my wife and me? My fucking bedroom! Kill my wife! Invade my damn house as if this damn killer of yours was invited into my home by me! Dammit! I'll get even with you if it's the last thing I do in life." Yurkowa growled savagely as he went to swing his feet off the side of the bed and ring for his security guards to come and save his life from this assassin threatening him so with its sword.

She did not understand but one word her target hissed at her in English, her master's name. But his uncontrolled rage brought her back from the confusing memories of the long ago past, and her mind focused in on what she was commanded to do by Hiromoai. She moved her killing blade out in front of his face, and she stopped all further movement from the angry man, as he saw the blade looming so dangerously close before his face.

Yurkowa followed the end of the shaft of the shining blade up the length until he saw the ugly looking Hoate mask staring threateningly back at him. The eyes behind the brass mask seemed to actually glow an angry red while glaring down at him.

"Who the hell are you, fucking murderer? Get the hell out of my god damn room while you can still breathe and live." He growled as he sat down on the side of the bed now.

"Speak Japanese so I understand your disgusting words of hatred aimed at my person, manure eating dog." She warned as she continued to glare at him from behind the brass mask.

"So, my assassin only speaks fucking Japanese huh? Are you a god damn woman? The woman assassin Hiromoai had warned me was coming for my life like a lowly thief as you have done."

"Hai! Your foul words have the ring of truth to them, detestable one that shall soon be walking with your worthless ancestors inhabiting the Floating World." Wind snapped angrily as she moved the deadly blade of Wind's Breath back and forth, barely inches before his face.

"I thought so bitch of the fucking night's darkness! Why the hell have you killed my wife? What the hell has she ever done to you or your lousy Master, god cursed assassin? If you were sent to kill me then why did you have to kill her? She was innocent of any wrong doing against your Master as you refer to that sonofabitch who sent you against me and my family. Do you have no soul in your worthless body? What the hell are you doing here? Are you going to kill everyone in my family? My children? Are you without any honor, Samurai? You come here as an angel of death, with her wings dipped in the blood of the kind. Do you quench your miserable thirst by drinking the blood of the innocent, after you have slaughtered them for no good reason but for Hiromoai's want and lust for my family's blood? If you leave my room this minute assassin, I'll allow you to escape with your life. Remain a second longer than now, and you'll die slowly, and I'll fucking dance on your dying body in merriment and pleasure."

"Foolish one with a biting tongue and angry words, I am your death! Your words are wasted on my ears. Can one negotiate with the Tiger? I'll answer that question, fool of fools. No! Just as you cannot negotiate with me foolish one, your destiny is written upon the breath of the wind on this night. Your time to make amends for your miserable life is at hand, my Master's teki." She snarled as she tightened her grip on the hilt of her sword, and aimed it at his chest again.

"Are you going to slaughter an unarmed man like you killed my wife, fucking murderer? Where the hell's the honor in that shit, Samurai filth? What kind of Samurai would slaughter an unarmed man in the night! Like you done to my wife, you successfully dug in the deepest abyss of my tortured heart by killing my wife, murderer. And for that you'll die on this fucking night."

She mostly ignored the angry words from Yurkowa's mouth, as she looked around the large room, while holding her killing blade against Tsutomu's heaving chest. She was still fighting the memories clouding her mind of the past. Spotting a set of old katana blades in their decorative holders hanging by a fire place hearth, she smiled behind the brass mask. With the tip of her blade, she pointed to the swords then waited for Yurkowa to move for the blade. She felt if this man was of the spirit of her lover, she would offer him an honorable death at her skilled hands.

"What's this? You're going to allow me to arm and defend myself? Whore of the darkness."

"Hai! The meaning of life is different for each mind and each set of eyes. I am your waiting death to visit your person." Wind hissed at the angry acting man.

"Huh, I see you're a fucking believer in Zen, and even dumber than I thought, bitch. I warn you witch hiding behind the mask of hatred, you'll live long enough to regret that stupid decision of allowing me to arm myself, foolish killer of the shadows. I'll avenge my wife's death on your body in ways you'll never believe possible. I'll win my revenge against you for invading my home and threatening my life. I warn you, you'll die long and painfully, this I swear to your soul.

"Then, my wrath will find and destroy the one who is behind this ruthless murder you have committed on this night. I know how to fucking handle the blades of my ancestor's very well, murderer. Beware evil one of the night, I warn you, leave now and live. Allow me to arm myself and I'll hack your body to pieces and then piss on your remains with joy and pleasure." The fuming Tsutomu was trying his best to scare the samurai into sparing his life, when he saw she didn't flinch an inch, he made a dash for the weapon in case his killer might change her mind.

He unsheathed the old blade and then quickly moved in on her. Feeling the full weight of the old katana blade locked in his hands, he felt he stood a little better than even chance of saving his life, against this murderer. He raised the deadly katana blade to the side and then he snapped it right at her face, hoping to catch her off guard.

She anticipated his opening sneak attack against her and easily side stepped his initial and wild sword thrust, and then she ran her sword's razor sharp edge across his exposed back, making a deep gash across both shoulders of his naked back. It was a wound not designed to kill, but to cause uncontrolled pain, bleeding and fear. She understood the wound would hamper some of the rapid movements of her intended target.

Yurkowa felt the pain and blood running down his back and legs, from the wide gash she inflicted on his back, and was already having trouble moving freely because of the wound. He realized this assassin was an expert with the blade. He was going to call out an alarm, but her swift move cut his scream off as he had to place his full attention on the attacking warrior.

She moved swiftly before the shaking with rage Yurkowa, and swiped at him with her blade. It felt good to once again be forced to use her outstanding sword skills in the heat of battle to the death with honor. He responded to the swing from his would be killer, by swinging at her momentarily exposed back with his sword. He missed his target, for his soon to be murderer moved too swiftly for his blade to catch her by surprise with his attack aimed against her.

She spun around and clipped him on his left arm, opening another bloody deep gash.

Yurkowa covered the wound with the hand holding the sword and then he glared at her, bouncing on the balls of her feet and staring in his eyes with all the hatred of the world in them.

Wind swung out and hit his sword up with her sword, and then she followed that attack by crashing the heel of her right foot in his exposed solar plexus in the same motion. Doubling him over in pain, and causing him to gasp for air and go down on one knee.

Yurkowa glared angrily at her while he held his stomach then struggled to his feet and moved the sword before his face. He was too weak from the kick to properly defend himself.

She wore the face that a cat would display when playing with a trapped mouse. She again slapped his sword from before him and nicked his face with the edge of her blade.

The searing pain caused him to roar with anger as he wildly charged the female assassin.

She moved with skill to the side and brought the back end of her blade down across the head of her attacker, sending him sprawling to the floor and crashing hard into the wall before coming to a stop in a heap.

His breath was knocked from his lungs as he painfully rolled over on his bloody back, while trying to get air into his starving lungs. With effort he used the wall to help him slowly inch his way up and help him get to his feet, leaving a bloody trail on the wall. His head was pounding, his eyes clouding over as unconsciousness threatened to overtake his exhausted and pained body, he glared again at the assassin who was like the wind to try and capture. He growled savagely at his attacker. "God and faith allowed themselves to be lead astray by Satan and your evil Master, to allow you to draw in another breath in this world, depraved murderer of the innocent."

She allowed him time to try and regain his senses while she ignored his threatening words aimed at her as he hissed them at her. She was beyond recognizing words from anyone as she prepared to take his life, and fulfill her master's orders demanding his death.

The moment his wits returned to him, the young businessman made a reckless lunge at his attacker. Hoping to crash his much heavier body into her, and knock her down to the ground where he could have at her much smaller body with his bare hands. He understood if he was able to get his hands on his attacker's body for just a moment, he would be able to defeat this slight of build assassin sent out to kill him. His mind was telling him there was no way he was going to best this attacker with the killing sword and his weak skill with the katana blade. The only hope he had of surviving, was to get his hands on her body. He thought she was no match for his greater strength and weight in the battle of death with their hands.

The suddenness of the unintended lunge from Yurhowa caught her slightly off guard for the brief moment, but she recovered quickly and used her sword to trip the wildly charging man. Again, he went tumbling to the floor, but this time he used the tumble to help him roll until he ended up back on his feet. Without thought of what he was doing, he charged the samurai a second time. Swinging his deadly blade wildly before him without control, he rapidly moved in on her. The swords clashed with her easily fending off his savage blow, and then whirring around and catching his sword a second time before it struck her slightly exposed back.

The force of his blade crashing together caused her to spin around. She was well trained and understood the willow remained strong after a storm because it was smart enough to bend with the blowing wind. So she allowed his force to turn her body sideways. She understood where and how she was going to come out of the slight spin. She allowed the momentum of her swing to turn her body sideways, when she came back face to face with him she struck without hesitation, catching him on the forearm of his right arm. A rip four inches long and deep was opened by her thrust of the killing sword. He used up every bit of his remaining strength to stop himself from dropping the blade, and attend to the new injury.

Wind ended up kneeling on a knee from her spin, with her blade tucked tightly under her left arm pointing up facing back, in case her attacker tried to charge her from behind unexpectedly. She then whipped around and held her blade out before her, and glared at the injured Yurkowa, as she warned him in an extremely threatening tone. "I shall send you on an endless journey to the land of fantasy and hope. Foul one prepare your evil self to enter the underworlds of ceaseless darkness and endless waiting and wanting, where you shall dwell for all eternity for daring any treachery against my Lord and Master! I shall kill you in such a terrible way that even the black Kami who eat souls, will not find enough of your worthless body remaining to feast its foul desires upon. Your soul will never be allowed to return to the living world, reborn Samurai pure. I curse you for your hatred of my faithful Lord and Master."

"Look bitch, I know who your repulsive Master is. What the hell have I done to Hiromoai to make him aim you at me, and order you to kill my wife and me on this god damn night? I want to know if he's your true Master, so I can right any wrongs I committed against him in the past times. Tell me the truth god dammit! Tell me Samurai who your foul Master truly is?"

Wind had endured enough of the sword play with her master's skillful enemy. She did not speak to Yurkowa as she leaped to her feet and then stabbed out with the tip of her sword. It caught him in the softness of his belly and she gave a twist and lift to her blade in one motion.

He had no choice but to drop his sword and try to stop the terrible damage to his body she was doing by the sword of his assassin, before his innards poured from the terrible gash the blade opened in his belly. He drew in his breath in an attempt to scream out an alarm to his security guards stationed outside his bedroom door. But Wind withdrew her sword from his body and again it sliced through the air with blinding swiftness, with the blade finding his throat and his head jumped in the air and then fell to the ground and tumbled across the floor.

Yurkowa was only able to strike at Wind's body once with any kind of a controlled thrust and attack, but the noise of the battle inside the master bedroom suddenly caught the attention of a security guard standing on duty out in the hallway. Hearing the noise he lightly tapped on the bedroom door and called out in concern. "Tsutomu-san, are you alright sir?"

When no reply came to his pleas, the now concerned security guard pulled his palm radio out and gave out the alarm to the other guards on duty, as he tried the handle of the bedroom door. When it would not open, he tried ramming his shoulder into the heavy carved thick wood door, while calling out his boss's name a second time, to see if he was okay in his bedroom.

Wind ignored the assault on the door as she hacked her enemy to pieces on the floor of the bedroom. She followed her orders to kill this man in a horrible and despicable way, to serve as a further warning to others who might seek harm to her master, or ignore his will. She picked up his head by the hair after she finished her assault on his body, and carried it to the center of the chopped apart body and placed it down right in the equidistant of the gore. His unseeing eyes staring at her as she bowed and smiled as she prepared to leave the bedroom.

Just as she finished her onslaught on Yurkowa's body, the bedroom door splintered and she came face to face with a bulky security guard holding a pistol aiming it at her chest. In less than a heartbeat, a throwing star soared through the air and hit the guard in his throat. Gagging on his blood, the guard dropped the weapon and tried to pull the star of death from his body.

Wind used this brief interruption to dip back out on the balcony. Once outside the room she heard rapid footfalls running up the marble stairs leading to Yurkowa's bedroom. As she headed for where she climbed up the side of the building before, two other security guards came charging around the statue of the woman with the dove and stepped over the body of the downed guard she killed moments before, both were armed with katana swords. The moment they saw this threatening woman dressed in weird shaped armor and covered with fresh blood, they prepared to attack this invader in the old way of defending oneself against any intruder. She attacked first without thought or hesitation.

Wind lunged at the first attacker, catching him in the chest with her killing blade, and she plunged it deep, cutting into his lung and completely disabling him for further fighting. She yanked the blade out of his body and spun it over her back in her attempt to block the assault against her body from the trailing second attacker. The swords clanged with the ring of a bell. She dropped low and swung her sword at the attacker's legs. Cutting the right leg in two below the knee, and her blade did massive damage to the other leg because of her over swing. Because she was not directed to kill anyone but Yurkowa, she held off her attack on the injured man.

She lifted her blood soaked sword across her chest then nodded to the downed man. It was the ancient way of honoring her enemy who she defeated after he done his best in battle for his master. The guard nodded, knowing he was going to be allowed to live on this mysterious night, conceding to the skilled assassin as he tried to stem the flow of blood from his legs.

She did not dispatch this guard because his wounds were not life threatening. She turned to the first attacker, and noticed that he was suffering terribly from his wound, dying slowly and hard. She swiped at him with her killing blade and dispatched him humanely, his head landing two feet away from its body. She then ran to the area where she used to climb up the side of the building and jumped from the balcony and quickly scurried down its side, grabbing hold of bricks that stuck out slightly further than others. She moved like a cat climbing a tree after an unsuspecting bird. When she landed on the ground silently, she hunched down in an attempt to get her bearing, and to make certain that no other security guards were coming at her from the darkness, and then she ran for the walkway and wall circling the grounds of the compound.

As she quickly ran for the wall where she climbed over she immediately picked up the guard who lit the cigarette when she first entered the compound. The guard stared at her, stunned he was frozen in place at the awesome sight of this chilling apparition with the brass grimacing face staring at him. He thought the shadow charging him was some kind of a joke being played out against him by his fellow guards, so they could see how he would handle himself in time of crisis. The thought to be joke suddenly smashed his body with the back of her blade, crashing it down on his head and dropping him to the ground out cold as she swiftly ran past him.

The thud of a falling body was the only sound of the swift one-sided battle on the compound grounds. Wind did not miss a step as she flew by the last guard and struck at him with the blunt end of her sword, as she ran passed him. She knocked the last man out cold with the hard blow and then she finally reached the lower six foot section of the wall with no further trouble, just as the blinding lights of the building snapped on, bathing the entire compound with glaring light, yelling men and barking dogs. She leaped up and easily pulled herself on the wall and then she silently dropped to the other side of the wall and instantly disappeared into the shadows of the night from where she came. It seemed as though her form was completely swallowed up by the earth, as she quickly disappeared in the darkness. In the far off distance the wail of police sirens could be heard as the squad cars screamed towards Yurkowa's home.

Wind quickly worked her way back to Hatanaka Towers and the safety the penthouse offered her. She had no problem with retracing the path she employed to leave the tower hours before. Her heart was pounded in her chest as she entered the sliding doors completely out of breath. She was still caught up in the thrill of battle and the death of a surprisingly well trained man who wanted to fight her, rather than die meekly and dishonorably by her killing sword.

The Lady Yoke was pacing the apartment while waiting for the ancient female warrior's return to the study, and met her as she entered the apartment like a stalking cat through the glass doors of the balcony. Her protective armor was sprinkled here and there with drying blood, and Lady Yoke helped her out of the body protection. She moved it into the bathroom and placed it in the shower and ran hot water and soap on the redesigned body armor as she slipped in a fresh kimono after washing her body of blood, grime and filth of the night and sweat.

Lady Yoke thoroughly scrubbed the altered armor with a hard brush and harsh cleaning solution, erasing any signs of blood and smallest flecks of skin and bone from the armor. She was making certain she did not miss a single drop of blood, or fleck of skin marring her armor.

Wind entered the bathroom and prepared for a soak in the hot tub. The second Lady Yoke finished working on the armor she bathed her even though she was already clean then helped her in the tub. Once she was comfortable and settled in the water, she moved the armor from the bathroom and placed them on the baskets after drying them.

She wanted nothing out of place in case the police visited the apartment to speak with Hiromoai over what had befallen Yurkowa.

Lady Yoke found her katana blade and scrubbed it free of blood and skin and then she placed a strong abrasive cleaning solution on the steel of the blade, to eat away any traces of blood and skin that might later be found by the police, if they took the time to examine the blade of the ancient warrior. Then she carried the katana sword to the special carrying case Hiromoai had crafted for the blade, and set it back in the box without placing it in its protective sheath.

CHAPTER ELEVEN
THE TOKYO HILTON, 1:20 A.M. WEDNESDAY, JUNE 5th, 1996

The young Hiromoai was a very cautious man, and he made certain he was surrounded by a bevy of beautiful young Japanese and American women, all the time he spent at the exclusive party. The women were all plying to be taken home by the rich and very handsome Japanese businessman. He shared drinks with some, and enjoyed their laughs and friendly grabs and jokes. All the while, he kept his eyes glued to the doors to the room. When they flung open and three police officers entered and they briskly walked through the crowd, he knew he was smart to attend the party. He had an air tight alibi to protect himself from suspicion of Yurkowa's death.

The police Lieutenant searched the many faces at the party staring at him with concern, until he finally noticed Hiromoai standing in the middle of a crowd of women, and he slowed his pace and made his way to him. The officer bowed correctly as if there was nothing seriously wrong, and he asked him in a friendly manner if he could speak to him privately for a moment.

Hiromoai nodded and smiled and then excused himself from the horde of women surrounding him, and then he fell in line with the officer as they headed to the outside verandah and privacy.

"Would you care for something to drink Lieutenant err...?" He asked as he picked up a glass of Champaign, and then tipped it at the officer and sipped it while looking at the Lieutenant as if he had no idea why the detective was wishing to speak with him.

"No thank you Hiromoai-san, allow me to introduce myself to you sir. I'm Lieutenant Kenzaburo Motoshima of the Tokyo Police Department, Homicide Division sir. I have to refuse the drink because I'm still on duty and its ag..." The Lieutenant offered as he handed him his card, but his offer and words were cut off by Hiromoai as he asked.

"Then I take it this is an official visit, Detective Lieutenant Motoshima-san?"

"I'm sorry for this intrusion into your private time at this party, Hiromoai-san. It is, there has been a terrible crime committed tonight, a heinous murder, a horrifying slaughter in fact sir, and we were asked to speak to you about the murder, and see if you had any idea who..."

"And you think I might have had something to do with this disgusting murder you speak of, Officer!" Hiromoai growled and threw his glass on the floor and glared at the officer. The glass shattered into a hundred pieces and went flying everywhere on the marble floor. The business owner was renowned for his hair trigger temper and bad moods, and he was making the best of his displayed before the lieutenant by carrying it one step further than good manners allowed.

Detective Motoshima bowed to the fuming man to take some of the sting of his presence from him and replied. "No, Hiromoai-san, not at all sir. That thought's the furthest thing from my mind sir. But it's just that you happened to know the murdered, actually slaughtered victim well sir, and we're asking anyone who might know him, if they were aware of any death threats leveled against him recently, sir. That's the only reason for my wanting to speak with you."

"I see, please Officer forgive me for my childish outburst, I lost great face before you tonight, Lieutenant. But so far you have failed to inform me who was murdered on this night, or as you say, slaughtered on this night, sir. So how in the hell can I possibly answer these troubling questions you pose to me, without knowing who the hell we're talking about, Lieutenant."

"Please excuse my stupidity, Hiromoai-san." The officer was trying to be extra polite to one of the most powerful businessman in all Japan, and he bowed low and held it for a moment and then he offered in a very polite voice. "Hiromoai-san, I'm terribly sorry to inform you, but the murdered victim was Tsutomu Yurkowa-san and his lovely young wife. It was a terrible murder, a slaughter as I said, sir. I'm afraid it's more like an assassination than a mur..."

"What!" Hiromoai interrupted the officer as he placed a stunned look on his face and stared at him and then he added. "My God in Heaven Lieutenant, I can't believe this. Do you think I might be next on this murderer's hit list sir?" He was good at acting stunned by the death of the man he so despised throughout all his life. He staggered to a chair and used the back of it to help support him momentarily, as he continued to stare at the officer and shook his head slowly.

"Why would you suggest that to me, Hiromoai-san? That you feel you might be next on the murderer's death list sir." The suddenly concerned officer asked as he cocked a wary eye at Hiromoai, wondering why he would ask such a question of him.

"Because Lieutenant, poor Tsutomu-san was in the construction field as I am. Could this believed assassin be some sort of nut who might be angry with the construction field in Japan?"

"Hmmm... that's a very interesting question and good point to make indeed to me, Hiromoai-san. I'm pleased you brought this thought up to my attention, because it could turn out to be a good lead in this most troublesome case, sir. It's defiantly something I'll look into I assure you, Hiromoai-san. Please forgive me again, but with all due respect offered to you Hiromoai-san. I do have a list of questions I'm bound to ask of you, sir. They're not asked to insult you in the least sir, it's just my job and I must carry out my work faithfully, Hiromoai-san. Please understand why I must ask you these most annoying and terribly insulting questions, sir."

"Yes, I understand why you have to ask some bad questions of me to further your investigation of the terrible murder of young Yurkowa-san, Lieutenant Motoshima-san. Please, feel free to ask any questions of me you want answered, sir. I'll try my best to answer them to your complete satisfaction, Lieutenant. I have nothing to hide from the law."

"Please Hiromoai-san, first, when did you arrive at this gala party you're attending sir?"

"Oh, I believe it was somewhere around six o'clock, Lieutenant. You can ask anyone here, I'm certain they all know when I have arrived at the party, Officer."

"And you were here ever since you first arrived at the party, sir? You didn't leave the party for any reason, not even for the briefest of seconds, Hiromoai-san?" Lieutenant Motoshima asked while looking totally embarrassed over his question of the powerful businessman.

"Only one time and that was to relieve myself I believe. But no, I never left the floor since arriving, Lieutenant."

"You have these people here who can attest to your presence since arriving at the party sir?"

"Yes, I've been with the same few women ever since I first arrived that you saw me with when you first entered the room, Officer. Please, feel free to ask them about my presence, sir."

"That won't be necessary at this time sir. I don't want to embarrass you further than I already done before your friends, sir. I'm embarrassed for bothering you at all sir. These people are of Japan's most influential and elite citizens. But Hiromoai-san, do me a favor and take names and phone numbers of the women you were with, err... in case I have to interview them in the future."

"Huh, I assure you Lieutenant Motoshima-san, I already have most of their names, and their shape sizes here." He snapped with a sneer as he lightly tapped his suit jacket breast pocket.

"In that case Hiromoai-san, I'll leave you in peace so you can get back to your party, sir. Again, I'm sorry for any embarrassment I caused you with your friends, sir. Please give my regards and apologies to the hostess and their guests, sir." The officer bowed then turned on his heels sharply and gave a few hand signals, and all three officers left as quickly as they arrived.

When the officers left the room, the flock of young women quickly circled Hiromoai and they hit him with a flood of questions and worries if anything was wrong. He smiled as he assured them it was only a business matter the officers were interested in. He picked up an American beauty and spun her around in his arms and then he kissed her on the neck. He was trying his best to act like nothing was wrong with him. He felt the officer might have planted a spy to keep an eye on his moves at the party, and he wanted to put on a good act.

As the clock ticked to two a.m., he began to make his apologies to the guests and beautiful women hanging on his arm, and then he quickly left the party. He wanted to get back to his apartment and see how Wind made out, and maybe share her treasures on what was left of this long night. As he got in his limo, he ordered the driver to take him home. All the way to the apartment he kept a constant watch behind him, and easily picked up the trailing police car trying to make itself invisible. He cursed because he knew the first thing he had to do, was send Wind back to the Floating World until the heat got off his back. He did not need her hanging around if and when the police came to question him further about the murder of Yurkowa.

He was certain he was going to be bothered by the police in the near future, until they grew bored tormenting him over the murder incident. He understood any roads leading them to his involvement, would be erased when he sent Wind back to her world of the dead.

The driver dropped Hiromoai off at the front of the tower and then he moved the car to the underground parking lot as Hiromoai entered the building. He cursed all the while he was in the elevator, and charged down the hall in haste to his apartment. He bellowed as he entered. "Lady Yoke, Wind, get out here, dammit!" He ran to the study and pulled the case for the sword from the couch and flipped it open. Wind was dressed in a kimono and Lady Yoke in a neat blouse and skirt. Both women seemed relaxed until they saw Hiromoai waiting for them.

"What's wrong Hiromoai-san? You look so upset, sir." Lady Yoke asked with concern.

"I don't have the fucking time or the patience to explain this shit to you right now, Lady Yoke. Wind! You have to go back to the Ukiyo World immediately for a few sticks of time. I'll send for you when it's safe for you to return to the land of the living again."

Wind nodded, she hated time she was forced to remain in the place of forever waiting Ukiyo.

Hiromoai slammed the ancient sword back in its wood scabbard, and watched as the glowing light quickly engulfed the beautiful body of the ancient female warrior. The glow disappeared and he placed the sword in the carrying case, and then placed it on the sofa. All that remained of Wind was the crumpled up kimono she wore, lying in a heap on the floor. He did not notice it until he finally calmed down that the once restored armor and ancient weapons looked like the discarded and worthless pieces of junk he originally found in the ancient crypt.

Yoke tried her best to help her boss, and when he seemed like he calmed down she asked. "What's wrong Hiromoai-san? You seem to have the fear of the gods chasing after you, sir."

"I think the god damn police might be paying us a visit tonight Lady Yoke, and I wanted to be ready for them to arr..." Even as he spoke the words, there was a knock at the front door.

"Hiromoai-san, change your clothes from the party and wash your face. I'll handle the police, if they're foolish enough to show up at our door." Lady Yoke ordered as she marched to the door.

Hiromoai followed her advice and shot up the stairs to his bedroom, taking two steps at a time to his master's suite as Lady Yoke opened the door. She acted like she was in a nasty mood, as she barked at the two officers after seeing their badges. "What's the meaning of this god cursed intrusion to my Wa, fools! Since when do police show up at my Master's home at such an ungodly hour in the morning? Do our worthless police no long possess the good manners their Mothers taught them from their foul birth? What do you want here? Ieeee, Hiromoai-san has no time to waste on the likes of such impolite visitors to his home as you two obviously are. Leave my door immediately before I report you to your superiors, and have you fired."

"Young lady please, my name's Detective Lieutenant Kenzaburo Motoshima, and this man to my left is Sergeant Toshihiro Okamatsu. We know Hiromoai-san has just arrived home, and we were wondering if we might have a few words with him in private. I spoke with him earlier this evening, and I'm afraid I have a few more questions that I must ask him, before I can leave him alone for the night, Ma'am. I'll not keep your Master long, this I promise. May we come in and see please?" The Lieutenant bowed graciously at the steaming and upset acting lady Yoke.

"I don't care one grain of worthless rice who you think you are, or who you think you might be in the flow of Japan's heartbeat, and what you might want with Hiromoai-san, Officer! You have no questions you must ask of my Master at this ungodly time of the day, fool. If he chooses, he might speak with you, but it will be on his terms and not yours. And no, you may not come in this apartment and pollute its sweet air and disturb its Wa!" She snapped at the officer then added. "If you want to speak to my Master, I suggest you come to his home at a more proper time during the day. I'll not allow you to upset Hiromoai-san's sacred Wa, before he turns in for the night. My Master needs his rest, and I'll not allow you to upset him this late at..."

"Who is at the door Lady Yoke?" Hiromoai asked as he came in the hallway tying his obi.

"It's the cursed and police who uncouth say they spoke to you earlier in the day, and they request permission to speak with you again. I won't allow them to upset you this late at night, Hiromoai-san. The two fools beg they want to ask you more quest..."

"Hiromoai-san, it's me, Lieutenant Motoshima who spoke to you earlier on at the party sir."

"Oh yes of course, come in and make yourself comfortable, Lieutenant Motoshima-san. Would you like a refreshing cup of tea, or maybe some coffee and something to nibble on, sir?" Hiromoai asked as he led the two officers in the living room.

Lady Yoke glared at the two police officers as they walked passed her as if she no longer existed. She lost great face when the one chose to speak to her boss over her objections. She lost further face when the two officers went over her head and acted like she was not there, and spoke directly to Hiromoai. She wanted to curse them to the evil of hell, and all their generations for the detestable insult they leveled against her personally before her boss.

"Thank you for the offer of tea, Hiromoai-san. I believe I'll indulge in a cup of tea if you don't mind, sir. This Officer with me is Sergeant Toshihiro Okamatsu-san. A cup of tea would be most pleasing sir. I'm afraid it's been a very trying night to endure, sir." Lieutenant Motoshima bowed over his offer of some tea and then he waited for it to be served, before he would start his questions of the powerful young Japanese businessman.

He nodded to the other officer and then they walked in the living room with Hiromoai acting like he had an air about him, and he sat on his favorite chair and motioned the two officers to the chairs directly across from him. He then looked at Lady Yoke and said to her pleasantly. "Please Lady Yoke I believe the Officers would like to enjoy a cup of tea."

"Hiromoai-san, I don't understand why you're displaying such polite manners to these ill begotten Officers who smell terribly, and they look worse, and they have dared to upset you so late tonight, sir. I think you should not have allowed the two foul fools in your home until a more proper time in the morning." Lady Yoke snapped as she disappeared in the kitchen while still mumbling loud enough for them to hear she was still angry at them.

The three men smiled as they listened to Lady Yoke to continue to complain all the way to the kitchen. The Lieutenant spun his hat absentmindedly in his hand, as he offered. "Please Hiromoai-san it seems I might have upset your help tonight, sir. I'm sorry for this intrusion sir."

"Don't mind her Lieutenant Motoshima-san, lately she's been acting more like my Mother than a helper, sir. What's the reason for this late night visit sir? I thought we spoke at length at the party earlier in the night, and I settled everything there was to be settled with this matter. Did you find anything else out about the terrible murder, err... slaughter of poor Yurkowa-san?"

"No, I'm afraid not Hiromoai-san, but I do have a few more questions I needed to ask of you tonight if you don't mind sir." All the while the detective spoke to him the other officer scanned the huge room, and the rest of the apartment he could see from where he sat. Looking for any possible evidence and he tried to glance into the darkened study.

Hiromoai ignored the second officer as he spoke with the Lieutenant. "And these questions couldn't wait until tomorrow morning I guess, Lieutenant Motoshima-san? I'm rather tired, the party lasted longer than I first expected. I'd like to turn in for the night if you don't mind, sir."

"I'm terribly sorry Hiromoai-san, but I'm afraid some things just can't wait for a proper time to be gone over, sir." Lieutenant Motoshima tried his best smile on the Japanese businessman.

"So you offered before Lieutenant." Hiromoai interrupted the officer nastily as he displayed his displeasure at being bothered so late. "Well, now that you're here, you might as well ask these important questions that couldn't wait until a more fitting time to be asked, Officer."

"Well Hiromoai-san, we saw you being driven home earlier, and we figured since you weren't asleep yet, we were hoping to try our luck and see if we could get these nagging questions out of the way, sir. That way they won't be hanging over our heads for who knows how long, before we got another chance to meet with you, sir. I was wondering Hiromoai-san, if you received any possible death threats leveled against your life lately, sir. It's been reported Tsutomu-san had received a number of death threats as late as yesterday, sir. Although he never told his security guards where the threats originated, he did pull more guards around him, sir. He also made mention something about a female assassin was coming to murder him. Evidently, the assassin was rather successful in her task sir, and the threat wasn't an idle warning to make Tsuto..."

"Evidently the possible assassin was rather successful at that Lieutenant Motoshima-san." Hiromoai snorted at the concerned looking police detective.

"Yes, right Hiromoai-san, but the remark you made at the party, if your name was on the killer's hit list, made me concerned you might have been threatened. We're aware Yurkowa-san had a meeting with you earlier in the day, sir.

We were wondering if the two of you were discussing recent death threats leveled against either of you. This is important we find out if either of you was receiving death threats, and if so who they might be originating from if you..."

"It was a mere business meeting, that's all Officer. Nothing more than that Lieutenant."

"We figured that much sir. Two busy people such as yourself and Tsutomu-san, would surely have business dealing in any meeting held between you two, sir. But since you're one of the last people known to see Tsutomu-san alive, I was wondering if he might have mentioned anything about an assassin's attempt on his life, and if you were receiving any of these threats as well, sir."

"No, I'm afraid Tsutomu-san never mentioned anything to me about any death threats he might be receiving, Lieutenant. I can't believe someone wanted the young man dead. Remembering his state of mind during our meeting though, he did seem to be unusually upset, sir. Edgy, unable to sit still, and his usual temper was more evident than ever during our meeting, Lieutenant. But no, he never mentioned someone coming after him sir. I'm sorry. However, I have received a few death threats of my own in the past few weeks. But I'm always getting them. Anyone who has money and is in charge of a large business is bound to step on some toes along the way, Officer. I never paid much attention to any of these threats. As you can see Officer Motoshima-san, I'm still here sir." He slowly spread his hands apart and grinned at the young police officer.

"Hmmm... I think it might be a wise idea on your part if you did start paying a little closer attention to any of these threats you might be receiving in the future, Hiromoai-san. Under the present circumstances that is sir."

"Yes, I'll do that from now on, under the circumstances, Lieutenant. I'll start taking threats more seriously from now on, sir." He replied as he grinned at the slightly older police officer.

The officer nodded and asked. "Have any of these threats been on the increase lately sir?"

"No, not really Lieutenant Motoshima-san, I think I receive a new death threat on the average of at least once or twice a week, sometimes more than that I believe, sir. I think it's some of my own lazy workers just busting my back, or trying to get a little more pay out of my ass. I'm quite certain I made many enemies along the way of life and business, Lieutenant."

"Was Tsutomu-san among the enemies you made along the way, Hiromoai-san?"

"Huh, don't be a horses' ass, Lieutenant. Of course we had our own problems and differences, disagreements, like all business people in our field do. But I never once considered him anything but a worthy competitor in business, sir. You're barking up the wrong tree with those questions, Lieutenant. Quite frankly sir, I kind of resent the implication you're hinting at sir. This is why I don't take threats against my life seriously sir. Ha, I laugh in the face of danger Lieutenant."

"Hiromoai-san, I don't think this is something to really be joked about so lightly under the present circumstances I repeat, Hiromoai-san. I have the son of a very powerful Japanese businessman slaughtered in a disturbing and savage way. But the damn killer wasn't satisfied with just killing Tsutomu-san. The lousy bastard went and killed his wife who never hurt anyone, sir. She was slaughtered also. Disgusting, I can't wait till I get my hands on this damn assassin's ass, sir. I'll personally teach him to offer his services in my area of protection, sir."

"I thought you stated this assassin was a female attacker, Lieutenant?" Hiromoai remarked sarcastically at the officer with a slight snap in his tone.

"I have no way of knowing that for certain, Hiromoai-san. To assume something as important as this before its proven right or wrong, could cause the foolish one some serious embarrassment investigating this terrible murder case, sir. Ahhh... the tea."

Hiromoai watched as the Lady Yoke carefully poured tea, he never touched his though.

The Lieutenant sipped his tea then placed the cup in the saucer and spoke in a matter of fact tone. "Hiromoai-san I'd be pleased to leave a few of my Officers in your apartment, and at your business, until we're able to capture this assassin, sir. I don't want anything to happen to you, you're too important to Japan's future to be lost to an assassin's deadly blade and evil skills of killing, sir. I'll be contacting the other construction firms, offering them the same protection.

"A police guard or escort if you will for them until we're able to capture this homicidal maniac carrying out his evil work in the heart of downtown Tokyo, sir. Judging by the disgusting way the evil executioner slaughtered poor Tsutomu-san and his lovely wife. We feel this one would stop at absolutely nothing to get at his targets, if there are more that is sir. Hiromoai-san, we don't consider this assassination as an isolated murder, sir. We believe someone very important and powerful is standing behind the assassin's actions, and I fear there are more deaths to come in the future of Japan, sir." Lieutenant Motoshima took a quick sip of tea.

"Dear God in Heaven, did the assassin hurt any of Tsutomu-san's children, Lieutenant?"

"No Hiromoai-san, thank the gods who protect us from harm and evil for that much sir, this senseless murder is weighing heavy on my mind. The children didn't wake by the assassin's visit to Tsutomu-san's bedroom, sir. I thank you for asking of Tsutomu-san's children's health, sir. The security guards had to wake the children, and remove them from the home until we arrived on the scene of the murders. The children are staying with their grandmother for the time being, she's looking after them until things calm down a little for the family. I'm quite certain poor Yurkowa-san's honorable father will be more than willing to take the children in his custody, once he's feeling a little better over the murder of his most honorable son and his wife, sir." Lieutenant Motoshima looked to the floor in respect of Yurkowa's death and his memory.

"Detective, do you have any idea where this assassin came from? What stable he or she might be hailing from?" He asked as he sat forward and allowed a mask of concern to cloud his face.

"No, but we're checking on all Ninja cults throughout the country to be certain this assassin didn't come from one of those cults, sir. By the skill this assassin displayed during the attack on Tsutomu-san and his wife, we feel whoever it was that committed the heinous murders, was a trained and experienced killer. The murderer was able to sneak by a number of Tsutomu-san's defenses, and some of his people were experts in self-defense, Hiromoai-san. The assassin killed two of his guards, and the assassin injured another two during the attack on Tsutomu-san.

"If the killer was out to kill just for the sake of killing, he wouldn't have just injured some of the security guards the assassin attacked. He would've killed everyone he came across in the compound during his attack on Yurkowa-san. This murderer we feel is one who spent years perfecting his or her evil craft of murder, sir. That's why we feel this act wasn't an isolated incident, sir. Anyone who would employ such a well trained killer wasn't only planning to kill these two people. We're confident the killer didn't take it on his own to kill Tsutomu-san either, sir." Lieutenant Motoshima relaxed and then waited for Hiromoai to reply to his response.

"I didn't know other people were killed or injured during the vicious attack on Yurkowa-san, Lieutenant?" He asked more than replied to the officer's information he released.

"Yes Hiromoai-san, there were these deaths also involved in the attack on Yurkowa-san's home and family, sir. We're trying to keep that part of the attack secret, and I must beg you to keep this information to yourself at this time, sir. That way, when we capture this crazed murderer, only he or she would know of the other deaths during the attack on Tsutomu-san and his wife, it's a novel way of trying to convict the damn criminal by his own trap, sir."

"I see what you're aiming at Lieutenant Motoshima-san. Yes, a smart move on your part sir."

"Errr... Hiromoai-san, do you have the list of names and numbers of the women who can attest to the fact you were at the party for the full time in question, earlier tonight sir?

Believe me Hiromoai-san, this is only a precaution I'm taking sir, for your benefit might I add. It'll clear you of any further investigation, or involvement in this terrible matter of tonight, sir."

He allowed his temper to rise for show as he barked. "What the hell is this crap, Lieutenant Motoshima? Am I to believe I'm a suspect in this murder of Yurkowa-san and his poor wife? How dare you come to my home and accuse me of killing a close and very dear friend of many years! I assure you Lieutenant I'll be lodging a formal complaint with your sup..."

"No Hiromoai-san, I assure you you're not a suspect in this case in the least, sir. This is part of my duties attached to this exhausting case and my investigation, sir. I want to remove all shadows of doubt that might be leveled against you in the future, before I turn my attention on someone else. Believe me sir I haven't the slightest doubt you were never involved in this deplorable incident, sir. But this is part of police work sir, good or bad it has to be done and done right, Hiromoai-san. I'm sorry, but it's something I have to do sir, it's part of my job, and I do my job very well sir." Motoshima bowed politely as a form of apology to his insulting remarks.

"I feel I must warn you Lieutenant Motoshima-san. I'm insulted you're daring to doubt my word or honor I offered over this matter. Here is the list of names and numbers of six of the prettiest women I told you I was with all night. They're the only women of the lot I considered a prospect for further consideration and also bedding. Are these six names enough proof of my innocence in this cursed matter, Officer? Or do you want me to get the names and numbers of the other women who I spoke with for even a brief time at the party last night as well, sir?

"The list might be longer than you suspect Lieutenant." Hiromoai glared at the officer, warning him to be careful in his choice of remarks or questions. He was carrying out his act of being offended by some of his questions, in his attempt to remove suspicion from his shoulders.

"These names will be more than enough for my needs I believe, Hiromoai-san. I'll be most discreet I assure you if and when speaking with them, sir."

"Fine Officer, I take it this is all you need from me on this never-ending night of bad news and terrible death, Lieutenant? I'm rather tired and upset as you can well imagine, sir. It's been a long and trying night to labor through, and I wish to place an end to it as soon as possible. I'll have to get in touch with poor Asahiko-san tomorrow, and give him my condolences for the terrible loss of his fine young son, and his beautiful wife, sir. I can't imagine how hard it must be for the old man to lose his first born son in this savage manner, Detective Motoshima-san.

"Terrible, it's terrible Lieutenant Motoshima-san. What a terrible loss to the construction field and to Japan's future in the world market, Officer. I fear that Yurkowa-san's position will never be able to be filled properly by any other person of Japan. He was a very formidable competitor. I'll surely miss the fine battles of mind and competition we were engaging in, sir. Lieutenant, it's getting late and I'd like to turn in for the night if you don't mind, sir." He grumbled as he glanced at his watch and noticed it was nearly three thirty in the morning.

The wise Lieutenant hesitated for a brief moment before replying as he stood, and then he bowed politely and then prepared to leave the huge apartment. "Yes Hiromoai-san, it's been an unending and most disturbing night for me to suffer through as well sir, and I too would like it to end this night. I believe I have the information I need to conclude this part of my investigation at this time, sir. Again Hiromoai-san, I must ask if you'd like to have some of my men remain, until we're able to capture this assassin at large in Tokyo, sir?" The Lieutenant committed all the comments about the battles he and Tsutomu engaged in the past to his memory for reference.

"No Lieutenant Motoshima-san! I believe I have enough security and bodyguards on my payroll to protect me from the very best of assassins lurking in the shadows of Japan, sir. I might as well allow them to earn some the money I'm paying them for their duty to my service, sir. Do you not think so Lieutenant?" He smirked at the officer.

"Yes, you have a point there Hiromoai-san." Lieutenant Motoshima replied as he gave an apprehensive laugh and then he added as if it was an afterthought. "Yes Hiromoai-san! I wish you wouldn't make light of this extremely dangerous situation facing us over this assassin, sir. We believe we're dealing with a highly trained and exceptionally ruthless murderer, sir. One who'll stop at nothing to get at its intended target and destroy them most savagely sir. The assassin might even be able to get through any defenses place against it, and around your person, sir. He or she has proved this point by killing Tsutomu-san, who was well protected all the time, Hiromoai-san. I'd surely like to leave some of my men behind, to better help protect your..."

The extremely upset Hiromoai glared at the officer again, as if he was wasting his time as he snapped angrily at him this time. "Lieutenant, you just finished saying this lowly assassin might be skilled enough to get through any defenses I might surround myself with. So why the hell should I consider taking on any of your men for my added protection, sir. If this assassin could work his way through your people as well as mine, Lieutenant Motoshima-san? I see no fucking sense to surround myself with even more people to get in my way, dammit."

Lieutenant Motoshima was forced to smile because he found himself trapped by his own words as he replied to the young Japanese businessman. "Hiromoai-san! I assure you sir that my people are better adapted to handling assassins, and the damage they wreak on the innocent civilians of Japan, sir. I suggest you allow my people to remain for your protection."

Hiromoai smile this time as he offered to the police detective. "Again Lieutenant, I find myself refusing this offer, sir. The last thing I'd need or want is a gaggle of police officers getting in my way, and clogging up my office and home with their constant presence and interference, sir. How the hell could I possibly conduct my usual business matters with uniformed officers trailing me everywhere I go, sir? Thank you sir, but no thank you for the kind offer Lieutenant, I'll be pleased to look after my health if you don't mind, Lieutenant Motoshima-san."

"Hiromoai-san, I assure you the Officers I'll choose, will be dressed in plain clothes and they will act most discrete in order to avoid any concerns you just brought up to my attention, sir. Arrrr... Hiromoai-san, no matter how I feel about the matter, I'm afraid this is your decision to make, sir. I can only caution you and hope you'll be wise enough to follow some of my instructions to the letter for your own safety, sir. Hiromoai-san, I must leave you now sir, but I'll keep you apprised of our progress in this most disturbing criminal murder case, sir.

"Please, if you receive any further death threats against your life sir, you're to notify my office immediately sir. Immediately I warn you Hiromoai-san. Whether or not you believe these possible threats to be a real danger against your life or not sir, I suggest you take nothing for granted sir. We have a highly trained killer now stalking the shadows of downtown Tokyo, sir. And until he or she's captured, no one is safe and my job will never end I fear, Hiromoai-san."

"Yes, yes of course I will Lieutenant, and I'll notify you the instant, if and when I receive any further death threats, sir." Hiromoai said as he stood and then he led the two officers to the door. Once the door was closed, he leaned against it and breathed out a deep sigh of relief.

In the hallway, the two detectives spoke to each other as they headed for the elevators.

"Well, what do you think about the conversation Sergeant?" The concerned Lieutenant asked.

"I don't know what to think Lieutenant. I felt as though he was hiding something from us this morning, sir. But for the life of me I couldn't think of one reason why he might choose to do so, Lieutenant. I couldn't get a good look, but it seemed like he had a pile of ancient Samurai armor and weapons stored in the next room, sir. I sure would've liked to have a closer look at what they were, Lieutenant. Some of the stuff looked old as hell and even crumbling, Lieutenant." Sergeant

Okamatsu offered with a touch of concern in his tone as he watched the numbers of the floors they passed clicking off on the elevator door, informing him the car was coming for them.

"Huh, you might get your chance at that to get a better look in the other room, Sergeant. I too believe that Hiromoai knows a whole lot more about this unholy murder than he's willing to let on. What if anything do you think he's trying to hide from us, Sergeant? Do you think he was involved in the death of poor Tsutomu-san and his wife? I'd hate like hell to think such an honored and well respected man as he, could possibly be involved in such ugly crimes committed against Japan, or one of her citizens. It'll sure remove all trust I ever had in the elite of Japan." Lieutenant Motoshima grunted as he stared at his sergeant while waiting for his response.

"Lieutenant Motoshima-san, I believe anyone who is involved in the construction field is guilty of some kind of crimes committed against humanity and some of our innocent civilians, sir. The whole lot of them are nothing more than a pack of liars and cheaters in one form or another, Lieutenant. They have to be in order to survive in their chosen field they endeavor in sir. I don't know about you, but I can't help but feel he's truly hiding something from us sir. I believe he knows a lot more about these appalling deaths than he's willing to admit."

"In that case Sergeant, it'll be your duty from today on to trail Hiromoai-san wherever he travels until we get the evidence either against or for him, or we capture this ungodly assassin and prove beyond a shadow of a doubt he's free of any guilt in this situation. He's to go absolutely nowhere without you walking behind him at all times

Sergeant." The Lieutenant smiled informing the Sergeant he had nothing further to offer him in the matter.

The Sergeant bowed slightly to the Lieutenant then smiled as they boarded the brass elevator, and watched the richly decorated doors close. Lieutenant Motoshima went on to explain what he wanted the Sergeant to do as he pushed the button for the lobby, as the Sergeant tailed Hiromoai around town. He left the Sergeant at a store stationed across from the Hatanaka Towers, and then he got in his unmarked car and headed to headquarters as fast as traffic allowed.

Hiromoai did not get sleep well since first discovering the female warrior and her horde of ancient weapons and armor and he was suffering from total exhaustion. He retired to his bedroom without speaking to Lady Yoke who stared at him as he walked by her as if he did not see her standing there. He turned in and quickly fell asleep, his mind did not think of Yurkowa or his wife he ordered to their deaths. He slept peacefully, and did not wake until eleven a.m. the following morning. His mind did not care for the two deaths he was the cause of.

The Lady Yoke remained awake all night, and made certain everything was cleaned in the kitchen and apartment. Paying close attention to Wind's armor that again looked as old and crumbling as time itself. She removed the three cups of tea remaining nearly untouched from the room Hiromoai spoke with the two officers. She made certain the police did not covertly sneak any listening devices in the room while they were visiting Hiromoai. Once she was satisfied everything was proper in the room, she picked up a magazine and put her feet on her bed and read the rest of the morning, waiting for Hiromoai to awake so she could prepare his morning meal for him. She was fast becoming concerned over his health she noticed the lack of sleep and rest he was going without, since bringing the ancient samurai home.

Her mind went off remembering the beautiful but ancient samurai warrior, and found herself wondering what she was doing in the land of the dead of wonder and myth. She could not believe she was actually talking to someone who had died so long ago, and not fearing her for what she was, a spirit from beyond the grave and death.

CHAPTER TWELVE

HATANAKA TOWERS, TOKYO, THURSDAY, JUNE 6th, 1996. 11:10 A.M.

Hiromoai Hatanaka slept in, and by the time he woke he was still suffering from exhaustion. Glancing at the clock he decided to go to work at twelve. He showered, ate and prepared to leave his apartment. He looked at the case containing the sword of Wind and smiled. He planned to place a call to Asahiko Yurkowa, and request a meeting at his earliest convenience. First, he was going to give him his condolences for the loss of his son then he was going to level the same threat against the old man as he did his son, if he was unsuccessful in talking the old man into selling him his company. He had no fear of the old man going to the police against him.

No one in Japan went to the police for anything until it was too late for the police to correct the problem. In Japan, everyone tried to work out their disagreements amongst themselves. If he could not talk the old fool into surrendering his company to him, he was going to turn Wind loose on him next. Once the old man was out of the picture, he knew he would take over Yurkowa Construction by a hostile takeover if need be, with none of the surviving officers and children putting up any complaints to his bid. With the deaths of the founders, the rest of the officers would come to believe the company was a bad risk. With a shadow of death hanging over the business, everyone in control would want to dump its stock to any buyer.

Hiromoai entered his office at twelve twenty in not a very good mood, and he was immediately swamped over with a flood of important messages from his highly concerned and worried secretary who copied them. Lady Meko began to tell him of Tsutomu's savage murder last night, but he cut her off with a simple wave of his hand, and then he ordered her to get Asahiko on the phone for him. Then he entered his office and closed the door for a little peace.

Moments later his intercom buzzed, his secretary was informing him Asahiko Yurkowa was on line one waiting to speak with him.

Hiromoai picked up the phone and then drew in his breath and said in a polite tone in the receiver. "Ahhhh... Asahiko-san, I'm so terribly sorry to hear of the tragic death of your honorable son. It's terrible, terrible, to think something like this could happen in the very heart of Tokyo. I fear for what Japan is fast becoming, to allow god cursed assassins to walk the streets of downtown Tokyo as if they own the night is simply unforgivable. When I heard of your son's death, I feared I woke in the United States, and I was suddenly surrounded by the gangsterism that inhabits that foul country." He smiled, not able to believe his lie to the old man.

"Huh, I must thank you Hiromoai-san for your kind words you offer for my poor son and his wife's savage death. It's a horror I must live with for all my remaining days." The old man tried his best to hide the anger etched in his voice threatening to take over his body. He hated Hiromoai as much as he hated him as he added to his words. "Hiromoai-san I fear we're allowing too much of the western bad attitudes to invade the youth of our country."

"Sir, do you believe this might have been a lowly American assassin who might be responsible for the untimely death of your most honorable son and his poor wife, Asahiko-san?" He asked, surprised over the way of thinking of the old man on the phone, and it was okay for him to mention Tsutomu's wife after the old man mentioned her death to him first.

"No, of course not Hiromoai-san, I'm not a foolish old man to dare think this so, the fatuous Americans would never be able to master the discipline displayed by this lowly assassin devil that soaked his lips in my son's blood to quench its thirst. This hated assassin had to be Japanese, who else could he have been able to show such skills in the art of killing my beloved son. But he could've been employed by the hated Americans for some reason unknown to me. If only the future will be kind and tell us who was behind this criminal act committed against my son. Then, I'll be able to wreak my revenge upon the head of the loathsome murderer and his control."

"True Asahiko-san, only the future will tell of the past. When will you be honoring your son?"

"The sacred pyre fire will be consummated the day after tomorrow, and then my beloved son's ashes will be released to the four winds that give flight to the wings of the birds, as is our custom Hiromoai-san. I shall order his ashes released just as the sun breaks free of its night sleep and soars and warms the Heavens once again. That's the proper time to allow my son's fine spirit free, to soar among the clouds and be with his ancestors and dear Mother. May I ask will you be attending the funeral of my son, Hiromoai-san?" The questions were more of a plea for him not to show up, than an invitation to attend the ceremony.

Hiromoai easily picked up the underlying tone, and he did not allow it to bother him as he replied to the old man's question. "I'm terribly sorry to offer Asahiko-san, I'm afraid I'll be otherwise engaged in many meetings on that saddest of days, and will be unable to attend the funeral, sir." He heard the unmasked sigh of relief from the old man's lips as he added. Asahiko-san, if it'd be possible I'd like to have a meeting with you at your earliest convenience. There are certain matters I must speak over with you. It's most important to both our interests, sir."

"I'm afraid this is a trying and heavy of the heart time for me to be involved in, Hiromoai-san. Is this requested of that much importance it must be held at this sad of times? I need time to anguish my son's death." Asahiko was unable to hide the exhaustion he was suffering through.

"I assure you Asahiko-san this is important I speak to you over this matter at your earliest convenience, sir." Hiromoai said his words almost as a demand for them to meet.

"In that case, I guess I can find a way to spare time for this demanded meeting to take place later tomorrow. What would be a good time for you to come by my office, Hiromoai-san?" The old man was trying to sound civil even though his heart screamed Hiromoai was somehow the cause of his son's death. He knew in his mind some way, he was behind the savage attack that killed his son and he would have his revenge on his head before retiring for his eternal sleep.

"Sir, I'll be free anytime in the afternoon, but I don't wish to meet in your office Asahiko-san. After all that happened to your son, I have to be cautious where I allow myself to travel. Even the police warned me in no uncertain terms, there could be an assassin stalking your wh..."

"You worry about nothing to concern yourself with Hiromoai-san. There'll be no such treachery played out against you. Not while breath remains within my old and aching body no harm will ever befall you." He interrupted the younger Japanese businessman.

"I'm not worried about treachery against my person. I worry about unwanted ears hearing what we have to speak of, sir. What I have to offer is far better if only your ears hear it first, sir."

"I can understand your caution, and it's a wise course to wander upon, Hiromoai-san. Where do you wish to meet with me?" He tried to hide the loathing he harbored for this man.

"If it pleases you sir, I can make plans to meet with you at the main park about half way between both our offices, Asahiko-san." He smiled as he heard the anger in the old man's voice growing again. He hoped it would be the cause of his old heart to stop beating, and that would make his takeover effort of the old fool's company much easier to accomplish.

"Yes, that seems like a good place to meet. The birds and trees will be soothing to my unraveled nerves and exhausted body. What time do you wish to meet, Hiromoai-san?"

"I'll be walking in the park at twelve noon. Will that be a good time for you, Asahiko-san?"

"Yes Hiromoai-san, this time will serve me well sir." Asahiko moaned barely over a whisper.

"Fine, then I'll see you tomorrow afternoon Asahiko-san. Alone I trust sir. We'll meet by the fifth bench on the south side of the park. It's very peaceful in this area, do you not agree?"

"Yes Hiromoai-san, I have been there many times in the past, and it's a very peaceful and beautiful place in which to hold a meeting, and I'll be alone Hiromoai-san."

"Fine, until tomorrow afternoon then Asahiko-san, I wish you peace of mind over your fine son's terrible death." He hung up before the old man could reply to his last statement. He opened the drawer and removed a spray can. It was a special formula designed to be sprayed in the hair. A mild chemical reaction between the formula and hair created a constant static cloud around his head, and any listening devices employed by Asahiko's security people, or anyone else for that matter who might try and listen to their conversation, would be rendered useless.

He stuffed the hair spray in his pocket and then left for his first meeting of this day. It lasted far into the afternoon, and he found himself dealing with lingering construction problems, staggering delays, and spiraling costs on a span bridge his company was building in downtown Tokyo. By the time the meeting ended, it was past five in the afternoon. He decided to return home and catch up on his sleep after canceling the rest of his meetings that he was already late for. He wanted to be as sharp as a knife for his meeting with the old, but sharp Asahiko.

He was so thoroughly exhausted by the time he reached his apartment he went to sleep without supper. He did not think of ordering Wind to appear from the Floating World, so he could enjoy her treasures a second time. He knew there would be plenty of time later for pleasures of the body to be enjoyed, once his was the largest construction company in the world. Morning came too quickly for his still exhausted body. He struggled out of bed and then went to the kitchen he plopped down before the table and rested his weary head in his trembling hands.

Lady Yoke was hovering around her boss dressed in a beautiful kimono like a colorful butterfly seeking a meal of nectar from a flower in a garden. She was dressed in one of her finest kimonos. He noticed how open the front of the fine garment was, and he settled back and enjoyed the slight show offered by his young and beautiful helper.

Lady Yoke prepared breakfast, and made certain he had enough to eat for this long day's work schedule. When Hiromoai finished eating she quickly cleared the dishes from the table as he walked into the study to relax before heading off to work. He was already washed, shaved, and dressed in the suit he was to wear for his meeting with Asahiko. For the first time since the police entered his apartment, he turned his attention to the case containing Wind's ancient Katana sword named Wind's Breath. He walked over to the lacquered box and opened it.

He cautiously fingered the crumbling Zutsu scabbard and smiled as he rubbed the fine dust layer picked up from the scabbard between his fingers. He could not believe the awesome power this sword, and now he possessed and controlled. His first instinct was to remove the sword and make her appear. But he knew he did not have the luxury of time to enjoy his new play toy and weapon. He snapped the lid closed and moved the long box more on the chair it rested on.

Lady Yoke strolled in the study carrying a cup of tea and three rice cakes and offered them to Hiromoai with a smile. He sat on the sofa and allowed her to serve him. Again, she bent low and lingered longer than necessary, allowing his eyes to behold the fine, young breasts fighting to be free of the exquisite silk fabric.

As he took the cup, he noticed a second cup resting on the tray and offered. "Lady Yoke, it'd be a wonderful honor if you'd share some tea with me on this fine morning. I feel today will be the beginning of a new era in the construction field of Japan, young lady."

"Hai, domo Hiromoai-san." She quickly poured her tea and sat across from her master. She smiled as she sipped her tea then spoke. "Hiromoai-san, you seem to be in a good mood on this fine morning. I was up early and decided to enjoy the sunrise it was a beautiful sight to behold. I wish I had someone I could've shared the magnificent sight with though."

"If today goes as I expect, you'll have someone to share tomorrow's sunrise with, Lady Yoke. I give you permission to wake me before the sun awakes for its long day of travel through the Heavens, and we'll enjoy tomorrow's sunrise from my balcony together. Hmmmm... Maybe we'll invite Wind to enjoy the sunrise with us if you don't mind that is."

"Hai, I'd truly enjoy that much Hiromoai-san. I thank you for the kind consideration sir."

"Well, what do you think about the female spirit of the ancient Warrior, Lady Yoke?"

"I think she's a proud Warrior and one of the most beautiful women I ever saw..."

"I wasn't referring to her beauty, Lady Yoke. Do you see anything hidden within her fine spirit that might cause you any alarm that she might be a threat against me?"

"Hai Hiromoai-san I'm afraid to offer this, but I happen to see an extremely dangerous female person, a well fearsome weapon if you will, sir. I also see in my eyes, a young and very venerable woman, an ancient Samurai Warrior loyal beyond belief to your wants and desires, beyond all understanding and free will of her own spirit, sir. I also see this female Warrior willing to do anything in her power for your pleasure and protection and interests, Hiromoai-san." She offered as she allowed her tea cup to hover over her body, locked in her hands.

"You see no treachery held hidden in her heart, Lady Yoke? Please, your honest opinion is important. Your eyes might've picked up something I overlooked because of her beauty and loyalty." He wanted to see if she truly trusted the samurai from the past as much as he.

"I'm afraid Yuriko-san can no more harbor any treachery against you than she can tell a lie, Hiromoai-san. She's an honorable person to deal with sir. Pure truth and understanding sir."

"Yuriko, huh? Yes Lady Yoke, I believe Yuriko can't have treachery harbored against me either. No hidden agenda. I think she might choke if she ever tried to lie to me. Lady Yoke, you placed my mind at rest over this disturbing matter I just spoke of. Thank you for the tea, I'll be leaving for the office now. Have a good day Lady Yoke maybe I'll summon Wind tonight."

She shot to her feet and picked up his empty cup and placed it on the carrying tray. She knew exactly what she was doing and she bowed low before him and held it as long as good manners dictated, allowing his eyes to wander into the soft folds of her kimono. His eyes easily exploring her treasures hidden by the exquisite fabric hugging her body like a second skin.

He enjoyed the interesting being display from her, and he made up his mind to invite her to his bed in the near future. He left for his office in a very good mood. He left his apartment nearly singing with a spring in his steps. He was that pleased over the way his future was shaping up for him. He was not going directly to his office though, as he offered to her. Instead he was planning to go to the garden like park and enjoy its beauty for a while in private, and then wait for Asahiko's arrival. He entered the park at eleven forty and enjoyed walking down one of the many flower shrouded petal paths, spread throughout the lush gardens in full bloom.

Where he chose for the meeting was not crowded, especially at this time of day, and he took the bench seat and waited for the old man to arrive. He barely got comfortable before he saw Asahiko walking down the concrete and gravel pathway. He was aided with a walking stick he was certain, hid a sword in the handle. Behind him, he could see a number of his bodyguards spreading out trying to disappear in the gardens. He was certain some of them were in possession of long range listening devices. He fluffed up his hair and the effect of the static hair spray began working. Almost instantly, the two portable listening devices went off line on the nearest security guards, and nothing but annoying static was being picked up by their machines.

He stood as the old man painfully approached him. Asahiko walked like he had the weight of the world pressing down on his fatigued shoulders, forcing him to lean heavier than normal on the bamboo walking cane, as most old men do at this time in their life. It was easy for the younger man to see the pain and hurt etched in the old man's eyes as he approached.

Asahiko did not smile or bow as he came up to Hiromoai who bowed politely to the old man who ignored his kind actions. Then he motioned towards the bench with his hand, and two of the richest and powerful men in Japan, sat in silence. They stared at the flowers blooming about them, and enjoyed their sweet fragrance as it filled the air. Asahiko was the first one to break the silence by speaking to the younger man seated by his side.

"Hiromoai-san, this is most confusing to my limited understanding and wisdom I fear. What is the reason that you have requested this meeting to take place between the two of us on this most sad day of my entire life? I don't deceive myself in the least by thinking you might like, or are willing to assist me or my family in any way, shape, or form in our times of need and sorrow, Hiromoai-san. We have too much of a bad past to offer any help to either of us.”

“Asahiko-san! Please allow me to tell you how sorry I am about your poor son’s death.”

The old man glared at him. In his mind, he talked himself into believing he was the man behind the assassin who had slaughtered his son and daughter-in-law so savagely in the night.

He gave a sigh, knowing the old man was not interested in small talk. He decided to be frank and get to the point. “Asahiko, this is the reason I called for this meeting. With the death of your son, I know your company is going to be placed in financial and leadership difficulties. I wanted to be the first to make an offer before the vultures make a hostile takeover attempt against your weakened company and self. I know your son was running the business and you wanted out. I’m also aware you’re too old to take command of the business any longer, sir. So I’m offering you the door to walk through with honor and face, that’d make you a rich man indeed, sir.”

“In case you’re unaware, I’m already a rich man at peace with the world, Hiromoai!” Asahiko decided to drop the san from his name, as the younger man did him earlier in the conversation.

“Well then old man, I’m offering you a peaceful way to spend your remaining days on earth.”

“Huh, what do you think you’re offering me I don’t already possess in my worthless life, Hiromoai?” The old gentleman moaned back at the younger Japanese businessman.

“I’ll give you fifty million dollars in American money for your foul company, Asahiko. I don’t think your company is worth anymore than this price I have just offered you.”

"Do you think me so old and feeble I'd allow your loathsome being take advantage of my person? Foolish! Very foolish of you Hiromoai! The sum of money you offer me won't make up for the machinery and other heavy construction equipment I have working in the field in Japan. My company is worth ten times ten that of what you so foolishly offer my old ears fool. This conversation is going nowhere, Hiromoai. I'm done with speaking to you, I should've known you'd try and steal my company out from under my worthless feet. You were unable to defeat me in the business world, and I'll not allow you to steal from me at this most sorrowful time in my life." The old man went to stand, but he was held back when Hiromoai roughly grabbed him by the arm, and held him in place with his painful grip as he hissed.

"You might be done speaking to me you old bastard you. But I assure you that doesn't mean I'm done speaking with your old ass, dammit. Listen to me you old fool you. Remember well what happened to your worthless son the other day, old man?"

"Neh, I was right! You were the bastard behind the death of my son! I'll split your evil heart in your body and then I'll be the one who absorbs your cursed company, and I'll have my reven…"

"And I'm going to be responsible for your death if you're not more careful with me, old man."

The old Asahiko's eye's narrowed to mere slits as he stared at the younger man for a few seconds before he hissed at him. "Huh, fool of life and death. Your empty threats are wasted upon my old and tired shoulders and ears, Hiromoai. I care not one worthless grain of rice if I live or die any longer, now that my faithful son has crossed over to the world of not before me. But I'll not die before you're brought to my justice and..."

"Like you old man, threats don't fucking impress me! I fear not your empty words spoken by an old man wasting his life waiting for death to visit his old bones. If you'll not think of yourself with this deal I offer your head. I suggest you think about your children and their children.

"If you'll not sell me your worthless business for the money I have offered you. You'll be the last to die, but not before you have witnessed the deaths of anyone important to your old ass. I'll not stop my attack against you and your family until I bring you and your company down to their knees. Old man you know if you die, the fools who'll be left will be begging to end your company's existence. Then, I'll pick up your worthless company for far less than half of what I'm offering. The money I offer you will make your heirs rich beyond their wildest dreams, old man. But this offer will end the moment I leave without a deal from you for your company."

"I warn you I'll go to the police and have them arrest you, you son of a milkless whore!"

"Don't make me laugh old man, neither you nor I will ever go near the police. That's why I chose to speak to you in this manner, Asahiko. You waste my time and yours with these idle threats and pig headedness to accept what I offer you, Asahiko." Hiromoai warned him nastily.

The old man's body shook with rage as he fought to control his temper, and accepted the way this pup was speaking to him as he barked. "Hiromoai, before I'm force to sell my business to you, I'll turn to the Americans. I'll sell my business to them, for years they struggled to get their greedy fingers into Japan's pulse. Your threats will force me to go to them if you insist on threatening me. Then, you'll be forced to deal with them to take over my company, fool."

"You'll die long before you can open any understanding with the hated Americans, old man."

"Again, you waste your idle and useless threats upon an old man's ears that no longer care if he lives or dies, fool. My world was stolen out from under my worthless feet by you and this evil devil spawn assassin of yours. But I'll fight you every step of the way to make certain that you never end up with my construction business. That warning will keep me alive long enough to see the death of your most detestable executioner, and yourself as well, my sole driving force will be to stop you from existing in this world as you have done to my son. I'll surround myself with the very best bodyguards Japan has to offer. Then, I'll go to the killers and turn them loose upon your foul neck. I'll seek my revenge on your head for my son's death. This much I swear on my son's soul and memory, Hiromoai." Asahiko snapped with surprising strength in his voice.

"And I promise you old fool of time, there's nothing you can possibly do that'll keep you alive longer than I'll allow you to remain breathing in this world. The assassin I'll send for you will be successful, no matter what you do to try and protect your foul self, or who you surround yourself with. Your death is as sure as the sun will rise tomorrow and tomorrow's tomorrow. You'll die swiftly old man, and I'll have your business as a result of your timely death as well."

Asahiko rose on shaky legs and then he glared and suddenly slapped him across the face.

Hiromoai refused to rub the slapped area as he sneered at the bent over old man before him.

The second he slapped Hiromoai, his guards charged forward to protect the old man, and surrounded him and took a threatening stance against Hiromoai. Seeing he was not going to react to the slap by the old man, the two large bodyguards quickly ushered Asahiko back to his limousine, nearly lifting the old man from the ground as they rushed him towards the car.

Hiromoai grinned as he stared at the old man being surrounded by his guards.

Hiding in the garden, Sergeant Toshihiro Okamatsu observed everything taking place between the two powerful business owners. Throughout the entire conversation it seemed peaceful enough, that was until the slap. His police reactions taking over, Sergeant Okamatsu's first instinct was to charge from behind the bush and rush to Hiromoai's side, to stop the guards from harming the younger man. He knew Asahiko had plenty of guards with him, and he was aware Hiromoai had no protection. He thought the guards were going to slaughter Hiromoai where he stood. But something stopped him from betraying his position, and now he was pleased he remained hidden, as he watched Asahiko's entourage climb in their cars, and leave in a rush.

Sergeant Okamatsu ducked lower behind the bush and watched him through the leaves of the bushes. When he saw Hiromoai made no attempt to leave the park, he decided to make contact with Lieutenant Motoshima back at police headquarters to see what he might want him to do next over this situation. The concerned Sergeant removed his radio and keyed it then spoke. "This is Sergeant Okamatsu, and I wish to speak with Lieutenant Motoshima immediately. Over."

"One second please Sergeant Okamatsu-san, and I'll have Lieutenant Motoshima-san come to the radio at once, sir." A sweet sounding female officer's voice replied pleasantly to him.

Sergeant Okamatsu checked Hiromoai while he waited for the Lieutenant to reach the radio.

"Sergeant Okamatsu-san, Lieutenant Motoshima here. What do you want of me? Have you discovered something of importance in this case for me, dammit?"

"Lieutenant, I followed Hiromoai-san to the park. He came here to meet with Asahiko-san. You could have knocked me over with a feather when I saw him come down the walkway to meet with Hiromoai-san. I never thought he'd be out so soon, not with his son's death..."

"Come on Toshihiro-san, I demand you get to the point for me mister. I don't have the time to waste on you I am very busy." Lieutenant Motoshima hissed angrily.

"Sorry sir, But I want t o report that the meeting between the two seemed to go peaceful enough throughout until it ended that is sir..."

"How did it end mister?" Lieutenant Motoshima growled in the radio mike, showing that he was getting extremely angry with his Sergeant.

"The old man stood and then he slapped Hiromoai-san across the face, sir."

"He did what! He slapped Hiromoai." He roared as he listened to the Sergeant's words.

"Yes Lieutenant, Asahiko-san slapped Hiromoai-san across the face sir."

"What the hell did Hiromoai do against the terrible insult from Asahiko-san, Sergeant?"

"Nothing much, Hiromoai-san remained seated and pleasant and smiled at Asahiko-san."

"He smiled! That's all he did, just smile." Lieutenant Motoshima nearly yelled in the radio.

"Yes sir, but that's only the half of it, sir. Asahiko-san's horde of bodyguards quickly circled the old man. They made certain none of Hiromoai-san's usual bodyguards came out to correct the insult. Then Asahiko-san's entourage quickly left the park, sir."

"Hiromoai's bodyguards did nothing about the actions against their boss, Sergeant Toshihiro?"

"That's the odd part about this meeting, Lieutenant. Asahiko-san showed up for this meeting with at least fifteen bodyguards I was able to count around him. But Hiromoai-san arrived with no protection around him at all, sir." The excited Sergeant explained to his superior officer.

"Hiromoai was out without guards surrounding his ass, dammit? Why the damn fool he is. I warned him of the assassin stalking Tokyo. He's playing around with a loaded gun that's going to end up blowing his damn head off his shoulders for the fool. What's he doing now Sergeant?"

Sergeant Okamatsu carefully poked his head just above the bush he was hiding behind and he could not believe his eyes over what he was seeing. Hiromoai was still sitting on the bench obviously enjoying the pleasures of the park like he had absolutely no fears in the world, while enjoying the flowers and chirping of the birds. The Sergeant ducked back down and replied to his commanding officer. "Lieutenant Motoshima-san, you won't believe this shit for a moment sir,

Hiromoai-san's still sitting on the bench enjoying the gardens."

"Ieeeee... Sergeant, these foolish rich people are a hard lot to understand. Hiromoai should be hiding under his foul bed shaking with the fear of the damn gods, surrounded by his horde of bodyguards until the damn assassin is captured. Yet here the fool is, exposing himself to the will of this assassin's aims. Sergeant, what do you think was the reason for the explosion at the end of the conversation between the two fools? I trust you caught it all on tape, right Sergeant? Maybe what they were talking about can shed some light as to where this damn assassin came from."

"Errr..." Sergeant Okamatsu hesitated before replying to the Lieutenant's question.

"God dammit! What the hell do you mean err? You have your tape machine with you right?"

"Yes, but for some reason, the machine refused to work properly. All I picked up was static..."

"Were you near florescent lights? You know they interfere with our electronics, Sergeant."

"Lieutenant, this isn't the first stake out I worked, sir. I know florescent lights can interfere with our electronics. I'm nowhere near those lights. I'm in the middle of the park Lieutenant."

"Then why didn't the damn recorder work properly for you, Sergeant? You did check it before you logged it out of special services, right Sergeant?"

"I have no idea why the machine didn't work properly for me, sir. I made certain it was in proper working order before I took it out of special services, sir. I can't swear to it, but it seemed to me like something was running some kind of interference against the machine, Lieutenant Motoshima-san."

"Do you think Hiromoai or his people had something to do with the jamming, Sergeant?"

"No Lieutenant, like I told you Hiromoai-san came alone to the meeting, sir."

"Then it had to be one of Asahiko's guards doing the jamming of the machine." Lieutenant Motoshima growled in the radio, not believing his bad luck with this case of murder so far.

"I don't think that was at all possible Lieutenant Motoshima-san. I checked out the closest guards to Asahiko-san's person, and it seemed like they were having the same sort of trouble with their own recording machines, sir." The Sergeant actually smiled, knowing the angry Lieutenant was just fishing for answers, where there were none to be found.

"Never mind that shit Sergeant we'll discuss this shit in detail when you return to the office. Sergeant, while everything's fresh in your mind, I want you to go over what you witnessed of their conversation. Try to remember everything and I'll have it taped from this end. Before you start your report, check on what Hiromoai is doing at this moment in that damn park."

The Sergeant poked his head above the bush a second time and checked on what he was doing. This time he was more stunned than before. He ducked back down and keyed his radio and then reported. "Errr... Lieutenant Motoshima-san, you're not going to believe this either, sir. It seems Hiromoai-san is taking a cat nap while sitting on the bench. He's sitting out in the open sir."

"Keep a close eye on the damn fool while you report what took place at the meeting."

"Yes Sir Lieutenant." Sergeant Okamatsu allowed his head to remain above the bush this time as he continued to stare at Hiromoai. When he was comfortable, he explained what he heard and saw of the meeting between the two. It took him ten minutes to finish his verbal report.

"Okay Sergeant, you stay on Hiromoai's ass like a flea on a dog's rump until he finally returns to either his damn apartment or his office, and he's out of harm's way. I'll have a replacement Officer standing by waiting to relieve you in either place. Once you're relieved, you are to report to my office immediately, Sergeant."

The concerned Sergeant remained hiding behind the bush for an hour before Hiromoai had his fill of the gardens and birds, and got up and left the park in no rush.

As he was seated on the bench pretending to be asleep, he smiled because he was aware the police officer was hiding nearby. Although he never saw him, he was positive at least one officer was assigned to keep his eye on him. He spent the hour of resting, thinking of excuses for the slap he had received from the old man. That uncomfortable point was going to be a problem to explain away to the police, if they questioned him over the incident.

The thoroughly bored Hiromoai rose from the bench and took the time to stretch his arms and then he walked away as if he had not a care in the world. He walked to the meeting because the gardens were in walking distance to Hatanaka Tower. Besides, he had no intention of braving the harrowing and maddening traffic of downtown Tokyo, to travel five blocks to his office at near noontime when everyone else was getting out of work for a half an hour to enjoy their lunch, and whatever else they do with the half hour off time.

He walked out of the park, making certain the trailing officer could keep up with him on the now crowded walks. When he entered his office building, Sergeant Okamatsu searched the outside of the building until he saw the other officer standing by a clothing store. The officer nodded in recognition to Okamatsu who returned the nod and headed for his car.

HIROMOAI'S OFFICE IN THE HATANAKA TOWERS. 3:30 P.M. JUNE 7th, 1996

Hiromoai Hatanaka rushed passed his secretary he was fuming and ignored her as she rose to greet him. He slammed the door, warning the secretary he did not want to be disturbed as he proceeded to take his office apart. In his wild rage, he picked up and threw anything he could pick up, across the room as he cursed Asahiko for not taking his offer for his business. Now, he was going to be forced to do things the hard way. Slowly, he began to calm down, and when the secretary heard no more noise from inside, she dared to enter the office cautiously.

She ignored the destruction and rubble covering the carpet as she cautiously approached her boss with the flask of warm sake. Lady Meko knew it was the only thing that would help calm him further and she was than concerned over his health because if his latest actions.

He sat behind his antique desk with his head resting in his hands, and he looked up while trying to control his breathing and roaring temper when his secretary called out his name. At first he was going to explode at the secretary for daring to interrupt his concentration. But when he noticed the sake she held in her hands, he smiled at the lightly shaking Lady Meko.

"Hiromoai-san, I noticed that you were upset when you came in for work, so I brought you some sake to help calm you." Lady Meko smiled as she held out the cup to him.

"Ahhh... you know me better than I know myself. Forgive my foul manners I believe I told you to take extra time for lunch didn't I? I'm certain you didn't take it, did you Lady Meko?"

"Iye, (No) Hiromoai-san! I felt I should remain at my desk in case you needed my services."

"I figured as much young lady. You're a loyal secretary. Look Lady Meko, why don't you take the rest of the day off as my gift for your attention to my needs."

"But Hiromoai-san, I was going to do..." The secretary went to offer in her defense.

"There are no buts about it Lady Meko. I'm tired and you must be exhausted. So go home and enjoy your husband's attentions, young lady. The day is almost over anyhow."

The secretary bowed and her expression turned to one of great sorrow.

He noticed the change in her attitude and inquired. "What's wrong with you now Meko?"

"This unworthy woman wishes to inform her boss things are not well with my marriage or my honorable husband, Hiromoai-san." She looked at the floor, as if looking for a place to hide.

"Is that so Lady Meko? Why is that? Please, maybe I can be of some help to you, Lady Meko. What happened to your marriage to make you frown?" He displayed the height of bad manners by asking about Lady Meko's personal relationship with her husband.

His secretary could not hide the embarrassment and she stared at him.

"Oh come on, we're both adults here and we have known each other for what? At least ten years now, Lady Meko. I didn't think there's one question I couldn't ask you without you replying truthfully to me, Lady Meko. Look, I don't have time to waste, so speak freely or leave my office!" He suddenly snarled, further surprising his stunned and beautiful secretary.

Hesitantly, she began what she believed was her sad saga. "Hiromoai-san, my husband has accused me on numerous occasions of working too many hours for your company, sir. He further accused me of sharing more than a working relationship with you. I tried to explain his fears were most unwarranted, but my mistaken and confused husband refused to believe my words of defense. Lately, my husband has been staying away from our home, sometimes even at night at times. I found out he's sharing a bed with his secretary. Spending money on her, terrible, I feel he has betrayed my love and loyalty to him, and I'll never forgive him for this terrible insult against my person, Hiromoai-san." Again, she sadly lowered her head and eyes to the floor.

"Sometimes, men can be stupider than the stupidest item on earth, Lady Meko. But in this instance I wish your foolish husband was correct with his foolish fear. Over we were enjoying pillowing between us, young lady." He smiled at her looking so scared of her future.

"Ieeeee... What was that you said, Hiromoai-san? I'm afraid I didn't hear you correctly sir."

"Huh Lady Meko, I said I wish your stupid husband was correct with his foolish assumption you were guilty of sharing my bed instead of working overtime, dammit." He smiled at his uncomfortable secretary standing before him like a female divinity.

She dropped to her knees and bowed as if she committed an infraction against her boss.

He did not know what to do over her actions as he offered. "What is this about Lady Meko?"

"Please excuse this detestable woman for her evil thoughts and wanton desires, Hiromoai-san. I have to admit I too wished on numerous occasions you'd invite me to your bed and pillow me, Hiromoai-san." She said as she held her head close to the floor and refused to look at him.

His eyebrows arched over Lady Meko's words. He stared at her kneeling on the floor before him for a few seconds then offered. "Lady Meko, stand and face me please." He waited for her to comply with his request then offered. "Please, remove that displeasing western world outfit, so I might gaze upon your beauty. So I can drink in the wonders of your fine body and soul."

With shaking hands, she stood and slowly undid the buttons to the blue silk jacket, and then she allowed it to slide sexily off her slender shoulders. She stepped out of the skirt while staring at the eyes of Hiromoai. Next, she removed her blouse, she wore no bra.

She looked in the lust filled eyes of her boss as he drank in her beauty. This gave her the strength to continue removing her clothes. Encouraged by his leer, she sexily wiggled out of her underpants, and stood before her boss with only her thigh high black stockings on her body. She turned to the side so he could enjoy the extent of her exquisite body from the different angle.

He drew in his breath he never realized how beautiful his secretary was until this moment. Yes, many times in the past he wanted to pillow her, but never saw the beauty she possessed until seeing her naked. Her breasts were the right size to fondle, her waist was tiny and rearend was small. He smiled again, for he noticed she was hairless on her body. This added to her unlimited beauty and his wanting of her. What finished off this masterpiece was her body was completely tanned. Her skin glowed golden light brown and when she allowed her waist length hair to fall around her shoulders, she seemed to be wrapped in a halo of black clouds.

Hiromoai stood behind his desk and walked around it to the lovely vision of Meko. He cupped her breasts and rolled them delicately, pinching her nipples between his fingers as he sought the nape of her neck, and kissed it and moaned barely over a whisper in her ear. "Lady Meko, I can't tell you how many times in the past I longed to take you in my arms and make love to you."

She did not hear a single word Hiromoai mumbled as she hungrily attacked his belt buckle. She undid his pants and allowed them to fall, wrapping around his ankles. She followed them to the floor until she was kneeling before him. She smiled and then she took him in her mouth and began working him over until he exploded.

"leeeee... such skill you possess in the art of bringing great pleasures to a foolish man with your well educated mouth, Lady Meko. I can't believe we never explored each other's bodies before this foul day. What a waste of lovemaking on our parts, lady." Hiromoai cried as his strength returned and he pulled her up to her feet by the shoulders. He went to return the favor, but Lady Meko refused to allow him to kneel before her.

"Why? Why won't you allow me to bring the same pleasure to you, Lady Meko?"

"Because I'm not ready for your fine attention, I'm thoroughly embarrassed because it's the time of the bleeding dragon for me to endure, Hiromoai-san." She blushed at being forced to explain her condition to him.

"Oh, but I don't mind Lady Meko. I can still bring you great pleasures to enjoy young lady." He offered as he flashed one of his best smiles at her.

"Hiromoai-san, I'll not allow you to entice me in such a manner when I can't fully enjoy our first meeting of passion. The bleeding dragon should fly within the next two days. Then we'll share the lovely experience of our first coupling, completely free to do as we please to each other's bodies. Please Hiromoai-san, I beg of you to be patient for a little while longer with me. Then I'll please you beyond your wildest dreams when I'm free of mind and spirit to do so." She cried as she continued to stop him from enjoying her body.

He did not know how to respond to her, so he allowed her to pull away from him. He was not in the right frame of mind to take his time with her. He breathed a sigh of relief as he watched her dress as he offered. "Lady Meko, I'll pray to the Kami of the unknown world there'll be uncountable couplings between us in the future, young lady."

She cocked her head to the side, wondering why he began using ancient words of Japan's past. She found this strange but interesting and pleasing to her soul, because she knew how he truly felt about Japan's wonderful past. He never showed interest in it.

"Hiromoai-san, I promise we'll couple until there are no more clouds to soar freely within the morning sky." She replied, still slightly concerned over his words.

"Thank you for that most interesting offer, Lady Meko. I assure you that I'll be looking forward to the next time we have a few moments to share together, young lady." He said as he sat down in his chair behind his desk and watched her movements.

She knew what she was doing and decided to remain topless before her boss for a few minutes, to tease him with her exquisite body as she began cleaning up the pieces of scattered destruction littering the floor of the office from his anger. She looked at him and then smiled as she placed the shattered bust of the golden Buddha in the waste basket.

The look made him understand he owed her an explanation for what he done to his office, and the items he destroyed in his wild rage. He cleared his throat and offered weakly to the beautiful secretary. "Please Lady Meko you must forgive this foolish wild man, but I allowed my temper to rule my feeble mind. Thus, this mess you see resting before you." He waved a hand over his office and shrugged in submission then added. "I lost my temper because of a deal I was planning on for countless years, has slipped through my hands and is eluding me further."

"Hiromoai-san, you don't need to offer explanations to this unworthy woman. I'm pleased to clean this mess without words of apologies from you." She smiled again as she straightened up and allowed her breasts to sway before his face while she worked on his disheveled office.

"Lady Meko, you're far from worthless to me and my needs and company. You're as beautiful as a butterfly born to ride the wind currents, and showered with nectar of love and desire. Your attention to my company and matters that concern me are beyond normal secretary's attention. I don't try to fool myself, I could never be in the position I am, without your constant guidance of my business, and now, love Lady Meko. I'm one of the luckiest men in the entire world. I thank the gods and you for the love both showered me with, young lady."

"Hiromoai-san, it's I who am the luckiest person on the earth today, sir."

He sighed as he groaned. "I'm not going to be drawn into a boring and long drawn out battle of compliments and wits with you, Lady Meko. What the devil are you going to do about your foolish husband? If he's willing to allow a pearl such as you to slip through his foul fingers then he's the foolish of men to ever walk on the soil that blessed Japan."

"I'm afraid that decision is up to my husband to make about our future. In my family, I'm not allowed to seek divorce under any circumstances. It'd kill my parents, and I'll become an outcast to them, and my family. We're of the belief, once we decide to take a husband he'll remain that husband until death releases one or the other, or both from our bond. I'm afraid my parents are of the old belief. That's why I gave you that look when you said Kami before. It's a word from the old beliefs long thought to be forgotten by most modern men of Japan, Hiromoai-san."

"Now I understand where you're coming from young lady. I guess lately I've been catching up on a lot of reading about our well honored past. I was lucky, and able to buy a number of ancient items of Japan's past glory a few days ago. I must admit I'm enjoying the thrilling experience of examining the ancient weapons and armor, Lady Meko." He grinned at her.

"This is most pleasing for my ears to hear, Hiromoai-san. Very good indeed sir, it pleases my sad heart to no end to know the honored past of Japan are once again being remembered by her loving people. Your thoughts are giving the ancient ones new immortality, and renewed life to their spirits and remembrance, Hiromoai-san. It's the only way to honor the worthy gods who helped to shape the past of Japan's history, and who'll continue to shape the future of our country, sir." She offered warmly as she slipped in her blouse sexily, and smiled lovingly at him.

Seeing this he announced. "Lady Meko, I fear I must be going, I have paperwork waiting at home I must attend to, before I start losing major commitments I have slated, and my business starts suffering from my lack of attention. Since you refused to take advantage of my offer for an extra hour lunch earlier, I'll make certain you take advantage of it tomorrow. If you don't take a two hour lunch tomorrow, I swear I'll personally chase you out of the office and lock the door behind you, and will not open it again for two hours, and that will be that young lady."

He bowed which was nothing more than a slight nod as he walked passed Lady Meko she slapped him lightly on his rump as he passed her and replied. "I guess I'll be going home then, but not before I cleaned up this mess you created, Hiromoai Hatanaka-san."

"Suite yourself young lady, you're more than free to leave the office right now if you care to. The lazy night cleaners will take care of my office as is their duty. After all, that's what they're being paid for. And remember my words of warning to you, a two hour lunch tomorrow or else, young lady. I'll take the matters in my own hands and have the foolish security guards escort you out of the building, and not allow you to return for at least two hours tomorrow." He warned her in a pleasant tone as he quickly left the office.

CHAPTER THIRTEEN
POLICE HEADQUARTERS, DOWNTOWN TOKYO

Detective Lieutenant Kenzaburo Motoshima waited for Sergeant Toshihiro Okamatsu to arrive back at his office. He wanted to check the recorder out himself, to find out why the machine was not working properly, and see if it was his foolish Sergeant who was responsible for screwing up his orders, or if it was the recorder's fault for the malfunction.

Sergeant Okamatsu walked in the stationhouse like he was trying to tiptoe through a mine field and the other officers watched him pass as if he was walking to his death. Some of the officers began to chant the death chant as the Sergeant slowly walked by them, and this caused him to give the other officers the finger. Everyone in the stationhouse knew Lieutenant Motoshima was fuming with rage, and he was angrily waiting for the Sergeant to arrive and report in person.

The worried Sergeant walked down the hallway to the Lieutenant's office smirking, knowing he was not in trouble with the police lieutenant. He stopped by the water cooler before entering the office, and from there he could see Motoshima behind his desk through the glass wall. He saw the look on his face and knew he was still angry as hell. He entered the office cautiously.

The angry Lieutenant Motoshima looked up from the report he filled out according to Sergeant Okamatsu's phone interview, at the same time the Sergeant looked in the office. The moment the Lieutenant noticed the Sergeant walk in his office, he tossed the report aside and then growled at his officer. "Well it's about fucking time you decided to show up back here Sergeant. Get in here and close the fucking door behind your ass. I want to talk to you mister."

Okamatsu moved in the office wearing the slight smirk and closed the door behind him.

The upset Lieutenant Motoshima waited until the Sergeant was in the office and the door closed then he laced into him as he rose to his feet, and leaned on his desk with both hands flat on the surface. "Okay Sergeant, I thought you were a professional when I put you on Hiromoai's tail, dammit. Evidently, I was wrong to assume such an unwise thought of you. Give me that damn tape recorder and let me see it!" The Lieutenant reached out and wiggled his fingers.

The Sergeant fished around in his breast pocket and removed the recording device and handed it to the Lieutenant. He examined the machine, checking the batteries first as he headed back for his seat. He placed the recorder on the desk and rewound the tape. When it stopped spinning, he hit the play button. Nothing but static and some unintelligible words could be heard on the tape. He stopped the tape and removed the spool, and placed a second tape in its place from the top drawer of his desk, and then hit the record button as he grumbled in the recorder.

"This is Lieutenant Motoshima, testing this damn recorder, one, two, three, four. Sergeant Okamatsu-san's in a load of god damn trouble if this damn machine is working correctly." The still upset Lieutenant looked at the Sergeant, and Sergeant Okamatsu smiled at him.

The Sergeant knew he was not really in any real trouble and grinned at the Lieutenant.

He stopped the recorder and hit the rewind button and when it stopped he hit play and heard clearly. "This is Lieutenant Motoshima testing this damn recorder, one, two, three, four. Sergeant Okamatsu is in a load of god damn trouble if this machine is working correctly."

The Lieutenant shut the machine off and dropped it on his desk and glared at the uncomfortable Sergeant. "Well, I see it wasn't the damn machine's fault for not working. It's working properly now Sergeant. Could it be as simple as you didn't know how to work the damn thing?"

The smug looking Sergeant refused to allow the Lieutenant to get under his skin as he replied. "It sounds to me like it was some sort of interference being used against us, Lieutenant. I think I heard some words though through the interfering static, sir."

"It was unmistakably some kind of interference was being worked against us, Sergeant. Dammit to hell, do you think

Hiromoai was aware you were tailing his ass? Could he have detected you lurking behind him, and he was the one who created the problems with your taping machine in some unknown manner, Sergeant?" Lieutenant Motoshima shook his head slowly in disgust for losing this opportunity to get something incriminating against Hiromoai.

"I seriously doubt that Lieutenant, I'm afraid there's no way for me to be certain of that, sir."

"Yes Sergeant, I know there's no way to be absolutely certain about that fucking situation, Sergeant. I'll tell you what I'm going to do though I'm going to have this damn tape sent down to the lab for possible enhancement of the damn thing. Maybe the lab boys can clean the damn thing up so we can at least pick up some of the conversation between these two fools. Dammit, do you know what we could have had here if the machine worked properly Sergeant? We might have been able to solve this miserable murder case with this damn thing, if it was working properly.

"I'd love to know why Asahiko slapped him, and why he didn't retaliate against the insult. Shit, I wish I knew what the hell was going on with those two jack rabbits, dammit. All of a sudden I'm beginning to think one of these men was involved in the slaughter of Tsutomu. Damn tape machine anyhow Sergeant." The Lieutenant griped as he flipped the tape in his hand.

"You really think the father might have had his son and his wife killed, especially in such a savage manner, Lieutenant!" Okamatsu asked surprised at what the Lieutenant just offered.

"Yes, and why the fuck not think the father might've had his son killed by a lowly assassin, Sergeant? Maybe the old man found out something about the kid, and he was about to cut him out of the business and do something…"

"Like what Lieutenant? What could cause a father such as Asahiko-san to slaughter his son, in such a savage way, Lieutenant? It doesn't make any sense sir. Why would Asahiko-san have this assassin go after his daughter-in-law? If it was Asahiko-san, he'd know when the daughter-in-law was home, and when to plan the attack so she wouldn't be involved in the slaughter, sir."

"Who the hell knows what drives the damn elite of Japan to do whatever the fuck they do to make themselves happy, Sergeant Okamatsu-san. I'll tell you this though he's not beyond any suspicion in this damn murder crime. Nobody is Sergeant. Maybe Asahiko found out Tsutomu might have been planning to sell the business out from under his ass. Believe me Sergeant there are many reasons for a father to go after his son over a business situation."

"Then what's our next step in this case, Lieutenant Motoshima-san? Do you have a plan?" Sergeant Okamatsu asked as he stared his commanding officers dead in the eyes.

"Hmmm… I think I want you to set up a meeting between yourself and Asahiko. I want you to pump that old man dry of any information, and find out why he slapped Hiromoai, and what he might be hiding, Sergeant. I need information, or this case will not be solved quickly, dammit."

"I have no problem with that Lieutenant. Tsutomu-san's funeral is not until the following day. I'm certain Asahiko-san will grant me an audience with him, sir. If not, I'll take it out of his hands and demand a meeting between us officially, Lieutenant." Sergeant Okamatsu announced.

Lieutenant Motoshima stared at the Sergeant until he smiled and then laughed.

"I thought so I didn't think you'd be demanding anything from that powerful old man, Sergeant Wise Guy." The Lieutenant taunted him with a grin.

"Yes, and I don't intend to turn up missing for daring to insult the old man either, Lieutenant. That one's too powerful to mess with unless he allows it, sir. What are you going to be doing while I'm meeting with Asahiko-san, sir?"

"I guess I'm going to have a meeting with Hiromoai-san. I'll see if I can trip him up, and find out why he was slapped by the old man. We have to find out what the hell these businessmen spoke about, Sergeant. Something's wrong with the sushi rolls if you ask me, Sergeant."

The Sergeant nodded and added. "I'm done for the day. I want to catch up on some sleep sir."

"I don't blame you Sergeant. I intend to leave myself as soon as I get this tape down to the lab boys so they can see what they can do for us." The upset Lieutenant Motoshima added as he dropped the tape he was playing with on his desk next to the tape recorder.

HIROMOAI'S PENTHOUSE IN THE HATANAKA TOWERS,
FRIDAY, JUNE 7th, 1996 5:30 P.M.

Hiromoai entered his apartment in a rush, the sexual experience he just shared with the lovely Lady Meko, placed him in a much better mood. He headed straight to the kitchen for water.

The Lady Yoke was in her sleeping room still resting, and she heard Hiromoai when he came in. She dressed quickly and then rushed out to be of assistance to her boss.

"Hiromoai-san, please forgive this lazy woman, I was cleaning my room and failed to look after you when you first entered your home. I should've been in the kitchen looking after my chores. Can you forgive my laz…" Yoke began to plea before she was cut off as he grumbled.

"Please, I'm not in the mood for a battle of wits. It doesn't matter where you were and what you were doing. I'm certain it was something that had to be looked after, if you were doing it. I can get my own drink once in a while." He interrupted her by waving his hand before her face.

"Hieeee… not when I'm supposed to be looking after your health, can you fetch yourself water, Hiromoai-san. Please allow me to place ice in it for your enjoyment. I can warm up a few rice cakes for your pleasure if you so desire?" She complained as she placed her hands on her hips.

"Are you making supper tonight, Lady Yoke?" He demanded in a harsh voice of her.

"What do you think I am a worthless old whore of the Tea House trash, sir? Of course I'm going to make supper for you to enjoy, Hiromoai-san. It's my duty to look after your health and well being." Lady Yoke mumbled as she busied herself with kitchen duties, after pushing him out of the room so she could look after things.

He walked to the sliding glass doors and scanned the area of the street below while sipping water. He stared out the doors until he accidentally located the police keeping an eye on him. The officer did not see him looking down at him because he was trying to light a cigarette.

He smiled as he moved from the doors and walked to the study then plopped on the couch and slipped out of his shoes and rested his feet on the table. No sooner did he rest his glass on the table than he was sound asleep. The mental drain of having Yurkowa and his wife killed, adding the stressful meeting with Asahiko, and now knowing police witnessed the slap, and his reaction to the old man, took a toll on him. He slept until Yoke came in to inform him supper was ready.

Silently, she walked to the restful sleeping Hiromoai, and softly called his name. "Hiromoai-san, please forgive this foolish old woman for daring to wake you from your needed sleep, sir. Your supper is ready for your enjoyment, and I don't want your food to get cold on you, sir. Please, you must wake to eat sir. I worry about your health which is..."

"Huh? What was that Lady Yoke? Dammit, I'm dog ass tired and you're waking me up for what again?" He said as his eyes open, and he found himself staring at Lady Yoke as he sat up.

She smiled as she moaned. "I'm sorry to be forced to interrupt your Wa and sleep. Your supper is waiting for what I fixed for your enjoyment. I'm concerned over your health of late, sir. Lately, you haven't ate enough or slept properly to live healthy. I don't want you to become ill on me."

"There's no chance of that ever happening, not with you hanging around me Lady Yoke."

ASAHIKO CASTLE OUTSIDE TOKYO. FRIDAY, JUNE 7th, 1996. 6 P.M.

The elderly and well respected Asahiko had long ago bought the ancient castle of the once powerful warlord once known as Lord Kawasomeru, when he was a much younger but very rich man. He loved the old place with its many ponds of carp and large flowering gardens and raised walls for his protection. He intended to die within the castle walls. He was mentally and physically exhausted from the terrible burden of the death of his son and his wife, and from his stressful meeting with the very threatening Hiromoai.

His hands shook as he was led to his oversized desk by his concerned leading bodyguard. The moment he was seated before it, the guard left to give the old man privacy so he could carry out his intentions on paper. He knew Asahiko had something troubling on his mind, something he had to do before he turned in for the night. He was always in bed by seven but not tonight.

He remained still as he tried to gain control over his body. Nothing he did would stop him from shaking. With a trembling hand he reached for the phone as his other hand removed the leather phone book from the desk. He held the phone to his ear as he thumbed through the pages heading for the names starting with 'B'. His finger traced the names down the list until he found the one he was searching for. Under the name was the number four. He punched the four on the phone and it automatically dialed the number he wanted for him. He was aware it was early in the morning in the United States, he also knew the man he was trying to reach, would take his call at anytime it came in. After the third ring, the phone was answered by a sleepy, husky voice.

"Yeah, this is Cal Batterman. I'm warning you whoever the hell you are that this better be damn important fella? Do you know what time it is around here, god dammit?" The American voice snarled in the phone receiver.

Although he knew and understood English well, he rarely used it when he was dealing with his Japanese competitors. He seldom allowed anyone to know he understood and spoke the language enough to get by. Through his dealings with the troublesome Americans of late, he remained silent as his bank of lawyers spoke for him. But the lawyers would not do or say anything until they checked with the old man first. He enjoyed listening to the way the Americans talked to, or about him when they felt he did not understand a word they were saying. He came out many times on the top of the deal by simply faking not understanding English. He drew in his breath and let it out in a rush of pained words to the American on the other end of the phone. "Calvin Batterman-san, of Batter and Batter Construction I trust?"

"Yeah, but I'm certain you didn't call me at three thirty in the fucking morning to find that bit of information out, buddy. Who the fuck are you, buster? And what the fuck do you want this early in the damn morning from my ass, fella?" Cal Batterman growled in the phone angrily.

"Ahhh... it's certainly pleasing to hear your voice once again my old friend."

Cal shifted the phone to the other ear because he quickly recognized the shaky voice and could not believe his luck the Japanese owner was calling him. He was one of the few people aware he spoke flawless English. He found out by accident the last time they spoke together. He left the meeting telling Asahiko personally, if he wanted to sell his company all he had to do was call the number he gave him on the back of his business card. He knew the old man understood his words by the smile on his face, and the quick nod he gave him before they parted ways.

Batterman's last conquest of life was to have the first American owned construction company in Japan. He spent a number of years trying to get his foot in the door but to no avail. The many years of greasing the palms of Japanese business owners or politicians, left him with nothing more than empty pockets, and further away from having his dream become a reality. The Japanese government would not allow an American in to own one of their businesses. The Japanese men that owned the businesses were harder than ever to work with or get anything out of than their unpredictable government, which seemed to be throwing new obstacles in his way of trying to buy one of their companies.

Batterman sat up and swung his legs over the side of the bed as he reached for a cigarette and tapped it on his wrist before lighting it. He prepared himself for the battle of wits he was certain Asahiko wanted to play against him. He waited holding his breath for the old man to speak. He understood if he was calling him this late at night, something important had to be up with the old man. He also knew he was on the line, because he could hear the labored breathing in the phone.

The old Asahiko carefully went over his words in his mind before speaking to the American. "Cal-san, the last time you were in Japan you made an interesting offer for my company. Ahhh... let's say I might be interested to hear again what you have to offer. Things changed in my life, and I'm no longer interested in carrying on in the construction field. I want to retire and live my remaining years out in peace and quiet. I'm too old to be involved in construction any longer."

He could hear the unspoken words in his tone as he stopped himself from cheering in the phone, as he thought it was about time the old man was hanging up his spurs and getting out of the construction field. A thought crashed in his mind and he offered. "Asahiko-san, what about your son? The last time we spoke, you said through your interpreter that he was taking over the business, and doing quite well with it sir. I knew you understood English, I saw it in your eyes sir." He was doing everything in his power not to insult the old man, even to remembering to add the honorable 'san' to the end of his name when he spoke to him.

Asahiko smiled over the poor way the American pronounced 'san' and replied. "I'm sorry for deceiving you in the past, Cal-san. It was a cloud I had to hide behind for the sake of my business, and future holdings. I trust you'll understand this minor deception by me against you."

He took a quick breath and let it out in a sigh then continued. "Alas Cal-san, my honorable son has met with a terrible accident. He now dwells within the lands of his ancestors and dreams."

His eyes lit up as he looked at the receiver locked in his hand, now he knew why the old man was placing this call to him. His mind instantly went in overdrive, thinking if he should low ball his original offer. He quickly placed that thought out of his mind. All he had to do was insult the old man and he would be screwing himself out of owning a construction company in Japan.

"Errr... Asahiko-san, my original offer still stands as I stated, sir." He offered cautiously as he held his breath while waiting for the old man to reply.

"Cal-san, you must forgive the memory of a befuddled mind of an old man. I cannot seem to recall your honorable offer of the past you made for my company, Cal-san. I think it's because I originally put the offer and thought of selling of my company to an American, completely out of my mind Cal-san." He was having a problem speaking to the American. He was suffering from total exhaustion, and struggling to keep his mind on the conversation.

'I bet you did, you old gook'. Batterman thought to himself, he did construction work in Saigon during the Nam war for the government and he picked up many mannerisms, attitudes, and ugly slang words harbored against the Asian people by the American servicemen.

Again, the cunning American businessman toyed around with trying to low ball his original offer to the old man. He thought maybe, if he truly did not remember his offer, he could change the price a little more in his favor. But the past dealing with this wise old Japanese man popped in his mind, and it sent a warning that he felt Asahiko was just playing with him that he remembered not only the price, but every word spoken at that meeting very well. He knew he should not try to bluff the old man or he would pay for the error. "Asahiko-san, my last offer was one hundred and seventy five million American dollars for your company, sir."

"Ahhhh so, I do seem to remember the kind offer you placed to me after all, Cal-san."

He smiled as he realized his thoughts were correct about the memory of the old man. Again, he held his breath while waiting for the old man to reply. The silence was deafening as he pressed his ear to the phone, and listened to the old man. All he heard was the labored breathing on the other end of the phone. At first, he feared the old man was going to have a heart attack and die, but the breathing continued. Not able to take it any longer Cal grumbled in the phone.

"Asahiko-san, did you understand my offer? And if so, what's your answer sir?"

"Ahhh so... the forever uncontrolled impatience of the Americans comes to the surface I see, Cal-san. Is it no wonder we Japanese don't choose to allow you Americans to own one of our businesses in our country, sir. I fear your impatience and presumptuousness rules your better judgment, and your tongues at most times. Cal-san, one must learn the important virtue life has to offer, if he wishes to deal with the Japanese businessmen successfully in Japan, sir. That virtue is patience Cal-san. If you master the exercise of patience than all things will come true for your enjoyment, Cal-san." The elderly Japanese owner offered over the phone.

His heart dropped when he heard him say his government did not allow any Americans to own Japanese businesses. Now, he felt the old man called him just to rub his face in the dirt another time. His hatred of the Japanese people began to grow anew within him. Feeling like he was being played a fool he growled. "Well Asahiko-san, what's it gonna be? Are you gonna sell me your business or what? Or did you call to hurt my feelings again over this damn matter, sir?"

After a few moments of silence, he growled. "When can I expect your check, Cal-san?"

Batterman actually had to shake his head in order to clear his mind and focus on what he just heard from the old man. He snuffed out his cigarette and then asked cautiously. "When do you want to consummate the deal between us, Asahiko-san?"

"I'd like to finish our dealing as soon as I can get your check in my hand. This would do very satisfactorily, Cal-san." He said with surprising strength and certitude in his voice.

"Asahiko-san, I can have a trans-continental draft in your hands in three hours I believe sir. Will that do, Asahiko-san?" He again held his breath waiting for his reply.

"That'll do nicely for me, thank you Cal-san. I'll have the necessary papers for the transfer of my company to you prepared tonight on my side, and I'll turn over the ownership of my business to you tomorrow at twelve o'clock Japanese time. Cal-san, you'll be dealing with my lawyer. I'm fearful my heart could not take the strain of the sale of my company to you, Cal-san." Asahiko let out an exhausted sigh, because he planned to join his son and his wife, by committing the age old custom and honor of Suppuku, suicide. He found it impossible to live on without his son standing by his side it was too much of an insult to bear on his aged and aching shoulders.

"If that's so Asahiko-san, when will I be taking over the ownership of the business, sir?" He asked the old man, his impatience showing again.

"Cal-san, in reality you have ownership of my business, I ordered the papers of the transfer to be drawn up before placing this call to you." Asahiko offered to the American businessman.

He cursed for not trying to lowball the old fool now. If he already had the transfer papers drawn up, he would have agreed with any price he offered him as he responded. "Asahiko-san, forgive me sir. If I'm to make the money transfer, I'm going to be forced to place a quick end to this interesting conversation, and get on my horse to the bank, sir."

Asahiko smiled over the interesting way he expressed himself as he added. "Please Cal-san, carry the business out on your end, and I'll do the same here. I'm praying to Lord Buddha to give wings of haste to this transaction. Japan no longer holds my heart and soul dear to its soil."

Batterman did not hear the last words of the old man as he hung up and charged out of bed and dressed like a wild man. He kissed his wife good-bye, who was used to him darting out of the house day or night on his dealings in the construction field. He shot out the door and jumped in his car and punched the gas pedal, and the car took off like a dart in the night.

HIROMOAI'S APARTMENT IN THE HATANAKA TOWERS.
FRIDAY, JUNE 7th, 1996. 8:30 P.M.

Hiromoai Hatanaka felt much better after his catnap and eating. He pushed away from the table and headed for the study. He turned back and saw Yoke clearing the dishes from the table and called to her. "Leave the dishes and come to the study, Lady Yoke. I'm feeling refreshed and want to send for Wind. I want you to look after her comforts and needs when she arrives."

"Hai Hiromoai-san, I'm coming." Lady Yoke replied as she followed him in the study. She was happy he was going to send for the ancient samurai called Wind. Although she was only sent to the Floating World for less than twenty four hours, she found herself already missing the warrior, and could not wait to see her again in what she calls the living world.

Hiromoai went over to the long wood case containing Wind's Breath, the ancient samurai's katana sword. He flipped the two latches up and then lifted the cover and picked up the well aged sword. He pulled the blade free of the crumbling scabbard in one swift motion, since he removed the sword many times now, it moved much easier out of the old scabbard. Then, he placed the killing blade on the floor where he was certain Wind would appear before him. Instantly, the light began to grow but it was far less intense and violent as the cloud instantly engulfed the aged old blade. Quicker, Wind stood holding the deadly katana blade in her right hand, and she was naked and seemed proud as she bowed correctly to her new lord and master.

Lady Yoke rushed forward and handed her one of her fine kimonos. She smiled as she handed Lady Yoke her sword as she slipped in the garment. When she tied the obi, Yoke went to hand her the sword instead of taking the katana, she dropped to her knees and bowed to Hiromoai.

"I'll take charge of the blade of this Warrior, Lady Yoke." He growled as he stepped back, remembering to speak more like the ancient Japanese leaders, as he held his hand out and wiggled his fingers while waiting for the katana blade to be placed in them.

"Which is your divine right to demand of me my Liege Lord, because without your sword I'm nothing but a mere breath that blows in the night." She responded and held her bow.

He took charge of the sword and leaned it against his shoulder. It had instantly returned to its past glory, the deadly point aiming towards the ceiling. "Wind-san, you may stand." He offered while tapping his shoulder lightly with the backside of the blade. He almost used the word please, but caught himself in time. He guarded himself against this, scared to display any form of weaknesses or politeness in front of this ancient and extremely deadly warrior of times past.

She stood, but kept her eyes cast to the floor until she heard his words again.

"Wind-san, you done well on your first mission, everything I wanted, you accomplished to my satisfaction. I'm afraid your work is far from completed, Samurai. The enemy you vanquished last night has been cursed by the gods to have a worthless father, who is as much my enemy as Toshihiro ever was, Wind-san. A stronger and far wiser enemy though, one who'll cause me great problems in the future, if he's allowed to continue to breathe, and remain living a day longer. But I see by your expression you seem upset tonight, what's bothering you Warrior?"

"My honorable Master, there is no part of the endless life that does not contain lessons hidden within them only to be found by the searcher, as long as one is alive there are many lessons to be learned. If this teki remains on the earth, his stay will be painful and short, my Liege Lord." She drew in her breath and held it, to calm her feelings and wants for revenge for her master. But she was asked a question, and she was bound by honor and blood oath of obedience, to answer that question. She decided to open with a compliment, in the past her master told her no one could argue with a compliment. She let out her breath then offered. "Hiromoai-sama, you have the ability to see in my soul. I have no escape from you. Yes, I am upset my Liege Lord."

"Why are you upset? What has caused you to be upset?" He ignored the fluff and waited her reply. He could ill afford having her upset with something, unless he knew what it was.

"I'm upset because of what I did last night in my Master's name, my Lord." She refrained from informing him Toshihiro reminded her of her past lover as she added. "I'm fighting with my soul, my Master over life and death. I feel like I have acted like a filthy Ronin, a follower of the filth eater. A stalker of the night, who thrives on visiting death on the unsuspecting innocent, I feel guilty of drinking the blood of the innocent ones I feasted upon last night, my Lord."

"What the hell are you talking about for Pete's sake? Look Samurai, I'll use one of your own quotes from Lord Buddha's teaching that I know. 'One cannot live one cannot breathe between such troubling thoughts'. To clear things up a little better for your fine spirit, you're what I tell you to be, nothing more and nothing less. If I want you to be a criminal, a Ronin that's what you'll be, and be proud of it Warrior, and if I order you to be a whore and waddle around with pigs, you'll smile while bringing pleasure to such lowly animals. Enough of this foolish talk, there's another of my teki walking the lands of Japan that needs your immediate attention, more than you being allowed to feel sorry for yourself, Wind-san." He growled at her, he was not going to display any possible weakness before this extremely threatening female weapon.

Knowing he was correct in his decree he aimed at her and she was truly his to command in any matter and fashion he may deem fit or needed from her. She bowed and then she mumbled very respectfully to who she believed to be her lord and master. "No one who stands against my honorable Liege Lord shall be allowed to live to his assigned death time, when the Kami call his soul to rest for eternity everlasting, my Lord of fate. What is the god cursed name of this eta who weighs heavily upon your mind my Lord? Where does this vile one reside in my Master's realm? Aim me in the proper direction, and your hated teki will be no further worry to your presence." She snarled as she locked eyes with Hiromoai, the fire of hatred burning bright within them.

"That's much better from you Samurai Warrior from past times. You'll succeed on your next mission equally as well, Wind-san?" Hiromoai grumbled at his female weapon.

"Hai Hiromoai-sama! To nourish one's soul is to fulfill one's ordained destiny, my Lord and Master. Hieeee, what do you think I am, I am not one of the chugen o kimono? (People of small account) I'll be as successful on this mission as I was on my last one for your demands. May the Monen, (Evil spirits) eat of my worthless soul if I fail your orders, my Master. May the mighty Shibi, (Sea monsters) nibble upon the brittle bones of my long dead ancestors, and I be disgraced before the mighty Hachiman-sama, the Kami of Warfare. And may he be allowed to rob me of all my great skills of making war, if I even dare think of failing my mission for my Liege Lord. I have taken before you many years past, the honorable

Kishomon, the sacred written oath of blood to serve you and to vanquish all your hated enemy regardless of whether they may roam within the land of the living world, or if the hunted ones have retreated to the vastness of the Ukiyo World, the floating world of non-existence to hide from my unfettered wrath. I shall piss on all who contemplate any treachery against my Liege Lord. I shall..."

Hiromoai had to raise his hands in the air in order to silence Wind's anger and ranting of hatred aimed against his thought to be enemy. He had no idea how long she would have gone on threatening his unseen enemy with her words of anger if he did not stop her in her tracks as he growled at the female samurai. "Wind-san, this enemy I'll send you out against this time, is most cunning and wise beyond his countless years of living upon the sacred soil of Japan. He's very well protected at all times by many highly trained and heavily armed security and bodyguards, and he also dwells within the protective walls of a and ancient massive Castle Keep. One thought to be impenetrable from all possible attack by any great Armies and even by you.

"The Castle stood since beyond the written times of Japan's proud history. This evil man has threatened my life on numerous occasions, and he has caused me countless problems in the past, along with vast wealth and job opportunities over the many years of his detestable existence. Twice in this year alone, he has sent out the Black Death against me. Only because of the attention of my security guards am I still here and able to describe my enemy to you. Asahiko Yurkowa! He's the hated one who has sired the enemy you have just killed, Wind-san."

"Ieeeee my honorable Lord and Master, what ill mannered enemy would dare employ the feared Ninja of the Black Death who own the night and shadows to carry out their evil work? No one from the past or the present times is prepared to defend his life against such filth as these disgraced and lost Samurai. No one but me that is, my Master of destiny! Courage is the price demanded by life for granting one peace. I shall dispatch his evil being with all the unfettered anger the underworld possesses." Wind vowed as she stood straight and stared him in the eyes, forgetting about the confusing thoughts plaguing her mind as she added. "When will you send me out after this loathsome soul, so I can rid and purify the earth of this eta's foul existence? I shall not rest at peace until I am able to erase this evil one's being from your memory, my Lord."

The very pleased Hiromoai suddenly let out his breath and then he nodded as he made a motion to get up from the couch. He smiled and offered to his ancient female warrior in a very calm tone of voice. "Wind-san, make yourself comfortable while I go and retrieve the papers that I need to show you the path of your travels you must take to find my hated teki on this night. Lady Yoke, you'll look after Wind-san's needs until I returned with the papers." Hiromoai leaned the ancient katana killing sword against the arm of the sofa, and then he headed for his office on the second floor. The moment he was out of the study, she allowed herself to relax and breathed easier, and Lady Yoke moved closer to her side as she offered to the ancient samurai.

"Yuriko-san, I would be most honored to get you a cup of cha if you care to indulge." Lady Yoke bowed ever so graciously to the beautiful female samurai. Then she knelt and moved her legs under her rearend and straightened her back until she was comfortable, and able to look right at the stunningly beautiful face of this dangerous ancient warrior.

"Hai Lady Yoke. Cha would be most pleasing to my Wa. The Floating World is a most arid place in which to dwell, and one thirsts constantly." She bowed politely to the young woman.

"Please forgive this most inconsiderate and lazy servant for my terrible lack of manners displayed against your person, my new sister. You must be famished, and if I was seeing with my eyes and listening with my worthless ears, I would've anticipated your needs for food and drink." The Lady Yoke bowed gracefully to the warrior. She was beginning to love this most mysterious woman, and enjoyed using the words and phrases of the ancient past. She never realized how much she missed the old ways of Japan, until this female samurai of yesterday entered her life. The polite and very respectful ways the old ones used to deal with each other, all but lost with the turn of the century, has been reborn in this spirit's respectful attitude. As she held her bowed, Lady Yoke discovered the only thing she resented about Hiromoai, was his using this woman as an instrument, a weapon of death instead of the find of the eon.

"Lady Yoke, we are not born with great wisdom set in place in our worthless minds. We must discover it from where it hides on the never-ending path of journeys that no one can walk for us, or spare us from carrying out for ourselves. Wisdom is gathered from every day we live upon the wonderful soil of Japan." Wind offered without looking at her.

Lady Yoke got up and then she bowed to the ancient warrior and then she rushed off for the kitchen to get the female samurai a cup of tea.

Wind heard her moving the plates around in the kitchen from their meal, and she smiled. She was also able to hear Hiromoai still looking for something in the outer room. So she used this time to meditate and relax a little, and prepare her mind and body for her master's next mission he was about to send her out on.

Lady Yoke returned with the tea, she carried the cup properly, to display to the one receiving it her hands were in sight and planned no treachery against her person. She carried the cup with two fingers of the right hand supporting the bottom of the cup resting on the out stretched fingers of her left hand. She bowed correctly to the resting ancient warrior before offering her the cup ceremoniously. She also smiled as Wind stared at her as she entered the study.

Wind took the cup gracefully, there was something special about the way she prepared the tea she enjoyed much, and she was looking forward to enjoying another cup of the sweetly flavored brew. Something different she enjoyed immensely. She had no idea Lady Yoke sweetened the tea with sugar for her enjoyment. A luxury she had never shared in her past life.

She looked to Lady Yoke and noticed she was not enjoying tea, and offered. "Lady Yoke, why do you not share cha with me? Do you not enjoy sharing the brew with me? It would be an honor to my person to sip cha with you, Lady Yoke. You are my most trusted and only friend in the living world, and a trusted friend always shares in what their friend is doing."

"Hai Yuriko-san! I'd be honored to share cha with you, my sister from the past of Japan's ancient history." Lady Yoke recited excitedly as she smiled and turned and then rushed for the kitchen. She returned with a cup of tea, and knelt on the floor by the left side of the beautiful samurai. She read much about Japan's past, and realized at no time is anyone supposed to sit on the right side of the warrior. This was so a visitor did not hinder the samurai's sword arm, in case he was attacked and forced to react against any enemy while entertaining friends.

As they sipped they spoke softly and giggled quietly. But their conversation was interrupted when Hiromoai returned carrying a cache of papers stuffed in his arms.

Wind placed the discarded cup on the floor and made a move to stand. But she was waved back to her resting place by Hiromoai, who knelt next to her and then he quickly spread out the bundles of papers he carried, before her on the polished wood floor by her knees.

Without being told to leave the study, Lady Yoke rose and walked to Wind's left side silently and picked up the discarded tea cup and then disappearing to the kitchen. While the excited Hiromoai and Wind spoke about her upcoming mission for her new lord and master.

Lady Yoke busied herself cleaning up the kitchen, mainly because she had nothing else to do with her time, and she did not want to be caught doing nothing in the apartment by Hiromoai. She placed the dishes in the sink and then ran hot water and soap over them. She did not use the dishwasher for fear of disturbing their conversation in the other room. All the while her mind was concerned about the beautiful samurai. The Lady Yoke was wondering what was going on in her mind and how she felt about killing men he sent her after. She wanted to be by the side of Wind, but with Hiromoai speaking with the warrior, she knew she could not be hovering around the two of them, and interfering with their conversation and plans.

It was impolite to be near a conversation that you weren't invited to be part of as a matter of respect offered to the people of Japan. Although she was not very pleased to be part of this scheme of plotting the deaths of some of the most powerful businessmen in Japan, she knew she would do anything for Hiromoai's sake and love, and now for the beautiful samurai known as Wind. Her every thought was revolved around the two important people in her life right now.

There was a knock on the door and Lady Yoke went to answer it while they continued with their conversation in the study. It was Utsumi and Lady Yoke invited the old man in, and led him to the kitchen where she briskly fixed him tea, after informing him Hiromoai was engaged in conversation, and was not to be disturbed. She had to place her finger to her lips to stop the old man from speaking loudly in the hallway, interfering with their conversation in the study.

Once they were in the kitchen, they spoke barely over a whisper not to disturb the meeting in the study. She made the old man some tea, and spoke pleasantly as she waited for the meeting to be concluded. Then, she would be able to be around the fearsome warrior, and better look after all her needs and wants. Because she wanted to, not that she was being forced to do so.

CHAPTER FOURTEEN

HIROMOAI'S STUDY IN THE HATANAKA TOWERS

Hiromoai Hatanaka laid out the pictures of Asahiko's face on the floor before the ancient female samurai. Along with pictures of the castle he dwelled in, he had a very detailed map of downtown Tokyo laid out on the floor, along with the outskirts where the castle was constructed.

Wind had to sit forward in order to see the material her master laid out before her. She was concentrating on the pictures of the old man's face, and did not notice the ones of the castle. She saw the old man standing with the younger man she killed a few days ago in one photo. Asahiko seemed very proud of the young man, with his arm protectively looped over his shoulder, and the both of them were grinning happily at the camera. They both seemed like they did not have a care in the world and loved each other dearly.

For a second, she wondered what possible threat this man of obvious great age and bent frame might pose against her much stronger and younger master. Then she remembered about Lord Wakatsuki's presence, he was old and yet he was the cause of Kawasomeru-sama and his realm's many problems for countless years of warfare and strife. She shook her head to try and cleared the troubling thoughts of doubt from her inquisitive mind. She was not visiting the world of the living to question her master's orders, but to carry them out without hesitation or delay to their final conclusion. Wind picked up the picture with the close up of Asahiko's face printed on it as it the picture might burn her fingers, and studied it intensely for several seconds.

Hiromoai watched as she stared at the picture then offered. "Yes that's the man who cost me much wealth in past times. I don't want him to be breathing after this night has run its course."

Wind listened expressionless to her lord and master's words of warning and anger for this elderly person, as she stared at the old man's wrinkled aged face on the picture and she replied. "Hai my Liege Lord, after tonight this great dung eating eta will be free of his worthless life, and would then be roaming in the Floating World of not."

"Good Wind-san, I want you to pay attention to my explanation, this enemy dwells in a mighty ancient Castle which proved to be quite impenetrable in the past history of Japan. Only the most cunning of Samurai will be able to breach the security this old one surrounds himself with."

"Yes my Lord and Master, I understand this and there's no place in all Japan that this worthless enemy of yours will be able to hide from my unyielding wrath and his final fate on this earth. I piss on his foul soul, as I shall piss on his ugly remains once I have dispatched him from your memory and the earth, my Lord." She snorted nastily as she turned to the picture of the old man in her hand, and stared at it tenaciously.

"Look, do me a favor and hold on to that thought for a minute. That's the way I want you to be when you go after Asahiko's soul on this night, Samurai. Anything short of pure hatred harbored in your heart against this most evil man will cause you to fail on your mission. I want you to pay close attention to these instructions very carefully I give you." Hiromoai moved the first picture of the castle over the snap shots of Asahiko on the floor. When he turned back to Wind, he was surprised by the expression on her face. For a moment, he thought she was angry with something he just said and he asked her with concern. "What's the problem now? You seem upset."

"Ieeee my Lord. Please excuse this worthless Samurai, but I do not understand this please?"

"You don't understand what? Now is not the time to be even slightly confused by anything I order you to do, Wind-san." He moaned as he stared at her.

"This my Lord! I do not understand what you are showing me on what you have called pictures." She actually growled as she held up the picture of the castle to show her master.

"This structure is where my hated teki dwells, Samurai. What's not to understand about the damn picture, Wind-san?" Hiromoai questioned as he looked from the picture to her again.

She stared at Hiromoai intensely for several long moments before hissing her response to him. "Why does your worthless teki dwell within your great Castle, my Lord? Has there been a war that I was not summoned to witness and be part of for my Master's sake, a cursed war that has obviously caused you to lose your great Castle to your lowly enemy."

Hiromoai could not hide his confused expression from her. He had no idea what was upsetting her so about the picture she was showing him, or what she was talking about. All of a sudden, he felt he was walking in dangerous waters with his eyes closed.

"Kawasomeru-sama, why does your enemy dwell within your honorable Castle?"

His mind raced, he was beginning to figure out what was her problem. Evidently, the warlord she worked for in the past times had lived in the same castle Asahiko now owned. His mind went in overdrive, and he offered to the extremely dangerous female warrior. "Err... Wind-san, my father was Kawasomeru-sama. He died many years past of old age and terrible injuries suffered in battles. During his rule over Japan, I was sent to school and was away when the last war raged between my honorable father and his hated enemy. When I returned home, much of my father's land and worth was absorbed by this evil man you see here on these pictures. Now, you can see why he's such an enemy of mine. He took advantage of my father in my absence of training.

"It's been so long since the last time I walked on the sacred ground protected by the great walls of the Castle, I even forgot what name my father gave to the Castle." Hiromoai was a very wise man and he knew it was impossible for his father to be still alive to be this Lord Kawasomeru and former lord and master of this ancient samurai, because this warlord ruled way back in the thirteenth century, long before his father was even born. But he was banking on her not making the connection in age. He believed she would believe anything he told her without thought.

"Hieeee Kawasomeru-sama, I am so thoroughly ashamed, because I was not summoned by either you or your honorable father, before this cursed dog eating fool moved into your great Castle. I would have protected your realm until you returned to take your proper place upon the thrown of Japan. I cannot believe an enemy of yours now enjoys the protection offered by the great walls of Engakuji Castle, my Lord and Master. This is unthinkable, almost too much for me to bear. I shall seek your great revenge on the head of this foul Kami who dares to keep what is my Master's property. By the sacred Aquene knot of the honored Samurai Caste, this loathsome enemy will not live past the hour of the next cock call.

"This I swear to my Lord and Master that I shall be his faithful kaishaku, his executioner from Night Wind. I will dispatch his filthy soul from the living world, and return to your hand what is truly yours to enjoy, Kawasomeru-sama." She was calling Hiromoai her Lord Kawasomeru, because the pictures of the castle brought her memory back as she took her killing sword resting against the sofa, and ran her finger along the razor sharp blade. Wind's blood coated the edge of the sword, but none dripped to the floor. Her blood was actually being absorbed by the shaft of steel, almost as if the blade was drinking her blood in thirst for revenge.

This action sent a shiver down his back. It was chilling to see the blood obviously being soaked up by the steel of the ancient katana blade. Hiromoai committed the name of the castle she called Engakuji, to his memory. He breathed in a deep sigh of relief he was worried because he did not know the name of the castle, before she spoke it. If she would have worked out the deception he was trying to carry out against her, he had no doubt in his mind that he would be dead. Then, a thought struck him and he turned to her and asked.

"Wind-san, how much time did you spend within the Castle walls in your past lifetime? Had you visited the Castle on many different occasions, Samurai?"

"I had the pleasure to spend countless sticks of time wandering through the great walls of your mighty Castle in the last times, my Lord and Master. Why do you ask me such a foolish question as this is my Liege Lord?" Wind asked him with concern in her voice.

"I wonder, perhaps, you might remember your way around the inside of the great Castle yet?"

"Hai my wise Lord and Master that was a very wise question to ask of me. But you above all others should know better of the many secrets the great Castle hides within its great walls, Hiromoai-sama." Wind went back to calling him by his real name as she put the worried and troubling thoughts out of her mind about this man who said he was the son of Lord Kawasomeru. As far as she was concerned, he was her liege lord and he always will be her lord.

"That's true Samurai from Japan's great past, but it's been too long since the last time I was allowed to roam the Castle

Keep with memories of my father and past times. I'm afraid I forgot much of the inner workings of the Castle Keep over the years that past, Wind-san." Hiromoai held his breath for a moment, hoping that the female warrior would not put the pieces together, and then she realized that he had nothing to do with this Lord Kawasomeru clan.

"Ahhhh so, I see because my eyes have been opened by your most enlightening words, I understand what you offer me now, Hiromoai-sama. The mind has many different ways of placing unpleasantness out of its memory, or to be hidden within its walls of the mind to avoid insanity from overtaking what we call the mind. It is the way the mind allows the Wa of peace to return when at rest, even though the soul is not at rest with the countless moods of the earth and gods we respect in life, my Lord. Rejoice in the wisdom of the mind Hiromoai-sama. By recognizing what is, what is just, only then can one understand the true key to unlocking the dungeon of self judgment which lies buried deep within our troubled minds, my Lord."

"Yes, I'm aware that the mind helps the body survive unpleasant memories. Wind-san, I was wondering, do you know of any secret passageways hidden in the Castle's walls? I believe my father told me of many hidden passageways throughout the Castle walls." He offered, allowing her to babble her Buddha teachings, as long as she was willing to do what he wanted of her.

"Ieeeee... many my Lord, I see where your mind is wandering on this thought, and it is an intelligent path to tread upon, Hiromoai-sama. Huh, if the Castle remains as constructed in the past, there are many secret walkways and escape routes hidden throughout its walls and rooms. With these passageways, I'll be able to roam the Castle walls unobserved. It was through your precautions, these passageways were incorporated in the construction of your Castle, to allow you to leave the walls without detection. It also served in the times of siege, to allow your Warriors to attack your enemy from their flanks. Or bring food and water in the Castle if the attacking army was too powerful to be destroyed in any other way but by attrition, my Lord."

"Yes yes Wind-san. I know why the passageways were placed in the Castle. I asked you if you remembered where any of these passageways were hidden, dammit." He shifted his weight on the floor while growing angry at Wind's constant babbling and interruptions.

"There are no inaccuracies or consonance's to be accepted as truth, my Lord and Master. All that takes place that makes up the many laws of Karma is a blessing from Lord Buddha, given to us to learn life's lessons we're allowed to wander through. I am terribly sorry for upsetting your peace with my confusing words, my Lord. I shall be more direct with my replies then wait your command to commit Suppuku for my god cursed transgressions against Master's will." Wind bowed correctly and then she waited for the order for her to kill herself.

"Gees Wind-san! You're becoming a real pain in the arse with your constant Zen babble you keep spouting back at me whenever I ask you a damn question." Hiromoai growled before catching himself. He was angry at the way she danced around his questions. He was beginning to believe she either didn't remember, or she was deliberately stalling for some reason.

"Forgive this undereducated and very foolish Samurai Warrior, Hiromoai-sama. My Master is again employing words of Japanese that I fear I am not familiar with." She moaned, hoping her master would not order her to commit the painful respect of Suppuku. She did not enjoy the experience when she committed the act before.

"Enough dancing around the damn issues, huh. Wind-san, I want you to look at the map before you, and point out any possible passageways you can remember from your past times spent at the Castle. I warn you Samurai, my patience is growing very thin with you of late."

"You do not wish me to commit Suppuku for my foolish infraction against you my Lord?"

"Why the hell would I want you to do that for, for Christ sake? But I warn you for the last time. If you don't get on pointing out these hidden passageways I want to know about, I just might be tempted to make that order against you. Wind-san, turn your attention back to the map." He moved the map over the pictures on the floor so she could see the map easier.

"Yes my Lord and Master, the well used secret entrance to the great Castle used by you lies printed here on your map Hiromoai-sama."She said as she pointed to the map and structure and the area she remembered hid one of the many secret passageways of the castle.

ENGAKUJI CASTLE, TOKYO, JAPAN

Once Asahiko finished speaking with the American, he left his downstairs office and headed for his master suite. If he was going to commit Suppuku, he was going to do it in his beloved castle. He went to the old meeting room of Lord Kawasomeru turned into his private sleeping and meditation suite. He had a desk and computer set up for late work he wished to accomplish. He sat at the desk and dialed his accountant, and placed him on hold when he answered the call.

Then he dialed his lawyer, once he was on the other line, he placed the receiver in the cradle and turned the conversation into a three way call. The old man spoke to his lawyer first, informing him that he wanted the papers delivered to the American as soon as they were drawn up. He did not like working from the smaller office when he was in the massive castle. From his interconnected rooms, he was able to see many gardens surrounding the great castle. His mind was brought back to the reality of life when he heard his lawyer's voice reply.

"Asahiko-san, I feel I must implore you again not to sell your honorable company to this arrogant and loathsome American, sir. He doesn't have the best interests of Japan, or your company, in his mind and heart sir. It'll not take long for him to completely destroy the great reputation your company has developed by your honorable actions of the past. Asahiko-san, you have to listen to my judgment, there are many good and honorable Japanese businessmen, who would continue to serve you and Japan, better than this Gai Jin. Japanese businessmen who'll protect the reputation you developed over the years of service and working in Japan, sir. I don't understand why you want to go through with this transaction, sir. As your lawyer and trusted friend, I must protect…" His lawyer offered but was cut off by the old man as he growled.

"Shigeru Nagaro-san! It's not for you to understand anything I do or say or request from you in my worthless life. I know you have my best interests at heart and in mind at all times. But I'm weary of this way of life, of the construction field, and the unending problems that comes with the company. I want to enjoy my remaining years in peace and in harmony with the world."

"I understand how you feel Asahiko-san, and sympathize with the pain you're suffering over the loss of your son. But you must reconsider this unwise thought of selling a well established Japanese business, to a lowly American fool, sir. One I don't like much, I must offer sir."

"Nagaro-san, I value your opinion and the way it's offered. In the past you never steered me along the wrong path to tread upon. It's important you be honest in this conversation, if I'm to make the right decision. Why don't you like this American? He made me an offer I can't refuse."

"I don't trust him for a minute sir. I know once this greet fool is in control of your honorable company, all the good will you once commanded will be lost forever, Asahiko-san."

"Thank you for your valued opinion my old friend. But I'm afraid it didn't change my mind one iota, Nagaro-san." The wise old man offered to his concerned lawyer

"If I might ask Asahiko-san, how much did the hated American offer for the construction company? I need this so I can fill it in properly on the contract, Asahiko-san."

"Nagaro-san, he offered me one hundred and seventy five million American dolla..."

"Hieeee... Asahiko-san. That barely covers the staggering cost of your heavy earth moving equipment, sir." Fumimaro Kakizawa, Asahiko's long time accountant cried as he cut in on the conversation. "I beg of you sir, is that all you're selling the lowly Gai Jin, Asahiko-san?"

Asahiko took exception to being interrupted so rudely by Kakizawa, but he chose to overlook the infraction by his overly excited accountant. He knew Kakizawa was only looking after his best interests, and that was why his words were uttered. The old man drew in his breath and then answered in a strained and angry tone. "No Kakizawa-san, I'm selling the Gai Jin everything I own and have. All assets are on the table in this transaction to the American. It includes my mining operation, cement company trucks, concrete forms, and all machines. Everything goes in the sale. Even contracts I have opened on the table for consideration. Everything."

"lieeeee... Asahiko-san, I fear someone might have crawled in and pissed in your ear, and has scrambled your brains. I know the death of your most honorable son weighs heavy on your mind and heart. But you must put this terrible tragedy out of your troubled thoughts, before it makes you commit a fatal error for your proud company and all its loyal investors and workers, and Japan's future, Asahiko-san. I must protest against this incorrect assumption of a deal with the god cursed lowly Gai Jin. Your construction company is worth double what he's offering you, sir. If you allow me a few months, I'm quite certain that I can easily find many a buyer living in Japan, who'll be more than pleased to pay you what your company is truly worth, sir.

"I can't see you just giving away your honorable construction company to the lowly Gai Jin at such a low offered price, Asahiko-san. I must protest this deal you're offering your trusted friends of many years, Asahiko-san.

Nagaro-san, you have to talk some sense into Asahiko-san's troubled mind before it is too late, and we lose his great construction company to the lowly Americans, sir." The overexcited accountant begged of the lawyer over the phone.

Asahiko allowed the insolence from his accountant to continue. He was only guilty of following orders to be honest in the conversation. He listened to Kakizawa angry words, but again he did not allow his words to sway the outcome of his decision. He hated Hiromoai so much he was willing to give his company to the American, to keep it out of his hands.

"Asahiko-san, I'm forced to agree with Kakizawa-san on this most confusing matter we are currently discussing here, sir. What the hell does the board have to say over this threat of yours to sell your business to the lowly American Gai Jin, Asahiko-san?" Nagaro asked calmly, his years of being a loyal lawyer controlled his temper during this trying conversation.

"I care not one foul grain of worthless dried rice what those great fools think, or have to say of my want and desire to sell my construction company to the Gai Jin for that matter, Nagaro-san. Their opinion doesn't interest me in the least I tell you. The great fools will do as I say, or they'll be removed from the board, even if I have to fire the entire board to complete this transaction with the hated American, sir. I'll not allow anything to interfere with the progress of this deal. It must be completed before the gods call me home to their bosom. Nagaro-san, I control fifty one percent of the stock of my company, and as the controlling influence I'll do what I please with it, and the fools will have to follow my lead like the dogs follow a bitch in heat. Or they'll all be fired and lose everything they once invested in my company, Nagaro-san."

"Asahiko-san, if you go through with this most unwise sale of your company at this poor offering price, your investors will lose everything they have invested anyhow, sir. I'm sorry Asahiko-san if you insist on going forward with the sale of your company to the Gai Jin I'll be forced to complain to government officials. You do understand you have to have their final permission to sell any Japanese company to a Gai Jin, a foreigner. I'll have the government protect your interests in spite of your misguided wants, sir. If your thinking's unclear, they'll clear it up for you Asahiko-san. No damn foreigner born to this earth will ever own a Japanese business while I draw breath in my body, sir." Kakizawa warned the owner of the company.

"Huh Kakizawa, if you try to block my attempt to sell my construction company to the lowly Gai Jin. I'll fire you on the spot, and if you continue to hinder my attempts about this deal, you might be drawing the few breaths you have left to breathe on this land." He said with surprising strength and conviction in his voice as Kakizawa interrupted him again. He eliminated the 'san' from his name, he was so angry with the man for not steadfastly backing his decision.

No matter what the accountant Kakizawa felt of that decision, one thing Asahiko demanded from all his staff was blind, total loyalty to any decisions he made or offered. Going against any of his decisions like he was doing during this conversation, completely destroyed that loyalty he once offered the old man. The elderly owner of the company made up his mind to fire Kakizawa, no matter the outcome of the sale of his business. He knew the government could block his wants to sell the company to the American, but over the years he had greased enough palms of Japanese politicians to actually force them to back any decision he made. That was why he was awarded more government projects than any other construction company.

"What is this you're offering against me now? Are you daring to threaten my life? Me! Your loyal and trusted friend of too many years to count on the stick of time, you dare threaten me like this! I don't believe this for one moment, what has come over your troubled mind, Asahiko-san. I'm worried about you, I'm afraid I no longer recognize you or your actions. You have changed drastically sir. To dare threaten such an old friend as myself is detestable. I fear what might've crawled in your ear and is creating inner turmoil in your brain, sir. I fear more than ever you're not sound of thought and mind, and this offer to sell your honorable company, my old friend."

"Kakizawa! I warn you you're taking our friendship for granted, for more than it's worth in your worthless eyes. To dare speak to me in this most insulting manner is beyond our friendship, beyond instruction, its deplorable you great fool. If I were a younger man, I'd challenge you to the field of honor, and battle you to the death. Once defeated, your bones would've been brought down to the sea to allow the lowly crabs and birds to feast upon your dishonored body. My mind is the only thing that remains sound and strong in my crippled body, sir."

The worried and deeply concerned accountant suddenly gave up over trying to talk sense to Asahiko. He turned to the lawyer on the phone and then begged him. "Nagaro-san, you must try and talk better sense to Asahiko-san's mind, or all is lost. He must be shown the many errors in his interest to sell his honorable company to a lowly Gai Jin from the United States. You know once the hated Americans' get a foothold in one of our companies it'll not be long before they pollute all our businesses with their foul manners and dishonorable ways of conducting business. I can see it all in my mind's eye, in a matter of just a few years time, the Americans will do to Japan what they have done to America. Destroy the company by creating nothing but turmoil, mistrust, and failing profits and inferior work ethics.

"Then the hated Unions will step in, endowing their brazing workers and giving them the power to dare to refuse to work, our day shifts will be cut down to eight, or even seven hours of work. Time and a half or God forbid double time on weekends. Workers demanding, can you imagine that horror, workers making demands of their bosses in Japan? Demands that'll threaten the very heartbeat of the company and cause it to fail, foul demands impossible to meet, strikes would follow the lazy American workers, further eroding the makeup of the mother company. Weakening that company further until it can no longer survive, or compete in the global market, sir. They, the useless workers of America destroyed the trust of the United States, now they want to come destroy the trust of Japan and our workers loyalty to the companies they work for.

"Besides what I'm telling you, the working conditions the Americans will bring to the shores of Japan. Asahiko-san's selling his company at so low a price for either of us to be pleased with. Please Nagaro-san, if Asahiko-san can be patient long enough, and allows me the time to work. I'm certain I can discover an honorable and loyal Japanese buyer for his company, who'd double, maybe offer more than double the price for Asahiko-san's company the American offers us."

Nagaro was doing what he did best. He was allowing both Asahiko and Kakizawa to get involved in heated words, so he could better judge the thoughts, and unspoken ideas of Asahiko.

Kakizawa and Asahiko fell silent and waited to hear what the lawyer had to offer them.

Nagaro knew they were waiting his reply to the accountant's plea, so he rushed himself in formulating his thoughts. Once he knew where he was going to drive the conversation, he began to speak after clearing his throat, he offered. "Asahiko-san, as I done many times in my service to you and your company, I'll continue to do for you now. Any decision you make concerning your most honorable company, I'll back your decision with my dying breath..."

"Why will you do that for Nagaro-san?" Kakizawa snarled, hearing the unspoken word.

Nagaro ignored the accountant angry outcry as he continued with his words. "On the other hand Asahiko-san, I'm forced to agree with Kakizawa-san. I don't like the idea of selling an honorable and extremely successful Japanese business to an American, especially this one of whom I know of quite well of, sir. I further think that you're selling your company at much too low a price. However, if this is your final decision over this matter Asahiko-san, I'll be most honored to have the contract completed by later tonight for you, sir." Nagaro continued with his words, overlooking Kakizawa's attempt at another interruption.

"By the gods who roam the black world, Nagaro! How could you back this decision to sell Yurkowa Construction to an American? A Gai Jin, Nagaro!" Kakizawa screamed in the phone.

"Kakizawa-san! How dare you address me in this foul a manner? No matter how angry I ever got at you in our countless conversations of the past. I have never once failed to add 'San' to your honorable name. I resent your omission of that honor, sir. I believe I have earned that respect from you, sir." Nagaro snapped angrily at the upset accountant over the phone.

Asahiko smiled as he enjoyed the small war waging between his accountant and lawyer. As long as they warred between themselves, they were allowing him to ride and avoid their great and angry wrath from descending down upon his shoulders for his decision to sell his business to the hated and mistrusted Gai Jin. He knew he was selling his company at a rock bottom price, but he did not care any longer. His overwhelming thought was to keep his company out of the hands of Hiromoai, no matter the cost to his wealth. Although he grew angry at Kakizawa's omission of the 'san', he overlooked the insult. He felt Nagaro was able to protect his own interests when dealing with the always troublesome accountant.

Kakizawa was ashamed of the terrible insult he just leveled against the lawyer unintentionally. In the heat of his argument he went unaware he made the omission. He bowed to the phone as he offered to the fuming lawyer. "Shigeru Nagaro-san, please forgive my unintentional insult I have just leveled against your person. I'll offer a bowl of uncooked rice and seven sticks of incense to Lord Buddha, to beg him for this terribly infraction to be erased from your honorable mind, sir. Its Asahiko-san's decision to sell his company to the lowly Gai Jin that kind of caught me a little off guard, sir. We can't possibly allow this sale to transpire as Asahiko-san has requested, sir. We have to block this misguided sale to the hated Gai Jin at all cost, sir. Nagaro-san, you must speak sense to Asahiko-san, he listens to you more than me. Tell him to find a young consort for the night that can suck the ill thoughts out of his mind through the end of his serpent.

"I feel Asahiko-san's in need of a long journey in the Jade Gate world to clear his troubled mind so he can rethink this ill begotten decision, sir. If he wants, I'll be more than pleased to go to the local Tea House, and bring him back any number of fine looking young Geisha girls who can accomplish this act for his pleasure, sir. Asahiko-san must be stopped from committing this fatal error with his company, one that'll destroy Japan over the coming future years, sir."

Again, Asahiko smiled over the offer of whores to open their young and waiting Jade Gate for his withered old and useless dragon that had spat its last fire years ago. It was a very appealing thought though, one he might look into before beginning the journey into the Ukiyo World by committing suicide. He heard many stories about life in the Floating World, soaring with the clouds and looking down on Japan, helping her in times of trouble from the beyond.

Nagaro laughed over the accountant's offer to get Asahiko some young women to sway his mind from the sale of his business to the American. But he knew anything he or the accountant would offer Asahiko, would not change his mind once the old man decided on a certain course of action, as he offered to the over excited accountant. "Alas, Kakizawa-san, I fear that I'll be as unsuccessful as you are, if I were to try and change Asahiko-san's mind. I know him as well as I do my own honorable father. The two are much alike, once they made up their mind, even the rumbling of Mount Fuji wouldn't sway it from its chosen course and belief."

The well aged Asahiko's chest swelled with great pride over Nagaro's last remark, because he knew of Nagaro's father very well. And to be respected by his son so honorably, was a great distinction offered him that was beyond an honor. He nodded in agreement to Nagaro's words over the phone. Even though Kakizawa's words were still upsetting to him, Nagaro's words robbed him of his anger he held against the overly excited accountant.

HIROMOAI'S PENTHOUSE IN THE HATANAKA TOWERS

Hiromoai stared at Wind's finger pointing to the map placed before them on the floor. He never dreamed an ancient passageway would go under the moat and to the interior of the castle complex. He pulled the map a little closer to him as he tried to see the hidden opening in the picture. It was impossible to locate on the poor print. He looked at Wind again, and smiled as he moaned at the ancient female warrior. "Wind-san, are certain the passageway may still exist after all these years? Do you think the years might have caved the passageway in on itself? Or it might have possibly been discovered by Asahiko, or one of his security guards and then filled in or somehow been blocked from entry, so no one could breach the walls of the great Castle against him? To hope the aged old passageway still exists seems to go against fate."

"Hiromoai-sama, although I have the pleasure to dwell within both worlds at the same time, I'm terribly sorry to announce for your ears, I fear that I do not possess the power of unlimited vision and knowledge in either. The only way I would know for certain if the passage still remains, is to travel to the opening and see if it is yet there, my Lord and Master."

"Hmmmm... this might create a problem for us. Until I know for certain if this passage remains, I'm going to be forced to hold you back on your mission against the old fool. I think we'll do the wise thing and put off this mission until tomorrow night, Wind-san. That'll give me time to travel to the Castle and see if I can locate the old passage. If it still remains, we'll go ahead as planned tomorrow night. But if it's been discovered and filled in or collapsed from age or war, we'll have to come up with another way of getting you inside the Castle. If this passage is still there, it's going to make your mission all that much easier for you to accomplish."

Wind was unable to hide the sad look that was suddenly etched on her lovely face from him.

"Why the look of sadness? What's bothering you now, Samurai?" Hiromoai asked as her.

"I am sorry to offer my Liege Lord that I suffer from the deplorable sin of greed and want. I'm guilty of wanting to stay in the world of the living for longer sticks of time, as long as I can visit the living world. I do not wish to be returned to the forever lonely endless Floating World of waiting and wanting my Master. I must admit to my Lord that this worthless Samurai is becoming rather accustomed to the innumerable luxuries that the living world has to offer one's peace. The sweet smell of countless cherry blossoms fills my mind with memories of long ago. Oh to sing the ancient songs of pleasures and lovemaking." She moaned as she stared in his eyes.

"Who said you're going back to the damn Floating World? I didn't say that Wind-san."

"You did not say so in words. But if you are going to put off my mission to rid this earth of your enemy until the turn of the sun in the Heavens. I fear I shall be sent to the lonely world of floating spirits until you have new need of my skills." Again she placed a sad look.

"Wind-san, you worry needless of these most troubling thoughts I assure you. Don't try to think for me I warn you, Samurai of the past times. I have no intention of sending you back to the vastness of the Ukiyo World. I have other needs of your expertise, whether it is today, tomorrow, or tomorrow's tomorrow. You'll not be returning to the Floating World unless you happen to fail or somehow anger me. Now I know you have interests in the land of the living, I'll find other ways of keeping you here longer. Does this satisfy your worries, Wind-san?"

"Hai my Lord, this lowly Samurai thanks her Liege Lord beyond words and thoughts, for the pleasing considerations. This I swear, I'll never flounder on any mission you dispatch me on."

"Wind-san, now we have that straightened out, how will I be able to locate this passageway you informed me of. I'm afraid I'm unfamiliar with the outside walls of the Castle Keep. I'll take a drive to the site tomorrow to make certain the ancient corridor exists in this world?"

"My Master, of course you would not be very familiar with the outside of your Castle Keep. The Lord of the Castle would never have reason to examine the outside of the Keep. To do so would be beneath your great honor. You had many loyal vassals and Samurai to keep an eye on your structure. My Lord, you'll have to walk around the moat on the east side of the Castle, always looking to the Castle walls. There, you will search for two stones turned sideways against each other in the wall. Once these stones are located, you must walk twenty paces in a straight line to the north. You must locate the great stone of Shibi, the mighty sea monster stone. If I remember correctly, this stone rests on a slight incline. You must shove the mighty stone aside, because it covers the very mouth of the opening to the secret passageway, my Lord."

"Why was the Shibi picked to protect the stone and passageway, Samurai?" He asked, almost confused by the sacred emblem.

"This was wise thinking to consummate, to seek the protection of the powerful Shibi Kami, my Lord. No Samurai of the past was willing to risk the dreadful wrath of the sea monster, even under times of siege and war. Thus, if the Castle was under assault and the enemy was looking for entry to the Castle, they would not dare to disturb the resting rock of the sea monsters of myth and wonderment. Too much of Japan's past rested on the waves that covered the Ocean, and the bounty of the seas offers to the children of Japan, to anger the protectors of the sea, my Lord."

"Well I got news Wind-san. How it was in the past, it remains the same to this day. Much of Japan's survival depends on the vast seas and its wonderful bounty offered us."

"As it should be always in mind my Lord and Master. The fearsome sea monster honors all who honor its forever presence in the world." She bowed.

"Wind-san, I'm unfamiliar with the shape of the Shibi carving. Can you draw the shape of the sea monster on the stone?" He asked the samurai with concern lacing his tone this time.

"Hai my Master, this is simple for me to accomplish for you, Hiromoai-sama." She put out her hand, displaying she was in need of a writing brush, ink, and paper.

He reached in his pocket and removed a ball point pen and handed it to her. She stared at it as if she was holding onto the tail of an angry snake as she looked back at him.

"Damn, what the hell's the problem now Samurai?" He snapped at her angrily.

"What is this you offered, my Lord? I'm afraid this foolish Warrior has no idea what this is."

He laughed as he shook his head. "Ohhh..., I forgot you're from the past. You never saw a pen, Samurai. Here, allow me to display its wonders to your presence." He took the pen and hit the button and the tip appeared. He moved the map and wrote her name on the back of the paper.

Wind stared at the print and then she touched it lightly and it did not smear under the swipe of her fingers. She turned to Hiromoai and placed a smile of victory as she exclaimed to him. "Hai my unbelievable Lord and Master, is there nothing that you have not learned to conquer in your honorable lifetime? This foolish Warrior of the past is in total awe that you have been able to subdue the unruly paint of writing, to where it will no longer smear under one's hand, and dry to the touch immediately when written, my wise Lord. Where is the paint well that you must dip this item in so one can write further with the wonderful writing stick?"

"You do have a lot to learn about this time you walk in now, Samurai. You no longer need brush and paint to write with, Warrior. Everything you need is held in the handle of the pen. It doesn't run out of ink for many sticks of time and writing many agreements, and when it does run out of ink, you merely replace the ink cartage and you can write further with it. Here, take the pen and draw the damn impression I must search for on the ancient stone, Wind-san."

She took the pen as if it was going to devour her soul, and held it as Hiromoai held it a moment ago, and placed the tip to the paper. She drew a quick picture of a sea serpent rising out of the water, while attacking an ancient fishing ship. When she finished the drawing she dropped the pen, and rubbed her hand as if it was burned by the modern day writing implement.

Hiromoai picked up the pen and placed it back in his pocket as he studied the understandable drawing Wind created and then he turned to the samurai. "Wind, how large is this stone?"

"My Lord, I believe if I remember rightly, it is about the size of one kolu of rice."

He cocked his head to the side and gave Wind a queer look because he had no idea what a kolu of rice even looked like. But he hesitated in asking another foolish question of the samurai.

She saw his dilemma and searched the room for something roughly the same size of the serpent stone. Her eyes settled on the coffee table then she pointed to it.

He looked in the direction she pointed and saw the table and remarked. "Ahhhh... I got it Wind-san, I'd say the stone is about two feet wide and around three feet long."

Now it was her turn to cock her head to the side, and stare at him.

"Never mind, I got it Samurai." He glanced at his watch and saw it was late. He looked to Lady Yoke and said. "Lady Yoke, I'm exhausted. You may turn in for the night if you please."

The Lady Yoke looked from Hiromoai to Wind and bowed to the warrior at the same time.

He saw the kind look and offered. "If you so desire, you're free to turn in for the night, Lady Yoke. Wind-san and I will be talking further on this night of her upcoming mission for me."

Lady Yoke knew what was on his mind. He was going to pillow with Wind for a second time and she rose like she had just lost her best friend and lover in the same night.

Wind picked up the pained expression pass over her face, and she instantly understood what she was thinking, and actually felt her pain in her heart. She felt terrible for her only woman friend of the living world. She felt very upset she was betraying her friendship to Lady Yoke by pillowing with her intended lover. She knew what was on his mind, and could not possibly deny she was praying to the Kami of love, asking her to have him pillow with her again.

CHAPTER FIFTEEN

When Lady Yoke was out of the room, he rose and held out his hand and she took it. He helped her to her feet and when she was standing, he undid the golden obi holding her kimono closed. She allowed his hands to glide over her shoulders as he forced the silk from them. She bent her arms, catching the cloud like silk garment in the bend of her arms. She was taught this by her older sister Estsuko. It was unflattering for a woman of class to stand before any man naked, unless they were engaged in pillowing. She remembered warmly her sister telling her to allow the silk to enhance her beauty by letting the garment surround her body like a cloud.

She smiled as she looked in his hungry eyes, and saw the lust growing in them and knew her sister was correct in her instructions. She melted in his arms as he pulled the silk garment from her body. Naked and stunning, she was drawn close to his warm hard body, his hands clutching her rearend as he pulled her closer. His breath on her neck made her tremble with desire.

Hiromoai released the grasp on her body and then he got out of his clothes.

Wind dropped to her knees and bowed until her forehead touched the toes of Hiromoai.

"Now what's this about Wind-san?" He asked as he looked down at the lovely Wind.

"I kneel before the feet of my Lord and Master because you are the center of all things in life and mind, and the heart and soul of Japan. From your breath the air of Japan stays pure. If my Lord happens to turn his back on Japan in anger, all life as we know it will disappear from her Eight Islands and Japan will be shrouded in perpetual darkness and upheaval. The Japan I love will be nothing more than a sad memory in my mind. Me! Yuriko Masahiko Tanizaki. Wind!

"I'm the luckiest being that dwells in both worlds. This unworthy Warrior to be so picked by the most powerful warlord in Japan's history, for pillowing is an honor thought to be beyond reach, beyond my worthless grasp. I thank your wisdom for sharing his pillow with one of such little worth and respect." She said without taking her forehead off his foot. She was so honored to be picked to pillow with her master that all thought of Lady Yoke and her want to be with him, slipped from her mind. All she wanted to do was pillow with her master and forget about time.

"Nonsense, you're of a worth beyond all treasures the world of the living has to offer, combined." He reached down and lifted her to her feet by the shoulders. He held onto her until he was looking her right in the eyes, and he kissed her as his hands rolled her breasts.

ENGAKUJI CASTLE

Asahiko allowed the kind words of Nagaro to fill his head with great pride and respect, and bring him the greatest of pleasure and inner peace. The pleasantness ended when the still upset accountant Kakizawa spoke with anger still filling his voice.

"Nagaro-san, I can't believe this for one minute, you're going to actually allow Asahiko-san to sell his honorable business to a lowly and hated American Gai Jin, sir? You know how wrong this foul decision is. You, above all men in Japan, have to talk Asahiko-san into changing his mind before all is lost, and his company will be disgraced by this Gai Jin's ownership, sir."

He spoke quickly, forcing the accountant and lawyer to hold their words as he offered. "Kakizawa-san, how many years have you been forced to suffer my worthless presence?"

Kakizawa laughed and replied. "Since my first son was born to the world, neh?" (Isn't it)

"Yes, and in all those years of dealing with me in the past, has anyone ever been successful with changing my mind once I have made a decision, Kakizawa-san?" He remained polite to the accountant, even though he was going to instruct his lawyer to fire him the moment he entered the next world. He hated this man as much as he did the killer of his son.

"No, never can I remember you ever changing your mind, once it was made up on a certain decision good or bad, Asahiko-san."

"Good. Then why in the devil are you still wasting breath arguing with my decision? You're guilty of arguing over shadows that can't be seen, fate, Karma, whatever drives the will of us."

"Because Asahiko-san, this decision is dead wrong and it must not come to past."

"Right or wrong, good or bad for Japan's future or her history, it's my decision to make which has been pissed upon, and the sand of truth kicked on it to seal its fate forever, and it'll stand the way I decreed it to be, so save your fruit. Do you think my mind would have been persuaded for the honor of a soft teat to suckle on, a moist Jade Gate to slip my shriveled and forgot serpent into, as you had suggested? No Kakizawa-san, leave Karma to Karma, life to life, to be is to be, so be it. What cannot be avoided must be for history to learn from. My business will be sold to the American, and there's nothing either of my friends can do about it, Kakizawa-san."

He suddenly understood his thinking nothing he tried would possibly sway the old man from selling his construction company to the American. With a deep sigh of total surrender he offered. "Asahiko-san, it's my fault if your Wa was disturbed by any of my angry words. I beg forgiveness sir. What is it you wish me to do in the assistance of the sale of your business, sir?"

"That's better on your part Kakizawa-san I want you to prepare a prospectus, complete with figures and balance sheets, include our expansion and future rate which is exceptional if I remember correctly. Encompass all my stock holdings, along with a thorough list of all my heavy equipment, land holdings, future deals, and all offerings we're interested in. I must bid you to use your head most wisely on this order you know how to make my business a must to be had by this Gai Jin. I'll leave this all up to your wise skills and knowledge, sir."

"Asahiko-san, I trust you want to include your private shares of stock in with this sale?" He asked, his voice betraying his want not to include Asahiko's stock shares in the deal.

"Yes, I demanded everything to be included in the sale of my construction company to the Gai Jin from across the Ocean, Kakizawa-san!" He growled at his accountant.

"Yes, I understand Asahiko-san. It'll be as you have instructed me my old friend."

"Very good, I knew I could count on you when help was needed by me, Katizawa-san. How long will it take for you to accomplish my request to be completed, and have the papers on my desk at the Castle, sir?" the old man groused, unable to hide the anger in his tone.

"Iieeeee... Asahiko-san, if I was to work throughout the entire night, I could probably have the documents prepared and on your desk by tomorrow afternoon at the earliest..."

"Tomorrow morning will be soon enough for my likes I assure you, Kakizawa-san!" He warned unpleasantly, hating the man more than ever with each passing word he spoke.

"Hai Asahiko-san, tomorrow morning at eleven you'll have the papers in your possession?"

"By nine you offer me!" He interrupted the accountant a second time as he waited again.

"Hai sir, nine o'clock it shall be, Asahiko-san." Kakizawa corrected himself.

"Very good, I thank you for your time and patience over this trying matter, sir. You may leave this conversation and get started with your weighted paperwork. I wish to speak to Nagaro-san, privately." Asahiko moaned, knowing he was forced to put off his death until tomorrow night.

"Hai Asahiko-san." Kakizawa replied sadly as he hung up as ordered.

"Nagaro-san!" He demanded angrily, startling Nagaro momentarily on the phone.

"Hai sir I'm still here sir, and am waiting for your further orders, Asahiko-san."

"Good Nagaro-san, prepare papers for the dismissal of the useless and weak will Kakizawa, sir. I have decided I'll not be leaving him a thing after I passed to the other world of wonderment. All he gets from my company is two week's severance pay and nothing more. I owe the old fool that much, but no other aggrandizement is he entitled to enjoy from the sale of my company, Nagaro-san. I'm deeply insulted by his disrespectful arguments, and lack of good manners and diplomacy he displayed during this conversation. I no longer trust a man who'd drink his own cursed urine with the future of my company and any other dealings of my world."

"I'm sorry to offer my old friend. I knew you had that in mind, Asahiko-san. I read your mind. I began a document while waiting for you to finish your conversation with the foolish Kakizawa. I too no longer trust the man as far as I can throw him. If he was prepared to fight you on this decision, he'd only create problems once you left this world for the

Floating World, sir." Neither man was honoring the accountant by adding the san to his name as they referred to him. All pretense of civility was erased from their conversation when they were referring to Kakizawa.

"What do you mean by that last remark to me, Nagaro-san?"

"My friend, when do you plan to commit the honored act of Suppuku, Asahiko-san?" He asked as he shifted his weight and waited for him to reply. He knew since the conversation began between them he made up his mind to end his life, and he wanted his company sold.

"Huh my suddenly all seeing lawyer, what makes you believe I intend to do away with my worthless old self by my hand Nagaro-san, who can now see my inner thoughts and plans for my future." He asked as he became concerned his lawyer was able to see what he had on his mind.

"Asahiko-san, you're selling your company to a lowly Gai Jin. At a price well below what you should attain for your most honorable company. Your honorable son and his lovely wife were slaughtered in the old ways, savagely. It's only fitting if one intends to follow his son into the never lands, he'd adopt the ways of the old to accomplish this great feat with honor and respect, sir." The lawyer warned, knowing these words were what he was looking to hear from him.

Asahiko's shoulders sagged as he gave up all outward signs of trying to deceive his wise lawyer in their conversation. "Huh! How well you understand my deepest thoughts I see, Nagaro-san. I should've known I couldn't hide a thought from your all seeing mind my old friend. I'd never defile the great honor of my respected ancestors by committing suicide in any other form. I'm afraid I'm ready to die because

I'm so tired of this worthless life without my son to enjoy. Life is no longer a pleasure to dwell in without my son to share life with my existence no longer holds my desire. Life and death is but the same. It's a terrible punishment to outlive one's son, unthinkable. I thank the gods for your kind assistance and diligence to your yoshi gi, one's duty to me. Without your wise mind, my company wouldn't be what it is today. Do I shame you by what I intend to do?" The concerned old man suddenly asked of his lawyer for many years.

"Quite the contrary, I have nothing but the greatest of respect and honor for what you're about to do, Asahiko-san. It takes a man of great love and respect for his child to want to follow his son to the unknown world, to once again be able to stand by his side and faithfully and help guide him in the new world of the afterlife, as you have guided his honorable life in this world. It honors your great ancestors to spill ones innards upon the sacred soil of Japan. It nourishes the mighty dragon's spine on which Japan rests its faithful soul upon. As I asked, when do you plan to carry out this act, Asahiko-san?" He asked concerned for the old man's spirit and mental state.

"Nagaro-san, I plan to do away with my worthless old self on this night. But since that great fool of a dung heap of an accountant of mine can't possibly complete the minor paperwork task that I have requested of him until tomorrow morning at the earliest, it seems that I'm suddenly forced to put off my worthless death until after that time my old friend."

"Errr..." Nagaro hesitated momentarily making it known he had something else to offer.

"No Nagaro-san, please do me a large favor and don't ask that question of me, allow me to make you the offer, sir." He said as if he was now able to read his lawyer's mind.

"Hai!" Nagaro offered kindly, he was surprised the old man knew what he was going to ask.

"Nagaro-san, I want you to secure the bonds that are safely locked away in my safe. It'll sustain you and your family until you finally grow as weary as I of life, and the pain of old bones cause one's self. I know you..." The old man's words were cut off by his lawyer.

"Asahiko-san, that's too much for my services. I can't in good conscience take such a fortune. Surely, you must have a relative, an old lover or friend you'd want me to share it with."

"Nonsense Nagaro-san. You're more than worthy of the worthless payment I offer your loyal services over the past years. I have no one in this entire world I'd trust with such a great fortune. No one I love more than you. You have earned every cent I offer you for your services Nagaro-san, for your unending loyalty and unending friendship of this old tired man. I'll leave you an envelope in my safe for the other worthless son I have dwelling on this earth. Even though I said time and again I'll never leave him anything from my company for his failure to assist in the running of my business. I decided before I leave for the other world, it might be wise if I mend bridges with him. You'll make certain the lazy one receives this envelope, Nagaro-san. Oh yes, one o nega, a favor I must beg from you before I enter the next world, my old friend."

"Asahiko-san, I'll make certain that your surviving son receives the envelope you're leaving for him. Sir, you can ask of me any favor and I'll fulfill that request, if it's within my power to do so." His lawyer replied with the greatest respect in his tone.

"It is Nagaro-san, it's within your power to grant and carry out this favor I beg of you. I want you to promise that you'll make certain the sale of my company with the American goes through without hindrance, you'll make certain of this deal, or you'll die forcing the deal to its final completion. You must not allow the worthless Kakizawa to disrupt my plans in any way, shape or form. You must even be prepared to kill, or have him killed if he goes to the government, and gets in the way of this deal. I have one important reason to sell my construction business to the lowly Gai Jin, rather than any Japanese businessman of this land. If something happens to this deal and my sale is blocked by any means, I'll never be able to rest in peace in the afterworld of never, Nagaro-san. I can't tell you how deeply important it is to me for this worthless deal to go through as I have planned for it to be completed."

"You need not explain anything further to this old fool but loyal of a retainer, Asahiko-san. I know why it's this important to sell your honorable business to the foolish American, sir." The old man's lawyer replied as he actually tried to see his face through the phone.

"Again my all seeing lawyer, you surprise me by proposing you have some secret window in which to look through, to see my inner thoughts and respects, Nagaro-san. If you possess the ability to see the unseen things so clearly then you must share this power with me for one minute of time. So before I die I can discover the detestable being that had my beloved son murdered so terribly, so savagely. Oh, to have revenge on his loathsome soul before I leave this world of pain and sorrow and disappointment." He moaned with sorrow and pain as he stared in the phone, trying to see his lawyer and friend's face on the other end of the line.

"I'm afraid it's no mystery in how I read your cunning mind, Asahiko-san. I know you want the Gai Jin to have your business to keep it out of the hands of that mongrel of a man, Hiromoai, sir. If it's the last thing I do before I die, I'll find the miserable one responsible for your son and his wife's death, and prove the foul killer to the world, so they could deal justice for the creature. So the proper authorities can melt out your final revenge and justice on his evil shoulders, Asahiko-san." Nagaro proudly boasted to the old man as he too looked in the phone, as if in an attempt to see Asahiko's aged and proud face over it, as he waited for him to speak again.

"Again my all seeing Nagaro-san, you surprise me by your uncanny ability to read my thoughts and desires. You're correct in your assumption of Hiromoai, and he's the reason why I want this lowly Gai Jin to end up with my honorable company. Bah, I grow so wary of this boring and most upsetting conversation we're presently engaging in. You'll make certain this deal reaches its achievement as I have ordered it to take place." The old man demanded of the lawyer as he sighed over the phone and struggled to get his breathing and trembling under control.

"Hai, this I swear with my dying breath and loyalty it shall be as you have requested of me, Asahiko-san." His lawyer replied as he calmed down and waited for his reply.

"I hope it doesn't come down to that kind of decision being cast upon your honorable head by the foul winds of fate, my old friend of too many years to count. Kon banwa, good evening Nagaro-san. I trust I'll see you tomorrow afternoon, before I start off on my last journey into the land we only dared to dream and wonder about. I'll only be relieved of this great pain and burden I'm forced to suffer with, when I'm able to rest my arse in a cloud seat, and see my most honorable son's face once more." Again, he gave an exhausted sigh.

"Kon banwa Asahiko-san. May the gods who control such things, help guide you faithfully to their protective bosom, and then assist you in your unending search in the afterlife for your well honored and loving son. My thoughts will be with you as always in the hereafter as it was when your world was right, Asahiko-san. I shall offer many sticks of incense and prays to the Lord Buddha to keep your fine spirit and the spirit of your honored son safe for all time to come."

HATANAKA TOWERS, HIROMOAI'S PENTHOUSE
6:30 A.M. SATURDAY, JUNE 8th, 1996

Hiromoai woke to the sound of Lady Yoke working in the kitchen, and again he slept on the floor with Wind tucked protectively by his side. He was still exhausted from their long night of lovemaking. She was like a wild cat unable to be satisfied, when they finished making love, she found other interesting ways of arousing him until they made love three times throughout the night. The last thing he remembered of the wonderful night, was she trying to get him ready for a fourth time with her mouth. But when he could not rise to the occasion, she reluctantly gave up and snuggled in by his side and fell asleep.

He felt her body pressed against his, but hers felt unusually stiff, almost as if she was on guard, aware of what was happening even while sleeping. The moment he moved, she sat up like a startled cat, and turned to him and smiled. "Huh, I see you didn't sleep a wink last night, did you? You have to learn to relax while visiting the living world, enjoying its countless wonders."

"Ieeeee! Does my Lord not think I would carry out my yoshi gi? My duty is to protect your life even while you are sleeping, my Lord." As she kept a watchful eye on her master during the night, her mind wandered, remembering the words Lord Kawasomeru said as she died. 'Wind-san, your brave life experiences and accomplishments will forever be written on the clouds of time and history, so they will be read about every time the sky nurtures the earth. For future lifetimes yet to be unfolded, your name will be spoken with the honor and respect it deserves'.

To remember these words from Lord Kawasomeru, forced her to attend to her duty of protecting her new lord with every breath she consumed, and every thought she had.

"When will you catch up on your needed sleep, Wind-san?" Hiromoai asked concerned as he got up on his elbow and looked into her delicious and caring eyes.

"My Master, I have no need of sleep like the spirits of the living world require in order to maintain their life and health. A short nap renews me, so I am ready to carry out your orders without hesitation. It is a gift showered on this worthless Samurai from the Floating World, and the Kami who dwell there. My Lord should not be concerned over my well being and health. It is my duty to protect you above all else." She bowed politely to him as he struggled to his feet.

He bent his back on the floor then stretched his arms over his head, to work out some of the nagging kinks and knots the hardwood floor placed in his body. Then he got up and stood over her, naked and proud. She reached up and began to play with him again.

"Please allow me to retain some of my strength in my body for the unlimited toils that lay ahead on this beginning day." He grunted with a smile as he turned his hip and she let go of him.

She smiled as she offered. "What brings you pleasure, you must do much my Lord, for pleasure gives light heartiness to your head, and works amazement for your soul and peace of mind, my Master. What does my Lord have planned for this worthless Samurai to accomplish for today while you're searching the Castle wall for the hidden entrance to the secret passage?"

"That's a good question Samurai. You'll do nothing but rest for your laborious mission later tonight. Lady Yoke will take care of you while I'm on my mission to see if the hidden passage is still there. You're free to take a hot bath, enjoy food and rest." He wiggled in his pants.

She rose like a mid summer breeze and slipped in her exquisite kimono.

Lady Yoke was in the kitchen working while trying to control the beat of her heart, she was angry and did not realize she was making a racket attending to her chores. When she woke, she looked in the study and noticed them lying side by side on the floor, they were naked and peaceful. She cursed the Kami gods that controlled all things in the world, for not making it be her sleeping under the protective arm of Hiromoai. Since that most disturbing vision assaulted her eyes she was unable to control her temper, and it grew with every duty she carried out. It was the noise she created that woke him from his sleep.

He walked in the kitchen as Lady Yoke slammed a pot on the counter and barked. "Lady Yoke! What has your blood boiling? I never saw you in such a state. I'm afraid if this keeps up, everything in the kitchen will be destroyed. Calm down and tell me what's bothering you."

Hiromoai was joined by Wind who got up and followed him into the kitchen. She stared at her highly agitated friend being glared at by him. She lowered her head in sadness the moment he spoke angrily at Lady Yoke because she understood what was driving the fire beneath her skin. The fact she spent the entire night with him, her wanted lover.

She bowed as she begged forgiveness from Hiromoai. "Please excuse the stupidity of this vile old woman, Hiromoai-san. It's my foolish actions that upset your Wa on this beautiful morning." She longed to share the peace of the sunrise with him as he promised the day before, but he forgot to share with her since this female warrior took up his spare time.

Wind saw the confrontation between Lady Yoke and her master and slowly backed out of the kitchen, and leaned against the hall wall and sighed deeply, sad she was the cause of the troubled mind locked in her new friend's body. She vowed she would find that special way to make it up to Lady Yoke. She tried to think of a way to bring the two people of the living world together, so she could share the joy of pillowing with her experienced lord and master.

"Will you never mind my Wa, woman! I repeat, what the devil has you upset, Lady Yoke? I never saw you act like this."

He demanded while allowing his voice to rise higher in anger now.

"Alas Hiromoai-san, I fear this ashamed woman woke in the most foulest of moods, and been taking my anger out on the poor pots of the kitchen. I'm not worthy to work in your home. I should be whipped, and turned out on the streets and shunned by every honorable Japanese person who crosses my worthless path. I should be marked on the face for all to see my disgrace for upsetting your great Wa. I'm an inconsiderate and vastly stupid vassal, Hiromoai-san." She cried as she looked up from her kneeling position, and looked into the staring and burning eyes of Hiromoai, her disgrace was written clearly across her lovely face.

"Lady Yoke, I don't understand why you're so upset on this day. You did nothing more than display a little anger for some reason I'm not aware of. Even though a show of anger is shameful and childish, it's nothing to beg such a harsh punishment for. Hmmm... Could it be that time of the month and you don't realize it as such, Lady Yoke?"

Her face flushed with embarrassment, it was the height of foul manners for any Japanese person to speak of such a personal problem as her period, especially from a male. She was shocked by the unexpected comment she was unable to respond to his words in her angered state.

"Oh come on will you please, this is the twentieth century for the love of God. Relax, the old taboos of the ancient past are long ago forgotten as they should be, as are the ways of the old, Lady Yoke. My question wasn't meant for your embarrassment, it was meant to give you an excuse for your actions. Ahhh... never mind dammit, I don't have time for this crap. Your infraction is nothing to be punished over, is breakfast ready?" He looked at his watch, it was ten of nine. He was dismayed it was so late he considered not going to the office at all today.

He did not know how long it was going to take to reach and search the walls of Engakuji Castle. He thought for a few seconds, trying to remember if any work meetings were scheduled today. He could not remember a single one important enough to force him to go to the office. He was exhausted, and sore as hell from sleeping on the hard floor for the night.

"Dammit, it's so late I think I'm going to put off going to the office today. Lady Yoke, I want you to call my secretary and tell her I'm feeling a little under the weather, and not coming to the office today. Tell her to cancel all my scheduled meetings for today, have her spread them throughout next week, the most important ones for early week. It's Saturday, and I think I'm entitled to take one Saturday off every once in a while dammit."

"Hai Hiromoai-san, if anyone deserves a day off from work, it's surely you sir." Lady Yoke replied kindly, relieved to be out from under the conversation of what was bothering her. She rose and then bowed to Hiromoai who nodded back over her politeness.

When everything calmed down, Wind entered the kitchen and looked at them.

Utsumi worked so late last night on detailing the paintings and engravings on some armor and weapons he ended up sleeping in one of the spare rooms. He entered the kitchen wrapped up in his favorite faded cotton kimono. His face needed a shave and he seemed to be dirty of body, and he sat next to Wind across from Hiromoai and then waited to be served by Lady Yoke.

Wind barely acknowledged his presence she disliked the old man so and did not trust him.

Hiromoai nodded to the old man as he seated himself and got comfortable and picked at his cooling eggs. He was unaware Utsumi was in his apartment. He was angered because of it.

After they ate, Yoke cleared the table and went to her room to call his secretary as ordered.

Wind wanted to follow Lady Yoke to her room, but did not dare because she was not dismissed by Hiromoai. She wanted to get out from under the upsetting gaze of Utsumi. She noticed him trying to look down the front of her kimono and pulled it tighter around her.

"Utsumi, next time you spend the night, you make damn certain I'm aware you're here, old fool. I don't like to be surprised like I was this morning, and especially this early in the morning as well mister." He glared at the old man until Utsumi lowered his head and then he stared at the table's surface to get out of his angry glare.

She picked up the anger in Hiromoai's voice and this sent her senses running wild. She would love to erase this old man. She stared at Utsumi, looking for any sign of treachery from him so she could react and kill him. None came as he sat remorsefully.

Hiromoai picked up the threatening look from Wind aimed at Utsumi, and understood his life was in serious danger. He was about to say something when there was a knock on the door. He looked to the door and turned to Utsumi and ordered. "Utsumi, take Wind to my room and stay with her until I find out who the hell this is. Don't make a sound up there I don't want anyone to know she's here. Take the sword with you in case you have to send her back to the Floating World. If I start upstairs without calling out your name first Utsumi, you must return her to her world of the dead before she's discovered inside the apartment."

"Hai Hiromoai-san." Utsumi nodded as he replied and stood and waited for Wind to stand, he went in the study and picked up the ancient killing sword and wooden scabbard and led the way as she followed him to Hiromoai's bedroom.

"Yoke! I have need of your services at once." He bellowed as he came out of the kitchen.

She rushed out of her bedroom with the phone glued to her ear. She wore a shocked expression as she stared at her master. The way he called out to her, she feared he decided to dismiss her after all, for her actions of earlier in the kitchen.

"There's someone knocking at the damn door. Answer it for me!"

"Hai." She finished with Hiromoai's secretary and headed for the door.

He got up and hurried to the study, he quickly cleared up the makeshift bed they had shared the night before from the floor and then he sat on the couch and picked up a magazine and slowly thumbed through it absentmindedly. He acted like he had no worries in the world as he carelessly flipped through the colored pages of the magazine, while sneaking quick little peeks at Lady Yoke walking to see who was at the door.

She opened the door while holding the phone in her hand, her smile left as she found herself glaring at Lieutenant Kenzaburo Motoshima. He smiled the instant she opened the door for him. But it was wasted on the woman who ignored the pleasantry and snapped angrily at the officer.

"Huh, what the devil do you want at my Master's door again, you foul fool? Take your foul manners and crawl back under the rock you have slimed your way out from underneath on this day. My Master has no time in his day to waste for the likes of you."

"Your Master?" Lieutenant Motoshima asked surprised at how she addressed Hiromoai.

She ignored the snide from the detective remark as she repeated. "What do you want Officer!"

"Is Hiromoai-san at home Lady Yoke? I'm sorry to announce but I must speak with him again." Lieutenant Motoshima had committed her name to memory the last time he visited Hiromoai as he added. "I checked with his office this morning and the secretary said she didn't expect him in today. It's imperative that I speak to Hiromoai-san at once, young lady. Please, if he's home, see if he'd indulge me with a few moments of his valuable time."

"My Master's far too busy to waste his time on you. Go from my door before I call security and have you thrown from the Tower. And don't dare to address me as your friend, sir."

The Lieutenant lost his cool and snapped at the young lady blocking the door. "Now you look here missy, I don't have the time to waste either. So if Hiromoai-san's home and you refuse to tell him I'm wishing to speak with him again. I'll return to the station and write out an arrest warrant for him then, you'll have no further say in the matter. You'll be forced to allow me in. Please Lady Yoke, I don't want to travel down that road against Hiromoai-san. Right now, this is an unofficial visit I'm offering him today. If I need a warrant then it's out of my hands and it becomes an official visit and in doing so, it becomes public information at the same time. You don't want a wave of nosy news reporters flooding your apartment do you, Lady Yoke?"

"No she doesn't and neither do I Lieutenant Motoshima-san is it?" Hiromoai asked as he walked up behind Lady Yoke and rested his hand lightly on her slender but tensed shoulder.

"Yes Hiromoai-san, you surprise and honor me by remembering my name. Thank you sir."

"Let's just say that you really impressed me on your last visit to my home, and let it go at that for the time being Lieutenant. To what do I owe the honor of this latest visit to my home, sir? You said something about it being an unofficial visit today, Officer. Please sir, come in and tell me what brings you back to my front door, Lieutenant Motoshima-san?" He had to actually take Lady Yoke by the shoulder to move her away from blocking the door.

"Hiromoai-san, I'm sorry for disturbing you on your day off, sir. But I was led to believe you always worked every Saturday, sir. That's why I decided to try my luck and meet you at your office in private, sir." The Lieutenant bowed to him for allowing him to speak with him again.

"Usually, I'm in my office every Saturday, but these past few days have been most trying on my shoulders Officer and I decided to take off for today and rest and regain my strength."

"You need not explain why you decided to take a day off, Hiromoai-san. Your business is your business to enjoy, sir." Lieutenant Motoshima offered as he took the chair.

"Thank you for keeping your nose out of my personal business, Officer!"

The Lieutenant picked up the underlining sarcastic tone lacing his voice, but chose to overlook it. He did not need an angry Hiromoai fighting his every question, while he was searching for answers and the truth from him. They remained silent until seated in the study.

Hiromoai sat back and clasped his hands together, and then he let out his breath as he stared at the Lieutenant for several long seconds then asked. "Why the hell are you here Lieutenant? I believe I told you all I know about the death of poor Tsutomu-san. I'm not very fond of these intrusions by the police in my private life, Officer. Have you had any luck discovering the yakuza (gangsters) responsible for the savage death of Yurkowa-san and his lovely wife, Lieutenant?"

"I'm terribly sorry but this visit has nothing to do with Tsutomu-san's death this time, Hiromoai-san. It's only a matter of time before we finally catch up to the killer of Yurkowa-san and his poor wife, sir. There's another reason for my wanting to speak with you on this day I'm afraid, Hiromoai-san." The detective offered to the powerful Japanese businessman.

"Is that so then why are you at my apartment, Lieutenant? And is this visit off the record as before, Officer?" Again, the sarcasm returned to his sharp tone as he stared at the officer.

"Of course this conversation's off the record unless I discover something that might help in my investigation, sir. I'm sorry sir, but I don't know any polite way of putting this Hiromoai-san..."

"Please, there's no need to stand on any false formalities here sir. I have absolutely nothing to hide from the police. Especially if this conversation is off the record as you have just stated to me sir. Are you having any progress with your investigation on Yurkowa-san's death, Lieutenant?" Hiromoai repeated, trying to get any information from the one seeking it from him.

"I'm afraid that I'm running into a stone wall on my investigation in Yurkowa-san and his wife's death, Hiromoai-san. It seems that no one in Japan knows the stable this contemptible assassin is committed to sir. I spoke to the Kaminari (Thunder tribes) to see if this kobun (soldier) was one of theirs. I also spoke with the Bosozoku, the biker gangs had no information they could, or were willing to share with me, Hiromoai-san. But I have no doubt this foul killer has left some clues behind, every killer always does. I never met one who didn't, and when I discover them I'll get him and make him pay for what he has done to Asahiko-san's son."

"Maybe this killer is a Gai-Jin, imported solely to carry out the horrible deed, Lieutenant?"

"I seriously doubt that Hiromoai-san, there's no honorable Japanese who would employ an outsider, sir. But I'll look into that suggestion, Hiromoai-san. Thank you for suggesting it. Japan and China have enough assassins to choose from, without importing any from America or Europe. Honor among thieves I guess sir. But I'll get him have no fear of that Hiromoai-san."

"I thought you told me you had some reports stating that this lowly killer was possibly a female killer, Lieutenant?" Hiromoai remarked as he looked the lieutenant in the eyes.

The confused Lieutenant Motoshima shook his head as if he was lost for a moment and then he stated. "That's what's making this damn investigation so difficult for us to solve. It seems none of the cult's who offer killers for hire, employs the services of a female assassin sir. I made numerous inquiries in China to see if any triads there might have sent this assassin to our shores, sir. There again I'm running into a block wall. When I asked the Hong Kong police if they knew of any possible female assassins working, they practically laughed me off the damn phone. But it makes no difference whether or not this killer is male or female, Hiromoai-san.

"I'm going to find the damn killer and when I finally do I'll bring him or her to justice but quick, sir. I just wish everyone I speak to would be honest with me for once in their worthless lives, dammit. The old ways of not trusting the police are so entrenched in the mind of the public of Japan, they fear for their lives if a police officer dares ask them any questions, sir. The gangs and cults have everyone so damn scared to death to even speak to the police. This fear of speaking to us is severely hampering my duties, sir."

"Again Lieutenant, I repeat I have nothing to hide from anyone, especially the police sir." Hiromoai replied as he allowed a bit of disgust and anger to enter his tone again.

"I didn't mean to hypothesize you had something to hide from me, or anyone else for that matter, Hiromoai-san." The detective offered politely as he bowed towards the seated Hiromoai.

"Please Lieutenant it's too early in the day to engage in a battle of social graces with you, sir. I repeat Officer, what the devil brings you back to my home this early in the only day I decided to take off for myself, if this visit has nothing to do with the death of poor Yurkowa-san and his wife as you just offered me, sir. Then what's this visit over Lieutenant Motoshima-san?"

"It'd be much simpler if I was able to speak more direct with you during this conversation, Hiromoai-san." He replied to the Japanese businessman.

"Please do Lieutenant, in that way, maybe we can conclude this troublesome conversation before the weekend is over with, sir. I have other matters on my mind I must attend to today Lieutenant Motoshima-san." He snapped at the young police officer.

"I understand you're a very busy man, Hiromoai-san. I'm deeply honored you allowed time so I might speak with you like this sir. Hiromoai-san, it has come to my attention that you had a meeting with Asahiko-san in the park yesterday afternoon, and the meeting was far from a very friendly one when it concluded, sir." The concerned Lieutenant offered.

"How the hell do you know about my meeting with Asahiko-san in the park the other day, Lieutenant Motoshima-san?" Hiromoai barked nastily as he glared at the detective.

"Please Hiromoai-san, it's like I said, there's no delicate or polite way of entering this troubling conversation, sir. Let's just say it came to my attention and let it go at that sir." The Lieutenant used the same phrase he used on him earlier in their conversation.

Hiromoai nodded as he replied to the officer's last remark. "Huh, I take it you must have had me trailed at my meeting with Asahiko-san yesterday, Lieutenant!"

Now it was Lieutenant Motoshima who nodded at Hiromoai, and allowed a slight smirk of a smile as he stared at the powerful Japanese businessman.

"I should've known you would've done something as crude as that, Lieutenant. I guess if I was trapped in your position, perhaps I would've have had you trailed as well, Lieutenant."

"Perhaps so Hiromoai-san." The detective snapped without thinking about it, allowing a touch of sarcasm to creep in his voice. He no longer felt he had to deal with Hiromoai with kid gloves.

"Please Lieutenant Motoshima-san, can we proceed with this unending and most upsetting conversation, sir!" Hiromoai moaned at the boring detective this time.

"Yes, by all means Hiromoai-san. The reason I returned to your apartment today, is because I'm aware of the slight confrontation that occurred between Asahiko-san and yourself yesterday, sir. I'm rather interested in what exchanged between the two most powerful and elite men in all Japan, to cause one to strike out in anger against the other, sir. It was a terrible insult delivered against your person by the elderly Asahiko-san, Hiromoai-san." Lieutenant Motoshima stared at Hiromoai to see if he was going to try and lie to him.

"As well you should be Officer. It's not often that I allow an old man to work out his deep frustrations upon the side of my face, Lieutenant. If you know what I mean sir?" He smirked as he rubbed the side of his face and then grinned at the Lieutenant.

"Then you admit Asahiko-san slapped you yesterday, Hiromoai-san?"

"Sure, why the hell should I try and deny it, especially if you had me tailed as you said, and the incident was witnessed by one of your people, Officer? The slap occurred because of my foolish indiscretion committed against Asahiko-san, sir. That's why I allowed it to go unanswered like I did sir. It was entirely my fault for the angry response by the old man, Officer."

"Indiscretion you say Hiromoai-san?" Lieutenant Motoshima asked with surprise in his tone.

"Yes Lieutenant, I believed Asahiko-san might be tired of his construction company, and I foolishly offered to take it off his hands, freeing the old man so he can enjoy his remaining years without the constant problems of the construction field weighing heavy on his mind sir. To be quite honest with you Lieutenant, I'm kind of looking forward to the day when I can finally hang up the stressing toils of construction life myself, sir. I'm growing rather tired of it, it's not like it once was in the past. Now, the government wants to know too much of my business, and they cut too deeply into my profits at the same time, sir. Anyway Officer, I offered Asahiko-san a fair and going price for his honorable company might I add, Lieutenant Motoshima-san."

"Of course you did Hiromoai-san. I never suggested you were an un-honorable man, sir."

"Of course you didn't Officer. Perhaps I'm being a little too sensitive over this matter and this conversation, sir." Hiromoai replied, his voice was laced with sarcasm.

"Perhaps, and this offer was the reason for Asahiko-san's rash reaction against you, sir?"

"Yes, I admit I was kind of surprised by the attack Lieutenant. I thought I was helping Asahiko-san out it was what I had in mind. But to receive a slap in the face for my kind offer was totally unexpected, sir. I guess it was one of the other reasons I didn't react against it, Officer."

"And the other reasons might be Hiromoai-san? To slap any Japanese person is a terrible insult, one that must be answered to." The police officer asked him cautiously.

"Lieutenant! I don't believe I like the way you're speaking to me, sir. Remove the nasty tone from your damn voice sir." Hiromoai shot a hot glare at the seated and young Japanese officer.

"I'm sorry Hiromoai-san, these questions must be asked, even if they cross the lines of good manners and taste, sir. I'm trying to finish my investigation, and to do that I must be meticulous, leaving no stone unturned, no bush unruffled, sir. I can't impress on you, how much pressure the government's placing on my shoulder to clear this baffling mystery up. It's not every day the son of one of Japan's most influential businessmen is slaughtered while he's asleep in his bedroom, and no one saw or could offer a description of the intruder, sir. With the trouble exploding in the Middle East of late, we have to make certain there are no international terrorists at work in Japan. I'm sorry if my questions are insulting, Hiromoai-san. But as I stated, they're questions begging to be asked and answered, sir." The Detective Lieutenant shrugged and stared at Hiromoai.

"Perhaps, but you can keep a civil tongue in your god damn mouth while speaking to me."

"Hai. Please forgive my foolishness Hiromoai-san." Lieutenant Motoshima replied as he bowed politely at the rather upset acting Hiromoai.

"Very well Officer, where were we in this unpleasant conversation, Lieutenant?"

"Hiromoai-san, you said one of the reasons for not reacting against the insult from Asahiko-san, was because it was unexpected, and I asked if there were other reasons for you to hold your temper against him." The Lieutenant let out his breath, he knew he was insulting Hiromoai, but he was determined to get to the bottom of this case no matter whose toes he might step on.

"Yes, quite right Lieutenant Motoshima-san. You're correct, there were other reasons that I chose to overlook the terrible actions of the feeble old and deeply troubled Asahiko-san. The main one was because I took into consideration of the old man losing his honorable son and daughter-in-law in a most savage way, by a hired assassin no less who works in..."

"I can understand that, are there any other reasons you might see, Hiromoai-san?"

"Yes Lieutenant, how could I possibly attack an old man such as Asahiko-san, and retain face in Japan? If I was to dare strike a man old enough to be my father, I'd have to fear my father's angry reaction, even from the grave sir. I was brought up much better than that, to respect my elders and ancestors, Lieutenant. Even if Asahiko-san chose to act like a wild dog snarling at the hand that's feeding him, it's not going to make me stoop to his level, Lieutenant Motoshima-san." He looked at the concerned officer as if to say the slap was of no big deal anyhow.

"Are there any other reasons you might have held your anger in check, Hiromoai-san?"

"What other fucking reason could there possibly be Lieutenant? Those few I offered should be more than enough for you to understand my lack of reaction against the suffering old man, sir." Hiromoai snapped angrily, not liking where this conversation with the detective was heading.

"I'm sorry Hiromoai-san. Please forgive me in advance, but I must make this comment to you, sir." Lieutenant Motoshima offered with caution lacing his voice.

"Then make your god damn comment and get it over with will you please. So I can finally get about my own business on this foul day, Lieutenant!" Hiromoai snarled, not trying to hide the anger building up in his body any longer, because this police officer returned to his apartment, and he was again bothering him with more boring and most insulting questions he had no intention of answering honestly for the officer.

"Like not striking Asahiko-san because you were remorseful for having his son killed sir?"

Hiromoai glared angrily at the Lieutenant, his body actually shaking with rage.

Lieutenant Motoshima had to sit back because the look was so chilling. Without a word, he rose and walked over to the wall covered with ancient swords. He picked out an old katana and removed it from the wall. As he walked back to the chair, he angrily pulled the aged sword from the scabbard, and pitched the wood cover on the chair, and then he stood menacingly before the worried looking Lieutenant with the killing sword locked in his hand.

With nothing but hatred burning in his eyes, he aimed the blade right at Motoshima's face. He dared to lift the officer's chin with the end of the tip of the blade as he snarled. "Lieutenant! It's only because I fucking chose to remain a civilized man that your head is still attached to your insulting shoulders. Here's advice for you to practice, Officer. Respect Lieutenant. Always make certain you respect the one you're speaking to under any circumstances sir. For the moment you become uncivilized to him, you erased the civilization from the other person's soul you were speaking with, fool. How fucking dare you try and lay the blame on me of such a crime, Officer!

"I repeat Lieutenant, how dare you ask such a fucking question of me! Me! One of Japan's most respected and powerful businessmen, I should demand satisfaction from your worthless body, sir." He pointed his free hand at his chest as he glared at the detective while leaving the sword dangle so dangerously close to the Lieutenant's face.

Lieutenant Motoshima sat frozen in place, the coldness of the razor sharp steel of the blade barely touching his throat, sent shivers down his spine. At first, he thought about reaching for his service revolver, but decided against it. He knew no matter what he said to him, the businessman would never kill or harm him with the deadly blade. What the officer was hoping for was if he was behind this assassin's actions, he could get him mad enough for Hiromoai to send the killer after him. Besides, there was something locked in his eyes besides hatred that interested him, and he read it to take he was angry, but not angry enough to kill him. He cautiously raised his hand and placed two fingers on the back side of the deadly katana blade, and with pressure he forced it away from his throat, never once taking his eyes from Hiromoai's.

He allowed the officer to move the threatening blade from his neck with his hand.

The Lieutenant relaxed when the blade was far enough away from his body.

Hiromoai aimed the blade at the floor, but held the Lieutenant locked in his angry glare for several intense moments, and then he spoke in a controlled voice. "Lieutenant, in all the days I walked upon the soil of Japan, never had I been accused of such a foul and despicable act. Yes, certainly I'm hell to fucking work with, or for. I'd try and bluff an old woman out of her finest kimono to get a god damn job or make money. But fucking murder, never Lieutenant, I happen to like and respect Asahiko-san. I loved his foolish son he never did anything to upset or anger me, never, Officer. I enjoyed the battle of wits I locked in with him over business reasons.

"But that was all it was, just business, Lieutenant. Not fucking murder! If I had to resort to killing all my competition in the construction field, where the hell would I be? There are five major construction companies in all Japan. Damn, if I killed one, wouldn't I have to kill them all for hell's sake and fury? No Lieutenant, I'm sorry, but you're wasting your fucking time and mine as well, if you think I had anything to do with the murder of poor Yurkowa-san. Where in the hell would I get a damn assassin from anyway, Lieutenant?

"I don't know the first fucking thing about that dark side of life, or where to go to acquire the services of one of these pieces of filth. I'm a construction man Officer, not a fool involved with drugs, or gangs and gangsters, or gun running and Ninjas lowlifes and the likes. If those insulting words came from anyone else but you, that fool would no longer be breathing in this world. I'm highly insulted by your evil words offered me, and I'll never forget them, Officer."

He hardened his glare aimed at the officer, making him shift nervously in the chair. His mind went to Wind and he mumbled under his breath. 'Fool, if Wind was in our presence when you first spoke those ugly words against me, your soul would be drawing its first breath in the Floating World. I have a good mind to allow Wind to visit you one night, and you'll see firsthand the power that's mine alone to control'.

Lieutenant Motoshima did not know what to do to relieve the tension between them. He knew he was going to push Hiromoai hard before he arrived at his apartment, but now he felt he might have pushed the powerful businessman too far. Feeling ashamed over how he spoken to him, he bowed with reverence and offered. "I beg you to forgive the ill mannered mouthing of a fool, Hiromoai-san. I believe perhaps I've been an officer so long I forgot how to act properly before a well respected man. I'm sorry for my unkind words, and the harm they caused you, Hiromoai-san. But it was a question that had to be asked and it was answered properly by you, sir.

"After all I'm certain you were expecting these questions to come from me sooner or later, Hiromoai-san. As I'm equally as certain if I didn't ask them, you would've thought I wasn't doing my duties to the best of my abilities, sir." The Lieutenant allowed his shoulders to sag as a sign of submission for his manners. He also ignored his omitted the 'san' from the end of his name as he was addressing him during this conversation.

"Perhaps, you're correct at that Officer, but it was stinging nevertheless. I'll never forget your hateful words, Lieutenant. The respect I once held for you as a person and police officer, and as a Japanese person of honor and good standing, is gone forever."

"Perhaps, I can regain your respect in the future, Hiromoai-san?" He replied as he tried a smile on the extremely angry Hiromoai.

"Perhaps, sometime in the future yes but not for now!" He hissed as he pitched the unsheathed sword at the chair. He had to turn his back on Lieutenant Motoshima as he struggled desperately to get his temper under control. Although the officer was correct with his question, he was not going to give him anything to poke his nose in. He felt he was acting in the manner of an innocent man, an act that was not wasted on the officer.

Lieutenant Motoshima judged every action and reaction of the businessman with rage burning in his eyes. He had to admit, for the first time since questioning him at the party, he felt he did not have anything to do with the death of Yurkowa. In his investigation he found never once in Hiromoai's life, did he or his father or brothers ever look for, or speak to someone who might be able to supply the services of an assassin. And the executioner used to kill Yurkowa, was a highly skilled and accomplished killer, and had to belong to one of the elite of Ninja stables. One who would have to be located by someone familiar with the inner working and dark world of the assassin cults that flooded Japan. He glanced at his watch and was surprised they spoke so long. He stood and bowed to Hiromoai's back, and held it until he turned and looked at him.

Without thought, the wise Japanese businessman automatically returned the bow with one of his own. His many years of dealing with the elite of Japan took over, and he was forced by honor and respect to return the politeness offered by the police officer.

The Lieutenant smiled as he politely offered with a slight second bow. "Hiromoai-san, again, I'm terribly sorry if I have insulted you with this most confusing conversation, sir. That was the furthest thing from my mind. But you know these detestable questions had to be asked of you, or they would've forever been floating above our heads and always be in our way, sir. You have answered all my questions in the fashion I come to expect from an innocent and honorable man, sir. I'll pray to Lord Buddha and burn ten sticks of incense in his honor that I'll never again have to upset your peace by asking embarrassing questions, sir. Hiromoai-san, I fear I have wasted enough of your valuable time on this day. I shall leave you in peace and hope you'll be able to recapture your great Wa on this fine day sir. Konnicha wa, good day Hiromoai-san."

"Konnicha wa Lieutenant. Perhaps, you're correct Lieutenant, it's better to clear the air of all doubt and concerns, than leave these questions unasked and hanging in the air. I'll try to forget the questions, and the way they were asked of me, sir. Good day Lieutenant, I have work I must attend to, sir. Please, find your way out of my home I'm still too angry to be the polite host."

CHAPTER SIXTEEN

Lieutenant Motoshima bowed and turned and then left the apartment as swiftly as he could. The moment he was out of the penthouse, Hiromoai collapsed on the sofa and battled to get his breathing under control. As quick as the officer had left then Lady Yoke stormed in the study, her eyes betraying her anger at the officer she held in her heart. Seeing the condition of Hiromoai, she darted back to the kitchen and placed cold water on a towel. She then rushed back to the study and placed the cool towel over his forehead to help him relax some.

"Ahhhh... that feels so good. Lady Yoke, what would I do without you to look after me?"

"Hiromoai-san, if you would've allowed me to take care of you that foul mouth filthy police officer would never have gained entry into your home. I heard the horrendous way the inconsiderate fool spoke to you. How dare he, the son of a dog eater, I don't know how he left your home breathing with his foul head attached to his foolish shoulders. If the fool ever spoke to me in the fashion he did you, I would've found some way to dispatch his useless breathing for the worthless police officer. I can't believe him, no wonder no one trusts them, damn police."

"Lady Yoke, you have the temper of a stalking Kotora, it's good to act like a hunting Tiger when angered, if you possess the burning desire of one. But one must remember when it's the proper time to allow the spirit of the Kotora loose on ones worthless enemy. Where's Wind?" He asked as he pulled the towel from his head and stared at the Lady Yoke with a smile.

"Wind-san is upstairs with Utsumi in your master bedroom, Hiromoai-san." She reported to her boss with little concern in her voice.

"Good, go get her. I have to leave for Engakuji Castle, and I want to make certain she's comfortable, and knows what to do while I'm away on my mission."

"Hai Hiromoai-san." Lady Yoke headed for the stairs leading to Hiromoai's sleeping quarters.

Upstairs, when Utsumi walked in Hiromoai's suite with Wind in tow, he was awed. He never visited his bedroom before. The room was the largest he ever saw in all Japan for just one person to dwell. He waved his arm out before his chest, and Wind rushed by the old man. There were two chairs facing the sliding shoji glass doors leading to a second floor patio that overlooked the very heart of downtown Tokyo, and the endless sea beyond. But she understood she should not be seen by anyone, so she walked to the bed and sat on the end of it.

He followed Wind into the massive bedroom. Everything he did was done in an effort to see into her loose fitting kimono, and the treasures it hid from his view. He was not being enigmatic about his attempts, and it was making her very self-conscious and uncomfortable about how she sat. She blocked his view at every step, so he decided to try a different tact against her to see what he wanted. He stared at her for several long seconds while quickly gathering his thoughts and then he grumbled at her. "Wind-san, is it not your sworn duty to do everything your masters command of you without thought or hesitation?"

"Hai Utsumi! You are correct in your words and thoughts you speak to me. Everybody who walks the face of the earth is governed by a master, some by the master of greed, others by the master of power, yet others by the foul master of greed. Who is your true master of life over you, Utsumi?" She snapped, refusing to honor the old man by adding the san to his name, as she kept her eyes glued to the floor, refusing to look up at him.

Utsumi ignored the insult by this beautiful female and continued. "That's right Wind-san. But I have no such master to answer to. I'm free to do as I please, Warrior. Although Hiromoai-san is your master, am I not your master when he places you in my charge for any time, Wind-san?"

She blushed and bowed to the old man as she was forced to agree with his assumption, still refusing to give him the pleasure of her looking into his weathered eyes. "Hai Utsumi.

You are most correct and I learned a lesson on this day. When one suffers the torments of pain, it is a lesson well learned. When one experiences the pleasure of joy, that one learns another of life's lessons. To live one day and learn wisdom from that experience is a day of great worth."

"Correct, and as your temporary Master, you're bound by your sacred oath to do as I say, and respect me in the same way and manner you respect Hiromoai-san. And learn from my wisdom, is that not right Wind-san?" He allowed a sneer as he looked in Wind's eyes.

"Hai, Utsumi-san, you're most correct again with the words that you offered to my soul. To improve is to bend with the wind, to be perfect in thought and deed one must bend often to the countless ways of the commanding wind and true destiny." Wind added the honor to the old man's name after listening to his logic.

"Fine that's better Samurai. Now you're beginning to understand. It's hot I wonder why Hiromoai-san doesn't have the air-conditioning turned up to make it more comfortable in the room? I'm in the mood for some entertainment. Would you oblige an old man's few moods?"

"It is long believed that moods are for cattle and love play, Utsumi-san. The richest of persons on the face of the earth, is the one who is content with what he possess in life, and longs for no further possessions to conquer and own." She offered to the old man in a polite voice.

"Yes, but this conversation's doing nothing to relieve the heat of this room, Samurai."

"Hai Utsumi-san, again you are correct, it is warm in this room, conceivably, maybe Hiromoai-sama enjoys warmth." She did not know what he meant by air-conditioning, but she refused to ask him questions for fear of having to engage him in further conversation.

"Maybe Wind-san, but I don't enjoy the heat as much as he does, and seeing you wrapped up in a winter kimono is making me warmer than usual. It'd help me cool if you were to remove such a heavy garment." The old man offered while allowing an ugly sneer to cross his lips.

Her face heated from embarrassment and anger she was suffering by the old man's request. Now she knew what he was up to, but she was powerless to deny him any wishes because her master's ordered him to control her. With her head bowed, she rose and slowly undid the obi and allowed the kimono to fall open. She was naked underneath.

He drank in the stunning beauty of her body that had the kimono caught up in her elbows. She was breathtaking as the old man drew in his breath. All fear of wrath from the extremely dangerous samurai left his body because he knew he was in control of the warrior.

"You may sit and be comfortable, but allow the kimono to slide off your legs when sitting, Wind-san." He mumbled while wearing an ugly sneer, staring at her body.

Again, honor forced her to do as ordered by the ugly foreman without hesitation or complaint from the ancient warrior. Sitting like he commanded made it completely impossible for her to cover her nakedness. She cursed the Kami god who made the laws that commanded her to follow this evil one's disgusting orders. She made up her mind that moment she was going to search the ways of the old for an honorable and just reason to dispatch this old man who was guilty of making her do things that went against her desires.

"Wind-san, you have something marring your chest." He walked to her and brazenly reached out and began to fondle her breast, sending shock waves down her spine, and hatred in her soul. She wondered how much she was going to be subjected to endure by this old man who made her skin crawl, and her stomach complain with anger. She had no choice but to allow him to assault her body in any manner he deemed fit, uncontested by her fuming anger.

It was like he protested that he was her master of her being when Hiromoai was not in her and his presence. She actually tried to will Hiromoai's mind to force his body to come upstairs and catch this evil one in his most deplorable act against her body. But her mind was not able to link to Hiromoai's. With a deep sigh of disgust, she capitulated herself to allow this terrible insult to continue, no matter what the old man did, or requested from her. She knew she was bound by her honor to the curse of the deadly katana sword, to carry out any act requested by this old man. She prayed to Lord Buddha to keep the old man's mind off any sexual acts with her. She had no intention of taking him in her mouth like she done with Hiromoai.

Wind was the first one to hear the light footfalls on the steps leading up to the bedroom suite. The second Utsumi heard them he jumped two feet away from her and ordered her in an excited voice. "Quick, close your kimono, I'm cool enough now."

She pulled the fabric around her exquisite body as if it was her protecting armor. Her cheeks remained red from embarrassment and anger, and when Lady Yoke entered the room, she saw her condition and glared harshly at Utsumi. She knew what the filthy old man was doing to her.

Utsumi turned from her accusing gaze. He knew she would never say anything to Hiromoai for fear of creating problems for his household. But he also understood he was no longer going to be allowed to be alone with Wind. He cursed the crafty consort for daring to interrupt his fun.

She turned to Wind and snapped at her. "Wind, Hiromoai-san is in the study, and he requests your presence before him immediately. I warn you it's not wise to keep him waiting long, Wind."

She watched her stand and shoot out of the room as if the Devil Kami was in pursuit of her, refusing to even glance at Utsumi standing in her way. Once she was out of the room, the Lady Yoke started on him. She crossed the few steps separating them like a ghost, and she slapped the old man hard across the face and then she glared as she waited for his response.

He grabbed her wrist and twisted the fragile arm to the side as he hissed in her face angrily. "I should kill you for that fucking slap, slut who spreads her legs for anyone willing to pay the price for the lowly privilege of pillowing with a bitch from the Soft World. If you ever slap me again, I'll kill you sure as I'm standing before you, bitch." He shoved her from him by the wrist.

She was not afraid as she snarled back at him. "Pig of the sludge you were born to, if you ever dare to place another loathsome finger on Wind's body, I'll personally chop your insulting paws from your detestable body. I'll separate your head from your worthless shoulders and use it for a piss pot for the lowly eta to enjoy. You're the lowest of the low old man, lower than even the foul eta class to dare take advantage of the honor and respect of that Samurai. If

Hiromoai-san ever found out what you did to her, he'd kill you slowly, old fool."

"But you'll never tell the fool what I did will you, Yoke?" He shot back in a taunting tone, almost daring Lady Yoke to inform Hiromoai what he done to his prized possession.

"No you old foul fool, not one ugly word of this terrible insult played out against Wind's person by your detestable presence, will ever come from my lips to Hiromoai-san's honorable ears, old man. Words that'll cause him to be upset by you, I'll never inform him of what you have done to Wind, or what you dared to call him behind his back, foul one born from the pits of hell on a dark and rainy night. But it's not for the sake of your worthless head that I'll refrain and remain silent over this terrible matter. I do it only to keep the Wa of Hiromoai-san and Wind at peace. I don't want to be the cause of possibly upsetting Hiromoai-san's Wa over the likes of you and your most detestable actions committed against Wind's sacred temple, you old fool. Return to your worthless room until you're being is needed by Hiromoai-san again, old man." Lady Yoke placed her hands on her hips and then she again glared angrily at the old man.

"Huh, and who are you to dare order me around like you're trying to do, filthy little witch of the dirty sheets. I'm the one who possesses the mightly dragon hanging between my legs, not you bitch. And that means I don't have to listen to one possessing a void, the den the home for the male dragon." The old foreman dared to gripe at Lady Yoke.

Lady Yoke moved a step forward until she was staring him dead in his face for a second time, and then she snarled at him in no uncertain terms. "If you don't return to your god cursed foul room immediately, it'll be I who'll own your shriveled and useless dragon, old one. I am not fooling with you old man, I will harm you if you don't move away from e at once." Then she pulled a razor sharp kogai she removed from the hidden pocket of a katana sheath, from the folds of her kimono and used it for her protection, and aimed it threateningly at his manhood.

He stared at the unwavering implement of harm held threateningly in her hand just a few inches from his body and offered her as if he was not the least bit afraid of what she was aiming at his body. "Hmmm... I believe I am tired at that, lowly witch of the filthy sheets. Maybe a short rest would do me a world of good today. It has been a very trying day at that, woman of the underworld." He moaned as he turned and rushed out of the bedroom.

She stared hard at him until he was completely out of her sight. Then she quickly straightened out the covers of Hiromoai's huge bed and neatened the throw rug, and then she checked the rest of the room to make certain nothing else was out of place in the massive room. She fixed what was in need of repair and then she quickly headed for the study herself in a rush.

Wind was sitting on her knees before her master as Lady Yoke entered the massive study. Her kimono circled her kneeling position like a fine, silk light blue mist surrounding her.

Hiromoai was seated on the sofa looking down at her. When he saw Lady Yoke enter the study he asked her with a snap in his tone. "Where the hell is that old fool of a useless foreman hiding at, Lady Yoke? The lazy bastard should be listening to this conversation, so he knows what the hell's going on about him, dammit. I want him to know everything of what's going on in case he has to go out and retrieve Wind, if she happens to get lost in the city, or might get caught by the police, or gets in any kind of trouble out there tonight, young lady."

"Utsumi was suffering from exhaustion and he has announced he was going to lie down for a while and rest, Hiromoai-san. He said he worked too long in the night yesterday, and he was from exhausted from his toils. I'm sorry to inform you I said it'd be all right for the fool to lie down, sir. I hope I haven't overstepped my bounds giving him permission to rest, Hiromoai-san." She offered as she lowered her eyes so he wasn't able to read the lie written in them.

"That's no problem Lady Yoke. It was very wise on your part to use your head when dealing with the old fool. Besides young lady, there are no bounds to your authority in my world when it comes to making any decisions for my best interests. I could always depend on you to do the right thing for me at all time, young lady." 'The stupid old man he is', Hiromoai mumbled under his breath while shaking his head slowly in disgust over the old man. He hated him almost as much as Wind did. Lately, since finding Wind and her horde of ancient weapons and armor, he was entertaining thoughts of eliminating Utsumi. He knew Utsumi was the one who found her when he located her crypt. Eliminating him, he would not have to worry about him getting drunk, and accidently slipping about the presence of Wind to the fools in the bar drinking with him.

He placed these troubling thoughts out of his mind for the time being, and began to go over his final orders for Lady Yoke and Wind to carry out while he was gone from the apartment. When he was certain she was going to be looked after properly, he checked his watch. It was almost ten a.m. and he wanted to get to the castle before the noontime traffic got heavy. He got up and left the room for his car parked in the underground parking lot under the Hatanaka Towers.

ENGAKUJI CASTLE, 10:30 A.M. JUNE 8th, 1996

Asahiko was meeting with the accountant, Fumimaro Kakizawa, since he arrived at the castle at nine a.m. sharp as he was ordered by the old businessman the day before. He went over the accountant's endless columns of facts and figures of his company's true worth. They were very impressive indeed to review, the ceaseless list of construction equipment, stocks and other property his company owned, or leased, pleased the old man to no end. But his review of his heavy equipment was interrupted when his man servant entered the room and announced that a young police officer was at the front door, and he was requesting to speak with him.

Asahiko allowed the concern over the officer requesting a meeting to show on his face as he ordered the servant. "Allow the uninvited Officer to enter my office, but detain him for five minutes before showing him to the room." He dismissed the man servant curtly with a flick of the hand, as he turned to his accountant. When the man servant was out of the room, he looked at Kakizawa before speaking. "I believe it's time for you to leave me, everything you worked up for me is in proper order. You did fine work on such short notice, Kakizawa-san. Have it typed up as it reads, sir. Have a copy sent over to Batterman at his office in the United States. Leave, but use the back staircase to leave by. I don't want this Police Officer to run into you here."

"Hai Asahiko-san. Hmmmm... I was wondering what the police might want of you? I never saw a Police Officer requesting to speak with you before, Asahiko-san." Kakizawa offered and then bowed to Asahiko as he prepared to leave his side to carry out his orders.

"It's none of your god cursed business what this Officer might want with me, Kakizawa-san." He snapped as he glared at his accountant and then added. "Your only concern is to make certain all my holdings are listed on these foul pages. The police are my concern, Kakizawa-san."

"Maybe, the fool found something out about the assassin who killed your son, Asahiko-san." Kakizawa ignored the mood Asahiko was in this morning and his stinging words aimed at him.

"Perhaps, but again Kakizawa-san, my private life is none of your concern. Leave my office before the Officer arrives and discovers your presence here." He grumbled as he removed from sight the papers they were just working on. He placed them in the top drawer of his desk and stared at his accountant until he started to move out of the office.

Kakizawa quickly gathered his papers and bowed to Asahiko a final time, and then left the room through a second door just as there was a knock on the main door of his room.

"You may enter my room!" Asahiko growled from where he was resting in the massive room at his man servant and the police officer he was escorting to his room.

The door opened quietly and the male servant came in first, followed by a second but much younger man as the servant announced. "Asahiko-san, this man is Sergeant Toshihiro Okamatsu-san from the Tokyo Police Department, Detective Division he states to me sir. Sergeant Okamatsu-san wishes to speak with you for a few moments if possible, sir. I'm afraid he said it was most important that he speaks with you on your day off, sir."

"You may leave, bring tea for us. I'm certain this young Officer would enjoy something to drink. He looks like he's been working too many hours, and not getting enough rest. Once the tea is delivered, we're not to be disturbed further under any circumstance." Asahiko snapped as he pointed at the chair across from him, and then waited until the officer was comfortable.

"Hai Asahiko-san." The servant replied as he bowed and quickly backed out of the room.

Sergeant Okamatsu did not reply to Asahiko's words, he did not know if the old man was honoring him, or trying to insult him by offering he looked tired, exhausted to him.

When the officer was seated and seemed like he was ready to begin his conversation with Asahiko, he asked ill mannered. "And what does the honorable Tokyo Police Department, Detective Division want with this old man on a Saturday morning that could not wait for a work day, so this interruption wouldn't be so bothersome to me, Sergeant? Usually, I see no one on my days off, especially Police Officers, young man. I cherish my private time and guard that time I add, Officer." He warned as he folded his arms across his chest and stared at the Sergeant.

"Please excuse me Asahiko-san I'm terribly sorry for disturbing you on a Saturday and your day off, sir. But a Police Officer never truly has a day off. There are important questions I must ask of you, in order to forward my ongoing investigation of your honorable son and his wife's savage deaths, sir. And maybe clear up some of disturbing instances that recently took place that was my misfortune to witness, sir." Sergeant Okamatsu bowed graciously as he moved in the chair to try and get a little more comfortable.

"Then I take it this visit is over that investigation of my honorable son's death, Sergeant Okamatsu-san? If that's the reason for this visit to my home then ask your questions but be quick about them I warn you, Officer. I have all the time in the world to help hunt down this loathsome killer of my honorable son and his lovely wife. I'll do anything in my power to find my honorable son's cursed murderer." Asahiko stared at the officer waiting for his reply.

"Thank you for the kind consideration, Asahiko-san. I'll try not to waste too much of your valuable time on this day off sir, and I'll make this interview painless to endure, Asahiko-san." The Sergeant removed a pad and pencil from his pocket, crossed his legs and began speaking again. "Sir, yesterday, I happened to be enjoying an afternoon walk in the park..."

They were interrupted by a soft knock on the heavy oak door.

"Enter." Asahiko remarked over his shoulder, not bothering to look at the door leading to his room. He was anxious because of this police officer's visit it was disquieting him.

The servant appeared with the requested tea. He quickly placed it down on the table separating the two, and then he bowed politely and left.

"Tea Sergeant Okamatsu-san?" Asahiko asked the officer.

"Please Asahiko-san. I'd enjoy that very much if you don't mind, thank you kindly sir."

"Please Sergeant, help yourself, I serve no one on this earth but myself, sir." He announced as he prepared his tea. Once he was done, he sat back and stared at the sergeant as he fixed his tea and said. "You were saying the reason for this visit was about my son's murder, Sergeant."

Sergeant Okamatsu picked up his cup of tea and sat back and let out his breath as he took a second, and looked about the room serving as Asahiko's sleeping quarters and workstation when he was in the castle. All he saw were a huge number of ancient weapons, armor, and extremely expensive hand painted tapestries of years long ago, decorating the massive room's stone walls.

Each exquisite paintings and reliefs represented some historical event, or a war that helped shaped Japan's proud history. The massive bed was made many years ago. The desk he used for work was from the Emperor's Palace in Kyoto, built in the sixteenth century, hand carved and huge. Everything in the room was from Japan's proud past. Sergeant Okamatsu was in amazement of everything he looked at in the room.

Asahiko shifted his weight and placed his cup down on the table and settled back before offering with a touch of sarcasm etched in his tone.

"Sergeant, I'm quite certain that you have not traveled all this way from your office in downtown Tokyo, just to look about my private living quarters, and view my outstanding collection of Japan's proud and ancient history, sir. Because if that's the true reason for this visit to my home then all you had to do was place a call, and I would've gladly set up a private tour of the entire Castle for your enjoyment Sergeant. Along with anyone else you might want to take with you on the expedition of my dwelling, sir. Again Detective Sergeant, when you first came to my room, you were saying something about your ongoing investigation of my honorable son and his lovely wife's untimely death?"

"Quite correct Asahiko-san. I'm sorry, but this conversation is not so much about our ongoing investigation of your honorable son's death, sir..." The Sergeant lowered his head to get his eyes out of the sudden glare of the older man staring at him with questioning and demanding eyes.

His eyes sharpened until he was glaring at the officer then he snorted. "Huh, then you're here under false pretenses I take it, Sergeant? Why the devil did you feel it was necessary for you to use deceptive purposes to gain entry to my home, Officer Okamatsu-san? I warn you sir I'm not used to having trickery employed against me in such a manner. You need no such tricks to speak with me any time, especially over anything to do with my son's death. I'm at your beck and call day and night, for you're helping to discover the yakuza, the gangster who killed my son."

"Again Asahiko-san, I'm upset if you believe I came here to deceive you in any way, shape, or form, sir. That was the furthest thing from my mind, sir. But in a way, this conversation will help clear up some rather confusing circumstances I had the misfortune to observe of late sir, and it may also make the investigation of your poor son's death proceed at a quicker rate, Asahiko-san." Sergeant Okamatsu tried a quick smile on the old man, but it was wasted.

His glare softened and he moaned. "I fear you're confusing me, Officer. Please, I don't need a disconcerting concoction of confusing words to help scramble my mind any more than it's already confused on this day. Get on with your questions so we can end this conversation and then I can return to work, Officer. Please, inform me, what brings a Tokyo Detective to my doorstep, begging entry to my home to speak with me on my day off, Sergeant Okamatsu-san?"

With a deep sigh, the Sergeant said in a contrite tone of voice to the old man. "Asahiko-san, I'm regretful to inform you sir, it has come to my attention that Hiromoai-san and yourself had a rather violent altercation in the park yesterday, sir. I was wondering why two such fine, well educated and highly respected gentlemen of Japan would lower themselves to come to blows in what seemed like a pleasant conversation taking place, sir. I don't mind informing you sir, when two of Japan's elite trade slaps with one another, it quickens the heartbeat of Japan for all of us. An action like this can actually send our stock market into a tailspin. I was stunned to see what took place between the two of you in the park yesterday, Asahiko-san."

"Huh, then it was your man who I noticed hiding behind the bushes yesterday, Sergeant?" Asahiko offered as he gave the police officer a quick smirk.

"No sir, I'm afraid that was me who you discovered hiding in the bushes, sir. I'm surprised that you were so easily able to detect where I hid, sir. I thought I was well undercover, Asahiko-san. I have failed my duty to this investigation I fear, sir."

"Please Sergeant you belittle yourself needlessly over nothing I assure you, sir. You had no choice but to be discovered. You see young man, there was no one living in this world that would've been able to get close enough to me to cause me any harm. I had more bodyguards and security personnel surrounding me in the park than there were visitors to the place. It wasn't I who detected your presence so near my person, Sergeant. It was one of my female security guards walking with the baby carriage that warned me a police officer was observing the conversation between Hiromoai-san and myself. She warned me by means of a small portable radio, I had the receiver placed in the left ear facing away from Hiromoai-san, so it went undetected by him when she placed the warning to me about your presence in the bushes, sir.

"I didn't want to be the cause of undue alarm to Hiromoai-san's presence. So you see Officer, you failed no one, it was impossible for anyone to get in a thousand yards of my person, without being observed by my guards. Since my honorable son's death, I trust no one, no one Officer."

"I can understand your precaution Asahiko-san, and now I search my memory, I did notice the female walking with the baby carriage. How did she know I was a Police Officer, sir?" Sergeant Okamatsu was resorting to small talk to relieve the tensions of the conversation between them.

"Huh, that was rather simple to accomplish Sergeant. The woman took your picture as you hid behind that bush, and she sent by means of her miniature computer hidden in the carriage. In less than a heartbeat, you were identified as a Police Officer, so she took no further action aimed against your person. If she didn't confirm your identification, she would've confronted you, and see why you were lurking behind the bushes and observing me and Hiromoai-san, sir. I have to admit, my communications were having problems with certain devices we were operating in the park. Our radio communications were being interfered by unknown systems, sir.

"Anyway Officer, you were within the zone to attack and kill me if you so chose to go down that path as an unknown attacker against my person, Officer. All my guards have standing orders to protect my life at all costs. Ever since my son's tragic death, my guards are more prone to be overly protective of my old life than usual, Sergeant. It's now my turn to offer I'm sorry, but you were marked for death by my people, until you were identified as a Tokyo police officer, young man. In these trying of times facing Japan and her people, one must know all stalking him."

"Yes sir, I also was having some major communication problems and I felt someone was interfering with my abilities to communicate with my department, sir. I'm very impressed by the protective ring you have successfully surrounded yourself with, Asahiko-san. It's a very understandable precaution that you have adopted for your own protection, sir. The system you speak of Asahiko-san, is a most interesting one at that sir. The department has no such portable computers to so quickly identify any person by means of a mere picture, or by any other means in the field for that matter I'm afraid, sir." The surprised Sergeant moaned impressed over the intricate detection equipment he had at his disposal.

"Maybe it's time that your police department thought about investing in such items to better assist them in their many investigations, Officer. It helped to protect my life when I'm out and about. It wasn't that expensive an investment to begin with Sergeant. What are we doing, we're getting way off the reason for your visit to my home on this day, young man? Besides Officer, I don't enjoy speaking with the police, especially on my days off. I'm like everyone else in Japan, and don't really trust the police for any reason. The only reason you were allowed entry to my home in the first place, was because you offered the reason for your visit was about my son's murder." Asahiko grumbled at the officer as he waited for him to get to the point of his visit.

"Yes sir, getting back to the point of this conversation, sir. I asked you why you traded slaps with Hiromoai-san in the park yesterday, sir. If you're honest with me Asahiko-san, it will help greatly with the investigation and move it along at a much quicker pace for us, sir."

"Officer Okamatsu-san! I'm always honest when speaking to anyone, even to the police. I have absolutely nothing whatsoever to hide from you or anyone else on the face of the earth, Officer. My entire life is like an open book, available for all in the world to read through the very boring of pages at their leisure about my worthless being and efforts of life, Officer." Asahiko snapped tersely while staring at the younger man harshly.

"Please, forgive my poor choice of words Asahiko-san. I didn't mean to offend or offer you might not be honest with me in the least sir, or with anyone else you might speak with for that matter Asahiko-san. It was a terrible poor choice of words on my part I fear sir." Sergeant Okamatsu bowed correctly towards the old man.

He nodded, accepting the officer's expression of apology as he began anew in his attempt to end this conversation. "Sergeant, I'm afraid you have some of your observations confused in your memory. Maybe some branches of the bush you hid behind blocked your view of the altercation that took place between us. We didn't trade slaps sir. No, it was I who slapped the honorable Hiromoai-san. I'm guilty of a terrible insult I admit one I must beg his forgiveness of, Sergeant. I don't know what ever possessed me to strike out in anger against Hiromoai-san like I did, Officer. It's not like me to resort to violence under any circumstances, sir."

"If anyone's entitled to be forgiven for rash actions, it surely is you Asahiko-san. I can't begin to fathom the horrendous shock and sadness you must be suffering over losing one's honorable son and his wife, sir. It must be a heavy millstone to travel through life burdened with around your neck, sir." The Sergeant displayed sincere sorrow and emotion for the loss of his son.

"Yes, you're being very kind and respectful to this old fool who wastes the air of the earth by breathing, Sergeant. Most kind indeed young man and I want you to understand I appreciate your words, and they served to relieve some of the pain of the murder, sir. I thank you from the bottom of my heart for your kind consideration and understanding, Officer. Yes young man, there's no way for you to understand the dreadful pain involved with the loss of a loving and honorable son, unless you had the terrible misfortune and Karma to have experienced the overwhelming loss, sir. Yes, yes young man, understanding is something hard to come by, Officer. I hope Hiromoai-san is in possession of such understanding for my foolish actions of yesterday, sir."

"Thank you Asahiko-san, but this doesn't explain why you have decided to slap Hiromoai-san across the face during your conversation with him in the park, sir." The concerned Sergeant pressed the old man for the answer for the reason of his slapping Hiromoai.

"I'm sorry Officer for the confusion I might have caused you and your department, sir. Officer Okamatsu-san, it was I who requested this meeting take place between us. Hiromoai-san was most concerned for my health and poor state of mind over my honorable son's terrible slaughter I believe." He lied to take some of the sting out of the observed confrontation.

"Yes, I can understand this easy enough Asahiko-san, but I must ask why did you slap him, sir? You must explain the reason behind this to me very carefully, Asahiko-san. To dare slap any Japanese person across the face is a terrible insult to that person, one that must be taken extremely seriously in Japan, sir." The Sergeant then cocked his head to the side as he waited for the old man's explanation to begin. He was sorry he was forced to question the old man in this manner but he was following his commander's orders to get to the bottom of the slap.

"I don't need such a young pup to dare inform me of the horrendous insult the slapping caused to Hiromoai-san's person and honor, Sergeant." Asahiko growled as he shifted his rearend in the chair to get more comfortable. The questions caused him to be extremely uncomfortable.

The Sergeant bowed with humility to the exhausted businessman. Sorry for the loss of face his words caused him.

Knowing he was being inconsiderate to him with these terrible questions.

The old man let out his breath in a painful sigh as he explained further for the police officer. "Well Sergeant, since you were there and didn't understand what your foolish eyes had witnessed of my most deplorable actions, I'll clear up your confusion for you. Hiromoai-san and I spoke at length about my poor son's horrible death. Then, out of the blue, he offered to buy my business as a friendly gesture by him. I was stunned and taken by surprise by the suddenness of the unsolicited offer for my construction company, and I just overreacted like a foolish old woman would who wanted the waning attention of her worthless lover.

"Once I found out the true reason for the offer by Hiromoai-san, I was sorry for my uncalled for and rather childish outburst aimed against his person and honor. But one's actions can never be erased once they were cast upon the seas of anger. I assure you Officer it was nothing for you at the department to be overly concerned with, sir. We're businessmen, and in the ruthless world of the construction business, sometimes, tempers flare and get the best of even the most civilized of persons in Japan, Officer. Such is what happened to this old fool as witnessed by you on that terrible day, Sergeant Okamatsu-san." He nodded a polite bow to the policeman this time.

"Yes sir, do you think there was anything behind the offer to buy your business by Hiromoai-san, Asahiko-san?" the Sergeant stared at the old man's face, looking for signs of deception.

"I don't understand what you mean by your last remark, Sergeant? Explain this question a little further for me so I better understand what you want of me, Officer."

"Certainly, I didn't mean to confuse you in any manner, Asahiko-san. What I meant was do you think that there was anything sinister hiding behind Hiromoai-san's sudden offer to buy your honorable construction company, Asahiko-san?" Sergeant Okamatsu held his breath in fear, hoping that he was not kind of overstepping his bounds in the manner he was trying to press his questions to the powerful and well respected Asahiko.

The old man smiled, because he still did not understand the officer's question as he added. "Again Sergeant, I remain slightly confused by your choice of words and request of me. Sinister Sergeant Okamatsu-san, what could possibly be sinister about someone trying to buy one's successful business from him, Officer? Businesses in Japan and across the world are bought and sold every second of the day and every day of the week, Sergeant. It's the way all businessmen expand their interest and opportunities, sir."

"Yes I understand this as fact Asahiko-san, do you think that his want of your honorable business was so overwhelming to him that he might have resorted to the elimination of your honorable son, to get a better price for your company, sir? Or maybe even force you into selling a business you had no intention of selling, sir?"

He leaned back and laughed as he stared at the officer, understanding it took courage to place such an insulting question before him. "Sergeant, I fear it's only because of your youth that keeps me from being insulted by that last question of yours, sir. If there's anything sinister about the situation that took place, I believe it lies within your overly active mind, Officer. No Sergeant, Hiromoai-san's offer was well within the boundaries of a very honorable and respectful proposal for my company I offer you, sir."

The old man began to sweat his body screamed for his mouth to inform this young police officer that he was correct in his assumption that Hiromoai was the evil entity behind his son and his wife's savage death, in an effort to take over his construction business. The old man fought desperately with himself not to cry out this information to the police officer as he continued to stare at the younger man for a few long moments.

"Am I to take the slight altercation was nothing more than just a normal business action and reaction, Asahiko-san?" Sergeant Okamatsu shrugged and he stared back at the old man while waiting for his reply.

"There's no other possible explanation that I can offer you other than that, Officer Okamatsu-san. It was only business, and the actions of a very distraught and rather confused father who is guilty of overreacting to a very interesting offer by his competitor."

"Then I take it your company is not up for sale Asahiko-san?"

"Quite on the contrary Sergeant, it certainly is available sir. In fact, I have a buyer for my company, sir. He's a very wise and keen and rather successful young American businessman. One I'm pleased to be offering my construction company to. All I'm waiting for is the signing of the papers, and I'll no longer be in the troublesome industry. I can't tell you how I'm looking forward to being a man of leisure for the rest of my worthless life, Officer."

"Huh, an American businessman you offer to me, Asahiko-san!" The stunned young police officer said, shocked that the old man would dare consider selling his vast construction company to an American Gai Jin. The detective understood the severe ramifications in place in Japan to protect the country from being invaded from outside companies, for such a rash move as an American obtaining an operating business in Japan. He found himself wondering how Asahiko was able to get around all the extremely oppressive laws protecting businesses from being purchased by foreigners, especially the American businessmen.

"Yes, an American businessman, one who'll command my company wisely I believe sir." Asahiko added, proud of what he was announcing to the young officer.

"I don't understand this and I must admit that it shakes me to my very soul, Asahiko-san. Why in the devil would you want to sell your rather successful construction business to a Gai Jin, an American at that sir? Especially after having a most interesting offer for your company from an upstanding, proud young Japanese businessman of honor and respect such as Hiromoai-san is, sir? Please sir, can you clear up this most troubling decision on your part that you..."

"You don't have to understand any of my actions I commit when it comes to my business dealings, Officer. I account to no man on this Island, or in the world but myself, and the daisho-jingi-guri, sir! The honored band of all Gods we respect Sergeant, all you have to understand is the deal is legal, and consummated. You must leave Karma to Karma and my business to me, young man." Asahiko replied while allowing a trace of anger to seep into his voice

"But why sell your honorable company to an American, Asahiko-san? There has to be a good reason for you to decide to go to the foreign shores to sell your construction company, sir."

"It's rather simple a question for me to answer for you, Officer. Is it not said that if one can destroy an enemy then he controls that enemy for life?"

"Asahiko-san, why would you ever think to classify Hiromoai-san as an enemy against you, sir?" the suddenly deeply concerned officer asked of the old man.

"Foolish young Officer, I wouldn't expect you to understand what I just said to you, fool. Hiromoai-san is every bit my eternal enemy, in the world of business that is. You see, outside our world of constant transactions and dealing, we're the very best of friends, sir. But in the business world, I'll do anything at my disposal in order to destroy that enemy, totally Officer. In this case, it happens to be the unsuspecting and well respected Hiromoai-san. I'll destroy him to the point of selling my construction company to the lowly Gai Jin, to keep my business out of the hands of my worst competitor in all Japan, Hiromoai Hatanaka Mining and Construction Company, Sergeant Okamatsu-san." Asahiko suddenly smiled as he slowly spread his hands apart, and then he shrugged while staring back at the young police officer.

"But Asahiko-san, there are so many laws forbidding a business to be sold to outsiders of our country. Especially an American, how can this be allowed by our government?" the Sergeant cried, upset an American was going to own an established construction business in his country.

"Again, you're trying to dabble in a world you're most unfamiliar with, and I suggest you concern yourself with the matters of police work you're properly trained for, and leave my business workings to me, and the others involved in that most confusing world. Now Officer if I have successfully answered all your troubling and offensive and unending questions to your complete satisfaction. I have to rush you out of my room because I numerous pressing matters I must attend to, immediately sir." He rose on shaking legs and waited for the officer to do the same. Then the old man skillfully guided him towards the door. Once the door opened, the elderly servant was waiting just outside in the hallway and he immediately took over leading the younger officer out of the castle in silence.

"I guess I'll never understand the confusing world of business, Asahiko-san." The detective offered in his defense, as he allowed himself to be led from the room by the servant.

"Nor should you try, and I promise you that I'll never attempt to understand the world of the police department, sir. So we're standing on an even footing in our understanding of each other's line of work, Officer. Konnicha wa Officer Okamatsu-san." The old Asahiko announced as he bowed to the officer for the last time.

"Konnicha wa Asahiko-san. I'm sorry you decided to sell your company to the American Gai Jin. If I have any further questions to ask of you, may I be allowed to call on you again in the future sir? Asahiko-san, I shall burn several sticks of incense and offer a bowl of cooked rice to Lord Buddha for your departed son and his wife's fine spirits, sir."

"You're most kind to remember my son in such a respectable way Sergeant, and I thank you for the kindness you displayed from the bottom of my heart. Please, you're more than free to call on me anytime of the day or night if you have questions concerning my son's death, or the investigation of their murders, Officer." He said as he closed the door behind the officer, not waiting to see him being lead away by his servant down the staircase.

He allowed the elder man servant to guide him from the castle, all the way to the draw bridge leading out of the castle. There, he stood on the tenth century steps, and took time to light a cigarette. His unconcerned eyes happen to pick up the stark white Mercedes Benz of Hiromoai, as it slowly drove by to the east end of the Castle Keep. He held the burning match between his fingers as he watched the snow white car slowly disappear around the side of the massive and ancient castle. Only when the flame finally reached his fingertips, did he react. He shook the match until it was out and then he merely pitched it in the dark moat to his left that surrounded the castle. His first instincts were to head out and follow Hiromoai to see where he was going in this area of town. But he corrected himself and decided against it.

He understood the businessman would have pursuits in this section of old town Tokyo. He went down the crumbling stone steps and headed for his car, but not before checking his recorder to make certain it worked. It did, and everything they spoke about was captured on the tape. He breathed a sigh of relief as he slid behind the wheel and started it then gunned the engine and pulled in the flow of traffic getting heavy, as workers headed out for lunch.

CHAPTER SEVENTEEN
HIROMOAI'S SNOW WHITE MERCEDES

The young owner of one of Japan's largest construction company, Hiromoai Hatanaka was so concerned with the maddening traffic of Tokyo he failed to notice the Police Sergeant staring at him from the steps of the massive castle, as he slowly drove by the ancient keep. He headed straight for the east section of the mighty and thick stone wall that protected the castle from invaders for centuries past. Hiromoai parked his car off the side of the road surrounding the castle, and he got out and began searching for the large stones with the carving printed on it. It took him a few moments to locate the oddly placed stones in the thick wall.

Once he located the turned to the side set of stones, he walked in the direction directed by Wind. The thick underbrush was heavy in this section, and it successfully hid the well faded white stone with the threatening Shibi, the long feared sea monsters carved deeply into the face of the well aged stone, from view. He had to stomp down the high, wild patch of weeds with his feet until he finally located the ancient rock. The stone was near the exact size that Wind told him it was and where it was supposed to be.

With effort and energy, he moved the heavy and slippery rock just enough to see the age-old opening of the passageway hidden behind the carved stone. He propped the rock open enough so he could peer into the damp void. He pulled the flashlight from his pocket, and shined it in the dark opening. The light ended, but the passageway continued beyond the light's ability to illuminate the interior. There were no obstacles that would hinder her progress to her target.

He allowed a quick smile of victory over Asahiko, and the castle he dwelled and protected him. Then he pulled his body out of the opening and slid the slippery rock back in place. He was pleased beyond words to find the ancient opening still remained where Wind offered it would be located after so many centuries that had passed in time. It went to show how well the ancient Japanese workers constructed castles in the past. A feat he understood could not easily be copied with the same precision in this century by the best of construction equipment available to the new generation of modern day builders.

Without thinking about it any further, he then scanned the slime and moss coated stone walls of the still very impressive castle and then he checked out the main building constructed right in the center of the large complex, nearly hidden behind the high walls of the castle because he was standing so close to the high wall. Hiromoai could only see lights in one room of the structure blazing, and he smiled and figured it was Asahiko's private living area. He made a mental note of the position so he could inform Wind of where she was supposed to head inside the building. Slowly, he walked around the hori or moat, spotting a lazy school of carp and many frogs in the water. A gaggle of ducks made a home on the bank and complained as he walked by them.

The smell of the ancient building filled his nostrils, and he wondered how it was to live in the past of Japan's history, when no wheeled carts were allowed on the dirt roads of the Shogun of the time. He thought of what he might have been back in that time. He was so conceited that he allowed himself to think of being the powerful Shogun, in control of many lives and destinies of all who served him faithfully. How he would have ruled the simple people of the time, and the shape he would have forced to form the future of Japan to his wants and desires.

When he had enough daydreaming, he walked back to his car in a much better mood and he climbed in and pulled the vehicle out into the flow of traffic. The traffic was less than when he arrived by the castle site. He was dying to get back to Wind and make preparations for her to dispatch the old fool standing in his way of becoming the most powerful businessmen in Japan.

SERGEANT TOSHIHIRO OKAMATSU

Sergeant Toshihiro Okamatsu fought the maddening lunch time traffic in his effort to get back to Lieutenant

Kenzaburo Motoshima's office downtown, and inform him of what he found out from the old Asahiko. The Sergeant was disappointed, because he was heading to the office with little if any new information that might shed any light on, and help them with their ongoing investigation of Tsutomu Yurkowa and his wife's murder. By the time the Sergeant pulled in the parking lot under the building, it was one ten p.m. He slid his car in his allotted parking slot, and then nodded at a few other officers shooting the breeze and then he headed for the bank of elevators in the building. He came out on the third floor and saw the Desk Sergeant, and bowed as he asked. "Sergeant Noguchi-san, is the Lieutenant in his office please?"

"Hai, Sergeant Okamatsu-san, but he's in the most foul of moods I ever saw him in I fear. He's been chewing on everyone's ass all day, ever since first arriving for work duty today, sir. If you don't have anything good to tell the Lieutenant, I suggest you get back in your patrol car, and make yourself scarce until he calms down some and is his old self again, sir." The concerned Desk Sergeant smiled at his fellow Sergeant after his warning to him.

"That's good advice Sergeant, but I have to go in the lion's den, and place my foolish head within its angry mouth, and make my worthless report to the Lieutenant." He smiled at Noguchi.

"Is it a good report you have to offer the Lieutenant, Sergeant?" The desk officer asked concerned if the Sergeant was going to upset the Lieutenant further than he already was.

"Naw, I discovered nothing new on the case I'm afraid." Sergeant Okamatsu said with a smirk.

"If you insist on going in the Lieutenant's office, can I have your parking spot Sergeant? Your parking area is closer to the elevators than mine, sir." Noguchi retorted with a smile of his own.

"The Lieutenant's in that bad a mood, huh Sergeant?" Okamatsu responded with a grin also.

"The worst mood I ever seen him in since I came to work at the department, Sergeant. I guess this murder case is weighing heavy on the Lieutenant's shoulders." The Desk Sergeant replied.

"Well, I believe my life insurance is paid up to date, Sergeant Noguchi." He replied smartly with his hand resting on the door knob to Lieutenant Motoshima's office. He rapped lightly on the glass door and then he waited to be summoned in the office.

"Yeah? You better bang on my damn door like you have a fucking pair hanging between your legs, Sergeant! Come in here and make your report to my ass mister."

Sergeant Okamatsu entered the office with a smile. It faded quickly the moment he saw the terrible scowl on the Lieutenant's face.

"Where the hell were you all day for crap sake? I've been eating my fingernails down to the nub waiting for you to get your can back here, Sergeant. What the hell did you find out from the old man? I hope you found out the reason for the old man to have slapped the other bird?"

"Please excuse me Lieutenant Motoshima-san, but I didn't find out more of anything from the elderly Asahiko-san at our interview, Lieutenant."

"It fucking figures, we haven't found out a damn thing about this murder case yet, Sergeant. It's like this assassin is a damn ghost who can appear at will, and slaughter whoever it chooses then disappear in the darkness from whence it came from without being detected by anyone. I cursed the Devil Kami, and his unholy spawn children, and all who chose to follow their unholy beliefs. Dammit, you couldn't find out anything positive from Asahiko-san, Sergeant?"

"Not very much sir, it seems that the slap Asahiko-san gave to Hiromoai-san was just an overreaction on his part he offered to me Lieutenant. I wrote it off to the stress he was suffering over the death of his honorable son, Lieutenant." The Sergeant shrugged, informing the Lieutenant that was all he was able to get from the old man.

"Yeah, I kind of got the same feeling from Hiromoai-san, when I spoke to him earlier today, dammit. You think the old man was holding anything back on us, Sergeant?"

"I don't know for certain Lieutenant. He's so damn sharp and hard to read, sir. I guess it comes from his many years of dealing with the general public. I did get the feeling that there was something more he could have told us if he really cared to, Lieutenant. But I don't understand why he'd want to hold anything back from us. He knows damn well we're trying to help him and find his honorable son's murderer, Lieutenant. I'm quite certain he understands if he holds anything back from us, he's only going to help to keep the damn assassin from being arrested then brought to justice. It just doesn't make any sense to me for him to hold anything back from us. This is one helluva a miserable murder case we got ourselves involved in, sir."

"Yeah, I can't believe we can't catch a damn break in this unending case. Just how much time did you spend with the old Asahiko today, Sergeant Okamatsu-san?"

"I don't know, a few hours at best I guess why Lieutenant. I didn't keep the time on the interview. He seemed relaxed enough with me. He did act like he knew more than he was willing to let on though. There was something about the expressions on his face throughout the conversation that kept catching my attention. I think he knew I was seeing something..."

"Like what? This might be something you could have zeroed in on, Sergeant."

"Well Lieutenant, I don't know for certain, like maybe some questions seemed to upset him more than they really should have. Others seemed to make him sad at one point, and then angry at others. At one time, I thought he was going to say something then he quickly caught himself and held back his words. Asahiko-san changed the subject if I remember correctly. I got it down on tape this time Lieutenant. I think it was the time when I asked him if he thought Hiromoai-san had anything to do with his son's death, sir." The Sergeant reported, not knowing for certain if this was the question that caused Asahiko what he believed was alarm and concern.

"You mean the damn machine worked properly for you this time around, Sergeant?"

"Hai Lieutenant, it certainly did this time sir."

"Dammit to hell Sergeant Okamatsu-san, did you try pressuring him further with any of your questions, Mister?"

"What! Me, a mere Police Sergeant hanging onto my job with my fingernails try to pressure a man who can snap his fingers and have my job taken out from under me, sir. No way in hell Lieutenant, I tried to be extra polite and indifferent at all times during our conversation, sir. If any pressure has to be placed on this wise old man's shoulders, it's going to have to come from someone who possesses much more clout than I have at my disposal, Lieutenant."

"I guess you're aiming that slug back at my ass, huh Sergeant Wise Guy?" Lieutenant Motoshima growled back as he pointed to his chest with his finger.

"Damn right you Lieutenant. He'd have to work at it to get you dismissed from the force." The Sergeant smirked at his commanding officer.

"You damn chicken shit Sergeant you." He shot back with a grin.

"Damn right I am Lieutenant. That's because I like my job and my balls hanging the way I'm walking around, sir." The Sergeant offered with a grin back to his commanding officer.

"Yeah, sure, right wiseguy." The Lieutenant stared at his Sergeant for a few moments while gathering his thoughts and he suddenly smiled, knowing he was correct. He wondered if it would not have been better served for the investigation for him to have questioned the old Asahiko, and leave Hiromoai to his Sergeant to interrogate. He shrugged it off because it was too late for second guessing anything he ordered now. What was done was done, and there was no way for him to correct it at this point. If he wanted to ask Asahiko any further questions about Hiromoai, he would have to come up with a good reason to bother the powerful old man for a second time over the same subject. There was still something about Hiromoai and his smug attitude rubbing him the wrong way over this murder case. The confused Lieutenant was stuck with no leads, and everywhere he looked, Hiromoai or his name kept cropping up in his face.

"Dammit Sergeant, we have to catch a break in this damn case sooner or later, if we want to solve the damn thing for Christ sake. We have to find this bitch spawn of the devil's swill, this whore of darkness and death roaming the very streets of downtown Tokyo. Hmmm... Maybe I can come up with a reason to speak to Hiromoai again. I can't help but feel that he had something to do with this damn murder case than he's letting on. Why else would he try to buy Asahiko-san's construction company out from him? If I was looking for a possible motive to murder someone, that one certainly fills the bill for my ass, Sergeant."

"Huh, if you want to question Hiromoai-san again Lieutenant, I suggest you take a ride out to Asahiko-san's Castle then, sir." The Sergeant offered without thought this time.

"Again that sonofabitch's name crops up, dammit. What the hell do you mean by that remark Sergeant Wise Guy? Did you see Hiromoai in your travels?" The Lieutenant snapped as he rose from his chair and rested his hands on the desk as he leaned over and stared at the Sergeant.

"What I meant by that remark Lieutenant is, when I was leaving Asahiko-san's Castle before reporting back to your office. I happened to stop on the bottom step of the Castle and lit a butt. I glanced at the flow of traffic and noticed Hiromoai-san driving his fancy ass white car around the side of the Castle." The Sergeant offered as he took a seat, kind of upset the Lieutenant did not have the good manners to offer it to him when he first walked into the office.

"Why the hell didn't you tell me about this discovery when you first entered my damn office Sergeant! This could be a very important bit of information you just offered me, mister." The suddenly angry Lieutenant barked at his smug looking Sergeant.

"Huh Lieutenant, you really think Hiromoai-san has something to do with the death of Yurkowa-san?" Sergeant Okamatsu asked as he tapped a cigarette out of the pack and lit it.

"Like I just said to you moments ago, Hiromoai's name is the only one that keeps popping up every god damn time I go off looking into this damn murder case mister. Yes Sergeant, I strongly believe that he has something to do with this unending case." The Lieutenant replied with a snap as he shoved an ashtray across his desk towards the Sergeant.

"I don't really know Lieutenant, I don't see why Hiromoai-san would have Asahiko-san's son butchered so brutally, sir. If he truly wanted Asahiko-san's business, he could've tried a hostile takeover of it, or something like that to gain the business from Asahiko-san without resorting to murder. It's done every day of the week Lieutenant. It doesn't make any sense if you ask me, sir. Hiromoai-san, resorting to murder, it's almost unthinkable, Lieutenant." The worried Sergeant complained as he stopped the sliding ashtray and flipped his ash in it.

"Dammit to hell, murder never makes much sense to anyone but the damn murderer, Sergeant. Let's look at the overall picture here. Who would have the most to gain if Asahiko-san sold him his damn business, Sergeant?" The Lieutenant snapped as he took a cigarette from Sergeant Okamatsu's pack he dropped on his desk when he walked in his office.

"I believe you might be dead wrong with your belief, Lieutenant Motoshima-san."

"How is that Sergeant?"

"Hiromoai-san has nothing much to gain, if that was his original plan and want, Lieutenant. I happen to know Asahiko-san's selling his business, but to an American buyer sir."

Lieutenant Motoshima suddenly leaned back in his chair and then he stared at the younger Sergeant, trying to digest the information he just received from his field officer, and organized his thoughts over the matter. He breathed out deeply and then grumbled at his Sergeant nastily. "What the hell are you talking about? You know damn well no Japanese business can be sold to an American, without obtaining the proper approval from the government first. If such a sale was pending, I would've been informed about the deal in its infancy, and asked to conduct an intensive investigation into the matter and the background of the American. I can assure you no such request has ever crossed my desk, so this sale is nothing but bull I'm telling you."

"I don't know about how the government would react to such a sale offered by Asahiko-san, but I do know what Asahiko-san said, and he was kind of positive about it might I add, sir. He stated he was selling his construction company to an American Gai Jin in no uncertain terms, sir." The Sergeant snapped as he crushed the cigarette out in the ashtray.

"Hmmm... it looks like we're going to be forced to widen our investigation a might of this damn murder case a little further if you know what I mean, Sergeant."

"Why is that Lieutenant?"

"Well, if an American is suddenly involved in this damn mess, it's a possibility we might have just found our smoking gun in the case. The Americans aren't afraid to apply any undue pressure when they're interested in a business proposition. The lowly Americans will stop at nothing to get their grubby little fingers locked into Japan's world of business mister. Yes Sergeant, even murder if necessary I believe. What better way to apply pressure on someone's head, than by having his honorable son killed in a savage way as this murder was committed? No wonder we weren't able to find any trail of this damn murderer after all this time, Sergeant.

"This daughter of hate who was walking around and killing important Japanese people and their family is no longer on Japanese soil, Sergeant. It looks like I'm going to have to notify the Minister of Foreign Affairs over this sudden turn of events. Maybe, he can shed some light on this supposed transaction you brought up to my attention. At least, find me the name of the American going to become a Japanese business person. That way I can start investigating his ass over this murder case. Maybe, we just got our first break in this damn case after all, Sergeant."

"Then you no longer feel that Hiromoai-san might be the one responsible for poor Yurkowa-san and his wife's savage murder, Lieutenant?" The stunned sounding Sergeant asked as he placed his cigarettes back in his pocket.

"No, Hiromoai-san name will not be removed from the narrow list of suspects I locked my eyes on, Sergeant. That is, not until I found someone else to aim my sights at over this confusing case." The Lieutenant growled as he looked at the tape machine on his desk.

"Who else is on this so called narrow surveillance list you command, Lieutenant?"

"Hiromoai, and now this foul American fool who has dared to invade our country and is thought to be buying Asahiko-san's construction company, Sergeant."

"Then you always believed Hiromoai-san was responsible for Tsutomu-san's savage death from the very beginning of this case, Lieutenant?"

"To be honest with you, yes, ever since the first time I questioned him at that damn party he was attending, I did Sergeant. He acted too damn smug if you ask me when I questioned him, too cock sure of himself, like he was above reproach. The news of Yurkowa's death didn't seem to upset him as much as I though it should. I had my doubts after I last spoke to him. But now, finding out he's hanging around Asahiko-san's Castle, and this American fool coming into the picture now. I lost all doubts. If anything, the two of them are in cohorts with each other.

"Sergeant, I want you to relieve the other officer I have trailing Hiromoai. I don't want you to let him out of your sight for a damn minute. Sleep in your car if you have to so you can remain constantly on the job. Take a second officer along with you so you can sleep while he watches, and then he can sleep while you watch our pigeon. Sooner or later, he's going to make a mistake, and when he does we're going to fall on him like a crumbling building. I can't shake the damn feeling that he's the one behind this damn assassin and his or her evil work."

"What about my girlfriend sir? You know I'd like to spend some time with her if you don't mind, Lieutenant. It's been so long since the last time I pillowed with her, she might start looking around for another warm body to spend her time with. She's been doing a lot of bitching at me lately she never sees me any longer." The Sergeant complained as he shifted his weight.

"I have some bad news for you Sergeant. If we don't crack this murder case in a fast hurry, we're both going to have plenty of time on our hands to play with our ladies, while looking for new employment, Sergeant." The Lieutenant snapped as he snuffed out his cigarette in the ashtray, and then he glared at the Sergeant to get him moving faster on his last orders.

The angry Sergeant glared at Lieutenant Motoshima while weighing his words then said. "Yes, I see what you mean Lieutenant. I guess love is going to have to be placed on the back burner for a while. I only hope she'll understand the extra time I'll be spending on this unending murder case, and she waits for this damn case to finally wrap up for us, sir."

"Damn right Sergeant, and I suggest you get on with your assignment, while I make contact with the Minister of Foreign Affairs office." The Lieutenant let out his breath in a disgusted sigh.

"Yes, I'll get on with it Lieutenant Motoshima-san."

The Lieutenant watched as the sergeant left his office. He hated dealing with the Minister of Foreign Affairs. Every time he got involved with the pain in the ass government officials, it always meant longer hours and very little sleep. If Asahiko was going to sell his business to an American, it was going to be a very sticky investigation on his part.

HIROMOAI'S PENTHOUSE, THE HATANAKA TOWERS

The ancient female Samurai Warrior was relaxing with a warm cup of tea and enjoying the fine company of Lady

Yoke. The two women got involved in speaking about Hiromoai, and when Lady Yoke found out she indeed spent the night with her intended lover and was chika, intimate with him a second time, she began to cry softly.

Wind felt terrible but did not know what to do about her spending time with Hiromoai that Lady Yoke longed for. Tenderly she reached out and caught a tear with the tip of her fingernail and looked at it for a moment, and said in a pleasing voice as she cursed her ari, her existence.

"Lady Yoke, you must remember that the tears are the diamonds of the eyes. They give birth right to the stars that soar freely within the Heavens above our foolish heads, and they give great pleasure to the spirits who guide our footfalls throughout life. Tears are meant to be shed often, so the sky can be lit up at night with a thick blanket of stars for our enjoyment. Never be ashamed to shed them for something you long for, you desire for Lady Yoke. The spirits that place the stars in their position in the sky, will, once they feel you have gave birthright to enough stars for them to enjoy, will answer all your longing dreams."

She stared at Wind with her mouth hanging agape and then she mumbled while drying her eyes. "Oh, how beautiful you truly are spirit of Japan's history. How beautiful your soul is, Yuriko-san. How clear and simple you see what is not supposed to be seen by another's eyes, but by the heart that's breaking within one's chest. I'm so blessed to have such a dear and close Tomo, a friend such as you Yuriko-san. I'll burn three sticks of incense in your honor before the statue of Lord Buddha tonight, and I'll thank the Kami of friendship for placing you within my path. You have made the unendurable most endurable for me my Tomo. Thank you for being my friend. I'll try to be as good a friend to you as you are to me, Yuriko-san."

"As it was said throughout the many ages I have wandered through, the only heart that is whole is the one that has been broken in the game of love fare, Lady Yoke. You are more of a friend to me than I could possibly hope to attain to you. You stood by me when the old one forced his self on my person, and I was powerless to stop his indecent assault of my body. I am cursed by my toda chu, my loyalty to my Lord, to carry out the bidding of my Master no matter who or what that Master demands of my spirit. I do not know how far the disgusting and lowly Utsumi would have gone with his assault against me in my Lord's bedroom.

"I thank Karma for giving you the great wisdom to enter Hiromoai-sama's room when you did. I wait in silence for permission to seek my revenge on the repulsive head of that old man. I know that day is fast approaching, all I have to be is patient and the gods will reward me with his foul head resting on the gunyoki spike for their viewing, and his rotting carcass brought before the Council of Kami for discernment and tenchu, Heavenly punishment. The lonely life of a Samurai is one of unending patience and waiting to be summoned by his Lord, or the Kami." She proudly announced as she placed the tip of her finger with Lady Yoke's tear in her mouth.

The Lady Yoke was truly enjoying the chance to use her Japanese. Lately, she used her native language less and less when dealing with modern day Japanese people. She was so pleased listening to Wind's wonderful words, and the pleasant way she pronounced them. Over the countless centuries, the Japanese language had suffered from the intrusion of many different dialects, and words of slang inserted that it so polluted the once pure language of the past and changed the old language terribly. She believed what she was hearing from Wind's lips, was the correct and true way to speak the forgotten Japanese tongue.

"You know so much of both worlds of wonder I understand and I'll never be as wise as you I fear. Will you teach me to have the eyes you see life through, and the ears you hear with? I have heard enough words spoken with nigon, double tongue of late, Yuriko-san." Lady Yoke asked of her friend as she smiled warmly at the ancient female warrior.

"It would give this worthless Samurai great pleasure and honor to show you the many ways of both worlds I travel in, Lady Yoke. I have witnessed much in my long and very exhausting existence. In that of the living world, and of the Floating one I dwell mostly within, there are many secrets withheld from the uncountable spirits who roam freely in the Floating World. If they are patient, and see with not only their eyes, but their ears and hearts, one will hear all the well guarded secrets the living camouflage their hearts with. The pain, hatred and killing, requests for help or revenge, and above all, the loving which is withheld from we spirits. We are doomed to a very lonely existence without love dwelling within the Floating World, even though we might come across a past love, a dear friend or a defeated once enemy to your person, we are not allowed to pillow with them." She smiled at Lady Yoke as she bowed to the young woman.

"Yuriko-san, if you don't mind, may I ask of you a question please?"

"Hai Lady Yoke, and if it is within my limited power to fulfill that question, I shall be more than pleased to answer it truthfully for your kind self."

"Yuriko-san, in all your endless days of dwelling within the Floating World of wonderment, have you ever come across your past lover, Captain Seisakajo-san? Have you ever seen him again in the other world?" She asked as she wiped the tears from her eyes.

Her heart immediately became saddened at the mention of his name, as she allowed her mind to fondly remember her one and only love, Captain Katsunoke Seisakajo. Her mind locked in on his ever smiling face, as she retraced the first night of lovemaking with him in her mind. How gentle he was with her, how she needed someone when he chose to enter her dwelling to see what was troubling her so. The terrible memory of her honored father dying so overwhelmed her, and she cried unashamedly. She missed her honored father, her mother, and two sisters as much as she missed her past life as the commanding samurai and respected General.

She fought off a shudder as she remembered embarrassingly how she nearly attacked Seisakajo when he entered her living quarters, with the need and want of a lover while he ripped her kosode from her body. She remembered how she struggled to get him out of his fundoshi, the samurai loincloth. How her desperate need for someone to hold, to make love to, to seek life giving warmth with and from, her need for love and understanding from anyone at that moment in time, gave her the forwardness to be so brazen, like a woman from the pleasure world.

She remembered speaking of this to Lady Yoke while she enjoyed a soak in the hot tub, but to revisit fond emotions was both pleasing and upsetting to her Wa and spirit. She chose to visit these memories often, because it gave the spirit of Captain Seisakajo immortality in the land of the living world, by her remembering his life so and in so loving a light.

The ancient female samurai allowed a quick smile to cross her lips, as she affectionately recalled the first vision of Samurai Seisakajo's mighty dragon swaying gently, once it was freed from the manly protective mantle, as it waited permission to enter her wanting Jade Gate. She remembered the wonderful experience of Captain Seisakajo's first entry in her void. The slight pain it caused her then how it so filled her, overwhelmed her being, opening the door to her womanhood and making her whole, wanted and loved. She retained how they made love on that night when her honorable father died by his own hand, and frowned unhappily when she came to her senses and forced the confused Captain Seisakajo out of her shoinzukuri samurai house, as if he had done something wrong against her. She allowed her fears to overrule her mind, leaving Captain Seisakajo questioning himself for what he done to displease her so.

A scowl caused frown lines to appear on her forehead as she remembered the loathsome warrior who killed her once lover on the field of battle. When she found out about Captain Seisakajo's death, she sworn an oath of blood to kill the hated attacker and all his lowly ancestors as she saw the ugly and sneering face of Tetsuo Hatanaka burned deeply in her mind's eye again.

Finally, after much time had passed between them, Wind was finally able to muster the strength she needed to answer Lady Yoke's last question of her as she replied calmly. "Gomen nasai, I'm terribly sorry for not responding to your question sooner than this time, Lady Yoke. But living in the Floating World of forever wanting, ever waiting, it is forbidden for all but the most powerful of Kami to seek out any worldly pleasures of body and mind with another spirit, or take the revenge of the soul and heart for one's self against ones cursed and hated enemy. I fear that it is a very lonely place in which to be trapped in for all eternity to come, Lady Yoke.

"I have prayed many times throughout my unending life to the Lord Buddha, begging him to end the terrible loneliness I have been forced to suffer through for so many centuries past, Lady Yoke. But he has never thought to answer my countless pleas for my release from my forever prison. I fear that I will never be allowed to be reborn a pure Samurai Warrior to the world of the living ever again, but for these very short visits I am allowed by the powerful Kami who control all destiny and time."

"Iye! gomen nasai. No, I'm the one who is terribly sorry and thoroughly embarrassed for my endless questions of your past life, Yuriko-san. Did something I say upset you my new friend? What's wrong, you seem suddenly distressed and upset my dear friend." Lady Yoke noticed the sudden change in her facial expression, and the sad and almost angry look she witnessed that had now covered her face.

"Iye, nane mo. No nothing you have mentioned has upset me in the least Lady Yoke. I was just remembering the loathsome and hideous face of the lowly and hated eta that had killed my lover in a most horrendous and terribly cowardly way in the dark of night, Lady Yoke. That is all, my friend." The female samurai allowed the troubled lines of out of control hatred to contort her lovely face into an ugly distortion for a moment.

Lady Yoke was about to ask her the killer's name, when Hiromoai suddenly entered the apartment in great haste. He was smiling from ear to ear, and he nodded pleasantly at both Wind and Lady Yoke as he rushed passed them so he could change into the more comfortable kimono, and he called out as he rushed by them. "Kon banwa. Good evening my two fair ladies. I hope that everything is well with you ladies on this lovely night. I have much good news to share with both of you on this fine night that I can't wait to tell you about my news."

They both looked at each other, even though it was late, it was not quite evening as Hiromoai's had suggested. The women giggled as they watched him climbing the steps leading to his master suite two steps at a time, as if he was going to be with his long wanted mistress after much time apart from each other. The two beautiful women prepared for when the lord of the house came back to speak with them. They knew he was excited about something and they could not wait to know what it was.

They were silently praying Hiromoai's good mood would last throughout the evening and night, for they too were in good moods. Although Wind was ancient in her time and age, she looked about the same age of her death, and Lady Yoke was finding it strange to look at someone so old, yet looked young enough to be her sister. She could not take her eyes off the lovely spirit's beautiful face from many years ago past.

CHAPTER EIGHTEEN

THE ANCIENT ENGAKUJI CASTLE IN OLD TOKYO

It was late and Asahiko had more things that he needed to complete before he went through with his final act of life, and committed Suppuku to relieve the terrible burden clouding his mind of knowing he had outlived his first born honorable son. The old man scanned the many stacks of papers delivered by courier from his accountant, Fumimaro Kakizawa. He signed the necessary papers without reading them over and then set them on the lacquered table he placed to his left for his trusted lawyer to retrieve, when he arrived to carry out his part of Asahiko's plan of selling of his company to the American, Calvin Batterman.

To Asahiko's right sat a specially prepared altar where a small statue of Lord Buddha rested peacefully on a base of fine sand. In the sand sat five sticks of incense burning, raising a slight cloud of rich scented smoke around the Buddha's head like a halo, filling his nostrils with the fragrance, the sweet rich scent calmed his nerves. A bowl of uncooked rice sat before the feet of the religious statue on the makeshift altar. This was offered because his hara-kiri was not going to be seconded by a friend who would assure he would not suffer long before the second lopped his head from his shoulders, and finished his act of Suppuku, and the pain involved in the act.

It was a terrible insult for any Japanese man of worth to commit Suppuku without a second at his side as witness, and a protector against the evil Kami forever prowling the underworld. If he did not offer rice, ancient law stated he would never be reborn to the world of the living. All Asahiko was waiting for, was the arrival of his lawyer with the papers from the American, and then to collect the papers delivered by his accountant. Then, he would be allowed to take his life once he signed the papers and relieve his constant suffering over his slaughtered son.

Time crawled by at a snail's pace as Asahiko went through the rest of the needed ceremony as he laid out the three pure white sheets of unwrinkled rice paper before his bent and aching knees. He turned to his right and gingerly lifted the small, teak box hon zogane with inlays of silver and gold decorating the fine wood box. He lightly touched the small box to his forehead and bowed to it in silence and respect as he mumbled time forgotten words of prayers to the Kami. Then he placed the box out before him beyond the rice paper. He could not yet open the box containing the chiisa gatana, the short stabbing sword reserved especially for the hallowed act of Suppuku, until he was ready to take his life with the honored weapon.

Next, the old man moved the wood shaped bowl containing pure spring water free of all contaminants, and placed that bowl next to the box. He picked up the bamboo cup that he would soon use to pour the clean water over the blade of the tanto knife, to purify the spirits of the fine blade, seconds before using it to open his innards for the honored Kami's appetite to feast upon.   He crossed his aged bent legs under him with great effort and then he entered into a period of deep meditation. He prayed for the good Kami to second his honorable death, and to keep the worrisome tengu, the ever present evil wood goblins known to be half man, half bird from stealing his soul before it had a chance to reach the Court of Final Justice of the Kami.

He feared the loathsome tengu spirits, because his death was not going to be seconded by a close and trusted friend, as the ancient laws demanded of the sacred act. If the tengu were able to capture his spirit before it reached the safety of the Kami lair, they would completely devour it, and his soul would be forever condemned to wander aimlessly through the vast void of never, without guidance, without true direction or support.

He was so deep in meditation he failed to hear his lawyer as he entered the room.

Asahiko's lawyer, Shigeru Nagaro walked into the room with a smile as he held the papers under his arm and the check from the American in his hand. The moment he saw the position Asahiko sat, he understood he was in the void of meditation, preparing for his honorable death. The lawyer stopped for a moment, and when he realized he did not interrupt Asahiko's prayers by entering the room, he moved forward as silently as a cat. He remained standing, barely breathing as he waited for his mind to come back to the present world, and acknowledge his presence. For nearly fifteen minutes, he remained standing in silence and awe of the old man.

Suddenly, Asahiko's eyes fluttered open and he stared momentarily at his lawyer as if he did not truly recognize him. Then he let out his breath and began to breathe normally as he smiled at the lawyer looking him in his eyes, to make certain he was still alive.

Nagaro bowed and held it, paying homage to the fragile old man about to do the noblest act to be carried out by any Japanese man of honor and respect. A man his family knew for countless years. Before his father died, he was the lawyer for Yurkowa construction. When he died, Asahiko was kind enough to seek out Shigeru, and asked him to takeover where his father left his company. It gave him pleasure and honor to take over his father's position in his company.

"Yokoso oide kudasareta, welcome to my house old friend of unquestionable loyalty and respect. Please Nagaro-san, sit and be comfortable for one last time in my worthless and aged life. You may join me at this place of honor and purity. I have not yet opened the box to seal my fate, Nagaro-san. Ikaga desu ka? How are you tonight?" The old man smiled with great effort, his lower lip actually trembling slightly because of the stress he was under.

"Domo genki desu, quite well thank you Asahiko-san. Ikaga desu ka tomo? How are you my old friend? You honor me now as you have honored me as always in the past years of long and unending friendship." Nagaro replied as he straightened from his bow and respectfully lowered himself to the floor with the greatest of care before Asahiko. Making certain no part of his body touched the wood box, rice paper, or bowl of water separating them. Once he was seated and comfortable, Asahiko said.

"Domo genki desu Nagaro-san. You have the necessary papers from the American for me to sign, huh?" he reached out his hand and waited for the lawyer to pass him the papers.

"Hai Asahiko-san, the necessary papers are prepared and signed by the fool and they're with me, sir." He offered as he held the papers above the sacrifice area as he went on with his words. "Asahiko-san, the check from the foolish American is with me as well sir. It's all of what you had agreed to with the American who I dislike, Calvin Batterman, Asahiko-san."

"Good, I knew that I could depend on your loyal assistance to me as always, Nagaro-san. Give me the page or two I have to finalize with my chop. You'll make certain that my honorable son's wife's family will receive the money for my company as was promised, Nagaro-san?" He asked making certain that his son's wife's family was going to be well looked after by the money he was going to leave them in his will.

"If that's what you want done with it then it shall be as you have ordered me, Asahiko-san. You don't wish to read the papers and check them and make certain they are as you have requested, before you sign them, Asahiko-san?" The lawyer offered as he bowed slightly.

Asahiko nodded in compliance with the lawyer's question. "Iye sir! I trust you with my very life as I have always done in my past my friend. If you wrote up the necessary documents like your honorable father before you then all has to be in order in my favor, Nagaro-san. Once I signed them, what will I care what happens to my business, or for the fate of Japan? I feel Japan has abandoned me at the time I needed her support the most. Soon, I'll be walking with my ancestors and my honorable son and his wife, and again enjoying myself Nagaro-san."

"Please, I wish I could talk you out of this most honorable act, Asahiko-san." The lawyer mumbled, already knowing it was impossible for him to stop Asahiko from taking his life.

"You cannot, what cannot be avoided must be history until the end of time as we know it, Nagaro-san. I truly appreciate your devoted interest in my worthless welfare and life. Nagaro-san, everything has a beginning and an end to it, and my end is waiting for my final summons to the laws of fate. I don't want to live in a world in which my most honorable and trusted son has abandoned before me. There's nothing remaining here for me of any further interest, no more wars to conquer, no more ventures I have not defeated, no fences to climb or crash through. The life in my old and bent body has left this worthless shell, and is now carried in the arms of my dead son, and he's guarding it faithfully until my arrival before him. I pray to the Kami to open the true path of meeting, so I might once again find my worthy and loved son in the next world, and again am able to walk with him shoulder to shoulder.

"All I want, all I crave in my remaining moments of life, is to once more lay my foul eyes upon Tsutomu-san's forever smiling kind face. To have this request granted by the Kami, will fill my worthless hollow shell with the full spirit of life, even in the Floating World, Nagaro-san."

"Asahiko-san, you're a man of great honor and respect and undying love and affection for your honorable son, and his lovely wife. Your fine spirit will carry my greatest respect with it for always, to lay it before the feet of the Judgment Kami. It'll help plea your request before them, Asahiko-san. What else can I say to ease your terrible pain and hurt, my old friend of countless years past?" The cunning lawyer Nagaro said as he lowered his eyes towards the small box that contained the razor sharp and blessed tanto blade.

"There's nothing you can say or offer that would cause me to delay my existence on this worthless rock we call Earth, for a moment longer than I'm forced to endure it, Nagaro-san. I hope beyond hope in my next life, I'll find a world of peace and love and understanding. I spent my entire life fighting, deceiving, and cheating everyone I was forced to deal with. Now, it's time I make amends for my past sins played out against humanity and the soil of Japan, and I'm finally allowed to rest in peace. Please pass me the papers so that I may sign them then leave this plain of misery and sorrow." He held out a shaking, old and wrinkled hand and waited.

Nagaro passed the sheet he had to sign and said. "Asahiko-san, you pay me great honor to trust me without checking what I have set to paper on your behalf. I'm deeply honored my old friend."

"Nagaro-san, if there's anyone who dwells on the face of this Earth who'll protect me and my interests with his dying breath it has to be you. You're a man of toda chu, total loyalty. As great as your honorable and respected father before you was to me and my company, son." The old man turned slightly and laid the paper on the floor next to his hip and placed his name to it.

Nagaro sat back, his chest swelled with pride over the compliment offered by this proud old man waiting to kill himself. He could not believe his ears when Asahiko called him his son. It was far too great a sign of respect the old man offered him. He searched his mind, trying to find another way to support, to help his old friend at this great time of need. Suddenly, a thought entered his mind and he offered in a polite voice to the old man. "Asahiko-san, please excuse this fool for interrupting you at this most sacred of times. But I beg an o negai, a favor of you sir."

Asahiko did not respond until he signed the paper, and then handed the page to Nagaro then he stared into his sad eyes and replied. "Hai Nagaro-san. What is this great favor you request of this old fool? Any request from you, forces me by honor to fulfill it my son."

The lawyer actually flinched and squirmed as he knelt uncomfortably on the floor before Asahiko. At first, he was not certain the old man heard his request for the begged favor.

Seeing the dilemma his lawyer was suffering from, he repeated his words impatiently to him. "Nagaro-san, I asked you what is this great favor you have requested from this old and feeble man who wastes the oxygen designated for the young and useful of the Eight Islands of Japan. I'm anxious to begin my sacred journey of the search for my honorable son, my friend."

HIROMOAI'S PENTHOUSE IN THE HATANAKA TOWERS.
6:30 P.M., SATURDAY, JUNE 8th, 1996

Hiromoai Hatanaka marched defiantly down the steps from his bedroom as if he were an ancient and feared Shogun of the past great times of Japan. He was dressed in a strikingly yellow and green kimono of victory and a wide golden obi held the exquisite fabric in place.

Both women remained kneeling while they waited for Hiromoai to come downstairs. When he entered the study, they both bowed to the good looking young master of the house.

Hiromoai did not speak until he dropped down like a sack of potatoes on the sofa before the two beautiful women kneeling peaceful on the floor. Hiromoai looked at Lady Yoke first, and he grunted in a commanding tone at her. "Lady Yoke, fetch me three cups of sabazuki, the good sake from my private collection is needed for this wonderful celebration between the three of us. I believe tonight is a time for great commemoration, especially when Wind has returned from her next mission. Ima! Now, at once Lady Yoke, I'm waiting your return."

"Hai Hiromoai-san." She replied as she jumped to her feet and rushed to the kitchen.

Wind remained locked in her gracious bow before the young lord of the house. She would remain that way until she was instructed to do otherwise.

He sat comfortably and closed his eyes and pinched the bridge of his nose for a moment as he collected his rampaging thoughts, and tried to organize them. He opened them when Lady Yoke entered the study and knelt before him as she offered the first cup of sake to him. She held, and then offered the first cup in the old way, with the porcelain cup resting comfortably on the outstretched palm of her left hand, two fingers of her right hand carefully guiding the cup so it would not spill, and show him she held nothing of a threat hidden in her hands.

Hiromoai leaned forward and took the cup from Lady Yoke with carefully respect and then waited for Wind to be served next by the Lady Yoke.

"Wind-san, please allow this worthless of vassals to serve you proudly and properly on this great night." Lady Yoke pleaded as she bowed politely towards the female samurai from Japan's proud and savage past. She did not call Wind by her chosen name of Yuriko because she did not know if Hiromoai would approve of the name or not.

She looked up from her bow, smiled and took the offered cup in silence as she nodded.

Lady Yoke bowed low while lifting the third cup, not knowing who it was ear marked for.

"What are you waiting for Lady Yoke? You don't wish to join us in drink and honor tonight, young lady?" He complained at the beautiful Lady Yoke, and smiled at her.

She stared at Hiromoai, surprised she thought the third cup was for the foul Utsumi to enjoy.

"Please forgive this foolish old hag of a lowly woman, but I thought this cup was for Utsumi, Hiromoai-san. I dared not take your kindness to me for granted." She was so angry with the old man she subconsciously omitted the san from his name.

"Nonsense, it honors me to share drink with my two most trusted and loyal friends in this world. Where the devil is the old fool Utsumi hiding at anyway? I haven't seen hide nor hair of the old man since yesterday afternoon." He hissed as he brought the cup up to his lips.

"Utsumi is still in his room. I can fetch him if you please Hiromoai-san?" She offered kindly as she left her bow and brought her cup towards her mouth slowly.

"No, there's no need for that old fool to be here and upsetting all three of us on this fine occasion between us. I want this celebration to be one of great pleasure and respect, and his boring presence might upset that pleasure for us. What I have to offer you two ladies is better served to remain between us, Lady Yoke, Wind-san. Gyoko, luck." He grumbled at the two women as he gulped the sake.

Lady Yoke and Wind repeated the phrase Hiromoai employed as they drank. Wind was proud to share drink with Lady Yoke and her Lord and Master at the same time. It was like old times as she stared proudly at the young Hiromoai.

When they drained their cups, he placed his cup on the coffee table and then snapped hotly. "Lady Yoke, where the hell do you have the map and pictures of Engakuji Castle placed? I have need of them, to go over what I have discovered there today with Wind-san."

"I shall get them for you immediately Hiromoai-san." Lady Yoke bowed and got up.

"Isogi! Hurry, we have much to go over on this night, and little time to do it in Lady Yoke."

"Hai. I shall return swiftly Hiromoai-san, with the requested papers you need, sir."

They waited in silence for Lady Yoke to return with the requested papers. When she did, she immediately handed them over to Hiromoai and then she swiftly returned to her kneeling position before him, and looked at Wind and smiled at her.

He quickly laid the pages out before Wind as he dropped to the floor to join the two women, so they both could see what he was offering them.

IN THE STREET OUTSIDE HATANAKA TOWERS

Sergeant Toshihiro Okamatsu of the Detective Division of the Tokyo Police Department, removed the last cigarette from his pack of American made Winstons, and crumpled the pack and pitched it to the rear seat of the unmarked police car both he and Corporal Tomiichi Hattori sat in. The Sergeant lit up the cigarette and moaned to the other officer with him. "I really hate this crap with a passion. Here we are, sitting in this damn police car sitting on our rumps while Hiromoai-san sits in a room no less than a Castle, while enjoying who knows what with who knows who. I can't believe Lieutenant Motoshima-san still believes Hiromoai-san has anything to do with the savage death of poor Tsutomu-san and his lovely wife. I think we're wasting our time sitting here like a couple of fish out of water all night long, Corporal. There has to be something more important we could be doing to help solve this damn murder case than just sitting on our rumps looking at a building like we expect it to up and run away on us."

"Whatever, as long as we're getting paid for it, who the hell cares? So stop your belly aching and count the money you're earning while we sit here like two fools, Sergeant." Hattori replied as he continued to look out the window of the squad car at the Hatanaka Tower.

"Yeah, you see things in black and white form, no color don't you Corporal? What do you care about how long we're cooped up in this squad car, you're married and you don't have to worry about your girlfriend dumping your ass because you're never home with her, dammit. If I didn't know any better, I'd think you're enjoying the time you're away from your wife, Mister."

Hattori shrugged as he continued to look out the window, keeping an eye on the Tower.

"I don't know about you, but I'd rather be spending my time exploring the many mysteries of the Jade Gate of my girl Miyako, than being stuck here wasting my time sitting here staring at this stupid ass building as if I was waiting for the damn thing to get up and walk away on us."

"So would I like to be exploring Miyako's mysteries of the Jade Gate, if I had the chance to Sergeant Okamatsu-san." He offered dryly without taking his eyes off the Hatanaka Tower.

Sergeant Okamatsu stared at the Corporal's back for several seconds, trying to figure out what the Corporal meant by his last comment about wanting to spend time with his girlfriend. Hattori took his eyes off the doors and turned to the Sergeant, smiled and then laughed at him.

"Funny Mister, real funny. You know something wiseguy. One of these damn days Corporal, that dry sense of humor of yours is going to get you in more trouble that you'll not be able to laugh your way out of. You better start watching your step before you really get into some serious trouble, fool." The Sergeant replied as he joined the Corporal in laughing.

"Can you see the penthouse from where you're sitting, Sergeant?" Hattori took his eyes off the Tower, and then looked at the Sergeant while he waited for his reply.

Sergeant Okamatsu then leaned forward in his car seat and lifted his eyes to the upper floors of the building. He could barely make out the five wide sliding glass shoji doors of Hiromoai's exquisite apartment only after he undid his seat belt and replied to his fellow officer. "Yeah Corporal, I got them in my sight and no one's going to get out those damn doors without my seeing them first I can assure you. I really hate like hell doing this damn boring stakeout duty, Corporal. It's nothing more than a pain in the ass, and is boring as hell like I said."

"Do you mind if I ask you a question Sergeant? Do you really think that someone's going to be foolish enough to try and get out of the apartment that way, Sergeant? The fool would have to be part bird and be able to fly in order to escape us that way." The Corporal said as he joined the Sergeant while looking up at the twenty-seventh floor of the massive Hatanaka Tower.

"Not really Hattori-san, but it's the only other exit from the damn building that we don't have covered by the other officers in the field, Corporal. I can't imagine anyone trying to get in or out of Hiromoai-san's apartment trying to work his way up the side of the damn building, or trying to leave his apartment this way either, Hattori-san." Sergeant Okamatsu had a second set of officers stationed at the rear exit doors of the Tower, just in case someone tried to get out or in the building that way, without them seeing the intruder.

"Hey Sergeant, would you want me to get you something to eat? Dammit, I'm starving and I think I'm going to hit the sushi bar next to us for something to eat, Sergeant. Every time someone opens the damn door to the restaurant, I get a good whiff of food and it makes my stomach growls with hunger. I just have to get myself something to eat from there. I can't stand the way my stomach is growling at me." The other police officer offered to his lead Sergeant.

"Naw, I'm fine, but you're free to go and get something to eat if you need to Corporal."

"No, I guess I can hack it for a little while longer if you can, Sergeant Okamatsu-san. I just offered because I thought you might be getting a little hungry like me, Sergeant. I should've had my wife pack me up something to eat though she knew I pulled stake out duty tonight, Sergeant. Damn, every time I get a whiff of their damn cooking it makes my mouth water."

HIROMOAI'S PENTHOUSE APARTMENT

Hiromoai had the map and pictures of the castle spread out on the floor. He showed Wind where he was able to locate the carved stone of the serpent covering the still hidden passageway leading into the great castle from under the moat on one of the many pictures.

"I believed it would remain in the world of the living, Hiromoai-sama. Anything that has the mighty sea serpent Kami guarding it is bound to have the powerful protection from the destructive elements of age and neglect, my Lord." She replied to the information as she stared at his finger and where it pointed on the picture of the castle.

"Yes Samurai, and I'm pleased it's still there Wind-san. It makes your mission much easier for you to accomplish. I believe I was able to locate the exact dwelling of Asahiko's living quarters in the Castle." He moved a few more pictures of Engakuji Castle over the map, and he looked until he found the location he was searching for on one of them.

"Yes, here it is, this room here was the only area in the entire Keep that showed any lights on while I was searching for the entrance of the hidden passage. I know Asahiko was in the Castle when I was near. So this has to be where the old fool is staying inside the Castle. Are you familiar with this area of the Keep, Wind-san?"

Wind closely examined the area where Hiromoai's finger pointed on the map. She realized it was on the third floor of the main structure of the castle he was drawing her attention to, and she immediately recognized the location to be the old meeting room of Lord Kawasomeru, his favorite room to be in whenever he was visiting the castle. She smiled as she remembered her last meeting with the Generals and the powerful warlord. When she offered to open her attack on Lord Wakatsuki's samurai from the Kii pass, in an effort to split his enemy forces in two so she could come in from his unprotected flanks, and then smash his main battle force in half on the dishonored warlord then defeat both smaller Armies with her mounted warriors.

"Yes Hiromoai-sama, I'm familiar with this certain section of the interior of your Castle. Once I made my way through the passageway guarded by the mighty Shibi Kami, I can make good use of the crossed yagara mogaro pole passage, to get myself up to the third floor where the location you're pointing to on this picture is, my Lord."

"There are more passageways hidden inside the Castle Keep, Wind-san?"

"Oh yes my Lord, there are many to choose from. The Castle is honeycombed with concealed passageways. All designed for the Master of the Keep to make use of at his leisure, and remain undiscovered while you were roaming the Castle. To visit rooms of your consorts, unobserved I trust by your other servants. Or spy on certain invited visitors to the Castle to destroy any possible treachery being considered against my Lord and Master, before these evil plans had a chance to succeed against you. They were also designed to enable my Liege Lord to roam freely when your mind was troubled, or to escape the Castle in times of siege and war. So you were able to meet with your Military Officers out in the field, while your enemy thought you to be still trapped within your Castle walls, my Lord." She bowed correctly to her master.

"This is good, very good indeed. This is going to make your efforts to destroy my hated enemy that much easier to accomplish. Tonight, I want you to erase this enemy from the face of the earth." Hiromoai smiled as he listened to her assuring words.

"Hai my Lord, to hear your orders makes me ready to do battle for your honor. I'm the prophet of my Master's wants and desires. Fear not Hiromoai-sama, tonight, this teki, this hated enemy of yours will draw his last breath in the world of the living and enjoyment of sense and smells. So will be the fate of all fools who dare plot treacherousness against my Master's sake."

The excited Japanese businessman suddenly clapped his hands loudly as he rose from the floor to stretch his legs starting to cramp up under the weight of his body. For some reason, he decided to stroll to the sliding glass doors that led to his patio. He glanced out the doors to the streets below with no thought in mind. A glare from a car interior light caught his eye. He watch as a Japanese man got out of the car and headed for the sushi bar. He watched the man, and knew by his mannerisms he was obviously a police offer assigned to watch his every move.

He realized who it was and moved away from the window as if his life depended on the quick move, and then he turned and headed for the sofa while his temper began to grow. Knowing he was under tight police surveillance, changed things drastically for Wind's mission tonight. Now, she would have to be extra careful leaving the Tower for her mission. He was not certain she could leave his apartment without being detected by the officers below in the streets. He sat deep in the sofa while staring at Wind, who was still kneeling on the floor before him.

SERGEANT OKAMATSU'S POLICE CAR

Just as Hattori got out of the squad car to get himself something to eat, Sergeant Okamatsu happened to glance up at the sliding glass doors of Hiromoai's penthouse apartment. He quickly picked up the silhouette of someone looking out at them. He tried to get Hattori's attention to stop him from opening the door and light up the interior of the vehicle, but he was too late because the other officer was already out of the parked car. The angry Sergeant turned back to the doors of the apartment and saw the shadow had already moved away from the doors. "Dammit", he growled, fearing they were just discovered by whoever just looked out of the sliding doors. He found himself cursing Hattori's constant hunger as he watched the Corporal enter the sushi bar, knowing he did not notice what just took place.

Now, he did not know what to do, his first instinct was to pull the surveillance teams from their stakeout of Hatanaka Tower, in an attempt to try and make Hiromoai think he was no longer under their observance. He knew the sly businessman would never be so foolish as to make a mistake now he understood he was under around the clock surveillance by his department. One thing he knew for certain he was not going to do, and that was to call Lieutenant Motoshima to inform him they were discovered by their target. He would never allow him to live this error down as long as he continued to work for the police department.

The upset Sergeant resigned himself to tough it out in hopes nothing was going to take place on this night anyhow. He still did not believe Hiromoai had anything to do with Tsutomu and his wife's death. The officer's attention was drawn again to the store, as Hattori came walking out the door carrying two containers of raw tuna and cups of cooked rice.

HIROMOAI'S APARTMENT

Hiromoai stared at her for a moment in silence and offered. "Wind-san, some of my enemy is much wiser than I first gave them credit for, and they're watching me in hopes they can discover your existence. We're going to have to be extremely careful about this exercise tonight. I'm going to need you to be no more than a kage, a shadow in the middle of the night. Do you think you'll be skillful enough to leave this apartment now you know there are eyes watching my every move? Or do you think it might be wiser to put off your mission for another time, another day. I don't want you taking chances on this night. I can't have the police capturing you, Wind-san."

"Hai my Lord, I do not think it is necessary to put off my mission of this night. I can be no more than a breath of air in the night's darkness if I choose, Hiromoai-sama. If you want, I can dispatch the enemy who disrupt your yasu, your peace, before I go after this other of your teki?"

"No that'll not be necessary in the least, I believe I want them to continue their observance of me, I need the damn fools to watch me so that way I can't possibly be connected to the soon to be death of this old fool you're about to dispatch on this night, Wind-san. The foolish police must be allowed to live so they can report to their superiors that I was at home minding my own business, when the worthless Asahiko finally met his offensive fate at your most honorable hands. Are you quite certain you can leave the apartment without being detected by the lowly ones who watch me at all times both day and night?"

"Hai my Lord, no one will see me leave your honorable dwelling for my duty. I shall be like the Night Wind moving through the darkness my Master." She proudly boasted to Hiromoai.

"Very well, we'll go ahead with our plan. I so want this old fool to meet his foul fate tonight, Samurai. I want the worthless fool dead so badly I can actually taste his wanted death in my mouth. The old man has more than out lived his loathsome days allotted on this Earth, Wind-san. I need his death I demand his death as I demand you to end his worthless life for him." He checked his watch it was nearing eight p.m. then added to his words for the female warrior. "Wind-san, we'll do as we did last time you went out against my enemy. We'll wait for the first stick of time that identifies the new day's beginning. That's twelve midnight in this time."

"Hai my Lord, your wish is my only desire to complete on this foul night."

"Well Samurai let's trace out the path that you'll employ to get you to the Castle undiscovered tonight, Wind-san." Hiromoai removed the pictures of the castle from the map of downtown Tokyo, and explained using the map and route she would take to get her to the castle safely.

The Lady Yoke remained silent as she listened closely to the orders Hiromoai gave Wind. She enjoyed listening to the old words being spoken between the two, even though those words would result in the death of one of the most powerful and honored Japanese businessman. It mattered to her, but her loyalty to Hiromoai meant far more than this man's death.

THE ANCIENT ENGAKUJI CASTLE

Asahiko could not understand the eerie look Nagaro offered while he waited without word for him to speak. His patience was growing thin, and he snapped as he repeated. "Nagaro-san, I'm waiting to hear of this favor you seek of me on this exhausting and unending night. I fear though I might die of age by the time you speak the words that has your tongue tied in knots."

"Forgive the stumbling of an old friend who wishes to speak, but is afraid to do so for fear of possibly insulting my old friend of countless years at this most important time in his honorable life, Asahiko-san." The lawyer moaned with the greatest of respect in his voice as he gathered his strength to speak to the old man glaring angrily at him now.

"Lawyer we've been friends too long for you to fear insulting me over any matter of interest to you, Nagaro-san. Ask of me what the devil you want of me, and if it's in my power, it'll give me great pleasure to offer it to you at this sacred of times in my life. But it must be quick about it because my destiny is calling these old bones to its bosom on this faithful night, Nagaro-san."

He did not know what to do, so he bowed deeply towards Asahiko again.

"Nagaro-san, you're still wasting my time over this matter that seems so important to you. I have to prepare my soul for what I must do on this saddest of nights in my life. I must complete my preparations by midnight, that way my spirit can be sent on its way by traveling in my body between the two day's life, and escape before the Tengu wood goblins realize a lonely spirit's traveling through their domain on its way to the mystical Floating World of wonderment.

"I must do everything in my power to fool the crafty evil spirits of the woods, if I hope to get my being before the feet of the Justice Kami, because I'm suffering an honorable death without a second to assist and send me on my last journey of life. Now Nagaro-san, ask of me your favor before I lose my temper and patience, and refuse to listen to your request, let alone honor it if it's in my power to fulfill." He glared at the hesitating friend he did not try to deceive himself, he understood if his lawyer had something he was begging to ask, he had to honor that request.

Without knowing it, he gave the lawyer the opening he was searching for, and he took advantage of the lead. "Asahiko-san that's what I wanted to speak to you about, my old frie..."

"What is it Nagaro-san!" Asahiko snapped, interrupting the one person he felt would never be at a loss for words. He believed if a lawyer ever lost his tongue for even one moment, he would lose his profession and mind at the same time. He allowed a smile over this most pleasing of thoughts, a lawyer without a tongue. Oh what a dream and a pleasure and peace that thought would bring to the Wa of the earth and its people. The old man even smiled over this thought as he continued to stare at his so concerned looking lawyer while waiting for him to talk.

"About committing Suppuku without the assistance of a loyal and trusted second, to help guide your honorable soul to the land of Kami, Asahiko-san." He offered cautiously to him.

"I see what's troubling your stumbling mind so, Nagaro-san. So what is it you're suggesting to me my old friend?" The old man allowed a slight smile again, as he stared at Nagaro.

"Asahiko-san, I'd deem it a great honor and privilege if you'd allow me to second your honorable death, sir." Nagaro stiffened as he waited for Asahiko to respond to his request.

"And you want to claim this is a favor you're begging of me, Nagaro-san?" He asked, not believing what his ears was hearing from his lawyer, as he shook his head in disbelief.

"Hai Asahiko-san, it certainly is that sir."

"Ieeeee, to what honorable Kami do I owe such toda chu to my worthless soul and being. I doubt even the great and fearsome Shoguns of past yore possessed such loyalty from any of their vassals and friends as I obviously enjoy in my wasted life upon this earth, Nagaro-san. I thank you for this kind offer you have just offered to me my friend." He returned his bow as respectfully, pleased his trusted lawyer wanted to assist him in this honorable manner.

"I take this to believe you're going to allow me to second your death, Asahiko-san?"

The stunned old man suddenly leaned on his haunches and stared at his lawyer while weighing his offer. After thinking it over, and feeling if he was to allow Nagaro to second his death, and lop his head from his shoulders when he turned the tanto blade in his innards, and began to work across his belly a second time. He might be held responsible for his death by the officials once the police entered his sacrificial altar. Releasing his breath, he replied.

"Nagaro-san, you offer me too great an honor to act as my second in death."

Losing his temper momentarily over the refusal of his request, Nagaro complained bitterly at the old man. "Why do you refuse me this great honor I beg for Asahiko-san? If I second your honorable death then there'll be no need to worry about the Tengu intercepting your spirit, before it had a chance to enter the Floating World for final judgment. Think about it further I beg of you Asahiko-san. Think of the pain and suffering you'll endure while waiting to bleed to death. Is it not better for me to take your head and relieve this great suffering as quickly as possible? Is it not commanded by the ancient tomo rin (Codes) for me to be allowed to assist you on this night?

"Does it not state in the Bushido teachings, the code of conduct, chivalry, and the Way of the Warrior, for the act of Suppuku to be seconded by a friend, or kaishaku, the executioner of the honored Samurai about to enter the Floating World by his own command? I beg you Asahiko-san, don't allow yourself to suffer needlessly when your friend is willing and is most capable of relieving this terrible pain you'll endure if you don't allow me to second your honorable death, Asahiko-san." The lawyer was almost on his feet as he struggled to help his friend's death.

Asahiko allowed himself to relax he knew it was against his best interest to get upset before committing Suppuku. He needed all his strength and cunning to carry out this last act of his honorable life. He did not need his friend draining his strength like he was doing, by placing this added stress and confusion in his mind at this certain time. He understood the pain he was going to suffer while waiting for death finally embraces his spirit. But he was aware he couldn't allow Nagaro to take the chance of being blamed for his death, by assisting him on this night.

Summoning what strength remained in his body, he replied weakly to his lawyer. "Nagaro-san, I'll never forget your offer to assist me in my worthless death. But I cannot allow you to take a chance for the sake of my spirit making to the next world safely, my old friend. As I said before to you, I must decline your kind offer of assistance. What must be must be, Nagaro-san."

"What chance Asahiko-san?" He snapped, allowing anger to creep deeper in his tone.

"Nagaro-san, dear friend, son of my only true friend of this world, I cannot possibly allow you to take the chance of being blamed for my worthless death by the hated police. If I was to allow this and you were arrested once the police investigated my death. My spirit would never be able to rest in peace while I roam in the Floating World of wonder, forever in search of my beloved son and his honorable wife. This is why I plan to take my life in the first place, to be relieved of this terrible burden of worry I must endure until I breathe no longer on the lands of Japan. Please, no more of this stressing conversation, it's late and I must prepare my mind and body for its final act. I thank you from the bottom of my heart for your kind offer, but this is why I must decline it again Nagaro-san." He looked into the troubled eyes of his concerned friend.

"Asahiko-san, you must remember, I'm a lawyer and a damn good one at that sir. There's no way in hell the police could possibly blame your death on me. Besides, I'm willing to take the chance of being blamed for it, if it'll help ease your suffering even a little bit. What a shame it'd be for your last memory of living on the earth, was that of unending pain and long suffering and a slow death. I care not one grain of worthless rice what the police can do to me. As I said, I'm willing to take this chance to assist you in this sacred act. Please, if I can't talk you out of this honor, and to walk with me as we search together for the murderer of your honorable son then at least allow me to offer you the safe and secured journey to the Floating Wor..."

"Well I'm not willing to take that gamble on behalf of a noble and honorable friend, and to insult his loyalty to me, Nagaro! Enough of this endless talk Mr. Lawyer, I'll do what I plan to do, and in the way I planned to do it on this foul night, and that'll be the end of it, my old friend." Asahiko knew if he omitted the san from his honorable name, Nagaro would immediately understand he was not going to change his mind over this decision.

Nagaro rose and began to pace the room before the still kneeling Asahiko.

CHAPTER NINETEEN

Asahiko wiggled his painful body until he was kneeling in the proper position to commit Suppuku again, while he watched his troubled friend struggle with his decision and anger.

He stopped his pacing and then he looked down at Asahiko who was kneeling so peacefully on the floor. He was doing everything in his power to try and control the mounting rage suddenly plundering his entire body. Shaking with anger at not being able to talk his old friend out of taking his honorable life, or allowing him to second his fine pending death, Nagaro suddenly roared, forgetting the great respect he harbored for this old man. "Asahiko-san! I curse Karma, and I curse all Karma as I curse the unholy Kami who created the circumstances that forced such a great man as yourself to be condemned to take his most honorable life, to try and make things right again in both worlds. I don't know of the countless and confusing ways of the foul Kami, nor do I wish to try and understand them, Asahiko-san.

"That belief is for the foolish and worthless priests to figure out, and help to guide our journey through life. But all I do know is if there was justice in the next world the Kami would find a way to stop you from taking your life. I curse the assassin who is the cause of this drama yet to unfold. If you don't allow me to second your death, I swear. I'll spend the rest of my life hunting down the filthy assassin, and the one who sponsored his evil acts carried out against you and your family. With every breath I breathe, I'll use that on my vengeance pilgrimage to find this assassin and the one who commands his spirit. I swear this to you by the blood of my honorable son's head." The lawyer raised his clenched fist up to the Heavens as it shook with rage.

He listened without expression or reaction to the ranting of his lawyer. Even though displaying anger was the height of bad manners to any Japanese male, he knew where he was coming from, and allowed his rage to continue unfettered. When he saw Nagaro was calm enough to listen to reason, he offered in an almost fatherly tone to the younger man. "Nagaro-san, you have as much chance of changing Karma as you have of controlling the weather when it rages in anger.

"Nagaro-san, I appreciate all you offered to this old fool on this night of his worthless life, but you must leave Karma to Karma. Life and death are but the same. What must be, will be no matter how much you roar anger at the Kami who make what is, is. I'll never forget the loyalty you have displayed to this fool. This gives me the strength to carry out this final act of my life. It's getting late and I must prepare my soul for my last action upon this earth, while strength remains within my worthless old body." He smiled at his friend, hoping to calm him further.

Nagaro was not going to give up the fight to aide his friend in his time of need this easily. "Dammit Asahiko-san, this is what's fueling my rage. I feel so helpless, I know I can't change what has to be, what has been preordained by Karma. But I resent your death will come by the hand of the assassin that killed your honorable son Tsutomu-san and his wife. Yes, I know your hand is the one that's going to take your life, but you're taking your life because of the actions of this loathsome assassin, and the lowly bastard who controls this evil one's depraved course and spirit. So it's like his hand is taking your life, and I resent that to the ends of the earth. Asahiko-san, you're going to allow this god cursed executioner to win and take your life as well as the life of your honored son and his wife? Take your life without a second to open the stairs to the Floating World is more than insulting to my person, sir. I'll find it extremely hard to live with this terrible stain marring my spirit until I finally cross over to the Floating World myself."

"Nagaro-san, don't concern yourself so about this loathsome assassin's foul deeds being played out against myself and my most honored family, and the one who is behind her vengeance hand. Once I'm home in the Floating World and if the Kami allow me to, I'll wreak my own vengeance upon the fool controlling this daughter of the darkness and hate."

He stared at Asahiko, he had the overwhelming feeling that he truly knew who was behind the assassin's evil ways, and waging death and destruction upon his honorable family. Now more than ever, he had to do was force the old man to tell him of the name, and he would do the rest.

Nagaro heard the unbelievable suggestion that the deadly assassin was that of a female killer. But knowing as much as he did about the ruthless gangs and cults polluting Japan's Eight sacred Islands, he understood there were no way any gangsters prowling the streets of Japan, would ever employ the services of a female killer. But hearing Asahiko also slip call the killer a she, he was forced to believe this unthinkable rumor might be the truth.

Shifting his weight on his feet, he watched Asahiko as he knelt before him as if he did not have a fear in the world. He knew Asahiko was at peace with all that must be before he committed Suppuku, but he still wanted the assassin's controller to be named, so he could seek his revenge in this world on the hated person, and leave Asahiko to deal with this madman once he appeared before him in the Floating World. Drawing in a breath and letting it out slowly, Nagaro asked in a controlled tone. "Asahiko-san, you know who is behind this damn assassin's evil missions?"

A smile slowly spread across his cracked chapped lips as he nodded ever so slightly yes.

"By the lower gods who crawl on their slimy and loathsome bellies, and leave their stink and waste on the ground as they slither along, you must tell me of this man's cursed name. So I could perpetrate my revenge and your retribution for his detestable actions committed against the house of Asahiko-san. I demand the right to confront this man who would drink his own urine, and enjoy its evil taste and smell of it. Especially if you won't allow me to second your honorable death, you must leave me some manner of respect and honor to carry on with. If you don't allow me to enjoy revenge on this controller of evil, you'll leave me with no honor. A man without honor is a man without a soul." His lawyer growled Asahiko would keep the name from him.

"Nagaro-san, I'll not be the cause of your shedding any blood for the want of revenge on my behalf. True, I know of the man who is truly behind the death of my most honorable son. But revenge is better off left to the gods who control such events to enjoy and melt out. You know the man because you shared many days working on deals between us. Even if you pull up the name of this man, I demand you give me your blood oath that you'll not seek revenge on this person's head. Nagaro, I demand this of you, and your sacred oath has to be performed by keppan. In case you're not aware of the old ways of the great past of Japan. Keppan is the placing of the blood from your index finger upon the Katana blade to seal your oath and bond to me for all times. I'm waiting Nagaro." He omitted the san from his name.

"Asahiko-san, at the risk of insulting your great honor and memory, I'll swear nothing of the sort to your demand of my loyalty, unless you give me the name of this dog eating madman who destroyed your family entirely, first." As he made his demand of the old man, he continued to search his mind to place the name to the evil man Asahiko described moments before.

"How dare you make any demands of me, you who stretches our friendship almost to the breaking point! It's only because of our long friendship, and your loyalty to me I don't have you pitched out the window to your death, Nagaro." Asahiko seethed, angry he would dare take such a demanding stand against him, especially at this sacred of times. If he was not planning to take his life, he would put great effort in destroying this man making particulars of him.

"Asahiko-san, why is it fair for you to make such overwhelming conditions and demands so hard for me to honor and accept, yet I can't make them of you? I only want to do what any self-respecting man of good conscious and respect would do when his friend of countless years is forced to take his honorable life because of what this assassin forced on your shoulders, Asahiko-san. Seek my revenge for that honorable death on the evil head of the foul one responsible for your honorable death, sir." He begged in his own defense to him.

Asahiko refused to back down from his decision and his demanded oath from his lawyer as he hissed angrily at him this time. "There'll be no revenge taken on my behalf on the loathsome head of the god cursed assassin, or on the one guilty of pulling its evil strings, Nagaro-san. But yes, forgive my foolish outburst. It's a fact you're the only man on the face of this earth who has the power to make demands of me. I believe you're entitled to know the name of the man who ruined my life so completely. I'll give you his name as long as you promise you'll take the Keppan for me. Please, allow this old fool his kabukimono." (Eccentricities)

"Huh, what is this you offered me to suffer, Asahiko-san who has successfully boxed me into a corner with no possible escape? You offer me a victory that is not a victory, crafty old one. You doom me to live out my worthless life knowing the foul one responsible for your honorable son's death, and yours, and he is allowed to continue to roam the earth, proud of his detestable accomplishments. What choice do I have left opened to my footfalls? Yes, I'll unhappily take the Keppan as you have demanded of me Asahiko-san." The lawyer replied in a giving up tone.

"In that case you'll know the name you seek to bring inner peace to your honorable mind and proud Samurai spirit and heart, Nagaro-san." Asahiko looked around the room and saw an ancient katana hanging by an equally ancient set of samurai armor. "Nagaro-san, you can use that Katana blade hanging on the wall there to complete your sacred blood oath to me."

Nagaro removed the blade as if the weight was almost too much to handle. He unsheathed the ancient blade angrily as he walked to Asahiko. He bowed to the old man, and extended his index finger from his right hand, the sword hand. He looked at the old man who nodded at him, and he slid his finger across the razor sharp old steel. Blood oozed from the slight gash then he placed the bleeding finger to his forehead and announced. "Asahiko-san, by the blood of my oath to you, I swear I'll not seek revenge of any type upon the unconsecrated head of the fool who drives the assassin's evil will and ways, and who has killed your honorable son and his wife."

"Thank you for the proud respect and honor you have shared with me on my last day upon this troubled earth. You have made what I must do, much easier to accomplish for these useless old hands of mine. The name you seek from me is Hiromoai. He's the one who is responsible for the death of my honorable son. I heard the words from his own vile mouth, as he bragged about having my son killed by his lap dog of Satan. I'll have my revenge upon this manure eating heap from the land of wonder and beyond." The old man allowed his shoulders to noticeably sag after relieving the truth that was weighing him down so heavily.

Nagaro dropped heavily in the chair, stunned beyond belief and understanding at the name that came forth from Asahiko's lips of the evil assassin's manager. He would have never though it possible for such a man of character and respect, but evil dealings in the business world to dare be part of the savage attack against Yurkowa and his wife. All he could think to say in reply was. "I don't believe it possible for Hiromoai being the one who is guiding this assassin's hand."

"Huh, I'm terribly sorry, but I have to admit it is true, and yes you do believe it as the truth in your heart, Nagaro-san. In your mind you have already known it was he, responsible for the total and complete destruction of my respected and honorable family. Nagaro-san, you had to have your suspicions of this loathsome man before I spoke of them before you my old friend." Asahiko declared strongly as he painfully straightened up his altar, and then he lit more incense to better insure his offering would be burning at the time of his death.

"I don't understand your logic at all, Asahiko-san. Knowing this, you refuse to allow me to take revenge on this treacherous of evil men terribly insulting Japan's honor by living upon her sacred soil, and continuing his existence in this world, Asahiko-san? Denying me a lowly and obedient Samurai Warrior's right for revenge against the one who caused my friend so much pain and sorrow, sir." The lawyer grumbled angrily while gathering his troubled senses.

"Nagaro-san, you're an otokodate, a very brave man who stands proudly against the injustices committed against your friends, by the evil actions of this lowly assassin and her worthless Master. But even if I were to allow you to seek your wanted revenge upon the loathsome head of Hiromoai on my behalf, your sacred blood oath taken before me on this night will forever forbid you to do any harm whatsoever to his god cursed being, Nagaro-san. I warn you once again dear friend, if you have these kind of betraying thoughts held within your heart and mind, you'd be forever cursed to the lower ranks of the Kami if you cause any harm to befall his worthless soul. Even if you're not physically responsible for this harm to befall him that means you can't give his name to the hated police, or a hired assassin you might think to employ to do the act of revenge for you, without breaking your blood oath to me and to the gods of yore."

"Yes Asahiko-san, you have so successfully imprisoned my wrath and fighting spirit locked forever within the sacred blood oath that you have forced upon my soul and head, old and wise friend. But once again I must beg your permission to second your most honorable death on this night. You must allow me at least this much to honor you by and to help protect your proud spirit until you are safely with the Kami for protection." Nagaro wasn't going to let up on this request.

"Again my ageless old friend of many years, I must refuse this very considerate request for the reasons I have stated before to you, Nagaro-san. I worry for your spirit and I don't need you in any trouble with the hated police." Asahiko snapped antagonistically at his lawyer and friend.

"Then what will you have me do to make my worthless existence more endurable to me to live with, Asahiko-san? To exist with no aims of honor and respect left open to me, is a very hollow and wasted existence that you have forced upon my spirit and head. My friendship and blood oath to you will destroy me in short years if allowed to fester without the taste of revenge and then I'll be with you again, but in the Floating World of awe this time. Unless I'm able to avenge your honorable death and the slaughter of your honorable son and his wife Asahiko-san I beg of you to allow me this much of my manhood to remain unaltered by your last decree sir." He spread out his hands in total submission towards the old man now.

"Your mind is too troubled by the want and longing for revenge for the evil sins of hatred that has been committed against me and my honored family. I want you to leave my presence at once so that I might get on with this final drama of my worthless and long life. Nagaro-san, you'll continue with your honorable life, with your manhood undiminished and proud. I, much like you, ask of you this one last favor in life. I want no correct that my friend, I demand that you call the worthless police tomorrow morning at exactly eight a.m. Don't be foolish enough to identify yourself to the crafty police, just tell the worthless fools that there's a body resting on the third floor of Engakuji Castle and say no more to the fools, Nagaro-san.

"Even if the foul police try to pressure you into telling them of your honorable name, you must refrain from doing so. In fact Nagaro-san, I wish you to make the call from a pay phone far from your office or home, so that the worthless police cannot possibly trace, or use the caller ID system to assist them in identifying your person. I warn you Nagaro-san, be most careful and extremely wise when speaking to the hated police, for they are most wise and very cunning, and they'll try anything in their power to gain your identification and whereabouts. I don't wish my body to be unattended longer than that short a period of time. I would be greatly dishonored if my body be unattended for too long a time. You must promise me this request."

"Hai Asahiko-san, if that's the last orders you give me, rest assured I'll carry them out faithfully for you, and your body will be attended quickly after your final sacred act of life." He bowed gracefully before the old man as he prepared to leave him for the last time.

"Very well then Nagaro-san, it seems our business has finally and at long last come to its inescapable conclusion after all these years of friendship and trust, and I must ask you to leave my side for the final time in my honorable life. I don't need a witness as to what I must do to gain inner peace and respect from the evil spirit who has slaughtered my honorable son, my friend whose name I'll carry upon my lips as I enter the Floating World of wonderment. So the Kami gods can see the friendship we have developed over the many years, still exists even in death between us. Some things in life are left better off served, if they're carried out in private. I need my space to honor Lord Buddha and beg him to clear my way into the Floating World for me." Asahiko graciously bowed towards his friend from his kneeling position. He had been kneeling so long he doubted he would be able to stand, even if he wanted to.

The lawyer returned the bow as courteously as he could to him, and held it as he slowly back stepped out of the room as silently as he could move. It was the last bit of honor and respect he could think of doing to display his total respect to his old friend, about to begin his faithful last journey to the world of the wonder and myth by his hand and desire.

Asahiko nodded as he watched and waited for Nagaro to finally leave the room for the last time. Once he was out and the door closed behind him, he made the final preparations for his date with destiny's outcry to his ears. Suddenly, he was at total peace with all his ghosts and fears that have long troubled his mind and being. Nothing now could possibly upset him, nothing could cause him any alarm, nothing could cause him any worry or stress in the life remaining to him. It seemed at long last, the world was at complete harmony and in total sync with his spirit, as he began to recite the mandatory prayers to open the gates to the Floating World before him with the gods who will this, and to inform the Kami that he was coming home to greet and be with them and his beloved son and his wife at long last.

All the stress fled from his body and the inner calm prevailed over his body as mumbled the prayers to Lord Buddha. Even the air about him was suddenly so relaxing and calm to him. His knees that had so long bothered and caused him such constant pain seemed to be at rest and hurting him no longer. With his prayers completed, all that was left for him to do was to wait for the proper time so he could end his terrible existence on the earth. Then start his long search for his honorable son and his wife who were waiting his presence in the Floating World.

HIROMOAI'S APARTMENT IN THE HATANAKA TOWERS

The young and crafty Japanese businessman Hiromoai Hatanaka, slowly traced his finger along the route that he wanted Wind to travel, across the map that she would use while heading for Engakuji Castle and Asahiko's soul. The castle was about fifteen miles from Hatanaka Tower and downtown Tokyo, which meant she would be on the ground and moving for a greater time than when she went after Asahiko's son, and she would be exposed longer to the local population as well. Which meant Wind would be more vulnerable to the police who roam this area of Tokyo, and that bothered him immensely. He did not like this part of her quest in the least, because it made her very susceptible to detection and arrest, or the slaughter that would follow, if the police tried to arrest his weapon from the ancient past. He went over the route for a second time to make certain she knew where she was to travel.

Wind stared at the route being traced out on the map by her lord and master's hand and she instantly realized the fear he was suffering about her possibly being detected by civilians while out on her mission. She drew in her breath and offered reassuringly to her master. "Hiromoai-sama, I see by the route that you have chosen for me to travel upon on this night, that it shall bring me in possible contact with the lowly people of the night's existence. What would you favor me do with them if I am somehow discovered by any of the night dwellers of this time?" She turned away from the map and stared at his eyes with concern.

"I don't know what you should do if this happens, what do you suggest you do if discovered by who you refer to as night dwellers?" He replied, knowing the answer to the question she would offer, but he wanted to hear it come from her lips before he gave her suggestions to follow.

"I can dispatch them without hesitation if they become involved, or try and hinder my mission for your wants and desires, Hiromoai-sama."She offered as she turned her eyes back to the map.

"Huh, I guess I have to leave that up to your discretion. If you see no way to avoid a person of the night, and you deem it necessary, dispatch anyone who crosses your path and you believe he's a threat to your mission. If you're forced to kill someone you weren't sent against, you must hide the body. No one is to stop your oserareru." He offered while looking in her eyes.

"Hai my Lord and Master, because it is written upon the faithful wings of destiny, no one or thing will keep me from dispatching your faithless enemy on this lowly night. I offer to you that I shall and will not fail your demand my Lord, or the Kami gods will eat my soul, thus destroying my spirit for all eternity Hiromoai-sama."

He relaxed his shoulders as he stared at Wind and announced, "Very good, is there anything you hitouyo, require to make your mission a success, Wind-san? One question Samurai, if the Kami gods eat your soul, does that mean you'll never be able to answer my call again?"

"Iye, no my Lord and Master, I just need to get in my body armor so I shall be prepared to do honorable battle on this faithful night in your honor and respect. Hiromoai-sama, I'm in fear your last question is most incorrect, because the Kami will never interfere with your ordered bidding of my spirit. This is because of the curse you have placed upon the ancient sword, and my foolish head. But having your soul eaten by the Kami gods is a worse fate than any possible death I could ever suffer at the hands of the living world."

"Very well, Lady Yoke will assist you getting in your armor. Since you have a long way to travel by foot, I suggest you leave when ready. When will you begin your attack on my teki?"

"My Master, I will not attack your hated teki until the moon cracks tomorrow's first breath. In that way, all the Kami will blink and not see what is about to befall your worthless enemy's evil head. It is the right of the feared Ninja, if the night warriors are sent to dispatch someone it is always done on the first breath of the new stick of time. This is to rob the dishonored dead of the beginning of the new day, and show him what he will be forever missing until the end of time, Hiromoai-sama. It is another evil way to punish one's enemy forever." She paused.

"Sometimes Wind-san, your forever wandering words are most confusing to my ears, we call that time of the first breath, midnight." He offered after he figured out what Wind meant.

"It shall be as you offered my Lord I will not dare insult your presence by arguing with my Master for the briefest of moments. What you say, I take to be the word of truth and justice, Hiromoai-sama. I shall not begin my attack on your enemy's head until midnight."

"Fine, I'll remain here in my living quarters for the entire night in order to avoid any further problems with the hated police lurking about outside this building. I'll make certain they see me at the fateful time of Asahiko's timely and called for death. This way, the police can't possibly place the blame upon my shoulders, Wind-san. I must protect myself at all times because the laws of the living apply to me only, not to your fine spirit. You're well above anything the police might do to you. There's nothing the authorities can do to your spirit, it's unconquerable. All I have to do is return your deadly killing sword back to its scabbard, and you'll fade before their non-believing eyes. Thus avoiding any punishment these weak fools may deem fit for one guilty only of following her master's orders."

"If that is your desire Hiromoai-sama, it makes my heartbeat happily in the living world. Anything you wish for is my duty to fulfill for you, my Lord." She bowed and held it.

Hiromoai turned his attention to Lady Yoke and snapped almost nastily. "Lady Yoke, you'll take Wind to your room and assist her dressing in her armor for this mission. She'll return before me when she's dressed and ready to begin her mission. Then, I'll send her on this commission and relieve me of this burden of Asahiko's presence once and for all on the soil of Japan."

"Hai Hiromoai-san, it'll be as you requested." She replied as she rose from her kneeling position and bowed then waited until Wind joined her at the doorway to the study. Together, they bowed again to Hiromoai and turned and disappeared in Yoke's room talking to one another.

Hiromoai was exhausted and sat back on the couch and waited for Wind to return.

They were laughing as she stuffed herself in the tight fitting, heavy body armor she designed for fighting in the world of the living. Even though she enjoyed a good laugh, her mind was deep in thought of her mission, and the seriousness of Hiromoai's commands. Nothing was going to take her mind off this latest mission until it ran its course and she carried out his orders.

SERGEANT OKAMATSU'S POLICE CAR

Sergeant Toshihiro Okamatsu sat staring at the doors to Hiromoai's apartment on the twenty seventh floor of the Hatanaka Tower, his eyes burning from the concentration he was doing. He decided to take a break from his vigil and make contact with the other officers he had guarding the rear exits of the magnificent Tower. As far as he was concerned, he had Hiromoai trapped inside the walls of his building for the rest of the night, and he was following his orders from Lieutenant Kenzaburo Motoshima to the tee. The other two officers reported to the Sergeant of seeing nothing out of the ordinary on their watch of the building.

Suddenly fearing he might have found another way to leave his apartment, Sergeant Okamatsu picked up his phone and quickly dialed his room, to make certain he was still inside the apartment. The phone rang three times before being answered by Hiromoai himself.

Lady Yoke, who usually answered all calls coming to the apartment while she was there, was busy helping Wind getting dressed in the battle armor for her attack on Asahiko's life.

Angrily, he picked up the phone to relieve this much from her shoulders, while she attended to Winds needs. Yes!" He actually barked into the phone angrily.

Instantly, the Sergeant recognized his voice, and immediately hung up. Now, he was certain Hiromoai was in the apartment, and again he relaxed in the squad car. He informed the other officers on watch of this fact. Once this was completed, he sat back in the car feeling it must have been someone other than Hiromoai who looked out the window fifteen minutes ago.

HIROMOAI'S APARTMENT

The call did not really upset him as much as he let on, because he was always receiving calls at all times of the day and night, wrong numbers, hang ups, or from people trying to sell him or his business something, or someone who he bested in the business world who wanted to curse him out because of what he did to him. No matter how well he guarded his private phone number, someone always seemed to be able to find it out and begin annoying him at home.

Hiromoai did not have long to wait until Wind appeared in her altered body armor before him, her weapons hanging from her implement of war like body in the proper positions. She looked like what she was designed for and trained to be an executioner of his enemy and in her eyes he could easily see the wanting to be set free to begin her mission for him.

He bowed and Wind returned it. "Wind-san, you look most threatening on this night."

"I am threatening in both thought and deed, to my Lord and Master's hated enemy on this night no matter where they try to hinder from my justice Hiromoai-sama!" She bowed for the compliment offered her from her master. She did not suffer from the sin of false modesty she knew she was the best samurai, now executioner to walk on the soil of the Islands of Japan.

"Yes, yes indeed you certainly are most threatening at that Wind-san, but I believe it's time you head out on your quest. Omi desu ka. Remember, I'll not embrace anything but complete success from you on this night. If you fail on this mission then you'll be expected to commit Suppuku before me to make amends for your failure to my orders. I waited too long to witness the death of this man, to accept anything but that. Free me of Asahiko's worthless presence."

"I have no intention of committing Suppuku on this or any other night because I have no intention of failing my Master on this or any other mission I am dispatched on by your command and desires, Hiromoai-sama." She actually glared at him for several seconds while referring to him as Lord Hiromoai in the old ways.

He ignored the slight insult of the glare from her, he was more concerned with the death of Asahiko than of any angry glare from this weapon he was about to turn loose on the head of his enemy. He was savoring the sweet taste of revenge for the times Asahiko and his bastard of a son had interfered with his business, or cut his throat on many a proposal for work.

Suddenly, Wind bowed, knowing it reached the time for her to leave.

He knew what the bow was about and he replied warningly. "Wind-san, you're to make use of the same path to leave this apartment as you did when you destroyed my teki's dishonored son. Remember, there are many angry and highly skilled eyes trained on this apartment, trying to discover your presence. You must be like the kage, a shadow of the night world when you're leaving this apartment. If you're discovered leaving here then you'll be captured and your mission will be a complete failure, and I'll not welcome that I warn you, Samurai. Do you understand what's expected of you while leaving for your mission tonight, Wind-san?"

"Hai Hiromoai-sama, I'll not be detected by anyone when I leave your dwelling my Lord."

"Very well then, you're correct and it's time to leave on your mission Wind-san."

She again bowed as graciously as her armor would allow. Then, without further words she went over to the sliding doors as Hiromoai shut off the lights in the apartment to give her cover of darkness to make her escape from the apartment unobserved by the police below.

She waited the few seconds it took until the apartment was bathed in darkness, as Hiromoai escorted her to the sliding door and outside the apartment. She took a moment to enjoy the sight as she looked over the width and breadth of downtown Tokyo, bathed in the constant glare of countless night lights of buildings, and marveled at the magnificent structures as she exclaimed in awe of the vision and remarked to her master. "My Lord, what powerful Shogun of this time is in command over Edo he can build such Castles, even threatening the clouds in the sky and as far as the eye can see? And develop marvelous carriages and carts that move with divine force."

"There's no Shogun in power that was until you came along to assist me, and gain my rightful place in Japan's order of things to come. With your unfettered loyal assistance to me and my desires, it's I who shall become the new Shogun of all Japan, which is my rightful place in this world. Once I'm in power over the decisions of such things, I'll return Japan to the years of great respect. I'll drive the polluting Gai Jins from our shores. Then I'll control all the trade and commerce in the country. I will return Japan to the old ways of great honor and respect."

She bowed to Hiromoai as she offered to her master. "To hear your proud boast is sweet songs to my worthless ears, and fills my heart with great pride to know you shall again be in control of all Japan, Hiromoai-sama. I shall follow your orders, or be cursed to the dreaded underworld for eternity. Who is the god cursed Gai Jin's that you speak of my Master? Did Kublai Khan finally establish a foothold in Japan while I was asleep for so long a time, my Lord?" She asked with concern, her sharp mind always working, always searching for knowledge and understanding, and what had transpired while she roamed within the Floating World of nothingness.

"Never mind that crap for the time being Wind-san, there's no time for any long winded explanation of what I suggest to you, Samurai. You have much more important work to perform on this unending night. I'll explain who the lowly Gai Jin's are when we have more time to speak of such things, Wind-san. Your task is now waiting your final justice and hand." Hiromoai snapped at her as he opened the glass door a touch then glanced out of it.

Wind nodded and silently slid out of the door open just enough for her to squeeze out onto the patio. Once outside the apartment, she made like the ghost and worked her way down the side of the building to the first rooftop, where she moved to the next building as she did when she was sent out to destroy Tsutomu, the son of her new target on this night.

SERGEANT OKAMATSU'S POLICE CAR

Sergeant Toshihiro Okamatsu was enjoying a soda and trying to relax the best he could being coop up inside the small and uncomfortable squad car when he happened to glance out the squad car window up towards the patio doors of Hiromoai's lush apartment, twenty seven floors above him. Suddenly, he noticed the lights go out in the main room, and he paid closer attention to the apartment and then he thought he saw something moving out onto the patio for a brief second. As fast as he noticed the shadow move, it seemed like it instantly disappeared into nothingness. The Sergeant put the soda down and moaned to the other officer with him. "Corporal Hattori, did you see that slight movement out on Hiromoai-san's patio?"

"See what movement Sergeant? I didn't see any damn movement in the area you're concerned with, Sergeant. I don't think anyone but us are still up if you ask me, all the smart ones are fast asleep by now." Hattori retorted as he looked in the same direction Okamatsu was staring in.

"Dammit to hell and back again, the lights went out in Hiromoai-san's apartment, Corporal."

"So what Sergeant, maybe he turned in for the night, or maybe and I hope he got lucky with that little spitfire he calls a housemaid, and he wanted it to be a little romantic for their coupling by shutting off the damn lights. If you look at the rest of the Tower, there are but a few lights still burning in the massive building, Sergeant. Everyone who is smart has turned in for the night, Sergeant. Like we should be doing right about now if we had any brains operating correctly that is, Sarge." The Corporal gave the Sergeant a wide smirk as he turned to him and waited to see if he said anything else over what he believed he noticed by Hiromoai's apartment.

"That's not what I'm talking about at all wiseguy. I thought I saw something moving on the damn patio of Hiromoai's room. I lost the damn thing in the shadows of the building, but it sure looked like someone went over the side of the rail of the patio, Corporal."

"You have to be shitting me Sergeant, that's twenty seven stories up there. Nothing but a damn fly could jump from that height and survive the fall. There's no way anyone could climb up or down the side of the Tower and hope to live to tell about it." The concerned Corporal nearly laughed, but when he picked up Sergeant Okamatsu was dead serious about what he said and possibly saw, the concerned Corporal concentrated watching the spot the Sergeant stared at.

After a few seconds of staring at the area, Hattori grumbled at his partner. "I don't see anything out of the ordinary moving up there, Sergeant. Maybe it was the movement from a passing cloud, or a shadow of a second building that happened to catch your eye Sarge. Who the hell knows what might have caused what you thought you saw?"

"Maybe so Corporal, but I'm going to make damn certain Hiromoai-san is still in his damn apartment, and he's alive and well. If he gets out on our watch, Lieutenant Motoshima will eat us alive and shit us out later. Then he'll have us guarding the seagulls as they pick through the garbage at the city dump for the rest of our lives, Corporal." Sergeant Okamatsu reached out for the cellular phone and quickly dialed Hiromoai's private number a second time. The moment Hiromoai answered the phone he immediately hung up on him again.

Hiromoai listened to the dial tone for a few seconds and then he smiled to himself. He knew who had just placed this call to him, and figured the police stalking his outside, saw something of Wind leaving his apartment, and they were just making certain he was still at home, and nothing happened to him. He hung up and sat back to relax as Lady Yoke brought him the tea he requested a few moments ago, shortly after Wind had left the apartment. He settled in to enjoy the sweet tea while waiting for Wind's return to his room after she dispatched the old man.

The Sergeant dropped the phone on the seat as he continued to stare at the shadows covering the south side of Hatanaka Tower, looking for the suspicion he swore he picked up moving on the patio of the apartment a few moments before.

Wind was making good use of the shadows covering this section of the massive building, as she carefully worked hand over hand along the window sills that stuck out a little further than the building's construction. She hesitated for a brief second while hanging onto a window ledge, there was no shadow for at least three feet in this particular area. She knew she was going to have to move very quickly in this area, or she was going to be detected by the eyes ever watching Hiromoai's apartment. With a quick breath and as quick movements, she crossed the unprotected area as fast as she could possibly travel in the darkness.

Corporal Hattori turned to the main doors leading into the Tower, but Sergeant Okamatsu continued to scan the side of the building where he thought he saw something moving along the front of the Tower. In a blur of confusing movements, he could swear he saw someone climbing down the south side of the building. The Sergeant grew frightened, fearing that maybe it was the assassin, and he or she was trying to get in Hiromoai's apartment and kill him, the same way the murderer did to Asahiko's honorable son a few days back. Why else would someone be so daring as to try and climb up the side of the massive Tower building?

"There it is again Corporal dammit, I just saw the shadow for a second time. Now I'm certain, someone is stupid enough to try and climb the side of the building. I think it's the damn assassin, and I'm afraid it's going after Hiromoai-san on this attempt, Corporal. We have to stop this killer, or I'll stop being a police officer and become a lowly street cleaner for the rest of my worthless life I tell you. Let's move dammit!" Sergeant Okamatsu grumbled to his other officer on duty with him as he picked up his radio and screamed excitedly in it.

"All units, all units listen up, this is Sergeant Okamatsu. There's an assassin trying to kill Hiromoai, move out. Move out, move out, move out! We have to protect his life at all cost. Move out! Get up to his apartment and protect his life from this killer, now dammit!"

The detective threw his radio down as he struggled with the door handle and seat belt, almost getting strangled by the belt crossing over his throat, as he left his car in a rush. Corporal Hattori was already out of the vehicle, and he was running wildly towards the main entrance to the elegant Hatanaka Tower building, as the rest of the officers rapidly closed in on the building.

The highly concerned Detective Sergeant quickly caught up to the Corporal just as he forced the brass doors of the Tower open. They ran as fast as they could for the elevators, as the second team ran into the lobby from the rear of the building, and they employed the service elevators to get up to Hiromoai's apartment.

As the worried officers hurriedly made their way up to the twenty seventh floor of the huge building, Wind reached the roof of the first building where she ran across it and then leaped to another but lower roof. She ran without making a sound as she leaped from the second building onto another structure two floors shorter than the one she just ran across. Shadows hid her from view of others who might be out and about on this night, and made it nearly impossible for her to be detected by anyone watching the surrounding area.

The detectives reached the door of Hiromoai's apartment at the same instant as the other officers did, and Sergeant Okamatsu began to pound on it wildly.

Lady Yoke watched from behind the curtain as Wind disappeared over the side of the patio wall and was startled by the sudden pounding on the door, and headed for it in a rush. Anger grew in her chest over the excited way the door was being assaulted by whoever pounding on it.

Hiromoai decided to allow the already upset acting Lady Yoke to find out who was banging at the door, although he already knew who it was. She answered the door with seething anger in her heart, and a rage in her voice. Instantly, the out of breath officers merely shoved their way into the apartment. Sergeant Okamatsu's gun held at the ready as the excited officers shoved the slight framed Lady Yoke rudely out of their way, and they tried to pass by her. He was of the rank and training to allow him to carry a weapon on the streets of Tokyo.

He heard shouts from the officers and Lady Yoke as she screamed at them for barging into the apartment. He got off the sofa and went to aid Lady Yoke as she dealt with the excited officers.

The officer pushed his way into the room as Corporal Hattori took up a protective stance by the door. He was joined by the other officers out of breath from their hard run to the apartment.

Hiromoai rushed up to the lead officer and growled angrily at him as he held his hands out before him. "You, what the hell's the meaning of this god damn intrusion into my home? What the hell are you people doing aiming guns at my help and me? I demand a fucking answer to this intrusion of my apartment in the middle of the damn night, or I'll complain to your superiors and have all of you suspended from the police force. What the hell is this, are you allowed to be armed Sergeant? Sergeant, am I to believe that I'm under arrest for some infraction I'm not aware I committed and remove that damn weapon from my person at once I tell you?"

"Hiromoai-san, I'm pleased to see you're alright sir. I was afraid for your life, Hiromoai-san. And yes sir, I'm allowed to be armed because I was trained on how to employ a weapon, sir. I was ordered to take up arms since the lowly assassin began her evil work of the night. Hiromoai-san, I'm the only one here with a weapon." The officer said as he lowered his weapon and then he calmed down and tried to gain control over his heavy breathing, as he stared at the powerful Japanese businessman standing in the doorway while glaring angrily at him.

"Of course I'm alright, Officer. What the hell else did you expect some harm would befall me while I'm resting safely in my home? This building has its own security personal and systems as you well know, Sergeant. Foolish thoughts!" He snapped as he tried to grab hold of the ranting and raving Lady Yoke, and stop her from trying to assault the group of officers physically.

Hiromoai had no fear of being attacked by anyone, because he knew who was behind the deaths soon to be taking place in the future. Besides, he had this female weapon protecting his life. He had to smile, this small woman was in the officer's face, and she was shoving and kicking at the larger man, actually forcing the much larger officer to step back and out of the apartment while she was reciting a string of curses and demands in Japanese at him.

Sergeant Okamatsu completely ignored the raving young woman dancing so crazily before him as he tried to get around her wildly swinging arms and legs, when Hiromoai suddenly grabbed her by the arms, and he tried to restrain her attack on the concerned police officers. He wanted to get control of the situation and then see where it went from there, and if he was able to confuse the officers trying to question and protect him.

"How dare you enter my Master's honorable home in this fashion, filthy one? Your ill manners make me believe you're lower than the lowest eta class who pollute the pure air of Japan with their existence. Officer, I warn you, if I were a man I'd have your disgusting head hanging on a stick, and your golden globes drying in the sand waiting their time to be fed to the seagulls. You dung eating manure heaps who call yourselves police officers make me angry and ill to my stomach and I am a Japanese woman of good standing and respect. Your dishonorable actions should be reserved for when you invade the Tea Houses of Japan looking for illegal drugs and filthy women, and a cheap thrill to please your foul desires. Get out of this apartment before I forget I'm a woman of class, and take proper action against you for this foul invasion..."

"Yoke please will you be still for a moment dammit, it's alright it seems there's something bothering this concerned police officer. Get out of the way and allow him to enter so we can find the reason for this deplorable invasion of my home." He tried to pull the wild Lady Yoke back, but again she resisted his efforts as she kicked out angrily at the officer standing before her.

"Please Lady Yoke it's alright, get the hell out of the way of the officers will you please before you risk my anger, young lady." This remark from him seemed to calm her as she allowed herself to be pulled away from before the gaggle of officers and door by her master.

"Hiromoai-san, that one's as wild as the Kotora who would be better served prowling the jungles in search of some raw red meat to satisfy her hunger and endless anger." Sergeant Okamatsu grumbled with a smirk as he slowly relaxed in the area that Hiromoai cleared by pulling Lady Yoke away from the front door of the apartment.

"How dare you call an honest and hard working young Japanese woman of great respect such terrible names, you dog eating Ronin filth? You don't know me, yet you dare insult my honor with worthless names that you cast from your foul breath." Lady Yoke roared as she swung her leg at the officer a second time, striking him high on the thigh and roared at him again. "I demand you leave this honorable apartment at once, at once I say to you fool! Before I send for security and have your ugly carcass removed from the building forcefu..."

"That's enough Yoke! You're acting unladylike. Go back to the kitchen and prepare some tea for the officers while I find out what the trouble is with them." He glared at her until she turned and disappeared in the kitchen. Then he turned to Sergeant Okamatsu and snapped nastily.

"Officer, forgive me, but I forgot your name. What's the meaning of this terrible invasion of my home? I thought I answered all your loathsome questions to your complete satisfaction yesterday. I don't have more time to waste on this never-ending investigation, Sergeant."

"Please forgive me Hiromoai-san." He bowed as he continued with his words. "I'm exceedingly sorry for this intrusion, sir. My name is Sergeant Toshihiro Okamatsu, I was orde..."

"Yes, yes, I remember you now. Why have you come to my home in this manner, Officer?"

"Hiromoai-san, I was concerned for your life, sir. We happened to stop at the sushi bar across the street from your building, and I believe I noticed someone trying to make his way up the side of the building, and feared it was the assassin trying to harm you while you enjoyed your home."

"Huh, that statement sounds absolutely ridiculous Sergeant Okamatsu-san, we're twenty seven floors from the damn ground. What type of crazy ass assassin could possibly work his way up the side of a building this high, and live through the unadvised and foolish attempt? Have you been drinking too much sake lately, Sergeant?" He snapped angrily at the officer, pleased that he found a way to have the police verify he was in his apartment at the time of Asahiko's death.

"The Monen, the evil and vile spirit who killed poor Yurkowa-san and his wife, and is currently stalking the streets of downtown Tokyo, might be able to survive it I offer to you, Hiromoai-san." The still rather excited detective replied, the way he said it took the wind out of Hiromoai's sails, and he calmed down and nodded at the concerned officer. The Sergeant added to strengthen his cause to be at his apartment this late. "After seeing what this evil spirit did to poor Yurkowa-san and his lovely wife. I don't place anything out of his or her abilities to kill the person that the assassin is aimed at, Hiromoai-san."

"Hummm, perhaps you're right Officer Okamatsu-san. I'm afraid this assassin stalking Tokyo is like the Night Wind's Breath, if she or he can make it past Yurkowa-san's security forces. I'm forced to agree with your concerns. Please, Sergeant, come in and search my home until your heart's satisfied, if you fear so much for my worthless life that is, Officer. I have nothing to hide from anyone, especially you, Sergeant." He stepped aside and then waved his arm out before him to allow the group of officers to get by him and enter his apartment for their inspection.

The Sergeant moved deeper in the apartment as he moaned. "Sir, it's not necessary to search your apartment. I just wish to make certain nothing happens to you tonight sir, that's all. I beg the privilege to protect your life on this most dark of nights, Hiromoai-san."

"Tell me again Sergeant, how was it you happened to discover there was someone trying to sneak up the side of this building. Are you certain you weren't observing my actions? Am I still a suspect in your eyes in the murder of poor Yurkowa-san? Why the hell else would you be stalking outside my building, Officer? There's no need to hide in the shadows like a thief in the middle of the night, Sergeant. If you want to ask me any further questions, all you have to do is knock on my door any time of day or night, and it'll be opened to you." He growled as he led the complement of officers to his study then added. "I promise you, if you ever appear at my door again, I'll have Lady Yoke out of your way and she'll not attack you again, Officer."

The officer laughed at his remark to keep Lady Yoke out of his way as he replied in a much calmer voice this time. "I'm afraid that's not correct, Hiromoai-san. I assure you you're above reproach in any illegal matter facing Japan, sir. It's the furthest thing from my thoughts, to believe you could have anything to do with the death of Poor Tsutomu-san and his wife. I was normally patrolling my area of my responsibility in my car, when Corporal Hattori here asked me to stop, so he could get something to eat at the local sushi bar. He's always hungry sir.

"It was only by normal patrol we happened to notice a shadow moving across the side of your building, and I immediately feared this assassin was trying to attack you in your apartment, sir. There's no one safe in all Japan until this skilled killer is brought to justice sir. That's the only reason for this intrusion into your home, sir." The Sergeant was lying through his eye teeth, hoping Hiromoai would not see through the deception he was playing against him.

"How lucky for me the sushi bar is open all night, or perhaps I might have fallen victim to this assassin who roams freely through the night and streets of Tokyo at will."He allowed a smile, knowing the officer was speaking untrue. He also knew he had leveled a terrible insult at the Sergeant by suggesting this assassin was free to roam the streets of Tokyo undetected.

"Yes Hiromoai-san." The Sergeant replied as he sat, the insult registered in his mind as he cursed Hiromoai under his breath over the harsh remark against his person. The other officers remained standing and silent, scanning the interior of the apartment for signs of treachery.

Lady Yoke entered the study with a tray of cups and tea for Hiromoai, and the officers.

He nodded and ordered. "Lady Yoke, would you pour tea for us please."

"Hai Hiromoai-san." Lady Yoke growled as she poured the first cup for Hiromoai, and offered it politely to him. She filled the four other cups, but refused to serve the officers. The insult was noticed by all in the room. Again, he allowed a smile over this new insult.

Hiromoai took a sip of his tea and then placed the cup on the side table, never to return to it as he said in a harsh voice to the still concerned police officer. "Well Sergeant Okamatsu, if you fear so much for my life then perhaps you wouldn't mind remaining for a while, you know, in case your fears are well founded and my life is truly in some danger tonight, sir."

"Hai Hiromoai-san that seems like a wise request, I'd be most honored to stay a while, sir."

"Fine, thank you Officer for your concerns over my welfare, can I offer you something to eat?"

"Iye, no sir, I'm fine thank you Hiromoai-san. I'm too excited to eat anyhow sir."

"Very well, what can I do to entertain you while we wait for dawn to arrive, Officer?"

The officer scanned the study and noticed the many items of ancient armor and weapons of the samurai, which were in incredible condition scattered about the room, and adorning the walls of the study as he offered. "Yes Hiromoai-san, if you'd be so kind, perhaps you can take time to explain some of these interesting weapons to me. I must admit that I'm really fascinated by age-old Japan, and the lifestyles of that time period, sir. Judging by these fine items I see, you must be knowledgeable of that period of time in Japan's history, Hiromoai-san."

Hiromoai nodded respectfully, accepting the kind compliment offered by the young Sergeant. He was pleased to show off his vast knowledge of the times of ancient Japan. He spent most of his spare time lately reading about the past since finding Wind and her amazing catch of ancient weapons. Besides, it gave them something to do while Wind was carrying out his orders. He checked his watch, it was ten thirty. He knew he had to get rid of the officers by no later than two o'clock tomorrow morning, or they might be there when Wind returned from her mission. He glanced at the clock he decided to use this clock to warn him of the passing of time.

CHAPTER TWENTY
WIND'S TREK THROUGH THE STREETS OF DOWNTOWN TOKYO

Wind was having no problem making her way across the dark streets of Tokyo unobserved. This late on a Saturday night had most civilians lurking in bars and dance halls, or home sharing their wives and families' joys. Twice she was forced to walk in the streets to get to the area she wanted to cross, employing the shadows and roofs to hide her forward progress. Once during her travel, she wandered across a group of young people grouped together in an alley smoking, but they were too involved in what they were doing to pay any special attention to her. Her nose picked up the pungent odor of pot burning, but she did not recognize the powerful odor as she stared at the young kids as she walked by them.

She kept her eyes on them just in case one of them decided to try and attack her from behind as she walked past the group.

Wind made up ten miles of travel by eleven p.m., but from here on out she would have to abandon the safety of the roofs and dark alleys and the security of the shadows of night, for the more open area separating Tokyo from the great castle. In this area of the city rested the homes of many of the elite and very powerful of Japan. Open areas and vast compounds dotted the land of the rich leading to the ancient castle compound. Few small homes where she would be able to make good use of their shadows and yards existed in this section of the city. Drawing in a deep breath she started her forward progress again.

She dropped down from the last rooftop and instantly crouched on to one knee and searched the area in order to get her bearings and direction. She looked to the night sky and checked the moon's position, and then scanned the area out before her a second time and knew what direction she had to travel. Slowly, she made her way across a large flat area of ground, but just as she moved out of the shadows she stopped her forward movement, because before her stood two concerned looking men and she knew immediately they were official in nature. She tried to drop back in the shadows of the night in any attempt to avoid their acknowledgment, but the two concerned looking men spotted her and were heading right at her quickly.

"Hey you, I see you trying to hide in the shadows back there, yes you there in the dark, come out of there at once and tell me what the hell you're doing in this area of the city. You don't seem to belong around here. Come out of there or we'll come and get you and drag you out by your heels! I need to check you ID and find out what you're up to hanging around in the shadows of the night. Come out of there at once and there'll be no further trouble for you on this night, stranger. Resist me and there'll be pure hell to pay I assure you, stranger." The officer warned her hiding in the shadows as he and his friend walked towards her in a rush now.

She stood full height and allowed the two police officers to approach her which they did very cautiously and professionally. The very moment they were within her sword striking distance, she threateningly pulled her deadly katana blade from its highly decorated scabbard, and then waited for the two men to close in on her.

The officers stopped in their tracks the moment they saw her remove her katana and take a threatening stance against them and one moaned at the spirit now seemingly stalking them. "Why the hell are you hiding in the shadows like that, stranger? Come out where I can get a better look at you, mister. I warn you we're police officers, and your actions are making us very suspicious of what you might be doing in this area of the neighborhood, night stalker. Come out of the darkness so we can see you clearly, and you'll answer our questions truthfully, or we'll take you down to headquarters, and then you can talk to our Lieutenant, and he's not a very nice fellow to talk to, especially this late at night I warn you. He'll make your life miserable for you."

"Be careful he's armed he has a sword and he seems like he's ready to use it against us." The trailing officer warned his fellow officer, and then he took a more defensive posture and added to his warning. "Will you look at the fucking armor he's wearing? What the hell is this person, a fucking nightmare or a throwback to times long ago forgotten? Okay my friend, you drop the damn weapon and come out of the shadows and you'll not be hurt by us. Do you understand Japanese stranger? Can you hear what I'm saying to you?"

"I warn you, you're stopping me from carrying out my sacred yoshi gi to my Lord and Master. I'm sent on a special mission of honor and revenge, and my duty demands that I carry it out to its final completion, and I'll not allow you two fools to interfere in that mission in any way. I give you this one chance to save your foolish lives. Leave me in peace and you will survive to see the light of tomorrow's morning. Persist in harassing me further, and you will pay with your worthless lives for your foolish folly, and you will then spend eternity with your foul ancestors trapped within the hell where all your kind belong." Wind warned angrily as she assumed a much more threatening stance against the two officers she believed were stalking her.

"Shit, this fucking Warrior's a female, I can tell by her voice and the shape of her body. Hey baby, you had your little fun and games with us, but we're too busy to play along with you any further. Where the hell are you going with that there old pig sticker anyhow? Dammit young woman, do you understand that you're threatening police officers, and we'll not accept that threat for a damn minute by you or anyone else in Tokyo. You can go to jail for just that reason alone by carrying that there sword on your person. Can she be the one we were warned about as we started work today?" The second officer suddenly asked his partner.

"Sure she is, look at the way she's dressed. Look at those weapons she carries on what she calls her missions in the middle of the night. As I just said, what the hell is she, a throwback to the ancient times of long ago past? Dammit, I wish we were better armed. You, you there, stand where you are and lay down your weapons at once, and then step away from them then you're to stand with your hands clasped behind your head and not move again please. You're under arrest for the murder of Tsutomu Yurkowa-san and his wife. Fukuoka, get on the radio and inform headquarters that we believe we found the assassin they warned us about at the briefing, and she's threatening us with a sword. Tell them we need backup out here and quick, weapons too."

"Foolish one who speaks to the other fool with you, a Samurai of honor cannot be guilty of any crime when that Samurai is only guilty of carrying out her Lord and Master's orders. My sword will not kill the right and the truth. All who are guilty of treachery against my Liege Lord must fear my sword, my presence and my unfettered wrath." She hissed through clenched teeth as she waved her deadly katana blade slowly out before her body while aiming it at the two police officers threateningly and standing in her way.

"Well we'll have to see about that there threat won't we murderer of honorable people of Japan in the middle of the night. Put the damn sword down and put your hands over your head like I told you, and don't move a muscle until we properly secure you. Who is your Lord and Master anyhow, person who thinks she's an honorable Samurai Warrior? We wish to speak to him as well as you. You were told a number of times to come out of the damn shadows, if you insist in ignoring our orders and don't come out of there immediately, we'll come in there and move you out of the shadows by force if necessary. Your evil dress and killing weapons don't scare us in the least, we're used to your type of lowlife hanging around here. I told you to come out of the shadows twice now, and you'll do it right now or else, stranger!" The first officer warned her again as he moved out before his partner by a few steps.

"My honorable Lord and Master's name is of no importance to the likes of you two fools, but your actions are of concern to me. Again, I warn you to step back if you value your worthless lives, fools. My quarrel is not with you, it's just my Lord and Master's hated enemy roaming the honored soil of Japan. Leave me in peace and live and enjoy what the Kami ordained for you to enjoy on this night, come any closer against me and you'll die without honor and face."

"Forget that shit woman, we have a job to do, and right now you're part of that job. Who is your Master's enemy that forces you to be out on this night hunting?" The first officer snarled while trying to find out who was the next target of this female assassin. He removed his baton and challenged her with it. It was the worst mistake of his life, and his last.

In less than a heartbeat of time, her sword sliced through the arm of the police officer holding the wood baton in his hand. Her second move lopped his head from his shoulders.

The second officer tried to get away to wait for backup to arrive on the scene and assist him in the arrest of this female assassin. But a throwing star ripped into the back of his neck. He crumbled to the ground in a heap in pain and paralyzed from the neck down.

Wind knew where to strike the officer with the star, to stop all movement from her target. She cautiously walked up to the struggling officer and saw the pain and fear etched deeply in his eyes and without thought or hesitation, she lopped his head from his shoulders.

She followed the ancient code of the samurai of not allowing a warrior felled in battle, to suffer pain needlessly. The police officer's death was as meaningless to her as were the cries of the birds soaring in the air. For she was a true samurai from the old ways and beliefs, and being so she was prepared to lay down her life as a proud warrior as she felt all samurai should be. These two officers had just laid down their lives in the line of their duty to whichever master owned their destiny and contract, as it should be in the world of samurai warriors. When she was certain the two challengers against her will were dead, she moved the bodies into the shadows of the building to make certain their discovery wouldn't happen until she was well finished with her mission. Once she was pleased that she hid the two bodies properly and well, she resumed her trek for her intended target of Asahiko, across Tokyo.

Time passed as she picked and chose her way across the terrain of Tokyo in silence. By the time she reached sight of Engakuji Castle, the moon was high nearing midnight as Hiromoai called this time of night. She increased her pace, knowing she had to make it to Asahiko's room before the turn of the new day, or the Kami would bear witness to her actions.

She ran like a deer running away from an attacking pack of hunting dogs to the side of the fifteen foot high, massive six foot thick stone wall of the castle keep. Then she ran alongside the wall to the east section of it. Frogs cried and disturbed her Wa as she moved with the skill of a tiger in search of the stone of the mighty shibo sea monsters imprinted on it. The ground under her tabis, the split toed socks was damp as the air she traveled through. This was because the hori, the moat was so close to her at this point. She decided to change from the high boots when she found them hard to walk in, before she left on her first mission to kill Asahiko's son and wife. It was a mistake on her part, a part of vanity that she wanted the high, pleasing to look at and fine feeling leather boots in the first place.

Her eyes searched the bank for the stone. The familiar smells of the castle bringing back pleasing memories of what was once her life in the ancient past. She looked at the stone wall and remembered how many times in her past she walked this muryogo no michi, never ending road carved out by war rounding the walls of the great castle keep. In her sharp mind she could still hear the countless screams of her attacking samurai warriors, as they charged wildly to battle under her orders. The cries coming from the charging horses and the fond memories and smells of the dust and blood filled her nostrils and mind.

She continued to move as silently as the Night Wind in continuing search of the foreboding stone. She suddenly scared a cat up from its hiding place as it searched the moat for prey of the many frogs by the water, and she cursed the cat Kami for placing such a vile and worthless animal in her path. Her mind fought with her spirit, and the countless haunting spirits of her past memory for attacking the once home of lord Kawasomeru, her true lord and master sent chills running down her back. For too many years to remember, her duty was to protect the master who dwelled within the very walls surrounding the mighty castle. Now, she was forced to kill the man who had replaced Lord Kawasomeru currently living within the castle walls.

She looked along the stone walls and saw all that remained of the yegura, the defense tower that once protected this section of the wall from siege, or invasion from their enemy forces. Three wood posts rose ten feet above the stone wall and the wood platform and fourth post long ago gave way to the ravages of nature, and the assault of unending time.

Pinpointing the crumbling remains of the ancient yegura stand was all she needed to discover, it gave her a pretty good idea as to where the sacred stone rested. She cautiously walked another twenty feet or so before starting to look for the stone in earnest. Years ago, the location of the hidden passage was imprinted in her sharp mind. Shown to her by the wise Lord Kawasomeru the night before she took her warriors and set out in search for her master's eternal enemy, Lord Wakatsuki. He wanted Wind as her name implied, to be able to come and go from the castle unobserved by the spies who kept the castle under continual observation. When she came on the patch of brush recently trampled on, she moved in that direction.

Over the years that passed since the last time she had the privilege to visit the castle, the once wide, clean moat shrank by yards and feet, making it harder for her to recognize the location of the stone until she was nearly standing on it. Seeing the stone hidden in the beat down brush, she smiled as she rushed for the nearly white stone. She had no idea the stone resembled a head stone for a modern day grave. As if finding an old friend, she touched the rock as if it was an important memory of her mind. She ran her hands slowly, almost lovingly over the cold stone.

Carefully tracing the almost faded shapes of the sea monsters with the tips of her fingers once carved so deeply in the hard faced stone, as she paid silent homage to the mighty and feared deity that roamed the darkness of the seas for time everlasting, for a moment of respect and honor. She brushed off some dead leaves and branches, and brushed dirt from the face of the stone, paying more respect to the stone that served her on many occasions in her past.

Again, she looked at the great walls of the castle proper, seeing the two oddly placed stones implanted in the wall, she smiled to herself as she struggled with the overwhelming weight of the hallowed and ancient stone. She wanted to make certain that no one had observed her actions from the castle, or the area surrounding the walls. She was no way near as strong as Hiromoai, so she had quite a bit of trouble trying to move the heavy stone from its resting place of centuries. With great effort, she was finally able to roll the heavy stone far enough away from the opening for her to gain entrance into the dark void of the narrow passageway.

Seeing how small the opening was, she instantly realized that she was going to be forced to leave her yumi, the six foot long bow along with her ebira, the open quiver she had strapped to her leg. She did not mind leaving these weapons behind, because she had no intention of having any true need of them in this attack against the old man. This mission was going to entail her using her katana blade to accomplish her orders from her lord and master.

Silently, she slowly slid her taught, slender body into the narrow opening and once inside it, she began to cautiously work her way into the castle proper. Foul odors and stale air made her breathing almost impossible, and it assaulted her nose as the dampness from under the moat made the cave sodden and slimy to walk through. The hundreds of tiny bones from countless small animals trapped in the passage over the years, littered the ground and cracked noisily under the weight of her feet as she trotted upon them. Moving inside the opening was treacherous as her feet slid on the muck coating the floor of the tight passageway. Seeing was another problem for her to struggle with. As well as she was adapted to work in the night and darkness on familiar grounds, without the light of the stars and moon to help guide her along, the cave was pitch black and hard to walk, or even see in and slowed her progress dramatically.

She closed her eyes for a few moments in hopes it would give her a little better vision in the darkness of the narrow cave. When she opened them again she realized that it did not really help her all that much and she was forced to move slower than she wished to travel through the tunnel. Inch by slow inch, she moved deeper into the dampness of the man made cave as her hands searched out before her, looking for the first signs of the slight incline that would lead her to the ancient stone steps and then the upper floors of the castle.

Countless noises from the outside world made her senses grow to a keener sharpness. Every muscle in her body was on full alert for any possible signs of treachery displayed against her. Or someone who might be waiting to intercept her inside the cave opening on the other side of the moat, with each step she took her caution and stress increased until she was at that point to be able to kill anyone without thought or hesitation.

She continued to work her way deeper through the pitch and very constricting tunnel running beneath the moat until she finally came to the first bend in the narrow walkway.

Drawing on the information from her memories of the route, she realized she was now past the moat. Here, the tunnel began to incline steeply and the ground was much better footing because of the dryness under foot, so she increased her pace forward. Her driving force was to confront Asahiko before the moon had entered the first moments of the new day's birth. She went another fifteen yards in the tunnel before she found the first split in the confining walkway. Now she had to draw on her memory on with path to take to get her to her target.

She remembered she had to go to her right if she wanted to get to the second passageway she needed leading to the upper floors of the castle, and the private living quarters of Lord Kawasomeru. She used her hands to help guide her along in the darkness, feeling for any signs of wood that covered some of the interior walls of the ancient castle.

The ancient female samurai went another twenty yards where she saw the first light filtering through one of the tiny peek holes carved from the passageway into the interior of the castle. She went to one of the openings and peered through it. What she saw on the other side was the main entryway, and first floor meeting room of the great keep. She could not help but wonder how many times in the past that Lord Kawasomeru had peered through this very hole, observing his enemy and friends alike, as they went about their business while visiting his castle. She knew the stairway she was looking for was near, so she moved deeper into the widening tunnel in search of the first steps to it and the floors above her.

She continued moving forward until she eventually located the first step of the stone staircase leading to the upper floors of the structure. She began to carefully climb the narrow, cold and steep stepping stones that were not built for comfort walking and covered with years of dust and tiny branches and more bones of small animals littering them. She knew when she reached the second floor level, because there was a large, flat stone landing with many small peep holes drilled into the wall. She peered through one and smiled to herself when she realized she was looking into one of the visitor's private bedrooms. Now, she wondered if her master used these holes to observe his guests while they made love to their wives and lovers. She smiled as she thought Lord Kawasomeru was quite the deceitful and wise master who must have enjoyed spying on his many countless visitors to the castle in this manner.

When she had enough of this section, she moved to the next staircase and climbed these twenty steps. In no time, she reached the third floor and had to choose from three separate passageways circling the interior of the vast castle. She searched her memory for a moment while trying to get her breathing under control, trying to commemorate which passage led to Lord Kawasomeru's room. The room he told her was the only one that had lights glowing.

This was the room that she was brought to when it was first discovered she was a female warrior on the great day of her Gembuku, the ceremony of commemorating her first entry into manhood, and she was trying to invade the long time sequestered lifestyle and conditions of the samurai class. She remembered kneeling before Lord Kawasomeru and his many wise but angry Generals, waiting for fate to befall her once it was discovered she was a female, guilty of carrying out a sinful deceit against her liege lord of the time.

She felt the damp stones in this area with her hands as she used them to move ahead, trying to remember the exact way, using her feet and hands to slowly guide her forward. Finally, she decided to take the left walkway. She moved along the concourse, peering through the many small holes drilled in the stone wall of the castle here. The faint light filtering through the holes made her progress slightly easier. Seeing some familiar items on the other side of the wall through the holes, led her to believe she was moving in the right direction. Suddenly, she stopped her movement as saw the faint glow bathing the passageway yards before her. Drawing in her breath and holding it for a second as she prepared her mind for mortal combat, she cautiously inched her way forward. She knew this light was coming from Lord Kawasomeru's private room.

She moved to the first observation hole and looked in the room. Instantly, she recognized it as the one she was in search of. The interior of the huge room was bathed with harsh light, and she could see the shadow of someone inside the room. She was surprised this room seemed like it was turned into a sleeping room for the new lord and master of the castle. She saw a shadow, and it looked like the person was kneeling and paying homage to a small altar resting peacefully before him. She moved further to her left and found the hidden wood panel that opened, and gave her stealthy entry into the large room.

With great effort on her part, she forcefully shoved the heavy panel, it slid slowly and moved to one side and instantly her eyes were assaulted by the harsh light filling the room. She saw the back of an old man kneeling on the floor. Forthwith, she realized what the person was up to in his efforts. Confidently, she walked into the room, passing the kneeling man on his left side in order to stay away from his sword arm. It was the sign of respect for what the man was about to do with his life. She realized he was of no real threat against her person, because he was unarmed except for the small tanto blade resting inside the closed box beside his leg, and he was too involved in preparing for his honorable death to even notice her presence.

The old man suddenly noticed the shadow of the murderess passing over his shoulder like the Night Wind, and it hover over him like an evil harbinger of death to come, as the shadow crossed his small altar then stopped moving and stood over him. But he refused to recognize the god cursed assassin's presence, as he or she stopped moving closer.

Wind cautiously passed by the old man while keeping a close watch of him out the corner of her eyes, to make certain he did not try any treachery against her, yet also respecting his honorable actions by not looking directly at him. She saw the wood box containing what she knew to be the blade of death. It was most disrespectful to look upon the eyes of an honorable man as he prepared his spirit for the sacred act of Suppuku, unless he recognized her presence first. Without word she drew her katana blade, the steel sliding along the wood scabbard sang its song of death to her ears. She then walked forward and turned until she was able to face the old man. Silently, she knelt down before him and bowed as she removed the heavy brass Hoate mask from her face so he could look upon his executioner's face and see her eyes.

Again, the old man did not recognize her attendance with his eyes as he continued mumbling with striving, the sacred prayers to Lord Buddha. His mind was locked deep in the depths of thought for the preparation needed for his pending death. When he finished his prayers, he finally recognized her presence by snarling savagely at her. "Ahhh... so, my most honorable son's cursed murderer has come to visit death upon these old shoulders of mine, and finish the disgusting job you have started of destroying my entire family on me? What intelligence possessed by the ancient ones of good will and foresight and understanding, could have possibly stumbled and erred in their way of thinking as to create something so monstrous so full of evil and hatred as your being, foul assassin of the night's darkness. Well evil one born from hell's fire, it's too late for you to entertain your loathsome lust for murder and blood on this night's darkness, for I'm going to visit the Floating World by my own honorable hand.

"By my own want and demand I tell you, foul one who slithered into my presence from the darkness of the night and the very pits of hell. There's no human blood for you to feast upon on this, the saddest of nights for me to labor through, evil one. I'm afraid you'll have to fast from your blood lust tonight, and the destruction of my entire world as I once enjoyed it. My throat swells in unwanted torment, and wants to burst violently forth from the mere sight of your foul existence standing before my tired eyes, evil loathsome one. What unseen madness without goal or meaning, what thoughtless, soulless Kami fed by the mystical faith of its believers, has allowed something such as you to crawl along the sacred soil of Japan? You should've never been allowed birth in the first place, evil thing of the night's madness and hatred."

"Hai old one! You may judge me as you deem fit which is your right to do at this most sacred of times in your wasted life. When one has reached the mountain's zenith, only then does the true climb of his life begins. Honorable old one, I see by my eyes that you're without a second to help guide your proud spirit forth to the world of unknown dreams and wonder of the Floating World." She studied the old man's well aged face, and read the overwhelming suffocating pain that was etched so deeply in the ancient lines on his face. Again, her mind was confused by what her eyes were witnessing as she looked upon the face of the one about to end his existence.

"Huh, it's as they have offered to my being and unbelieving ears and eyes, I see that the loathsome beast has awakened from its cursed sleep. But the heart beating within your putrid and evil chest is the sum of all the agony and deep despair of suffering, with humanity patiently waiting your death to call upon your head, and send you back to the very pit of hell you were spawn from to again be with your own kind of evil kin." Asahiko looked to the face of the killer, but he still refused to look her in the eyes, and he knew then by the unnerving pursing of Wind's lips that her mouth contained not one single word of comfort or guilt for what she did to his honorable son and his wife, or his life. He hissed through clenched teeth at the assassin.

"Gall doesn't have to be enjoyed from a beautiful vessel to be displayed, and you foul one constructed from the foulest and lowest of sinful flesh and filth, are consumed by all the unmitigated gall the world has ever witnessed in her long and lonely existence in history. To dare show up before me after what you have done to my honorable son and his wife. Even now the vile sin you have committed against my noble house and family germinates from within your foul presence, and the stink it emits is festering like an open sore that will not heal until it has successfully eat away your very worthless soul, ancient Samurai Warrior. Then, the ones who gave your being foul birth, will feast upon this putrid extract, and all will follow you to the depths of the hell where you belong, evil one of the night's call.

"The honorable Kami who the good people of Japan respect, will become ill with your evil presence, and they'll shun you like all civilized persons will, and you'll find yourself alone even in the underworld life of the red hell. Your detestable evil being has so overwhelmingly invaded my domain so completely, it sickens me to my very soul, my very being, you have absolutely destroyed, fully penetrated, totally occupied, and have taken over, and laid unholy siege against my most well guarded, well protected, most cherished places of my ancient body and mind.

"I curse your loathsome existence back to the angry pit of hell that gave forth your insignificant birth. Bah! All this evil and hatred is too confusing for my befuddled old mind, and it's for the foul Kami to sort out properly at the great Council of Kami. But I will honor you by answering your one question of me, evil one of the night's darkness. That's very observant and surprising decent of you evil one, because I'll not force one of my most honorable friends to assist me in my respectable death, my hated Kaishaku (Executioner) from the red hell's fires. I have too much respect for my faithful friends to have them get in trouble with the police, but what the devil do you know of true respect and honor, foul one?

"Old one, I see your tears and feel and understand what you feel locked deep within your ancient and breaking heart, honorable old man almost as ancient as myself. I suffer with you because of your all consuming anguish at this most sacred of times in your honorable life of the living world. Old man of vast knowledge and age, a wise Samurai Warrior knows well when to coil like the dragon, and when to strike like a stalking Kotora. (Tiger) Why do you wish to take your great experienced life on this night, ancient one with the angry tongue?" Wind refused to honor him by using his proper name while speaking to him, thought she knew it well.

"Vile murderer of my honorable son and his loving wife, I'm forced to take my life because it's been ordained by your evil hand and fate that I have been cursed by pain and hatred, and the unscrupulousness of all Kami who control Karma, to outlive my beloved son. A most horrendous insult that's too hard for any self-respecting man to endure. It's an extremely low and foul curse of absolute meanness to be condemned to outlive one's honorable son, one meant to punish its victim well beyond good conscious and belief. Your filthy and deplorable actions will come back to haunt and feed upon your worthless evil soul. By all the Kami great and small, respected and hated by men and women of fair conscious, I can feel you as plain as if the devil's own breath was falling upon my being. Evil thing born from the devil's vile flesh and urine."

"Yes old one, I understand the harsh words of pain and anger that you speak out against me. When cruel demands are made of one's honorable spirit, one must faithfully weigh and measure all his options very carefully. Old one of many years upon this earth, our greatest weakness lies within giving up one's faith and our beliefs. The most certain of ways to carry on one's most honorable life, is by fostering the will to always try that once more in life's destiny. Hai, this pain I understand all too well, because I too have lost all who I once held dear to my bosom and heart. It's a very noble reason to desire to take one's sacred life, honorable old one." She settled her weight on her legs as she looked deeply into Asahiko's sad eyes.

For the first time since she entered his room, he allowed his eyes to meet those of his assassin of the night. Seeing her face without the dreaded Hoate brass mask hiding it from his view, he moaned barely over a whisper at her. "So, it's as was believed by all who speak of your hated and vile presence in this world that my honorable son's assassin is that of a lowly ancient female Samurai Warrior, neh? Tell me bloodthirsty evil spirit born from all the hatred trapped within the filthy pits of the red hell. Why have you visited death upon my honorable family so viciously, so completely, evil breath from the depths of the lowly black underworld and red hell?

"What has my honorable son and his very respectful wife ever done to the likes of you, or to your foul Master who is without honor and face, for him to deem it necessary for you to be sent out in the middle of the night, to take their lives in such a savage manner that you chose to destroy their lives, whore of the dark world? I swear by everything I believe and honor and respect, if I was a younger man I'd fight you to the death, and it'll be your death that I'd be celebrating on this night, not mine. I so detest your vile being forever being allowed to draw life giving breath meant for the faithful and respecting of the earth and the sacred land of Japan."

Wind understood and respected the strength and anger possessed by this old man, for him to speak while his mind was so preoccupied with the sacred preparations that were needed for his praiseworthy death. Drawing in her breath out of respect for this old man, she replied solemnly to him. "Wise one who has forgotten more than I fear I shall ever know and understand, sacrifices are demanded by fate, and the victims must be provided in order to appease my Lord and Master's great wrath and want for revenge against you and your entire family. For is it not said that the hardest lesson to be learned from life's enlightenment and endurance, is not to allow one's self to become too attached to the known facts of one's own faithful deeds, old man? It was not by my wish or want, but by my hand that your honorable son and his wife were sent to float forever together for eternity within the clouds that crown Japan with their ancestors of yore.

"If it is of any peace to your wise mind, your most honorable son fought valiantly against what was preordained by fate's hand against me. I had allowed him to arm himself and enjoy his last battle for survival on this earth. You have trained him very well old one of countless years of wisdom and existence. He was a most worthy adversary to do honorable battle with. I was forced to employ all my vast skills of warfare to defeat his fighting spirit and skills."

Asahiko was stunned that this evil spirit had allowed his son to arm himself and do just battle with his killer sent to destroy him and his wife for reasons unknown to him. It was a sign of deep respect offered by this evil thing staring back at him as if his life did not matter a spec to her being. An honor that he did not believe existed within the foul killer's honor, as he replied to the evil apparition speaking with him as if he was not about to die by his own hand. "I'm honored that you had allowed my son to arm and fight the daughter of Satan to his death. By whose foul desire do you practice your evil work of death, evil demon of the darkness of night?" He knew the answer, but he wanted to hear it said by the assassin's own lips to set his mind at peace.

"It is well within your right to request and even demand this knowledge from my lips, and I'm bound by the honor of history great past for what you are about to accomplish by your own hand, to answer that request of yours, old man. My Lord and Master, Hiromoai-sama has deemed it necessary, for you and your entire family are his hated teki for life. As teki against my Lord commands that I must erase all of you from fate's memory, in order to appease his great wrath." She did not hesitate with informing Asahiko of her master's name, because she knew he was soon destining to be walking among the great ancestors of Japan's proud past. The name of her master would surely follow him to the next world, and forever silence his lips against any possible deception or revenge aimed against her master in the living world.

"Yes evil thing that pollutes the pure air of the living world, I'm conscious of your god cursed Master and his depraved intents harbored against me and my honorable family. It's a terrible shame that he has sought to take the battle existing between us, and he has now extended it to my honorable son and his family, evil lap dog of Satan's will and demands."

"I am upset to be forced to announce for your understanding that there is not one single ear that can hear the silent scream of the breaking heart that yearns for a loved one's kind understanding and warmth. The sorrowful scream of the dead deafens with its hardness, and hardens with its deafening silence. Old man of endless time and unlimited experience, when your mind has stopped comparing what is right with what you wish, or believe or deem is right, only then do you begin to enjoy what is truly ordained by Karma and the Kami for us to endure and enjoy. As it is believed, what cannot be avoided must be set in stone for life everlasting, honorable one. I know not of the true reason for my Lord and Master's want nor his need and desire of your honorable son's death. I only followed orders as received by my Master's lips to my faithful ears, and to see them through to their final conclusion, that is my destiny."

"So say all the cursed killers ever born to the earth of the past and present times of great pain, death and sorrows. I'm not guilty of my sins, because I was only guilty of following orders of the worthless ones who command my being forward. Huh! You try to sound like you're a righteous and just entity, but you're nothing more than what you were born to be from the start of your evil life, a savage murderess doing hell and the devil's business for him.

"You're devoted solely to no one but your own evil self, and your depraved ways and desires of dishing out that death and destruction of the innocent who populate the earth in an honorable and respectful manner, evil black spirit of yesterdays past. You, who have been anointed by all the evil that the red hell possesses to carry out its lowly ideas of hate and blood lust, you're the most wretched and loathsome foul being the sun and earth have ever witnessed to birth. So hated one, are you going to interfere with the sacred act of Suppuku that I have planned for myself to endure on this night? Are you going to rob my faithful spirit of its final dignity and respect for my dead and honorable son and his wife, inferior one from the depths of hell?"

"Iye! No, old one possessed with the stinging tongue and biting words aimed at my heart and soul! What do you think I am, a lowly Ronin, a hated and worthless criminal who kills for the sake of killing alone, and suffer from the lust of blood and death in my heart? No ancient one with the angry words cursing my honorable spirit! I need no artificial embellishments to increase my being, my fate, my pulse to the things that shape the past and future of the two worlds that I am allowed to travel within. For I am an honorable and well respected Samurai Warrior who respects the sacred and forever guarded ways of the ancient past, and of life pure for Japan and all her faithful children, old one who enjoys aiming words of pain and anger at me for no good reason, in hopes of hurting my person as if those words were the biting edge of a killing sword."

"Then you shall allow me to commit Suppuku, evil one born of the foul dragon's evil breath?"

CHAPTER TWENTY ONE

Wind completely ignored the terrible insult of being called evil by the old man. Normally, she would have attacked and killed anyone who dared to insult her in such a foul manner as he was attacking her being. But she felt he was trying to draw her ire to weaken her strength against her, but she was a well trained samurai, and she understood not to give in to the iniquitous prodding from the wise old man kneeling before her in respect for the great Lord Buddha. The state this old man was locked in, informed her that he was well within his right to call anyone whatever he wished. For in the throw of the sacred act of Suppuku, the honored one was beyond insulting anyone. His words were taken as law, as the truth of ages. Again, she drew in her breath before replying to Asahiko who was still kneeling at her feet.

"Old man of aged and endless time and anger, I shall honor what you are about to accomplish to accolade the respected Kami gods of the past, and your most honorable son's fine memory. It is a very noble way to nourish the Kami who prowl the sacred soil of Japan, to feed it your blood and clear the way for your entrance into the Ukiyo, the Floating World respected by the living and dead alike, in constant search of loved ones and peace of mind. I respect you ancient one to the point where I would be most honored to second your virtuous death. In that way proud one, your soul will have no worries as it searches for the chosen gate of entry to the Floating World." Wind finally relaxed her threatening stance and waited for him to reply to her offer.

Asahiko leaned back on his legs and stared with his mouth agape back at the female murderer, he was stunned that this loathsome creature of the night's darkness, would know so well of the ways of respect and honor of the past of Japan, as he barked angrily back at her. "You! You who were born to transport the loathsome pitch fork of evil in which the despised Devil Kami employs to destroy the scared ship of humanity and honorable life upon this earth. You would offer to second my pending death for me, evil one of the night's darkness?" The old man mumbled barely over a whisper at the female warrior who removed the hatred from her eyes.

"Hai honorable old one, because my war is not with your honorable spirit, or its future fate within the Floating World, my war with you is only with your worthless body of being and existence upon the earth. I care not one lowly grain of valueless rice what the Kami do with your honorable spirit once it is resting peacefully within the Floating World. I believe that decision is left up to them to accomplish and ordained. My only concern and interest is in your earthly presence, old one about to honor the gods of the past with great respect." Wind replied to the old man as she bowed politely back at him and even gave him a slight smile.

"Huh, how could my black angel of death and evil be so willing to honor me, vile one with the evil heart waiting to drink my blood? How could you be overflowing with such great respect and honor, and the faithful ways of the ancient past of Japan's great history, and yet slaughter the innocent without thought or hesitation or it disturbing your evil mind in the least?" The old man asked as he stared at this woman who was a beauty, but deadly being.

"As I have stated before for your knowledge old Warrior of many past battles and victories upon this world, my war is not against your fine spirit. To honor one, even though I must kill that one's earthly form, is the highest respect any respected Samurai Warrior could possibly offer to his enemy. As it was in the past of Japan's history, to honor one's enemy for his accomplished feats displayed upon the battlefield of his choosing, makes that honored Warrior everlasting and immortal for all time to come. His noble spirit would be sung in the entertaining Nolt plays, so his name is spoken in the future in order to give his name forever immortality sought by all who dwell upon this rock of the earth. Thus, I offer your outstanding warring spirit the same great and deep respect and honor, old one of the modern times."

"Huh! What kind of evil spirit that knees before my worthless eyes are you spawned from, Satan's pet and toy? You offer to assist my honorable death, yet you have destroyed my honorable son and his loving wife as if their existence didn't matter to the wonder of things that be, and you're so willing to end my worthless life, even if I wanted to continue living on in this world that offers me nothing but pain and sorrow and terrible regrets. Bah! The most confusing ways of Karma are most befuddling to my feeble old mind as I have stated.

"You have forced me to honor the most unworthy of evil existence kneeling before me. I thank your evil spirit for your kind offer understanding and assistance in my pending death, daughter of the devil's vile spawn. Because I was in fear of the cursed Tengus, worried the evil things would kidnap my spirit before it could enter the safety of the Floating World, in search for my most honorable son and his wife. To lay eyes upon his face once more in either life, is all the immortality I'll need to rest at peace with the world forever, daughter of death and darkness."

"Then old one, allow this worthless Samurai Warrior the honor to offer you this great peace of worldly things that you seek on this last night of your most honorable life." Wind bowed graciously at the kneeling old man this time.

"I'd deem it a great honor for you to second my pending death, Samurai Warrior of the past times that once glorified Japan's proud past of long ago." Asahiko offered the ancient female warrior spirit kneeling before him and offering to assist him in his death.

"Huh, then you know that my being is not of the world of the living, wise ancient one with the all seeing eyes, and enough anger within your chest to forester a dozen men's foul ego?" She asked, surprised by the knowledge and wisdom possessed by this crafty old man.

"Certainly I understand this as a true fact, evil one who has feasted in the dark of night on sour mother's breast milk and has greedily eaten upon the devil's unholy and filthy flesh. Why else would someone so young as you appear before me, knowing so much of the well respected and guarded ancient ways of the past glory of Japan's proud history. I have heard often over my many years of existence upon this foul rock we call the earth, of honored Samurai Warriors coming back to earth from the Floating World, in order to serve their Lord and Masters of the past times in further of their need and wants upon the earth. But I have never dared to dream the foolish allegory might be born within truth until laying my tired and burning eyes upon your black evil spirit, Samurai of yesterday's past! It's a terrible shame for all humanity if, that only the evil doers of our great past history might be granted this honored privilege to revisit the living world, when requested to do so by their once masters of long ago.

"Why in good faith you would persist in wanting to visit the world of the living is beyond my puzzling thoughts and knowledge. For all you have ever known and all you have ever loved in your evil life, are gone from your eyes and this earth forever. Gone is your entire family from the face of this earth, as well as is all those who respected and honored you in your past. Your whole world is dead your honored ancestors are dead. Huh, to dare to beg existence within a world of no acknowledgment and love but the only acknowledgment you own is of being a god cursed murderer, and evil harbinger of death, a hired and hated killer for another's evil intent. This I cannot understand for one moment of time in my wasted life, evil witch of the past times.

"Dead things cannot hurt the living world. What do you dare hope to accomplish with the murder and death forever stalking your foul wings of evil, Angel of death and of the devil's smile?" He stared in her beautiful eyes seeking her answers to his questions he put forth on this night of sadness, yet of hope and wanting to him. His sharp mind demanded the answers to her continuing want of life, if that life was only to bring death to the living of this time.

A flush of angry embarrassment suddenly washed over her face momentarily as she fought desperately with inner herself against allowing her anger to strike out and react against this old man's terribly unkind and extremely hurtful words that he was aiming at her in this unending conversation. She wished she was still wearing the protecting and ugly heavy brass mask of anger. Thinking the thick brass mask would deflect most of his appallingly stinging words he was growling at her from her ears and heart. All she could think of replying to the old man's very upsetting words was. "You are wrong with your angry words of hatred that you foolishly aim at me being, Master of the venomous tongue. Dead things can kill from the past of times as you are about to witness for yourself."

"I must admit ancient Samurai Warrior from the great past of Japan you honored and served your most repulsive Master so well, foul spirit of the forgotten days. I hope you'll serve my death equally as well, Warrior of the past. Will not your dishonorable Lord and Master be upset with your spirit for daring to aid me in my death so honorably, Samurai of yore?"

"If you are trying to test my loyalty to my Lord and Master then you will only end up testing my patience for your presence in this world, old man with a tongue as sharp as the sharpest Katana blade. My loyalty to my Master is heavier than the world's weight in its entire, yet my life is lighter than that of one lowly plucked feather from a goose hide, honorable old one. If my life is of so little importance and value to the existence and pulse of the world and dreams that be. Then my enemy's life is far less than worthless to me in both thought and deeds. Death will slay with her Wings of Justice, for I am the wind that generates the very lift to those vengeful currents. My Lord and Master is a most honorable and kind man, and he will not be angry with me if I were to open the true path for your proud spirit to tread upon, on its long and lonely search and journey to the Floating World of wonderment, and unanswered dreams and wants.

"Your death is the only thing of any importance to my Lord and Master's want and desire. How you achieve your most honorable death is of little concern and interest to his sacred Wa. I am ready to assist your proud death on this respectful of nights, time is short for you. There is a preordained time of night that your fine spirit must be set free from its earthly bonds, to make things right with the sacred act that you must carry out for yourself on this night of wonder and respect." Again, she bowed graciously towards the kneeling old man.

"Oh, pen up your pits of hell and desire for a blood feast, foul witch of yesterday's past. Yes evil spirit of hatred and pure disgust. I believe it's the time at hand for me to depart this land of sorrow and unending pain. But before I leave this cursed world of the living forever, there's one last question that I must ask of you, Samurai Warrior of yesterday." The old man said as he now glared openly and very angrily at her.

"As I have stated before in this conversation to you old one, it is within your divine right to ask upon my presence any question of favor of this lowly Samurai Warrior at this most honored time in your long and respected life, and I am bound by that honor and my sacred oath as Samurai of the past, to fulfill that request for you, old man. Ask your question my Lord and Master of the moment, and I shall reply truthfully if I have the knowledge to answer properly. If I know the answer to the requested question you seek from me, respected one. Time grows short and we must accomplish this sacred feat in the time allotted to your last act of life." She said this with humility and respect for the old man kneeling before her, as she bowed again to his presence.

"I thank you for the honor you offered to my being on this earth. Samurai of the past times, I want to know your once proud name given to you out of the purity of respect and loyalty by the one who had sired your most villainous presence to this, the world I inhabit so sadly and long. It's important for me to know this name so peace can follow me into the Floating World. Your name that is the evil thing who has killed my beloved and honorable son before I die, age-old Warrior of yesterday?" Asahiko glared into the shining green eyes of the samurai.

"Yes old one, it is your right to ask me of this want and desire, but I fear that you are in error in your concerned thoughts and belief that you speak to me of. I am not a murderer to be so feared by you in this world. I have killed your honorable son true, but the act was committed to avenge my Master's honor. That is not the action of a lowly murderer old man, but of a Warrior of worth and understanding." For the first time, she allowed a touch of anger to creep in her tone.

"Yes, that much I give you my hated Angel of death and darkness. You are not responsible for my honorable son and his wife's death. It's as you have stated to me ancient one, you were only guilty of following your Lord and Master's orders faithfully, something that is expected and demanded by any honorable Samurai Warrior of true worth and loyalty, past or present." Asahiko bowed because of his insult to the ancient warrior.

Wind nodded politely and then offered respectfully to the old man. "Asahiko-san, my true name and the only name I will respond to is Wind, given to me by Lord Kawasomeru of the past, to honor me for my loyalty to his orders upon the battlefield. I am the first and only female Samurai ever allowed to war side by side with his great male Samurai Armies. My most wise Lord Kawasomeru's mind was always searching to make his rule just and improved. That was the reason I was allowed to live and fight for my true Master's needs and desires."

"Yes ancient Samurai of hatred and evil, in searching my feeble mind I seem to remember the old foke lore explaining of a once well honored and feared female Samurai Warrior fighting for a great warlord of our ancient past. You are obviously that Warrior of myth I take it, Samurai of history's past?" He asked while continuing to stare at her in awe.

"Hai. I believe I am that Warrior you have learned and remembered of, old one. I am deeply honored in your proud mind I have once lived and was respected by you. It is as I have said before old one, to speak of the dead gives that dead immortality to enjoy forever."

"Huh, then it's a great honor of mine to be seconded in my death by such a noble Warrior of vast value of the past times and glory. But surely, Wind is not your given name at birth, Samurai. Who was your honorable father in the time long ago?" Asahiko asked as he relaxed and allowed himself to calm down a bit and be more civil to the ancient female warrior.

"To know of this demand baffles me beyond my limited understanding, my concern and knowledge ancient one. Why do all those who dwell and take up breathing space in the living world, demand of me my many names of respect and honor, and the name of the fearsome proud Samurai who had created my being? The Warrior who had sired me, who gave me life to breathe, I do not understand the driving force that compels you so to demand to know of my many names of the past times, old one. But since you have asked this of me, I am bound by the honor of past times to fulfill that request, old one. My honorable father was the Master Trainer of all times, Nitaro Tanizaki-san of the Ninth Village of the eight central provinces of Japan.

"I fear that my names are as many as there are the branches to the wise old willow tree. Masahiko-san was the name I used throughout most of my honorable life, employed to hide the fact that I was of the female kind from my respectful Lord Kawasomeru, until my deceitful sin was discovered. My family name was Yuriko Tanizaki, and my guiding Kami god is Fujin-sama, the fearsome and always angry God of Wind. Old man of time and vast experience, you have as much chance of changing fate, as you do of changing the patterns of the stars that soar freely within the Heavens for our enjoyment. I am ready to assist you in your honored death, for your proud spirit must be sent on its way before the moon enters the tomorrow's breath of the new day's beginnings, Asahiko-san." Wind gave a smile to him for the first time since she entered his room, in her mind she was trying to show him she was not as evil as he thought she was.

Asahiko bowed to her, pleased that she was showing him noble respect by adding the san to his name. Perhaps, in another time, in another world, he could have become friends with this feared and highly skilled female samurai assassin once again kneeling and speaking so respectfully before him as he offered to her as he finally gave into destinies call of his fine spirit to come home. "Yes, you're correct respected Samurai Warrior of old. It's time to release my withering spirit from the world of the living to the dead, Samurai."

She watched in silence and respect as the old man recited his final prayers to the statue of Lord Buddha in a rapid whisper of words. She remained soundless as he then slowly unrolled the two sheets of snow white pure rice paper. Then he reached out for the small highly lacquered box and snapped the seal open with a mere flick of his thumb of his killing hand. The respectful old man carefully removed the small tanto blade and held it out before him, to honor the fine blade while allowing it to breathe the clean air of this final night of his life. Then he bowed to the blade and then he lightly touched it to his forehead.

She leaned forward and respectfully dipped the bamboo dipper into the bowl of pure warm water resting by his right side, and poured the water over the small, exposed shining blade.

Asahiko nodded pleased she was assisting him with honor and respect.

She rose and moved her deadly katana blade known as Wind's Breath, out before her body and then she poured the rest of the dipper of water over the ancient blade. She flipped the razor sharp blade over in her hands to show him the water had washed both sides of the great blade at the same time, fulfilling her duty to this sacred act he was about to commit.

Again he nodded with reverence to the deadly and threatening spirit of the past times he ever witnessed in his long life on the earth.

She moved to his left side and took the best stance that would enable her to lop his head from his shoulders with the first blow from her deadly sword, and then she waited silently, patiently for the old man to carry out his final respects to the act of Suppuku. All the while she watched his right hand, to make certain he did not try to attack her with the blade before he died.

Asahiko took time as he properly straightened up his old painful body resting on his knees the best he could, as he pulled apart the silk fabric of his exquisite white kimono. He pulled his arms free of the expensive fabric like a blossoming flower and then he tucked the fabric properly under his legs then he sat on the cloth in an attempt to lock it and his body in place. This was an act to try and stop his body from falling off to either side once he was dead. It was a great loss of face to his spirit, if the one who was about to commit Suppuku, fell from his kneeling position during the final act of his life. He made certain the folds of the fine kimono were proper.

Once this was accomplished, the old man then picked up the small tanto blade with the razor sharp edge, and he brought the blade slowly and respectfully to his forehead and lightly touched it lightly a second time. He mumbled his final prayers to Lord Buddha, and the blade while lowering it towards his waiting body, and then aiming it threateningly at his exposed stomach. The old man suddenly straightened his back to expose more of his belly to the call of the blade's silent whisper. He then drew in his breath and held it, and with the inner strength and courage he needed, he plunged the razor sharp cutting edge full depth in his exposed guts, and drew the blade swiftly through his body from right to left. He was so excited that he put so much of the blade in his body. Usually only about an inch of the tip of the blade was used to open his belly.

In a fine spray of blood and saliva, he let out his breath in a grunt as the knife ripped through the innards and the muscles of his belly. His life and innards poured out of the nasty gash and fell on the sheets of rice paper lying before his kneeling position. When he paused for a moment then pulled the knife upwards, and turned it in his body after he pulled most of the knife out of his belly, and began to work his way slowly across his body a second time, he gave the first signs of pain to the sacred act. This was her time to react to his honored action.

In a blur of a blinding silver streak, her katana blade cut through the air with the shrill call of death, the blade striking his exposed neck as she let out with a terrible roar. Without the slightest hesitation or delay, the keen edge of the deadly sword cut his head free from his shoulders. His head landing at the grovel of his body. His lips were still mumbling the final prayers to his selected Kami, to allow his spirit to reside in peace until the time of his rebirth was at hand, he was allowed by the gods who controlled such things.

Blood gushed a few feet from his body, as it slowly sagged to its final resting stance. She had to place her hand tenderly on his shoulder in an attempt to stop his body from falling over and disgraced in his final act of life. She then bowed towards the body with great respect and without thought she tenderly lifted his head by the hair and looked deeply in the unseeing eyes for a moment. She bowed to the head as she carefully wiped some blood from the face with another sheet of rice paper she had picked up from the floor along with Asahiko's head.

Carefully, she set the head properly resting before the kneeling body on another clean sheet of rice paper. She took the time to fix the head so it could stare back at the body from which it was separated from. Before she left the room, she straightened the remaining hair of his head and fixed the head just so, to display to the world that this well honored man had died a very noble and respectful death, and he was seconded by someone who had immensely respected the old man, to make his travel to the Floating World easy for him to accomplish.

With one final display of respect for the old man, she bowed to his body she hated so, and did not understand the reason why she did, and uttered her last words of honor to his fine spirit. "Honorable Asahiko-san, anticipation of death is worse than death itself as you have just found out on this night." Then she backed out of the room, refusing to turn her back on the honored one, to maintain the greatest of respect to his memory on the earth and his body. Then, like the ghost she was, she instantly disappeared back through the narrow passageway and rapidly worked her way out of the castle. In no time, she was again making good use of the shadows of the night and its darkness, as she headed back to Hiromoai's apartment in the Hatanaka Tower, after picking up her long bow and quiver and arrows she had left resting at the mouth of the passage. She glanced up at the moon it was in the proper position to inform her that Asahiko had met his honorable death at the appropriate time he was supposed to die on this glorious night.

HIROMOAI'S PENTHOUSE APARTMENT IN THE HATANAKA TOWERS

The young Japanese business owner Hiromoai Hatanaka was bored to death with the annoying and inquisitive Sergeant Okamatsu, who refused to leave his home along with his constant stream of endless questions about Japan's ancient weapons and armor that adorned the walls of his massive study. He kept a close eye on the clock, it was nearing one a.m. and he knew he had to get rid of the four police officers if he wanted them out of the apartment before Wind's return. He suddenly rose from the sofa, but the officer made no effort to follow his lead, the Sergeant was so enjoying their conversation too much to allow it to end so easily. He did not know what else to do to get rid of the young detective. Giving a deep sigh of total exhaustion, Hiromoai moaned he was getting tired as he yawned and stretched and stated he wanted to go to sleep.

Again, Okamatsu refused to read the hint he was passing that he wanted him to leave.

THE LAW OFFICES OF SHIGERU NAGARO

The lawyer sat in silence in the darkness of his office, three miles away from Asahiko's castle, as he waited for what seemed like a short lifetime for his friend of many years to answer faith's beckoning to take his life. He was well aware of the exact time the old man planned to commit Suppuku, and he was faithfully following orders from him, by not allowing his body to remain unattended for too long a time after his death. With a trembling hand he reached for the phone that seemed miles from his hand, and quickly dialed his private number. The phone rang three times before the old man servant Makoto Ishikawa, answered in a tired and bored voice.

"Asahiko-san Castle. Who is this please?" The old man recited in the phone as always.

"Yes Makoto-san, good evening, this is Shigeru..." The lawyer offered to the old man calmly.

"Kon banwa, good evening Shigeru-san. And how are you doing on this lovely night, sir?"

"Kon banwa Makoto-san, I'm fine, thank you. By any chance is Asahiko-san still up please?"

"I'm afraid I don't know the answer to that question, Lawyer Shigeru-san. It's been several hours since I last witnessed the Master's presence when I saw him resting uneasily in his quarters, sir. He seemed to have something weighing heavy on his mind, and he was acting rather strangely tonight might I add, Shigeru-san. I'm very concerned over his health tonight sir."

"How is that Makoto-san?" Nagaro asked, displaying false concern for Asahiko's condition.

"Asahiko-san was quiet most of the day, almost secretive if you will, and tonight he was beyond trying to figure out, sir. He seemed to be in an agitated state and distant. Nothing seemed to please his angry mind on this night. He stayed in his sleeping quarters and entertained from there, instead of coming down to the first floor to entertain his few visitors of the day, sir. Asahiko-san also gave strange orders most of the day. Even repeating some of the orders a second time as if I didn't hear them the first time he ordered me, sir. Many times he told me he didn't want to be disturbed for any reason whatsoever. He didn't even eat anything all day, not even taking in water I fear. I'm deeply concerned over his health, Nagaro-san. Do you have any suggestions to offer me to follow in dealing with the strange acting Master tonight, sir?"

"None that I can think of offhand that might help you out any Makoto-san. Maybe Asahiko-san is still upset over his honorable son and his daughter in law's savage murder. Makoto-san, it's extremely important and I must beg you to interrupt Asahiko-san's sleep if he's sleeping. I must speak to him immediately. This way I can see if there's anything seriously troubling his mind I should be concerned over myself, Makoto-san." The lawyer said wanting someone to get to his body as soon as possible as he promised the old man he would do.

"I'd be in your debt if you speak to Asahiko-san, Nagaro-san. He has me that concerned over his health on this day, sir. You're the only man in all Japan who can possibly bring peace to his troubled mind I believe, Nagaro-san. I'll knock on his door and if Asahiko-san refuses to answer then this conversation will have to wait until he wakes tomorrow morning, sir."

"I'm sorry Makoto-san, but I must insist that you wake him if at all possible. It's that important that I speak to him at this time." The wise lawyer pressed the old man servant harder as he nearly barked his words at him this time.

"Yes Lawyer Nagaro-san, I'll wake the Master of the Castle for you, sir. I know he'd be extremely upset if I didn't inform him that you were requesting to speak with him on this night, Nagaro-san. If the Master's angry over the intrusion to his sacred Wa. I'll blame it on your shoulders, Shigeru-san. Please remain on the line while I go and see if Asahiko-san is willing to speak with you this late at night, Nagaro-san." The old man servant laughed in the phone.

'Huh, see how long you're laughing when you discover Asahiko's body, you old fool you'. Shigeru growled under his breath as he waited for the man servant to carry out his duty.

Makoto left the phone resting on the table and slowly waddled up to Asahiko's room in no great hurry. The elderly man servant moved with indecision, he did not really want to wake him, knowing the old man needed his sleep. When he reached the door, he was surprised to see it slightly ajar. He cautiously peered into the well lit room and was shocked to see the slaughtered body of Asahiko kneeling on the floor with his head missing from his shoulders. He didn't stay long enough to see where the head rested. The man servant ran down the stairs for the phone.

Nagaro waited when suddenly Makoto was back on the line, he was excited and completely out of breath as he nearly screamed his words into the phone.

"Shigeru-san! You must come and help me immediately sir. I'm afraid that Master Asahiko-san is dead! His head has been chopped from his body, and his innards are scattered all over the floor before him, sir. You must come and help me, please sir! I don't know what to do for Asahiko-san." The old man's shaking voice reported to the lawyer.

Shigeru's eyebrows arched in surprise as he listened then offered. "Calm down Makoto-san, I fear you might hurt yourself. What the devil do you mean Asahiko-san's dead? Have you been drinking his prized sake behind his back again? If you have, I warn you I'll inform him, and also of this most insensitive remark he's dead, slaughtered as you have put it." He knew what he was doing he was taking the eye of blame from his shoulders. He could not believe his head was removed from his body. That meant he allowed someone of respect, to second his death.

"No sir, I have not been drinking and have never drank while I was caring for Asahiko-san's health and needs, sir. I resent the suggestion you have aimed at me sir. Asahiko-san's upstairs in his sleeping quarters, his body's been slaughtered beyond belief, Nagaro-san. The devil is the right word for what I have just seen Nagaro-san. Asahiko-san was murdered much like his honorable son and his wife, sir. What shall I do? Please, I'm scared, there's a cursed killer stalking the Castle, and you must direct me what to do next, sir. You must help me, please sir."

"Makoto-san, hold your water and get better control of your mind along with your wits, before you end up hurting yourself. You must pay strict attention to my words, and follow them exactly as I order them of you. I'm on my way over to the Castle. I'm leaving immediately right after I'm off the phone with you. I want you not to touch a thing in his room, and the entire Castle for that matter and call the police immediately. Do you understand my orders to you, Makoto-san?" The wise lawyer informed the old man in a rather excited but commanding tone of voice.

"Yes sir, I'll do as you have suggested Nagaro-san. I thank you for your wise guidance, sir."

"Good Makoto-san, I'm on my way over to the Castle, call the police. You have to call them immediately. Remember not to touch anything inside his private room until the police arrive and they take control of the situation from you." The lawyer warned the old man as he prepared his mind for what he would see when he arrived at the castle.

"I assure you Nagaro-san, I'll call the police as soon as I'm off the line with you. I promise I'll not enter Asahiko-san's room ever again in my lifetime, sir."

Shigeru hung up and took a stiff drink of rye and belted it down then headed for his car.

As soon as he was off the phone with the lawyer, Makoto phoned the police as ordered by the lawyer. As he began explaining the reason for his call to the Desk Sergeant who answered his call, he was placed on hold while the Sergeant tried to locate Lieutenant Motoshima. He was forced to wait a few minutes before the excited Detective Lieutenant finally answered his call in an excited tone. "Yes, this is Lieutenant Kenzaburo Motoshima of the Tokyo Police Department, Detective Division, who is this please? Tell me what this call to me is all about."

The Lieutenant was not informed what the call was about by the Desk Sergeant who went looking for him. He was only told there was an important call he must attend too quickly.

"Lieutenant Motoshima-san, this is Makoto Ishikawa, I'm Asahiko Yurkowa-san's man servant at his Castle, sir."

"Yes, yes I remember you from a dinner party I once attended at the Castle a few months ago, what do you want of me, sir? I'm quite busy at this moment as you might guess, sir. We're searching for an assassin working in the area and the search is taking all my time, sir." The Lieutenant smiled as he remembered the old man being in his way at the dinner party.

"Lieutenant Motoshima-san! I must report to you that Asahiko-san is in his sleeping quarters, sir. He's been murdered and his body was terribly slaughtered beyond belief and understanding on this terrible night, sir! I'm afraid the lowly assassin that your Sergeant warned us about two days ago, has struck again and this time massacring poor old Asahiko-san in his stateroom. I don't know what to do and I am afraid to remain in the castle alone with his body."

"Dammit! Are you still at the fucking Castle, Ishikawa-san?" Lieutenant Motoshima angrily asked shocked over the news of Asahiko's death. Again, he found himself cursing this wanted assassin running loose in downtown Tokyo.

"Yes sir I'm staying at the Castle both day and night now to better take care of poor Asahiko-san's many needs and wants sir. I have been staying at the Castle ever since last year as I was ordered, Asahiko-san has demanded this of me so I can look after him and make certain he was enjoying good health sir."

"Good, stay where you are and don't leave the castle for any reason, and don't allow anyone to enter or leave the building until I arrive at the castle, sir. And above all, don't touch anything in the room of Asahiko-san's death, sir. I'm leaving for the castle immediately, Makoto-san."

"Lieutenant Motoshima-san I'll not enter Asahiko-san' stateroom until you arrive, I believe I shall never again enter his stateroom in my life sir. Lieutenant Motoshima-san, Lawyer Nagaro-san is coming to the castle. He's the one who ordered me to phone your office, sir." Makoto added when he remembered Asahiko's lawyer was on his way over to the castle.

"That's fine and he's the only one you're to allow to enter the castle until I arrive at the site. Understand?" the detective barked at the old man as he prepared to head for the ancient castle.

"Yes Lieutenant Motoshima-san, I understand this and I'll follow your orders, thank you sir."

"Fine Ishikawa-san, I'm on my way over as soon as I make contact with my Sergeant, and order him to go to the castle. Remember sir not to touch a damn thing in the room. Keep your eyes open for any sign of the damn assassin, in case he or she might still be lurking inside the walls of the castle. Don't try to stop him, just get a good description of the evil one and then stay well out of the assassin's way." The concerned Lieutenant warned the old man.

"I understand Lieutenant Motoshima-san, and I shall follow your instructions, sir."

Lieutenant Motoshima immediately called Sergeant Okamatsu on the radio the moment he was off the phone with the old man staying and reporting from the castle.

"Sergeant Okamatsu here." The Sergeant moaned into the radio when he felt it vibrating in his pocket, and he answered his small handheld radio.

"Sergeant, it was just reported to me that Asahiko-san has been murdered at his damn castle. Where the hell's Hiromoai at for crap sake?" The Lieutenant growled into the radio.

"He's sitting right in front of me at this moment, Lieutenant Motoshima-san."

"What the hell do you mean he's sitting right in front of you, Sergeant? You're not outside standing your post guarding his god damn home from this damn assassin?" The Lieutenant roared into the radio because he could not believe what his Sergeant was reporting to him

"No sir, I'm in Hiromoai-san's apartment, I'm sitting before him as we speak, sir." The Sergeant reported to his commanding officer.

"What the hell are you doing inside the god damn apartment with him, mister?" the Lieutenant growled as he snapped a pencil he was twirling in his hand in half.

"I'll explain this to you later when I meet you at the castle, Lieutenant Motoshima-san." The concerned Sergeant replied to his commanding officer over the radio.

"Yeah, right, good, okay, drop whatever the hell you're doing with him and get your ass over to the castle immediately, Sergeant. I don't know what the hell's going on yet, I just hope it wasn't the damn assassin's work again, if it was, maybe the miserable executioner's still in the area and we can finally get our hands on the lousy bastard's neck. Damn, this case is pure hell I tell you, Sergeant." The angry Lieutenant groaned as he broke off the communication with his Sergeant, still refusing to believe the killer was possibly a female murderer.

Sergeant Okamatsu rose and placed the radio in his pocket after he removed the ear piece as he bowed to Hiromoai. He used the ear piece so the business owner could not hear what his Lieutenant was ordering him. He was stunned by the news of Asahiko's death, and he wanted to get over to the castle as soon as possible, so he could see what truly happened there. The Sergeant tried his best to keep his facial expression passive as not to alarm Hiromoai that there was new trouble facing downtown Tokyo and his police department.

Hiromoai was easily able to see the sudden strained look clouding over the Sergeant's eyes and asked him in concern. "Is there a problem Sergeant? You seem suddenly upset sir."

"No, no, not at all Hiromoai-san, it was just my Lieutenant and he was informing me that my shift was completed for the day, and I'm allowed to go home and see my girlfriend for the rest of the night, sir. I'm terribly sorry for taking up so much of your valuable time tonight sir. I really enjoyed our talk though Hiromoai-san. I have learned quite a lot about the ways of the past of Japan from you tonight, sir. Your unlimited understanding of Japan's most honorable past is impressive, most impressive indeed Hiromoai-san. I hope in the future we can continue our enjoyable conversation about Japan's ancient history, sir." There was something the Sergeant liked about Hiromoai, and this made it impossible for him to believe that he might have had anything to do with the now, three deaths of the very powerful Yurkowa clan.

As the Sergeant rose from the chair and he bowed politely, the other three officers with him only nodded and then fell in step with the Sergeant without word, as they quickly filed out of the massive apartment. Once in the hallway, the Sergeant informed the other officers what took place at Engakuji Castle. He ordered the others to resume their surveillance of Hiromoai's apartment, and his protection while he went over to the castle to see what happened to Asahiko.

It took him twenty minutes of weaving in and out of the heavy flow of traffic to get over to the castle with his lights flashing and siren screaming in the night's warm breeze and darkness. By the time he finally arrived at the latest crime scene, the front of the castle was swarming with a gaggle of police cars and other officers stopping anyone from entering the now restricted area surrounding the massive castle. Countless news reporters were also showing up at the main doors of the castle. They picked up the countless police calls stating there was trouble at Asahiko's castle and they were asking annoying questions of the officers trying to set up a perimeter line, or the reporters were attacking anyone else standing by and watching what was going on at the ancient castle, trying to get some information over the situation.

The Sergeant saw the Lieutenant pulling up behind him, and he waited for him to catch up to him before they both entered the castle proper together.

Many reporters followed the police cars and were flooding the castle area, and already setting up their broadcast vehicles, tape machines, powerful lights and microphones. The reporters were making real pests of themselves to the police, as they shoved each other trying to find out what the police was doing at Asahiko's castle so late at night. The officers were doing everything in their power to keep the reporters at bay, but it was impossible work to accomplish. The reporters were ignoring orders being shouted at them from the police, in search of their next story.

CHAPTER TWENTY TWO

Lieutenant Motoshima picked up Sergeant Okamatsu entering the area and rushed over to him. He growled as he placed his hand on the Sergeant's back and then lead him towards the crime scene and bitched at him at the same time. "What the hell were you doing in Hiromoai's god damn apartment with that sonofabitch, Sergeant? Gees man."

"Lieutenant, while we were keeping his apartment under constant surveillance, I thought I picked up someone or thing, trying to climb the outside of the building. I feared it was the assassin trying to kill him. So I pulled all units in, and we charged his apartment. When I informed him of what I believed I saw outside his building, he offered to allow me to remain in his apartment to better protect his life for him. I felt it was the easiest way to keep an eye on him, Lieutenant. It's a good thing I did, because this proves beyond a shadow of a doubt he had nothing to do with Tsutomu-san's murder. And Asahiko-san's murder now, Lieutenant."

"Sergeant, I want you to take a minute before you answer this next question for me, to think this over very carefully. Hiromoai-san never once left your sight while you were with him?"

"No Lieutenant, never once was he out of my sight for even one second sir."

"Not even to go to the damn bathroom, or get something to eat, anything Sergeant?"

"No Sir Lieutenant. As I just stated, he never once left my sight for a second sir."

"What about what you thought you saw climbing the side of the damn building? I can't believe this daughter of Satan would possess the skills needed to climb up the side of Hiromoai's building. What the hell do you think it might have been you noticed, Sergeant? Do you think the assassin was hiding in his apartment, and he dispatched the evil thing to do his bidding?" The Lieutenant asked as he stopped walking, and stared in the eyes of his young Police Sergeant.

"Iye! No way in hell Lieutenant, I think what I saw, might have been just the shadows of other buildings playing some tricks on me, sir. Corporal Hattori was with me and he pointed this fact out to me when I asked him if he saw anything moving on the side of the building. He was at my side the whole time, and he said he saw nothing out of the ordinary sir."

"I can't believe that Sergeant, there's no way in hell anyone could possibly work their way up the side of the damn Tower and live to talk about it. There's no hand holds to grab on to to help assist the damn assassin, Sergeant." He replied as he resumed walking into the castle.

Lieutenant Motoshima walked right past Makoto as if he was not even standing near him as he headed right for the main staircase of the castle, and started up the marble stairs as if he owned the castle. The Lieutenant knew where Asahiko slept in the castle and he headed right for his private sleeping quarters. Sergeant Okamatsu was polite and he nodded to the older man as he acknowledged his presence, and then he followed the Lieutenant upstairs.

A horde of police were running up and down the stairs frantically. Lieutenant Motoshima was the first one to enter Asahiko's private quarters on the third floor. He drew in his breath as he viewed his slaughtered body, still locked in a kneeling position in death, and his blood was spattered all over the highly polished wood floor and his body, the head was missing from the prone body. The way his corpse was positioned at the time of his death, hid his head from the Lieutenant's view for the moment as he entered Asahiko's sleeping quarters.

There was a medical examiner already in the room checking the body of Asahiko out. He paid little attention to the other officers as they entered the room and closed in on him.

"Do you have any idea yet when the murder of Asahiko-san might have taken place, Doctor?" He asked as he looked over the doctor's shoulder and watched what he was doing to the old man's body. The Lieutenant looked at where the head was severed, and noticed it was a clean neat cut, obviously done with one swipe of the blade.

"The body's still warm Lieutenant, eight-six degrees at the throat area sir. But I'm not entirely convinced that this is a murder scene in the least, Lieutenant. I'd dare to offer that the death occurred at or about midnight, sir. It's still too early to tell with any certainty though sir. I can have a positive answer for you in a few hours, after I can make a more thorough investigation of the body once I get it down to the lab. Will this do for your concern Lieutenant? It's the best I can offer you at the moment." The doctor turned to look at the angry lieutenant to hear his reply.

The concerned Lieutenant leaned forward and looked in the unseeing eyes of Asahiko's head lying on the floor resting on the sheet of rice paper and grumbled at the doctor examining the body. "It looks like the damn assassin was at work again tonight. Dammit, look at how clean the head was severed from the body, Sergeant. That took someone who knew what the hell he or she was doing with a fucking sword. No jagged edges, it was one clean swipe of the damn sword. I'd give a month's pay to get my hands on this filthy executioner for just five minutes for crap sake." Lieutenant Motoshima grumbled and then he noticed Sergeant Okamatsu was bowing towards the terrible carnage and the body of Asahiko in the room.

"What the hell's wrong with you Sergeant? What the hell are you doing now mister?" The upset Lieutenant growled at his officer as he placed his hands on his hips and watched what he was doing and his anger was hiding the most obvious clues from his view.

"This isn't the work of any damn assassin, I can tell you Lieutenant. I believe the medical examiner's correct with his assumption. This is not a murder scene in the least, sir." The

Sergeant replied as he straightened from his bow and turned to Lieutenant Motoshima.

"Oh, and you know this for a certainty I take it Sergeant?" The Lieutenant snorted as he placed a smirk on his lips and then glared at the other officer while waiting his reply.

"Yes Lieutenant Motoshima and you would feel the same as well if you allow your eyes to read over the lifelong honored events that has taken place over this situation." Sergeant Okamatsu smiled at his commanding officer, as he looked over the Lieutenant's shoulder to Asahiko's slaughtered body, while continuing to honor his last act of life.

The Lieutenant turned to Asahiko's butchered body, and studied the scene of death more carefully. Seeing the terrible gaping gash across his belly and his innards lying on the rice paper at his knees, and the way the head was positioned before the old man's slaughtered body away from the gore of his guts and blood, made the lieutenant understand the scene more clearly. Strangely, there was little if any blood left on the head, even though it sat in the middle of the pool of Asahiko's blood. Almost as if someone took time to clean the blood from the head.

"Good Lord Sergeant, you're right. Asahiko-san committed hari kiri. What the hell would make such a well respected man do some stupid thing like this?" The commander grumbled at his Sergeant as he shook his head slowly and rubbed his chin with the back of his hand.

"I don't believe it was that difficult to understand his actions, Lieutenant Motoshima-san."

"How is that, my Sergeant who suddenly seems to know all the answers to this murder scene?"

"Someone had to have helped the old man commit Suppuku, Lieutenant. He couldn't possibly been able to cut his own head from his shoulders after opening his belly like he did here, sir." Sergeant Okamatsu offered the Lieutenant with his own smirk this time.

"All of a sudden you seem to know one hell of a lot about the old ways of ancient Japan, Sergeant. Is there anything else I must know about this damn case?" The Lieutenant again glared at the Sergeant as he moved closer to the slaughter to get a better angle of Asahiko's body.

The Sergeant laughed as he went over the death scene with the Lieutenant one step at a time, and then he offered. "Lieutenant Motoshima-san, someone had to have cut Asahiko-san's head from his shoulders at the proper time of his death, sir. You can see by the expression locked in Asahiko-san's eyes that he was just beginning to suffer the pain from the sacred act of killing himself. Whoever aided Asahiko-san in his death, the assistant knew when it was the appropriate time to intervene in the act, and strike with honor and respect with the sword. Also Lieutenant, if you were to look at the head, you'll realize this unknown assistant had placed his head carefully on the rice paper in the correct position to watch over his body protectively for all eternity, sir. The assistant whoever he or she was even took time to wipe blood from Asahiko-san's head and face. Someone knew what he was doing in this final act of Asahiko-san's life, Lieutenant." The Sergeant proudly announced for his commanding officer's information.

The concerned Lieutenant followed Sergeant Okamatsu's words and hand movements with his eyes and then asked.

"Who the hell do you think assisted Asahiko-san with his death, Sergeant?"

"I don't know the answer to that question as yet, Lieutenant Motoshima-san."

"Well Sergeant Wise Okamatsu, allow me to inform you of what I know a lot about. Whoever the hell assisted Asahiko-san in his death is as guilty of murder as if he slaughtered the old man himself. We don't condone assisting someone in suicide in Japan. Do you think Makoto might have something to do with this murder of his boss, Sergeant?" The lead detective asked of his Sergeant as he glanced at the old man waiting outside Asahiko's private room in the hallway.

"Like I said, I don't think this is a murder scene at all Lieutenant, least wise not yet sir. I seriously doubt if the old man would have the courage or the strength to carry out the finer details needed to assist someone to commit Suppuku. Especially not the way it has been carried out in this case, Lieutenant. It takes a person with great inner strength and know-how, to cut one's head from his body and at the right time in the middle of the act, particularly when there's so much blood and guts coming out of the honored one's body, Lieutenant. It had to been someone with a damn strong stomach, and little heart to assist Asahiko-san's death in this manner, and offer Asahiko-san with the proper respect and honor over what he was doing as his last act of life, sir." Sergeant Okamatsu allowed a small smile of victory to slowly cross his lips as he waited for Lieutenant Motoshima's next question of him.

"Yeah, I see what you're driving at here Sergeant. Nevertheless, I want Makoto detained for the time being. He had to have seen something of the damn murderer, or he might have even somehow assisted the old man in his honored death. Have one of the other officers bring him down to the station for further questioning and..."

"Why the devil are you arresting Makoto-san for, Lieutenant Motoshima-san?" The lawyer snapped nastily as he walked in the room and placed his hands on hips and stared at the officer.

Both officers turned at the same time and saw Nagaro walking into Asahiko's suite proudly.

"Because someone had to have helped Asahiko-san kill himself Mr. Lawyer, and until I know any better, I'm classifying this death as a murder case, sir. And that makes anyone in the castle at the time of Asahiko-san's death, a prime suspect in that death, sir. May I ask you what the hell you're doing here so late, Nagaro-san? Do all lawyers always work so damn late into the night, sir?" Lieutenant Motoshima hissed nastily, allowing his anger to rule over his better judgment. He did not try to hide from the lawyer the fact he was angry. He was fuming Asahiko was dead on his beat, and he still had no positive suspect in his, or his son's slaughter. He cautiously eyed the lawyer as he entered deeper into the large suite and began to view the death scene.

The lawyer was shocked at the way Asahiko killed himself and wondered who he allowed to assist him in his death. He too was angry because Asahiko obviously allowed someone the honor of sending him off to the next world, protected from the evil spirits by taking his head from his shoulders. Something he was quite prepared to do for his old friend as he moaned while looking at Asahiko's slaughtered body. "My

God." Was all he could think to utter as he stared in disbelief at Asahiko's body, and then at his head on the floor in the middle of the blood.

"You don't seem to be too upset by what you're viewing here, Lawyer Nagaro-san. It's almost as if you were kind of expecting to see what's lying before you sir. Were you expecting Asahiko-san to take his own life tonight, Mr. Lawyer?" Lieutenant Motoshima growled nastily at him.

"Lieutenant Motoshima-san, I don't believe I like the tone in the way you're choosing to address me. You better remember who the hell I am, and who I represent here, Officer. One complaint from me and you'll be back walking a damn beat at the Tsukiji fish yards, keeping an eye on the rotting fish and the flies from landing on the damn fish for the rest of your miserable life, Lieutenant." The suddenly fuming lawyer fired right back at the Lieutenant, as he placed his hands on his hips again, and then he glared angrily at the insulting officer.

The Lieutenant thought about the warning by the lawyer for a few seconds, and then he bowed his apology to him. The last thing he needed was this lawyer complaining to the commander about him and his actions during this murder investigation.

"That's much better Lieutenant, I repeat for your benefit just in case you didn't hear me the first time sir. I ask you again, why are you arresting Makoto-san for, sir? Hasn't he been put through enough on this horrible day, Officer?" Nagaro waited for a reply, impatiently tapping his foot on the floor while continuing to glare angrily at the Lieutenant.

The equally angry police lead detective stared at the lawyer for a long moment and then he snapped nastily at him. "I'm not arresting anyone over this damn situation yet sir. I'm only placing him in protective custody for the time being that's all Mr. Lawyer. I want to take him down to the station to ask him some further questions about the murder of Asahiko-san, Nagaro-san. Its procedures whenever I'm investigating a murder scene, sir. Nagaro-san, this you should know better than me or anyone else for that matter, being a lawyer yourself that is sir. He was the only one in the Castle at the time of Asahiko-san's death, sir. Thus, it makes him a prime suspect, or possible witness to the murder act or the assassin, Nagaro-san."

"Nevertheless Lieutenant Motoshima, if you're taking Makoto-san down to the station, I'm going to accompany him to better protect his legal rights for him, sir. I have no intention of allowing your Officers to browbeat him into making any false confession or statements. I know how you people work when you want something from someone, especially a confession from an innocent man, an old man at that might I add sir. I'll protect his legal rights all the time you're detaining him, Lieutenant Motoshima-san."

The Lieutenant smirked back at the lawyer as he hissed at him in no uncertain terms. "Now you look here Mister smart ass fucking lawyer. My god damn Police Officers don't go around browbeating anyone into making any god damn false confessions or statements, Nagaro-san. I deeply resent that last comment by you sir, and I expect an apology from you this instant sir. If we have the guilty party then he'll confess without any hard tactics being employed against him by any of my Officers, sir. We don't water board anyone despite what you might think of us Police Officers, sir. Err... excuse me Nagaro-san, but you still didn't answer my question of a few moments ago, sir. What the hell are you doing at the castle so late at night, Mr. Lawyer? Is this normal in your course of actions and work for Asahiko-san, sir?"

"If you feel that you must know my business affairs with my client Lieutenant Motoshima-san, I'll inform you of the reason for this late night visit to Asahiko-san's castle, sir. I was working on closing the sale of Asahiko-san's construction company to the American buyer, and I had a few troublesome questions for him that needed to be answered tonight, before I could finish the contract for the sale to go through at its earliest convenience, sir. In fact Lieutenant Motoshima-san, the American, a Mr. Calvin Batterman is due to arrive in Japan sometime tomorrow morning, so he can take command of his new company. I personally handed Mr. Batterman's check to Asahiko-san earlier today, sir. I placed a call to the castle and Makoto-san told me Asahiko-san was acting rather strangely all night, sir. I pressured him into disturbing Asahiko-san's sleep, so that I might speak with him before the American's arrival.

"That's when Makoto-san made the grizzly discovered of the body of Asahiko-san, and he informed me over the phone of his horrible death, Lieutenant. I was the one who ordered him not to touch anything in the room, and informed him that I was coming over to the castle to see what he was telling me was the truth, I also told him to phone the police immediately, sir. Does this answer your question to your complete satisfaction, Lieutenant Motoshima-san?"

"For the time being it certainly does, thank you Nagaro-san."

The Lieutenant's last angry remark brought him another harsh glare from the distinguished and powerful Japanese lawyer. He was about to get in it with the Lieutenant, when a second officer called out to him.

"Lieutenant Motoshima-san, come here please sir. I think I might have discovered something by the wall you should know about, sir. It seems to be another one of those split towed small footprints we discovered at the other crime scenes, Lieutenant."

The Lieutenant turned on his heels and rushed over to the two concerned police officers to view their new discovery as the other officers looked at the floor. Sergeant Okamatsu and the lawyer Nagaro followed him to see what was causing the other officers concern.

"What did you find there Officer?" The Lieutenant asked as he looked at the floor.

"Lieutenant Motoshima-san, I believe we found a slight trace of a muddy footprint on the floor here, sir. I believe it might be of the same type of split toe type footprint we found at the Tsutomu Yurkowa-san's death site by the stone wall, where the assassin went over the wall to escape the compound where we found the pair of altered leather boots, sir. Please, be careful and don't step on the print and destroy it on us, sir." The officer reported as he knelt on the floor, and protected the footprint with the bulk of his body.

"Sonofabitch, it was the assassin's evil work after all tonight! Dammit to hell and back, now we have the evidence linking the two murder sites together, Sergeant. I knew all along that this mess was the work of that damn murderer. I just knew it in my heart Sergeant." Lieutenant Motoshima growled as he stared at the faint muddy footprint on the highly polished teak floor. He could see the executioner obviously walked on tiptoes as she entered the massive room. Most of the muddy print was of just the upper part of her foot and toes.

"Where the hell did this damn assassin come from dammit? The footprint is clearly heading right for Asahiko-san's body from this direction, sir. It almost seems like the assassin came right through the damn wall someplace. It seems this assassin not only knows her work, but she also knows things that no one should know about, dammit." The Lieutenant growled angrily until he was interrupted by the other officer standing near him.

"This is nonsense if you were to ask me Lieutenant Motoshima-san. Why the hell would someone who slaughtered poor Tsutomu-san so savagely a few days ago, possibly offer Asahiko-san the respect demanded by seconding his honorable death, sir? If it was the assassin who create this act then why the hell did she or he not slaughter him in the same terrible manner she did poor Yurkowa-san?" The lawyer mumbled as he stared at the muddy footprint.

"Beats the hell out of my ass Nagaro-san, I don't know the answer to that question, Mr. Lawyer. This footprint was the only evidence left at the crime scene of Tsutomu-san's horrible death. It looks like it's the same size and shape as that slight footprint we found back there, sir. Officer Furuta, you're correct, it seem like the murderer came from behind the wall somewhere near here, dammit. Get the crime scene people up here on the double and get a copy of the damn footprint and then check out the walls, there has to be a hidden passageway some place near here. I heard numerous stories about many possible hidden secret passageways honeycombing the damn castle in the past. I guess they're true from what we just found here, find it Officer.

"Nagaro-san, to answer your last question of me sir, I don't know why any god cursed assassin would offer the respect and honor it did to Asahiko-san. I don't know why any damn assassin does whatever the hell it does for a living for God's sake. But this meant Asahiko-san must have had to spoke to this murderer face to face to get the murderer to assist him in his death. What the hell next is going to take place with this damn murder case? This case is getting weirder by the minute sir. Check out the rest of the wall Officer, and let me know what you find."

Officer Furuta and his partner started lightly tapping on the exquisite wood panels of the wall as the lab technicians started making a copy of the footprint they discovered on the floor, while the other officers continued searching for an opening in the wall. Lieutenant Motoshima went back over to the body of Asahiko because he wanted to see if there were any signs of a struggle he could discover, or if Asahiko's death was rushed in any manner. Now, he felt Asahiko was in the process of committing suicide when the assassin entered the room on him. Maybe, he killed himself to avoid being slaughtered like his honorable son was by this hired killer. Or he decided to kill himself upon laying eyes on this cold blooded murderer who suddenly appeared before him from behind the wall of his room, and the assassin scared him into the final act. Either way, he felt certain the assassin was the cause of Asahiko's death one way or the other.

The confused and upset Lieutenant checked the body more carefully this time, and he could not discover any signs of a possible struggle or fight, or any marring marks of rushing the honored act to its final completion. On the contrary, everything he noticed of the latest crime seemed peaceful, almost serene like. Like the death of Asahiko took place with the needed time and preparation, before the sacred act was perpetrated by his own hand. Could it be that the assassin actually helped the old man kill himself so honorably out of respect for him and the act itself. Now, he was at a total loss as to where to go next with his most confusing case.

"Lieutenant Motoshima-san, I think I found something over here sir. I believe it seems hollow behind this section of the wall panel, sir." The concerned officer offered as he continued to tap lightly on the wooden wall section.

Lieutenant Motoshima, Nagaro and Sergeant Okamatsu rushed over to the other officers staring at the wood panel. The young Officer Furuta cautiously pointed to a certain panel in the wall and Lieutenant Motoshima and his Sergeant took over the search, and they started to lightly tap the same panel. Suddenly, the wall moved ever so slightly under their constant probing and pushing. The Lieutenant immediately stopped tapping and he pushed with all his might on this section of the wall, and the large panel slowly slid out of his way.

"I got you you miserable little sonofabitch you. Tonight's the last time you'll ever do your loathsome work of murder in Japan I assure you, lowly assassin. Get me a god damn flashlight! We got the bitch of darkness trapped, all we have to do is catch up with her, and find out where the hell she's hiding at, and we got finally her ass." The excited police detective roared as he waited for someone to hand him the requested flashlight.

The moment he had the flashlight in hand, the lead detective entered the narrow dank opening and cautiously inched his way deeper in the passageway, he was followed closely by Sergeant Okamatsu, and the lawyer Nagaro, and the other four police officers, including Furuta. Two officers had hand guns and knew how to use them. Mindfully, the small group of police officers followed the disturbed ground in the tunnel. In no time, the group came up against the heavy Shibi stone, and Sergeant Okamatsu had to help Lieutenant Motoshima try and shove the heavy stone out of their way from inside the tunnel. When the officers came out on the outside of the walls of the castle after the moat, the Lieutenant mumbled aloud to the others with him.

"Well, at least we know how this believed to be female assassin got in the castle unobserved tonight. How the hell would she have known this ancient passageway existed? I wish I had a damn crystal ball to help me with this murder case. It seems that's the only way we're going to get any kind of breaks in this damn case. Okay people, I want everyone to fan out and check the ground surrounding the tunnel. I want to know which direction this assassin escaped. Nagaro-san, you stay close by my side, I can ill afford to have anything happen to you during this investigation, sir." The Lieutenant growled as he waited for the lawyer to move to his side.

Everyone involved in the ongoing murder cases, was taking it for granted because of all the evidence they had discovered so far, that the dangerous assassin stalking downtown Tokyo, was that of a hired female killer.

Sergeant Okamatsu was the first one to find the second series of small split toed footprints outside the castle wall, and he immediately gave out the alarm to the other officers with him. "Lieutenant Motoshima-san, I found more of those small footprints over here sir. They seem to be heading off in that direction, sir." He pointed towards the very heart of downtown Tokyo.

"Okay everyone, close ranks on me and we'll follow these damn footprints right back to this lousy assassin's fucking lair. If Karma is truly with us on this night, we'll place a quick end to this killer's evil act of late, and we'll also find out just who the hell is the one responsible for this murderer's actions plaguing our city, gentlemen." Lieutenant Motoshima allowed the officers armed with hand guns to lead the way for the rest of them. He did not want the unarmed officers coming across this assassin first, just in case she was somewhere ahead of them waiting to attack them because they were trailing her. Not as deadly as this one was to their presence.

The officers continued following the footprints in the soft ground, only losing them momentarily here and there when the assassin crossed a hard surface of the road, or cement sidewalks leading around the massive castle. The small gaggle of police officers moved forward in a loose and attentive group. They followed the footprints for about a quarter of a mile until they finally disappeared right at the base of a two story masonry building.

"Now don't try and tell me that the damn assassin has disappeared right in the wall of this building?" Lieutenant Motoshima mumbled angrily as he stared at the last footprint marked that was found almost right up against the side of the building.

"I don't think that's a fact at all, Lieutenant Motoshima-san. If you look here sir, you'll see what I mean, sir. I believe I can still see her trail and it's going right up the side of this wall, sir." Sergeant Okamatsu offered as he pointed to a slight mud spot left on the side of the building just about eye level. There were also a number of fresh, deep marring scratches cut in the cement wall. He and Lieutenant Motoshima immediately looked up towards the roof of the building. Their hearts started pounding for want to capture the assassin as the commanding officer suddenly growled at the rest of the group following him.

"It seems the damn assassin has some kind of climbing device with her to enable her to climb up the side of a wall. Okay everyone, the killer got up to the roof, in the building and get to the roof on the double quick. This murderer's heading for some place in downtown Tokyo, and we're going to stop her this time around, before she reaches the safety of her damn hideout and eludes us again. If we're lucky enough tonight, we can follow her trail up there and cut her off before she's able to escape in the clutter of downtown Tokyo. If we get close enough to her, maybe we can figure out where the hell the killer's heading." He ordered the officers as he took the lead of them. The group rushed inside the building and charged up the stairs, scaring people who owned the building as they rushed passed them without explanation.

The officers crashed through the dilapidated thin wood door leading to the roof. Again, the officers with guns took the lead for the rest, in case the assassin was trapped on the roof and was waiting in ambush for them so she could attack them. The Lieutenant was hanging back, trying to protect Nagaro as he stood in his way, and allowed the armed officers to assume the lead again.

Once the officers gathered on the roof, the smudges from the drying footprints disappeared half way across the tar covered roof. The mud and dampness wearing off the assassin's feet, and leaving no further traces of the direction the assassin headed, it was impossible to detect further footprints on the asphalt tiles. There was nothing else disturbed on the roof, making it impossible to figure out which direction the assassin went off in.

"Dammit to hell and back Sergeant Okamatsu-san! This damn assassin has given us the slip once again I see." The Lieutenant grumbled angrily as he studied the clutter covered roof in search of any other possible traces of the assassin or the direction she headed off in, or anything that was disturbed by her passing. Nothing out of the ordinary was detected by him or the other officers with him. He placed his hand over his eyes to shield them from the harsh glare of the countless night lights from downtown Tokyo, but he was still unable to detect any further movement from the assassin as he stared out in the darkness of the night.

The fuming lead detective stared at the many roofs in the area in hopes of catching a possibly glimpse of movement created by this assassin's fleeing the scene of death and savagery. Not seeing any movement from the assassin, he then looked at his watch and discovered it was twenty after two in the morning. If the murder of Asahiko took place like the medical examiner checking Asahiko's body had suggested, around midnight then the killer had plenty of time to make good her escape from the area. By now, the assassin would be hiding back in its lair, waiting patiently until the next time to strike at some unsuspecting person of worth of Japan. The Lieutenant could not help but feel that the assassin was settle down some place and was more than likely laughing at them as they continued to search for any clues to her identity, and this was driving his anger forward. To feel a dangerous criminal such as this one was, was laughing at him and his efforts to capture her, made this a personal murder case for him.

The lead detective was about to call off any further search for the assassin, when he suddenly noticed Sergeant Okamatsu looking at something with concern in his face. Almost as if he was trying to align something up from where he stood, using himself as the center of this alignment. The Sergeant seemed slightly troubled at what he was working on, causing the Lieutenant to bark at him. "What the hell do you have going there Sergeant?"

"I don't know for certain Lieutenant Motoshima-san, it might be something, and then it might not be anything. If you were to look at the castle then line the tower from the castle up to where we are then look to downtown Tokyo, sir. What's the first building you see?" the Sergeant turned back to the castle and then he looked at downtown Tokyo, and studied that area again.

He did as suggested by the Sergeant, and when he turned to the center of the capital, the first building he saw in the distance, was Hatanaka Towers looming above the surrounding buildings.

"Sonofabitch!" Was all he could think to grumble.

CHAPTER TWENTY THREE
HATANAKA TOWERS, 1:45 A.M., SUNDAY
JUNE 9th, 1996

The highly agitated Hiromoai Hatanaka paced the apartment almost in a wild rage while waiting for Wind to return from her mission to kill Asahiko. He snapped at Lady Yoke on numerous occasions and then at Utsumi who came out of his room when he heard him raising all sorts of hell with Lady Yoke. Hiromoai even thought about going over to the window to see if he could see her returning. But then he remembered about the police officers keeping an eye on his apartment from outside and thought better of this move. He did not want to draw any further attention to his apartment while Wind was still outside roaming around the streets below.

He snapped the TV on, and then quickly drained his sake as if he was angry at the harsh liquid and then demanded more. Before she could refill his cup, there was a soft sound on the patio outside. Everyone in the apartment held their breath as they turned and looked to the sliding doors. Lady Yoke ran around and quickly turned off the few lights and TV in the apartment. The door slid open just enough for her to squeeze her exquisite body through the opening when the apartment was bathed in complete darkness. It was a good thing he did not turn on lights in the study, or it would have illuminated her as she entered the apartment.

Wind was totally out of breath and covered with dirt, sweat, and blood from head to toe that sprayed on her when she lopped Asahiko's head from his shoulders, and she was spent out from her labors. She moved deeper into the dim room as she started to remove her altered yoroi hitatare heavy armored robe, but not before she looped her long bow off her shoulder. She then dropped down to her knees before Hiromoai, and she unsheathed her killing sword and allowed him to view the blood ominously staining its fine steel shaft, as she let out with a deep sigh, and then she bowed until her nose barely touched the hardwood floor before him.

Hiromoai nodded, pleased at the evidence she returned with as he mumbled to her. "Wind-san, it seems you have accomplished your mission and served me well on this night, and for this I'm grateful to you, Samurai. Give your sword to Lady Yoke and she'll clean it of any blood and dirt for you. Did you have any trouble on your mission, Wind-san?" He relaxed as he stared at Wind.

"Hai, once on my long travels on this night my Lord and Master I was forced to dispatch two soldiers who call themselves Police Officers. I'm terribly sorry that it took me so long to return to your side. I believe I was being trailed by more of these Officer soldiers that seem to be everywhere I travel, and I had to take some extra precautions not to be discovered by them, or lead the pursuers back to my Master's Castle. I do not believe the followers were able locate my movement, my Liege Lord." She let out with an exhausted breath again.

Hiromoai turned to Utsumi and ordered him to get her some Sake. He was not the least bit concerned over the officers' violent deaths as he led her deeper into the apartment. Utsumi hid his glare, angry he was now reduced to waiting on this ancient female warrior hand and foot, something beneath most male Japanese persons.

Hiromoai put off any further questions until Wind had a chance to rest a little, and enjoyed some Sake. When she seemed ready to speak, he asked with much concern lacing his voice. "Wind-san, was there any trouble with Asahiko's death?" He looked deep in the face of Wind, her beauty indescribable in his mind, yet disturbing to him at the same time. Her skin was flawless a golden skin free of any wrinkles or sags. Her teeth were as white as snow, and her round face was absolutely perfect. Her nose was beautiful, small, her mouth surrounded with blood red lipstick, perfect, small and tight. He remembered when his serpent shaft parted those wonderful lips, sending a shiver of delight down his spine over the fond memory. Her neck was slender and her ears covered by the black, shinning silk like hair that worked free of the restrictive braid the Lady Yoke wrapped her hair in, before the start of her mission.

But the most striking feature about her exquisite face and body was her captivating eyes. Her eyes were narrow, long, and circled with a delicate black Lady Yoke applied, and dangerously piercing. He allowed her to place the desires of the female world on her beautiful face, because it pleased him to see this extremely threatening warrior as a female weapon.

She stared at him with a set of eyes he was certain could see in the both worlds she shared at the same time. He wondered what secrets those marvelous eyes and memories could betray, the time guarded secrets of the Ukiyo, the Floating World of dreams and wonderment. Try as he might, he was unable to look away from those piercing and phenomenal eyes of this ancient and beautiful female warrior. Eyes that made her the most stunning woman he had vision of. Only her words broke the bewitching spell he was falling victim to. He could understand how easily she was so successful in attacking his enemy. If she looked at him with those eyes, he would have been unable to protect himself until it was too late for him to react against her charms.

"I'm proud to report the foul one died as your desire, painfully and alone Hiromoai-sama."

Lady Yoke returned with the cleaned killing sword to the study and laid it down before Wind's knees on the floor not certain who was going to pick it up. Hiromoai allowed the sword to remain resting on the floor as he pressed his words further with the ancient warrior.

"What the hell do you mean by he died as I desired, Samurai? That doesn't seem like the way I wanted him to die. You did attack the old man in the same manner you did his worthless son, correct Samurai?" Hiromoai glared at her as he demanded a quick answer to his question.

"He is dead Hiromoai-sama and that should answer your question to its fullness as you demanded of me, my Lord." Wind dared to display impatience to her master as she kept her eyes glued to the teak floor, and hoped that he would not press his question any further with her.

"That's not fucking good enough of an answer from you. I warn you Samurai, take care in your tone whenever addressing me. If not, it could end up being a most unpleasant experience for you to endure for your insolence. How did the dog eating Asahiko meet his fate?"

"Hiromoai-sama, forgive this foolish Warrior for her insolence displayed against her Lord. I'm more exhausted than I realized, and have not responded with the respect due my Mast..."

"Never mind the damn niceties, I piss on niceties. I demand you tell me how the old fool died. Omit nothing from your explanation I demand to know everything, right up to his last seconds of breathing of this world Asahiko enjoyed." He suddenly bellowed at his female weapon.

"Hai! Hiromoai-sama, it shall be as you have demanded of me, this is your right as my Lord and Master. When I first entered Asahiko's room, he was locked in the process of committing the aged old honor of Suppuku. I did not know what to do, so I allowed him to continue with his honorable act unabated. I was bound by the ancient Code of the Samurai, to not dare interfere with the sacred act, or I would displease the Kami god the old man was honoring with his death. I felt how did it matter the old man died, as long as your wish was fulfilled as demanded. I'm sorry my Master, but I seconded his honorable death, but not before allowing him to suffer for as long as good manners had allowed." She lied, but she knew somehow he was going to find out how the old man died. She felt it was wiser to be almost honest with her master.

"What the hell do you mean by that load of crap you seconded his fucking death, Samurai? Who the fuck told you to honor this old man in that fashion? I wanted the old fool dead for daring to challenge me throughout his worthless life, and dead in the most hideous of ways possible by your sword. What lesson did it serve anyone from his death, if he was honored by you in that death? What effect will his death have on my other enemies lurking throughout Japan? You were supposed to dispatch him in a way serving as a warning to anyone else that might go against my desires. I wanted him savaged like his worthless son and his bitch of a wife was! Why do you think I sent you out against him, to honor him or to send a warning to all others? I'm disappointed by your actions. I thought you knew what I wanted. I guess not. How could you honor the lowly dog, Samurai?" He turned from her and began pacing the room.

Wind understood the rage in his voice and lowered her head closer to the floor and then stretched her neck out further, giving him clear access to it if he wanted to take his revenge against her. One she was certain was going to cause the wrath of Hiromoai to fall on her soul. She stared at her katana blade as he picked up the cleaned sword and then hefted the weight in his hands until it rested perfectly balanced in them. She feared that he was so angry at her he was going to lop her head off her shoulders for her failure to his orders. She waited for what she felt was an eternity, but the bite of the sword never fell on her neck. Stunned, she listened to his next words in wonderment, as he began speaking to her again.

"You know something perhaps you're right at that course of action you adopted with Asahiko's death Wind-san. What the hell does it matter how the dog eating old fool died, as long as he's dead and is no longer a threat to my future plans?" He was hesitant to demonstrate harsh actions aimed against the dangerous warrior, for fear he might lose her loyalty.

"Hai my Liege Lord that is the way I saw it as well." She let out her breath in a rush. Painful memories of the past invaded her mind, reliving the time she waited for Lord Kawasomeru's rage to fall down upon her shoulders for the sinful deception she carried out against him, when he first found out she was a woman. Hearing his words relieved her as much as when lord Kawasomeru refused to follow the suggestions of his General, and the samurai who demanded her head for the mendacity. Now, more than ever did she believe Hiromoai was the reborn Lord Kawasomeru in her mind, why else would he show the same kind honorable judgment of sparing her life, even though he was unable to truly take the life of her ancient spirit.

"Wind-san, I'm interested in the manner of how he died. I never believed for an instant the old fool possessed the strength and respect needed to commit such a sacred act. Please, take time to tell me how the old fool died." He asked in a much calmer tone this time.

LIEUTENANT MOTOSHIMA'S SQUAD CAR

Lieutenant Motoshima rushed to Engakuji Castle when they lost all traces of the assassin's trail on the roof. He ordered Sergeant Toshihiro Okamatsu, Corporal Tomiichi Furuta, and another officer to get in his squad car as they headed for downtown Tokyo at breakneck speed. The Lieutenant believed he knew where the assassin was heading, and he intended to capture the murderer, and discover the face behind this executioner's murderous rampage throughout Tokyo.

Sergeant Okamatsu knew right off what Hiromoai was thinking and did not agree with him. They sped through the traffic in silence until he could not take it any longer and offered. "Lieutenant Motoshima-san, I believe you're still dead wrong with your thoughts, sir."

"Oh and how is that, Sergeant?" He growled at the officer, not taking his eye off the traffic.

"You seem to be of the same thought that this lowly assassin's heading for Hiromoai-san's apartment. I believe you still feel Hiromoai-san's somehow behind her evil actions, sir. But suppose you're wrong with these thoughts, sir? I can't see how in the hell he could possibly be in league with a murderer, a hired assassin at that, sir. What the hell purpose would this alliance serve him? Why the devil would he be forced to turn to use assassins, when he can buy and sell anyone or business in Japan any time he desired? It doesn't make any sense, Lieutenant.

"You know I rarely go against anything you believe, but I think you're still wrong looking at Hiromoai-san as the instrument behind this killer's blood lust. Suppose this damn assassin's on her way over to his apartment to murder him? Not to return to him after carrying out his thought to be bidding, Lieutenant. If you're wrong in your judgment sir, it could well prove to be most embarrassing to the department, and the Chief will take it out on all of us, if we allow anything to happen to Hiromoai-san. I can hear him now when he finds out about Asahiko-san's suicide. If he falls victim to this lowly assassin's blade, and we failed to stop her he's going to be uncontrollable, and that rage will fall down on our shoulders."

"Sergeant, I appreciate where you're coming from. But you've been on enough murder cases to understand where the finger of truth usually points to, is the guilty one. So far, we haven't been able to capture this assassin, but every time we get a lead on him or her. It always seems to bring us right back to the front doorstep of Hiromoai-san. What more proof do you need dammit? Do you need to find Hiromoai-san actually in bed with this damn murderess? No, too many arrows point right back at him. He has to be the one behind this assassin's murder rampage."

Again, Lieutenant Motoshima did not look at Sergeant Okamatsu as he spoke. But his mind screamed back at him maybe the Sergeant could be correct. Maybe this hired killer was going to visit death on Hiromoai, rather than return to him after carrying out his evil bidding and wants. Subconsciously, he increased his speed in case the concerned Sergeant was correct and his life was truly in danger by this killer. He smiled to himself, knowing if the Sergeant was right, he would never admit he was to the Sergeant under any circumstances.

The lead detective recklessly wove his car in and out of the light flow of traffic he did not have the siren or lights on, because he did not want to alarm Hiromoai, or the killer. He reached for the radio and snapped it on and made contact with the officers still on guard at Hatanaka Towers. "Officer Noguchi, Lieutenant Motoshima here. Come in."

"Yes Sir Lieutenant Motoshima-san, this is Officer Noguchi, sir. Go ahead please sir."

"Noguchi-san, this is important so listen closely to my orders, has Hiromoai been in his damn apartment all night?" he asked his fellow officer, hoping the powerful Japanese businessman made a blunder he could capitalize on.

"Yes sir, as far as I'm concerned, he never once left the apartment tonight, Lieutenant."

"Noguchi, have you and the other Officers been keeping your eyes open all night?"

"Of course we were Lieutenant Motoshima-san. We kept our eyes on the building and all exits to the building all night long, sir." Noguchi snapped insulted by the innuendo he and the other officers might not have been carrying out their duty like the professionals they were.

"Noguchi-san, calm down a little and listen up, have you seen anyone lurking around in the shadows of the damn building tonight?" he ignored the angry tone of the officer.

"No sir, though at one time Officer Miyamoto thought he saw an out of place shadow on the side of the building. But after calling our attention to the suspected area, we saw nothing but the shadows of couple of clouds passing overhead, and the shadows of other buildings crossing over the area in question, sir. Nothing was out of the ordinary all night, Lieutenant."

"Good, we're coming to the Tower, I want you to go into the building and be ready to act, in case this assassin's coming after Hiromoai now." He ordered the other officer over the radio.

"Yes sir, we'll be ready for anything that might turn up, Lieutenant Motoshima-san."

"You armed Officer?"

"Armed sir? Heaven forbid, no sir, no one here is of the rank or qualified to carry a weapon on their person, sir. Why Lieutenant Motoshima-san? Are you expecting that type of trouble from this lowly murderer tonight?" The young officer replied, stunned at the thought of being forced to carry a weapon, and taking someone's life with a weapon hated by all officers of Japan. In all his years on the force, he had only one incident where he was forced to carry a weapon, and since that day he thanked the gods who controlled what had to be, because he didn't use the weapon.

"Dammit, do you have any weapons in the trunk of the damn squad car, Officer?"

"Yes I do, Lieutenant Motoshima-san, but I really hate the damn things sir! I don't like them one bit sir. I wish to hell all the damn weapons of the world were..."

"Noguchi-san, I'm not the least bit interested in how you feel about the damn things. I'm giving you permission to arm yourself and the other Officers with you. No, correct that, I'm ordering you to arm yourself and the other Officers. This evil assassin has killed enough people in her life span, we have to stop her here and now, and we're going to do it tonight if I have any say in the matter! I don't want you going up against this blood thirsty assassin without weapons to protect each Officer with you. If you corner the damn killer in the building, don't take any chances with her. We already have two officers down tonight, both dead, slaughtered by this miserable assassin, and I don't intend to have any other officers added to this evil one's tally.

"If you confront the murderer, use the damn weapons without hesitation if she displays any hostile intentions against your person. Don't get involved in any hand to hand combat with this devil. She's far too dangerous with her trade and skills to try and take her in alive if cornered. Be prepared to react with lethal force against the assassin if you come across her and she doesn't give up to you. I'm giving you this order, so if anything happens tonight the end result will fall down on my shoulders alone. Is this understood by you Officer Noguchi-san?"

"I read you loud and clear sir, I just gave the order for the others to arm themselves while we were speaking, Lieutenant. Even though I still disagree with that order, we'll be ready if and when the killer turns up to carry out her repulsive work of the darkness."

"I'm warning you in no uncertain terms Officer Noguchi-san, don't take this killer lightly or underestimate her or you'll pay dearly for that mistake with your life, Noguchi-san. I don't want any of you people hurt on her account. I'm telling you Noguchi-san, you have never come up against any such an entity as this one before in your life, sir. She'll kill without thought or mercy anyone who gets in her way. Be prepared for anything tonight, Officer."

"We're on our way in the building, Lieutenant." Noguchi gave out a number of hand signals to the other officers with him as he continued speaking with his commanding officer.

"I'm warning you Mister, be extremely careful in this present situation and this assassin, Officer Noguchi-san. We should be arriving at the Tower within five to seven minutes at the latest. Hold back with checking out Hiromoai-san apartment if you can, until we arrive on the site unless you detect Hiromoai-san's life is in danger, Officer. Then you're allowed to act on your own accord against the possible threat against Hiromoai, Noguchi-san. Out."

"Out!" Noguchi growled back in his radio. All of a sudden, he was fearful of what he might be walking into. Who was this killer who caused such fear in Motoshima's heart?

HIROMOAI'S APARTMENT

Hiromoai, Lady Yoke and Utsumi listened to Wind's words as she described how it was Asahiko killed himself, and how she had assisted him in the final part of his death.

He hated to admit it, but he found himself respecting the old man more with every word she whispered about the honorable way he killed himself. He found himself wondering if he would be in possession of the strength needed to take his life in this same fashion if the need arose. He wondered what it was like to take your life with the call of the blade.

When she finished her story of Asahiko-san death, he rose and stretched, raising his hands over his head and grumbled at the ancient female samurai. "Wind-san you have shown wise wisdom to allow Asahiko to take his own life, perhaps it'll take some heat off your shoulders and mine as well, Samurai. I don't see how the police can possibly suspect you were part of this old fool's death now. Suppuku is recognized and accepted even today as an honorable way to seek one's death. Yes, you were most wise indeed to allow the fool to kill himself. Tomorrow, I'll speak to Asahiko's lawyer under the guise of offering him my condolences for Asahiko's noble death. In this conversation I'll slip and offer to buy Asahiko's company. Knowing the old fool as I did, he must have given this lawyer power of attorney over his foul company. Lady Yoke!"

He turned to his servant and growled at her this time. "Lady Yoke, take Wind to the bathroom and bathe her properly. Allow her to enjoy the soothing waters of the hot tub for as long as it takes to relax her. Then, you'll dress her in your finest kimono and present her to me when she's well rested and relaxed. I believe I'll enjoy her treasures once again on this exciting night. A sort of celebration of my becoming one of the most powerful construction companies in all Japan. Lady Yoke, I'll be a man to be feared by all who have to deal with me in this country."

He suddenly clapped his hands together loudly to get the two women moving on his orders. A cloud of sadness immediately washed over Lady Yoke's face, as she bowed in an effort to hide the sadness in her eyes. She was hoping he might partake in her treasures tonight.

As she rose to follow Lady Yoke to the oversized bathroom to enjoy her soak, her ears heard the subtle movement from outside the door and she froze in place. Her actions instantly caught the attention of Hiromoai and his eyes went to where she stared as she took a threatening stance against the door and prepared her body for battle. She still retained the short wakizashi stabbing sword on her body. It was out in a flash and held expertly in a defensive position, as she moved in front of Hiromoai in order to protect his life from the unknown invaders.

"What do you hear Wind-san? Is someone standing outside my front door, Samurai?" he moaned as he tried to see around his female protector.

"A person is lurking outside the closed wood shoji door, Hiromoai-sama." She pointed to the front door of the apartment with her chin, as she waited for the intruders to act against her master's life, so she could defend him against the intruders.

"Who do you think is it Samurai?" he asked as he rushed to her side.

"My Lord, I believe it is one of the men who call themselves police soldiers in your time of life. I feel the lowly intruder is one of those people." She snapped low, never once taking her eyes off the front door of the apartment for a moment.

Hiromoai's eyes went back to the door, without thinking he picked up her killing sword and went for the scabbard as he said to the warrior. "Wind, I don't want to take any chances of the police discovering you in my apartment. I think it might be a good idea for you to rest in the Ukiyo, until I can rid myself of these nosy Police Officers. I bet it's that damn Lieutenant Motoshima again. He's like the biting cold of winter, never letting up for a moment."

She nodded her agreement to be sent to the Ukiyo for her escape. She knew Fujin, the Kami of Wind would be pleased with her actions, of allowing Asahiko to commit Suppuku, and of her seconding his sacrifice to the honored Kami. This fact would entitle her to relax peacefully in the Floating World as long as it took for her strength to return in the land of wonder and myth.

"I'll send for you the moment when time is right and safe for you to return to the world of the living, Wind-san." He offered with concern as he slid the sword in its resting place of centuries.

Wind was relieved, she was not looking forward to sharing his attentions, knowing that the pleasures she would be enjoying would insult and rip the heart out of her trusted friend. Before her spirit disappeared in the harsh light suddenly filling the apartment, she turned to Lady Yoke and smiled pleasantly at her as her spirit quickly faded from the land of the living. All that was left of her swift departure were the weapons she carried on her body, and the armor she was dressed in when she left to destroy Asahiko. Instantly, the weapons and armor stored in the study were again returned to their deteriorating state. Again, the stale odor of decay and ancient dust filled his apartment, threatening to take their breath from them.

The Lady Yoke knew why Wind smiled so politely at her before she disappeared, and she nodded her response, silently thanking the ancient female's kindness. She was pleased beyond words that Wind would give her the honor of the last face she witnessed, before she disappeared back into the world where she truly belonged, she picked up the pieces of armor and weapons and quickly returned them to the stands in the study as her spirit disappeared.

Lieutenant Motoshima and the other officers with him joined the original officers bunched up just outside of Hiromoai's plush apartment. He glared at Noguchi and then demanded from the officer. "Did you hear anything going on in there Noguchi-san?"

"I don't know for certain Lieutenant Motoshima-san, but it seems like there was a slight commotion and rush of words inside the apartment a few moments ago, but everything seems to have calmed down now, sir. I heard them talking then there was this blinding light filtering out from under the door, but it's gone now. It lasted for only a few seconds, like someone was shinning a light directly under the door. The talking stopped as well, but I was unable to make out what they were saying inside, sir." Noguchi bowed slightly to his superior officer.

"Very well Officer Noguchi-san, I'll take over from here. Take your officers and return to your posts outside the building and be prepared to lend any assistance if we run into some trouble in his apartment. Don't allow anyone to enter or leave the damn building until you hear from me. Detain anyone you come across and check them out thoroughly. If they have no reason to be around this building, hold them until I had a chance to interview them. I guess we beat the assassin back to her suspected lair. Keep an eye out for the killer because she's bound to be returning here. We followed her trail as long as we could, she had a good jump on us but she was on foot. We should've easily beaten back her here if this was where her sanctuary is, or her next target." Lieutenant Motoshima ordered as he knocked on the door to Hiromoai's apartment.

Inside the apartment, Lady Yoke returned from the study and stepped in front of Hiromoai and then snapped angrily at the person standing behind the door. "Who is the foul beast banging on my door at this ungodly hour of the morning? There are good people in here trying to sleep. Be gone from my front doorstep before I curse you to the underworld for eternity, foul one."

"This is Lieutenant Kenzaburo Motoshima of the Detective and Homicide Division of the Tokyo Police Department, and I wish to speak to Hiromoai-san if he's home, young lady. It's of the utmost importance that I speak with him at this time, Ma'am. Something terrible has just taken place, something he must be informed of immediately. Please open the door immediately, fiery one who displays nothing but hatred and disdain for the Police Department."

"You again Officer huh, I should've known it would be you begging entry at my door this early in the morning, you foul mannered evil thing you. You never appear before my Master's door at a more respectful time of the day. Be gone with you Officer Motoshima, my Master has no further time for the likes of you. Anything you have to inform him of can wait until a more proper time tomorrow to speak to Hiromoai-san. I'll be placing a complaint with your superiors in the more honorable hours of the day." She hissed at him.

"Look young lady, I grow tired of locking horns with you every time before you finally allow me to speak with Hiromoai-san. I told you this is of the utmost importance that I speak to him tonight, dammit. Now if you don't allow me entry in the apartment instantly, I swear by the gods we respect that I'll return to my stationhouse and swear out a warrant for Hiromoai-san's immediate arrest, and then I'll have him brought down to the station where I can speak to him without your constant interference, woman. What's it going to be lady, open the damn door at once, or I'll have him brought down to the station, and you can then explain to him why he was dragged down there instead of speaking to me in a private manner in his apartment.

"I don't believe he would think very highly of his servant, if you were the cause of his being arrested, just because you were too stubborn to open this damn door, so that I might speak with him in a much more friendly atmosphere. I have no further time to waste on you, open this damn door immediately I tell you, or you'll be the cause of Hiromoai-san's being arrest." The angry Lieutenant snapped as nastily as he could possibly growl, displaying the importance of his mission by being so foul mannered towards the young woman behind the door.

AMERICAN AIRLINES, FLIGHT 714

The American businessman, Calvin Batterman was trying his best to sleep on the long boring flight from the United States to Japan. He enjoyed the short stopover on Hawaii, but this part of the flight was going to be an endurance trial. Even though he was exhausted, he was unable to get a moment's sleep on the flight. He was worked up over buying the Yurkowa Construction Corporation. He already had his eyes trained on Hatanaka and Sons Mining and Construction Company once he took over Yurkowa's Company. He had no way of knowing he was sharing the same dream of Hiromoai of becoming the most powerful company in Japan.

The beautiful young female Japanese stewardess attending to the first class passengers on the aircraft noticed Batterman was having some problems resting, and she went over to him and offered politely in a whisper to him. "Mr.

Batterman Sir, can I offer you something from the bar please something that might help you relax a little better on the flight so you might be able to fall asleep for a while, sir." The stewardess believed he was a little afraid of flying, and she was trying to make it a little easier for him to relax on the aircraft.

"No, I'm alright little lady, thank you for the consideration though sweetheart. Do you have any books to read on this here flying death trap, honey?" He gave the stewardess a threatening wink, warning her he was on the make.

"Please Mr. Batterman Sir I don't want you upsetting the other passengers on the aircraft sir. You must refrain from statements like that, and keep your voice lower, please sir. Some of our passengers are trying to sleep on the flight sir. I assure you sir if you fall asleep, you'll be in Japan before you know it sir. A drink from the bar will help you Mr. Batterman?"

"No, just a book to read if you have one and you don't mind fetching it for me, little honey." The American businessman replied to the concerned acting stewardess.

"What kind of book would you be interested in reading, Mr. Batterman Sir? We have quite a variety of novels and magazines to choose from on board the aircraft sir. If music will help you relax a little sir, all you have to do is place the earphones on and dial the type of music you might desire to listen to on the flight, sir. There are fifteen music channels to choose from, Mr. Batterman Sir." The stewardess offered pleasantly as she smiled at him.

"You got one of them there juicy little novels with plenty of sex and crime in it, young lady? One of them there sex novels would do real nicely for me to enjoy honey."

Batterman replied as he continued to leer at the young and beautiful Japanese stewardess.

"Why Mr. Batterman, please sir. I'm afraid we're not allowed to carry such books on board the aircraft, sir. It's against all FCC regulations, sir." The stewardess gave him one of her best smiles, in an attempt to hide the fact she was embarrassed by his request of the book.

"I'd be pleased to show you why little missy. If you spend just one night with me, I assure you that you'll forget all about these little Japers you spent the night with before me, honey." He flashed one of his best smiles at her, trying to coax her into his bed when they got to Japan.

A flash of anger flushed the pretty stewardesses' face she did not like being referred to as a Japer. It was a terrible insult against her heritage and person. But she knew this crud and rude American man was rich beyond dreams, and he was good looking and young. She was tempted to take him up on his offer of spending the night with him, just to see where it might lead.

The wise American construction owner noticed the slight glint of anger flash across her face, and thought for a second and knew he had the stewardess right where he wanted her as he added to his words aimed at her. "I'm sorry if I insulted you just then, young lady. Please, allow me to make it up to you by offering you a fine supper tonight with all the trimmings in Japan. Any choice of restaurants you desire, and anything on the menu is my pleasure to share with you. It's all on me to make up to you for my foolish mouth little lady. After supper we can dance, and maybe have a couple of drinks and see what comes up after that, huh? The entire night will be ours to share and enjoy." He had the audacity to scratch his crotch to show her he was interested in her. The bulge in his pants attested to this fact.

"Why Mr. Batterman Sir, I'm afraid you're a man without much honor or proper respect for who you're speaking with, sir." The pretty stewardess even blushed over his interesting offer, but she remained at his side and smiled at him again.

"And damn dangerous about it as well little missy, and I'm rich enough to be without any honor, and still be respected by everyone I meet honey. Well, whatdaya say to the offer I made you young lady, supper tonight with me and who knows what after supper?" He grinned at the pretty young Japanese beauty while waiting for her reply to the offer of supper that night.

"I'm terribly sorry Mr. Batterman Sir, but I'm scheduled to be staying with a friend while I'm on layover in Japan for the next five days, sir." The stewardess offered in her defense, while showing she was a little interested in spending the evening with the American businessman.

"Oh, I'm sorry to hear that little missy, because I didn't know you were involved with someone here in Japan. I'm certain there are a few other young women in Japan who'd jump at the chance to have a good time with a rich American alone on a trip to your country, honey." He was trying the hard sell on the young stewardess now because he wanted someone to help celebrate with him when he took over Asahiko's construction company.

"Please sir, I'm not involved with anyone as you put it sir, with a man or lover, Mr. Batterman sir. I'm staying with another female stewardess while she's on layover in Tokyo along with me, sir. We're sharing a room together to save some money on our stopover, sir. We do it every time when we're both in Japan at the same time and are stuck on a stopover together, sir."

"Great then it's simple to solve honey. Just bring her along with you. Money's no object when you're out on the town with me, little missy. There's enough here to go around for everyone to enjoy, honey." Again, he dared to scratch his crotch in front of her.

The stewardess blushed a second time at the thought of spending a little time with Batterman and her female friend at the same time. She never experienced making love to another female, but she had to admit to herself that the thought always intrigued her a little. She placed her hand to her face and moaned at the American businessman who was staring at her while waiting for her to reply to his last offer to her. "Mr. Batterman, I never..."

"Well then little missy, it's about time you did. When and where should I pick you and your girlfriend up tonight?" He gave a lingering smile which was more a sneer than anything.

"We're staying at the old Edo Hilton Hotel for the five days that we're on layover in Tokyo, and then we shall..."

"Great, I'll send a car for the two of you, errr... let's say around eight o'clock tonight." The American offered as he cut the stewardess off in mid-sentence.

"That'll be fine with me and hopefully with my girlfriend at the same time, Mr. Batterman Sir." The stewardess replied with a pleasant smile, pleased that she was able to recapture his interests again. She knew there were many young Japanese women who would gladly give up their sexual treasures to spend some time with one as rich as this American man obviously was. She was due for a good time anyhow, and what better time could she possibly have than spending it with an American multi millionaire and her girlfriend.

"Great that's real great then it's settled between us little missy, but let me clear something up for you while I'm at it, its Cal to you from now on if you don't mind, sweetheart. Don't eat anything and tell your girlfriend the same not to eat, because there'll be plenty of food and drink where I'll be taking you two tonight. Be prepared to spend the night and get plenty drunk while you're at it, baby. Do you girls do the drug thing here in Japan, missy?"

"Please Mr. Batterman Sir not so loud. I don't want you upsetting the other passengers, sir. Or them hearing what we're talking about, sir. If one hears us and turns me in about err... that, I'll lose my job, sir." The stewardess glanced around to make sure no one was listening to them.

"You got it, remember, Cal young lady from now on please. And you don't hafta worry about your job either little missy. If you lose it, or you quit for any reason, all you have to do is look me up, and I'll find you a damn good position in my new Japanese company. I could always use someone who understands the damn lingo around here, honey."

The stewardess let out with a deep sigh and then she allowed her shoulders to sag a bit before she replied. "Please Cal-san, not so loud sir. Do you want the other passengers hearing what we're talking about, sir? Yes, some I'm afraid to admit, sir." The stewardess blushed as she smiled at the American shyly and informed him she was into the drug scene.

"Fine, I'll have whatever you do available for you to enjoy tonight. It's going to be one helluva crazy night for us tonight I assure you, missy. I have a lot to celebrate." Batterman answered her wearing a smile informing her, what he intended to do to her and her girlfriend's bodies.

"You seem to have something special to celebrate tonight, Mr. Batterm ...errr... Cal-san."

"I sure as hell do little lady, but the only way you'll find out, is by coming along with the wave that's going to be sweeping over Japan in the near future." He gave her a second lingering leer then dared to lick his lips as a further warning to what she and her girlfriend was in for tonight.

"I guess we'll be there and ready to party then Cal-san, do you want us to wear something special for your entertainment? I have plenty of dresses with me in y luggage sir." The stewardess asked while trying to keep the conversation going, cementing his attention to her so he would not think of inviting someone else to his party, and cutting her and her friend out of all the fun and games of the night. She glanced around the first class compartment. Most passengers were sleeping, or otherwise involved in conversations, or reading books or papers.

"The less you wear the better I'll like it, little missy." The American smirked.

"My name is Fumiko Kojima, and my friend's name is Tomoko Harada and we'll be wear..."

"Is she on this flight, Fumiko?" Cal asked interrupting Fumiko, hoping to get a look at this other female he was going to be spending some time with later on tonight.

"No Cal-san, she's doing duty on Flight 711 out of Hong Kong. She's been in Japan for two days already and has a layover of another three days, sir. We know how to dress that'll keep your attention on us, Cal-san. We'll surprise you when you have us picked up for our date sir. I'm looking forward to having a good time tonight, sir. It's been quite a while since the last time I was able to let myself go, Cal-san." She replied as she fluttered her eyes at the American.

"Great, I can hardly wait, and you'll have one helluva time tonight, this I promise you."

"I assure you sir all your wildest dreams will bear fruit on this night, Cal-san." Fumiko dared to reach out and rest her hand right on Cal's crotch. She smiled slyly and gave him a quick wink of her own and then she went to check on the other passengers in the first class section on the flight. All the while she attended to the other passengers she kept glancing back at Cal and smiling at him, trying to further cement his attention to her and tonight. It worked, Cal was drooling all over her every move. She made certain she bent low allowing her dress to rise so Cal could have a sneak preview of what he was in for later in the day.

CHAPTER TWENTY FOUR
HIROMOAI'S APARTMENT AT THE
HATANAKA TOWERS

Hearing the warning from Lieutenant Motoshima standing out in the hallway of his building about having him arrested, Hiromoai quickly moved out in front of Lady Yoke and opened the door while growling at the police detective, while forcing Lady Yoke to stand behind him at the same time. She was angry as hell again, but took the warning from her boss to heart and she remained silent as he handled the police officers from this point on.

"Huh, I take it that this is an official visit. Do I stand accused of doing something wrong?"

"Hiromoai-san, I must beg of you to give me permission to search your apartment..."

"Why? Do you have a search warrant to carry out this requested search of my dwelling, Detective? Am I under arrest as you offered to my housekeeper, Lieutenant? If so Officer, I want the right to have my lawyer present on this search of my apartment and my pending arrest. I demand to know what I stand accused of doing wrong that caused my arrest and search of my home by you and these other Officers for a second time, Lieutenant Motoshima." Hiromoai growled at the detective as he held him in his angry glare for the moment.

"I beg your pardon for that unwise statement, Hiromoai-san. By all means you're not under arrest at all, sir. I said that in an attempt to quiet that hell fire you call a servant, sir. Hiromoai-san, the request to search your apartment isn't an official request, sir. It's a request, a courtesy if you will sir. We have reason to believe that the lowly assassin who killed Asahiko-san is..."

"Asahiko Yurkowa-san is dead Lieutenant Motoshima!" Hiromoai cried as he interrupted the detective's words and then he asked. "How? When did this terrible dream of a nightmare take place, Officer?" He offered convincingly, as he faked a slight stagger and moved deeper in his apartment and leaned against the wall to help support him.

"Yes Hiromoai-san, that is correct sir and I must report that Asahiko Yurkowa-san was slaughtered tonight, and we believe it's the handy work of this god cursed assassin still stalking the streets of downtown Tokyo, sir." The detective offered as he followed Hiromoai deeper in his apartment and then waited until he got controlled of himself.

Gathering his strength for show, he snapped at the interested officer in a very angry tone of voice. "Surely, you don't expect to find this hell's spawn assassin hiding within my damn apartment, do you Lieutenant? I assure you detective, no such criminal is a friend of mine, sir. I'm not noted as making friends with these types of people and criminals, mister."

"Hiromoai-san, we have reason to believe that the devil assassin is on her way here, sir. I fear you might be marked for death by this evil nightmare, as was Asahiko-san and his honorable son were, sir." The Detective Lieutenant replied as he made some room for Sergeant Okamatsu and Corporal Furuta to follow him deeper into the massive apartment.

"And you believe this miserable assassin was somehow able to gain entry into my apartment? How? We're too high up from the street to make it possible for any assassin no matter how well trained and skilled they might be, to get to my apartment from the outside of the building. And seeing how many police officers you have, err... protecting me from inside my own building, Lieutenant. I seriously doubt that any hated assassin would be able to gain entry to my apartment from inside the building. I'm afraid you're following an impossible dream here, Lieutenant."

The Lieutenant spoke, but in a rush of words this time. "Hiromoai-san, I don't know how this damn assassin is able to get into the buildings the way she does, but judging by her past actions and successes killing two of Japan's most powerful and very influential people. I don't really think anything is impossible for this daughter of the darkness to accomplish, if she truly wanted to kill the one she set her evil eyes on, sir. I must ask you again for permission to search your apartment, sir. It's for your own safety I offer you this request, sir." The worried detective looked around the room they were standing in, and found nothing out of the ordinary in it.

"Perhaps you might be right at that after all Lieutenant Motoshima. Seeing what this lowly assassin born from hell was able to accomplish since first surfacing to stalk the nights of downtown Tokyo, while under the very noses of tight police security might I add to you sir. Maybe I shouldn't be so damn smug about this murderer. Yes by all means Lieutenant, search my apartment until your heart's content, sir. May I offer you some tea or something stronger to enjoy while you're conducting this second search of my apartment, Lieutenant? I was just about to turn in for the night, but I fear after hearing the disturbing news of Asahiko-san's death. I don't think I'll be able to sleep for a week after this news now sir. Was poor old Asahiko-san slaughtered in the same terrible manner as his honorable son and his wife was?"

"Thank you for the offer of some tea sir, but nothing to drink for me I'm afraid, sir. I have to pay attention to my duty and don't have time for such luxuries, sir." The Lieutenant offered as he gave the other bunched up police officers a number of quick hand signals. Immediately, they separated and began to search the many rooms of the huge penthouse apartment as he added to the owner. Hiromoai-san, Asahiko-san committed Hari Kari..."

"Now I'm really confused, Officer. When you people first entered my damn apartment, you mentioned to me that Asahiko-san was slaughtered. Now you state to me he committed suicide. Which was it Officer? And if I might ask, why the hell do you think this damn assassin was responsible for his death then, Detective? To hear you speak now, Asahiko-san took a very noble way of death out of this world. No assassin I ever heard about would allow such an honorable act, if she was sent supposedly to kill the old man, Lieutenant. Which was it now mister? Was he killed by this damn assassin I keep hearing so much about lately, or did he die by his own god damn hand, sir?" He actually barked at the officer, allowing anger to creep into his tone.

"Hiromoai-san, Asahiko-san died by his own hand tonight sir, but we believe he was seconded by the assassin..." The detective went to offer, but Hiromoai cut him off in mid sentence.

"By this lowly assassin's hand you offer to me, Officer?" He suddenly hollowed with a smirk, and then he grumbled at the officer. "Oh come on and get real with yourself for a damn minute will you please, Lieutenant. I might have been born at night, but I assure you it wasn't last night. This type of action is not what is usually expected by any cursed assassin I ever heard about sir. What the hell makes you believe for one moment that the murderer seconded Asahiko-san's honorable death? From what I know of the act of Suppuku, a close and very trusted friend, is the only one allowed the honor to second anyone about to commit suicide, Lieutenant?"

"Normally that's a fact Hiromoai-san, but we have gathered evidence that the assassin was in the room along with Asahiko-san when he was preparing to kill himself, sir. How we know this as a fact is, the assassin left the same type of evidence that she left at Tsutomu Yurkowa-san's death scene, sir. It's the only indication that we have of linking her to both scenes of deaths so far, sir. Yes, thinking about it a little further sir, I believe I just might indulge in a cup of tea after all, if you don't mind, Hiromoai-san." Lieutenant Motoshima was trying to take the fire out of his tone by asking for the offered cup of tea.

The Lieutenant noticed Sergeant Okamatsu was staring vacantly into the study. He seemed disturbed by something he was witnessing inside the room, maybe even scared by what he was looking at. He made a mental note to himself to question the Sergeant over his reaction to what was wrong in the large study. He did not want to ask him in front of Hiromoai in case he noticed some incriminating evidence he failed to remove before they arrived at his apartment. The concerned lead detective hoped it was evidence finally linking the assassin to his employ.

Hiromoai turned to Lady Yoke who was more or less trying to guard him against the police officers who just invaded his apartment by her trying to stand between him and the gaggle of police officers invading his apartment and he asked her. "Lady Yoke, please get these fine police officers some tea to enjoy. Bring some rice cakes and other food in case they might be hungry." He turned back to Lieutenant Motoshima who bowed his thanks to the offer.

Lady Yoke turned with a snap in her step and she angrily stormed out of the study without uttering a word of protest to Hiromoai or herself.

"Huh Hiromoai-san, that one's something to behold sir. If I ever find myself in need of someone to fight on my side, I hope you'll allow me to borrow that little wild cat to help assist in my defense, Hiromoai-san." Motoshima mumbled as he watched Yoke disappear in the kitchen.

Hiromoai bowed slightly, accepting the fine compliment by the officer about his young female helper. But he kept a wary eye on this officer also. The mention of Wind leaving some evidence behind at both death scenes shook him to his soul. He thought she was far better than that. Now, he had to find out what that evidence was, in case it might be able to link him to Wind.

They waited in a strained silence for Lady Yoke to return. The Lieutenant was really waiting for the officers to return from their search of the apartment. When they did, he looked at Officer Furuta and waited for his report. He did not mind him speaking in front of Hiromoai.

Furuta picked up the silent message and reported there was no one hiding in the apartment they did not know about, and there was no sign of the assassin, or of her ever being in the apartment.

The Lieutenant then turned back to Hiromoai and placed a rather passive look on his face and mumbled in a polite tone of voice to him. "Again it seems that I have successfully interrupted your Wa over nothing, sir. I'll pray to the Kami who make us happy that you'll forgive this rude intrusion into your apartment, Hiromoai-san." The detective bowed but inside he was fuming. Angry his officers were unable to locate any possible evidence of the assassin being hidden or working for Hiromoai. When the tea arrived, it seemed to relieve the tension filling the room.

Hiromoai took a sip of his tea and then asked the detective in a contrite tone. "Err... Lieutenant Kenzaburo Motoshima-san, you made mentioned of something about some evidence being left by this lowly assassin at both death sites.

Do you mind my asking you what kind of evidence the assassin had left behind that you're talking about, sir?"

'Ahhh so, it seems to me that you're awful interested in learning what your daughter of evil and blackness has left to enable us to link the filthy thing to both murders, huh Hiromoai? It's only a matter of time before I discover the proof you're the one behind the actions of this assassin and when I do. I'll take great pleasure in dragging your smart ass off to jail, Mr. big shot'. Lieutenant Motoshima thought as he stared at him for several seconds before answering. Now, he understood his anger he held against this man, he was jealous of his position in the Japanese higher class. He felt this man was given everything he owned served up to him on a silver platter. The officer wondered if Hiromoai even knew what a good, honest day's work was about.

Lieutenant Motoshima's mind was brought back to the conversation when Hiromoai suddenly cleared his throat. He refused to ask the question a second time of the detective for fear of drawing any special attention to his inquiry about the evidence left behind by Wind.

"Errr... yes, please forgive me for day dreaming a might on you, Hiromoai-san. It's been a very trying day and night for me to endure sir, and I'm thoroughly exhausted by my many toils, sir. Yes sir Hiromoai-san, I don't mind telling you in the least what the god cursed assassin has left behind at both murder sites. At both scenes of death we discovered a simple and small muddy footprint sir. Both were of the same size and shape, sir. Both prints were identical in nature same size and stride as well, sir. You see Hiromoai-san it seems this assassin takes some of her lessons from our past history sir. When she's out for the hunt for blood, she wears a certain kind of special foot coverings, the ancient tabis Hiromoai-san."

"I know what that is, that's the split toed sock made popular by the hated Ninja's I believe, Lieutenant Motoshima-san. Am I not correct sir?" he offered while wearing a smile of victory that stated he knew of the old ways of Japan's past.

"Very good Hiromoai-san, you surprise me by knowing this fact, sir. The Ninja had made the tabis famous, but it was originally used by the ancient Warriors of Japan's past as well, sir." The Lieutenant corrected, pleased that he knew something Hiromoai obviously did not.

Hiromoai bowed slightly to the correction by the detective, but he did not challenge it. This meant absolutely nothing to him, because he knew what the tabis were and who was using them to carry out his biddings. Inside, he was fuming that Wind was careless enough as to leave such a telltale mark behind to link her to both murders. He was hoping to make the police believe that Asahiko died by his own hand as Wind suggested. That way he would not draw further attention to his actions of trying to buy Asahiko's company a second time from the old man's lawyer.

Drawing in his breath in a deep sigh, he begged of the police officer. "Please Lieutenant Motoshima-san, I'm rather exhausted myself, and this horrible news about Asahiko-san killing himself for some reason tonight, and him maybe putting in league with the murderer, has drained me beyond my strength and endurance. If there's nothing else I need to answer for you, I'd like a little time to myself so that I might burn some incense to Lord Buddha, to pray for him to open the Gates of Heaven for Asahiko-san's honorable soul to enter, sir."

"I take it that you don't believe in the rebirth as a Samurai's soul, Hiromoai-san?" Suddenly, the detective was intrigued by Hiromoai's absentminded suggestion that maybe Asahiko was the one working with this assassin, and that's why she assisted him in his death. The more he got involved in these two murder cases, the more confusing they became. Now, he had something else to check out on this ever expanding case. Maybe that was why Asahiko took his own life. Maybe he felt the police were closing in on him, and rather than be arrested like a common criminal, the old man chose to take his life. A most interesting turn of events he thought.

Hiromoai felt the officer was thinking and offered to move the conversation along at a quicker pace as he offered. "Dead is dead as far as I'm concerned Lieutenant. I don't allow myself to get caught up in the romantic thoughts of the fools who wish for the impossible to be true for them. Lieutenant Motoshima-san, have your Officers satisfied your interest that this lowly assassin isn't hiding or stalking me in my apartment, sir?" He asked as he looked at the other officers gathering in his hall, and they were kind of staring at their commander obviously for orders.

"Yes, I must admit I too believe as you, Hiromoai-san. This nonsense of being reborn to a better life, a better Warrior is just what it sounds like, an impossible dream thought up by those who wish to be immortal, sir. Despite what Lord Buddha preaches, I too believe dead is dead, Hiromoai-san. Yes, I'll be going sir, and I must admit when I first entered your apartment sir, I had my doubts about your involvement in this murder case, sir. Now, I'm not certain of anything about the damn case any longer. I'll be in touch with you in the future I'm sure, Hiromoai-san. If you have any questions, please feel free to phone my office, here's my business card sir.

"I'd be most pleased to share any and all information I have of this murder case with you sir. Assassins, influential businessmen being slaughtered in their damn sleep, or taking their own lives by their own hand, and leaving no clear cut clues behind for me to sink my damn teeth in, has me chasing my damn tail all around downtown Tokyo in a circle sir, is enough to drive me nuts. I thank you for your time and kind patience and also your hospitality over this most trying of matters, sir. Good night and good health Hiromoai-san." Lieutenant Motoshima rose and bowed politely to the seated Hiromoai who merely nodded back at him.

The Lieutenant was dying to find out what was upsetting his Sergeant while in Hiromoai's apartment looking in the study. He turned to his people and aimed them out of the exquisite apartment with a swift head movement and guiding hands. In the hall, the concerned Lieutenant quickly caught up with Sergeant Okamatsu and moved him a little away from the other officers, so no one would hear his words. "Sergeant, what the hell did you see in there that upset you so much? You looked stunned looking into the other room."

The Sergeant stopped walking and looked at the Lieutenant as he offered in a confused voice. "It's the damest think I ever saw in my entire life, I don't get it Lieutenant. I was in Hiromoai's apartment just a few hours ago sir, and the ancient armor and weapons and other crap he had in his study, looked as if they were just made by their craftsmen. The gold and silver inlay shining so brightly it almost hurt the eyes, sir. But now, they seemed to be as old and neglected as time itself, sir. Most of the gold and silver was missing, and the paintings that once adorned the armor, was well faded and marred sir. I wonder what the hell happened to all the equipment, sir. It has me baffled and wondering if I saw what I believed I saw the first time I was in the apartment, sir. It's scary as hell, and I don't know what to think of it Lieutenant. I'm certain it was all like new a few hours ago, but now it looked like it wasn't worth hanging on to the ancient stuff."

"I don't know either Sergeant, but judging by what I'm seeing of this ongoing murder case so far, nothing about it surprises me any longer my friend. Let's get down to the station, I have a new lead from Hiromoai and he doesn't even understand he gave me this damn lead to follow." Lieutenant Motoshima moved the officers along towards the elevators.

"What new lead is that Lieutenant Motoshima-san?" The concerned Sergeant asked as he fell in step with his superior.

"Hiromoai-san didn't realize it, but he pointed out a most interesting item when we were speaking together a few moments ago. Why the hell would any assassin assist in a death as Asahiko-san committed? Even you said a second had to be someone the honored one trusted and respected and knew and might have even worked with, or for, or was otherwise employed by the honored one, Sergeant."

"I'm afraid I still don't see what you're driving at here, Lieutenant?"

"Sergeant, you surprise me if you can't see where I'm going with this thing. Why else would the assassin assist Asahiko-san in his death, unless he and she were working together? As confusing as his death was, it suddenly makes sense to me now. Maybe he felt we were closing in on him, and the only way out was to commit Suppuku. Something had to make the assassin assist him in his honored death, and that something might be the two of them were working togeth..."

"If that's so then why in unholy hell would Asahiko-san kill his own honorable son and his poor wife, Lieutenant?" The surprised Sergeant replied to his commanding officer.

"I don't profess to have all the damn answers to this most confusing murder case, Sergeant. I don't have answers to many of the damn questions of this perplexing case as of yet. But I'm sure as hell going to run down this latest lead from Hiromoai-san, and prove Asahiko-san was either working with the assassin, or he was killed by this god cursed murderer. Why the hell couldn't this damn case be a simple act of murder? Assassins, the evil of hell's own spawn hatred, dammit." Lieutenant Motoshima grumbled as he waited for the elevator.

TOKYO INTERNATIONAL AIRPORT.
SUNDAY, JUNE 9th, 1996 11:30 A.M.

Calvin Batterman's 747 aircraft landed as scheduled at the Tokyo's International Airport. He was handed a phone number by the beautiful Fumiko with a smile, and a quick wink of the eye, as she said when he was preparing to depart the plane. "Please Mr. Batterman-san, you'll not forget your kind offer to call me when you get comfortable in your hotel room tonight, sir? I'll be patiently looking forward to hearing from you a little later on tonight, sir."

The mid-aged American businessman returned the smile with one of his own, but his was more a sneer and warning as he replied to the stewardess' remark. "Remember baby, its Cal to you, and you'll be hearing from me later tonight I assure you young lady. Remember to bring your pretty girlfriend along with you little missy."

Again, the stewardess smiled sexily at Batterman as she was forced to turn her attention to a second passenger having a bit of trouble getting her overhead luggage down.

Batterman went down the ladder to the tarmac wearing a smile from ear to ear, because he could not believe the change in his luck in just a few days. Two days ago he cursed the Japanese government for not allowing him to buy a working construction company in Japan. Today, not only did he own one of the best and largest construction companies in all Japan, but he was going to be sharing the night with a pair of beautiful young Japanese girls, who could have been his daughters rather than his private little play toys. He nearly skipped over to the waiting limousine, and once inside the car he checked his watch. He had a meeting scheduled with Shigeru Nagaro, Asahiko's lawyer at four forty that same afternoon. At that meeting, he was supposed to take over complete control of Yurkowa Mining and Construction Corporation.

He found himself wondering why Nagaro informed him that the old Asahiko would not be attending this meeting with them. He shrugged it off because he understood the Japanese were a strange lot, and anything they did not surprise him in the least. Besides, he did not care who attended the meeting, as long as he ended up with the construction company under his control with the blessing of the Japanese government. He sat deeply in the lush leather seat of the car because he was exhausted and suffering from jet lag. He intended to sleep until the meeting, and then celebrate with the two women all night long once he owned the company.

HIROMOAI'S APARTMENT IN THE HATANAKA TOWERS.
9:30 A.M. SUNDAY, JUNE 9th, 1996

Hiromoai did not sleep a wink because he was so upset over Wind's carelessness at leaving some traceable evidence behind for the police to discover at both scenes of death he sent her to. He was worked up thinking of the meeting he was going to request to take place with his age old nemesis Shigeru Nagaro, Asahiko's despised lawyer later on today. He went into his bedroom, allowing Wind to remain for a while longer in the world of wonder and dreams, while he prepared for the meeting with Asahiko's cunning lawyer.

He shaved and showered, feeling refreshed he went to the kitchen and found the Lady Yoke preparing something to eat for his morning meal. He wondered why he did not approach her, to share her treasures last night. Perhaps, it would have helped him relax a little better if he had. He thought about this suggestion and decided if he did not summon Wind from the Ukiyo to help him celebrate his buying of Asahiko's construction company tonight, he would surely share the experience with Lady Yoke. One way or the other, after getting his hands of Asahiko's construction company, he was going to celebrate it with one of the two women later on tonight.

Lately, Lady Yoke seemed to be trying everything in her power to have him notice her. This morning, she was dressed in a sleeping kimono, short, barely covering her sculptured rearend and the front of the kimono just about hiding her wonderful breasts. Each time she leaned forward, he easily enjoyed the beautiful view of her breasts that seemed to be struggling to be free of the fine silk fabric, or her rearend. He found himself getting interested more and more in her lately, and he had to force his attention away from her loveliness. He had to stay focused on Nagaro and Asahiko's construction company and the matters at hand, if he wanted to be successful in acquiring the business. Tonight, there would be plenty of time to enjoy sexual merriment with the two women in his life. He held a thought of maybe even having sex with both Wind and Lady Yoke at the same time tonight. A smile quickly crossed his lips over the most interesting idea as he took a moment to enjoy that very pleasing thought.

Lady Yoke placed two eggs, toast, and hot rice cakes before him, with a cup of strong coffee and a glass of ice cold orange juice as she asked him in a pleasant voice. "Hiromoai-san, what are you going to be doing on this fine day, sir?"

"I'm going to place a call to that pain in the ass Nagaro and request a meeting with the great fool. Why? Did you have something planned for me, Lady Yoke?"

"That is nonsense Hiromoai-san, you know how that old fool feels about your presence, sir. He has made this known to everyone who witnesses meetings between the two of you in the past. If you request anything from that arrogant man, he'll try his best not to give it to you in a terribly insulting way against you, Hiromoai-san. I think that it'd be a very wise idea on your part if you merely showed up at his worthless doorstep, and made your business and presence known to him. So he couldn't possibly put your requested meeting with him off and never meet with you."

He stared at her with her hands resting on her hips, while weighing her words. She was correct that Nagaro would never give an audience to him, even if he begged him on his hand and knees. What better way to force a meeting with the crafty lawyer than by just merely showing up at his office. Once there, good manners would demand that Nagaro meet with him.

"Huh Lady Yoke, you're wise beyond your young years I believe. I like that idea, I like it very much and that's what I'm going do, young lady. I know no matter how much the dog eating fool of a lawyer hates me, he'd be looking to sell Asahiko's white elephant of a construction company to just get it off his hands, and then he can sit back and enjoy the many profits that sale would reap him. I'll be leaving for the fool's office after I finish this meal you prepared for me."

"What about Wind, Hiromoai-san? Are you going to summon her back from the lonely land of the dead? You know how much she hates staying there for any length of time since you have discovered her presence." Lady Yoke asked, hoping her boss would call Wind back from the dead so she could be with the ancient female warrior while he was with Nagaro.

H looked up from his meal into her eyes before replying to her. "Yes, but not right away Lady Yoke, I'm angry as hell with her blunders of leaving a set of footprints behind at both actions I sent her out on, dammit. Besides, I believe she needs the added rest and fear that the damn police might still show up at this apartment any time they want to question me again over these nagging deaths they're investigating. This time we were extremely lucky that Wind heard the police at the front door of the apartment before they entered. Next time, we might not be as lucky Lady Yoke. No, I think I'll allow her to remain in the land of the lost for a little while longer. Errr... tonight, I want you to prepare a very special meal, a meal for two people to enjoy. Some candles, a dish of fine food and plenty of sabazuki to drink, young lady."

"You'll be bringing someone home with you from work I suspect, Hiromoai-san?" Lady Yoke asked with concern, her heart breaking with want of the young Japanese man sitting by her.

"No, I believe the one who I'd like to share this special meal with, is with me right now, young lady." He stared at her until his words sank in and then he smiled kindly at her.

"Ieeeee! You mean you wish to share this special meal with this foolish and most undeserving woman?" Lady Yoke exclaimed as she pointed at her chest with her finger, and then she placed the largest smile Hiromoai had ever seen in his life on her lovely face.

"And a lot more if everything goes as well as I plan today Lady Yoke. I believe it's time we got to know each other a whole lot better. No young lady?" He gave her one of his best smiles.

The smile could not be hidden behind her delicate hands as she brought them up to her mouth and hid behind them. She knew it was terribly impolite to bare one's teeth to an intended lover. It was believed in Japan that the act of exposing one's teeth to another person was done usually during times of a confrontation or stress, or warring with one's enemy.

"I take it that you'll make certain everything's perfect for us to enjoy tonight, right Lady Yoke?" he asked as he pushed himself up and away from the small table.

"Huh my future lover, I promise that tonight will be beyond your wildest dreams. I swear this to you Hiromoai-san." Lady Yoke bowed and her breasts was again trying to struggle free of the light restricting colorful silk fabric of her kimono.

Again, he enjoyed the lovely view of her beautiful breasts trapped so unwillingly in the fine silk fabric as he wiped the corners of his mouth on the napkin, and then dropped it on the plate along with his half eaten eggs, and then he complained at her. "I'm warning you Lady Yoke, if you keep teasing me like you're doing this morning, you'll make it impossible for me to walk, or leave the apartment while trying to keep my dignity." He displayed the worse of manners by reaching out and running his hand inside the silk garment. To his surprise, Lady Yoke did not flinch an inch or resist his terrible lack of manners. She even allowed him to pull the fine fabric apart so he could enjoy the view of both her breasts at the same time. She rose and stood straight, he rose and placed his lips to one nipple and drew it in his mouth gently.

"Oooo Hiromoai-san, you suckle like a starving newborn first finding the offered teat of life, my soon to be lover." She purred sexily as she enjoyed his skilled attention to her body.

Again he complained as he struggled to make the crotch of his pants more comfortable for him to endure. He was aroused and made her well aware of his growing problem, and the interest he was showing her, and enjoying the effect she was having on his manhood as he grumbled. "Lady Yoke, you're making it awful difficult for me to even walk at this very moment, young lady. I'd stay and enjoy your treasures a while longer, but alas I have very pressing matters that I must attend to on this day. You'll be ready when I return tonight, right Lady Yoke?"

"Hai Hiromoai-san, I'll be waiting with open arms with a wanting heart for your return." She bowed gracefully but she did not straighten the front of her kimono. She was determined to make the most of this her first real opportunity to capture his long sought after attention and heart.

"You make me desire to return home more than you'll ever know, young lady." He replied as he headed for the door, followed closely by Lady Yoke. Her breasts swaying gently as she walked behind him in a rush. He left the apartment without further words.

In no time he found himself standing in the underground parking lot of the Hatanaka Tower in search of his car. This time he did not have the attendant or guards move it out beforehand for him. He was in such a good mood he decided to fetch his own car for a change. He started the snow white Mercedes and roared out of the parking lot right out into the flow of morning traffic, that was very light at this time of the day.

It took him half an hour to get across downtown Tokyo and over to Asahiko's lawyer's office. He stormed into the waiting room and walked right up to the seated secretary who bowed and held it in recognition of his presence before her. She was astonished at seeing this powerful young Japanese businessman standing before her unannounced, while grinning at her like he was a school boy looking at his teacher after she had given him a compliment. Straightening up she asked politely of him. "Hiromoai-san, it's a pleasure to see you on this fine morning, sir. What is it I might do for you on this fine day, Hiromoai-san?"

"I'll tell you what you can do for me I want to see Nagaro-san immediately. It's most important that I do, is he in his office this morning young lady?"

"Do you have an appointment set up to see Nagaro-san this morning that I am unaware of, Hiromoai-san? I didn't see your honorable name printed in his appointment book for a meeting with you today, Hiromoai-san." The stunned secretary asked as polite as she could offer as she quickly checked her appointment book again right in front of him, knowing for certain that he did not have an appointment to be with Nagaro this morning. If he had it would have been her who penciled in the requested meeting. She was sorry she had insulted him by asking him such a question. The secretary knew he must have spoken to Nagaro in private, and he invited him to over his office and he had failed to inform her in advance of this unknown appointment. Even Hiromoai would not be so arrogant as to merely show up at the office without an appointment scheduled between the two of them as she offered. "Hiromoai-san, if you'll be so kind as to wait for a moment, I'll see if Nagaro-san is ready to meet with you sir."

Hiromoai nodded and stood as she sat and placed a call to Nagaro over the phone. "I'm terribly sorry for disturbing you so early this morning sir, but Hiromoai Hatanaka-san is here to meet with you, sir." The secretary purred in her sweetest voice over the phone. She decided to use the phone instead of the intercom to keep the conversation as private as possible.

"What! Hiromoai! What the hell is that sonofabitch doing here for hell's sake? Did you tell the great fool I was in?" Nagaro growled angrily at his secretary as he wondered why Hiromoai had shown up at his office unannounced or uninvited.

"Yes please." The secretary replied, stunned at Nagaro's angry outburst against her.

"Dammit, I guess I'm stuck seeing what that foul one wants of my ass. I'll have to see him now he's here and knows I'm in my damn office. Give me five minutes and then escort the lousy sonofabitch in. Don't forget to interrupt us so I can get rid of him as soon as possible. I don't want the likes of him polluting my office for a moment longer than is absolutely necessary." Nagaro hissed in the phone, angry at his secretary for telling him he was in.

"Do you wish for me to remain at the meeting between you and him, Nagaro-san?" The concerned secretary asked barely over a whisper in the phone so Hiromoai could not hear the question, trying to save face with the upset Nagaro, by offering to stay in the office with them. Knowing there would never be a confrontation between the two if she was in the room.

"No! That'll not be not necessary young lady I don't want you to be insulted like I'm going to be forced to be by this evil man's foul presence on this damn morning." The upset lawyer snapped angrily at his secretary as he hung up the phone and then darted off for his private bathroom. He quickly shaved and splashed some aftershave lotion on that nearly burned his face off. Then he changed into a clean white shirt, and redid his tie. He was just coming out of the bathroom while slipping into his suit jacket, when the secretary entered the office with Hiromoai following her.

Nagaro was still in the same soiled clothes he was in yesterday and last night, when he was called over to the castle to view what Asahiko committed with his honored death, and he did not bother to change the clothes from the exhausting night before.

"Ahhh... Hiromoai-san what a pleasure it is to see you once again, sir. And what is it that brings you to this part of downtown Tokyo, sir? We have to be quick about it, because I have numerous meeting scheduled for this entire day sir." The lawyer grumbled, unable to mask the anger he held towards Hiromoai, as he put out his hand and shook with the younger man.

Hiromoai completely ignored the civility acted out by the cunning lawyer, and he spoke with a trace of anger lacing his own voice this time. He was not there for any pleasantries but business as he offered with a snap in his voice. "Nagaro-san, I'm here because I heard about the terrible news of Asahiko killing himself last night. How deplorable this is to learn. What could have possibly possessed such a great man as he to take his own life in the middle of the night, sir? A man with so much to live for, I lit five sticks of incense in his honor before Lord Buddha."

"Yes Hiromoai-san, it's a terrible loss for his construction company and for Japan as well, sir. I fear the appalling loss of his honorable son and his lovely wife was too much for Asahiko-san to endure. I thank you for your kind offering to his honorable memory, Hiromoai-san. I'm certain the offer has lit the way for his fine spirit to find its final resting place in peace and harmony with the Kami, sir. Is this why you have turned up at my office unannounced on this day, Hiromoai-san?" the wise lawyer placed an emphasis on 'unannounced', to display for him that he was upset over the unscheduled visit by him to his office. The lawyer successfully hid the fact he was fuming at the loathsome Hiromoai, for omitting the san at the end of Asahiko's proud name when he was addressing his fine memory before him.

"That, among other reasons Nagaro-san." Hiromoai snapped dryly, displaying more ill manners by taking a seat without it being offered to him first by the upset lawyer.

His secretary silently backed out of the office as soon as the two men were seated and began speaking with each other pleasantly.

Nagaro realized Hiromoai wanted to have an extended meeting with him, and he was powerless to refuse his unasked request, now the man he despised the most in all Japan, sat before him with his legs crossed and staring back at him. Reluctantly Nagaro gave in and took his seat behind his desk and then clasped his hands together while intensely studying Hiromoai's young and nasty looking face. It was eating him up inside to know the man responsible for the deaths of Asahiko and his honorable son and wife was daring to sit so brazenly in front of him, as if he was guiltless in the deplorable and foul deeds of these three people.

"Now we're speaking sir, are you not going to inform your secretary you don't wish to be disturbed while we're meeting this morning, Nagaro-san?" Hiromoai snapped smugly, knowing he trapped the lawyer into listening to his words for the full time he wanted to speak with him.

"Yes Hiromoai-san that seems like a very wise idea to execute, sir. I'd surely hate like hell to start a conversation with you only to have it interrupted by questions by my secretary, sir." The upset lawyer was fuming inside more than ever now, because he understood his secretary once she realized Hiromoai was here without his permission, would find a way to call and remind him of a prior meeting for the day. Something she has done whenever he wanted to get rid of a certain client he was stuck speaking with.

Hiromoai understood this age old ploy because he employed the very same ploy on many different occasions himself and that was why he suggested for Nagaro inform his secretary they were not to be disturbed under any circumstances during this meeting. He smiled more to himself, pleased at how easy it was for him to bend this highly respected lawyer around his finger. He waited for Nagaro to finish speaking with his secretary on the intercom, and the moment he did, Nagaro offered Hiromoai in a polite tone of voice.

"Hiromoai-san, now that you're here, you said something about there were other reasons for this unscheduled visit to my office, sir. May I inquire as to what those other reasons might be, sir? As you must be aware of, I represent Asahiko-san, and his construction company's interests, and it might not be proper or very ethical if I'm meeting with you privately like this, sir. I'm afraid this meeting may have the air of iniquitous interests involved with it, Hiromoai-san." The lawyer complained as he leaned back and stared Hiromoai dead in the eyes for a moment.

"At the risk of being rather presumptuous with you today, but what the hell's there to represent with Asahiko's god damn company any longer Nagaro-san? Asahiko's dead, what the hell does he care how you act and with who at that might I add, sir? Yes, one other reason I wanted this meeting held between the two of us, was to find out what you're going to do with Yurkowa's worthless construction company, Nagaro-san. I piss on how this meeting might look to any other fools of Japan, I care absolutely nothing for what others think or say for that matter. I'm certain the old man must have given you the power of attorney over this damn situation, Nagaro-san. If so, I'm inquiring if his company is up for sale. If it is, I'm here to say that I have interests in acquiring his company. I'll make a most honorable offer for it, that way you'll have a good retirement to live out the rest of your life on, sir."

Again, he was angered by the horrendous way Hiromoai was disrespecting Asahiko's memory and construction company. He was further angered by Hiromoai's assumption that he would be willing to betray Asahiko's best interests, now he was dead. His next words were going to give him the greatest of pleasure to deliver against him, and he was going to savor completely destroying his want to acquire Asahiko's honorable company. Nagaro remembered what Asahiko told him about the opportunity for revenge. 'Revenge was something that had to be nourished until ripe for the picking, only then could it be seized upon and enjoyed properly. One's advantage over any situation had to be savored like that of a bottle of fine Sake, slowly rolled around in one's mouth before being acted upon, to thoroughly break the back of one's enemy. The presentation of devastating news had to be delivered with the punch intended by it'.

CHAPTER TWENTY FIVE

The lawyer slowly drew in his breath and hesitated for a moment, drawing out the delight of how he was going to crush Hiromoai's dream. He shifted his weight and began in his deepest and positive tone. "Hiromoai-san, you're correct in thinking that Asahiko-san was wise enough to place me in the position to look after his company after he was gone on his last journey of life. Yes, I was well aware of what Asahiko-san was planning last night, and I followed his last instructions to me to the letter. To the letter I tell you, and you're right in thinking that Asahiko-san's honorable construction company is up for sale, sir. But it's my sad duty to inform you that his company has already been sold, sir. The deal was closed, and money had changed hands and the necessary papers signed, and Asahiko-san's chop set in place on those papers, sir.

"In true fact in the matter Hiromoai-san, I have a meeting with the new owner of the Yurkowa Construction Company scheduled for later on this afternoon, sir. I know the new owner's in Tokyo already, sir. He had arrive by plane some three hours ago, Hiromoai-san." Nagaro lied he knew Batterman was scheduled to arrive near twelve. But he was enjoying crushing Hiromoai so much that he chose to stretch the truth a might for his own delight.

"What the hell are you trying to fucking hand me, Lawyer? What the fuck do you mean that Asahiko's god damn worthless business was already sold? To who dammit! When? I met with the old fool just a few days ago, and he told me in no uncertain terms that his miserable company would never be on the selling block as long as he was alive. What the hell changed in so short a time, Nagaro?" Hiromoai could not hide what this news had done to his overinflated ego. He was crushed beyond words and thoughts, his shoulders noticeably sagged and his cockiness rapidly abandoned him. He looked like a young child who just lost his favorite toy.

"In case you haven't noticed it as yet Hiromoai-san, Asahiko-san's dead. So that's what changed and has forced the sale of his honorable construction company. Errr... please forgive me Hiromoai-san, but what Asahiko-san had meant at that meeting held between the two of you, when he said his company was never going up for sale, was his company would never be on the selling block if you could get your miserable filthy hands on it. Asahiko-san made that point painfully clear to me on many different occasions, before he took his own life.

"I'm terribly sorry to inform you, but it's already too late for you to entertain any such dreams of purchasing Asahiko-san's construction company to add to your worthless trust. I must admit, if you had acquired his honorable company that would've surely made you the most powerful construction businessman and company in all Japan. That's a real pity there Hiromoai-san. It seems that you'll have to look elsewhere to expand your loathsome dreams and want to command all the construction taking place in Japan." Nagaro had all he could do to avoid smiling at the dilemma Hiromoai was suffering through. He completely ignored the fact that Hiromoai had failed to add the 'san' to his name the last time he mentioned it.

"When? How in hell did this sale come to term so quickly, Nagaro? To whom did the old fool sell his damn business to? How the fuck could he have possibly sold his cursed company so rapidly? How the hell did the old fool get around all the confusing laws of selling a business in Japan so quickly? Something's wrong with this supposed transaction Nagaro, and I'll get to the bottom of this damn sale if it's the last thing I do, dammit. I demand to know the coward's name of who slithered behind my back to rob me of Asahiko's miserable construction company!" he actually stuttered a bit and allowed his tone to rise as he glared at the smug looking lawyer who seemed to be thoroughly enjoying himself at his expense.

"Again, I'm really sorry to inform you Hiromoai-san. But I'm bound by professional ethics not to divulge the buyer's name to anyone at this time, especially to you. That privilege is up to the new owner of the Yurkowa Construction Company, if and when he wants to become known in our country. It'd be highly unethical for me to do so. Not only would I be betraying Asahiko-san's trust in my loyalty to him, but I'd also be betraying the privacy and trust of the buyer. Now was that all you wanted to speak to me about on this day, Hiromoai-san?" The lawyer shrugged as he slowly parted his hands and looked at Hiromoai, signaling him the conversation along with the meeting was over in the lawyer's eyes and interests.

"I warn you lawyer, you try my patience most unwisely. I piss on all ethics as I piss on the worthless feet of all lawyers who pollute Japan with their loathsome presence. I demand to know the name of this lowly god cursed buyer of Asahiko's foul company! From what part of Japan was this person spawned from, Nagaro-san?" he hissed through clenched teeth and balled up fists as he leaned forward and openly glared angrily at Nagaro, as if trying to burn a hole through in his forehead, to see the information he sought.

"Don't waste your breath with trying to intimidate my ass here, Hiromoai. I'm not some old man who has just lost his honorable son along with his will to live. I assure you, you'll find I don't scare as easily, mister." Nagaro suddenly snarled in the same tone that he was being spoken to by Hiromoai. The upset lawyer added the further insult of omitting the san to Hiromoai's name, to drive the hatred that he held against the man home.

"Mr. Wiseass Lawyer, I don't intimidate anyone. My threats have an uncanny way of becoming reality. I warn you further lawyer, don't underestimate my warnings against you, or the harm that they could do to you and your entire worthless family, or you'll pay dearly for that error in your judgment. Again, I demand to know the name of the fucking fool who bought Asahiko's worthless business out from under my feet, and I demand to know it right now, Lawyer." He growled savagely as he rose from his chair and then rested his hands flat on his desk, as he leaned over it and stared right in Nagaro's unblinking and angry eyes.

"Hiromoai, what the hell could you possibly do to my ass that has not been tried before against me that you think would scare me in any way, shape or form? As you can plainly see for yourself, no one before you has succeeded in hurting me in any way. Besides mister, I'm but an old man waiting patiently for death to wrap its icy fingers around my soul, and bring me home to rest with the gods of our country and ancestors. Huh Hiromoai, are you going to release your devil's kin against me as you have done against Asahiko-san and his honorable son and his respectful wife? Take that foolish look off your loathsome face this instant, Mister!"

Hiromoai was stunned Nagaro was aware of the power he held over Wind's spirit.

"Yes Hiromoai, I know all about this daughter of darkness under your evil control. Asahiko-san told me about this female assassin of yours yesterday, before he took his honorable life, along with your confession to him of having the power over this god cursed assassin, and sending it out to dispatch poor Tsutomu-san and his wife. Believe me Hiromoai, I begged Asahiko-san with all my might and heart before he killed himself, to allow me to seek his revenge for Yurkowa's death on your worthless head. It's only because of my blood oath sworn to Asahiko-san that you still breathe life. I'm not without my own contacts in the world of revenge, Hiromoai."

Now it was his turn to rise from his chair, and likewise he laid his hands flat on his desk and hunched over as he glared directly in the angry eyes of Hiromoai, with their faces only mere inches apart, and he hissed at him as nastily as he could possibly muster. "Take your fucking hands off my god damn desk, before I lop the fucking things off their repulsive stalks!" The strength in the lawyer's voice actually forced Hiromoai to back away a step.

"It's fucking time that you know what the hell I and Asahiko-san thought of you, and this detestable and evil spirit you called back from the fires of hell and damnation. I hate you with all my breath I hate you for what you have done to poor Tsutomu-san and his wife. I hate you more for what you forced on Asahiko-san's honorable soul and spirit. The only reason he decided to kill himself was because he couldn't live with the marring stain and terrible shame of outliving his beloved son. And it's only because of my sworn oath to Asahiko-san that I don't go to the police with this information I possess, and have you arrested like the common criminal that you are. But I warn you in no uncertain terms Hiromoai, send out your hell's spawn hatred born from the armpit of the Devil Kami's body out against me, and see what happens to her and you. I'm not without connections to the underworld of my own I warn you a second time, Mister!

"I swear on the book of the Gods before this evil assassin successfully kills me, your foul and loathsome body will be sliced in so many little pieces that the hated and feared Tengu wood goblins wouldn't find enough of your worthless soul left to rob and feast upon. I fear not your unholy assassin or your evil stare! My loyalty to Asahiko-san is all that stands in my way of placing the revenge you so rightly deserve upon your loathsome shoulders, Hiromoai. Get the fuck out of my god damn office before I forget I'm a gentleman of respect and honor, and have you picked up and then pitched out of my office by your miserable heels!

"I said get the hell out of my god damn office and never return, because if I even see your face in my presence again, I'll have you arrested for trespassing. It gives me the greatest of pleasure to sell Asahiko-san's construction business before you were able to work your hostile takeover on it, if that was what you planned to do in that worm ridden evil mind of yours. And the further insult I offer you is the business was sold to an American, Hiromoai!" The lawyer glared so angrily at Hiromoai as the information of an American buying Asahiko's business hit him with the force of a sledgehammer to the side of his head, and it caused him to take his seat and stare back in awe at the lawyer who was staring at his with so much anger locked in his eyes.

"Ahhh so Hiromoai... I see by the stupid expression stuck on your cursed face that you don't like the fucking idea of an honorable Japanese business going over to an American, huh? That's right Hiromoai, I can't tell you the great pleasure it gave me to sell Asahiko-san's construction company to a fucking Gai Jin, fool. A fucking Gai Jin, Hiromoai! Remember that word for the rest of your miserable existence upon this earth, Hiromoai, Gai Jin! Allow it to eat into your befouled soul and dishonored spirit, because it's going to haunt you for all the remaining days you survive on this earth, and never leave your foul ears for a second of time until your timely death has wrapped its fingers around your worthless soul. Not even you would dare to send out your female killer against a Gai Jin in our country, Mister. I warn you Hiromoai, every second of the rest of your evil life, the word Gai Jin is going to be repeated in your worthless ears, until the word finally drives you insane with its echo, you sonofabitch you.

"As far as I'm concerned, you're nothing more than a god damn Yakuza, a fucking gangster Hiromoai, and this miserable assassin of yours is nothing more than your Kobun, your soldier of death. Before I die, I'm going to put a stop to both of you pieces of vile filth who pollute Japan's sacred air and soil with your worthless presence. I swear this to you Hiromoai with all my breath that I'll not rest at peace until the both of you lay rotting in your graves. Now get the hell out of my fucking office before I lose my better judgment and have you removed physically from my presence. Get out, god damn you to the fires of hell!" Nagaro suddenly roared as he pointed to the door as his secretary rushed in the office to see what the matter was. She never heard Nagaro raise his voice in such a fashion, let alone scream and curse as he was doing at Hiromoai.

"A fucking Gai Jin you offer to me, Lawyer?" Was all he was able to moan in a low whisper back at the fuming lawyer, because he was that stunned an outsider was now the proud owner of his most prized desire of Asahiko's construction company.

"You heard me right damn you, a fucking Gai Jin, a fucking Gai Jin Hiromoai. Nothing you can do because a fucking Gai Jin i9s the new owner of Asahiko-san honored construction company. Remember this until your dying day, mister. I'm going to shove this Gai Jin right down your miserable throat until you lose your foul innards over his taste. Now get out of my fucking office, dammit!" The lawyer roared again, this time in front of his stunned secretary, as he straightened up and waited for Hiromoai to get up and leave his office as ordered.

Nagaro's secretary was so upset by his sudden and extreme outburst she moved forward and placed her hand lightly on the shoulder of Hiromoai. A further insult aimed at him in an effort to guide him out of Nagaro's office as he ordered.

He spun his head around with such force at the secretary and glared savagely at her with all the hatred he could possibly muster as he snarled at her. "Take your filthy whore hands off my person before I have them hacked from your violated body, pig of the lowly Tea House!" He roughly pulled his shoulder free of her light grasp. He then rose from his chair, but before he left the office he turned to Nagaro and he snapped at Hiromoai.

"Go ahead and take you anger out on my poor secretary now. I'm certain you delight in beating up defenseless women as you delight in destroying honorable Japanese men by dispatching your devil from hell to kill the proud of Japan. As I just ordered you mister, get the hell out of my office and never return if you value your worthless life, Hiromoai."

"Lawyer, don't allow yourself to become too certain this fucking outsider will enjoy Asahiko's cursed company for any length of time. And don't think for a second you'll be alive to see the destruction of this loathsome outsider either, Lawyer. I assure you Nagaro, my revenge is vast and complete, and it'll fall upon many heads before I'm finally laid to rest in my foul grave."

"Huh, I told you before your vile and empty threats are wasted on me, Hiromoai. Why do you not try them out on someone who truly fears your loathsome thundering and ranting? Get out of my office gangster! Murderer!" He glared at Hiromoai until he was out. Then he turned and saw his secretary flushed over the terribly insulting words leveled against her.

CHAPTER TWENTY SIX

As Hiromoai stormed out of his office in a wild rage, Nagaro turned to face his extremely upset secretary and announced to her as he tried to get his rampaging emotions under control. "That will be all for now, I'm terribly sorry that you had to endure those terribly disgusting words of anger that I aimed at the worthless Hiromoai on my account, young lady. Why don't you take the rest of the day off? I'll handle the meeting with the American myself later on today."

"Thank you so much Nagaro-san, I'll do as you have suggested sir." The shaken secretary bowed, pleased she was able to leave the tension filled office for the rest of the day. She wanted to go home and pray to Lord Buddha to cleanse her spirit of what she heard said today.

What the lawyer and his secretary did not know was, Hiromoai hesitated in the outer office, and he heard Nagaro when he told his secretary he would handle the meeting with the American alone for later this afternoon. This information added to his wild rage and anger. He stormed out of the office in an uncontrollable rage. He headed for his car and slammed it in gear and spun the tires and swerved out in the flow of traffic, cutting off two cars and almost causing a pile up, as he shot past the cars trying to avoid his speeding vehicle. He wildly sped down the streets not watching the traffic, cutting cars off and going through red lights and carving his way through the traffic. His rage controlled his car, along with his wild actions.

He raced back to his apartment seeking the comfort only the ancient killing sword of his female weapon could offer him at this point. Wind's Breath was his only lover now, his mind screaming over and over the one phrase the lawyer yelled at him while he was leaving the office, ringing so loudly in his ears, as loud as if he just heard the words shouted at him from Asahiko's hated and worthless lawyer. 'Gai Jin'. Once inside his building, he marched over to his private elevator, raging curses and actually punching and kicking the walls of the brass elevator, as he waited for it to deliver him to his apartment. He charged into the apartment, ripping his jacket from his shoulders and threw it angrily at the floor with such force, if it had any real weight to it, it would have possibly gone right through the floor.

Lady Yoke saw the wild rage locked in his burning eyes and she rushed to his side, but what she received stunned her beyond her belief and understanding. When she got up to him, he spun around and without hesitation slapped her hard across the face, the force of the blow knocking her down to the floor. His rage was out of control and he kicked her in the chest with all his might. Then he pulled her back to her feet by her hair while screaming in her face, his face just inches from hers while he shook her head violently using her hair.

"Fucking worthless whore of the sinful world, the fucking Asahiko sold his putrid company to a cursed Gai Jin. God dammit, a fucking Gai Jin now owns the dead Asahiko's construction company, bitch of hell! I should've had the lawyer killed first like I wanted in the first place, but nooooo, you had to talk me out of that killing, bitch. I curse the fucking gods who control the world of Karma to the hell they have placed me in." Again, he slapped her hard across the face while still holding her head by the hair with his other hand.

Her lip split and blood flowed freely from the small gash caused by his hand. She was in shock from the way he was treating and beating her. She never dreamed he would ever lay his hands on her in this terrible manner. Lady Yoke stared in the eyes of her thought to be lover, not believing what was happening to her.

"This is all your god damn fault, whore of the pillows! Yours and that fucking ancient whore from the land of forgotten souls and wasted dreams, I should've never sent for her again in my life, dammit." Hiromoai roared as he continued to shake her head violently by the hair, all the while he slapped her across the face repeatedly with his free hand.

She made no attempt to protect herself for fear of making him even angrier at her. All she could do was try her best to protect her body from his onslaught.

"Your fault god dammit, and the fault of that bitch from wherever the hell she comes from, caused this damn nightmare to fall down upon my shoulders. Get the fuck out of my sight before I beat you to death for your failures to me. Your presence makes me sick to my stomach!"

He violently shoved her back by her hair and struck out and grabbed her by the shoulders and flung her to the floor by the kimono. The light and delicate silk fabric did not hold up to his powerful assault against her body. It ripped and this encouraged his attack further on her body. He pulled and tugged on the easily ripping fabric and in seconds she was naked and he rained blows down on the exposed flesh of her unprotected and battered body. It gave him pleasure to strike the naked and cowering young woman begging him to stop punishing her so. All he saw was the lawyer's angry face as he yelled 'Gai Jin' at him in his office.

Lady Yoke was covered with marring black and blue marks and bleeding from many scratches from his fingernails as she tried her best to cover her body from the beating from Hiromoai, now fearing for her very life. It was still an accepted fact in Japan, that a master had the duty to beat a servant in any manner if she or he was negligent in their duties to him, and he was making the best of his attack on the defenseless woman.

Exhausted, Hiromoai finally relented and stopped beating the nearly unconscious Lady Yoke. All the while he beat her he kept screaming Gai Jin over and over at her in his rage. While she was lying on the floor completely helpless, he kicked her in the stomach as hard as he could kick, and then turned and went into the study. There, he plopped down on the sofa and picked up the sheathed sword of the ancient female warrior, and he began to finger the crumbling zutsu wooden scabbard with his finger nails. He thought about summoning Wind from the Floating World of dreams so he could bring down his anger on her shoulders. He thought about sending for her only to order her to commit Suppuku in front of him. But his anger was starting to settle down on him, reduced from his terrible attack on Lady Yoke's body. Instead of summoning Wind, he slowly rolled the once so deadly ancient sword over in his hands while drawing strength from the mystical powers possessed by the sword of the deadly female samurai.

His thoughts were interrupted by Lady Yoke who was trying to struggle up to her feet. Every inch of her exquisite body was in pain as she stumbled forward trying to cover her nakedness with her bruised arms and remaining strips of the destroyed kimono she was able to cling onto. She was unable to straighten her body completely and remained hunched over slightly.

"Get on your damn feet and make me something to eat, whore of the lowly fucking world." He growled while not bothering to even look at the poor girl bent over in pain and agony.

"Hai Hiromoai-san." She cried in a weak and trembling voice. She was crushed beyond thought. She dressed in her finest lounging kimono and was looking forward to spending her first night with her dream of a lover. Now, the kimono lay scattered about on the floor, ripped to tatters and hanging in strips from her aching and battered arms and body. Her always dreaming of sleeping with Hiromoai was gone from her mind. She slowly walked to the kitchen and prepared rice cakes, raw fish and rice for her master's enjoyment. She never realized that she was naked her mind was numb from the terrible beating she received from her master. She did not dare take time to clean her minor wounds or dress properly for fear of rekindling his anger. When his meal was prepared, she carried it to him on a tray and knelt before his feet and offered him the tray.

This brought a sarcastic smile to Hiromoai's lips, this was the first time he was offered a meal by a naked woman. He forced her to hold the tray aloft while he picked at the food on the tray. All the while he stared at her bruised and battered body. He slowly slipped his foot out of the shoe and forced it between her legs, spreading them apart with his force. He raised his foot high and ran it over her breasts and when he could not take it any longer, he attacked her. He raped her violently, taking his anger out on her a second time. It thrilled him to so dominate her fine spirit. He did things to her he never did to any other woman before in his life. When he had his fill of her, he slapped her across the face and ordered her to dress and get out of his sight.

H was exhausted from his attack against Yoke and sat back on the couch, he still could not get the word Gai Jin still ringing in his ears out of his mind for an instant, it was eating him up alive inside. The other thing gnawing at the pit of his stomach was the fact that an American bought Asahiko's construction company out from under him. He could not understand how the old fool was able to get around the many confiding laws governing the sale of a Japanese company to an outsider, especially an American. He cursed Asahiko and what he had done to his once dream of becoming the most powerful businessman in all Japan.

He knew he was now going to be forced to deal with this American in the near future, if he had any chance of getting some kind of control of Asahiko's business. He gave a quick thought of going to the government and complaining over what he was certain was the illegal sale to the American, but this would open up too much speculation of his intent to get control of Asahiko's company. He was convinced beyond belief if he continued this unwise route, Lieutenant Motoshima would start poking his nose into his business more than he was already doing. He knew time was his enemy now. The longer this murder investigation went on by the police department, the more likely it was he would make a mistake and expose the fact he was the one in command of the female killer stalking the men he aimed her wrath at.

The young Japanese businessman gave into his mounting anger again, and he suddenly threw the ancient sword at the chair across from where he was sitting as he closed his eyes and pinched the bridge of his nose, in an effort to try and relieve the pounding headache that was consuming his entire body now. In no time he was fast asleep on the sofa, totally exhausted from the meeting with the lawyer, and then his uncalled for attack on Lady Yoke.

Yoke changed after bathing and cleaned her many nips, cuts, scratch and bite marks. When she was dressed she returned to the study and noticed Hiromoai was asleep. She covered him with a silk covering and then she returned to her bedroom to rest, and looked after her many wounds.

THE TOKYO HILTON, 3:10 P.M., ROOM 1041 SUNDAY, JUNE 9th, 1996

Calvin Batterman showered and then dressed in his finest power suit and red tie for his meeting with the Japanese lawyer of Asahiko. All the while he dressed and preened himself he kept an eye on the clock and cursed it for ticking time off so slowly on him. He was in a great mood and nothing could possibly change it, and he did not know what he was looking forward to more. Acquiring Asahiko's successful Japanese construction company, or spending the night with the two beautiful Japanese women who were just old enough to be his daughters. He was combing his hair when he heard a knock on his door. "Yeah, come in and put the damn towels on the bed for me will ya boy. It's about fucking time you showed up with the damn things, I called for the extra towels nearly fifteen minutes ago, buddy."

Lieutenant Kenzaburo Motoshima and Sergeant Toshihiro Okamatsu entered the luxuriant suite and waited in silence in the living room for Batterman to appear.

"You bring me any extra fucking bars of soap with those damn towels, buddy? I asked for more of the small shitting things." He barked from the bathroom.

"No, I didn't sir!" Lieutenant Motoshima barked back at the American in the bathroom.

"Gees, and why the hell not dammit, I told the fucking front desk that these pussy ass tiny bars of soap you keep leaving in the bathroom, don't last me a full shower, man. I shoulda brought my own damn soap with me from America for Christ sake." Batterman grumbled as he came out of the bathroom after placing the finishing touches to his hair. Seeing the two official looking men standing in the room he stopped dead in his tracks and said. "Oh."

"Mr. Calvin Batterman-san?" The Lieutenant asked politely of the stranger.

"Yeah, and who the hell are you, sonny? And whaddaya fucking want with my ass anyway, man?" Batterman snapped at the good looking young Japanese man speaking to him.

"Allow me to introduce myself, sir. I'm Lieutenant Kenzaburo Motoshima, and this man is Sergeant Toshihiro Okamatsu from the Homicide Division of the Tokyo Police Department, sir."

"What the fuck do you want with my ass for dammit? I didn't kill anyone, yet that is Mister." The American offered while trying to be funny with the police officer.

The smirking Lieutenant enjoyed a slight chuckle over his foolish remark as he offered to the American. "I'm sorry but we know you didn't kill anyone in Japan, sir. Yet that is! I'm here to inquire about your acquiring of the Yurkowa Construction Company, Mr. Batterman-san. Do you have a little time to spare for some questions I need to ask you, sir?"

"Now you look here buddy, I know how you fucking people don't like selling one of your businesses to an American, what the fuck do you people call us strangers in this country, yes, Gai Jin I think it is. Names don't hurt me in the fucking least, sonny. But having the damn homicide division investigate my ass just because I bought one of your damn companies is just incredible to believe, buster." Batterman almost called the police officers Jappers before catching himself.

Again Lieutenant Motoshima gave a slight chuckled as he offered to the angry looking and acting American businessman. "Yes sir, Gai Jin is the correct words for a stranger to Japan, Mr. Batterman-san. You surprise me over your knowledge of our language, sir. I was unaware you understood Japanese, sir. And no, we're not here to investigate the sale of Asahiko-san's construction company to you, sir. We're here to ask you some questions we wanted to know what if anything you might know of Asahiko-san's honorable death..."

"Asahiko's fucking dead, dammit man! I just spoke to the old man last night over the phone, Officer. When the hell did that happen, Lieutenant? Gees, I can't believe the old dude's fucking dead for Pete's sake. I kinda like the old gentleman you know, Officer. He was a wise and very shrewd businessman." Batterman offered as he stopped wiping his hands with the towel and then stared at the two Japanese police officers looking back at him.

"Yes I understand how wise and shrew a man Asahiko-san was and thank you for the respect you have offered for Asahiko-san, Mr. Batterman-san. Asahiko-san has met his death earlier this morning I beg to report to you sir. We believe he killed himself, Mr. Batterman-san." The Lieutenant replied, seeing the American was stunned and obviously did not know what happened to Asahiko. Already, he felt this route was a waste of time and effort on his part.

Batterman quickly got control of his thoughts and grumbled at the officer. "This morning you say, Lieutenant. God damn, he knew damn well I was coming to Japan today to take control of his construction company, sir. You think the sale of his business to me was enough to push him over the fucking falls enuf for him to kill himself, sir? I know it wasn't because of his company, Officer. I looked at his prospective, Lieutenant. His company's solvent as concrete sir, and it was making damn good money and rather large profits at that, and Asahiko was about to land some very lucrative contracts to boot with your government, Officer. Those open contracts were in the processing stage and as good as done with, sonny. The job's a given to his, err... my company now sir. Why the hell did the old man kill himself for, god dammit? I can't believe it, I just spoke to the poor man on the phone just last night, sir.

"Shit, I hope to hell there was nothing hidden in the selling his company to my ass now I got his business from the old gentleman. I got a mind to stop the transaction until I can find out why the hell the poor bugger killed himself last night, Officer. Suddenly I don't like this crap in the least, Lieutenant. I worked too fucking hard at trying to get control of one of your Japanese construction companies, and now that I have it, the guy I brought it from killed himself..."

"I assure you Mr. Batterman, there's nothing wrong with the sale of Asahiko-san's honorable construction company to you, sir. I only stopped here to see if you were aware of Asahiko-san's death, or if he might have informed you of his plans in advance to kill himself, sir. That's all Mr. Batterman-san." The concerned Lieutenant Motoshima pleaded as he interrupted the American's complaint, sorry he decided to approach him in the first place, and ignoring the terrible way this foul man was speaking to him about Asahiko.

"Yeah, I got a meeting with Asahiko's lawyer scheduled for a little later on today, Officer. I believe his name's Naga something or other like that, sir. Damn, Asahiko's dead, gees sir." Batterman grumbled as he slowly shook his head and ran his hand over his chin.

"That's Nagaro-san Mr. Batterman-san. Shigeru Nagaro-san is errrr... was Asahiko-san's lawyer, sir." Lieutenant Motoshima offered politely to the American businessman.

"Yeah, that's the bugger's name alright, thanks for clearing that up for me sonny." Batterman nearly bit his tongue, wishing he could retrieve the insult he just leveled at the Japanese lawyer. He knew how the Japanese were about being insulted, especially from an outsider.

Lieutenant Motoshima smiled to himself as he ignored the rude remarks from the uncouth American a second time as he asked him. "Do you mind if I ask you what time this meeting's scheduled to take place later today, Mr. Batterman Sir?"

"Look Lieutenant, if you wanna keep talking to me fella, you gotta do me a favor and start calling me Cal, if you wanna keep my attention. The meeting's scheduled for four forty this afternoon, sir. Why Lieutenant? You want me to not go to the damn meeting, Officer?"

"No Cal-san, please keep your appointment with Asahiko-san's honorable lawyer, sir. What's scheduled to take place at this meeting?"

"Man, that's worse than that fucking Batterman-san crap you keep calling me, Officer. Look Lieutenant, at this meeting we're scheduled to finalize the contract that'll give me complete control over Yurkowa Construction Company. Why sir?"

"Just wondering Cal." It was strange for the Japanese Detective to omit the 'san' from anyone's name he respected.

"Is there any reason I should put off the meeting with the lawyer? I don't want to cross you guys up in your investigation of his death, if that might be a consideration from you sir?" Batterman stated as he continued to stare at the officer while waiting his reply.

"No Cal, by all means you must go through with your scheduled meeting with Nagaro-san for later on today, sir. He's a most honorable and just man to deal with I assure you sir. It'll be most interesting to have an American businessman running a Japanese company in Japan for a change, sir. I'd like to see how well you'll do with the company, sir. We wish you good fortune in all your endeavors in Japan, sir. Please excuse me for wasting so much of your valuable time and causing you any alarm, Cal. Welcome to Japan, Mr. Batterman-san." The Police Detective bowed as he and the Sergeant backed to the door of the apartment.

"Hey man, it's no fucking problem sonny. You can come by and speak to me anytime your heart desires, pal. I have nothing to hide from the cops, especially the Japanese cops, sir. You guys wanna drink or something to eat before you takeoff? I have a well stocked bar in this dump, Officer." He made a motion with his hand towards the wet bar in the corner of the living room.

"No Cal, we're fine sir, thank you for taking time to speak with us over this terribly disturbing matter, sir. We'll not be bothering you again unless you have need of our services somewhere along the line, sir." The Lieutenant bowed a second time as he handed Batterman his business card, and cursed himself for not offering the card to him when he first walked into the suite. He hoped the American did not pick up the minor insult he made against him.

When they were finished speaking, he and the sergeant turned and walked out of the apartment as quickly as they had entered. After he checked his watch and noticed it was nearly time for Batterman to leave, to make it to his meeting with Nagaro in time. The last thing he needed was the lawyer being angry with him for detaining his American friend and disrupting their dealings.

Once in the hallway, Lieutenant Motoshima complained at Sergeant Okamatsu. "Well Sergeant, I believe that was a complete waste of our time and effort. Batterman doesn't seem to know a damn thing happening here. I should've known better, but we had to speak to him anyhow, so it's good we got that much out of our way. But I'll tell you this much Sergeant, if the fool tries to talk to our Japanese businessman or his future Japanese clients the way he spoke to us, I don't give his company two years before it goes out of business. No self-respecting Japanese person would ever allow themselves be talked to in such a disrespectful manner."

"I know that for a fact Lieutenant. What's our next move on the Go board, Lieutenant Motoshima-san?" The Sergeant asked his commanding officer as he smirked at him.

"Sergeant, I believe we're going to check out the background of Asahiko-san very carefully. To make certain that he was not the type of person to be controlling this evil assassin's despicable actions? I hate like hell to think he might have lowered himself to deal with god cursed assassins. This case is getting to be one royal pain in the ass, that's costing me much sleep and a lot of overtime." The Lieutenant let out his breath as they headed for the elevator.

Batterman heard the elevator stop on his floor and knew the officers were gone, and he started breathing properly. At first, he thought this was a ploy on Asahiko's part to renege on the sale of his business. Then he thought about it and felt killing himself was pushing the plot way too far in this rapidly unfolding drama. He shrugged it off for he did not care a lick if Asahiko was dead or not. All he knew was, he owned the prime Japanese Construction Company, and only an act of God was going to change that fact. He waited a few moments longer to make certain the officers were gone, and then he headed for the elevators for his meeting with Asahiko's lawyer.

Outside his hotel, Batterman jumped in a taxi and ordered the driver to go to Twenty Four, Terukiyo Drive. The driver nodded and drove off without replying to Batterman's orders. It took fifteen minutes to reach his destination. He checked his watch as he got out of the cab and flipped the driver an American twenty and told him to keep the change.

It was four thirty and he was ten minutes early for the meeting. Rather than enter early and showing the lawyer he was anxious about closing the deal, he decided to walk over to a newsstand and kill off some time. Batterman looked around for some girlie magazines, but found none. Everything was in Japanese so he made like he knew the language as he picked up a newspaper and checked the headlines. It was telling of Asahiko's death, but he did not have the slightest idea what he was looking at. When the operator growled something at him in Japanese, he dropped the paper down on the stand and quickly walked away. He checked his watch, it was four thirty five and he decided to enter Nagaro's building. His office was on the third floor and by the time he arrived, he ended up being a few minutes late for the meeting.

Nagaro was in the outer office waiting for Batterman to arrive. The moment he saw the large
American come in the room he smiled as he put his hand out and they shook hands.

"Mr. Batterman-san, it's a pleasure to meet you at long last, sir. I have heard so much about you from Asahiko Yurkowa-san that I feel I know you already, sir." Nagaro offered as he bowed to the American and then led him to his office. His hatred of Hiromoai was making it so much easier for him to show more than gracious kindness to this American invader to his country.

"Yeah, it's good to place a face to the voice on the phone I wanna tell ya, sir." Batterman snorted as he handed his business card to the lawyer. Instantly, the lawyer gave him one of his cards and smiled because he was surprised the American knew the importance of giving him one of his business cards. To be first to offer a card gains face over the other.

The lawyer did not know what the American meant by the remark about a face to the voice, so he let it go unchallenged. Nagaro did not allow the ways of the foolish Americans to make him question himself. He waved his hand out before him and then lead Batterman to his office, once seated, he snapped eagerly at the lawyer.

"Nagaro, what's this crap about Asahiko killing himself last night sir? Is it true shit sir?"

Nagaro disregarded the insult of omitting the 'san' to Asahiko's honorable name by the rude American as he offered calmly. "Yes Mr. Batterman-san, I'm terribly sorry to offer the story you heard about Asahiko-san committing Suppuku is true sir. It's terrible, just terrible Asahiko-san took to end his life in the ancient ways of our proud past, sir."

"Why in unholy hell did he kill himself for? Dammit, with all the cash I just gave him, wow. He coulda lived on the top of the world with that much money for years, sir."

"It's a long and most sad story to offer to one who is so new to our great country, Mr..."

"Give me the short version." Cal interrupted, not really interested why Asahiko killed himself.

"Very well sir, you see Mr. Batterman-san, it started a few days back when we were..."

"Let's hold the horse in the stable Mr. Nagaro. If we're going to do business together, do me a favor and call me Cal, and hang onto the san crap for your Japanese pals, please."

"As you wish it Cal." Nagaro mumbled with a slight bow, already disliking the crude American immensely as he continued with his words without missing a beat. "I'm sorry to inform you sir, but Asahiko-san chose to take his honorable life because his number one son was killed in a frightful accident, sir. The pain of outliving his son was too much for Asahiko-san to bear. Terrible, it's terrible for a father to outlive his honorable son. There were also some pressing medical problems that caused Asahiko-san to take his life as well, Cal."

"Yeah, I guess I can understand that easy enuf I believe, Mr. Nagaro. Does this hamper the sale of his business to me in any way, sir?"

"No, not in the least Cal, I have everything ready for your signature to be placed in the proper positions on the contract, sir. All you have to do is sign these two pages, here and here, and the company and all assets of that company will be yours to enjoy, sir." The lawyer spread the pages out before the American on his desk, and pointed to where he had to sign them.

"Once they're signed you'll be in complete control of Yurkowa Construction, sir. Will you change the name of the company, and the board once you take command of the company, Cal?"

"Naw, I think I'll leave the name the way it is. Sort of pay some special honor to the old man and his poor kid." The American replied without showing much compassion in his voice.

Nagaro's eyebrows arched slightly, he was that surprised to see anything resembling honor and respect coming from this insulting and crude American person. Perhaps, there was hope for the Gai Jin's from across the sea to become civilized in the future years of their existence.

When the papers were signed to the satisfaction to both parties, Nagaro turned over the personal chop of Asahiko, his seal as he offered. "Mr. Batterman, you're now the proud owner of Yurkowa Mining and Construction Company of Japan, sir. A very successful and strong construction company that carried out business most honorably in Japan for over thirty five years, welcome to Japan sir." The lawyer rose and bowed to the American. In another show of respect, the American rose from his seat and returned the bow as graciously.

CHAPTER TWENTY SEVEN
HIROMOAI'S APARTMENT IN THE
HATANAKA TOWERS

It was late by the time Hiromoai was able to get his temper under control. Thinking of his actions, he felt terrible that he took his anger out on Lady Yoke's poor body. He was looking forward to spending the night exploring her sexual treasures. He was ashamed to even look at her, when she entered the study to see if he needed something, or wanted her to do something for him. He pretended he was asleep.

The moon's faint shadows danced across the floor of the study and he looked at his watch. It was nine forty five p.m. He was amazed it was so late and found himself questioning where the time had gone. He was starving, but did not ask Yoke to fix him something. Absentmindedly, he searched the study for Wind's sword. The only thing that gave him peace was Wind's Breath.

When he was in his rage he threw the magnificent sword at the wing chair, but the ancient weapon hit the chair with such a force it flipped in the air and ended up tumbling over the back of the chair, coming to rest on the floor behind it. He got off the sofa and walked around the chair in search of the fearsome killing sword of Wind.

The moment she heard some stirring from in the study she rushed to the room, she immediately dropped down to her knees and bowed before Hiromoai. She remained locked in that position and would remain that way until he chose to address her. She was scared to death he was still angry with her, and if he was she was prepared to take her life in the old way by plunging a knife into her throat over the shame of failing her master. She was not allowed by ancient law to address her lord if he was angry with her. Her destiny was resting solely in his hands. To have her wanted lover angry at her would be too terrible an insult to live with.

He ignored Lady Yoke locked in her bow as he continued to hunt for the missing sword, seeing the handle protruding from under the chair he reached down and freed the weapon from the chair's grasp. He walked around the chair flipping the sword from one hand to the other, as he moved to his perch on the sofa. He still ignored Lady Yoke locked in her respect of him.

From her kneeling position, the trembling young woman sneaked a quick peek at what he was doing. The moment she saw him moving the sword in his hand, she closed her eyes and feared he was going to lop her head from her shoulders, because he was still angry with her. It was his right to take her life if he felt she failed him in her service to him. Tears squeezed from out of her tightly closed eyes as she shivered, and prayed to Lord Buddha. It was not too much of an insult if he chose to kill her, because he held Wind's ancient sword in his hands. If she had to die to make amends for her errors, she was pleased she was going to die by Wind's sword. In her mind, she believed this would make it easier for Wind to find her once she entered the Floating World of forever waiting, and then she could assist her in searching for her resting place.

When he finally recognized her presence in the study, he noticed she was shivering and crying in fear. He went to her, using the sword to lean on as he reached down and lifted her chin with his fingers and said in a calm tone. "What's wrong Lady Yoke? Did I hurt you that much? I'm sorry I acted like such an uncivilized monster. I pray to the gods that you find it in your heart to forgive me for my criminal actions committed against you. I was so enraged I took my anger out on the one I trust more than life. I hope you can find it in your heart to forgive me, young lady."

Lady Yoke suddenly lunged forward and she wrapped her arms around his feet and hugged them to her, as she cried and laid her body out flat on the floor. "No Hiromoai-san, you must never apologize to this old woman who should be serving the lowlife of Japan's back streets, for her terrible sins committed against your person. I have failed in my duties to you, and for this I was justly punished by your hand for my failures. It's I who must apologize to you for my failures to you. Please Hiromoai-san, you must forgive this lazy old woman. If you don't forgive me, I'll throw myself upon the fires of hell, Hiromoai-san."

He drew in his breath and then he mumbled softly to her. "Nonsense Lady Yoke, you have done nothing you need to apologize to me for. Get on your feet because it's not necessary to bow to me." He helped her to her feet and hugged her.

She melted wrapped in His strong arms, sobbing against his powerful chest. In her mind she thanked the Kami for allowing him to forgive her failures committed against him. She was so in love with him that her eyes no longer recognized any wrong he could have possible committed against her or anyone else living in Japan, he was perfect in her eyes.

"How about I take you out for supper? I feel you deserve spoiling after what I done against you. I have much I must make up for." He asked her as he placed a warming smile on his lips.

"Hiromoai-san, I prepared a meal for your enjoyment. I prayed to the Kami who control such things, to make the meal to your liking. I'd be most honored to serve you as you desired earlier this morning, Hiromoai-san." She cried as she looked in the eyes of her lord and master.

"You'd still honor me after the horrible way I have acted towards you earlier today, Lady Yoke?" He asked, stunned she would want to do anything for him any longer.

"Ieeee... Hiromoai-san, am I a mean old woman of the lowly dogs I wouldn't serve my Master on any day he desires? No, I'm a proud Japanese woman with the proper upbringing and manners. I know how to serve my Master. Please, allow me to serve the meal I prepared for you to enjoy, the way I think it should be served for your enjoyment." She offered with a slight bow.

"Very well then Lady Yoke, I'll enjoy any meal you will prepare for me. Perhaps we can still explore each other's desires. I need to be with someone tonight, I fear I feel so alone and used, Lady Yoke." He replied as he returned the smile she was offering him.

"Please, you must allow me to be that someone you need to lean on and be within your time of need, Hiromoai-san." Lady Yoke offered as she led him to the kitchen. The meal was set out on the table sitting on warming trays. She smiled as he placed himself in her hands.

He allowed her to lead him to where he was to sit. Once he was seated, she stepped back and stared at him. When he smiled, she went in action for her soon to be lover. Slowly, she sexily wiggled out of her kimono. There, she stood before him naked except for the pair of thigh high black nylons made in the United States, something she was aware he enjoyed whenever he saw a woman wearing them. She reached out her hand and took a spoon of warm Sake from the cup, and she smeared it across her nipples and then she moved to Hiromoai, and allowed him to lap up the wine with his tongue.

Lights exploded in her mind as he paid attention to her breasts with his tongue then his hands. He was enjoying playing with her breasts and making the most of it.

The night was nothing more than a blur of twisting bodies covered in sweat and burning with wild desire, with Lady Yoke and Hiromoai enjoying each other's sexual charms for many hours into the night. He awoke the next morning lying on the study floor for the third time in less than a week. This time he was sleeping with the battered Lady Yoke who snuggled in close to him to steal some of his body warmth, because she was naked and the night was a bit cool. He tried to remember how they ended up on the study floor. Try as he might he could not remember anything but the long hours of wild lovemaking of last night between them. He tried to sneak his arm out from under Lady Yoke's head, but the movement immediately woke her. His arm was on pins and needles and he needed to relieve the intense pain it was causing him.

Lady Yoke looked in his sleepy eyes and smiled as she purred in a dreamy state. "What's my lover trying to do, start my motor running again on me? Hiromoai-san, you have worn me out to a frazzle with your wonderful knowledge and skills of pillowing one for pleasure."

"I'm sorry little one, but my arm's asleep and I have to go to the bathroom. Besides young lady, I want to find out what time it is and read the morning paper, so I know what's happening in the world. I want to see if the paper has anything written about Asahiko's timely death." He offered as he got up on an elbow and ran a finger along the side of her smiling face.

"Please Hiromoai-san, allow me to make you breakfast before you leave for the start of your work, my wonderful lover." She purred at the powerful Japanese businessman.

"Thank you kindly, that'd be nice, I'm starving. I haven't eaten or slept right since finding this ancient Warrior, and starting my revenge trip against Asahiko's family and worthless company." He replied with a hint of anger etched in his tone as he struggled to get up and headed for his bedroom. When he came down wrapped in an expensive kimono, he walked to the kitchen. He was surprised to see Lady Yoke cooking with just a lap apron on. It was thrilling to see her firm breasts swaying gently as she whipped the eggs on the stove. He walked up behind her and ran his hand down her rearend, one only the gods could have perfected by their handicraft.

"Hmmm... you are spawn from the devil's armpit, Hiromoai-san. If you're not careful my lover, I fear you'll have me wanting to lay with you again, though I feel my body will not be able to keep up with you, my lover. You have worn me out in ways never imagined by this foolish woman. It was lovely, a pillowing I'll remember for as long as I live, Hiromoai-san." Lady Yoke purred happily trying to build his ego by admitting he worn her out last night making love.

He smiled as he gently cupped her breast and then he sat at the table and was surprised to see the morning paper folded neatly on the table before him. He stared at her and asked at the same time. "Little one, don't tell me you have dared to step outside my apartment dressed like that? If you did I fear for my neighbor's health."

"Huh, why not Hiromoai-san, if anyone outside has never seen a naked woman then they wouldn't know what they were seeing this morning, if they did then they enjoyed themselves, and I set their day off perfectly for the fools, no my lover?" She snickered as she sexily wiggled her hips and smiled at him over her shoulder, as she went back to caring for his breakfast.

"Huh little one, and you call me the devil's armpit? Your sexual appetite has out surpassed mine." He retorted as he scanned the headlines of the newspaper. Instantly, his eyes locked on the paper. In bold print it screamed out the name of the American who bought Asahiko's company. Anxiously, he read the article as his temper rose, committing the name to his memory.

He stared at the American's name highlighted so boldly in the newspaper, 'Mr. Calvin Batterman, the proud new owner of Batter and Batter Construction Company of the United States. It was even placed above the story telling the world about Asahiko's honorable death. In a huff he angrily crumbled up the newspaper and was about ready to throw it to the floor, when he realized he did not find out where the Gai Jin was staying while visiting Japan. He smoothed out the paper as best he could and then finished reading the article until he found out Batterman was staying at the Tokyo Hilton. Controlling his rage, he dropped the paper on a second chair and then looked at Lady Yoke as he cursed the American invader under his breath.

She finished his eggs and carried them to the table and placed them before him. Her breasts smiling seductively as if whispering to enjoy their pleasures again and he cupped her breast as she placed the eggs before him and said. "Yoke, I think I'll be going out today after all. I intend to pay this lowly Gai Jin a visit. I want to see what his intent with Asahiko's business might be.

"Maybe, if Karma is on my side, I can wrestle the worthless company out from under the fool's feet before the Gai Jin has a chance to pollute it. I curse the old Asahiko's worthless soul to the fires of hell for all eternity, for daring to sell his worthless company behind my back, especially to a hated American of all people to sell his foul business to. I'll have my revenge on Asahiko's loathsome head if it's the last thing I do, even if I have to dig up his rotting bones and have them crushed beneath the wheels of my machinery, and the dust from his disgusting body scattered to the four winds of the earth. Then, I'll show this hated American fool the error in his ways for placing his nose where it doesn't belong."

Remembering the beating of yesterday at his hands, she flinched when she heard the rage returned to his voice. As much as she loved the man, she also feared him now.

He rose from the table without touching his eggs and then announced curtly to his new lover. "Lady Yoke, I have to dress, I believe I'll pay this repulsive American invader to Japan a visit without being announced, like I did with that miserable lawyer of Asahiko's yesterday. That was a very wise suggestion of yours Lady Yoke, and I'll use it again. But this time I'll use it against the American fool. I'll teach him a lesson when dealing with an aggressive Japanese businessman. If he's anything like a wise Japanese businessman, he'll see me. If not, I'll force my intentions on the foreign fool and see what he does about them, young lady."

"Will you be returning home for supper tonight, so I know what to prepare for your enjoyment, Hiromoai-san?" Lady Yoke asked, showing some concern while keeping her distance from him as long as the anger still showed in his eyes and voice.

"Yes, and I think I'll be sending for Wind later on tonight as well Lady Yoke. I fear that she might have a rather busy and most interesting night ahead of her, if my meeting with the detestable American dog eater doesn't go as planned." Hiromoai offered with anger in his tone as he turned and headed for the stairs to shower and dress properly.

"I'll be waiting your return home with bated breath, Hiromoai-san." Lady Yoke replied as she bowed and then watched him head for his bedroom again to change.

ROOM 1041, THE TOKYO HILTON, MONDAY, JUNE 10th, 1996, 10:20 A.M.

Calvin Batterman, Fumiko Kojima and Tomoko Harada were enjoying the soothing warm waters of the huge hot tub in his hotel suite, when there was a knock on the apartment door. All night long they celebrated his taking over of Asahiko's company. The endless supply of wine, beer and drugs flowed, so did sex and wild times enjoyed by the three of them.

Batterman was nursing a throbbing headache, and was busy watching the two women servicing each other from the rim of the tub. He heard the knock and thought about ignoring it. Then he remembered the police visit yesterday, and answered it himself. In case the police returned with more questions for him. He did not want to get on the bad side of the Japanese police, especially with him taking over Asahiko's company, and wanting to carry out business in Japan.

He wrapped a terry towel around his lower half and then he stumbled his way towards the front door of his room, but not before he made certain there was no trace of cocaine remaining out in plain sight. He then opened the door while rubbing his burning eyes, his body begging him for sleep and relief from the pounding headache. His eyes opened when he saw the tall Japanese fellow in the doorway. Just by his suit he knew this person was not a police officer.

"Yeah, what can I do for ya fella? Who the hell are you and what do you want with my ass? It's plenty early in the morning for a stranger to be paying me a fucking visit, what the hell brings you round here, buddy?" Batterman barked angrily at the tall Japanese stranger as he stiffened his body and assumed a linebacker's stance, ready to get on this stranger if he did not have a good reason for bothering him so early in the morning.

"Mr. Batterman I trust?" The good looking young Japanese businessman offered while ignoring the upsetting way the obvious foreigner just spoke to him. He knew this man was an American just by his looks and did not expect anything more from his putrid presence.

"Yeah, and thanks plenty for not adding that damn 'san' crap to the end of my name like the rest of you people do all the damn time. Like I asked, who the hell are you and what do you want from me, I'm rather busy, man?" He grumbled at the Japanese stranger at his door.

As if to empathize his remark, Fumiko suddenly ran out of the bathroom while giggling and naked, with Tomoko chasing right after her. Both women were soaking wet and Tomoko was trying to snap at Fumiko's rearend with a towel as they continued running through the suite.

Hiromoai omitted the san from his name as an intended insult aimed against him, not a favor as he looked over the broad shoulders of Batterman, and noticed the two young and beautiful women running around his room naked. He smiled, thinking this American businessman was not smart enough to know when he was being insulted. Again, he cursed Asahiko for selling his construction company to this ugly foreign man, and then he mumbled at him. "Yes, I see that you're rather busy at that, Mr. Batterman." The way he pronounced Batterman's last name, made it quite evident he was trying to be antagonistic towards the stranger as he added to his words. "Mr. Batterman, I'm pleased you were able to find some of the many luxuries and delights that Japan has to offer her businessmen and visitors to our country, sir."

"Hey look here pal, who the hell are you and what the fuck do you want with me, bugger! And what the hell do you know about my fucking business in Japan anyhow, pal?" Batterman suddenly snapped nastily at Hiromoai as he stepped a little away from the door, and then he took a more threatening stance against the newcomer standing in the doorway still smiling at him. One of his two large Japanese security guards moved nearer to the front door to intercede on any trouble aimed at his boss, but he was immediately waved off by Batterman. The American businessman wanted to see what this man wanted at his door.

"Please Mr. Batterman, I beg you to forgive my terrible lack of manner, and allow me to introduce myself. I'm Hiromoai Hatanaka of Hatanaka and Sons Mining and Construction Corporation." He immediately handed Batterman a business card with a smirk on his lips.

"Sonofa fucking bitch well why the hell didn't you say that in the first place, pal. C'mon in and make yourself comfortable, buddy. I know you won't believe this shit in the least friend, but I was intending to linkup with you sometime later on in the week, pal. You must be a fucking mind reader or something there to just show up like this and visit my ass here, man." The American snorted as he flipped the business card in the apartment, and dared to slap Hiromoai on the back. The card landed on the floor and remained there throughout their meeting.

His face turned red searing with anger over the American's insulting actions for daring to place his hands on his person. It was a horrendous insult for anyone to touch a Japanese person, unless it was in the act of love or of war making with him. He followed Batterman to the kitchen in silence and sat while he poured himself a cup of coffee and slurped it noisily. He never once offered Hiromoai anything to drink, nor did he really expect him to. He was aware of the lack of manners possessed by most Americans from across the water when they visit his country.

Fumiko stumbled into the kitchen in a drunken state and still naked as the day she was born, and she leaned all over Batterman's strong shoulders and back, totally ignoring the Japanese stranger as she complained at the American. "Cal, you come back to the hot tub and enjoy us again, we have more that we plan to teach you while we're entertaining you."

"Hey look honey but I'm kinda busy at the moment little missy, I'll come back to the room when I finish my business with this guy sitting here, okay honey." He actually shoved Fumiko rudely off his back with his shoulder away from him as he grumbled at her at the same time. "Beat it until I'm done with this one, but keep yourself hot and your motors running at full steam ahead in the meantime, young lady."

"Okay, but I must tell you Cal, it's your loss because you don't know what you're missing speaking with this man. Tomoko's motor is running." Fumiko looked at Hiromoai and she gave him a smile then ran off to join Tomoko, but not before she took another bottle of wine with her.

Hiromoai glared so angrily at the beautiful young female with raw hatred emitting from his eyes, silently warning her he felt she was betraying the honor of Japan by bringing pleasures to this filthy American newcomer. Fumiko ignored the terrible look which she seen on many occasions by Japanese men, and left the kitchen wiggling her naked rearend back at him.

When Fumiko was gone, he snapped at the American. "Mr. Batterman, you said you wanting to linkup with me later on this week. May I ask you why you intended to speak with me?"

"Yeah, sure pal. As you know by now friend, I just brought Yurkowa's Company." He grumbled and took a swallow of coffee and made a face, it was already cold.

He nodded, refusing to allow his anger to be displayed before the foul American.

"Fine, then I don't hafta go into that boring ass part of this conversation with you, buddy. The reason why I wanted to meet with you later on this week is because I'm planning to make a rather lucrative offer to purchase your company from you as well my friend. What the hell does the Japanese know about construction work anyhow, man? You people are better off playing with your fucking computers and little games for them damn things. Leave construction to the men with all the know-how to build things properly, pal." Batterman stared at the glaring Hiromoai, he liked it when he was able to read his adversary's thoughts, it made it so much easier to deal with this man, knowing he hated him enough to kill him right where he sat.

Hiromoai could not believe the sheer arrogance and forwardness being expelled from this uncouth American's filthy mouth, to assume he was going to meekly sell his construction company to him, was the most insulting notion he had ever heard in his life. It was a terrible insult and he was having some serious trouble digesting the offer. He suddenly leaned back in his chair and smiled more of a sneer and laughed as he stared back at Batterman.

"What's so fucking funny with you pal?" Batterman demanded hotly because he hated being laughed at by anyone as he stared so intensely back at the young Japanese businessman as he placed his cup down on the table, and then clasped his hands together.

"What's so funny sir? I'll be pleased to inform you what's so funny with me, Mr. Batterman. It's strange, but I came here to speak to you over the same matter..."

"That's great, so you're willing to sell your company to me, huh pal?" Batterman interrupted and quickly added. "That'll make it a lot easier for me. I hate when I have to resort to a hostile takeover, and the crap that goes along with such a shit move. Keep talking fella I'm listening."

Hiromoai again ignored the detestable manners being displayed by this loathsome American foreigner by his constant interrupting of his words, as he chose to speak with the Gai Jin even though he despised him as much as he did Asahiko already. "Quite on the contrary to your thoughts Mr. Batterman, I was planning to make you an offer for Asahiko's crumbling construction company, and relieve you of an Albatross bound to bankrupt you in the future. You're going to find Japan is an extremely hostile place in which to conduct your business, especially for a foreigner, sir. I assure you Mr. Batterman that there are not many honorable Japanese people who'll be willing to entertain dealing and work with an American in their own country, sir. Many will resent the fact that you brought Asahiko's business in the first place, sir."

"Well I got some bad news for them and your ass also pal. They and you better get fucking used to dealing with me a Gai Jin as you people like to call us, because I'm here to stay. So let me get this straight, you have no intention of selling your fucking company to me, huh pal?"

"None in the least, Mr. Batterman. Do you intend to sell your Japanese company to me, sir?"

"Not in the fucking least buster. I intend to become Japan's only fucking construction company in the entire nation, mista." Batterman replied wearing an ugly sneer.

"Then I believe we have come to an understanding between us, and we have no further business to conduct at this time. I'm sorry I took up so much of your, err... play time Mr. Batterman." He snapped sarcastically as he cast a quick glance in the direction the woman disappeared in, and added to his angry words. "One suggestion I have to offer you before I leave your presence, Mr. Batterman. Maybe, in the future we might even try and work together on a joint project that'd be most beneficial to both our companies, sir."

"Huh? Yeah, sure, now you're talking more to my liking, why the hell not work together to better both companies, buster. I'm only in this thing to make money, and expand my interests in your country, pal. Errr... nothing personal about it mind ya. But you know how we Americans are, and what we can't get with money, or a deal. We take it, even if we have to resort to hostile takeovers and the likes, pal." He warned as he rose with Hiromoai and led him to the door.

"Certainly, it's as they say in all countries, all is fair in the world of corporate business, Mr. Batterman. But don't be surprised if you find a hostile takeover bid for your company lying at your feet as well, sir. We have an old saying here in Japan, 'if you want it, go and get it by all means possible'." He made no bones about it as he openly glared at Batterman for a long moment, making a mental note of the two large body guards standing in the archway between the living room and kitchen. He was surprised to see the security men staying in the American's apartment. It informed him that this Gai Jin did not trust the Japanese either.

Batterman returned the angry look with one of his own, and then laughed as he slapped Hiromoai on the back a second time as he led him towards the door. "Sonofabitch, I like ya fella. Yes sir, I sure do like ya a lot, pal. If both our companies survive what we intend to do to them then I'd be looking forward to working on a joint project with ya, man. Thanks for paying me a visit buster, but as you stated moments ago. My play time is waiting for me in the hot tub."

Batterman practically shoved him out of his room and once he was back in the hall Hiromoai blew his nose, convincing himself he was getting rid of the invading stink of the American from his nostrils. He spotted another man standing by the elevators, obviously a security guard there who was also assigned to protecting the American's life.

Fuming, the obvious wise American businessman had surrounded himself with professional and very attentive Japanese bodyguards, and he headed for his car in anger. In the garage, he noticed another pair of Batterman's guards milling about the area, watching every move he made while getting in his car. He was already going over the different ways on how he was going to release his female weapon against him. This was going to be a problem, noting the security surrounding the American invader. He got the feeling the police were going to be keeping a closer eye on Batterman as well. And to kill him so close to Asahiko and his son's death, was going to point the finger of guilt his way. He knew he was going to be forced to make himself an airtight alibi for this American's death, and find some why around his security at the same time.

LIEUTENANT MOTOSHIMA'S OFFICE

Lieutenant Kenzaburo Motoshima from the Detective Division was busy reading the very complicated file on Calvin Batterman's background, and his work ethics he employed back in the United States. He received the file from the helpful American FBI operating in Japan. He made the request for the file when he first discovered the American's name, and he was buying Asahiko's honorable construction company. The Police Lieutenant wanted to know as much as possible about the stranger to his lands. Nothing written in his jacket caused him any undue alarm, twice in his life he was involved in some rather shady activities, but he was never brought to court over the supposed minor business infractions.

His company was very large and it was sued fifteen times for work not completed, and the company lost two of those cases in court, one cost his company nearly three million dollars, the second suit cost Batterman, three hundred and fifty thousand dollars. There was nothing strange for a construction company being sued, even in Japan it was a common practice. Lieutenant Motoshima smiled to himself as he remembered the young FBI Agent, and how cooperative he was to get the requested file for him. He wrote the name of the agent down on his rola-desk for future reference, just in case he had reason to contact the agent a second time over Batterman or this murder case. He glanced at the name, Robert Rossie.

He knew he was right about the boring American businessman ever since he first laid eyes on him. He did not and could not have had anything to do with the deaths of the Yurkowa clan, another dead-end for this endless murder case. The detective cursed as he threw the file down on his cluttered desk. Sergeant Okamatsu smiled, knowing he was not going to find anything on the American in the stack of papers he just read through to help him with this case.

"What the hell are you smiling like a jackass for, Sergeant? Don't you have anything to do around here to earn your damn pay, buster?" Lieutenant Motoshima demanded hotly as he glared at his Sergeant sitting across the desk from him.

"Nothing at the moment I'm afraid, Lieutenant Motoshima-san. It was a rather slow start for today's workload sir." The Sergeant offered as he smiled at him.

"Well take that nothing and go home and do your lady good. I'm giving you the rest of the day off, Officer. Are you going to attend Asahiko-san's funeral tomorrow, Sergeant?"

"Is that a question or an order Lieutenant?" Sergeant Okamatsu asked with a grin.

"An order."

"Then it looks like I'll be attending the funeral tomorrow, sir. What do you want while I'm there, Lieutenant?" he asked and then stared at his Lieutenant while waiting for his response.

"I want you to keep your eyes open and make note of all who attend the funeral. You know how it goes in these types of cases, Sergeant. Nine times out of ten, the damn killer or in this case, the killer's control might or will show up to view his handiwork. I want to know particularly if Hiromoai happens to show up at the funeral. Keep a sharp eye out for him there, dammit." Lieutenant Motoshima ordered his Sergeant as he held him in his angry gaze.

"Lieutenant, I'd really expect Hiromoai-san to show up at the funeral, sir. It'll be a terrible lack of good manners and a serious loss of face to him if he failed to attend it, sir. Hiromoai-san's father knew Asahiko-san for many years, and he has also worked with him on a number of construction projects throughout those years, sir. Even though they didn't much care for each other, they both respected and continued to work together, and once Hiromoai-san's father retired. Hiromoai-san ended up working on a number of projects with Asahiko-san's son..."

"Hate each other is more like it if you want to be correct about their relationship, Sergeant Okamatsu-san!" The Lieutenant snapped at his officer.

"Is hating each other enough to employ hired killers one against the other, sir?"

"Hate's a powerful strong emotion, one strong enough to cause the one harboring it to do things that he wouldn't normally do, Sergeant. As I believe is the case here."

"Then you still think Hiromoai-san's in league with this murderer, Lieutenant?"

"I don't know what to think about this damn case any longer Sergeant. Everywhere I look in this murder case, all I see is cement walls staring me back square in the face, and Hiromoai's name printed on those walls might I add. This loathsome killer's good, damn good and she leaves no damn clues that we can really sink our teeth in, and use against her that'll identify her or her damn stable. A footprint isn't going to get the job done for us in this fucking case." He complained as he took a quick breath then went on with his complaint. "Hiromoai's the only target I have, and until someone else comes along that's more convincing, I'm going to believe that he's the murderer's control, and I'm going to concentrate my efforts on his ass. Errr... how many officers do you have keeping an eye on his damn apartment, Sergeant?"

"Four each, day and night Lieutenant Motoshima-san." The Sergeant was a little upset because the Lieutenant was omitting the 'san" from Hiromoai's name when mentioning it.

"Good work there Sergeant, keep them on him like a flea on a dog's ear. If Hiromoai's guilty, sooner or later he's going to screw up, and that's when I'll pounce on his damn neck like a starving cat, and then I'll place a quick end to this damn murder case. We have to find the one doing hell's dirty work before she's able to kill again. Who could he possibly send this creature from hell after next I wonder, Sergeant?"

"Err... Lieutenant Motoshima-san, I was informed that Hiromoai-san visited the American who brought Asahiko-san's construction company earlier this morning, sir. One of my officers reported this to me before I came here, sir." The Sergeant offered shyly to his commander, afraid because he did not bring this fact up to the Lieutenant's attention earlier in their conversation.

He stared at the Sergeant for several long moments with his mouth hanging open while trying to collect his thoughts, and then he growled at him. "Well why the hell didn't you tell me this shit before now, dammit? Was there a confrontation between the two fools during the damn meeting, Sergeant? Why the hell would Hiromoai want to visit with his new competition so quickly? I'd think he'd want to stay far away from this new guy for a long as possible. "

"No, not at all sir, my Officer reported it seemed like a rather friendly enough meeting between them, although he was unable to tell what took place inside the American's apartment between the two, Lieutenant. But he did state that the American was smiling at Hiromoai-san as he left the apartment. I wasn't going to report it because it was so brief a meeting, sir. The American had two young women and a number of large bodyguards inside the room with him, sir. I figured the American invited Hiromoai-san there for the meeting. Why else would he show up at his room if he wasn't invited by the new owner of the construction company?"

"I can't believe this shit for a fucking minute because these two damn murder cases are going to be the fucking death of me yet, Sergeant Okamatsu-san!"

CHAPTER TWENTY EIGHT
HIROMOAI'S APARTMENT IN THE HATANAKA TOWERS

Hiromoai arrived home fit to be tied from his upsetting but brief meeting with Batterman. This time, Lady Yoke quickly disappeared to her bedroom to allow him a chance to work out his anger privately. Utsumi made himself scarce the moment he heard him beating Yoke yesterday, he left the apartment after Hiromoai, and he did not intend to return until tomorrow. He knew his boss well enough to know when to disappear to protect himself from his well noted wrath.

Although he was fuming, he was able to control his rage this time. He did not know what to do next. Asahiko took him by completely surprise by selling his company to the Gai Jin, but he was not going to give up on acquiring Asahiko's company that easily. He wanted to send for Wind and turn her wrath loose upon the American and the hated Nagaro. He wanted Nagaro's death as much as he wanted Asahiko's death now. He vowed to himself that he would get even with the hated lawyer for the way he had insulted him at his office yesterday.

Drawing in his breath he bellowed out. "Lady Yoke, I want to see you immediately!"

She rushed out of her room as if she was about to lose her life, trembling, tears already building in her eyes, and she was scared to death she was going to receive another terrible beating at the hands of her wanting lover. She rushed before him and threw herself to the floor and bowed, allowing her back to be exposed to him, in case he wanted to beat her again for any reason he deemed fit to strike her. She knelt before him and held it until he moved away from her body shaking uncontrollably, and she asked him with concern. "Hai Hiromoai-san. What is it you desire of this lazy and worthless person?"

He noticed her body being assaulted with trembles and asked while feeling bad. "Why do you tremble so before me, I have no intention of beating you ever again, Lady Yoke. I told you yesterday that was a terrible mistake on my foolish part. One I'll never allow myself to repeat against your person for the rest of my foolish life. Please, get to your feet, you must prepare for Wind's arrival on this cursed day. I believe I have further needs of her services very soon, and I must draw from her vast knowledge on how to attack this new enemy suddenly stalking me. Draw a hot tub for her and prepare some warm food and a cool drink also. I'll be sending for her momentarily, let's get a move on it young lady." He smiled pleasantly at her.

Lady Yoke let out the breath she did not realize she was holding. Hearing his calmer tone relieved her fear, knowing he was sending for Wind for work and not pleasure, served to relax her spirit further. As much as she loved Wind, she resented her spirit for sharing the bed with him. She rose and rushed to the bathroom to turn the temperature up slightly on the hot tub.

As she prepared for Wind's arrival, he went to the study. He picked up Wind's sword, and rolled it in his hands, while his eyes intensely studied the sword. He enjoyed the awesome power emitted from the antique blade, even though the weapon was in such dire shape at this time. Even now, it warned him of the deadly power it held in the dated weapon of death for countless years.

Slowly, he forced the steel shaft of Wind's Breath from the wood scabbard dungeon, and as the very tip of the blade pulled free of its prison, almost instantly a slight breeze arose in the large room. Loose papers drifted in the soft, blowing current. A light developed in the center of the disturbance and within a few seconds, he was able to see the first signs of the turning mass taking the form of the lovely woman. With each appearance of the ancient samurai warrior, the turbulence seemed to be a lot less violent. At the end of it, she stood before him naked and beautiful. He could tell she was well rested and ready to carry out his bidding.

The second her eyes focused on her new lord and master, Wind instantly dropped down to her knees the moment she was whole and bowed to Hiromoai, who was sitting on the couch waiting for her to take solid form again. He drank in her stunning beauty and then snapped at the warrior. "Wind-san, I have further work for you to accomplish for me on this night coming, but first we must discuss how you're going to carry out your next mission I'll send you out on. There are two enemies to be dealt with this time I offer you. Rise and face me so I can look in your eyes as I speak with you, Samurai. I have something I must discuss with you."

"Hai my Liege Lord, I have waited patiently for what seemed to me as a lifetime for your summons demanding my presence before you to do just cause against all those who have dared to insult you, my Master." Wind rose, unashamed of her nakedness and she walked towards Hiromoai still sitting on his couch watching her.

"Ahhhh... It's good to see you my weapon from the ancient past of Japan's glory. You're most pleasing to my eyes and desires, Wind-san. Your presence brings me great relief and pleasure."

"It is a pleasure for my spirit to once again be before your honorable presence, and breathe the sweet perfumed air of the living world, Hiromoai-sama. This is why I longed for a summons from you to be in your honorable presence again, my Liege Lord. What bidding does my Master have for this worthless Samurai to carry out for you?" the spirit announced to her master.

Lady Yoke appeared without being ordered and she offered Wind a clean light green kimono and obi tie to put on. Wind thanked her for her kindness and quickly wrapped the pleasing silk garment around her body, thoroughly enjoying its wonderful feeling of the fine fabric against her bare skin, but she failed to place the obi around her body to hold it closed. This action did not displease him he thoroughly enjoyed seeing her outstanding treasures.

"Enough wasting my time like this Wind, Lady Yoke. Wind-san, you made a foolish mistake on your last two missions for me. These mistakes have me extremely upset with your foolish actions. I don't know what to do about them yet. I thought you were much wiser than to leave something behind that the hated police can use against you and worse yet, use against me as well, Samurai." He growled as he glared angrily at Wind.

Her face turned to a mask of confusion, as far as she was aware, she made no mistakes carrying out her master's orders. Both men he sent her to destroy were dead in the fashion he had demanded from her. She bowed as she offered with concern lacing her voice. "If this foolish Warrior has erred on her missions and my Lord and Master is upset with me by my mistakes. There is only one course of action I must follow as deemed proper by my blood oath to you. I shall commit Suppuku to make atonement for my foolish mistakes, my Lord and Master."

"Yes, I assure you that course of action will be considered as punishment for these foolish mistakes in the near future, Samurai. But you spoke of atonement for these mistakes. You'll be able to erase these marring stains from your past actions, if, and only if you carry out my next orders faithfully, without errors this time Wind-san." He barked at the ancient warrior.

"Hai my wise Master, this I shall accomplish as surely as the wind shall blow on this day." She replied as she looked deeply into his angry eyes, waiting for him to tell her how she could make compensation for her past mistakes.

"Wind-san, you left a muddy footprint at both actions I sent you out on, and these footprints caused the nosy police to believe that you were responsible for Asahiko's death, as well as his worthless son's death. This mistake must never be copied on any future mission I dispatch you out on. You understand this Warrior?" he demanded from the female warrior.

"Hai, it shall be as you have just ordered of me." Wind repeated as she bowed to him.

"Very well then we shall lay this error behind us for the time being. Wind, the first of your next missions will be rather easy to accomplish for you. I want you to dispatch the disgusting lawyer who has so thoroughly betrayed me, by assisting a lowly Gai Jin invader to Japan to buy Asahiko's worthless construction business from under my feet. The second mission's going to be a little more of a challenge for you to accomplish. Your second target chose to surround himself with an active and very attentive security force. I fear he's wise and goes nowhere in Japan, does nothing, entertains no one without his security guards standing about him at all times."

"Then my Lord and Master, we'll have to devise a plan on how I'll breach this tight ring of security surrounding your next teki. I was taught that the only way to defeat an idea is with a better idea, my Lord. Nothing is impossible to accomplish if at first, one empties his mind of all thought and foolish restrictions. To think with a clear mind and eye will enable me to succeed in any venture I'm dispatched against, my Liege Lord."

"Yeah, that's why I wanted to discuss this future target a little further with you, before you hunt his evil soul down for justice. Before allowing you to move out against this target, you must know and understand everything there is to know about this worthless target. Come with me, I have some pictures of your first target to share with you." He grumbled with little patience in his tone as he waited for Wind to stand and then move over to his side.

She looked at the picture of the older man trapped on the glossy paper. He sort of resembled the one she seconded in death a few days before, but much older than this man in the picture as she questioned. "Where does this filthy one exist in the land of the living, my Liege Lord?"

"We'll get in that request a little later on in this conversation. First off Samurai, I want to go over the more troublesome target you must dispatch for my pleasure. He's a god cursed Gai Jin, a filthy outsider who has invaded Japan and wishes to deprive me of my just rewards in this life. Your first target is responsible for bringing the worthless Gai Jin to the shores of the Eight Islands of Japan. That's why he has to pay for his countless sins and disrespect, and for his disloyalty he displayed against me and my interests with his worthless life. I have met with the loathsome Gai Jin earlier in the day and he..."

"My Lord and Master, you offer to my worthless ears that you have just met with the lowly Gai Jin earlier in this day, my Lord?" she asked surprised.

"Yes that's how important Asahiko's loathsome business was to my future plans and company and my wants, Wind-san. It was a brief and most disturbing meeting that I carried out with the Gai-Jin at that, it informed me of where he stood and what he intended to accomplish with his..."

"My Lord, forgive my foolishness for daring to interrupt you like this, but you must inform me of everything spoken between the two of you at this disturbing meeting you spoke of earlier. I need to know everything that was said so that I might find something in this lowly Gai Jin's weakness." Wind dared to interrupt him a second time, showing him that she had concerns with the Gai Jin, and wanted to know more about him and their meeting. Her feeling she was helping her master, gave her the inner strength to dare interrupt him in this manner.

He ignored the lack of manners she just displayed before him by interrupting him twice in their conversation. It was more important for him to work out a plan of attack for her to utilize, than it was to respect one another during this troubling conversation. He thought for a few seconds while reliving his upsetting meeting with the lowly Gai Jin, because he felt it was not necessary to inform her of his attempting to buy Asahiko's construction company from the disgusting American, because he already alluded to that before. That part was his business was of no concern to her anyway. He told her of the words of no consequence, hoping she would be able to put something together for her attack on this man. There was no reaction from her until he reached the part of the talk when he offered to work on a joint project with the Gai Jin.

Again, Wind dared to interrupted her master by requesting of him not waiting for him to finish speaking to her first. "Hiromoai-sama, you have already opened the door in which I shall employ to destroy this unwanted invader to Japan's soul. It was a rather simple item to discover in the words you have offer this worthless Warrior, my Lord and Master."

He reacted with surprise to Wind's words, because he did not see any doors he might have opened for the samurai's use against this hated Gai Jin as he replied to her. "How is that?" Was the only thing he could think to reply to her.

Wind smiled at him as she offered in a rush of words, because she felt she was assisting her master much like she did her feared warlord of the ancient past. "Hiromoai-sama, you have offered for my knowledge to work on what you called a joint project with this one from another land. That is good and a most wise offer to make to the lowly Gai Jin, my Lord. If he survives wrapped up in this tight ring of security he surrounded him with. Then we'll have to bring him out of that protection through a very deceitful and cleaver plan. What better way to do this than by offering his greed as a medium in which to explore his weaknesses with, Hiromoai-sama."

This time He interrupted the ancient female samurai warrior as he snapped at her angrily this time. "What the hell do you mean by that load of crap you're offering to me, Samurai? I have no idea what the devil you're driving at in this endless conversation you're spewing forth at me. Explain yourself more clearly to me or fear my angry wrath falling down upon your head. I warn you Samurai, don't try my patience unwisely. I'm not in a good mood as it is, to be toyed around with in this foul a manner you're introducing to this conversation, could be extremely costly to your presence to dabble in words with me. I'm still very angry at you for your past mistakes Samurai, so don't add to that anger by stalling me any further, Wind-san."

Wind immediately bowed to her master, afraid she might have insulted her liege lord again. She decided to reply with one of her ancient proverbs. "Hai Master, a man can create a physical separation from the everyday world, and still be most attentive to its pulse, its life giving heartbeat. He can go to the remotest mountain cave in the world and still carry the world's knowledge with him. Hiromoai-sama, if you had the wisdom to offer this detestable one a joint project you are willing to share with him, I shall be successful on my new mission to destroy your hated teki wherever they hide in the world of the living. Call him and inform this lowly Gai Jin of the offered joint project, and then all you have to do is hide my killing sword in the area where you will be at large, and allow him to discover where it rests. The fool suffering from greed will dislodge my katana and then I shall react against his presence and eliminate him from your world and memory." Again, she bowed while waiting for him to digest her words.

"Hey wait a fucking minute here, Wind-san! I though you told me whoever held your damn sword, controlled your spirit and you had to obey that person no matter what. Why the hell would I want to turn over command of your services to my worthless teki? What the hell are you trying to pull off here Wind-san? This is a terrible suggestion you offer me, Samurai. Are your thoughts suddenly turning against me, instead of working for me? Are you turning against your true Lord and Master of this time, Wind-san?" Hiromoai glared at the nervous young yet ancient woman.

Wind dropped down to her knees again and bowed, allowing her neck to be exposed to the bit of the killing sword, because she was so stunned by Hiromoai's angry words aimed at her. She never dreamed to ever turn her back on who she believed was her lord and master.

"C'mon Samurai, now's not the time for that kind of crap. Explain yourself to me in most detail report so I understand where the hell you're coming from with these most confusing words you're speaking to me with, Wind-san." Hiromoai growled at her.

Now it was her turn to be confused by some of his angry words he was firing back at her so rapidly they were hard for her to follow. But she was still able to understand he was angry at her last suggestion. Wind dared to look at him from her bow, wanting to calm his anger for him.

Hiromoai was fuming and he hissed at her with rage lacing his tone of voice this time as he continued to hold her in his angry glare. "Get on your damn feet and explain to me why the fuck you want this god cursed lowly Gai Jin to control your great weapon of truth and justice, and over your fine spirit, Wind-san. Are you preparing to betray me with this loathsome Gai Jin, Samurai from the ancient past?"

"Ieeeee... my Lord and Master of time and existence, may my worthless spirit be laid upon the honored Do Dan, the ancient mound of sand used to support the body of a common criminal for the first sword test used to check on the weapon's sharpness. And the Kami who seek final justice against a dishonored Samurai, and they take turns chopping at my detestable loathsome body until there are no parts large enough to be recognized human, if I dare to plot any treachery against my Master of life and death. May my Kofun, my honored burial mound be desecrated by a gaggle of homeless Ronin filth if my heart is not true and pure, and I remain totally loyal to my Master of life. I live and I shall die in the spirit by the code of Bushido and I'll also…"

"Samurai, will you spare me the fury of your fucking righteousness for a few seconds, dammit. C'mon, I have no time for this kind of crap I warn you again, Samurai. Why the hell did you make such a thoughtless and foolish plan as to the one you have just put forth before me? I'm waiting for a good explanation from you, Samurai." He growled angrily, allowing his anger to grow further while he stared at the samurai from beyond life.

Wind was stunned by his angry words and she drew in her breath to help calm her rattled nerves as she offered in a rush. "I'm sorry if my confusing words have caused you bewilderment, or disturbed my Lord and Master's Wa. When I suggested that you allow this foul Gai Jin to discover my killing sword, it was the proper offering to make as I see it, Hiromoai-sama. As long as my Master draws breath while dwelling within the land of the living, you control my spirit no matter who may hold my Katana blade. It will take a special understanding by all the Kami who control what must be controlled to keep me just, to allow any worthless Gai Jin to command my warrior's spirit. I am of Japan, I am of all Japanese thoughts and beliefs, and only a Japanese person of the utmost honor and respect, can possibly order my spirit to do his bidding. Unless, like I have just offered to you Hiromoai-sama, the Kami deem it fit that I am to answer to any Gai Jin's call and orders."

He worked out her confusing words in his mind, and now he understood what she was trying to put forth to him as he replied in a much calmer tone this time. "Oh, I see what you're offering me Wind-san, and this plan's starting to take on good shape in my eyes. If I hide your Katana sword on the site and allow the filthy American find it. When he gives your spirit birth to the land of the living, you'll attack the fool without mercy and without his security standing in your way. I like it, yes I like it a lot Samurai. Good, very good, I'll do as you have offered to me. I knew I could count on you to come up with a good plan of attack, Wind-san."

"Forgive this worthless vassal my Lord, but I fear the security people protecting this loathsome man will have to be your problem to handle for this situation, Hiromoai-sama. You must find the way to make this foolish Gai Jin desire to leave his protective warriors behind, so you can discuss certain business conditions with him in private. Unless you wish me to eliminate his security forces before I deal with his worthless head, Hiromoai-sama?"

He shifted his weight on the couch, while he went in thought and after thinking about it for a few moments, he offered the extremely dangerous warrior of the past. "No, that'll not be good for you to consider. I can't possibly allow a blood bath to take place right in the center of downtown Tokyo, Samurai. It'll arouse too many police and politician's interests and anger I'd have to deal with if that were to take place. Hmmmm... I believe I can tell the foolish Gai Jin I want to show him a special construction project, a site I've been working on with Asahiko before he killed himself. A site that must be kept a secret if we want to land the job while keeping it from our competition, this move will force the fool to leave his security behind. Secrecy is an absolute must in our line of work, and I'm certain this fool understands this need. This is a good plan you have come up with, you solved my problem well, Samurai. We'll do this at the end of the work week. A Saturday is a good day to discuss business with my competition, Samurai."

"Hiromoai-sama, is this nefarious Gai Jin, this invader to our sacred land be that foolish that he would be so trusting of your words uttered to him?" Wind refused to use the word Hiromoai used when he was describing her target with. Besides, she doubted she could even pronounce the word 'American' correctly, and rather than chance insulting him by making another error before him, she chose to use the term she better understood, Gai Jin.

He allowed a slight smile to slowly cross his lips as he replied in a sarcastic tone to the ancient female warrior. "This American will do anything in his loathsome power to further his unlimited greed and evil wants as you have suggested in Japan. I had another thought though Wind-san, I think I'm going to allow the miserable lawyer of Asahiko to enjoy his worthless life for a little while longer, while we deal with the foolish American invader first. I believe it might be a much wiser idea to go after the worthless Gai Jin first. Then, when things cool off a little for us, you'll then be sent out to deal harshly with my other betrayer in this world of treachery, faithful Samurai Warrior of the past times of Japan."

"Yes my Lord and Master, it's a much wiser General who shapes the will of others to his desires and needs, while he prepares to take advantage of that foolish one and his evil interests. If it is as you have stated to me Hiromoai-sama, this most repulsive lawyer will have to wait for a better moment in which to meet his finally fate, and count his seconds of worthless life left to him to enjoy further until I stalk his detestable worm riddled soul, and rid this earth of another one of my Master's hated teki."

He glanced over at Lady Yoke for a brief moment and she nodded, informing him her hot tub was waiting her presence. He returned the slight nod as he turned back to Wind and said in a much calmer voice this time. "Wind-san, are you hungry? Are you in need of anything the living world has to offer its children who serve their Master's interests faithfully, Samurai? If you need anything, I'll be pleased to provide it for your enjoyment, Wind-san."

"Hai my Lord and Master, there is no need to eat in the land of the Ukiyo, but breathing in the cool air of the living world makes my body depend and require the necessities the living world endure and enjoy." She lowered her head she was ashamed to admit she was in need of anything.

"Fine Samurai, Lady Yoke has prepared an excellent meal for your enjoyment, but first you're free to take advantage of the soothing waters of the hot tub if you care to indulge in a soak." Hiromoai offered as he smiled pleasantly at the ancient warrior while he waited her reply.

Wind was placed in a dilemma by her master's last words she did not know which of the soul's face robbing sins she wanted to please first, the sin of the pleasure of the body, or the sin of feeding her soul of life giving nourishment. It was a samurai's belief that they must be willing to carry on with their master's bidding without the need for any food, sleep, or water if necessary. The master's needs were more important to the soul of the samurai than was life itself.

He saw she was having a problem trying to make up her mind and offered as he smiled a second time at the female warrior. "Wind-san, may I suggest you take time to enjoy the soothing waters of the hot tub first? While you're resting in the tub, Lady Yoke will place your meal on the table and when you're done enjoying a soak, you can then enjoy your meal at your leisure."

Wind bowed and then mumbled with respect to her lord and master. "Thank you for making up the mind of this foolish Samurai who was so blind to the many pleasures the living world enjoy Hiromoai-sama. It is as Lord Buddha preaches always, 'When walking, just walk, when sitting, just sit and above all, do not move unsteadily.'"

He had to shake his head because he was not certain if she was trying to force her Buddha beliefs on him or not. Although he was a Buddhist himself, he rarely paid much attention to the teaching of his age old religion, as he replied to this female weapon he summoned from Japan's past. "I told you before to keep your Buddha beliefs to yourself, Samurai. I see I'm forced to repeat this order a second time to you. What we have to accomplish in the next few days leaves no room for religion, or compassion to be respected, Warrior. Go and enjoy your soak, Samurai. Lady Yoke, you'll assist Wind-san, until she gets comfortable in the waters of the tub, and then you'll prepare her meal and return to my presence after that. I have some special needs of your services as well." His words showed Wind he dismissed her.

Lady Yoke's chest swelled with pride, hoping he was going to share her romantic interests when she returned to his side for the night after she looked after Wind's needs. She rushed the bathing of Wind's exquisite body, so she could sit in the waters of the bath. While she was bathing her, the samurai noticed the angry bruises on her face and shoulder, and decided to display ill manners by offering to the young woman attending her needs in a slightly harsh voice.

"Ieeeee... Lady Yoke, I see you have suffered with a minor accident to your body." The warrior was trying to strike up a conversation with her new found friend from the living world.

At first Lady Yoke did not understand what she was referring to, until she noticed what the ancient warrior was looking at. Unconsciously, her hand instantly went to her face to cover the bruise on the side of her cheek. She was thoroughly embarrassed by the dark and angry looking bruise, and the beating she suffered at his angry hands. Now, with this woman samurai making comments about the injury hurt her feelings further.

"Huh, do not be ashamed of awards won in battle of one's will trying to overtake that of another ones determination, Lady Yoke. It is a proud award for one who demanded from another to obey her wants and needs forcibly." Wind was trying to make light of the injury to her face, now she was sorry she drew attention to the mark marring Lady Yoke's lovely face, after seeing her reaction to her words.

"I'm sorry to announce for your knowledge, but the injury wasn't received in a battle over wills, Wind-san." She replied as she lowered her head and stared at the floor as if seeking to find a place where she could crawl under. She was ashamed of the marks adorning her body.

Wind stared at her for a long moment in silence, informing her further explanation was necessary for her understanding now. The warrior displayed her want to avenge the injury visited upon her friend's body in the land of the living by the unforeseen and unknown attacker.

Lady Yoke's eyes clouded over by sadness as she pleaded barely over a whisper to the suddenly concerned samurai, as she offered her friend. "Please Wind-san don't look at me with such anger held in your eyes. With terrible disgust and loathing locked in your honorable eyes aimed at me. It scares me to my soul when you look like that, Samurai."

"Now I demand to know who is the cursed animal who dared to lay hands on my friend in anger! Lady Yoke, I'll send his foul soul to the land of the dead for the gods to feast upon his repulsive being, until he can no longer exist even in the Floating World of wonder." Wind demanded of her as she continued to start at her.

Lady Yoke understood that she had to be completely honest with this extremely dangerous warrior, or this might get out of hand on her and she explained. "Wind-san, I'm terribly embarrassed to be forced to announce that it was by Hiromoai-san's honorable hand I was beaten for an infraction I had the misfortune to commit against his will and honor." Lady Yoke bowed the best she could to the ancient samurai sitting in the bath, and staring so intensely at her with demanding eyes, and a rage for revenge burning within her soul and heart.

Immediately, Wind's lust for revenge fled her body as she snapped nastily. "Huh, if the Master has chosen to beat you for this infraction you admit to then you deserved the beating he has delivered upon your person. I have no pity for someone who dares to insult their Lord and Master's honorable will. Hiromoai-sama was just to lay hands against you for this reason!" Wind almost turned her back on Lady Yoke, but she caught herself in time and with effort, she did smile pleasantly at Lady Yoke. Showing her that her friendship was more important than this minor infraction she obviously committed against Hiromoai.

Lady Yoke smiled back at her, glad the fearsome samurai was not angry at her any longer. She tried to get Wind to relax in the warm water. She gently applied pressure on her tight shoulders to get her to lean back in the tub and rest, and to regain her strength and calmness. Wind followed the suggestion of Lady Yoke's guiding and skilled hands. She did not want to be angry with her friend for any reason while visiting the living world.

While she was resting in the warm water, Lady Yoke nearly ran to the kitchen and heated her food and sake to enjoy when she finished her soak. When this was done she returned to Hiromoai resting on the sofa enjoying one of his expensive cigars while seemingly daydreaming.

Hiromoai turned to Lady Yoke as she entered and asked. "Is Wind taken care of Lady Yoke?"

"Hai my Lord, she's within Yasu, (peaceful) and in total Wa." (Harmony)

"Fine, Wind's Wa is important, I need her well rested and prepared to carry out my bidding against my teki. Tomorrow, I want you to deliver a message to the hands of the Gai Jin polluting Japan's consciousness with his presence in our country." He offered nastily to the young woman.

"Hai, it'll give me great pleasure to be of service to your needs and wants, Hiromoai-sama." Again Lady Yoke addressed him in the manner Wind spoke to him. She was unable to hide the hurt she was suffering, realizing he was not interested in her sexually this time. It made her sad, and she felt she was less than a woman, because she was unable to arouse him as any good women of Japan can usually entice their intended lover to pillow with them.

The rest of the day went by uneventfully, almost uninteresting. But the following morning Yoke left at exactly eight a.m. armed with the note, offering Batterman a joint venture to take place between his company, and that of the newly acquired Yurkowa Construction Company.

ROOM 1041, THE TOKYO HILTON, 8:30 A.M., TUESDAY, JUNE 11th, 1996

Calvin Batterman allowed the two young and beautiful Japanese women to return to their apartment for the day for a change of clothes, and to rest from their long night of drugs and sex. The women were going to return to his apartment at eight o'clock tonight for a second round of sex and fun. He was suffering from exhaustion from trying to conquer the two unconquerable women's endless sexual desires and youth. He was sitting at the kitchen table trying to regain some of his strength and absentmindedly stabbing at the eggs with his fork he ordered from the lobby kitchen. His head was resting painfully in his hand, pounding from too much drugs, booze and sex. His uninterested bodyguards were in the living room, one was reading a novel, the other watching TV. He intended to take this day off to in order rest and tomorrow, he was going to start to get down to business with his new construction company.

While he was suffering he was suddenly disturbed by the gentle knocking on his door. One of the guards rushed out of the living room and went to answer the knock. But he was waved back by Batterman, he opened the door and to his surprise, there stood a pretty young Japanese woman. Instantly he flashed one of his best smiles that left nothing to the imagination of what he was thinking of Lady Yoke sudden appearance, or of her exquisite body.

She blushed over the leering stare as she offered the folded paper to the American.

"What's this crap you're giving me here pretty one? Who the hell are you anyhow kid? Why the hell were you sent to my ass? Are you a gift for my enjoyment while I'm in Japan, missy? Who the devil are you working for anyhow sexy?" Batterman smirked as he threw open the door and bid her to come into his apartment while holding onto the paper she just handed him.

Again, Lady Yoke blushed from embarrassment as she offered with heat in her voice this time to the rude acting American. Reacting as she was, insulted with him for daring to believe that she would ever enter his apartment like a common whore of the night, she snapped without covering her anger aimed at the American businessman. "Mr. Batterman, I must remain standing in the hall because I'm an honorable single Japanese woman of great trust and loyalty, and I must think of my reputation at all times, sir. My Master has ordered me to deliver this message in person to you and I was furthered ordered to wait your reply. That's the only reason for my presence at your doorstep. If you please, would you read the letter I delivered on behalf of my employer. I do not enjoy being in your foul presence for a moment longer than I am forced to endure it."

"Wow, I guess I told you, huh?" Batterman snorted while trying to be funny with her as he added to his words. "Well little lady why the hell didn't you tell me that in the first place? I'll tell ya this much honey. If you want me to take time out of my busy life to read this here letter from your so called Master as you put it. Then I demand you come in my apartment and wait for my damn reply in person. I don't conduct my business while standing out in the middle of the hall like this for no one, baby. What the hell type of people are you anyway that you still allow one person to own your lovely little ass lock, stock, and fucking barrel, woman? No man's that damn important to the pulse of the world in this day and age, little missy. Come on in god dammit, I won't conduct my business standing in the damn hall like this, little missy."

The Lady Yoke thought about his angry words for a moment, and then she bowed within the limits of politeness, and kept her eyes cast to the floor as she cautiously entered the apartment. She moved as if every step might be her last. His two large bodyguards rushed in the kitchen, and instantly surrounded the tiny Lady Yoke, and scared her to death.

"What the hell is this crap, dammit? You two tree trunks think this pretty little lady here is a threat against my fat ass? Not a chance in hell of that ever happening, man." He growled at the one he knew understood English the best out of the two guards.

"Mr. Batterman, please allow me to offer you this in my defense sir. It's believed in Japan that a female assassin is loose and working her evil craft in Tokyo. We trust no one at this time for any reason whatsoever, sir. And if you know anything about Japan's past history sir, anyone who walks the soil of Japan, could be a serious threat to your life, male or female sir. You hired us to protect your life, and that's exactly what we're doing sir."

"How the hell are you going to accomplish that feat buddy?"

"Mr. Batterman Sir, we're going to take time to search this young woman, and if we find any hidden weapons on her person, we're going to use them on her, sir. Unless she gives them up willingly to us before we start the search of her. If she refuses to be searched then I suggest you have nothing to do with her, and allow us to call the police and they can search her, sir. They'll come here and search her against her will if needed, Mr. Batterman." The large bodyguard stepped forward and stared at the slight Lady Yoke, completely blocking her from moving any further in her defense, or against Batterman or trying to escape the apartment.

Lady Yoke understood what the bodyguard wanted from her because she was warned in advance she might have to suffer the embarrassment of being searched by the concerned bodyguards surrounding Batterman at all times. Without uttering a word of protest or hesitating, she slowly undid her obi and then pulled the two halves of her kimono apart. She had nothing on under it and she turned her body in the silk fabric so the two upset guards could see she was in no possession of weapons. She understood if she wore any underclothes, the guards would force her to remove them, thus exposing more of her body to their view longer than needed.

One of the insulting bodyguard's went so far as to pull the fabric up, further exposing her exquisite body to their glaze. She turned red from the embarrassment and anger.

When the bodyguard was done examining her body for weapons, he turned to Batterman and offered him calmly. "It's safe to say this young woman has no weapons hidden on her person, Mr. Batterman. But nevertheless we'll keep a close eye on her every move as long as she's visiting your apartment, sir. It seems this one was obviously beaten recently by someone, Mr. Batterman. And this makes us very wary of her intent sir. This assassin stalking Tokyo is able to kill with anything she picks up, even her hands I was told." The guard warned.

"Yeah, thanks a helluva lot for the report there pal. I can see that crap for myself, buster. All this caution's starting to get on my dick nerve I tell you, fella." The American businessman snapped nastily as he took the time to enjoy the lovely view her naked body offered them.

Lady Yoke closed her kimono as if the search meant absolutely nothing to her, and she retied the obi and bowed as Batterman unfolded the tri folded paper, and read it.

"Who the hell is this note from anyway little missy? Who is your master, young lady?"

"The letter is from Hiromoai Hatanaka-san, Mr. Batterman-san." Lady Yoke replied flatly without any emotion in her voice, refusing to even lift her eyes and look in his face.

"Oh, that fucking bugger again huh? I thought I was finished with his lousy ass for the time being, honey. It didn't take the man long to get back to my ass, did it missy? What's this, a proposal of a hostile takeover attempt on his part against my new construction company, honey? Well let him try that fucking move against my ass and see what it nets him for his trouble, little missy. I'm prepared for anything that master of yours tries against me and my new company, dammit." Batterman waved the page at Lady Yoke like he was angry with it.

"I don't know what it is my Master has no need of informing me of what he's doing in his life, or in the world of business. I'm here only to serve my Master's will to deliver that letter to you."

"Yeah sure, spoken like a true loyal little Jap nipper at that, honey." He snorted at hearing Hiromoai's name mentioned so soon, filled him with anger and warning. He carefully read the letter and then looked at Lady Yoke with surprise in his eyes. He was amazed he had such command of the English language that he was even able to write it so clearly on paper.

"Sonofabitch little lady that crazy ass Master of yours wants to work with me on a joint venture between our two construction companies. When he made this offer to my ass yesterday mind you missy, I thought he was kinda pulling my pud on me, because there was no way in hell I would ever sell him the damn business I just acquired from Asahiko. Sonofabitch, maybe we can work something out between us after all, little missy." Batterman refolded the letter, and then he handed it back to her as he added.

"Look little missy, if you ever think of dumping your stuffy ass Jap Master of yours, I sure can use a fine looking little woman like you in my corporation. One who understands the lingo and people of this here country so well baby. And I promise you lady, you won't have to call me Master or any of that uther crap you slaves always call your masters of this country." Again, Batterman flashed his best smile at the beautiful Lady Yoke.

"Huh, and I should be damned to the everlasting fires of torment for all eternity if I dared contemplate leaving Hiromoai-san's honorable employ to join ranks with the likes of you, Mr. Batterman. I'm loyal to only one Master throughout my life as is the belief of any honorable Japanese servant in their employ." Lady Yoke refused to add the san to his name again as she cast her eyes to the floor and stopped speaking.

"Yeah a real noble little dog you are, huh bitch?" He snorted barely loud enough for her to hear his insult aimed at her. Already, she hated the American with all the emotion trapped in her body. Now, she understood why Hiromoai wanted this ugly loathsome American fool to be dead, and floating with his worthless ancestors of the past.

"What's it your Master really wants from my ass, little missy? C'mon baby, you know damn well what he's up to with this damn letter of his, and you can tell me what he truly wants from my ass with this offer. I won't inform him if you tell me what he really wants from my can, missy. C'mon will ya for Christ sake, I'll make it well worth your betrayal of this Japper of yours, missy." He gave a smile that was more of a sneer than a grin as he waited for her to betray her so called master. Batterman knew enough money offered to this woman, would force her to pay homage to a new master. Him.

"Sir, my Master has requested me to wait until you had a polite answer for him to understand and enjoy, Mr. Batterman." She replied as she bowed respectfully. Still refusing to reply to the insult this man would think she might ever betray his trust in her for the briefest of moments.

"Cold ass fish huh, it figures missy. Look baby, you tell your stinking boss err... Master that I'd be happy as hell to meet him on this damn construction site, and help him figure out a proper price for the proposal we'll hafta offer for the damn job. Does anyone else in Japan know of this job's existence?" Batterman asked and then stared at her.

Lady Yoke tried desperately to confine her rampaging anger growing in her chest after having this filthy American call her baby, as she nearly spat at him with vinegar in her tone. "My Master doesn't tell me of his business dealings, nor do I see any need to inquire of them, Mr. Batterman. But in this case sir, I accidently overheard him when he was discussing this venture between the two companies. Hiromoai-san told the one who informed him of the job that this venture had to remain a secret until he had a proper proposal worked out for the project. Does that answer your question to your satisfaction, Mr. Batterman?" She even removed the sir from his name now.

"Hmmm... that was very wise on Hiromoai's part I must say, little lady. If we can get a bid in there before anyone else even finds out about the damn job's existence. There's a damn good chance we can land the project before anyone else even bids on the damn thing. Okay missy, you tell your Boss I'll give him a call on Thursday night, and we can work out the finer details of the deal then. I find it awful hard for me to call your Boss your damn Master though, baby. Thank you for delivering this letter to me, errr... can I offer you some tea, maybe a spot of Sake? Do you have to return to your Master immediately, little lady?

"Or can I offer you some fun and games before you hafta return to work and you so called Master. I saw what you got and quite frankly honey, I'm very interested in seeing a lot more of it and you at the same time. I have a hot tub just waiting to have a beautiful female like you to enjoy it with me. What do you say baby do you wanna earn yourself a little extra cash today or what? If I'm pleased, I'm very generous you know little lady." Batterman was operating under the assumption that money made it possible for him to sample any woman's sexual delights he came across, especially while visiting Japan.

She could no longer contain her anger and disgust of this detestable Gai Jin and his want for lust, and enjoying her body and she snapped before she was able to control herself. "Huh, do you think I'm a filthy one from the land of sin, a lowly whore from the last Tea House of the Willow Branch that I'd be even the slightest bit interest in giving away my sacred body for some filthy American cash. No foolish one who has slimed his way to the honored shores of my honorable ancestors from the foreign land of sin and disgust. I'm not of the foul chugen o kimono class, the people of small account to Japan that I would ever entertain such a foul offer from you.

"I offer to your being from across the Ocean, that I'm an honorable woman of high standing of the well respected yukakasa class, and if you don't know what that means, I'll be most pleased to explain it for your foolish understanding, Mr. Batterman. I'm an honorable woman of high value, respected and honored by many of the elite in Japan. I don't spend my wanting days by being carried around Japan in a worthless highly decorated wooden palanquin, to be enjoyed by the next highest bidder where I'd dare part my honorable legs for his foul member to assault my holy temple. I must go before I soil myself with a fool's blood, Mr. Batterman. This is all I have to say to you, are you finished speaking with me?"

"Hey baby, I didn't say I wasn't gonna pay you very well for your damn time and pleasures. If you're anywhere as good as you look in what you people call the art of pillowing, I'll tell you what I'll do for you honey. I'll let you set the damn price for your sexual services for just a stinking hour of your precious time, honey." Again, he gave her another lingering leer.

And again she replied before she even tried to get any kind of control over her raging temper harbored for this ugly man from America. "leeeee..., do you really think for one second of time that I'd be guilty of daring to defile the sacred honor of my respected ancestors, by sharing my desired bed with a filthy Gai Jin such as yourself? All the foul money you possess or will ever possess in your future will not be enough money to bribe me to part my legs willingly for the likes of you. Save your worthless money and your foul and disgusting desires of sharing my pillow foolish one, there are many worthless women in Japan who don't care who they bring sexual happiness and pleasure to. I save myself for my only one true love and no others, and my love is not of money or greed, Mr. Batterman. But be aware for your own sake fool, for if you partake of the pleasures of some of the women of the lower class, because your peerless pestle might be placed in dire peril if you pay to enjoy their sexual delights, fool.

"I have heard many worthless women who take money for pride and sex, have the affliction that'll cause your mighty dragon to wither and never be seen again by your foul eyes or hands. Although Japan is the land of great pleasure and true understanding the matters of nature and of the body, it's also the land of revenge, and the worthy gods have many disturbing ways of exacting that revenge against insult of their laws, Mr. Batterman." Though she was fuming at the ugly Gai Jin, her proper upbringing forced her to remain somewhat polite and respectful to the man by calling him 'Mr. Batterman' when she was addressing him, even though it disgusted her to offer him any form of respect and honor.

Batterman had to smile over the sheer anger being emitted from this slender woman as he moaned at her this time. "Whew little lady, a simple no would've done very well thank you very much. Sweet Jesus in Heaven, not for nothing baby, I just wanted to as you people say here, pillow with you, what's so bad about that want huh? Is it so bad for you to partake in pleasures where and when you might find them waiting for you?" Batterman mumbled as he kind of absentmindedly rubbed his member to make certain it was still swinging between his legs, fearing her words of warning, and wondering if the two young Japanese women he was sharing time with, were free of any diseases. He never gave that fear a thought until hearing Lady Yoke's terribly threatening warning aimed against him.

"I'll not dignify that most insulting question of yours with an answer from my honorable lips, Mr. Batterman." She was able to get a little better control of her rage and added. "You'll have me tell my Master that you intend to call him Thursday to make preparations to visit the construction site he's concerned with, Mr. Batterman." She actually growled her words in her most commanding tone while still staring at the floor. She refused to look at the American in the eyes.

"Yes, you can tell your lousy Master exactly that, I'll call him Thursday as he had requested in his letter, little lady." Batterman snorted at the beautiful lady, displaying a little bit of his own anger towards her this time for the way and angry words she was throwing at him.

"Then I believe that our conversation and time has finally come to its faithful conclusion Mr. Batterman. I'll therefore inform my most honorable Master that the next time he has any further need to communicate with your worthless being, he should consider sending the old and much wiser Utsumi-san to deliver his message to you. You might not be so interested in pillowing with him I offer to you. He's much more use to speaking and dealing with the likes of your kind of the construction field, Mr. Batterman. Konnicha wa." She snapped sharply and dryly as she bowed just within the limits of politeness, as the guard opened the door for her and then she turned on her heels and hurried down the hall, acting as if this meeting had never occurred between them.

Batterman closed the door while laughing at the young woman actually running down the hallway. The guards who searched Lady Yoke before their meeting started, was smirking as he headed to the living room. Batterman followed the two guards as the one who searched Lady Yoke offered over his shoulder with a smirk to his temporary boss. "Mr. Batterman, I bet that one possesses a fire that'd be impossible to control between the sheets, sir."

"Yeah, a real spitfire that little one is, huh? But think of all the fucking fun one would have with her exquisite body, if he was able to mount her without her burning him to death before he reached his pleasure with her body. She was sure a real pretty one there, wasn't she?" He snickered as he looked at the closed door she left through.

"She sure was Mr. Batterman." They laughed as they moved deeper into the large living room. The bodyguard in command of the rest of his security remarked to his boss. "Mr. Batterman, I'll take it to inform my boss we'll have a need of a few more body guards to accompany you on your upcoming trip to the construction site and your next meeting with Hiromoai-san, sir."

He stopped dead in his tracks and stared at the large Japanese guard for several seconds while wearing a frown. He was surprised the guard knew of the supposed meeting. He was angry as hell the man had dared to listen in on a conversation that did not concern him as he barked at his security guard in no uncertain terms. "Look here pal, if you heard so much of the god damn conversation then you had to have heard the little lady say that this job site was a secret. If I go dragging a gaggle of tree size bodyguards along with me, someone's gonna put two and two together and know what the hell we're up to. You two birds are gonna hafta be left behind, so me and Hiromoai can speak openly without any ears listening in on our conversation. I have a feeling there's a helluva lot more to this meeting than his wanting to work with my ass."

"That concern is exactly why I feel we should have more people surrounding you for this meeting, sir. Mr. Batterman, you must remember at all times while visiting Japan, sir. There's a wise and extremely successful assassin at work in Japan, sir. I believe she's responsible for Asahiko-san's death even though the police and everyone who knows of his death believe the old man killed himself. I know she's definitely responsible for poor Yurkowa-san's death, sir. Mr. Batterman, you hired my security company to protect your life at all times while you're visiting Japan, sir. You must allow us to carry out our assignment properly, sir." The extremely concerned guard stared at Batterman, while he digested his words of warning.

"C'mon man and be real about yourself for a moment, will ya huh? Not everyone in Japan's a marked man for this god damn assassin o yours pal. What the hell would any assassin want with my ass? You're gonna hafta remain behind as I said and that's it. I decided I'm going to meet with him alone, dammit. If I go dragging a bunch of you tree trunks along with me, I'll never find out what the hell's really on Hiromoai's mind. And that's the only reason I consented to this damn meeting with him in the first pla..."

"It could very well be the cause of your death, Mr. Batterman. You should reconsider and allow us to follow you to this meeting with Hiromoai-san, sir."

"Look pal, if you're trying to scare me, forget about it man. I've been involved in two different wars, and my ass is still wagging and ticking, my friend. No bitch assassin alive is gonna do the job real soldiers were unable to accomplish on my ass." Batterman bragged to the bodyguard.

"I'm afraid you have never come up against the likes of this assassin, Mr. Batterman."

"Give it up man, no matter what you say you're not going to change my damn mind. You people will hafta stay behind, and that's that. You got it?"

"If you command so it shall be carried out, Mr. Batterman Sir. If you're set against having at least one of your guards accompany you on this meeting with Hiromoai-san, sir.

Then allow me to offer you a weapon so you might protect yourself if the need arises, Mr. Batterman."

"I was under the impression it's illegal for anyone to have a side arm in Japan, pal? Especially what you people love to call people like me, a Gai Jin I believe."

"Normally, this is correct sir. But since you demanded to meet with Hiromoai-san alone, I think I can overlook this crime to Japan's laws. Just this one time mind you, Mr. Batterman."

"By the way pal, how the hell come you people are allowed to be armed in Japan?"

"Mr. Batterman, we're allowed to be armed because we're in the protection field sir. Japan doesn't want her visitors to our country to be harmed in any way, shape, or form sir. And instead of allowing the visitors to arm themselves, they give us the power to be armed, sir." The guard handed him his extra pistol after setting a round in the chamber and then he added. "I trust you know how to use the weapon, you did say you were in the military service sir."

"Yeah, buddy I know how to use the damn thing alright. Thanks for the weapon and if the need arises, I'll sure use the damn thing, pal."

CHAPTER TWENTY NINE

THURSDAY, JUNE 13th, 1996. JOB LOT 11657
ON THE OUTSKIRTS OF DOWNTOWN TOKYO

The young Japanese businessman Hiromoai Hatanaka, got out of his Mercedes he parked just off the side of the road like he owned the world, and then he began to slowly walk around the large vacant plot of roughly cleared land, he was going to use against the American in his ploy to deceive, and then have Wind destroy him on the site. He tried to hide the ancient katana blade under his overcoat, so as not to draw any attention to him or his actions. As he struggled along the plot of scheduled land to soon have a multi level commercial building erected on it.

He was well aware this project was going to be turned into a skyscraper sometime in the near future. Because he held papers for the job in his office safe for three months now, but he also understood there were already too many other bidders on the project to hold much hope of landing the job for his construction company. He carried the crumbling sword of Wind in his left hand hidden under his coat, as he carefully picked his way over the upturned ground. Stones and heavy clumps of raw earth made walking rather hazardous at best on the site.

He recalled the conversation he had with the new owner of Asahiko's construction company an hour before he headed out for the site. He felt the American was overly anxious to work with him on the false project. He smiled as he remembered the old Japanese saying that haste opened the door for foolishness, mistakes and failures. And this unintelligent American fool was walking with his eyes wide open into one of those mistakes that'll cost him his life.

When they first spoke, he told the Gai Jin to meet him by the old drinking well, that spot was a mile away from the proposed site, at six thirty in the late afternoon of tomorrow. He knew the police lightened their surveillance of the Gai Jin already. This fact insured the American would be able to travel the streets of Tokyo, without the police trailing his every movement.

Being that tomorrow was a Friday, he was certain any local civilians working near the site, would be more interested in getting home for the weekend than what was going on in a litter filled plot of empty land. There were enough debris and used building supplies lying around the site to shield them when he summoned Wind to dispatch the disturbing American's life.

Hiromoai cautiously walked this vast project site many times over the past few months, and he examined every square inch of the proposed site. He looked for one place in particular he noticed on one of his prior visits on his number of investigations of the project site, a place to safely hide Wind's deadly katana sword until he arrived tomorrow night with the foolish American in tow. When he spotted the area on one of the previous checking out the area, for some reason he knew he was going to make use of it in the near future.

He finally spotted the place he was searching for last week when he paid another visit to the site under the request of the owner, in hopes he would offer more money for the soon to be project than the owner received from other bidders for the project. It was a slight depression in the earth with a number of heavy timbers called railroad ties dumped on the slight incline. He knew he could easily hide the deadly sword there safely, and it wouldn't be discovered until he dragged the foolish American to the spot, and led him to the sword without his knowledge.

The large clearing of the land was no big thing because throughout Japan many huge plots of land in this area of the city were being leveled at an alarming rate, damaged by the earthquake that had destroyed much of this section of Tokyo. The land was already inspected by a Shinto priest, and it was blessed and determined that the site was placed on the proper position on the so called spine of the dragon for future construction success.

Japan's many beliefs were of such if the Shinto priest said the site offended the sleeping dragon of the earth. No building would ever be erected on the site, and it would be left in peace and baron or turned into a garden park. Japan was believed to be constructed along the dragon's spine, thus the curve of the Japanese Islands. And the fool who did not follow the Shinto priest's warning, usually had that building destroyed by a sudden violent earthquake, or any other angry acts of nature. The revenge of the sleeping dragon it was believed by many in Japan.

He was one of the few men in Japan who was aware of the planned skyscraper for this construction site. Once, seven, two story four family homes stood on this site. This section of Tokyo was one of the densest living quarters of the entire city. But the out of place earthquake killed nearly one hundred civilians and destroyed many building in the area. Many of the damaged building were rebuilt, but this one site was too heavily damaged and the buildings were raised. This area of Tokyo was usually never hit by the dreaded earthquakes plaguing much of the lands of the Eight Islands of Japan. The plot of twelve square acres were condemned, and the earth moving equipment had long ago leveled what was left of the all but destroyed civilian homes, and removed much of the carnage created by the rage and power of mother nature.

It was rather rough walking over the upturned uneven ground, with pieces of destroyed building material littering the land. Boards with rusted nails stuck ominously out of the dirt, and rubble once covered the boards they were driven into. He cursed for waiting so long before looking for the area he wanted to plant Wind's ancient sword in. The small flashlight did not illuminate the area enough for him to see many of the hidden dangers in the fill and uneven ground. But he knew if he was to come to the site during daylight, his mere presence in the area would have created interest by many of the nosy civilians, always involved in searching the land for items of worth, or lost memories because of the earthquake.

The cautious Hiromoai headed in the direction he remembered the depression and stack of timbers lay in, as he carefully inched his way forward in the closing darkness of the oncoming night. He suddenly tripped over an old water pipe sticking six inches out of the ground, and it caused him to tumble on his right shoulder and he ended up sitting on his rearend on the ground. He immediately checked Wind's sword and when he found it to be alright, he rubbed his aching shoulder and cursed again. He cursed Asahiko for forcing him to resort to this ill mannered deception so soon to be played out against the unsuspecting American as he struggled back to his feet. He thought if the old fool would have done the right thing and sold him his construction company then this next death would not have had to take place. In his mind he was blaming Asahiko for the forthcoming death of the American, and his lawyer soon to follow in death.

The young Japanese businessman pushed himself off the filthy ground using Wind's sword for slight assistance, and he took time to brush the dirt from his expensive overcoat. Then he picked up the flashlight he let go of when he fell moments ago, but he held onto Wind's sword and shined the light out before him, and moved cautiously forward again on the cluttered site.

After five minutes of walking the dangerous site, the light finally shined on the large stack of timbers he was searching for. He saw many times in the past, numbers of people walking on the site with flashlights, carefully picking through the litter once homes before the earthquake hit the area.

The police stopped a while ago from driving any of the scavengers away from the site. There was nothing left on the site of worth, so instead of wasting time running the civilians off the property, the police started ignoring anyone carrying off pieces of scrap wood, or other building materials and belongings they might have found under the ground they were searching.

A smile crossed his lips in the darkness and he headed for the large wood pile. He rested his hand on the heavy timbers with a light coating of dirt and dust covering it, and looked over the pile that seemed like it was ready to tumble into the slight depression on its own accord. As he remembered it, the depression was still there, but it looked a little deeper than he remembered it before, and he figured the scavengers were at their work again on the site.

He walked around the wood then carefully slid into the depression, remaining on his feet as he skidded forward on his expensive leather shoes. Once he was standing on the bottom of the pit, he checked out the rest of the area while looking for the proper place to hide Wind's killing sword. He picked out a wide timber half stuck in the side of the bank of the depression, and it was mostly covered over with a light coating of loose dirt and other timbers from the large pile. He smiled to himself as he carefully studied the wide chunk of wood.

He bent over and shined the light under the wide timber. There was a narrow hole that seemed just deep and long enough to hide the sword properly under the beam. He was forced to clean some of the loose dirt from the opening with his hand, and then he slid the mystical ancient sword in the enlarged opening. At one point the sword stopped moving easily and he was forced to work the tip deeper into the soft dirt, by adding more pressure to the handle of the sword as he pushed harder on the blade, to get it far enough in the dirt to hide it from view.

When the sword was placed to his liking, he brushed the dirt from the top of the timber and allowed it to lightly coat over Wind's deadly sword, further hiding its ancient and crumbling handle from view. He did not want it too simple for the hated Gai Jin to locate it. But he was certain once the American got the hunting fever for some ancient items of war of Japan's past history, he was sure to locate the blade with little if any trouble or guidance from him.

He understood he had to start the hunting fever burning strong in the greedy Gai Jin's heart. To insure the foolish American would be looking for the ancient keepsakes of Japan's honored past. He reached in his pocket and removed a bag of small items. He rested the flashlight on the edge of the timber, so he could see what he was doing without being forced to hold the light as he opened the bag, and then he removed some of the content. He pulled out the six ya no ne ancient brass arrowheads and cautiously fingered the old and still extremely dangerous items of war with the respect due them. Three age old arrowheads were of the highly sought after brass karimata, or forked, broad head arrow tips. The remaining three arrowheads were a mixture of different shaped arrowheads of lesser worth of iron and interest.

The wise Japanese businessman checked the ground beneath his feet in search of good hiding places for the arrowheads when he noticed the tip of a stone sticking out of the ground and he placed the first arrowhead up against it.

This one he was going to leave mostly in plain sight just slightly covered over by a little loose dirt. He smiled again, knowing each arrowhead was worth its weight in gold on the black market. It was a small price for him to pay for acquiring Asahiko's long sought after company no matter what h had to do to get it. Items from Japan's ancient past were commonly traded on the black market for small fortunes, as long as the government did not find out about the offerings and stopped their sale before it was consummated. It was forbidden to sell any items from Japan's ancient past, especially articles from the samurai warrior era. The Japanese government did not want any items to get out of Japan if they could stop them.

The construction owner salted the bottom of the pit with the remaining arrowheads, making certain the hidden brassheads would force the excited Gai Jin to search every inch of the bottom of the pit along with the sides of the depression in his search of greed and articles of Japan's past.

When the arrowheads were hidden to his satisfaction, he picked up the small flashlight and tried to find the hidden items with the glow of the light. The only arrowhead that stuck out was the one resting up against the rock as he planned. The other five arrowheads had small sections of the aged brass or iron heads exposed just above the ground. The dirt was so dry and loose it looked as if the arrowheads were there since first being dropped by the samurai, during their many battles for their Shogun's honor of the time.

When he was pleased with his salting of the shallow pit with the items he was certain would create the hunting fever to glow strong in the Gai Jin's heart, he then scurried up and out of the depression. His flashlight was held between his teeth in order to give him use of both hands as he crawled up the side of the constant shifting fill of the pit. The soft ground made climbing out of the pit rather hazardous as it continued to give way under his feet and weight. Once he was out of the pit, he turned back and glanced into the depression a final time, and shined the light where he hid Wind's blade under the piece of heavy timber.

Only because he knew right where it was hidden, he was able to locate the very end of the tuska, the hilt of the ancient sword. He put the light off and quickly scanned the entire site to make certain no one had observed his actions. The last thing he needed was for some fool to follow him to the depression, and the follower discovered the treasures he planted before they served their purpose. He was afraid of losing Wind's sword along with her awesome power to some lowlife walking the streets of Tokyo, looking for something to steal or find.

He had no fear of being trailed by the police to the site, because he ordered both Lady Yoke to dress to go out and Utsumi to dress in one of his finest suits, to go out moments before he left his apartment for his mission over to the construction site. The young owner of the construction company waited in the hall of Hatanaka Tower and watched as the police assigned to watch his every move, took off and followed them as they got in his backup Mercedes and then drove off for a shopping expedition with lady Yoke. He waited until he was certain all the police officers fell in line, and they followed his other car and Lady Yoke and Utsumi down the road.

They were supposed to go to the largest shopping center in downtown Tokyo, and Utsumi was going to remain in the car, hiding his face while pretending to read the newspaper while she bought fruit and necessities for the apartment. They were ordered to spend an hour driving around Tokyo enjoying the sights the city had to offer. This was to give him the time to plant the items and sword then return to the Tower before they returned with the police trailing them.

He laughed over how easy it was for him to out flank the gaggle of police officers assigned to watch him. He sped back to his apartment as fast as the night time traffic would allow, and then he checked out the area where he picked up the police squad cars parked earlier in the day. Their cars were nowhere to be seen, which informed him they were still trailing his servants in his other car. Again he smiled as he pulled into the large underground garage and parked his baby far from its usual slot way in the back of the large parking lot. This was so if the police followed his other car into the lot, they would not notice his car already parked there. He rushed across the parking area and jumped into his private elevator using the collar of his overcoat to hide his face from view in case there was an officer left behind with orders to keep his apartment under further surveillance. In seconds, he was in the safety of his exquisite apartment.

Once safely back in his apartment he opened a Budweiser beer and sipped it while waiting for Utsumi and Lady Yoke to return to the apartment. All the while they drove around the streets of Tokyo, Lady Yoke refused to speak to Utsumi she did not even look at the old man. She was still steaming over his deplorable attempt to enjoy Wind's favors, by using the temporary command he had over her fine spirit when he was ordered to watch her in Hiromoai's bedroom, as the police interviewed her boss downstairs in the massive study.

Lady Yoke kept a close eye on her watch and at the ordered time to return to his apartment, she snapped angrily at Utsumi. "Foul one from the lower depths of the slime world, I believe it's time for us to return to the apartment. Don't you dare even cast your loathsome eyes in my direction for a second lowly dog, because your wicked eyes make my skin want to flee my bones, and your filthy face makes my stomach ill to look upon." Lady Yoke was relieved she was going to soon be able to remove herself from Utsumi's dishonored presence.

Utsumi let out his breath in an angry sigh as he grumbled nastily back at her. "When the hell are you ever going to get off my damn back about that night, Yoke? I was only trying to have a little innocent fun with Wind for Christ sake. You can't blame me for trying to take advantage of her. She has an exquisite body and I'm a lonely old man who has forgotten how nice it was to look upon a young naked female body, witch of the filthy bed sheets. I didn't mean any harm to her or you by my actions in Hiromoai-san's bedroom. I'm only guilty of being a man trapped in the presence of a beautiful and nearly naked and fine looking young woman born from the flesh of the devil. I can't believe that you're still holding a gru…"

"Filthy old man who dares to speak to an honorable woman who has no interest in what you are allowing to spew forth from your worthless mouth. I'll never be off your despicable and evil back for the rest of your foul life, adulterated one. You should pray every night to the Kami who protect the evil spirits that I don't inform Hiromoai-san of your terribly disgusting attempt to have sex with Wind. You're beyond loathing and disgust you're even lower than the filthy slime that covers the swamps of the leper filth. You're married old one, and when the fever of lust fills your worthless heart, you should turn to your honorable wife waiting your return to her. Not to Wind." Lady Yoke hissed as she interrupted and she glared at the old man driving the car.

"I'm warning you Yoke, you better get the hell off my back about that damn night if you know what's good for you, or you just might not wake up one morning from your sleep, Ama." (Bitch) Utsumi warned her threateningly as he refused to take his eyes off the traffic, so he could glare at Lady Yoke sitting beside him in the car.

"Don't you dare try and threaten nor curse me with your foul breath and evil wagging tongue, you contaminated old man. Fear me and fear what I can have let lose upon your worthless head, evil one. Fear the awesome power of death that I possess at the very ends of my honorable fingertips, you old and worthless fool. I can own your loathsome head with one command from my honorable lips, detestable fool. I have a power that could easily end your evil presence upon this earth once and for all." She replied with a devastating threat of her own.

"Huh, and what the hell could you possibly do to me with such worthless words you spit out of your worthless mouth, threatening me like this Yoke? You're nothing more than a bitch placed on this earth to spread your foul legs and give pleasure to man. What little harm can you possibly release upon my old head, bitch?" This time he turned to glance at her.

"Wind will be the deliverer of my wanted revenge upon your good-for-nothing repugnant old head, if you insist on carrying on with this conversation a moment longer, and continuing your wasted threats against me and my person, foul one!"

Utsumi could not hide the sudden fear that instantly wrapped its icy fingers around his heart at the mere mention of her ordering Wind to kill him. He understood Wind would do anything for her if she asked her. The fear of the ancient female samurai stalking him in her search of his soul and blood, forced him to lower his head and turn the car and head for Hiromoai's building. The rest of the trip was completed in a very strained silence and in haste.

SERGEANT OKAMATSU'S UNMARKED SQUAD CAR

Sergeant Toshihiro Okamatsu was riding in the lead unmarked squad car as the officers continued to trail the Mercedes they thought had Hiromoai and his housekeeper Lady Yoke all over downtown Tokyo. He smiled as they kept the expensive car in view. He felt Hiromoai was playing a game of cat and mouse with them, by taking them on a wild goose chase all over town. The Sergeant knew Hiromoai never took his servant out shopping like this, but yet here he was, acting like he was married to the beautiful little spit fire. The police officers waited outside the store as the thought to be Hiromoai was doing while waiting for Lady Yoke's return to the car. Sergeant Okamatsu tried his best to get a better look at the driver, to make certain it was Hiromoai driving the machine. But the crafty one was keeping his face well camouflaged by the newspaper he was supposed to reading in the front seat of the vehicle.

Lady Yoke strolled out of the store like she had not a care in the world while carrying two paper bags full of groceries, and she climbed into the car as if she completed her chores. But to Sergeant Okamatsu's surprise, instead of going straight home, who he believed was Hiromoai continued to drive around the streets of the city as if out on a joy ride. At first he thought the two civilians were going to stop at another store, but they never did. It was like Hiromoai was giving the officers a private little tour of downtown Tokyo.

Over his radio, many complaints started to flood in from the other police officers involved in the small caravan of police vehicles trailing the expensive white car. They wanted to head back to Hatanaka Tower, and leave their Sergeant to follow their target alone. The Sergeant stopped all the complaining by ordering the officers to get off the radios and follow him in silence until they found out what the business owner was up to. After over more than an hour and a half of driving aimlessly around the heart of Tokyo, Hiromoai's car suddenly turned and headed right back for the Tower like a homing pigeon. In a matter of moments, the three police cars fanned out and circled Hatanaka Tower and parked at their assigned positions as the Mercedes disappeared inside the underground parking lot of the massive Tower.

The Sergeant pulled his car across the street from the Tower, and stopped it just outside the sushi bar opened all night and took up position there. From this location, he could easily see the entrance to the underground parking lot, while also able to observe Hiromoai's apartment doors that led to the balcony of his room on the twenty seventh floor of the building. He never saw Lady Yoke and Utsumi enter the Tower, or he might have been able to determine the driver was not Hiromoai from his height and the way he walked. As he settled down and found him staring at the sliding doors to the apartment once again, he reached for the radio to make his report.

He was instructed to report to Lieutenant Motoshima whenever Hiromoai left the building for any reason whatsoever. Sergeant Okamatsu understood Lieutenant Motoshima was going to be fuming because he waited so long before informing him that Hiromoai's servant visited the American earlier in the day. This was another reason why he decided to place a call to his commanding officer in hopes of soothing over his pending anger.

IN THE UNDERGROUND PARKING LOT UNDER THE HATANAKA TOWERS

Lady Yoke got out of the car and made certain she walked in front of Utsumi. This was not because she was still angry with his ugly actions carried out against Wind's person, but she was following Hiromoai's orders using her body to shield Utsumi's identity from the officer's view parked outside the building. They walked fast to the elevators, shifting their weight on their feet waiting for the elevator. They got in when the doors opened, only then did either of them relax.

Utsumi again tried to get back in favor with her, by trying to strike up a pleasant conversation with the pretty young woman. But she continued to refuse to listen to anything he had to offer her. When they got out of the elevator together on Hiromoai's floor, she led the way and walked faster than the old man could move. She entered the apartment and saw Hiromoai drinking a beer and felt something went wrong with his plan. She rushed into the study and dropped to her knees while Utsumi brought the groceries in.

He smiled the instant he saw Lady Yoke looking at him, and this made her believe everything went according to plan as he grumbled in a calm tone to her. "Get up Lady Yoke, there's no need for you to keep kneeling every time you come into the damn apartment, young lady. I need another Bud if you don't mind getting me one." He held the empty can out before him and shook it to show her it was empty. He was nearly drunk and in a good mood.

When she returned with the beer, he smiled as she bowed and offered the beer in the correct manner to the powerful Japanese businessman. He stared at the beauty, lust instantly filling his heart. He wanted to share Wind's pleasure tonight, but since it was necessary to send her back to the Ukiyo World so he could plant her deadly sword on the construction site, he was left with the want of a woman almost any woman would do to spend the night with. In a slightly slurred voice he asked Lady Yoke while he continued to leer at her. "Lady Yoke, I'd like to enjoy what we once spoke of the other day if you don't mind. I'm very interested in you and wanting to pillow with you lately." He flashed a beer induced half a smile at her this time.

She stared at him for a long moment, not knowing what he was talking about. It was so hard for her to understand because he was slurring his words so badly.

Utsumi sneaked passed the door to the study in a rush. He wanted to stay well out of Lady Yoke's way for fear that she just might slip and tell Hiromoai what he tried to do to Wind in his bedroom. He needed his job too much to throw it away by risking Lady Yoke or Hiromoai's ire raised against him for his crime he tried to carry out against the ancient female samurai warrior. He was really worried over the words Lady Yoke threatened him with while they were driving.

Hiromoai laughed over the confused look from Lady Yoke as he explained what he wanted from her while continuing to slur his words as he offered. "Please Yokeeee, you rememberrrr when I first asked youuuuu to shareeee my bed for the nightttttttt a few days agoooo?" He belched loudly and his head swayed a little on his shoulders as he went on with his words. "I'dddd like to enjoy spendinggggg a loving nighttttttt wit you tonighttttt, young lady."

"Hai Hiromoai-san, I remember well." She replied as she finally made out what he was trying to say to her, her heart beating wildly in her chest as she blushed from the embarrassment his words had caused her. Even though she was still getting over the painful bruises she suffered in the beating at his hands, she overlooked them. She would have snubbed anything for the privilege of sleeping with the powerful and good looking Hiromoai.

"Are youuuuu still interestedddddd in sharing your treasuresssss?" Another loud belch, followed this time by a fart as he continued to offer. "Wit meeeee, Lady Yoke? I'd do anything to haveeeeee that special nightttttt with you as I promiseddddd youuuuu, Lady Yokeeeee." He stuttered and again flashed the funny half a smile at her.

"Hai Hiromoai-san, it'd be my honor to keep you company tonight if you so desire of me." Lady Yoke replied, not attempting to hide the huge smile on her lips this time.

He could swear he was able to feel the beating of Lady Yoke's fluttering heart vibrating the air about him as he replied with equal enthusiasm this time. "I'dddd reallyyy enjoy sharinggggg my pillow with youuuuu tonight, my little wild flowerrrr. Lady Yoke, I enjoyed the firsttttt time we pillowed togetherrrr and I want to pillow wit you tonighttttt again."

Without replying with words to her lover, she rose and sexily removed her outer garments. She was still dressed in her street clothes to go shopping. When she stood before him dressed in just a black half bra, black panties, and thigh high black nylons, he drew in his breath in heavy little pants over her outstanding beauty. She always wore these types of undergarments since she first found out he was interested in seeing a woman dress so. Besides, they made her feel more like a woman of desire dressed in this fashion.

Her beauty was almost beyond compare, the only other woman he saw any prettier than Lady Yoke was Wind. This was because Wind was slightly taller and had larger breasts and a slightly smaller waist. Her skin was as flawless as Winds, and as golden. He reached up and pulled a bra cup down, exposing her wonderful breast. Carefully, he rolled the tip of her nipple between his fingers, making her sigh and purr with pleasure and want. He then moved to the second breast and exposed that one to his sight and touch.

Slowly, she dropped to her knees before him and worked with excitement on his belt buckle. When she had it undone, she unzipped his pants and pulled them down to his knees.

He was rock hard and waiting as his member swayed right before her face, and she drew the swaying member in her mouth. He let out a sigh as she worked him over expertly with her tongue, teeth and mouth. When she felt he was about to come she let him go. Then she stood and sexily wiggled out of her panties before him. Then she straddled his legs and guided his waiting dragon into her. Instead of Hiromoai making love to her, she was the one making love to him on this night, controlling the act of pillowing completely for the both of them.

He reached behind her back and undid her bra and threw it to the floor. Then his hands returned to playing with her breasts. He was unable to control himself and came while she skillfully rode him. Exhausted, she collapsed on his powerful chest and rested her head against him and listened to his breathing and heart beat in pleasing silence.

"Hmmmmm... That was absolutelyyyyy wonderful my little wild oneeeee. To think of all these years you workeddddd for me, I was so afraid to approach you for sexual desires, my ladyyyy. A foolish mistake on my part I tell youuuu, because you have satisfied me beyond my wildest dreams tonightttt." He said as he flinched after seeing the angry red welt high on her shoulder. He knew he was responsible for the ugly injury, and was thoroughly embarrassed for it. He was also speaking much clearer, making love to Lady Yoke sobered him up quite a bit.

Lady Yoke suddenly looked up from his chest and said in a dreamy voice. "Hiromoai-san, it's as Wind have offered on one of her visits to the living world, 'What gives you pleasure, do often.' I fear we'll repeat this pleasure many times, my lover." She offered as she climbed off his lap, she knelt before him and drew him back in her mouth. In no time he was ready again.

SERGEANT OKAMATSU'S PARKED SQUAD CAR

Already bored to death with the endless and terribly boring stakeout duty of Hiromoai's building, and the questionable drive that he and his servant just took them out on, Sergeant Okamatsu finally placed the mandatory call to his commanding officer, Lieutenant Motoshima. When the Lieutenant answered the call, the Sergeant quickly informed him of Hiromoai's confusing drive around downtown Tokyo.

The Lieutenant was unimpressed by his Sergeant's lack of information and the boring story of trailing Hiromoai around the city. But he paid closer attention when his Sergeant informed him of the female servant going to see the American who brought Asahiko's company, alone. Lieutenant Motoshima was suddenly upset, but he did not know why. He was confused as to why the young female worker and not her boss went to see the American invader to Japan's shore. What was it he had his servant offer to the Gai Jin he thought to himself then grumbled at his office? "Sergeant Okamatsu, what the hell do you think this stunt was all about on Hiromoai's part? That lousy sonofabitch has to be up to something here, and I'll not rest peacefully until I find out whatever the hell it is, dammit." The upset Lieutenant bitched at the Sergeant.

The stunned Sergeant flinched because Lieutenant Motoshima called one of the most powerful and influential men in all Japan a sonofabitch. It was very insulting and it displayed the terrible lack of manners the Lieutenant was falling guilty of over this horrendous and ongoing murder case. The Sergeant let out his breath in a rush and replied as crudely in an effort to cover his shock of the name calling. "Beats the hell out of my ass sir, it could've been anything or nothing at all Lieutenant. I feel it might have had something to do with business though, sir. Now that the American owns Asahiko-san's honorable construction company, I'm quite certain Hiromoai-san would want to open up some form of ties with the Gai Jin as quickly as possible, sir."

"Hummm... I wonder if it could be something as simple as that, Sergeant. Nevertheless, I want you to keep your eyes glued to his butt every second of the day and night, mister. I don't trust that one for a damn second, Sergeant." The Lieutenant moaned into the radio.

"Hiromoai-san?" The Sergeant asked as if he was not sure who he was talking about.

"Of course Hiromoai, who the hell else were we talking about, fool? Remember Sergeant Okamatsu-san, every criminal always takes something from the crime scene. Maybe as a sort of keep sake of the evil deed he had performed, as well as leaving something behind to help convict him with. Well when we find that something we're looking for is when we'll find out who's truly responsible for these horrendous deaths of late, Sergeant."

"After all that has transpired in this case, I can't believe you still think Hiromoai-san might be responsible for the three horrific murders, Lieutenant? It has to be someone else who committed the terrible crimes, someone who hasn't surfaced in this ongoing drama, Lieutenant."

"Yes, I still do Sergeant! I believe everyone involved in this damn murder case, has shown themselves to us so far. That's why I still believe that the smug ass Hiromoai is the one who is responsible for this murderer and her foul actions, Sergeant. Do you have anyone watching the American?" The Lieutenant asked his Sergeant over the phone.

"No Lieutenant, I pulled the surveillance teams from the American a little earlier today as per your instructions, sir." The Sergeant could not help it as he placed a smirk on his lips, knowing the Lieutenant was regretting that move now.

The lead detective shook his head slowly as he cursed himself for what he believed was a dumb order on his part. He had no idea Hiromoai was going to make contact with the American, if he had, he would have surely maintained the surveillance of the Gai Jin longer as he offered. "Okay, I guess we'll have to leave it that way for the time being, Sergeant. I don't have enough officers available to me to keep an eye on everyone living or visiting Tokyo, dammit. Where the hell is Hiromoai at this time Sergeant?"

"Hiromoai-san's back in his apartment Lieutenant, as far as I'm to understand, he's in there along with his little spitfire of a housekeeper and his old foreman, sir." The exhausted and bored Sergeant said as he shook his head over the fact Motoshima believed Hiromoai was still somehow responsible for the murders taking place in Japan.

"I wonder if he's tapping that always angry one, Sergeant." Lieutenant Motoshima offered with a sneer, trying to change the subject to one of a more pleasant one with his sergeant.

"I'd sure like to tap that one myself, Lieutenant."

"Huh, you would, you'd like to make love to every woman living in Japan I fear, Sergeant." Lieutenant Motoshima grumbled with a snap in his voice in an attempt to lighten up the mood he was mired in, and then he added for the other officer. "Okay Sergeant, keep your mind on the business at hand and out of the damn gutter will you please. Look Sergeant, don't allow Hiromoai to get out of his damn apartment or your sight for one moment. It's been too long since the last attack by this lowly female assassin. I feel she's about due to surface again, and soon at that, and anytime she's out and about people have a habit of dying, Sergeant."

"Believe me I have Hiromoai-san well covered on all sides, Lieutenant. There's no way in hell he's going to give me the slip while I'm on duty I can tell you, sir. I'm going to pull twenty four hour duty until we finally capture this damn assassin, sir." Sergeant Okamatsu offered as he glanced up at Hiromoai's windows twenty seven floors above him.

"Why the hell do you want to do that for? Look Sergeant I don't want you falling asleep on the damn job on me mister. I can ill afford you missing something Heromoai might pull off against us. You can't be on duty twenty four hours a day and be on the top of your game, Sergeant."

"That's easy enough for me to deal with sir, I can always sleep in the damn car when Corporal Noguchi relieves me and he takes over the surveillance of Hiromoai apartment in my stead, and when I relieve him from his watch then he can catch up on his needed sleep, Lieutenant Motoshima-san." The suddenly slightly excited Sergeant offered his commanding officer, trying to get the Lieutenant's permission to remain on the job for the full twenty four hour duty call.

"I don't know about you any more, mister. What the hell was all this bull you were handing me the other day about you wanting to spend a little extra time with your lady? All of a sudden it seems like you had enough wanting to spend more time with your girlfriend, mister."

"Well Lieutenant..." The Sergeant offered lamely to his commanding officer.

Now he felt he just trapped his Sergeant and snapped at him, keeping the conversation going a while longer. "Well what Sergeant?" The Lieutenant interrupted, wanting to find out a little more of why his officer was so interested in pulling a double work shift all of a sudden.

He knew his Lieutenant had him cold and offered in a contrite tone of voice to him this time. "Well if you have to know the reason why I just requested the extra duty, we kind of had a little squabble the other day. I think it's better for me if I give her some more time in order to cool off a little better, before either of us says something and can't take back."

"Ahhh... that mighty good thinking on your part Sergeant, I guess I'll approve the extra shift and overtime for you and your partner, until you feel your lady has cooled off enough, and you want some more time off to be around her again. To be honest with you Sergeant, I wanted my best man on the job, in case this damn assassin gets hungry for more blood, and she goes out on the hunt again in Tokyo." Lieutenant Motoshima broke off the communication without further words to his Sergeant and laughed as he mumbled to himself. "Yes, a bit of trouble in paradise sure gives my damn Officers renewed interest in their jobs, dammit."

HIROMOAI'S PENTHOUSE APARTMENT

Hiromoai and Lady Yoke made love twice more during the night before they finally collapsed in exhaustion. Like he did with Wind when he enjoyed her sexual treasures, he slept on the floor with his arms wrapped around her exquisite body. He was listening to the rhythm of her breathing, wondering who she was dreaming about, hoping it was him. He gently stroked her silk like long black hair, and when it moved away from her shoulder, he noticed the angry black and blue mark he inflicted on her, and he cringed again.

He still could not understand the awesome power he commanded over this beautiful lady, for her to sustain such a terrible beating at his hands, and yet still wanted to sleep with him. He wondered why she bothered to speak with him at all, yet alone want to sleep with him on this wonderful night. He kissed her shoulder gently, and it caused her to sigh sexily as she wiggled her rearend a little closer to his body, placing her rearend up against his crotch.

Hiromoai, as weary as he was, was having a bit of trouble falling asleep. His mind was working in overtime, cursing Asahiko for selling his construction company to a Gai Jin, and now he was forced to kill this American businessman. He found himself further cursing Asahiko's lawyer in the same breath. The fool of a lawyer had the power to sell the company to anyone he chose, yet he decided to dump it on a foolish American. He, as well as Asahiko was guilty of causing the death of the innocent American by Wind's revengeful hand, and her killing sword.

He found himself praying to the Kami of the underworld to wreak their revenge on the soul of Asahiko now dwelling in the Floating World, for daring to introduce the invading Gai Jin to the very shores of Japan. He feared if one American successfully landed in Japan and rose to own an honorable Japanese company, how many more hated Americans would follow, before they were able to completely destroy Japan, as surely as they have done to their country of the United States. In his mind's eye, he saw Tokyo being flooded with illegal drugs, guns and ruthless gangs, and the hated blacks and slums they always seemed to surround themselves with.

His unpleasant thoughts were suddenly interrupted by Lady Yoke who rolled over on her side as if she felt his troubling thoughts, and she began to play with his manhood. She was able to sense he was having trouble sleeping and he was worried about something. She was told many times in the past by her honorable mother, the best way to ease a troubled lover's mind was sex. Try as she might, she was unable to arouse him enough to engage in love play again.

He pulled Lady Yoke's body a little closer to him and kissed her lightly on the forehead and then on each eye as he purred just above a whisper to her. Thank you my little wild flower for the want of pillowing with me again, but I'm not in the right frame of mind to enjoy more of those wonderful pleasures of yours, young lady."

"Then what else can I do for you to help relax your needed Wa, Hiromoai-sama?"

He was rocked to his soul, here this young beauty referred to him as a lord. She had in the past, but tonight. Under these upsetting circumstances gave the response more power, more meaning as he replied. "All you have to do is hold me, and that'll help to relax me Lady Yoke."

"Hmmmm... my able lover, I wish all my duties were as pleasurable to carry out as what you have just requested from me, Hiromoai-sama." She returned his hug with surprising strength as she kissed him with a new passion he never experienced before. He looked in the almost angelic like beautiful face staring at him from her hug, and realized he could be very happy living the rest of his life with such a fine looking young and pretty Japanese prize as Lady Yoke was.

As if reading her lover's thoughts, she purred. "It's not necessary for you to make further comments. I'll be here even if I had to share your pleasures with another woman, my lover."

Her words did not have to be explained who she was willing to share his bed with. In his mind he knew she was offering to share him with Wind as he replied. "You're a strong, wise, and very understanding woman. Perhaps, once this mess is over with, and we can resume our normal lives and desires once again with a clear mind. We can make some special arrangements for you to stay with me on a much more permanent basis, young lady." He offered as he was getting caught up in his growing love for this woman laying nearly right on top of him now.

"Hmm... that would please me to all ends." She bowed while locked in his powerful embrace.

Her comforting words sounded so much like Wind's he found himself wondering what Wind was doing in the Floating World. He did not have the luxury of time to figure it out. The change of fortune and tribulations of the day took their toll on his exhausted and battered body. He fell asleep wrapped up in Lady Yoke's arms. What was left of the night passed quickly for them.

CHAPTER THIRTY

Utsumi was the first one to wake in the apartment and he walked cautiously into the darkened study to see what was going on in the room. He was aware Hiromoai did not leave the study last night. There he saw the two of them sleeping naked on the floor. He took in Lady Yoke's exquisite treasures as he studied her perfect body, with lust lurking in his aged heart. The way she was sleeping left nothing to the imagination of the old man's weather beaten eyes. The only thing he could not see of Lady Yoke was one breast because it was covered by his hand as they slept.

Again Utsumi cursed the outstanding luck Hiromoai seemed to always enjoy no matter what he was involved in. Here the great fool lay wrapped up peacefully in the arms of Lady Yoke, yet he was able to explore Wind's perfect body at will, and he was rich beyond his wildest dreams. And to add further insult to the anger eating away at his soul, he controlled one of the most powerful and deadly weapons to have ever walked on the sacred soils of Japan.

Fearing Hiromoai might wake up and see him staring at them on the floor, he decided to go to the kitchen and wait until they both woke. He knew Hiromoai set the time to meet with the American, although the time was far off, he was aware Hiromoai wanted to be up well before the meeting between them was to take place. He glanced at the clock it was nine twenty, so he decided to make some noise in the kitchen to wake them. It worked.

Minutes later, a very groggy, exhausted and sore Hiromoai staggered into the kitchen while rubbing the sleep from his eyes so he could see what was going on. The smell of freshly perked coffee drew him like a moth to the flame, and made his mouth water for some brew. He had his silk kimono looped over his shoulders open in front. He was not the least bit shy, and he did not care if Utsumi saw him in this condition as he entered the kitchen.

"Ieeeee... Hiromoai-san, I fear soon there'll not be one woman in all Japan you didn't pillow with, sir." He offered in an effort to hide the ill feelings he was harboring against his boss.

"Allow me to tell you something, Utsumi-san. Its mighty hard work, but someone has to do it, no old fool?" He complained with a smirk as he struggled to pick out a pubic hair that lodged between his front teeth during last night's lovemaking, it gave him a little trouble until he finally got it out. He plopped down in the chair as Utsumi poured him a cup of his strong coffee.

As he enjoyed his cup of coffee, Lady Yoke strolled into the kitchen. She was naked and in such a mood she did not care who was with him, as she took the cup from Utsumi's hand and started to drink his coffee on the old man.

Hiromoai noticed what Utsumi was staring at what he could not possibly be allowed to enjoy, and he decided to make the best of his wanting by cupping Lady Yoke's breasts right in front of the old man, and he gently rolled them in his hands. That made her purr like a wild cat that just got into the catnip bush, and getting his head scratched at the same time as she looked dreamy eyed up at him.

The old man finally had to turn away from the two of them when Lady Yoke brazenly straddled Hiromoai's lap and sat down right on his soft member. Utsumi thought she was going to make love to Hiromoai right at the kitchen table with him watching them going at it like two dogs in heat. He again cursed the two of them to the fires of hell under his breath for this terrible insult the both of them just aimed at him and he understood Hiromoai was actually taunting him.

Hiromoai looked in Lady Yoke's eyes and saw the desire and love they contained, and he moaned in his defense. "Lady Yoke, as much as I'd dearly love to share your sexual treasures again on this most enchanting of morning. I'm afraid I'd never be able to rise for the occasion. Besides, I have too much work to prepare for on this beginning day, young lady."

She placed a fake pout on her face as she cried and leaned her lips near his ear. "I understand my lover. Is there anything I can do to help make your troubles any easier for you to endure on this beautiful morning, Hiromoai-san?"

"Huh, there are some things in my life that I'm forced to look after for myself, my little wild one." He grumbled as he shifted himself under Lady Yoke's light weight. This action caused her to get off his lap and go to her room to clean herself and dress properly. Both men listened to the water running as she showered and hummed. Hiromoai allowed his mind to wander as he listened to Utsumi's words pounding in his ears.

"Huh, by all the Kami who force the Japanese Islands to remain held together, and be what they are today and all the tomorrows yet to come sir, you're lucky and truly a very successful man, Hiromoai-san." Utsumi mumbled as he tried to make light of the situation being played out right before his eyes as he sat across from Hiromoai at the table. The business owner was unable to get the troubling thoughts of how lucky he was out of his mind.

The powerful young Japanese businessman smiled as his mind went over his plans of the day, and the coming slaughtering of the foolish American invader to the shores of Japan, and his newly acquired Japanese business. The first thing he had to do was to prepare for his meeting with Batterman that was scheduled for later on that late afternoon. In his mind he could see the American's body lying hacked to pieces in the bottom of the slight depression on the clutter filled construction site he was to meet him at. With Wind hovering like a stalking tiger over his massacred remains, her killing sword locked in her hand and blood dripping from the very tip of the razor sharp shaft, turning the dry ground underfoot into a muddy crimson red.

He had to shake his head in order to get the horrible picture out of his mind of the slaughtered American's gruesome death. As much as he wanted this to happen, he longed for this in fact, he did not want to witness the bloodshed and death of this unknowing and innocent man, about to die only because he brought a business he wanted for himself. When his head cleared of these troubling thoughts, he decided to go to his master suite and shower, and then change into a fresh suit for the day's work, in hopes of feeling a little better about himself.

He informed his workers downstairs he was not going to come to work for the entire day, and he may even take tomorrow off as well if he so chose. If everything worked out as he planned tonight, he intended to celebrate his great victory over Asahiko's last wish, with both Lady Yoke and Wind at the same time. He was dying to see what the two women could teach each other about the art of making love to a woman, and a man. He wanted Lady Yoke to learn the respect of ancient Japan, and he wanted Wind to learn the pleasures modern day women bring to their lovers at night. Already armed with Lady Yoke's permission to share him between her and Wind, he planned to make the best of it and bring the two women together in his bed.

Lady Yoke returned to the kitchen when Hiromoai headed for his bedroom. He patted her lightly on the rearend, her short kimono the only thing she wore as she quickly passed him in the doorway of the kitchen. He enjoyed his shower, and shaved and splashed aftershave on. He went to his closet and found his best suit and dressed. He came downstairs with a slight spring in his step and went to his briefcase, opened it and removed the information he had about the skyscraper at the proposed construction site they were to meet at tonight. It cost him a fistful of cash under the table to get his hands on the plans, along with the promise from the inspector, to keep the job from the public until he received the okay, and another fistful of cash from him.

He unrolled the building blueprints and scanned the drawings of the building site, so he could get a better feel of the job. It was a very impressive offering, but he was more interested in using this site in his effort to kill the American, than he was of landing the future project for his company. He checked the proposal the government was looking for, before they would award the job to the bidder who came closest to their wants. It was a ridiculous low number, and to meet it would insure the builder of making little if any real profit from the venture.

He smiled, knowing full well with the papers he had in his possession, if he truly wanted the authority for the project, it would be a simple feat for him to accomplish. He shook his head knowing working for any government project was nothing more than trouble and little profit at the end of an exhausting major project such as this one was. That was why he was not very interested in the proposition. He rolled the blueprints up in a tight roll, and stuffed them in the cardboard tube. He had a government inter-office copy of the prints, and all inside proposals which explained everything the government wanted for the building, included in the bidding for the project from any company interested in work.

He was well aware when the blueprints were finally given out to collect the offers for the work they would contain little more than half the proposals he had in his possession. This was how the government always trapped the unknowing builders who dared to work for them, into a no win with very little profit situation always in the government's favor. If a builder wanted to make little profit, but always have steady work for his crews, all he had to do was follow up on any government offers which were easy to discover, and he was assured of plenty of work for his company that would be slowly bled to death working for the government.

When he had everything to show the American in order, he stuffed the papers into his briefcase and then snapped it shut. Then he laid the tube containing the blueprints on top of the case to ensure he would remember to take them along for his meeting with the Gai Jin.

Utsumi and Lady Yoke stood behind him as he prepared for his meeting with the American, waiting orders, or to offer in his toils of preparing for the meeting, if they saw he was in need of help. When no requests came, and he was finished preparing for his meeting, she asked if he would like another coffee, or maybe some tea to enjoy before heading out on this meetings.

He took the offered coffee and then not so patiently waited for the time to pass by so he could finally get on with his meeting with the already hated American business owner. The rest of the day passed at a snail's pace for them, and keeping everyone in the apartment in a heightened state of affairs. Hiromoai was getting a little snappy and rather anxious to begin his plan in motion, waiting to leave to meet with the highly insulting and always obnoxious American fool to ever visit his country of Japan and take over a Japanese business.

Utsumi, seeing his mounting anger, decided to disappear for a little while, telling his boss he was going to check on a project currently running a few blocks away from the Tower. He wanted to be out of the apartment and this gave him the perfect excuse he was looking for.

Lady Yoke likewise tried her best to stay out of Hiromoai's sight, by busying herself cleaning up the kitchen and the rest of the huge apartment, and looking after his wash and the dishes from the morning meal. She could also feel the tension emitting from his excited body as he waited for the time to come so he could finally leave for the meeting with the American.

He killed off much of his time by sitting on the couch, while staring at the clock as it slowly ticked off the minutes, as the recording of Japanese drums beat out their enjoyable song. He was relaxing the best he could, for his meeting with the American.

As the clock headed for time to leave for his meeting with the Gai Jin, he rose and announced it was time for Utsumi to dress in one of his suits again, and then leave with Lady Yoke. Utsumi had returned to the apartment from the job site at the time ordered by his boss. He was an important cog in Hiromoai's future plans and today, he was going to take Lady Yoke over to the famed Tsukiji Fish Market down by the docks of Tokyo.

It was always so overcrowded with the crazy mayhem from the countless bidders trying to buy the caught fish at the cheapest price possible, and the poor fishermen screaming back at the buyers while trying to get the best price for their wares. It would be such an easy matter for them to use the time he needed for Wind to kill the lowly

American invader, and then for him to safely return to the apartment before Utsumi, Lady Yoke, and the police officers to return to his building. Besides, with the wild mayhem always present at the Tsukiji Fish Market, it would make it completely impossible for the officers to get a good look at Utsumi's face, and realize they were being deceived by Hiromoai and his two workers, and the businessman successfully deceived them and he could be anywhere in the city.

Utsumi went to his room after returning from the other construction site, and he quickly dressed in the suit Hiromoai gave to him to wear this time. It was the only suit that nearly fit him properly. Hiromoai was much larger than the old man, and his shoulders broader. The suit made Utsumi feel most important in his mind than he was to the pulse of Japan. The fine silk fabric felt so good against his aged and always aching body. When he was dressed, he looked in the mirror and realized just how foolish he looked in the expensive suit.

An exquisite silk suit was not the kind of outfit the aged construction foreman would pick for himself to dress in. No matter how good he looked in it, the suit just could not fully hide it was covering the body of someone more comfortable in the work field running crews of workers than he was in trying to resemble the rich and famous of Japan's elite upper class, as he struggled with the ill fitting suit that was making him feel very uncomfortable.

Lady Yoke rushed to her room and quickly dressed in her usual traveling clothes and hat. When they came out of their rooms, Hiromoai nodded at them, pleased at the way they looked dressed in the fashion they were in. Hiromoai threw a hat to Utsumi, it was daylight and he did not want the police to realize it was not him driving his car and Lady Yoke over to the fish market. The hat threw enough shadow over the old man's face to keep his identity pretty well hidden from the police officers. The only way they would possibly know Utsumi was not him, was if they got right up in his face and saw it, something he knew they would never do if they were honorable police officers. It was terribly insulting for a Japanese person to walk up and stare at the face of another person, and he knew the officers would retain the custom.

He next checked his watch impatiently and told the odd looking pair to get on their way so they could follow out their orders so he could begin his own mission for the day. He followed Utsumi and Lady Yoke to the elevator and waited in the hallway of the Hatanaka Tower, for them to pull out from the underground parking lot in his second car. He did not start breathing properly again until he saw all three police cars parked around his building, quickly lined up behind his second Mercedes at a modest distance, while leaving the parking lot. When he was certain the police were gone from the area, he made a quick dash for his other car and pulled out of the parking lot and went the other way Utsumi headed off in.

Time was getting late and beginning to pressure him slightly, the unusual heavy flow of downtown Tokyo traffic this time of day was causing him to slow his speed down more than he cared to, or he figured on or allowed for in his plan to beat Batterman over to the place where he was supposed to meet on the side of the road. By the time he finally reached the meeting place with the American. Batterman was already parked at the place waiting impatiently, and lightly tapping his foot on the ground while he leaned up against his rented car. He was glaring at him as he pulled up behind his car. His security guards were nowhere to be seen in the area.

The master of Wind smiled to himself as he realized how easy it was for him and Wind to bring the foolish American out from under the protective ring that he had surrounded himself with since first arriving in Japan. This was going to make it much easier for Wind to accomplish her mission and slaughter the American for daring to buy an honorable business in Japan.

He mumbled as he pulled up behind Batterman's car and looked at the impatient looking American and placed his car in park and growled so only he could hear his own words. "That's right foolish Gai Jin, I see I was correct in my assumption of you, you're what I thought you were all along you great fool you. Impatience makes the anxious heart do extremely foolish things to survive in this world, or carry out one's hopes and desires. And I hope for my sake that today you're the fool of all fools to breathe Japan's air, Batterman."

As soon as his vehicle pulled up behind the American, he climbed in the Mercedes and openly glared at Hiromoai for running a little behind for this meeting. Hiromoai never offered the angry American a reason for his being a little late to linkup with him, nor was one asked for by the American either. Then he glanced around the interior of the expensive car and grumbled at the younger Hiromoai as if criticizing him for owning such a luxurious vehicle.

"Man, you sure know how to fucking live here in Japan I see Hiromoai."

"You don't drive an expensive car back in the United States, Batterman? I'd be surprised if a man of your position and wealth wouldn't allow himself to enjoy a luxury car. Sort of use it as a status symbol for yourself and any women you might be interested in pillowing, no Batterman?" He asked, trying to make pleasant conversation while getting into the flow of traffic.

"Naw, give me my good old trusted red Pontiac Grand Prix Wide Track vehicle over all these lousy foreign made buses any time of the fucking day and night, man. I hate these foreign pieces of crap, besides I only buy American made crap in my country, Hiromoai." Batterman retorted with a proud smile for the American made car he drove.

Hiromoai completely ignored the boring American's insulting words while maintaining his composure, as he offered back to him. "Batterman I have the papers and blueprints you need to review in my briefcase on the job we're heading out to visit, resting on the back seat. Please, feel free to help yourself and review the pages while I get us over to the proposed construction site. I have nothing to hide from a possible business partner and hopefully a friend. I'm sorry we have to visit the project at night. It's just a caution I must carry out if I show up anywhere in Japan, reporters and people seem to show up from out of nowhere, trying to find what I'm up to.

"Besides Batterman, if we're to work together on this possible joint project together, we must keep the venture a secret for as long as possible between just us. You don't understand the proud hearts of the Japanese people. If they find out an American and myself are going in on a project as partners, they'd do everything in their power to try and block that partnership," he had to take a quick breath before continuing. Besides, he was constantly using his last name as an insult aimed against the American fool. "Or they'll try to bid against us in an effort to become part of my endeavor. You see Batterman, everyone living in Japan understands if I bid on a project, it's a given that project will become a very good money making proposition for all involved. And let's face it Batterman, everybody is in business to make money. Is that not correct Batterman?"

The American had no idea Hiromoai was trying to taunt him with his mocking tone and ideas of his power and control he though he enjoyed over other businesses in Japan. He ignored most of his contemptuous words from Hiromoai as they drove along. He was only interested in this the first possible project for his new Japanese company, with him at the helm. He reached back and opened the briefcase as Hiromoai wove his way in and out of the flow of traffic. He was having a hard time trying to read the pages in the moving car, and the rapidly fading light.

The excited American businessman did not read all the pages it would have most likely taken him two days to do so. He was only interested in the bottom line of the contract, as he was on any potential project. The size of the job and what they were going to share at the end of the project in the way of profits between them was his only interests. He understood working for the Japanese government everything was going to be kept close to the vest in order to cut costs on the project. But he was willing to forgo huge profits on his first project in Japan, to get his foot in the door so to say with the government. Pleased Hiromoai had the forethought to have the Japanese contract converted to

English, so he could understand what he was reading and at what he read so far on the contract. He dropped the pages back in the briefcase, and turned and offered his soon to be associate. "Okay partner, now I see where you're going on this project. How are we going to split the profits at the end of the project if we work together that is, Hiromoai?"

Without taking his eyes off the road for a second he shot back at the smiling Gai Jin. "That's simple my friend, we'll share the profits at the end of the project evenly, fifty fifty I believe. As all good business partners should do at the end of any job they're working on together." He believed the American would trip all over himself to accept that offer.

"Fifty fifty, you say to my ass huh pal? Sonofabitch man, I can live with that easy enuf I guess, Hiromoai. You surprise the hell out of my ass buddy. I never thought for a stinking second to get a fifty fifty deal with you on this project you're bringing in for our two companies to work on together, man." Batterman offered with surprise in his voice, and he was taking what Hiromoai was doing to him and turned it around and started calling him Hiromoai.

"And how is that Batterman? There should be no surprises withheld between two trusting partners in any project they decide to work together on, no?"

"Because, I thought for sure you'd try and rape my ass over our first project together, man. I never dreamed you'd wanna share the profits of the project evenly, Hiromoai." Batterman placed a smile on his lips as he looked out the window at the swirling traffic ahead of them.

"And why the hell not Batterman, if you're planning to be my partner on this project, then you're equally entitled to half the profits we'll make at the end of the job." He offered with a smirk as he pulled onto the very edge of the soon to be construction site some hundred and fifty yards from the depression and heavy timbers on the site. Both he and Batterman remained in the car and spoke together for a few minutes. He was finding it much easier to refer to the American as Batterman. This was keeping him from getting to know the man any closer, and in that matter he would not feel that bad when Wind ended his life.

"Crap Hiromoai, I can't believe you're not trying to rape my stinking ass over this fricking first project we're putting together, buddy. I'm really surprised and rather pleased at the same time, man. If we can work this easily together on any other projects like we're gonna do on this one, maybe there'll be no need for either of us trying to wipe out the other's company." Batterman offered as he quickly scanned the grounds from the car.

Hiromoai drew in his breath and then offered confidently. "Batterman, I can assure you that there's more than enough money to be made in Japan to please both our companies. As long as neither of us gets too greedy over the matter, that is. Batterman, the true reason I thought to offer you this joint venture, was so that we could start to work together, and I can get your foot in the door on how to work for Japanese companies, and the government. It's much easier to work in the United States than it is here in Japan, Batterman. If we're able to work in peace and harmony together and make some profits while we're at it, we'll be able to drive out the other companies in Japan, and then we can absorb the broken construction companies into our businesses.

"I see it as a simple solution to a complicated problem, if we intend to be successful working together, Batterman.

Besides, I have an ulterior motive held in the back of my mind as well. One I'm quite certain you'll be most beneficial in helping me out with, Batterman." He turned his head to face the American while staring at his cold blue eyes.

"Shit, I fucking thought you might have something held up in the back of your stinking mind, buster. Let's hear the bullshit line pal. I knew this damn deal had to have some fricking strings attached to the damn thing, pal." Batterman snapped at Hiromoai, as if saying here it comes.

He completely ignored Batterman's sarcastic remark as he replied to the concerned looking American. "Yes Batterman, my plan is that I'd like to expand my interests to the shores of your country one day, and what better way to accomplish this great feat than by having an American as my partner here in Japan. In that way I can help you in Japan and in return, you can repay the favor and help me working my company in the United States, Batterman. Who knows how far we can go with this thing, if we're working together peacefully that is Batterman."

"Sonofa fucking bitch, and all along I thought all you damn Japers hated us Americans with a friggin passion, Hiromoai." The American replied as he stared at him in disbelief.

"Yes, that's true, we generally do at that Batterman, but that'll not stop the smart ones living in Japan from working with the disliked Americans in my country, in the name of profits that is, Batterman. Is not the bottom line to the madness that drives our never-ending efforts on this earth, named profits Batterman?" For the first time since they first met for the meeting, Hiromoai flashed a smile at the American.

"Damn right that's the bottom line man, now you're fricking talking my lingo loud and clear to my ass. If we work out good here in Japan, I'd be happy to help you get a foot in the United States, pal. Whatdaya say we get the hell outta this here Nazi built car, and check out this damn site. I wanna see what's facing us on the site. If I like it, I don't see any problem with working together on this project, Hiromoai." Batterman announced as he pulled the handle of the door and opened it and waited for Hiromoai to prepare to get out of the car with him.

Together, they climbed out of the car and began to cautiously pick their way across the baron and cluttered field. In the background of downtown Tokyo, the rush of cars could easily be seen and heard, as the drivers tried to get home for the weekend, and place an end to their week's work and relax until they had to report back to work on Monday. Those were the lucky ones, in many companies, the workers were expected to work on Saturday's, and most for free.

Hiromoai was certain the traffic and so many civilians walking around so close to the construction site, would make Batterman feel he was in no danger of being attacked from any unforeseen assassin who might be lurking in the darkness on the vast site.

That was what Batterman thought as well, as he glanced at the nearness of the cars speeding by them, and the open stores he noticed in the distance. He also saw many people walking around on the sidewalks, and going in and out of the stores to do some last minute shopping and speaking together, or rushing around to either get their last minute shopping done, or rushing home.

As the two powerful businessmen walked over the littered spewed ground of the roughly leveled site, Batterman suddenly tripped over a loose piece of wood he did not notice lying underfoot in the fading light of day, and he almost tumbled hard to the ground. If Hiromoai had not reached out and grabbed him by the arm and helped support his weight. He would have surely hit the ground hard and possibly hurt himself, placing a quick end for Wind to claim Hiromoai's desire to have the worthless American's life ended on this night, so he could then take over his company. Batterman looked at Hiromoai and nodded as he grumbled.

"Sonofa fucking bitch, I almost broke my fricking neck on that one, you woulda thought after all this stinking time, the damn buggers of your country woulda cleaned up some of this shit full site a whole lot better than they have done so far, dammit. Someone's gonna get killed walking around this here mess in the damn dark, Hiromoai." Batterman growled in a huff as he got his footing back and he straightened his body so he could move on.

Hiromoai saw his chance to forward his craftiness and offered smugly to the American while trying not to allow his sneer show. "Batterman, I heard tell there's a history to the very ground we're walking upon. When the earth moving machines finished clearing the plot of destroyed dwellings from the earthquake damage, it was in a fine graded condition. But when it was soon discovered many ancient arrowheads of the Samurai era were uncovered by the excavation work on the site. A horde of greedy civilians descended on the once level and well cleared land like the locus armed with pick and shovel, and they created this dangerous situation you now see here. Not a day goes by the police don't chase someone carrying a pick and shovel away from the site." He took a second and waved his arm out before them and they looked at the pot marked ground that clearly showed signs of someone recently digging in the field recently.

Batterman was extremely interested in antiques and his home attested to this fact, because it had many items of worth and ancient craftsmanship adorning its walls and floors of the structure. The mere mention of arrowheads of the samurai era started him subconsciously searching under foot. He slowed his pace down even more than necessary to walk safely on the darkening site, and he kept his eyes cast down to the ground as he cautiously walked on. Even taking a little time to brush some lose dirt away with his foot every time he thought he noticed the glitter of metal on the ground before him. The more he thought about finding one of the ancient brass samurai arrowheads, the more he slowed his pace and started to look more carefully on the ground for any of them. Even in America, it was well known of the great worth of one of the aged old brass arrowheads from the samurai time in Japan's great history.

Hiromoai smiled as he watched the foolish American looking for one of the prized items of the ancient past out of the corner of his eye, knowing how easy it was for him to get his attention. Greed and the fatuous Americans walked the same road hand in hand towards self-destruction and foolishness. Slowly, he skillfully guided the unsuspecting American towards the depression, even taking a little time to help him look for the old arrowheads he hid along the way. All the while they walked forward, Hiromoai did everything in his power to drive the American's interest and greed in the ancient weapons wild.

"Yes Batterman, I believe it's said during the reign of Lord Kawasomeru's era, a major land battle between his massive Samurai Army, and that of another fearsome warlord took place on this very here spot where we're currently walking. It's further believed that well over three hundred thousand loyal Warriors were sent on the path to greet their ancestors in this great battle that lasted for many days and nights. I know of at least three times, excavation on the site was forced to stop because the digging machines uncovered ancient weapons and armor. It was interesting to watch as the government fools held up progress on the site to retrieve the items of the ancient Samurai. The government is in everything that goes on in Japan, Batterman."

"As it is in the United States Hiromoai, my government has their grubby fat fingers in every damn thing you do in the States. Armor you said to me Hiromoai!" Batterman related as he turned and stared at the younger Japanese businessman, to make certain he was not giving him a pile of bull. All his life, he dreamed of owning a set of ancient samurai armor and weapons. Now, he was more excited than ever in finding something of Japan's great past.

"Don't be so surprised by my last remark Batterman. One is apt to find many such ancient items of warfare from the Samurai times beyond worth and belief, almost anywhere they happen to dig in Japan's sacred soil. At one point or another, about every square acre of Japan was once a field of battle in the past. There have been countless stories about a poor farmer turning over the ground of his farm for planting his crops for the year, and accidentally stumbling across a set of full ancient armor, Katanas and other trivia of ancient warfare and times. That once poor farmer is now one of the richest men in all Japan, Batterman.

"His farm was discovered to be a once encampment for a massive ancient Samurai Army. That Army was attacked while they slept, and everything of the slaughtered was left where it fell, along with the fallen bodies of the dead warriors and their faithful horses. You see Batterman, in the ancient times of Japan it was long believed it was bad Karma to use the sword of a Warrior killed in battle. Sometimes the lowly eta class was allowed to clean the battlefield of the dead, and while they were doing that, their job was to also collect the discarded swords and armor, and they were then melted down and recast for new weapons of death, after the steel was purified by a Shinto monk. But there were so many wars fought in the past of Japan's proud history, it was impossible to collect all the discarded now ancient weapons, and that's why they're so easy to find while digging in the soil, Batterman."

"Sonofabitch man! You're giving me the fricking heebe jeebees, and a hardon about this ancient crap you keep talking about at the same time, man. What the hell happens if I chance to be lucky enough to stumble over one of these damn things lying around here someplace, man?" His eyes were darting wildly all over the vacant site with a new interest, in an all consuming effort to find something from the slaughtered samurai fighters of the long ago past of Japan.

"Well Batterman, if Karma is good on this night and is truly on your side, and you're pure of a heart, soul, and mind, and you're an honorable man in life. You'll likely find one, maybe even two of the ancient items of warfare exciting you so. And, if you don't say anything to a government official about finding any of these items, I can see you returning to America with the items you were lucky enough to discover on this trek. I'll never tell the government if you find something of our great past. The walls of my apartment are covered with such items of great worth that I had the good Karma to discover while excavating sites throughout Japan.

"Yes you see Batterman, you're allowed to buy certain ancient weapons of Japan's honorable past at astounding prices on the open market and keep them for yourself to enjoy, as long as you reside and maintain these items here in Japan." He drew in his breath to make Batterman more excited over the items he was speaking about, by hesitating before he went on with his story to continue to the interested American.

"But alas, I'm sorry the government of Japan forbids any and all removal of such ancient weapons and other items of our great past to any other land in the world, with punishments ranging from heavy fines to even jail time if the infraction is severe enough. And if you happen to know anything about Japan, our jails are some place you truly don't want to visit under any circumstance I assure you. In all of my years of life, I know of only one authentic ancient Katana blade allowed to leave Japan in her history, and that sword was proudly given to your famous President Teddy Roosevelt, as a special gift from our honorable Emperor of the time.

"Most of these weapons in the United States are poor and worthless copies of real items, usually made in Spain, China or elsewhere. Unless someone was able to smuggle the genuine weapon passed our foolish Customs Officers, which is not impossible to accomplish mind you, Batterman. Yes, of course it's also true Batterman, a number of your museums have some ancient weapons of Japan, but they were given them by collectors or from my government as special gifts. Please, keep looking while we check out the rest of the construction site further, if Karma is upon your shoulders, you'll find what you seek on the ground.

"There was another way some of our ancient swords of my country were able to leave Japan. That was through the World War, where some of our Officers who carried their great ancestor's Katana swords to battle the Americans with. When these Officers were killed in battle, the foreign soldier who killed them was able to keep the Officer's sword as a keepsake for his accomplishments during that battle. So I'm forced to correct myself and offer there are many authentic Japanese swords that left my country, and many have ended up in the United States."

"Sonofa fucking bitch Hiromoai, I'm beginning to sweat between my stinking nuts thinking of these damn arrowheads you keep speaking about hanging around this damn site, man. You got me going about these damn things I don't mind telling ya, man. I gotta find me one of them stinking things if it's the last thing I do tonight." Batterman repeated in an excited voice.

"Please my new partner in the construction field, I think you might very well be successful in your search for these items if you were to wander in this direction that is. Because I'm aware there was a huge bivouac of Warriors in this area from reading the ancient maps of the past time, Batterman. Here is where most of the ancient items we speak of were located in abundance may I add for you." He guided the American towards the lumber in easy sight. He was trying everything in his power to make the American look for the arrowheads, that way he would be ill prepared for Wind's assault against him when she was called back from the Floating World.

The excited American businessman actually allowed Hiromoai to lead him towards the large wood pile. He would have allowed him to lead him to the gates of hell if it could be littered with the weapons he was searching for on this construction site. Forgotten was all thought of checking out the site for their joint business project. Batterman was now too wrapped up in his search for the ancient weapons of the past and he lost all interest in the project he was there to judge.

He was drooling all over the thought of possibly finding an ancient samurai arrowhead as he kicked at a small pile of dirt out of his way with his foot as he walked by it. He indeed wanted to actually get down on his hands and knees and search the littered ground with his hands, but he fought off this wild desire for the time being. He wondered if he could buy a metal detector somewhere near this site. That was going to be his next suggestion, but he quickly shelved that thought when they both ended up leaning against the scattered stack of heavy timbers.

He smiled at the American as he offered in a matter of fact tone to him. "Here is the exact position where it's believed to be the very heart of the once ancient encampment I spoke of moments ago to you. In fact Batterman, it's believed an ancient hearth was discovered in that slight depression not long ago. That's why the dirt was removed from the spot that created that depression we're looking at. Since the digging stopped, the rains have uncovered many other undiscovered arrowheads and the likes in the depression. Every night, the depression seems to expand further by illegal searchers who use the cover of darkness to hide their pillage of Japan's proud and ancient history." He allowed a smile to cross his lips as he stared at the excited and overly interested American, as he wanted to move off in the direction he pointed in.

"Say Hiromoai, do you mind if we check out the depression a little closer for a few minutes? I wanna see if I can find one of these damn arrowheads you keep speaking about tonight, man." Batterman requested as he stared into the eyes of Hiromoai.

"What about our business proposition we're at this construction site to discuss, Batterman? That's the true reason for why we're here in the first place I believe, Batterman. Though the thought of searching for some of these ancient items of war is most thrilling, I'm more interested in coming to some sort of conclusion on the deal that I'm trying to forge between our two construction companies, Batterman." He grinned at the overly excited acting American as he nodded yes to answer Batterman's request, and then he waited for his reply.

"The hell with the damn business project man, whatever the hell you want we'll do if I find any of them fucking arrowheads down there, buddy." He grumbled as he stared in the depression while leaning against the stack of heavy timbers.

"Then by all means Batterman, I'll be most pleased to help you search the depression until we have the luck of the gods to find any of the items that you're in search of. Can I help you down the side of the depression? I was in the depression just the other day and it was rather slippery area to climb in and out of, so please watch your step as you're going in it. I don't want anything to happen to you while we're visiting this construction site." He offered to the excited American businessman as he put out his hand to help him get down into the depression.

"In a pig's ear you can help me get down there, buddy. Get the hell outta my way and watch my dust, buster." He snorted in an excited voice as he nearly leaped into the hole. He actually fell forward from his momentum and the jump in the hole, as the loose ground underfoot shifted under his weight. It did not stop him for one second as he remained on the ground on his hands and knees, and he actually started to dig in the soft dirt with his bare hands, like a rutting pig in search of edible roots to enjoy.

He followed the American into the slight depression and moved to the side out of his way, until he was almost standing right on top of the rock with the arrowhead he planted earlier leaning against it. Without looking down to make certain the arrowhead was still there, he offered smartly to the wildly searching American. "Here Batterman, I believe this is one of the rocks from the ancient hearth I just spoke to you of."

He eagerly looked at where Hiromoai was standing and then warned him in a thrilled voice. "Holy shit man, don't move your stinking hoof an inch, man. I think I see something by it, buddy." The American actually crawled on his hands and knees over to Hiromoai's feet.

"What is it you see lying there Batterman? I just looked at the exact spot before I moved here and I was unable to locate anything of worth in this foul hole. Perhaps, your eyes are better than mine, Batterman." He asked and offered at the same time as he tried his best to hide the smile covering his face. He was having a bit of trouble trying not to laugh at the well dressed American fool crawling on his hands in knees in the dirt in his expensive suit, where he and all Americans belonged as far as he was concerned. A Japanese man would never allow himself to be lowered to such a state of greed and want. Again, his anger for the Americans rose in his chest and mind. The fools made it so easy for anyone they were dealing with, to dislike them so much.

"Hiromoai, I think I see one of the damn things you just told me about. It looks like one of them there ancient arrowheads I think. Or at least it looks like a chunk of stinking brass or something just like it man." He said as he picked up the piece of dull brass and sat down right on the dirt as he closely examined the arrowhead by slowly rolling it over in his dirt covered hands, while beaming from ear to ear as he carefully studied the old weapon.

Hiromoai bent down by Batterman's shoulder and examined the ancient item he found as he offered in a sort of excited voice to the pleased American. "Ahhh... sooo, Karma is truly resting upon your side on this fine day, Batterman. That's a Karimata tip, the ancient forked broad arrowhead commonly used in and around the thirteenth and fourteenth century, by many warring Samurai of the time. You're very lucky on this day, because it's worth maybe ten thousand of your American dollars on the black market I believe, Batterman."

"Sonofa fricking bitch man! You don't say Hiromoai. But I got stinking news for you fella, I'll never sell the damn thing no matter what's offered for it back in the States, man. I'd never offer it for sale when I get back home I assure you man." He mumbled as he greedily stuffed the small arrowhead in his pocket like it was his right to claim as he added. "Do you think there could be anymore of the damn things hanging around here someplace, Hiromoai? You know what they say in the States, where there's one there's usually more of the damn things hanging around, man."

He again smiled, knowing he had the greedy American right where he wanted him, as he thought he would when he decided to act against him, and it was time to begin closing the trap surrounding the foolish American's fate. This was so he could leave the area and be home long before the police, Utsumi and Lady Yoke returned to his apartment, and the police following them had again resumed their tight surveillance of him and his luxurious penthouse room.

"Huh, I feel I must warn you of something else I believe you're forgetting about my new friend from across the sea, don't be too greedy about yourself, Batterman. You have just discovered more than most Japanese people living on the Island have ever found all their lives of endless searching for such ancient things of worth and want. If there are anymore age old arrowheads resting in this area, why not leave them for the next man blessed with good Karma, and the honored Kami who enjoy control such things to discover."

"The hell with that load of bullshit fella, and fuck them where they breathe from, man. If there's one of the damn things in this here hole then there has to be more of the damn things hanging around here. And I'm gonna find them all while I'm at it, buster. I want as many of the damn things as I can find, Hiromoai. One never knows when I might come across them again in my lifetime, if ever again man. So I might as well make the best of what I can find right now." The American warned as he started to crawl around the bottom of the depression a second time.

The Japanese businessman wanted to continue feeding the fever now consuming the greedy American's soul, and he stealthily uncovered a second arrowhead with his foot, but again he allowed Batterman to discover it and take it in his greed. The raging fever of covetousness was taking over his mind and body, as he continued to dig wildly in the loose dirt with his hands, until he found a third Karimata brass arrowhead in the soft ground.

He waited not so patiently until Batterman found five of the six hidden ancient arrowheads he had planted earlier in the day. He cared little if the sixth arrowhead went ever undiscovered by the greedy American fool. He felt he lost all six of the rare arrowheads to Batterman, or anyone else that happened to find the missing last one. For him, it was of no great loss, not with him looking at stealing Asahiko's business out from under the foot of the greedy American fool. He wanted Wind brought back to the world of the living so she could rid Japan of this ugly Gai Jin's foul presence. At a leisurely pace, he moved Batterman over to the piece of timber sticking out from the side of the bank of the hollow with Wind's sword hidden under it.

Slowly, Batterman worked his way towards the timber pile, not knowing this was what he was supposed to do under Hiromoai's careful guidance.

He drew Batterman's attention over to the spot where he wanted him to look next, by trying to see around him as the greedy American continued to dig in the ground before him.

The overly excited American businessman was so consumed by greed for the ancient artifacts he finally looked to where Hiromoai stared, in an effort to try and cut him off before he went after what he was looking at. In case he spotted something hidden in the dirt he wanted and he did not see it yet. Batterman just could not believe the outstanding luck he was having with finding so many of the ancient samurai brass arrowheads.

He tried to get around Batterman, but the greedy American was quicker and covered the timber log with the bulk of his large body. He thought what Hiromoai saw was on the floor of the depression and he started to drag frantically with his fingers in the dirt of the pit, raising a small cloud of dust and a pile of dirt by his knees for his efforts.

As the ground under his hands moved, the slight covering of dirt resting over the hilt of Wind's ancient katana fell free, finally exposing more of the crumbling hilt, now he noticed the sword hidden under the timber and he stabbed his hands into the soft dirt. His hands instantly wrapped around the handle of the ancient blade, and he pulled the sword free of the earthly dirt prison. His eyes opened wide as he stared at the well aged ancient sword.

"By the wonderful gods who control such luck over the matters as this, what did you just find there, Batterman?" Hiromoai asked as if he was truly amazed at the stunning discovery when the rude American tried to clean the clinging dirt free from the ancient weapon of death.

"Sonofabitch man, I found me one of them there fricking old Samurai pig stickers, Hiromoai."

"Please, allow me examine the obviously ancient weapon, Batterman. I know of such ancient things of my country's honorable past. I have the knowledge needed, for I have many years of studying Japan's ancient past under my belt, Batterman." He wiggled his fingers in hopes the foolish American would relinquish his hold on the ancient killing sword of Wind, so he could have it again and control her revenge aimed against this American Gai Jin.

CHAPTER THIRTY ONE

"Hell I'll give this damn thing to your ass Hiromoai, its mine I found the damn thing man. I found it and it's mine to keep buster, so no way in hell am I going to give it to you." Batterman pulled the ancient sword closer to his body as if he was trying to protect it from Hiromoai outstretched hands. In case he tried to take the once deadly weapon from him by force.

"Yes, yes of course, it's yours to keep for all times to come, Batterman. I won't argue with you over that point you have just made. But without my assistance and knowledge, you'll never get the ancient Katana blade out of Japan to add it to your private collection back in the United States. You'll be arrested as a smuggler if you try to get the weapon out of Japan without my assistance my new friend. Let me see it, so I can tell you what you have discovered on this night of wonderment, and if it has any true worth to its ancient history." He again put out his hand and wiggled his fingers at the American. He knew what he was doing, although he was aware Wind stated no matter who unsheathed her ancient sword, as long as he lived and breathed. She was still bound by the laws of the ancient curse placed upon her soul by Lord Kawasomeru, to answer any request Hiromoai demanded of her powerful spirit in the land of the living.

He wanted the sword back so he could unsheathe the weapon and release Wind's wrath on the unsuspecting greedy American. Now he regretted allowing the American to find the weapon, he should have never allowed the greedy fool to ever get his filthy hands on the sword. His anger was also aimed at Wind for convincing him to allow the foolish American to find the sword, he should have found it. Then this slight argument would have never took place and Wind would already attacking the American if he found the sword first. His patience was wearing thin and he dared to give Batterman a nasty glare as he waited for the sword to be placed in his hands.

"Look here man, I told you before that I'm fricking in with you on this god damn project, even if we don't make a thin stinking dime on the proposition working for your lousy government, pal. So if you want me to stay in with the damn project then you better help me get this shitting thing the hell outta Japan in one stinking piece, or I might be forced to reconsider my offer to work with you on this joint project together, buster." The American looked at the Japanese businessman as if he was trying to steal the ancient sword from him.

"Yes, yes by all means, of course I'll help you get the seemly ancient blade out of Japan safely my new friend and future partner. It'd be my pleasure to assist you in this most unwise endeavor, Batterman. But first I'd like to examine the ancient looking sword first hand. Do you know how much this thing could possibly be worth on the black market, if it's as old as I believe it might be? If it's old enough and happened to belong to a certain Samurai or even a powerful Shogun or the blade could even identify the Master Crafter of the ancient looking weapon, and if he was one of a certain few honorable Crafters. You could name your price for the obviously ancient weapon." He waited for him to hand over Wind's sword as he requested from the American.

"What? Are you trying to tell me that you think the damn sword might have the name of the big shot Jap bugger who might have owned the damn thing, or even the maker of the ancient sword engraved on it somewhere I can't see it, do you Hiromoai?" He asked stunned over the possibility of actually knowing the samurai's name who might have owned the sword, and who used it in the heat of battle in the past. He glanced at the sword, as his mind went deep in thought over the last words Hiromoai uttered at him.

"I truly have no way of knowing this for certain, until I had a chance to closely examine the ancient sword of the Samurai, Batterman. Only I'd know where to properly look for the Warrior, or the maker's name imprinted on the great weapon, if one truly exists on the blade that is, Batterman." He was desperately trying to act like the ancient sword might not even be as old as it looked to the hated American.

Reluctantly, Batterman finally surrendered the ancient katana blade to Hiromoai.

He took Wind's killing sword greedily from Batterman's hands, and for the briefest of moments held it in a threatening manner, and dared to even aim the sword against Batterman's body. He felt his strength return to his body, now he was again in possession of Wind's sword and her spirit again. He never understood until this moment how much he was becoming to rely on the ancient weapon, and, or on Wind's help until the aged weapon was no longer within his command. Then, with a smile that was more of a sneer, he slowly lowered the great blade and then worked the steel shaft out of the wood prison of the scabbard. He took his time releasing the sword because he wanted Wind to appear slowly before the stunned eyes of this loathsome Gai Jin invader to his country. He wanted to make it last as long and slow as possible, before Wind stood before them both and he released her to slaughter this hated American fool.

"C'mon, C'mon man and get the damn thing out of the damn holder will ya man. I wanna see what the fricking shaft of the damn thing looks like, Hiromoai." He barked at the young Japanese businessman while he looked over his shoulder, and waited for him to pull the deadly sword free of the crumbling wood covering.

"It's believed throughout all Japan that only good things happen to those who are patient, and wait their announcement and birth anew, Batterman. In this case, you'll be treated to one of the many wonders and myth of the ancient and honorable great past of Japan in one blinding flash of memory and wonder. Behold fool of the sacred things of awe that I lay bare at your worthless and loathsome feet. For I give you the ancient and only true female Samurai Warrior to have ever walked upon the sacred soil of Japan ancient past.

"Batterman, allow me to introduce you to Wind! She'll be your truth, your justice, your final vision while the gods of who allowed you to continue to draw another breath within this world, watch as your last judgment befalls your worthless presence in Japan." He snarled nastily as he aligned the deadly sword where it would easily pull free of its wooden prison, and then he pulled the sword free of the scabbard with one mighty tug, and then he held it high over his head as he stared intensely at Batterman with wildness burning in his eyes. Almost instantly, the small hollow was filled with an eerie, bright growing cold light expanding outwards every second.

Batterman was stunned by the suddenness of the growing light and fell down against the side of the bank of the depression, his feet trying desperately to find a good foothold in the loose shifting dirt, so he could get out of the pit and flee what was trying to take shape before his eyes. Fearing the boiling mass of light was going to burn him as it completely engulfed the shallow hole in the earth in a blinding flash. He even tried to protect his eyes with his arms from the harsh glow as he continued to back away from the eerie light and growled at the Japanese businessman.

"What in the unholy hell's going on here, Hiromoai? What in fucking hell are you up to and what's this damn light about, dammit? What is this damn thing, man? I'm warning you..." He roared with anger as he stared at the center of the boiling light. A shape of a person was slowly struggling to take form within the boiling glow. He continued to try and get away from the glow by crawling backwards up the slight dirt slope. But the soft ground continued to kick out from under his feet, and it stopped him from getting out of the pit to safety from what it was, and Hiromoai obviously controlling what was taking place before him.

"You'll find your cursed destiny dealt to you on this fateful night, and on your last worthless day living on the earth at that, Batterman. All you have feared throughout your loathsome life will come true on this single night of wonderment and justice, Gai Jin invader to the sacred Island of my ancestors." Was all he replied to the scared American as he slowly lowered the ancient katana sword, and stared at the shape now rapidly taking form within the dimming light of the hollow. The sudden bright radiance seemed to be concentrating its efforts around the very tip of the weapon of death held in Hiromoai's hands.

For the first time in his life, Batterman was scared to death, scared enough to cover his eyes with his hands, and for his body to tremble in fright from the glowing light so near his person. He had no idea what was happening, all he understood was something not in his favor was taking place before him. He understood he had to get out of the pit, if he wanted a fighting chance of saving his life against whatever it was Hiromoai had summoned from the pits of hell, with the power of the ancient sword locked so tightly in his hand.

Suddenly, a sweet sounding obvious female voice instantly calmed his fear, as he heard the words of ancient Japanese almost being sung by what he took to be a possible spirit lingering within the glow of the old sword. They were the words spoken by a female voice, and he was not afraid of any female, living or dead.

The voice completely ignored Batterman's presence and it was speaking only to Hiromoai standing near him. "Hiromoai-sama, I thank you for releasing me from the lonely world of the dead and endless waiting." Her naked body fully appeared in all its beauty before the two men.

Batterman, who ended up sitting on his rump on the side of the pit, sat forward in the dirt and smiled as he stared at the breathtaking apparition of the beautiful naked woman, standing before him and Hiromoai without a hint of shame. Quickly, his strength and confidence returned to his large frame, and he mumbled to Hiromoai. "Sonofa fucking bitch, does she come with the damn sword I just found buddy? Who the hell is she anyway man? Where the hell did she come from?"

He did not bother to answer Batterman's request as he allowed the spirit to take command of the ancient sword. Once Wind held her killing sword in hand, her exquisite form took on a more solid shape the instant she was in possession of the deadly blade, as she purred sweetly to her master as she continued to ignore the other man in her presence and the swords returned to its original luster like it was just created by the master sword maker who forged the great sword.

"Do not be in fear of my person, everything that revolves around the eye of all creation is preordained, as ordered and as it should be throughout history's past. It is not possible to bend the true fate of man, nor of his existence. Everything that takes place in life has a beginning and an ending. It is I, the force who shall drive back the will of the feared Devil Kami, and all his evil desires. Death will slay the unholy workers of the world with its wings of revenge and justice, and it is I who am the wind that gives lift to those currents of vengeance. I am vengeance pure and total to all those wayward fools who dare to plot treachery against my Lord and Master in the living world." She then turned and instantly took a more threatening stance against the stranger standing so near her lord and master as she aimed her unsheathed sword directly at his body, and slowly waved it menacingly before the American who again was trying to back out of the slight depression as she offered to the stranger to her eyes.

"Neither Heaven nor the red hell is at peace on this night of true justice for my Lord and Master to enjoy, foul one who pollutes the pure air about my Lord and Master's presence."

She froze in place the instant Hiromoai spoke, though the words he said were foreign to her ears. She understood her master was speaking words to the Gai Jin trying to escape her presence.

"Batterman, I truly regret that you're about to die through no fault of your own, you're nothing more than an innocent bystander who finds himself caught up in the matters that concern only Japan and her faithful sons and daughters, and the people who control such things in my country. A mere pawn if you will in the fate of things bound to take shape on this night, Batterman. It was only by your hand and greed, and your acquisition of Asahiko's cursed construction company that placed you in the position you now find yourself mired in, fool.

"Asahiko's dishonored company was to be mine to control, to own, but the crafty old bastard found a way to keep his worthless company out of my hands, for what he thought would be forever. But only until your timely death is consummated will I not own his foul company. Since you're totally guiltless in this matter, I'll give you a few seconds to make peace with your God, I owe you at least that much for you are guiltless in this rapidly unfolding drama, Batterman." He offered to the American businessman as he actually grinned at him.

Batterman stared back at Hiromoai with is mouth hanging open in stunned disbelief as if he had just lost his mind, and what was happening was nothing more than a terrible nightmare taking place that he would soon awake from. All he had to do was wake and the nightmare would be gone from his mind and view. He drew in a breath and hissed at Hiromoai while continuing to stare at him. "What the fuck are you talking about for crap sake? My fucking death you say, Hiromoai? That's pure bullshit and bad manners man! No way in hell will that happen to my ass I tell ya, buster. Look buddy, I have no fricking intention of lying down and dying for anyone, especially a stinking Japper like yourself, or his lousy bitch slave standing before me waving that there pig sticker in my stinking face like she's going to use it against my ass, buster.

"You just try and send your animal's mother at me and see what the hell I'll do to her damn ass, Mac. I'm prepared to protect myself from anyone who tries and attack me, Hiromoai. You think I came here unable to protect my fucking self from everyone or thing alive or dead, buster? Not on your stinking life Hiromoai. I got news for you pal. I can take care of this bitch and you at the same damn time, buster." He pulled a 9 mm automatic Colt pistol from his pocket and aimed it directly at the naked woman as he continued to try and get a foothold in the loose dirt behind his feet.

He then turned his attention towards the woman aiming her killing sword at him. In his confused mind, he could not fathom the idea that this beautiful naked woman was dead, a spirit from the world beyond thought and understanding, here to do Hiromoai's bidding against him, or anyone else he aimed this female weapon at. He stared at the beautiful woman before growling at her in a savage tone of voice. "Now you look here bitch, I'm warning you, I don't particularly like killing a fricking woman, especially a naked one who looks as good as you do, baby. But you take one more fucking step at my ass with that there fricking pig sticker, and I'm going to blow you in fricking half and send you back to the hell from where you came." It was here he noticed the once marred and rusted sword looked like it was just made.

"Hey what the hell gives around here anyway dammit, I though you told me that was an ancient sword that looked like it was so rusty it'd crumble in your damn hands, Hiromoai? Look at the damn thing it looks as good as new man."

Although she did not understand one word the angry American just hissed at her master in anger, she did not like him aiming the harsh sounding words of hatred at Hiromoai's person. And when she saw the outsider suddenly aim the weapon that made the loud noise of thunder, and sent the dragon's tooth soaring through the air to kill without vision of the thing killing. She reacted without the slightest bit of hesitation to her actions on order to protect her master's life as she roared at the stranger standing before her.

"Lowly dog eater from a far off land, save your repulsive and unflattering words and actions for the eta class, your words are wasted speaking to my Lord and Master in such a loathsome manner. His honorable ears no longer hear, nor will they listen to what evil you offer him, foul one. Your waited destiny no longer concerns him who is of greatness and light. It is I, Wind who shall melt out his finally justice on all fools who do not respect and heed my Lord and Master's faithful word." Wind took a step at the American, putting her body between the gun and her master's body in her attempt to protect him from harm.

Batterman moved his weapon and aimed it right at her chest and held it. He was daring her to make any further threatening moves against him, and he was going to fire without hesitation of his own if she continued to move at him in the pit.

Wind warned as she moved more at Batterman. "Your thunder making stick that fires dragon's teeth causes me no fear or harm. I am above all earthly harm you can possibly do with your weapons of uselessness against my person or my Master presence, fool of the living world."

Batterman understood enough Japanese to know what she just hissed at him as he snorted back at her. "We'll hafta see about that there stinking threat little lady, won't we?" He then aimed his weapon at her chest again and waited for her to stop her slow advance towards him. When she did not stop coming at him, he warned her for a third time in a much more harsh and threatening voice laced with sudden fear and anger. "I told you to stay the fuck away from me with that damn pig sticker of yours, didn't I bitch? I won't tell you again. Take another fricking step at me with the damn thing, and you'll be back with your dead ancestor's, honey. Hiromoai, if you value the life of this bitch, you betta stop her from coming at me with that damn sword of hers. I don't wanna kill a bitch, but I will if I'm forced to man."

Wind continued to close in on him while showing no fear as she warned again in a threatening voice at the American. She had no idea if the stranger was not capable of understanding her words, nor did she really care as she snarled at him. Foul one who pollutes the clean air of Japan with your detestable presence and evil breath. My soul has been prepared for my death for countless years now, is yours? If it is not then you shall be ill prepared for the death that I will soon unleash upon your unholy soul. I believe I smell fear from your worthless being, evil one. Fear is what makes you weak of will and mind. Fear turns a faithful and brave Samurai into an already defeated foe. Repent while you still have worthless air within your cursed lungs, and life in your body to do so. Make your body pure so the Kami will allow you a most pleasing place in which to wait out your eternity, and see if they shall allow you to be reborn to the living world."

Batterman had enough and realized this female truly meant to kill him and he stopped hesitating and fired once to protect his life. Then he waited for the beautiful woman to drop the sword and tumble to the ground in agony from the bullet entering her body. Although he did not aim to kill the beautiful female, he hit her high in the shoulder only to wound her. To his stunned amazement, the female warrior did not even flinch an inch, as the bullet passed right through her being as if she was made of the air she was born from countless years past.

"Sonofa fucking bitch, what the hell are you, bitch!" he suddenly roared as he emptied the rest of the rounds in the gun at the beautiful naked woman, once he realized she was more of a threat against him than he realized.

She ignored the slight stinging sensation the bullets briefly caused her as she swung her sword effortlessly, lopping off the arm with the weapon in it from his body.

Hiromoai had to jump out of the line of fire, he was standing directly behind Wind, and the bullets traveled so easily through her body that he was afraid of getting hit by them. After he moved, the rounds dug into the soft dirt where he once stood. He stared as she began her finally assault on the American's body.

Batterman thundered from the pain as he grabbed his injured arm with his other hand and again moved his feet frantically behind him, trying desperately to back out of the pit soon to become his grave if he did not get out of it in time, as he bellowed in rage at her. "You fucking murderesses you! How dare you attack me with that damn sword of yours, bitch!" He turned to Hiromoai and roared at him this time. "Stop your stinking bitch from hell! Stop her before she kills me, dammit! I did nothing to be killed for to her or you!"

Wind prepared herself to take pleasure in offering the stranger to her lands a slow and very painful death to endure. She was angered by his loud and terribly threatening tone of voice he aimed at her liege lord. She realized this lowly Gai Jin was probably cursing at her lord and master, and this angered her and she was not going to allow it to continue. But she was forced to turn to Hiromoai as he loudly called out her name from behind her.

"Wind-san, I bid you don't play with the Gai Jin, I order you to dispatch him quickly and as painless as possible. He's absolutely correct, it's not his fault he finds himself trapped in the position he finds himself locked in, and we must remain civilized at all cost to him. Be merciful, he warrants that much from us, my murderess. I believe if we met under different circumstances, in a different world and different time, we would've been able to work together and possibly become friends in both business and social life." He offered in flawless Japanese to Wind. Causing Batterman to wonder what he was saying to this woman about to kill him, because he did not catch all his words spoken in Japanese to his female weapon.

"Hai my merciful Lord and Master, it shall be as you have commanded. I shall dispatch this man beast with the foreign tongue and rude manners with little pain to his earthly body. I will not punish him needlessly for my Master's sake." She bowed as she committed the Japanese word for murderess to her memory. Then she turned to the American who was still trying to back out of the slight depression, while hanging onto his injured arm with his other hand attending to his bleeding. She stared into the eyes of Batterman for a brief moment as she slowly approached him with her ancient killing sword held at the ready.

"Stop her Hiromoai you better fucking stop this bitch of yours. For the love of God man, look, anything you want man, you got it as long as I'm allowed to live and get the hell out of Japan. You want Asahiko's fucking company, fine, take the damn thing and choke on it for all I care, buddy. I'll sign the fricking company over to you for nothing if that's what you want." He was reduced to pleading for his life, as he held on to his arm minus his hand.

He did not reply to Batterman's pleading, he turned his back on the American which to her sharp mind was his death warrant. She again moved at the scared stranger to her country.

She stopped moving and then bowed to the American staring at her wild eye while still trying to back out of the pit, paying her respect to Batterman for what she was about to do to his earthly form. She hesitated and then lifted her blade to a proper strike angle, allowed it to hover for several seconds as she watched the shaking American's frantic struggle for his existence on the earth. Then she swung her killing blade with all the might she possessed in her rock hard body, as she took the last few steps at the frightened American again.

"Noooooo... don't fucking kill me bitch from wherever the hell you come from." He suddenly bellowed in his defense, as he raised his good arm in hopes of deflecting the sword strike. The words echoed in the night air as he tried desperately to protect himself and also try and fend off the assault from the sword and this mystical woman moving to attack him at the same time. His efforts were for naught, for Wind's blade sliced swiftly through his neck and bone and good arm in one motion, as easily as it did the air surrounding her perfect body.

His head was still screaming its cry of death as it tumbled through the night air. When it rolled to a somersaulting stop, forehead over chin at her feet she again bowed towards the non-seeing eyes of Batterman as his lips continued to quiver until they fell still. Then she announced to her master. "Your command was carried out as you have requested, Hiromoai-sama."

The young Japanese businessman turned and studied Wind's handicraft with the sword. He was pleased that Batterman was offered and had received a swift death. As his chest swelled with pride, he nodded to the ancient female warrior called Wind. He knew with the American's death, Asahiko's foul construction company would be placed on the selling block, and he would have first shot at acquiring it for far less than he was originally willing to pay for the company. He allowed a slight smile to cross his lips as he stared at the dead American's form.

She was deeply troubled and spoke in a rush to her master with a trembling and questioning voice. Seeking his wisdom to help ease the worries she was suddenly suffering through. "Hiromoai-sama, you called me a murderess when speaking to the lowly Gai Jin before his death. Why was that word spoken to me my Master? I am guilty of following your honorable orders of destroying your enemy no matter where they are in the world of the living, Hiromoai-sama.

"How can I possibly be considered a murderess, if you are the one who ordered me to commit these deaths in your honorable name, my Liege Lord? A faithful Samurai cannot be considered a murderer if he or she is guilty of obeying his Lord and Master's commands faithfully that is my duty. Please, explain this confusion to my non understanding soul, so that I might rest at peace once I am returned to the Floating World of wonderment and myth and forever waiting. How can this be so in the land of the living, Hiromoai-sama? I am in need of your vast wisdom and guidance so I might sort this problem out in my foolish mind, my Master over life and death."

Hiromoai was absolutely furious at being questions by Wind in this manner, his supposed faithful servant and he snapped savagely at her before thinking of his words of anger aimed at the extremely dangerous spirit. "Shut up whore of the dark world and give me that damn sword of yours, so I can put it and you back to sleep until you learned how to obey my command without hesitation or question. You dared to question me! Your Lord and Master! What treachery do you offer against me? Has your stay in the Floating World confused your cursed mind, and made you forget who your Master is in the land of the living, Samurai? Has the Kami of evil been able to corrupt your once obeying mind against me, Wind? I'm your Lord and Master, and until you finally realize that I'm the one who commands your body and soul Samurai, you'll find yourself rotting in the damn Floating World of forever waiting."

She was now familiar with many of the terribly stinging words he harshly aimed at her being, but his delivery of those words angered her more as she hissed at him without thought. "Huh, I know of this hateful word you speak at me, Hiromoai-sama. Whore! It is an old word used in my times of life. That means I am the lowest of the low, an eta of the lowly class of filth to pollute Japan's pure air." She actually growled, her anger growing in her body.

"Yes Warrior and that's exactly what you are. You're nothing more than that without my guidance and control. You don't exist without my command and want. You're what I say you are and nothing more. You're less than a fucking whore, an eta who threatens treachery against her Lord and

Master." He snarled, allowing his anger at being questioned by the dangerous spirit to control his better thoughts. He felt he had to put her in her place, or lose her to the doubts suddenly flooding her confused mind. For her to question him once, would give her the confidence to question him again, and this went against everything she told him of the past and her supposed loyalty to who she believed was this Lord Kawasomeru. A loyal samurai warrior would never dare to question his master, and expect to retain his head.

"Then it is true what I was called in your name. By your honorable lips you uttered those words at me, Hiromoai." Wind cried in frustration as she took a few steps from him and nearer to the body of Batterman lying on the ground by her feet as she stared in disbelief at him.

"What's true? Look Samurai I don't have the fucking time or the patience for this kind of shit from you. I have to leave before the damn police arrive on the scene, and they find me standing in the middle of this mess and arguing with you. I'm certain someone must have heard the shots fired by Batterman's weapon, and by now they have notified the police. Give me that damn sword, right now!" Hiromoai growled as he glared angrily at her. Ignoring the fact she insulted him by omitting the sama or lord from his name.

"Then it is true what you called me, and what the honorable Asahiko-san and his son called me before I released them from their earthly bonds. Their words I thought were words of hatred and pain aimed at me to cause me hesitation, to maybe allow them to continue to live their foul lives before I interfered with it. I see they were true words spoken against me in all accounts. I am nothing more than a murderess for the wants and desires of my unjust

Lord and Master. I am a worthless tool of destruction for your greedy gains I understand, Hiromoai."

Angered by her accusing words and failure on her part to add the 'san', or 'sama' to his name, he threw caution to the wind as he smiled at the upset warrior and then bellowed and lifted his fist to the Heavens. "Whether you like it or not, you made me, Hiromoai Hatanaka, Japan's most powerful and fucking richest tycoon to walk the lands of Japan. For this I thank you Warrior."

Hiromoai was still of the belief that she was unable to attack his person, for fear of what the Kami of vengeance of the hidden world would do to her body, if she dared to give harm to him. But he was ill prepared for what next happened to his body by the outraged female samurai.

His raging words of anger rang with the force of the roaring thunder storm in her ears. He just dared to utter the one name of her sworn enemy of life and death. Hiromoai roared the name of the repulsive warrior who had killed her one and only lover on the field of battle, like a filthy Ronin, a criminal stalking the night. Captain Katsunoke Seisakajo's smiling face instantly flashed back in her mind, and it seemed to be guiding her anger and killing sword forward without thought, as Hiromoai's last name was repeated over and over in her pounding ears.

Her body was nothing more than a petrified bundle of taut muscles and upset nerves as she glared angrily at Hiromoai's detestable form standing before her, and she was forced to stand as if rooted to the very ground under her feet. Her mind drowning in the consuming darkness of revenge, rage, and hatred of the man she thought as her honorable lord and master. An all consuming and suffocating hatred that tightened in her constricted dry throat as her body prepared to attack her once believed lord and master.

She remembered the cursed assassin who had killed her lover like a coward in the middle of the night, too many years to think back. Samurai Warrior Tetsuo Hatanaka was the criminal she sworn to kill along with his entire bloodline, past and future. She even saw Tetsuo Hatanaka's evil face in her mind's eye as plainly as if his disgusting being was standing before her, instead of his cursed kin of a lowly offspring, Hiromoai Hatanaka.

Her throat issued such a strange, crude, non human eerie sound, and her anger forced her eyes as if on command, to overflow and pour forth tears of hatred and unendurable pain and disgust. With the roar that had never come forth from her being before, she screamed as she wildly charged Hiromoai's defensibly body without thought, sightless with rage as she dared to hiss violently at him. "Woe to he when the servant becomes the Master of life and death over him!"

She screamed such words of hatred at Hiromoai as he became overwhelmed with fear of this extremely dangerous spirit suddenly charging at him with her killing sword held at the ready to kill him, as she roared without respect. "Foul and nauseating lowly one born from the evil arm pit of a cursed coward and dung eating murderer who had killed the only true love of my life! I cover my eyes with the stones that once weighed heavily upon my aching heart, and long ago buried the unending pain and heartache of my lover's death from my vision and memory. I seek my lover's honor and respect from your most detestable and hated spirit, and its unending greed and want for things of worldly needs. I shall take back what your loathsome ancestor once stole from his honorable spirit for all these years I searched for you and the rest of your worthless kin.

"Once I have dispatched your evil life from the land of the living, my lover's soul will finally be released from its bonds, and I shall find him and share his pillow for time's end." She seethed as her killing blade was turned into a blur of silver death ripping through the air, and then into Hiromoai's unprotected body, as he begged for his life. Over and over she savagely assaulted his defenseless body with her razor sharp blade of justice, powered by the rage she held for her once lord and master, as he fell to the ground and cried and begged for mercy, as it was now his turn to try and back out of the depression in his attempt to save his life. Not one muscle on his strained face could ripple out of fear of this angry spirit.

She attacked him with wild madness and rage that did not subside until there remained not one large enough piece of his slaughtered body to be separated with another sword strike from her blood soaked killing blade. All the while she hacked and chopped at his body she roared with all the anger and hatred she could muster, and she called the name of her long ago lover out over and over as she paid him loyalty and respect by killing this evil offspring.

Finally, suffering from total exhaustion, she dropped down to a knee right in the middle of all the blood and gore, and she tried to gain control of her breathing and unfettered anger. She paid no attention to the body of the Gai Jin, or to the fact she was still naked and covered from head to toe with the blood of the descendant of the hated murderer of her lover in life.

Over her shoulder a second light unexpectedly appeared in the pit's confines and all the gore it contained from the two bodies. She began praying to her protective Kami, Fujin-sama the angry God of Wind. She feared he was going to visit a terrible and unending punishment on her unconquerable spirit, for daring to kill the one who commanded the ancient sword, thus, her life and spirit for the past number of months while she was visiting the living world.

She stared into the bubbling, churning mass of angry cloud and boiling flames trying to take shape before her stunned eyes. Tears of fear and sorrow were streaming down her flawless cheeks, and washing some of the blood and grime from them, while she waited for the horrifying wrath of Fujin to befall her head and soul. Instead of unimagined punishment and pain, from within the boiling mass of turbulence, a voice she had long ago remembered, called out tenderly, charmingly, protectively to her. It caused instant harmony and peace to come from within her troubled and confused spirit, as she stared at the cloud in awe and waited for the spirit causing the turbulence starting to surround her being.

"My Wind, it is I, Lord Kawasomeru of countless years past, my loyal Warrior of all time. I dwell within the honored Floating World as does your uncontrollable spirit, but separate from you and the other Samurai who have served me throughout my life upon the great battlefield, and on the earth. I dwell in the land placed aside in the never, an honored and sacred place, and served by the honored Kami who protected all Shoguns who have served Japan's past so honorably and true. I command your fighting spirit do not be angry with yourself my faithful Samurai Warrior of countless years past. I have returned from the place without thought and being to guide you back home, Wind, my Wind.

"My honorable and beyond loyal female Samurai Warrior of time long ago forgotten and honored by all the children of Japan, Wind your unhampered and forever wandering spirit is still unable to be confined by the mere traps of mortal man, or the Gods who command them so. Wind, my Wind, I want to tell you, Fujin-sama is not angry with your spirit in the least, because you were only guilty of following your sworn oath, and it was by my curse that had caused you this indecision you have suffered from over your deed of honor. You were bound to the land of the living and earth by your sacred oath to kill the one who has destroyed your noble Samurai Warrior and only lover, Captain Seisakajo-san and all who were sired by the detestable murderer of the night who dispatched your lover.

"It was a just and most honorable oath you sworn long ago to the gods of wonderment, as it should have been uttered, an honorable curse that overrode even my curse that I rested upon your head and sword of justice and vengeance. An oath of vengeance is important, more powerful than any curse from I, could hope to attain Wind. Come with me your true Lord and Master of fate and time, my female Samurai Warrior of forever, give me your honorable hand. I shall be proud to safely take you home, to rest among the clouds until the next time you're needed by the next Lord and Master of the Sword dwelling within the land of the living. Yes Wind, your curse has not been lifted from your faithful shoulders, or has it been fulfilled by time and honor, for the sword remains as whole. As One my Wind."

With a strength not equaled on the face of the earth, Wind reached down to retrieve Lord Kawasomeru's katana. But she was stopped in her motion by her master of the sword's words.

"No Wind, you must not, do not dare try and pick up the sword in your hand again, because the sword of justice will no longer recognize your faithful touch and respect. You must leave the great blade lying behind because I am the only one in the entire universe who can possibly touch it now. Wind, you shall exist deep in the hearts and mind of all honorable Japanese people until the last star gives up its endless existence within the Heavens, and falls from the night sky to be silenced of its light. And the earth begins its everlasting sleep of death and non-existence. Come with me my loyal and most honorable Samurai Warrior Wind!"

The powerful Lord Kawasomeru tenderly reached out his hand from within the fine mist of the cloud that engulfing Wind's spirit and the slight depression she stood in, and when she greedily extended her hand and lightly touched his comforting hand with hers. When their hands touched, her ungovernable spirit instantly disappeared in the still boiling cloud of mist. Her spirit was bathed in a cool, refreshing relaxing light, and she was placed in a special waiting area for Lord Kawasomeru to be finished with his short visit to the living world. All the blood and gore that once covered her exquisite and naked body instantly vanished, the instant her spirit entered the cloud of mist. She was now cool, refreshed, and comfortable, and was dressed in the most exquisite kimono she ever saw in her long existence in both worlds of greatness.

When her spirit was gone from the blood soaked death scene, the once mighty and well feared warlord known as Lord Kawasomeru, took a more solid earthly form, and he picked up Wind's blood soaked katana blade. The very blade he used to dispatch Wind's life so many centuries back in his living life. It was good for him to once again feel the fine heft of his fearsome killing sword locked in his hands. The katana blade served him so well on many past battlefields, the one he buried with her body.

Lord Kawasomeru took a few moments to look around and view the terrible carnage created by his female warrior until he noticed the scabbard of his katana resting on the ground. Before retrieving the sheath for the blade, he moved a piece of Hiromoai's head out of its way with the tip of the ancient sword, as he growled at the piece of ugly flesh on the ground before his feet.

"Fool of evil fool's, how dare you to believe that you, a mere worthless mortal of this earth, a foul man as desperate as you could possibly control, tame what was not meant to be tamed and controlled by any mere mortal dwelling within either worlds. You have received your just reward in this life for daring to use the wonderful gift that the gods have bestowed upon Wind's fine spirit, for all your evil and personal gains, your evil wants of this earth. I shall find the proper way to dishonor your cursed memory correctly in much the same way that you have dishonored my faithful female Samurai Warrior of the past of Japan."

The once powerful warlord walked over the gore without care or concern for the remains of both slaughtered men, and respectfully picked up the scabbard and placed the sword back in its ancient home. For the briefest of moments, the indescribable warlord allowed himself a few seconds to enjoy the sweet smells of the living world, before he was called back to the Floating World forever. It felt good for the great stalwart warlord of myth and wonderment, to again tread upon the dismembered bodies of the fallen enemy to his realm and laws. These two killed honorably by one of his warriors forever loyal to his commands over these many centuries.

When the killing sword of Lord Kawasomeru was set in its rightful place in its ancient wood sheath, he took the time to hide the weapon in the same place where Hiromoai had placed the blade earlier in his ambush of the unsuspecting Gai Jin invader from another land. Then the warlord of the past left it for the next master of the sword to discover, and then control his Wind's spirit honorably. He was aware Hiromoai was a dishonorable and detestable man, and he used her great power and spirit for his evil gains on the land of the living world. The angry warlord wanted his own revenge played out against the man who hurt his Wind so badly, and it overrode his will to leave the land of the living, as the laws that commanded him to do at the allotted time of his departure.

In one final act of disgust and disrespect and loathing he could possibly display against the disrespected Hiromoai's despicable memory and remains, the great spirit of the powerful warlord slowly hitched his fundoshi, his loincloth to the side, and he desecrated his remains scatted about the depression by pissing on them. It was the only thing the well respected warlord could think of doing to the evil man, to insult the enemy of Wind for all eternity, and to honor his warrior for her faithful service to his commands.

The wise Lord Kawasomeru fondly remembered Wind doing much the same thing when she caught up with and killed the cast down assassin who murdered her beloved sister so terribly in Master Trainer Tanizaki's home so many centuries ago. It was a proper and most deserving of insults, one worthy of repeating for the sake of his honorable Wind's spirit to witness from her waiting area, locked in the fabled Floating World of amazement and wonderment.

Once he was finished disgracing the remains of Hiromoai, Lord Kawasomeru turned and found the head of the slaughtered and guiltless American Gai Jin, and he muttered to its spirit as he picked the head of the Gai Jin up by the crop of almost white hair. Then he looked into the non seeing eyes of the stranger to his lands, and the ancient warlord said in a commanding voice. "You, Gai Jin from another world, from another land, from another wonder, from another time, you are about to be honored as no other Gai Jin of the past has ever been honored by any Japanese Shogun. For your worthy spirit will be allowed to dwell within the great lands of the wonderment of the Ukiyo World in peace and harmony, and with the greatest of respect by all spirits that give worth to the Floating World, and all who honor the Kami of the Ukiyo.

"It is a special place in which to dwell for your eternity, and it was solely reserved for the honored and respected Japanese Samurai of the great past, and of the future years yet to be displayed for Japan's history, Gai Jin. Since you were killed by Wind's hand, an honorable Samurai Warrior of the past times, for reasons beyond your blame or control, or of your own fault or cause. The Kami who rule over such decisions, have deemed it proper and correct for you to be allowed to dwell in peace forever with me in the great void of life. You shall be by my side so we can watch the future of the world yet to be played out before our eyes.

"I shall take care of your honorable soul for all eternity yet to unfold in your memory, Gai Jin. I shall teach you of the many fine ways and great respect of the honorable Japanese Samurai Warrior Class. Come with me Gai Jin, for it is time you come home to fulfill the final destiny to your honorable memory and spirit. Together, we shall collect my beloved Wind's unconquerable spirit, and then we will bring her to stand before the great Council of Kami, so they might honor her spirit justly. Because she is still my most loyal and trusted vassal, my retainer of for time ever, and it's time an unknowing and unwise Gai Jin witnesses, and learns of the proper respect a true Lord and Master expects, and deserves from his loyal Samurai. Who serve him faithfully in life and in death, and how that Master repays the loyal Warrior who has honored him for the so many years of his useless existence upon this great rock of earth."

When the powerful and ancient Lord Kawasomeru finished speaking to the hovering spirit of Calvin Batterman through the unseeing eyes of his severed head, the warlord's spirit likewise rapidly dissolved into nothingness, while guiding the newly forming spirit of Calvin Batterman to its final resting place within the clouds of wonder, with his lovely Wind. Batterman's head was held tightly in Lord Kawasomeru's right hand as the ancient laws demanded it be carry to the Council of Kami, left the earth with them both. Once the warlord's spirit left the earth to be reunited with the many honored spirits of the past of Japan that once owned the unseen world of wonder and legend. Lord

Kawasomeru led the two honored spirits forth until they stood before the great Council of Kami, and the lords of the past began to honor them properly.

CHAPTER THIRTY TWO

The gun fire from Calvin Batterman's weapon fired so near to the very heart of downtown Tokyo, brought a flood of police cars responding to the latest crime scene to befall Japan. The call came in to the detective division by a concerned civilian, and Lieutenant Motoshima was immediately notified about the gun fire situation. He immediately pulled Sergeant Okamatsu from his surveillance of who he thought was Hiromoai driving throughout the many streets of Tokyo, and ordered the Sergeant to report to the scene of the recent shooting. Lieutenant Motoshima also informed him he was coming out to the scene, and he was to meet him at the crime scene as soon as humanly possible.

As yet, Lieutenant Motoshima had no idea what the shooting was about or who might have been involved in the shooting, but since there was little crime in Japan committed with a firearm. He was acting accordingly, ordering most of his detective division to report to the new reported crime scene. The concerned Japanese Police Lieutenant left the office as soon as he was finished speaking to Sergeant Okamatsu over the radio and headed for his vehicle.

By the time he finally arrived at the latest scene of death and bloody gore after fighting with the madding civilian traffic, Sergeant Okamatsu had already arrived and was checking out the terrible carnage they discovered in the slight depression of the earth. A score of interested civilians quickly gathered around the death scene, all trying to see what happened in the field, and see if they could discover who was killed in the vacant lot in the center of Tokyo.

The Lieutenant was suffering from exhausted because before the shooting was reported to his office, he was toying with going home and catching up on his sleep. Since the first murders of Asahiko's honorable son and his wife, the murder case was constantly expanding and causing him to lose much sleep investigating the situation and search for the female assassin believed to be responsible for the murders. But when a shooting report came in, he shelved that idea and headed for the reported crime. He saw his Sergeant as he pulled on the site, and headed for him. Something about where the shooting occurred was making the short hairs on the back of his neck stand on end, and he walked up to his Sergeant and barked.

"What the hell do you have going down over here, Sergeant? A gang killing this time I hope? I'd truly enjoy investigating a regular gang murder for a change. All this crap about an ancient female samurai running around and savagely murderering the elite of Japan has worn real thin on my ass, I tell you Sergeant." As he stopped at the very edge of the depression and looked down into the mess, and then at his Sergeant trying not to step on the dismembered parts of a human being slaughtered so savagely in the shallow pit. The nosy civilians tried to move even closer to the ugly scene of death to get a better look at the gore, and they caused Lieutenant Motoshima to yell at a few police officers hanging around the death scene doing nothing but looking at the same thing the troublesome civilians wanted to see.

"You two police officers over there gawking at this foul mess, get these damn civilians the hell away from this site, and set out some crime tape, and keep the pain in the ass civilians the hell out of the damn area. I can't have them people walking all over a crime scene and possibly destroying evidence, dammit." He stared at the officers until they got some kind of control over the gathering nosy civilians then he looked around the death scene again.

The area was already well lit up with temporary lighting strung out from a portable generator they set up, and some police officers were having a problem with the news reporters already starting to show up at the scene. The horde of reporters was trying to sneak under the crime tape, and get some pictures of what just took place in the pit. They were ignoring the officers' orders, and this made the police react harshly against the reporters. They were being shoved nastily back by the angry officers, along with a few more aggressive civilians, and they were resorting to a flood of curses at the police over being stopped from seeing what happened.

"Terrible Lieutenant Motoshima-san, it's terrible to witness such a savage slaughter as this one here is right in the very heart of downtown Tokyo, sir. It's a real mess down in the pit we have on our hands this time, sir." Sergeant Okamatsu looked at his fuming Lieutenant as he shook his head sadly as if to empathize the horrible state the murdered victim was in.

"Dammit to hell and back again, talk to me Sergeant. I need some answers to this mess and I need them this minute." Lieutenant Motoshima growled as he carefully slid into the pit of death with is Sergeant, and then added. "Who the hell is that one lying against the side of this pit? Where the hell's his god damn head at? Has anyone found this one's head, Sergeant? Have you been able to identify this one with no head and was he the shooter or the other victim, Sergeant?" The Lieutenant's mind was troubling him over where the shooting occurred.

"Lieutenant, he's the victim, he's the American, Calvin Batterman who just bought Asahiko-san's construction company, sir. Terrible sir, it's terrible." The Sergeant lit up Batterman's body with the flashlight, so the Lieutenant could get a better look at what the killer did to the man.

"Godddd dammit! Not the American this fucking time. Shit, dammit! Now I know why this damn site was bothering the hell out of my ass, Sergeant. It seems lately anyone murdered in Japan is somehow involved in one way or the other with the damn construction field." He roared at no one in particular as he carefully bent down, and looked at the lifeless body of the murdered American. He suddenly looked around the pit for his head and growled at his Sergeant at the same time. "How the hell do you know for certain that this one is the American who brought Asahiko's company? Where the hell's his damn head at anyhow, Sergeant?"

"That's the strangest thing about this murder, Lieutenant Motoshima-san. We looked all around the entire murder scene, and no one was able to locate the American's head, sir. It's seems to be missing from the crime scene, as if someone had carried it off with them for some reason, sir. Also Lieutenant, although the call came in as a shooting, neither dead person as far as we can determine so far, was killed by a firearm sir."

Lieutenant Motoshima started to search the pit for the American's head. He was likewise having a serious problem watching where he was stepping. It seemed there were human remains covering the entire area of the depression. He pointed with his flashlight at what looked like scattered raw meat covering the ground and snapped at his Sergeant. "What the hell's this other shit lying all around the damn crime scene, Sergeant?"

"I don't know as yet Lieutenant. What I do know is this mess is all parts of one human being, sir. We haven't been able to identify the remains as of this time, Lieutenant. We're waiting for the doctors and crime scene investigators to arrive on site, sir. Maybe they might have some luck identifying the remains of this second slaughtered one, sir. I have a thought as to who it might be though, Lieutenant. I think it's the remains of Hiromoai-san, Lieutenant."

"You have to be shitting me Sergeant. God dammit! What the hell's going on around here for the love of the gods? I was positive Hiromoai was the mastermind behind the assassin's evil actions of late. How could this one be Hiromoai, I thought you were trailing that bastard, Sergeant? Did you find any evidence this act might have been committed by the assassin we're searching for, mister? What the hell am I asking you, of course it was that bitch from the red hell, dammit? This damn assassin loves to waddle around in all the damn gore it creates at any crime scenes she leaved behind for us to investigate.

"Keep searching the area, the foul assassin had to have left some evidence behind, especially because she carried out her evil deeds on soft dirt of this pit. And I want the American's head found before anyone leaved this damn site, Sergeant! No one goes home until we found his missing noggin, is that clear, Sergeant?" Lieutenant Motoshima growled angrily as he began moving around the depression in search of any possible clues to what truly happened in the pit.

"I don't know how the hell Hiromoai got here we followed who we thought was him for over an hour. I'll find out who was driving his car if these remains are those of Hiromoai-san. I think we have to notify the American government about this murder case, Lieutenant. I believe they have a stake in this case now sir. One of their people was murdered by this damn female assassin this time, Lieutenant Motoshima-san. I still can't believe these remains are those of Hiromoai-san's, sir." Sergeant Okamatsu offered dryly while still trying not to step on any of the remains of the slaughtered Hiromoai, and the American.

"I agree, you're right with that assumption Sergeant, and I know just the man I'm going to call about this damn expanding case. Secure the entire scene and seal it off to everyone but the damn doctors and crime investigators, Sergeant. I have to make a call I can probably have the American Representative here within ten minutes at the latest I believe. Get everyone the hell out of here, especially them damn nosy ass reporters. The last thing I need around here is for any of them fools trampling all over the murder scene, and screwing up our investigation and possibly destroying evidence while they're at it. I repeat I don't want any Officers leaving this scene until the American's head is found. I hope someone will find the damn thing before the American Agent arrives. I'd hate like hell to be forced to tell him the head's missing, and no one was able to locate the damn thing on the site. Get hoping on my orders Sergeant.

"Damn nosy ass reporters anyhow, I'd love to know how the hell they find out about our business even before I find out about the shit myself, dammit. When the FBI Agent arrives on the site, I want the Agent to have unfettered access to the entire crime scene in private if he so requests it, Sergeant. Keep the damn civilians and reporters far away from the area until we're done with it. I wish it was fucking light out so we could see what the hell we're doing here. And find the damn American's head will you please! I don't believe anyone would want to walk off with the damn thing for some stupid reason. The lowly assassin has never removed anything from a crime scene before, and I don't think she'd start now. A criminal never changes his act in the middle of the damn crime."

Lieutenant Motoshima snapped again at his Sergeant as he carefully climbed out of the slight depression and headed for his car while rubbing his feet on the dirt in an attempt to try and scrape off some of the gore he picked up in the depression stuck on his shoes. He yanked the radio from its cradle like he was angry at it and keyed the mike.

"Sergeant Kayanuma here goes with your report Lieutenant Motoshima-san." Kayanuma was manning the front desk at the Tokyo police station along with the radio, and he was bored to death until this call came in from the Lieutenant.

"Sergeant Kayanuma-san, I need you to get in touch with an American FBI Agent working in Tokyo. He helped me in the past with a robbery case the Agent was working on, and he was also instrumental in getting me the report on the American who just brought Asahiko-san construction business. Once you have him on the horn, inform him I need to see him at this latest crime scene, as quickly as he can possible arrive here, Sergeant." Lieutenant Motoshima waited for the Desk Sergeant to digest his words before continuing with his orders.

"Yes sir, can I have the Agent's name and number you want, Lieutenant?"

"Yes, sure, I believe it's Agent Robert Rossie if I remember correctly, yes, it's Bob Rossie alright, and you can reach him at this number I'm going to give you, Sergeant. Inform him where the crime scene is located and inform him I need his assistance with it immediately. You know where I'm working it's in your damn log, Sergeant." Lieutenant Motoshima read the phone number to the Desk Sergeant from the agent's card given him when he requested a background check on Batterman and his business history in America a few days ago then he broke off the connection. He took a moment for himself and watched from his car as Sergeant Okamatsu quickly cleared the civilians and reporters away from the crime scene.

Lieutenant Motoshima took a moment to himself and he lit up a cigarette and breathed the smoke deep in his lungs in a rush, while waiting for the American Agent to respond to the death scene. It took over an hour before the young FBI Agent appeared on the site of death and gore.

FBI Agent Robert 'Bob' Rossie pulled up to the location the Desk Sergeant gave him over the phone and immediately recognized Lieutenant Motoshima standing by his unmarked police car while smoking and he headed for the officer the moment he pulled onto the scene. He was kind of caught a little off guard by the phone call from the Tokyo Police Department Desk Sergeant. Rossie was enjoying watching the spectacular fireworks display going off after watching a Japanese baseball game conclude. It was at that moment he received the message from Tokyo Police Headquarters, and he immediately headed for his car to find out what the problem was with Lieutenant Motoshima.

As the agent reached the Lieutenant, Rossie tapped out one of his American made cigarette and offered it to the Japanese Officer and then he bowed politely to the Lieutenant. This act was about the same as Rossie offering the officer his business card. He understood how well the Japanese people loved the American cigarettes.

SAF Special Agent in the Field Robert Rossie noticed the crime tape ran out in the field and realized this situation was probably a murder case, because of the way the gaggle of police officers were trying to secure the crime scene. He waited for Lieutenant Motoshima to explain why he wanted him at a murder in Japan. Something he felt was none of his business. But he knew it was bad manners to speak first to the officer.

"Ahhh so... Thank you Agent Rossie-san and thank you for responding so quickly to my call for your assistance, sir." The Lieutenant said as he took the offered cigarette and then continued with his words to the American Agent. "I'm terribly sorry to be forced to inform you Agent Rossie that one of your American businessmen has come to a terrible end in Japan, sir."

"Oh, I was wondering why you wanted me to assist you in what
I believed was a local crime, sir. Who was it you believe was murdered tonight, Lieutenant?" Rossie asked as he lit the cigarette for Lieutenant Motoshima.

"I'm sorry to inform you Agent Rossie-san, the murdered American is Mr. Calvin Batterman-san we believe, of Batterman and Batterman Construction of America. I spoke to you over this same man a few days back if you remember correctly, sir." The concerned Lieutenant offered and then exhaled the smoke and flipped the cigarette to the ground and shoved off the side of his car with his backside. He walked towards the murder scene with Rossie following him. The Lieutenant was adding the mister and san to Batterman's name to show the agent he was displaying the proper respect for the dead American.

"Damn, that's going to cause quite a stir back in the States I can tell you, Lieutenant Motoshima-san. He was one helluva big shot back in my country, sir. Any idea how and why he was murdered tonight, Lieutenant?" Rossie asked as he fell in line with the Lieutenant as they headed for the center of the scene.

"Yes Rossie-san, I believe Mr. Batterman-san had the misfortune to fall victim to the devil's own kin of a female assassin working her evil craft on the streets of downtown Tokyo in recent weeks, sir." Lieutenant Motoshima grumbled as he took a flashlight from a second police officer sort of standing guard over the depression, and the carnage it contained. Then he shined the light in the hole so Rossie could see the death in the pit. Rossie and Motoshima stopped five feet away from the edge to allow the other officers checking the depression to exit it before they got in the other officer's way.

"Damn! I heard something about that one doing her dirty work in Tokyo just the other day, sir. Any idea who the assassin might be in your ongoing investigation, Lieutenant? I heard your department was having quite a deal of trouble trying to identify and capture the damn assassin, sir. I can't believe a female killer was responsible for such terrible slaughter as this, sir. Damn, this one must not have much of a conscience and a heck of a strong stomach to be able to create such gore out of a human being, Lieutenant." The concerned American Agent offered as he drew in smoke from his cigarette as he stared at the death in the pit.

"No Agent Rossie-san. I'm stuck at a dead end in my search of this believed to be female assassin, sir. To tell you the truth about the matter though, I'm not all that certain this evil assassin is a female at all sir. No one is left alive who had the misfortune to come across this loathsome assassin to be able to positively identify her or him to us. This miserable assassin is good, damn good Agent Rossie-san. But I'll get her or him sooner or later, that you can bet your life on sir. It's only a matter of time before I finally capture her ass and bring her or him to final justice, Rossie-san." He was angry the agent was aware they were having trouble identifying, and capturing the assassin giving him such fits.

They moved a little closer to the side of the depression after the Lieutenant and agent stepped aside to make room for the two police officers who walked up to the side of the pit, stopping at the rim so they could get a better look into it.

Rossie let out a low whistle and whispered more to himself than the Lieutenant "Christ" as he looked at the remains of the slaughtered men scattered about on the bottom of the pit. He could not believe in this day and time people were still being slaughtered so savagely in Japan, especially by the sword as he mumbled to the Japanese Police Officer. "Whew, this damn assassin sure does love her work, Lieutenant."

"More than you'll ever know, Rossie-san. We believe in this particular criminal incident, the assassin even took the time to piss on her victim's slaughtered remains, a terrible insult to be taken to the grave with the dead one's soul. Come with me Rossie-san, and I'll show you what we have been able collected so far from the crimes scene as evidence we can work with sir." The Lieutenant was the first one to slide carefully into the depression. When he was comfortable he reached out and offered to help the agent in the pit.

Agent Rossie followed Lieutenant Motoshima in the pit of slaughter and death as he quickly surveyed the area. "Wow, there's not much left of one of the poor fuckers, Lieutenant." Rossie complained as he tried to watch where he was walking while trying not to step on any remains.

"Yes, we believe all the slaughtered bloody remains are parts of the body of the respected Japanese businessman

Hiromoai Hatanaka-san, Rossie-san. As you have just offered sir, I'm afraid there's not much left of him, and we're waiting for the coroner to arrive to positively identify that body as his, sir. Hiromoai-san was my only lead in this ongoing investigation, dammit. But now he's dead I have no one left to point the finger of guilt at, Rossie-san." Lieutenant Motoshima took Rossie's cigarette from his hand and flicked it out of the depression to preserve the crime scene in a better state for the inspectors.

"Why do you believe these remains are of those of Hiromoai-san, Lieutenant? I heard of this man before, I believe he was extremely important to Japan, as much as Batterman was to America, sir. I saw his picture more than once in the local newspapers, sir. This mess sure doesn't look anything like the man I remember though, Lieutenant." Rossie griped as he ignored the officer taking his cigarette from him and throwing it away. He cursed himself for taking the cigarette in a crime scene in the first place, he knew better than that.

"Come with me and I'll show you why we believe the slaughtered remains are those of Hiromoai-san, Rossie-san. Please, try and be as careful as you can be where you're walking, sir." Lieutenant Motoshima led the American over to the side of the pit and then he bent down and rolled over a severed hand so it could be examined better. He pointed to the watch on the wrist and announced. "There Rossie-san, you see that watch on the severed arm, sir?"

"Yes Lieutenant, it looks like a Rolex to me, sir." The agent offered back.

"You're correct Rossie-san. I happen to know its Hiromoai-san's because I looked at his watch just yesterday to see what time it was, while I questioned him over the recent death of the honorable Asahiko-san who he visited and tried to buy his business...”

“Then you believe this Hiromoai fella had something to do with the recent murders plaguing Japan, Lieutenant?” Rossie asked as he interrupted Motoshima.

“Yes, I hate to admit this to you but as I stated Rossie-san, he was my only suspect in the ugly murders of the Asahiko-san clan, sir. But now he has obviously fell victim to this lowly killer, I might be forced to change that opinion, sir. You see Rossie-san, in Japan a hired assassin could never go against the one controlling her or his evil events. It’s not done that way, respect and all the other crap that goes along with it you know. So now I’m forced to believe someone else is pulling the fucking strings of this damn murderer enjoying killing the elite of Japan, Rossie-san.”

“Hiromoai-san didn’t remind me of the type of guy who would be involved in murder, and employing the services of a hired assassin to help him with who knows what, Lieutenant Motoshima-san.” Rossie offered as he looked closer at the expensive watch still wrapped around the wrist on the severed arm and noticed it was still working.

“Don’t take me wrong, Rossie-san. I didn’t mean to make you believe that Hiromoai-san was the one doing the murders. No sir, not in the least. What I believe is Hiromoai-san was the one possibly controlling this assassin’s evil actions, sir.”

Rossie scanned the area where the hand laid, and noticed something and brought it up to the Japanese police commander’s attention. “Say Lieutenant, what’s this over here sir?”

He bent a little closer to the ground to see what Rossie was pointing at, and then he grumbled once he realized what he just found. "Dammit Rossie-san, it looks like a footprint, one of someone not wearing shoes. Hummmm..., it's small, like that of maybe a woman's foot. Rossie-san, it seems you might have just found the evidence I've been searching for in this mess of murder, sir. If this footprint's that of a female then I believe it shows the woman killer is the one guilty for these horrendous murders, sir. Sergeant Okamatsu-san, I need a cast technician over in this area immediately. He has to make an impression cast of this footprint that Agent Rossie-san just discovered in this damn pit." The Lieutenant and Rossie moved away from the small footprint, so the technician could get to work on it.

"Yes sir." Sergeant Okamatsu offered as he waved one of the technicians over to the pit.

Rossie straightened up and then asked Lieutenant Motoshima with concern. "I see Lieutenant now with Hiromoai-san's death do you think you might have seen the last of this assassin, sir? If it's like you just say, that Hiromoai-san was the one behind her evil actions, sir."

"I'll pray to the Kami who control such things that this shall indeed become a reality, Rossie-san. I couldn't fathom this crafted murderess running wildly in downtown Tokyo, killing without anyone to control her evil actions if her control is the one dead in this pit, sir. At least with believing Hiromoai-san was the one controlling the damn killer, she was keeping her body count low and to a very narrow field of victims, sir. I believe she was only killing the ones who he sent her out after. Now, I don't know what to think about this murderer any longer Rossie-san. I hope Japan will not witness a wave of terrible bloodletting, now that the assassin's possible control was destroyed by her hand in this damn case, Rossie-san." Lieutenant Motoshima offered as he was forced to turn his attention to another police officer who walked nearer the pit, and said something to his Sergeant.

Rossie took this break in their conversation to begin checking the pit for his own clues.

Lieutenant Motoshima quickly finished speaking with his officer and then he looked at Rossie checking the pit. He allowed the agent to look around on his own, believing a new set of eyes might discover something that his officers might have possibly overlooked on the scene he was investigating. Rossie carefully searched the body of Batterman, removing his wallet and other papers he found on the headless body. He also took control of the discharged weapon found in the pit. When he finished searching the body he scanned the rest of the pit for any other clues. As he searched, he offered to the Lieutenant because he could not locate Batterman's head nowhere in the area. "Where the hell's Mr. Batterman's head being held at, sir? I wish to examine it if you don't mind Lieutenant. I might find something on it, sir."

"That's another strange part of this most confusing murder case we're struggling to solve, Rossie-san. It seems that the murderer might have carted off Mr. Batterman-san's head for some reason unknown to me, sir. In all my days on the police force, I've never heard of such a foul thing happening, unless the head was to be displayed for private viewing by a powerful Shogun in control of his Warriors and land, sir."

"What? Why the hell would she wanna go and do something as foolish as that, Lieutenant? Take his head, for what possible reason, than to stop us from burying him whole, sir. That would be a very cruel thing to do to his family." Rossie asked the officer as he stared in his eyes.

"I don't know why the hell she might have carried Mr. Batterman-san's head off for. Maybe she wanted to keep it for some kind of keepsake, or maybe a fucking trophy or something. It's her first Gai Jin she murdered in Japan, Rossie-san."

"Shit!" Rossie hissed as he unloaded Batterman's weapon of spent rounds, and placed them in his pocket while searching the pit, he asked the officer again. "Lieutenant Motoshima-san, how the hell was it possible for Mr. Batterman to enter your country with a weapon, sir? I had a helluva time trying to convince your government to allow me to remain armed with my service weapon while I was on duty in Japan, sir."

"That is a good question that has to be answered by someone, Rossie-san. I looked into that when I first met Mr. Batterman-san, sir. I was informed he brought a weapon from one of his security guards he was using to protect his life while he was here in Japan, Rossie-san. I already complained to my people, but they ordered me to overlook this minor infraction by him, sir. My Commander took into consideration that the assassin stalking the night was a serious threat to everyone living or even visiting Japan, and he felt it might be a good idea if the American businessman was armed to better protect his life, sir."

"I can agree with that very easily, however, I believe this gives me another question that I have to ask you, Lieutenant Motoshima-san. If Mr. Batterman thought the threat from this assassin was that serious that he needed to surround himself with a gaggle of security guards from your country.

Then where the hell were they while he was being slaughtered by this murderer you keep speaking about while we're investigating this crime scene, Lieutenant?" Rossie stopped looking around the pit and turned to the Lieutenant while waiting for the reply.

"You're a wise and attentive investigator, Rossie-san. It makes me pleased you're so mindful to your duty, and helping me with this murder investigation, sir. Again Rossie-san, the moment I was informed it was Mr. Batterman-san slaughtered tonight sir. I immediately contacted the company that supplied the bodyguards for his protection. Their boss had informed me Hiromoai-san had a meeting scheduled with Mr. Batterman-san for tonight at this construction site, sir. And Mr. Batterman-san wanted, and further demanded to meet with Hiromoai-san in private, and he ordered the guards to remain behind.

"But yet Mr. Batterman-san was wise enough to order the security guards to become suspicious of the meeting and time, if he didn't return to his apartment by midnight, sir. The boss of his security guards already notified our department that Mr. Batterman-san was late returning from his scheduled meeting with Hiromoai-san. This is another reason why we're almost certain these slaughtered remains are those of Hiromoai-san's body, Rossie-san." The Japanese Police Officer reported to the American Agent.

"But if you believe it was Hiromoai-san who was the one controlling the assassin then how come he's the one slaughtered along with Mr. Batterman, Lieutenant? I believe I read somewhere, or at least I heard something about a Japanese assassin working for one man was willing to sacrifice his or her life carrying out his orders faithfully to the one who had hired his evil services, sir. That it was against some kinda special code of rules and conduct for this assassin to turn his wrath against the one controlling his or her evil actions, Lieutenant. In fact Lieutenant Motoshima-san, I believe you had already mentioned the very same thing while we were speaking about the actions of this damn assassin a little while ago, sir."

"Ahhh so... there's another question that has to be asked and answered by someone, Rossie-san. One in which I'm unhappy to reply that I have no positive answer to offer you at this time, sir. Maybe, the honorable American businessman was able to turn the assassin's head, before he died by her disgusting hand, and he had the assassin turned his wrath loose against Hiromoai-san. It's not that uncommon for one Samurai to turn his allegiance from one master to another, if the second master was believed to be just, or the Warrior was trapped in a no win situation, and the second master offered the Warrior life instead of death. Arrr... who the hell knows any longer, all I know is that nothing about this damn murder case surprises me any longer, Rossie-san." Lieutenant Motoshima grumbled in a tone displaying surrender on his part as he gave out with a deep sigh to the FBI Agent's last question.

Rossie shrugged to the Lieutenant's last words as he stared back at him.

"Thank you again Rossie-san. Your questions gave me other questions that I must pursue on this endless and most confusing murder case, Rossie-san." The lead detective complained then he began searching the pit in hopes this would end Rossie's confusing questions being aimed at him and he could not answer.

Rossie also went back to searching the depression again, trying not to trod on any of the remains from either man slaughter tonight. His eyes carefully scanned the inside of the pit and stopped when they focused in on the heavy stack of timbers that looked in danger of sliding into the depression and he called out. "Hey, what the hell's that thing over there Lieutenant, that thing sticking outta the dirt by that mess of timbers, sir?" Rossie asked as he went over to the timber sticking out of the bank of the hollow.

Lieutenant Motoshima followed the excited agent over to the timber stack as Rossie pulled the crumbling sword free of its prison trapped under the wood in the dirt bank.

"Ieeeee... Rossie-san, you are truly blessed with the four eight's of good luck and Karma in Japan, sir. You have just found an ancient Katana blade of some unknown Samurai from Japan's past, sir. Please Rossie-san allow me to inspect the blade. I fear it might be the murder weapon we're searching for, sir."

Lieutenant Motoshima took the well aged sword from the agent's hand and tried to free the blade of the crumbling scabbard, it would not budge an inch for him. This was because Wind was still being escorted before the Council of Kami by Lord Kawasomeru's hand and guidance. As long as she was in the presence of the Council of Kami, her sword was forbidden to be freed of its scabbard until the gods had finished questioning and honoring her spirit if honor was to be bestowed on her person.

After not being able to remove the ancient sword from the scabbard, Lieutenant Motoshima checked out what he could see of the old blade through the missing pieces of the wood scabbard. The sword's blade seemed totally useless, pitted beyond repair, rusted, and had countless chips missing out of the once fine cutting edge of the blade. At first, he thought it to be the murder weapon, but seeing the terrible condition of the ancient sword he knew he was wrong with that assumption. He handed the sword back to the American agent, feeling it had nothing to do with the murder of the two elite businessmen, and it was worthless as a collector's item, and knew the government would not be interested in the weapon because of its terrible state.

"You mean I can have the sword, Lieutenant Motoshima-san?" Rossie asked excitedly as he stared at the ancient katana. He was stunned the Lieutenant handed the sword back to him and then turned his back on him.

"Huh, sure, why not, though I should really turn the worthless blade in to the pain in the ass Artifacts Committee for Japan's antiques for further examination and possible restoration by them, Rossie-san. They demand every ancient weapon found anywhere in Japan to be turned over to them without exception, sir. But it's in such terrible shape I seriously doubt even they would be very interested in having the ancient sword to examine or possibly be restored by them, sir. Here's what I'll do for you because of your help in this murder case, Rossie-san. I'll give you an evidence bag so you can keep the sword and get it passed our Customs Officers easy enough when you decide to return to your country.

"From what I can see of the ancient blade, it seems absolutely worthless to us and maybe if you work on it, you can polish it once you destroyed the wood prison of the old sword. Then you can place the weapon on your mantle, something to talk about with your lady friends back in the

States I would offer, no Rossie-san?" Lieutenant Motoshima said with a wink of his eye and a smile. For some reason he liked this young FBI Agent, and wanted him to have the sword so he could think of his own lies to tell his young female friends. Maybe even tell them how he disarmed a feared samurai warrior and took his sword from his dead hands.

"Damn right I'll do just as you offered, Lieutenant Motoshima-san. Thanks, thanks a helluva lot for the sword Lieutenant, I'll take good care of it. I can't tell you how much this thing means to me, sir." Rossie told the Japanese police officer, as he tucked the sword protectively under his arm and then he went back but only half hearted, searching the shallow pit that now held little interest for him. He was dying to get back to his apartment to see what the ancient blade looked like once he removed the scabbard from the old weapon.

Lieutenant Motoshima was a lone child brought up in a well honored family that deeply respected many of the ancient ways of the past history of Japan, although he rarely practiced those respects. But seeing the antique blade reminded him of what his father always told him. 'My son, a Katana blade should never be allowed to breathe the pure air of life, unless it was doing what it was made for, killing your honorable enemy on the field of justice. The Katana's place dwells within the darkness of its scabbard, unless it's working for its master's sake and honor. This you must remember for all times to come, respect the old ways of your country, and you will become an honorable and well respected man'.

Rossie was so excited about being given the ancient katana blade that he thanked Lieutenant Motoshima a second time over the gift. "Gees, thanks a helluva lot Lieutenant, I'll clean it up and stick it on my mantle as you have suggested, sir. It looks like there's nothing else for us to find in this pit of death and slaughter tonight, Lieutenant. Perhaps, we should search better when it gets light out sir. If Mr. Batterman's head turns up, I wish to be notified at once about it Lieutenant Motoshima-san. I'll start the wheels in motion to get his body shipped back to the States, so his next of kin can have his body buried properly for him, Lieutenant. How long do you think it'll be before his body can be released, sir?"

"You're correct, now is not the time to continue searching this latest crime scene looking for any further possible evidence, Rossie-san. I believe while everything is fresh and undisturbed, the darkness might cause us to lose or otherwise overlook some evidence, Rossie-san. At first light we'll resume our search with conviction for any evidence, but I'm going to stay on the scene and carry out a minor search until its light enough for me to resume the full scale search of the scene. And if Mr. Batterman-san's head is located, I'll notify you immediately Rossie-san. Err... about releasing his body, it can't be released until the medical examination has been completed which should take about two weeks at the most, sir. Then we'll have to hold the body in case further examinations are orders by the courts. Yes, yes I can see his body should be released to the next of kin within four and no longer than six weeks at the longest, Agent Rossie-san." Lieutenant Motoshima replied with a snap in his tone as he went off in another direction, continuing his search of the crime area again.

After another hour of searching, the lieutenant finally decided to give it up and wait for the light of day to continue his search, and grumbled to Rossie who decided to continue helping him until the lieutenant finally called it a day by announcing to the American agent. "There's nothing more to be discovered at this scene until we can see better what the hell we're doing out here, sir. Shall we go and get a cup of coffee and compare notes to see if either of us has discovered something the other one might have missed, Rossie-san?"

"By all means Lieutenant Motoshima-san, I'm really exhausted and I want to turn in for the rest of the night. I saw enough of this blood and gore to last me a lifetime, sir. I can never get used to the foul smell of blood in the air, sir." Rossie complained as he followed the Japanese police officer out of the area of the slaughter.

Agent Rossie allowed Lieutenant Motoshima to lead him away from the murder scene. The two officers enjoyed a coffee and compared notes and then Lieutenant Motoshima excused himself and left the American agent sitting in the coffee shop. The agent had a second coffee and then left for his office. The moment he got back to his office in Japan and he made a report to FBI Headquarters in Washington D.C. His superior immediately ordered him home to make a more detailed in-depth report over the death of the powerful American businessman.

MONDAY, JUNE 10th, 1996.   FBI HEADQUARTERS, WASHINGTON D.C.

Agent Robert Rossie entered FBI headquarters from the Reagan International Airport while carrying the ancient sword of the only female samurai warrior in Japan's history wrapped up in the evidence bag. He was totally exhausted from his long flight back to the United States. It was late, and later by the time he finally finished with his report about Batterman's death in Japan to his boss. He also informed his superior that they had no solid leads as to who the murderer was, and his head was never found at the scene or anywhere else for that matter. The young agent kind of refrained from informing his boss that the Japanese Police Lieutenant believed some kind of god like woman assassin was running around Japan killing anyone who happened to stumble past her, or who she was sent out to kill. He did inform his boss that it was believed a woman assassin killed Batterman.

Rossie's commander grumbled in a sarcastic tone at the exhausted agent. "If Batterman was going to die, I believed he was going to die at the hands of some insulted young woman. I believe this because of the way it was reported on how he always treated women he was around, or with, Agent Rossie. I sure wish his damn body was complete though, or at least his dick was missing, so we could return his body as complete as possible to his wife and children. As it stands, it looks like the coffin will have to remain closed for viewing. It ain't good to look at someone about to be buried without his noggin resting on his shoulders, dammit."

This caused Rossie and his commander to laugh a bit and then they ended their conversation and he was allowed to go home and rest, with the next two days off as a gift for his extra work in Japan. The young agent appreciated the time off because he was spent out and exhausted, and needed rest to help recharge his batteries and catch up on his life in the United States. Especially his love life that suffered drastically since he was assigned to the Japanese FBI office for a year's overseas service. He had no wife to answer to, and he was too excited to go to sleep anyway, this was the first time since returning to the United States he had a chance to closely examine the katana sword he found in Japan in private. He still could not believe the lieutenant gave him the ancient sword to keep for his own.

Rossie's heart was pounding wildly in his chest as he grabbed hold of the crumbling wood scabbard in one hand, and the hilt of the ancient sword in the other and then he applied pressure to the both ends of the sword at the same time. He was dying to see what the steel shaft of the weapon looked like. He was also trying to be careful about it though, if the old sword did sudden release itself from the case. He did not want his hands to be sliced open by the blade no matter how bad a shape it was in, if the wood crumbled in his hand, and he ended up holding on the cutting edge of the old blade. He had no doubt in his mind that the edge would still do what it was designed for, cutting.

Rossie always wanted to own a samurai sword antique, but he never dared to dream that he would ever find a real one, and get it home free with the lieutenant's help. Under his pressure, the crumbling wood penitentiary finally released its death like grasp on the shaft of the ancient katana, and the sword started to pull free of the wood scabbard.

THE COUNCIL OF KAMI

The ancient Samurai Warrior known as Wind, just finished her meeting with the Council of Kami, and the gods who ruled over their Japanese subjects gave her special permission to speak for a short time with her former lord and master, Kawasomeru. But no sooner did they become comfortable and begin their conversation together, than Wind's form suddenly disappeared from his presence. The once so powerful and deadly warlord knew immediately that someone must have discovered her great sword, and the new owner and master of the weapon had just summoned her for a private appearance before her new lord and master from the depths of the Floating World. The once so feared and respected warlord was totally powerless to stop her from answering her summons by the new master of the ancient sword.

AGENT ROBERT ROSSIE'S APARTMENT

Agent Rossie was finally able to work the blade free from its crumbling wood sheath with little damage to the fragile and breaking wood sleeve. To his astonishment, the well aged blade began to return to its original beauty and luster the moment the air began to bath the badly damaged sword while it was still locked in his hand. The once frayed silk wrapped hilt was perfect as he held on to the handle and he actually felt the movement from the sword's handle in his hands. He stared at the blade in stunned disbelief as it changed condition right before his eyes. He felt the old silk wrapping moving under his hand as it rapidly returned to its original condition. Gone were the once heavy pitting and marring rust spots that were really blood stains that once scared the shaft of the ancient blade. The deep, scarring nicks and scratches also disappeared, and only the brilliant shine from the highly polished steel blade, replaced the once damaged sword.

He could actually feel the life growing within the steel of the sword emitting from it, as Wind's powerful spirit was again being called back to the land of the living of sense and smells, and causing the katana blade to indeed vibrate slightly while still locked in his now shaking hands. All of a sudden, he was afraid to release his death like grasp he had on the handle of the sword he held on the ancient weapon.

A blinding and all consuming light suddenly bathed his entire room, and he found himself wanting to scream out in fear and terror, as his free hand searched under his arm for his service weapon to defend himself with against whatever was happening before him in his room. But he also found himself standing and staring in awe of what was happening around him, freezing him in place as everything began to play out rapidly before his eyes in a blinding, confusing rush of light, breeze and action and smells.

A cool breeze gently crossed over his neck like a soft breath of wind, and numerous papers and other light items spread out about in his room. Were softly tossed in the air as the vision of a stunning and naked young Japanese woman slowly began to materialize from the center of the glowing, golden light, rapidly expanding before the very end of the ancient blade still locked tightly in his hands, and it was filling him with the fear of God. Suddenly he could swear he smelt dust, horses and heard the clanking of steel swords crashing against each other. He was also able to hear muffled sounds of screams and felt that he was overlooking a field where soldiers armed with swords and protected by their armor were doing battle with each other.

"Who the hell are you! Where the hell did you come from, and what the hell do you want with me!" Rossie demanded in flawless Japanese, as he drew on his strength at the cloud of the woman as he lowered the great sword, and aimed his service weapon at the chest of this naked and beautiful goddess of the glowing light. All the warnings from the Japanese lieutenant flooded back in his troubled mind, and he found himself wondering if he just found where the female assassin once stalking Japan, was hiding. He was wondering if this spirit like woman was coming before him, to kill him as the others were killed so terribly in Japan, as he waited for a reply to his words from the spirit taking on a more earthly and solid form.

"HAI, I AM WIND, MY GREAT LORD AND MASTER…"